Praise for *Some...*

Kallypso Masters has a way at breakin␣ ␣of us to see their deepest issues. We've ␣␣un't worked through in his past that were interfering ␣␣ngelina. We started to see in the previous book, but to see ␣ ␣␣␣w broken their relationship really was in this book broke my heart...*Somebody's Angel* was full of healing, heartbreak, love and family. It took me low, it broke my heart, it picked me back up and let me see hope. And let me feel love. That love, that bond, that deeper thread that connects the characters in this series and shows me they can all help each other.

~ **Francesca, Under the Covers**

~ ~ ~

Somebody's Angel "teaches even the most non BDSMer about the power of a submissive. It was an emotional ringer. I loved it! ... This saga may be about the people orbiting a BDSM club at least on the surface but in reality it's about a family. Individuals who have bonded together to become something more. Beautiful and powerful!"

~ **Shauni S., Tea and Book**

~ ~ ~

[This book] was one novel I have been eagerly anticipating. It was well worth the wait and is probably my favorite book of the series because of the myriad of emotions it brought forth from tears and sadness to laughter and joy. I was drawn into the story from the first page and long after having finished it I am still thinking about each person and their journey to happiness. I just wish I had more than five stars to give to this amazing book...While *Somebody's Angel* focuses on Marc and Angelina's story, we are able to revisit those friends we have made in the previous books. I am so glad that we were able to spend time with Karla and Adam as they work through their issues typical to first time parents. We also were able to see more of Savi and Damien's story.

~ **Robin, Sizzling Hot Books**

~ ~ ~

An exciting journey/roller coaster ride that has romance, kink, past secrets revealed, action, emotional catharsis, and a happy 'ending'.... Of course, with Kallypso Masters' saga, it never really ends because we can look forward to reading more about our Masters lives in her next book! This book is completely different than the first [three]—keeping the series more interesting, yet still giving the reader important snippets of the other Masters lives. *Somebody's Angel* is fulfilling yet makes you hungry for more!

~ **Eva M., Amazon Review**

Rescue Me Saga
Reading Order

Not stand-alone novels
(These love stories can't be contained within one book! In a saga, of course,
characters recur to continue working on real-life problems in later books.)

These four titles are available in e-book and print formats, and will be coming
in 2014 in audiobook form (digital only), narrated by the award-winning team
of Phil Gigante and Natalie Ross.

Masters at Arms & Nobody's Angel (Combined Volume)
Nobody's Hero
Nobody's Perfect
Somebody's Angel

Next expected title in series:

Nobody's Dream

Also available in Spanish editions:

Sargentos Marines (*Masters at Arms* in English)
El Ángel de Nadie (*Nobody's Angel* in English)
El Héroe de Nadie (*Nobody's Hero* in English)

Additional titles are being translated into Spanish as quickly as feasible, but it
takes time to do a good translation!

Somebody's Angel

(Fourth in the Rescue Me Saga)

Kallypso Masters

Somebody's Angel
Fourth in the Rescue Me Saga
Kallypso Masters

Copyright © 2013-2014, Kallypso Masters LLC
Print ISBN: 978-1941060056
First e-Book Version, December 22, 2013
Revised April 6, 2014
First Print Version, April 10, 2014

ALL RIGHTS RESERVED
Edited by Meredith Bowery, Fiona Campbell, Jacy Mackin, Rosie Moewe,
and Ekatarina Sayanova
Cover design by Linda Lynn
Formatted by BB eBooks
Cover image licensed through RomanceNovelCovers.com;
Image graphically altered by Linda Lynn

This book is a work of fiction and any resemblance to persons—living or dead—or places, events, or locales is purely accidental. The characters are reproductions of the author's imagination and used fictitiously.

To discover more about the books in this series, see the *Rescue Me* Saga at the end of this book. For more about Kallypso Masters, please go to the About the Author section.

Dedication

To one of my earliest readers (way back in 2011), Linda Thurmond DeCristofaro, who helped me discover what Marc had been hiding from me in the first three books in this series (even if she forgot what she told me later on).

To Lisa SK, who helped me see some serious problems with both Marc and Angelina and fix them before it was too late—and to Ekatarina Sayanova, for helping me teach them both discipline and the power of the submissive and the Dominant.

And to author Siobhan Muir, my roommate at Authors After Dark 2012 in New Orleans, who realized I needed to give Marc and Angelina another book, even if it did mess with the promised line-up of books. I know there are people picking up this book expecting it to be about Luke and Cassie, but I couldn't stand to leave Marc in so much pain now that he was on the threshold of finally deciding to change.

Acknowledgements

It takes a continent to put out one of my books, one of my editors said while working on this book. Among those who contributed this time (on *two* continents) are:

My editorial "dream" team (in alphabetical order because each is a vital part of the team and brings her own expertise to content and line edits)— Meredith Bowery, Fiona Campbell, Jacy Mackin, Rosie Moewe, and Ekatarina Sayanova. Each has helped bring out the best book I had in me (and all have helped in the past on various books, as well). I continue to improve and grow as a writer because of all that you awesome professionals teach me. Of course, it's those things I change *after* my editorial team and subject experts sign off on the book that usually lead to errors. So, as always, all typos and errors are solely *my* responsibility.

Rosie Moewe for keeping track of my series timeline and series bible, which was extremely helpful in writing this story because there were so many important parallels with events in *Nobody's Perfect* (Rescue Me Saga #3) to keep straight. Her hard work continues to help me move forward in the series without losing track of all those important details (and even the important minutiae).

Caterina L. who seemed to channel both Marc and Luke while I was working on this book. She's also begun to help me understand how Luke's work with his horses will eventually translate into helping Cassie heal.

Mountain_Jewel and Teckla Satterlee for providing invaluable help on the ice-climbing scene.

My awesome beta readers, Khriste Close, Margie Dees, Kelly Mueller, and Lisa SK who read through the entire book (several times!) and helped me fix some major problems. Also to Kellie Hunter who beta read some of the early versions before life intruded.

My proofreaders who found many typos and errors, thanks to Sandy Davis, Alison K., Eva Meyers, Christine Sullivan Mulcair, Annie Van Camp.

Eric Pride, a "master" at the BDSM interrogation scene, for that wild cab-ride conversation where we discussed mindfucks, torture, kidnapping, and more. I wonder what the cabbie was thinking. Thanks also for taking time to check over my scene and offer suggestions for improvements.

Top Griz for once again helping me channel my inner master sergeant (Master Adam). Thanks for your help with the intense interrogation scene that probably reminded you too much of SERE School! And thanks, once again, for expanding my Marine vocabulary to include the awesome word "unfuck."

Kayla Proctor for her help with my Navy questions. Your Navy Corpsman cracked me up with the "they're just psycho" comment, but I played it safe and went with the psychO usage that matches up with other "officer" nicknames in the Navy. Oh, and thanks for helping me get Marc dressed properly for the big day!

Psychologists Jennifer P. and Ruth Reid for helping me understand the psychological aspects of Marc's inner pain and for advice on how to help him overcome that cycle of coping that just wasn't working for him or giving him any peace and happiness. Also to Ekatarina Sayanova, whose knowledge of psychology helped me understand Marc (and intense interrogation scenes) much better, as well.

Cynthia Gonzales for giving me the details necessary to get a certain couple hitched in this book! Your knowledge and attention to detail made that chapter so much more meaningful and many readers have thanked me for helping them picture the scene so well. (I hope my Catholic readers will understand that this is still fiction and I took a few liberties with the traditional ceremony, but I tried to stay as close as possible to reality.)

Irene Eneri, one of my Italian experts, who lives in Italy and provided so many of the translations to Italian in the words and phrases sprinkled throughout Lombardy native Marc's book. And to Maria Cristina Robb, also in Italy, who gave me some "quickie" translations when I was on a deadline crunch for a blog and this book.

My Facebook friends and fans who chimed in over the last year at least on countless questions I asked on my Facebook group Rescue Me Saga Discussion Group or on my Facebook timeline or author page. You always are there to help me out when I just don't have one more brain cell left! With thousands of Facebook friends, there are way too many to name here without leaving too many out (or adding 100 pages to this book), but I thank you for joining me on this amazing journey and for helping me whenever I got stuck on something. I like to imagine your "squeeeee!" when you see something in here that you suggested, too!

The Kallypso's Street Brats who always entertain me with their pimping exploits. And to my Masters Brats (fans) the world around. Without you all telling all your friends about my books, I never would have reached so many readers.

My awesome new personal assistant, Charlotte Oliver, who helped keep me sane since August of this year. I had quickly come to see I couldn't keep up with business and marketing and still have anything left to write, so she freed up so much of my time to allow me to focus on writing.

Thanks also to my marketing assistant, Leagh Christensen, owner of Romance Novel Promotions, who has helped me with marketing; online things like newsletters, blog tours, web site; and my street team for almost two years now.

And to the heavy metal musicians who helped me torture classical-music loving Marc—namely, Mirror Mirror (*Farewell, My Love*), Stone Sour (*30/30-150*), and Korn (*Adidas Uncensored*).

Author's Note

Masters at Arms & Nobody's Angel (now referred to as the Rescue Me Saga #1) was a struggle to write because Marc D'Alessio was the most emotionally closed off character I'd ever encountered. I knew there was some inner pain that made him that way, but just couldn't put my finger on it. When Adam and Karla decided enough was enough and hijacked the ending of *Nobody's Angel* to continue their own journey, I decided to come back to Marc later in this saga when he was ready to talk. At least Angelina found significant growth and development on her journey of self-discovery in that book.

I originally thought I'd be able to crack him open in a subplot in *Nobody's Perfect* (Rescue Me Saga #3). Unfortunately, a bombshell was dropped over that New Year's weekend in Aspen that made it difficult for me to resolve Marc's own inner pain without bouncing back and forth too much between the two couples. Eventually, I realized Marc and Angelina needed a separate book to sort out their issues and move forward. Now the time has come here in *Somebody's Angel* for you to discover what makes Marc who he is.

If you haven't read the prior books in the saga, I urge you to do so, now more than ever. This is a saga, not a series, so each book builds on those that came before it. I can't contain my characters to one book, although I love it when I am able to get a couple to Happily Ever After.

Let me warn readers that Marc is a risk-taker and will engage in activities in this book that go way beyond the Safe, Sane, and Consensual (SSC) rules you've come to expect in my earlier books. Expect to find a Risk Aware Consensual Kink (RACK) scene in this book. While more militaristic than kinky, it takes readers and the characters involved to a very dark place.

Please enjoy Marc and Angelina's continuing journey as you once again enter the world of the Masters at Arms Club family, because you *will* get to revisit favorite characters from other books within these pages—plus get to know better some characters who will return in future books and spinoff series.

Cast of Characters for
Somebody's Angel

Marisol "Mari" Baker—Savi and Damián's daughter

Savi Baker—see **Savannah Gentry**

Evelyn Begali—Mama D'Alessio's executive assistant

Carmella D'Alessio—Marc's sister (the youngest D'Alessio)

Gino D'Alessio—Marc's older brother; killed in action in Afghanistan

Marc D'Alessio—Navy corpsman ("Doc"); co-owner of the Masters at Arms Club; has been dating Angelina since *Nobody's Angel*

Natalia Zirilli "Mama" D'Alessio—Marc's mother

Papa D'Alessio—Marc's father

Sandro (Alessandro) D'Alessio—Marc's younger brother

Luke Denton—Marc's search-and-rescue (SAR) partner who adopts rescued, abused mustangs; he is an artisan who makes furniture, including pieces for the kink community

Rico Donati—Owner of daVinci's bar in Aspen Corners and a high-school friend of Angelina Giardano's and her brothers

José Espinosa—Damián's nephew

Rosa Espinosa—Damián's sister

Teresa Espinosa—Damián's niece

Patrick Gallagher—Adam's half brother

Savannah Gentry—a social worker on the run; in a relationship with Damián Orlando, the man who rescued her from a brutal scene in *Masters at Arms*. (Also see **Savi Baker**)

George Gentry—Savannah's father who molested and abused her from the age of eight

Angelina Giardano—Marc's girl; a chef by trade; nicknamed Angie by Karla and Angel by Luke

Franco Giardano—Angelina's brother; a fire fighter

Mama Giardano (Angela)—Angelina's mother

Matteo (Matt) Giardano—Angelina's brother; a fire fighter; likes to go skijoring

Rafe Giardano—Angelina's oldest brother; a fire fighter

Tony (Antonio) Giardano—Angelina's youngest brother; a fire fighter

Lyle Gibson—business partner to George Gentry and responsible for being her "handler"; nicknamed Cabrón by Damián

Anita Gonzales—a mother-figure to Savi; organist at San Miguel's who took Savi into her home when she showed up in need at the church

Gramps—Marc's grandfather, a US Marine who served during World War II in northern Italy

V. Grant—a Lance Corporal communications specialist who joined the "family" when she served on special assignment with Adam's recon unit in Fallujah; she turns up at the Masters at Arms Club months years later shrouded in mystery about her activities after Iraq. She spent time in Black Ops after her discharge and has trained as a Domme with Gunnar and Adam, her mentors.

Pamela Jeffrey—Marc's last girlfriend; he broke up with her a year before meeting Angelina

Kitty—Nickname for Karla Paxton Montague

Gunnar Larsen—a sadist whip master who trained Damián, Grant, and others; retired Army Delta Force

Cassie Lôpez—Karla's friend from college who now lives in Colorado, a reclusive artist who hasn't dealt with the aftermath of a gang rape in her homeland of Peru while on a break from college

Allen Martin—Angelina's former boyfriend who abused her in the club leading to Marc's rescuing her (in *Nobody's Angel*); also known as Sir Asshole

Father Martine—priest at San Miguel's the church where Savi/Savannah took refuge after escaping from her abusive father's home

Doctor Robert McKenzie—a friend of Marc's who runs an inner-city clinic in Denver

Mrs. Milanesi—Natalia's friend from secondary school; babysat Gino and Marco as children in Brescia, Lombardia, Italy

Adam Montague (pronounced MON-tag)—Marc's master sergeant;

patriarch of the Masters at Arms Club "family"; surrogate father to Damián; husband and Dom to Karla Paxton Montague

Karla Paxton Montague—wife and collared submissive of Adam Montague; singer in the Masters at Arms Club; nicknamed Kitty by Cassie and Kitten by Adam

Damián Orlando—served with Marc in Iraq; rides a Harley; Patriot Guard Rider; in love with Savannah/Savi

Doctor Palmer—Karla's obstetrician

Vivian Paxton—Karla's grandmother

Melissa Russo—Marc's old girlfriend from before he enlisted in the Navy; he found her in bed with his brother Gino (aka Queen Bitch of the Universe to Angelina)

Emiliana Zirilli Solari—Natalia "Mama" D'Alessio's sister; wife of Paolo Solari

Paolo Solari—husband of Emiliana and brother-in-law to Natalia

Playlist for the Rescue Me Saga

Here are some of the songs that inspired Kally as she wrote the books to date in the series. Because each book isn't only about one couple's journey, she has grouped the music by couple, except for the first one.

Spanning Multiple Rescue Me Saga Characters

Darryl Worley – *Just Got Home From a War*

Angie Johnson – *Sing for You*

Evanescence – *Bring Me To Life*

Dan Hill – *Sometimes When We Touch*

Adam and Joni
(backstory in *Masters at Arms* & *Nobody's Angel* and *Nobody's Hero*):

Sarah McLachlan – *Wintersong*

Rascal Flatts – *Here Comes Goodbye*

Aerosmith – *I Don't Wanna Miss A Thing*

Marc and Angelina
(*Masters at Arms* & *Nobody's Angel* and *Somebody's Angel*):

Andrea Bocelli – *Por Amor* (and others on *Romanza* CD)

Sarah Jane Morris – *Arms Of An Angel*

Fleetwood Mac – *Landslide*

Mary Chapin Carpenter – *The King of Love*

Air Supply – *The One That You Love*

Air Supply – *Goodbye*

Lacuna Coil – *Spellbound*

Air Supply – *Making Love Out of Nothing at All*

Styx – *Man In The Wilderness*

Keith Urban – *Tonight I Wanna Cry*

Michael Bublé – *Home*

Leighton Meester – *Words I Couldn't Say*

Halestorm – *Private Parts*

And a "medley" of heavy-metal music cited in the acknowledgements of *Somebody's Angel*

Adam and Karla
(*Masters at Arms* & *Nobody's Angel*, *Nobody's Hero*, and *Somebody's Angel*):

Tarja Turunen – *I Walk Alone*

Madonna – *Justify My Love*

Sinead O'Connor – *Song to the Siren*

Paul Brandt – *My Heart Has a History*

Rascal Flatts – *What Hurts The Most*

Marc Anthony – *I Sang to You*

Simon & Garfunkel – *I Am A Rock*

Alison Krauss & Union Station – *I'm Gone*

The Rolling Stones – *Wild Horses*

Pat Benatar – *Love Is A Battlefield*

The Rolling Stones – *Under My Thumb*

Lifehouse – *Hanging By A Moment*

Leighton Meester – *Words I Couldn't Say*

Air Supply – *Lonely Is The Night*

Beyoncé – *Poison*

Randy Vanwarmer – *Just When I Needed You Most*

The Red Jumpsuit Apparatus – *Your Guardian Angel*

Oum Kalthoum – *Enta Omri* (Egyptian belly dance music)

Harem – *La Pasion Turca* (Turkish belly dance music)

Barry Manilow – *Ready To Take A Chance Again*

Paul Dinletir – *Transcendance*

Damián and Savannah

(*Masters at Arms & Nobody's Angel, Nobody's Perfect*, and *Somebody's Angel*):

Sarah McLachlan – *Fumbling Towards Ecstasy* (entire CD of same title)

Johnny Cash – *The Beast In Me*

John Mayer – *The Heart Of Life*

Marc Anthony – *When I Dream At Night*

Ingrid Michaelson – *Masochist*

Three Days Grace – *Never Too Late*

Three Days Grace – *Pain*

Drowning Pool – *Let The Bodies Hit the Floor!*

Goo Goo Dolls – *Iris*

John Mayer – *Heartbreak Warfare*

Three Days Grace – *Animal I Have Become*

The Avett Brothers – *If It's the Beaches*

Leonard Cohen – *I'm Your Man*

A Perfect Circle – *Pet*

Pink – *Fuckin' Perfect*

Edwin McCain – *I'll Be*

Prologue

As Marc D'Alessio followed his girl Angelina Giardano into the bedroom, he tried to shake the trapped feeling that had hounded him all day.

What the fuck was wrong with him? This had to be one of the best Christmases he could remember. He and Angelina had played Santa's elves to his buddy Damián Orlando's newfound daughter this morning. Well, that had been a high until the orphaned kitten they'd brought the little girl had triggered an emotional meltdown for her mama. Did witnessing that have something to do with his mood?

Angelina rested her head against his chest, and he wrapped his arms around her. He'd found the woman of his dreams a few months ago and couldn't believe his luck that she was still with him despite a huge mistake on his part. They'd been together almost three months, closing in on his record with Pamela Jeffrey, his last girlfriend.

He crushed her closer to him, as if afraid she'd leave. Or perhaps his unsettled feeling had him worried he'd leave her; he'd certainly done that enough times. How could he even think of doing such a thing? They weren't even having any issues worth fighting over. Why these unbidden thoughts about someone leaving?

Marc decided to make sure she wasn't sending some vibe he was picking up on. "You okay, *cara*?"

"Better than okay, Sir. You got me to a very good place, but I'm exhausted." She pulled away and stared up at him, a bliss-filled smile on her face, before placing her hand behind his neck and dragging him toward her face. Her lips were warm, inviting, and promised this evening wasn't going to end in them rolling over and going to sleep right away.

Angelina broke the kiss and stepped back. "I'll join you in bed after I take a shower." She hadn't bothered to dress from their time in the tower room. Watching her strut toward the head gave him a renewed sense of pride in the red marks he'd placed on her ass. The sashaying of her hips conveyed her pleasure in them, too. Angelina brought out the Dom in him as no woman had before.

He began undressing and hanging up his clothes as he continued to analyze what had him so off-kilter. Dinner with Angelina's family had gone well, considering her brothers didn't think much of anyone she dated. The setting had been the picture-perfect, Italian-American family gathering. Shit, despite his being born in Italy, that dinner had been an eye-opener. Meals with his family were formal, stately affairs—seating charts, waitstaff, and course after course served precisely on time. The Giardanos, however, sat wherever they liked at the table for eight after filling their plates to overflowing from a buffet stocked with enough food to feed a platoon of Marines.

The noise level had been mind-numbing, too. At one point, Angelina interjected a comment into a conversation happening at the opposite end of the table before going right back to her discussion with her youngest brother, Tony, seated next to her. How she had picked up on two separate conversations at once without missing a beat both impressed and confounded Marc.

Still, nothing that would account for the way he felt. They'd come home to top off the day with an intense, satisfying session in the playroom. He loved getting kinky with his girl. It relaxed them both. So why did he feel...disconnected?

He loved Angelina and wanted her in his life more than his next breath—no, not wanted, *needed*. What was keeping him from proposing? Angelina had made no mention of leaving him, and yet the thought haunted him, as if he expected it to happen any day.

Tonight, he planned to focus on her completely, worshiping her body. Reminded how sore her ass would be, he walked over to her vanity and retrieved the tube of lido.

Beside her hair clip, he noticed her red hairbrush had been replaced by one with a wooden handle and back. A vague feeling he couldn't even name washed over him, and he picked it up. His friend Luke had branded his artist's mark on the front of the wooden handle.

"*Marco, spazzolami i capelli.*" The older woman's disembodied voice asking him to brush her hair sounded oddly familiar, as if coming from a place deep inside him. Who was she? Definitely not Mama's voice.

"*I'm sorry, little one...you didn't mean for me to get hurt.*"

His chest grew tight, and he dropped the brush as if it had grown red hot. But the voice echoed in his head.

*   *   *

Angelina, don't even go there.

Marc had seemed so distant when she'd come out of the shower. He'd applied the soothing ointment to her burning butt. However, before they could make love, he pleaded exhaustion and rolled over. His uneven breathing made her doubt he slept despite the hours they'd lain here, which only left her to wonder what had changed his mood.

The day had been so good. Even her four brothers had played nice at Mama's for Christmas dinner. Although they never liked anyone she dated, they knew she was more serious about Marc than she had been about any past relationships.

So why did she get the feeling Marc was retreating from her?

From the night they'd met at Rico's, he'd gone hot and cold on her. Sometimes she wondered if planning a future for them might just lead to heartache. Could he ever commit to something more than living together?

She reminded herself again not to be so pessimistic. Marc just happened to be a very private man. He shared himself with her in amazing ways, becoming more creative the better they got to know each other. Hard to believe they were living together already having only met in September, well not counting that time she had no memory of in August.

Maybe they'd just moved too quickly. She yawned, and her eyelids drooped. She'd give him time…

"*Mamma, no!*"

Angelina jolted awake and turned to find Marc lying on his stomach, punching at the pillow underneath his head.

"*Scusami! Scusami!*"

"Marc, wake up! You're dreaming."

Her words had no effect. His face turned toward her, perspiration plastering his hair to his forehead. The light from the bathroom showed the torment on his face.

Marc had always been plagued by nightmares but had never called out to anyone in Italian before. Other nights, she'd always thought he was remembering combat duty in Iraq. He'd taught her soon after she moved in here never to touch him while he slept without announcing herself, but his

3

continued thrashing told her he wasn't hearing her.

Without warning, he rolled toward her and onto his back. His swinging arm sucker punched her. Regaining her breath after a moment, she straddled his waist, her sore butt burning against his skin as he tried to buck her off.

She grabbed his wrists to hold him down. "Marc! Wake up! You're scaring me!"

His brows scrunched in confusion. Had he heard her now? His eyelids fluttered open, and he stopped struggling. He'd come out of it. Thank God.

"You had a nightmare."

He reached up to brush the hair from her face. "Are you okay, *cara?*"

"I'm fine, but you scared the crap out of me. What was that all about?"

His face grew puzzled. "Strangest dream. A woman I called *mamma* who wasn't Mama. And Gino and I were in combat but on opposing sides. Then there was a wolf."

She grinned at him. "No more leftover lasagna before bedtime." She bent to place a kiss on his cheek before stretching out beside him. She needed to comfort him rather than go back to sleep, as if she could sleep now anyway.

He stroked her belly, and she winced when he touched where he'd punched her.

"What's wrong? Did I hurt you?"

Angelina stroked his chest, fingers running through the sprinkling of hair. "I'm fine, Marc. You scared me more than anything. I've never heard you talk in your sleep before. Or scream like that."

"What did I say?"

"Mostly yelling at your mama not to leave you. You said you had a different mama in the dream?"

He nodded before shrugging. "Maybe not. She looked a bit like Mama, only…younger than I can remember her."

She felt his heartbeat returning to normal under her hand. "Oh, and you kept saying you were sorry about something."

He stopped breathing. "Did I say who I was speaking to?"

"No. Do you remember from the dream?"

He shook his head. "No, I don't remember much of anything now." He turned on his side and pulled her against him. "Sorry I woke you, *cara*. Let's go back to sleep."

A kiss on her shoulder blade sent a thrill down her spine. Did he really want to sleep—or was he finally going to make love to her the way she'd hoped he would after her shower?

The way his arm grew heavier gave her the answer. Soon his breathing was slow and even.

At least one of them could sleep. Visions of a wolf now invaded her thoughts—specifically, the wolf mask Marc wore the night he rescued her at the club. She hadn't told him what she'd done to it yet. He hadn't replaced it, thank goodness.

Maybe Marc's days of wearing a mask were over. *Dio*, she hoped so. Slowly over the months he'd given her more and more tiny glimpses into his soul while still keeping so much to himself. The man was more private than anyone she'd ever met.

What secrets does that mind of yours hold back from me, Sir?

Chapter One

ngelina's heart fluttered wildly as she got out of Marc's Porsche. She stared up at the imposing resort lodge while Marc gave the keys to the valet. So far out of her league. What if they didn't like her?

"Breathe, *cara*," Marc whispered, wrapping his arm around her waist and holding her against his side.

She gained courage from his touch but couldn't remain plastered to him all weekend. With a smile, she glanced up at him. "I'll be fine."

"They're going to love you, *amore*. Stop worrying."

Easy for him to say when he belonged here. He'd grown up in this place; she was the interloper. What if his family thought she'd just latched onto Marc for his money? Or worse, that she was a kinky deviant? After all, they already knew about his predilection to kink, from what Marc had told her.

Had he told his mama where he'd met Angelina? Her heart thudded to a momentary halt. They weren't going to like her. Not one bit.

"Here they come."

She spotted a doorman approaching before noticing Marc's gaze was focused on the driveway where Savi Baker's car was pulling up, driven by Damián. Reinforcements. They could help convince his family she was a nice, normal, loving person.

Of course, as the Masters at Arms Club's sadist Service Top, Damián might not be the best one to vouch for normal. She smiled, remembering the first time she'd seen Damián at the club that disastrous night Allen Martin had taken Angelina there to introduce her to his twisted brand of BDSM. Now she understood Allen's actions were nothing short of abuse. When she shuddered, Marc drew her even closer. She'd been forbidden to think about Allen again, so she let him believe she was just chilled by the mountain air.

Luckily, their friends provided an excellent distraction. With a wave, Damián handed his keys to the valet and immediately moved to the open trunk to remove his family's luggage before the bellman came back with a cart.

Marc cleared his throat. "Damián, why don't we all get checked into our rooms and meet down here again in about two hours?" He squeezed Angelina's hand and grinned at her before leaning down to whisper in her ear. "That should give us time to relieve some of your tension, *amore*."

Angelina's clit sparked to life as heat infused her face, and her body began anticipating his offer of some much-needed release during those two hours. At the thought of being turned over his knee for an erotic spanking, she relaxed a little and grinned. She'd come to love those for…stress relief. Just what she needed—provided her screams didn't bring any family members running to the rescue.

She turned and watched Savi brush Marisol's bangs away from her eyes. What a beautiful little girl. Savi turned her gaze toward Angelina and Marc. "Perfect. Mari's been so wound up about this trip; she could use a little rest before we take to the slopes or whatever it is you all want to do." She looked at Damián, who only nodded. Skiing wasn't an option for him, but the proud new papa insisted that Marisol take a lesson or two from Marc on the bunny slope.

Twenty minutes later, they were upstairs in their suite. Angelina released a huge sigh. Everyone in the lobby had seemed to be watching her. Uncertain which were Marc's family members, if any, and which were hotel staff or resort guests, she'd felt even more lost. Apparently, the family hadn't been alerted about their time of arrival. Odd, but it wasn't as if they had shown up unannounced at Mama's little house in Aspen Corners. The Bella Montagna resort was huge, opulent even by Aspen standards. They could probably hide out on the grounds for a week without being found.

Wishing such a thing was useless, though. Sooner or later, she'd have to face his family. Dinner tonight, Marc had said.

"Enough."

Angelina looked up at Marc, furrowing her eyebrows. "Enough what?"

"Enough worrying. They are going to love you as much as I do, *cara*. This tug-of-war in your head has to end. Now."

"But…"

"The only butt I want right now is yours over my knee. Strip."

Her heart thudded, and her coat puddled at her feet. "Yes, Sir."

She pulled the heavy sweater over her head, hearing the static crackling through her hair. He'd insisted she go braless this morning—and he'd copped a few feels on the drive to Aspen. In seconds, she was half naked. His gaze lowered to her breasts, and her nipples puckered.

Marc reached out to touch one. The buildup of static electricity discharged, causing her to inhale sharply and jerk away from the pain. He laughed. "We'll have to explore the violet wand in the playroom or club sometime."

While not on her list of hard limits, she'd never liked the idea of Marc using kinky electricity on her body. If that tiny spark had hurt so much, imagine what it would feel like with heavier currents coursing through her!

Angelina shuddered, reaching for her pleated skirt's waistband before he stayed her hand. "Leave the skirt. Lose the tights."

Her pussy muscles tightened. *Mio Dio.* At the thought of his hand on her bare butt, her breathing became rapid and shallow. She needed this badly after stressing since Christmas over meeting his family. Well, she'd stressed about it long before Christmas.

Reaching beneath her skirt, she snagged the waistband of her black tights with her thumbs and quickly shimmied them over her butt to her knees. She plunked down on the four-poster bed to remove her shoes and take the tights the rest of the way off. She wore no panties, another of Marc's commands this morning cluing her in that he intended to play at some point today. But on cold days like this one, he allowed her to wear tights if they'd be outside.

He always seemed to know how uncomfortable and unsteady she was in fuck-me stiletto heels, though, and never asked her to wear them. A very considerate Dom.

When she dropped the tights onto the floor, his gaze roamed over her bare breasts and legs, heating her.

"Stand and present yourself."

Angelina stood, cast her gaze to the floor in front of her, and planted her feet slightly more than shoulder-width apart. She grasped her elbows behind her back, causing her breasts to jut out. Marc's warm hands cupped them, and he pinched her nipples until she hissed.

"I love your tits."

So I've noticed. "Thank you, Sir."

Marc lowered his mouth to one, taking the nipple between his teeth and tugging until she nearly lost her footing. He straightened and sighed, as if he, too, regretted not having time to continue his exploration. Walking over to his toy bag, he pulled out one of his paddles. She almost took an involuntary step back. The paddle? Why? She hadn't been bad.

Marc sat down on the edge of the mattress and laid the wooden paddle beside him. The turquoise-colored duvet enhanced the mirror image of the word "M-I-N-E." That word would soon be imprinted on her butt. She hated the sting of that paddle. Damn Luke for making it. But she couldn't put all of the blame on him; Angelina had chosen to present the gift to her Sir on Christmas night. She could have withheld it, but the sentiment seemed sweet at the time. Someday she would get her revenge on dear, sweet Luke.

"Kneel." He tossed a pillow from the bed down in front of him, between his feet.

She was permitted to use her hands to get into a new position, so she released her elbows and eased herself down onto the pillow. Once steady, she clasped her hands behind her back again.

"Remove my shoes and take care of your clothing." She reached out to untie and slip off the Guccis he rarely wore, setting them aside. Then she neatly folded her coat and sweater and placed them on the chair before resuming her position. Marc was particular about not leaving things lying around.

After reminding her of their safeword, as if she'd need it for one of his spankings, he said, "You need to take your mind off dinner tonight. Please me with your mouth."

Releasing her elbows again, she eased down the zipper of his black Armani pants and pulled out his penis. She'd never grow tired of the sight of him, large and stiff for her.

Leaning back on his elbows, he grinned down at her. "No hands."

Angelina scooted closer to better control the depth at which he could penetrate her mouth. No point letting her gag reflex steal the scene. As if licking a melting ice-cream cone, she let the tip of her tongue trace the engorged vein along the length of him before returning to the head. His hiss and the bobbing of his penis told her she pleased him. Maybe he was a little tense about this visit, too, and needed this session as much as she did.

Banishing from her mind all thoughts of meeting his family, Angelina leaned forward as far as she could and wrapped her lips around the head of his penis. Her mouth pulled him toward her as she sucked him deeper. At this angle, it would be difficult to bring him as deeply down her throat as she'd like, so she concentrated on flicking her tongue around the rim and paying special attention to the sensitive notch on the underside. His cock bobbed again, and she tasted his salty pre-cum. She grew wet thinking about having him inside her. Soon, she hoped.

"Your mouth is so hot, *amore*."

Emboldened by his words, she sucked him harder, and he hissed again, pumping his hips up until the tip of his penis hit the roof of her mouth. She loved pleasing her Dom this way.

Suddenly, he placed his hands on either side of her face and moved her off of him. Puzzled, she blinked and looked up.

"I don't want to come in your mouth or on your face. We don't have a lot of time to clean up before we meet up with Damián and Savi."

The man's ability to postpone coming was much stronger than hers. She hoped they'd have time for her to reach orgasm.

"Stand, pet."

She maneuvered herself to her feet and took a step back before resuming her presentation stance, unsure what he wanted her to do next.

Marc stood as well, kicking away the pillow and unbuckling his belt. He released the button and dropped his hands to his sides.

"Remove my pants."

Unclasping her hands, she hooked her thumbs in the waistband of his pants and lowered them, taking his boxer briefs in the same motion. His penis bobbed out, fierce and erect, surrounded by tufts of dark curly hair. Impulsively, she placed a kiss on the tip as she continued to remove his pants.

"You did not have permission to do that, pet."

"Sorry, Sir." *Not really.*

Marc sat down so she could shuck the pant legs the rest of the way off. She fought the urge to straddle him, because they were being formal now. Living with him these last few months, she'd learned a lot about discipline. He'd trained her to do as she was told during a scene, not to allow her impulses to get the better of her and not to clutter her mind with thoughts that pulled her out of the scene. Otherwise, there would be consequences. She glanced at the paddle again. Sometimes, though, she couldn't help letting her inner brat out to play.

"Across my lap. Now."

Angelina swallowed hard as she did so, his penis poking into her stomach. Her body was evenly distributed on either side of his thighs, hair hanging loose and curtaining her face. She grew wet anticipating the sting of his hand on her butt. He always started with his hand.

"Hands flat on the floor."

Shit. She didn't like that position, because it left her with very little control—so open and vulnerable. However, she did as he ordered. His penis now pressed against her pubic bone, and each swat of his hand would send a jolt to him, as well.

He lifted her short skirt and his warm hand caressed her butt. She squirmed when his fingers traced a path from her crack to the swollen folds of her pussy. "So damned wet for me, pet. Thank you."

"Thank *you*, Sir, for making me wet." Her voice sounded breathless to her ears. *Hurry, Sir. I need this!*

His finger slid into her opening, and she squeezed him in welcome. They hadn't made love this morning, and she wanted him inside her so badly. However, it wouldn't happen for a while at least. Perhaps not for hours— even days. Sometimes he preferred to leave her on edge for long periods before he gave her the relief she craved desperately. As he removed his finger, she hoped he'd touch her clit and give her release.

Smack!

Not expecting the spanking to start so suddenly, her breath hitched in surprise.

Smack!

His hand came down on her other cheek equally hard, and she squeezed her butt cheeks together. Several more swats rained down on her in quick succession, and she held her breath as the familiar warmth spread over her bottom.

"Open wider for me, pet."

Oh, no. She hated when he struck directly on her pussy or clit. Knowing it would only be worse if she didn't respond quickly, she angled her left leg toward his knee, exposing herself to him fully. He must want to send her straight into subspace.

Swat!

"Ow, *mio Dio!*" His hand struck directly on her clit, and she jerked, trying to avoid the next blow. *Swat!* No such luck. Tears ran down her nose. The release of tension as he continued to spank her left her sobbing; then the familiar euphoria sent her floating.

Bliss.

Whack!

The paddle landed on her left cheek and surprised her, stinging her sore skin and bringing her back to the present with a vengeance. How long had she zoned out?

Whack!

The pain burning in her butt from the impact of the solid wood caused her to clench her cheeks together, making the fire burn even hotter. New tears flowed.

Cool air blew over her burning butt; Marc had finished with the spanking. His breath only caused gooseflesh to break out, increasing her pain. He knew it, too, damn him. She jumped as the cold ointment he applied after spankings made contact with her sore ass, but it soon eased the sting away. His hand stroked her back in a soothing manner as he waited for the ointment to dry. She hiccupped.

"Shhh, pet." Marc helped her up, and she melted against him as he sat her on his lap and enfolded her in his arms. Her butt stung worse with the friction against his legs, but she needed to be held. He stroked her hair, and she laid her head against his shoulder, accepting his gentle ministrations.

"You're mine, pet."

Mine.

"Always, Sir."

A peaceful calm came over her; her eyes drifted shut, and she relaxed…

"Time to wake up, *amore*."

Angelina blinked awake and found herself still in Marc's arms. "I'm sorry, Sir." She tried to sit upright and felt the sting in her butt. His hand held her tightly in place.

"Talk to me. How are you feeling now?"

"Better. Extremely relaxed."

"Good girl."

"Just one problem."

He grew tense. "What's that?"

"How am I supposed to sit down through dinner tonight? You really walloped me."

"Brat. You know you loved every stroke."

"Yes, Sir. I did. Thank you for taking such good care of me."

"You're the one to thank. I can't imagine what my life would be without you. You have given me something I didn't even know was missing."

"What's that?"

He thought for several moments before shrugging. Would he elaborate or was she digging too deeply? "A need to…be needed, I guess you could say. You need me. I like that."

Angelina, needy? Hardly. She'd fought too long to gain independence from her big brothers only to let this man steal her heart away. Ready to argue the point, she opened her mouth.

"But it's mutual, Angelina." He leaned back and gazed into her eyes. "You also take excellent care of my needs, *cara*. You fill a void in my soul."

His acknowledgement of her need to nurture, one of her best traits in her opinion, reminded her why this complex, sometimes infuriating man was worth loving. One day she hoped to see beyond the mask he wore to protect himself—or to hide whatever he didn't want to face.

Marc controlled and kept his emotions hidden most times. So private. Every now and then she'd catch a glimpse of yearning coming from him, a look telling her something remained locked inside. Often, those times came after a restless night with him where he was tormented by something from the past that he never could name upon waking. Maybe someday she'd help him identify and release that pain, just as he'd helped her find release from so many hurts in her life.

Angelina couldn't understand how he could have grown up male in a big Italian family without feeling he had the world on a platter. She reminded herself that his family was very different from hers, though.

Thoughts of meeting his family tonight sent another flurry of "what ifs" rampaging through her mind. What if she couldn't impress them and…

"Why did you tense up again just now?"

Shit. She really could have no secrets from him. He read her body like a book. "I'm sorry, Sir. I let my mind wander where it shouldn't."

Marc sighed, stroking her cheek. "*Mio angelo*, please stop worrying. My family will love you."

"Yes, Sir." But she still had a niggling feeling of doom. If they didn't accept her, she could lose Marc. So much was riding on this meeting with his family.

She couldn't wait for this dreaded dinner to be over.

* * *

"Marco! Marco D'Alessio!"

In the lobby of the condo building that adjoined the resort, Angelina turned. A curvaceous Italian woman approached, long black hair fluttering loose over her shoulders, and her enormous boobs arriving a half-second before the rest of her. Something in the way she devoured Marc with her eyes raised Angelina's hackles. The woman was drop-dead gorgeous, but her eyes were empty, cold, and calculating when she cast a disdainful glance Angelina's way.

Marc tensed as well, causing Angelina to shift her focus to him. His nostrils flared as he narrowed his gaze. Angelina curled her fingers around Marc's elbow before realizing she was being territorial. Not to mention more than a bit insecure.

Oh, as if that's something new.

Angelina glanced back at the woman and caught another cold glare aimed at her.

Bitch.

The word popped into Angelina's head, surprisingly accurate.

"Melissa. How are you?" Marc's cold response and stiff posture told Angelina all she needed to know. He didn't like her, whatever their history might have been. Plus, the perfect globes protruding from the woman's chest had to be silicone.

Okay, now who's being the bitch?

Angelina plastered a smile on her face and squeezed Marc's elbow. As if suddenly remembering her presence, he stared down at her but didn't smile as he made the introductions.

"Angelina Giardano, meet Melissa Russo. She was Gino's fiancée."

Gino's? With the emotion sizzling between these two, something more than an engagement to his dead brother lingered between them. But did she really want to know about the women in Marc's past?

Yes.

No! As long as they remained old flames and in the past tense, she didn't need to know.

When the woman tried to kiss Marc, he turned his face away, and her red-slathered lips branded his cheek. Angelina released his arm—uncertain whether she was trying to put distance between herself and them or to deck this brazen bitch making a move on her man. But Marc wrapped his arm around her waist and drew her closer.

Mine.

Angelina relaxed.

"If you'll excuse us, Melissa, we have dinner plans."

Ignoring Marc, Melissa glared at Angelina again before adding, "Mama asked me to join the family for dinner tonight to welcome you home."

Marc's arm jerked reflexively against her back before he relaxed it again. Angelina wished the floor would just open up now and swallow her whole if she was going to have to sit through this meet-the-parents meal from hell with not only Marc's intimidating family but a woman who might be an old flame, too.

Ever polite, Marc held his arm out to indicate that Melissa should precede them across the lobby. Angelina got the full impact of Melissa's perfectly shaped ass and fuck-me stilettos as the woman undulated toward the elevator alcove. Melissa didn't wobble at all on the heels; Angelina would have fallen flat on her face.

Brass-encased, filigreed mirrors on three walls of the alcove made it impossible to look anywhere without seeing Melissa's absolutely stunning body. Tearing her gaze away from the woman's perfection, Angelina looked up at the floor numbers above the elevator doors, watching as one of two cars made its way slowly to the first floor.

She wished she'd gone with Damián and Savi to dinner at the lodge, not wanting to be here. The red floor numbers blurred, and she blinked away tears of frustration and trepidation. When the bell dinged and the door opened, Melissa walked into the elevator with her head held high, as if she owned the place. She turned and pushed the button for the floor she obviously knew by heart, giving Angelina a smug look that clearly stated, "*I belong here. You don't.*"

When Angelina would have followed her into the elevator, Marc's arm around her waist held her back. Puzzled, she looked up at him as he grinned at Melissa. Angelina followed his gaze.

"Tell my mother we've been detained a bit, but we'll be there shortly."

The doors began to close on a glaring Melissa, who realized too late she'd been outmaneuvered. Angelina smiled back at her as the doors closed.

"Come, *cara.* We need to talk."

Oh, Dio. Her triumphant joy was short-lived. Would he tell her what this woman meant to him?

Leading her back toward the lobby, he guided her into a secluded corner where burgundy velvet covered an expensive-looking empire sofa set between two matching wingback chairs. The furniture surrounded an inlaid mahogany coffee table. The Aspen cityscape shimmered beyond the windows. Marc turned her toward him. Seeing Melissa's lipstick still marred his cheek, she quickly reached down to pluck a couple of tissues from the box on the coffee table before wiping that woman's mark off her man's face.

Memories of the marks he'd placed on her ass from her earlier spanking made her smile.

Mine.

Her smile softened the muscles in Marc's jaw, which had been hard as steel under her ministrations. The corners of his eyes crinkled as he grinned. "What questions are scurrying through that busy mind of yours, *cara?*" Angelina looked down, but his hand on her chin forced her to return her gaze to his face. "Ask me what you want to know, and I will answer your questions."

"Who..." Angelina cleared the frog in her throat and started again. Over the past few months, Marc had insisted she tell him truthfully whatever was on her mind. He'd be forthcoming with her, too, as long as she asked the right questions. She'd never needed to ask the right questions more than now.

"Who is she? What does she mean to you?" *Did.* She meant did, not does.

Dio, please don't let the woman mean anything to him anymore.

Marc's warm fingers brushed a stray hair off her forehead. "She's nothing to me now." He glanced away, making her nervous. "But there was a time I almost proposed to her."

Mio Dio. Angelina didn't want to know that he was attracted to someone that perfect. That beautiful. Angelina could never have a body like that without serious reconstruction. She wouldn't do that for any man. Not even Marc.

Marc grabbed her upper arms as she struggled in vain to pull away.

"The operative word, *cara*, is *was.* I found her in bed with Gino the day I planned to propose."

She searched Marc's eyes. More relief than regret showed, so she let herself relax a little more. "Did you love her?"

He grinned and shrugged. "I was young and horny and mistook that for love. In these past few months, by exhibiting real love you've shown me how stupid I was back then. Let's just say I was a young man unable to get beyond the woman's surgically enhanced body to see the phony person inside." A glint of mischief shone in his eyes. "Besides, you know I prefer yours to plastic ones."

He reached up, and Angelina looked toward the hallway as she hissed, "Don't you dare!"

Marc ignored her embarrassment and tweaked her nipple sending heat pooling to her core. "Marc…"

He lowered his face to hers and captured her lips in a searing kiss that only left her wanting more. His teeth pulled at her lower lip, sucking it into his mouth. Their tongues tangled before she broke away, both of them drawing ragged breaths.

He'd already left her on the edge of an orgasm once today. If she made it through this dinner without yanking him into the bathroom for a quickie, it would be a miracle. She could just imagine how swollen and well-kissed her mouth must look now. She hoped it was obvious to Melissa when they got upstairs.

Meow.

"*Bella*, I love everything about your body, because it's real, not the result of multiple surgeries. But most importantly, I love who you are on the inside. You're nurturing and kind, incredibly sexy in and out of the bedroom, and cook like a goddess—everything a man could want. Everything *this* man wants."

He gave her a peck on the cheek and took her hand. "Now, be prepared for Melissa to say things that will upset you, but please don't take her word for anything. She's never been particularly honest. If you have questions, our signal will be that you will touch the necklace you're wearing. When I see that, I'll know to find us a quiet place to talk before you let that fertile imagination of yours go hurtling off a cliff."

Marc understood her insecurities so well and always tried to allay her fears. She wished she could keep her mind from automatically discounting herself, because she saw only acceptance, encouragement, and love in his eyes.

"Thank you, Marc. I needed that—and I'll try not to yank you away from the dinner table more than once every fifteen minutes or so." She grinned.

His pupils dilated, as if he was thinking along the lines of having that quickie she'd been fantasizing about a few minutes ago.

"We'll get away as early as we can, *amore*. I believe there's the unfinished business of one beautiful woman's orgasm that needs to be taken care of."

Her clit pulsed as he bent to nibble the side of her neck. *Mio Dio*, how was she ever supposed to sit through dinner when all she wanted to do was sit astride Marc's lap and let him fill her completely as they both rode toward a satisfying climax?

Marc broke away, breathing a little harder himself. "We'd better go before Mama thinks I've tied you to the bed and am having my way with you."

"Marc! You don't think she knows...well, how we met, do you? I mean, that I...we...like to...you know..." Angelina looked around and whispered, "...do bondage and stuff."

Marc laughed long and hard as he took her hand and steered her back toward the elevator. "I think my mama assumes anyone I'm with is into that after my little brother told her about an...incident I was involved in here at Bella Montagna in my younger days."

Angelina wondered what type of incident, but he averted his gaze, giving the impression it was better not to ask. Heat crept into Angelina's cheeks as perspiration broke out on her forehead thinking about the implications for her. Oh, *mio Dio*. She really wasn't going to be able to look his mother in the eye now.

Maybe there would be a supply of good wine to ease her discomfort.

Chapter Two

Marc's confidence in his parents' judgment waned slightly when he and Angelina arrived at the penthouse to find Mama deep in conversation with Melissa. Why that gold-digger was hanging around after all these years he couldn't understand. Mama must think the woman needed the D'Alessio family's support to get over her "grief" from Gino's loss. Clearly, the only loss Melissa felt was that of the family's bank account. Then again, if his mother had supported her all these years, Melissa hadn't lost much at all. Coming after him on the day they buried Gino told him what little regard she had for his big brother.

Marc guided Angelina over to where they stood, keeping his arm around his girl's waist. He could feel her trembling and wished he could ease her nervousness. Ignoring Melissa, he said, "Happy New Year, Mama." He bent to kiss Mama on both cheeks. "I'd like you to meet my girlfriend, Angelina Giardano." As Angelina hugged his mother and kissed both cheeks as well, he thought that *girlfriend* didn't begin to describe what she meant to him. Still, he couldn't very well describe her as a fiancée yet, even though he wanted to declare that soon. He hoped taking her to meet his family would help her to understand how special she was to him.

He'd bought an engagement ring a few weeks ago for when the time was right. Would that time be at midnight tonight? What better time was there to start a life together than on New Year's Eve? He just needed to be sure he'd get the answer he wanted. Making himself so vulnerable to a woman wasn't something he did—ever.

"So tell us how you two met." Melissa's claws came out quite naturally. She waited for something salacious, if not embarrassing. Angelina stiffened. He hated that his sweet girl had to suffer through the added stress of dealing with Melissa tonight.

"*Il mio angelo* was in need of rescuing, so my SAR partner, Luke, and I did the honors."

Angelina smiled up at him. Melissa didn't need to know about the first rescue at a kink club. Instead, he'd referred to the night at the bar near her home where she was trying to avoid Sir Asshole, the abusive poser Dom he'd rescued her from a month earlier. But Melissa would probably interpret it as a rescue by his unit in the mountains.

Relief showed in her eyes. "Marc really was quite heroic." She glanced back at Mama. "Mrs. D'Alessio, you did a wonderful job raising your son."

Mama beamed.

Melissa seethed.

Marc groaned.

His mother took Angelina's hand and led her over to where Papa was pouring drinks. "He was a hero in the war, too, you know..." Her voice trailed off.

He couldn't take his eyes off Angelina's backside, knowing he'd marked her as his own just a couple of hours earlier.

"Well, isn't she just the perfect little submissive, Marco?"

Merda, if only he could banish this woman to his sordid past! He turned to face the one person he wished he'd never met.

"How is life treating you, Melissa? Any new prospects for nabbing a rich husband here in Aspen?"

Her eyelids narrowed and what barely passed for a smile crossed her lips. "Alessandro and I have dated a few times."

Oh, hell no. Marc stood taller. "Stay away from my brother."

"You had your chance, Marco. If you choose to be with that fat sow, then...."

He followed her gaze to Angelina, who laughed at something Papa said and hadn't heard Melissa's vitriolic remark. Angelina's body was nothing short of perfect—and natural—and he wouldn't trade her for a thousand Melissas.

He turned back to the bitchy woman, glancing over her implants before he pierced her with a look colder than the ice outside. "You listen to me, woman. If you *ever* say anything to hurt her feelings, I will make it my life's mission to ruin you. I can and will have you cut off from whatever financial arrangement you have with my parents. I only have to tell them what happened between us the day of Gino's funeral to show them your true colors."

Melissa's eyebrows shot up in surprise, but Marc chose that moment to rejoin Angelina before he did or said something to upset the peace and harmony Mama desired in her home. He hoped she had seated them far enough away from each other that Melissa wouldn't bother Angelina. Melissa would love nothing more than to boost her self-worth at the expense of Angelina's self-esteem, and he wouldn't stand for it.

"Hey, bro!"

Marc grinned with relief and dismissed Melissa as he turned to watch Sandro approaching. He hadn't seen his brother since Sandro came to Denver on business more than two months ago. Sandro wore a three-piece suit. Dress shirt and pants were as far as Marc would go most times—and only for Mama or special occasions.

Better you than me, little brother.

The two hugged, and Marc clapped his brother on the back. "How's life?"

"Not bad." They discussed business at Bella Montagna a while, and Marc congratulated Sandro on some of the improvements he'd noticed, knowing his siblings were responsible for modernizing the resort. Seeing Carmella and Sandro take the reins of the business and thrive in the process made it clear that Marc's decision to join the Navy was the best one he could have made for them, too. Being the youngest of three brothers, Sandro would always have been in the shadow of an older brother, not taken seriously or given much authority. Some of the guilt that had kept Marc away from his family in the past lifted from his shoulders.

"Come meet my girl, Angelina. You're going to love her."

"Alessandro, it's good to see you again."

Marc hadn't noticed Melissa nearby until she spoke. Sandro glanced her way but didn't smile. He gave her a perfunctory, "Melissa. Nice to see you, too." If that's how Sandro treated someone he wanted to date, Marc wouldn't want to be…well, Melissa. Apparently his brother knew what Melissa was after. Maybe Marc didn't have to warn him to stay away from her after all.

Smart kid.

Marc turned to Melissa. "Excuse us, but Sandro hasn't met the guest of honor yet." She glared, none too happy about being supplanted as the center of attention, but Marc took Sandro by the elbow and steered him across the room without a backward glance.

Sandro pulled free of Marc's hand and slapped him on the back. "Thanks for getting me away from her. She's a real piece of...work."

"I'll say." Marc laughed to hide the shudder at the thought of how close he'd come to asking that woman to marry him.

When they reached Angelina's side, Marc waited for a lull in the conversation before introducing his little brother. Angelina smiled at Marc before turning to Sandro. Her face lit up even more. She seemed relaxed now, thank goodness, and stretched her hand out to shake Sandro's, but he wrapped his arms around her instead and welcomed her to the family properly with European-style kisses. When the hug lasted a little longer than Marc thought appropriate, he tapped on his brother's shoulder.

Sandro laughed and pulled away before saying to her, "Thanks for taming this big guy, Angelina. I've never seen him so happy and relaxed."

Angelina's eyes twinkled as she looked up at Marc. "He makes me really happy, too. I'm not so sure how tame he is—yet—but I'll keep working on him."

More than taming, she had brought a sense of peaceful contentment to his life. He'd never been so comfortable in his own home before—hell, in his own skin, for that matter.

Most of the time.

Sandro grinned at Marc. "You were right. I like her a lot."

Marc watched a blush spread over Angelina's cheeks as she looked down. *Damn, woman. Cut that sexy shit out or we aren't going to make it through dinner.*

"Happy New Year!"

Marc turned at the sound of Gramps's booming voice. He hadn't seen the man since Adam and Karla Montague's wedding a few weeks ago and went to give him a bear hug. Just like at the wedding, Karla's grandmother, Vivian Paxton, was by his side. This must be getting serious. Marc grinned. Good for them.

"Angelina, I don't know if you had time to stop catering to the guests long enough at Adam and Karla's reception to meet my grandfather, but let me be sure to introduce you now."

"Ah, the fair Angelina! Of course, we've met." Gramps took Angelina's hand and bent over it, planting a kiss on her knuckles. "Vivian and I still haven't stopped talking about that wonderful meal you served at the reception."

Marc loved seeing the light shining in her eyes at the compliment, or perhaps it was there because of the charm the old Marine exuded. He'd always had a way with the ladies.

A little later, Mama guided everyone to the dinner table. Marc was pleased to see she'd seated Angelina on Papa's right, as the guest of honor, but he hated that, as the oldest son at the table, he had been relegated to Mama's right at the opposite end. Keeping his girl's nervousness at bay with under-the-table touches was out of the question, but Mama was nothing if not formal and Old World about such things.

Gramps sat across from Marc while Angelina faced Vivian. Marc commiserated with Gramps who wouldn't get to cop any feels with his girl, either, in this seating arrangement. Seeing how demonstrative the two were, Marc had no doubt the hot-blooded octogenarian did so at every opportunity.

Sandro and Carmella sat across from each other, Sandro next to Angelina. Thankfully, his little brother separated Angelina and Melissa. He would protect Angelina from any barbs shot by Gino's former fiancée. Melissa clearly was the odd person out, with no one in the seat opposite her, showing her current status in Mama's eyes. Perhaps tonight wouldn't turn out as badly as he'd expected when Melissa had shown up in the lobby earlier.

Marc grinned down the table at Angelina who smiled back. He watched her relax as Papa engaged her with a question that seemed to require some thought. Unlike her, he couldn't hear two conversations at once the way she had been able to at her family's smaller table.

Course after course was presented over the next hour, and conversations flowed around him. An occasional few words drifted to him as Angelina mentioned one of her brothers and Mama Giardano. He loved watching the joy on her face when she talked about her family. Sandro teased her about something, and she blushed. Perhaps he needed to take his little brother aside and be sure he knew the boundaries when it came to Marc's girl.

Sandro isn't Gino.

And Angelina certainly wasn't Melissa. He trusted her. Marc relaxed.

After dessert, Marc returned to Angelina's side; Papa beat him to pulling out her chair, but Marc took her hand and helped her up. Wrapping an arm around her waist, he leaned down and whispered, "How are you holding up?"

She smiled up at him. "I love Sandro, your parents, well, your whole family. They've all made me feel so welcome."

While she excused herself to go the head, Marc reflected on how important belonging was to Angelina, as were family connections. Marc understood that need better now, but during his younger years he hadn't felt connected to his own family. He'd never been as stable or obedient as Gino, who always seemed to do what their parents wanted. Earning a Bachelor's in Recreation and Leisure Studies rather than pursuing a Master's in Business Administration like Gino had disappointed Mama especially. Abandoning his role in the family business to join the Navy had nearly gotten him disowned.

He'd come to realize their objections to his enlistment were more about his safety and possibly losing another son to the war, which became clear when Mama and Papa traveled all the way to Germany to visit him after Marc had been injured in Iraq. They'd sat by his bedside at a time when they should have been at the resort gearing up for the height of the ski season, and they stayed with Marc until he'd been flown back to the States.

While he hadn't spent a lot of time here in Aspen after his discharge from the Navy, he tried to keep up with family more than he had before. But he stopped short of returning to live here and helping run the resort. Guilt over not wanting to take on responsibility for his family's business had plagued him his entire adult life.

Perhaps now that he was with Angelina and had seen what a close relationship she had with her family, he would spend more time up here. Although nothing would tear him away from Angelina, knowing his family accepted the woman he'd fallen in love with lifted a weight off his shoulders.

This was going to be a memorable weekend; he could feel it in his bones. Tomorrow he hoped to get Angelina out on the slopes with him. She still didn't enjoy the outdoors the way he did, but he'd work on helping her feel more comfortable there, little by little.

He touched the ring box he'd been carrying in his pocket since Christmas. He didn't know what was keeping him from popping the question; he'd been planning this moment ever since Adam's wedding.

Sandro's voice intruded on his thoughts. "Thirty seconds to the New Year!"

He let go of the box, glanced around, and found Angelina standing next to Mama. While the others grabbed for noisemakers, Marc walked over to Angelina and wrapped his arms around her. They locked gazes. Not waiting for the New Year to begin, he grabbed her hair and tugged it back, tilting her head and opening her mouth. He lowered his mouth to hers, nibbling on her succulent lower lip, feeling her warm breath mingle with his.

Angelina's hands reached up to encircle his neck, and Marc's tongue delved inside to tangle with hers. With blood rushing through his brain, the cheers of "Happy New Year!" barely registered.

Remembering where he was, he fought the urge to grab her breast and twist her nipple. However, he could wait until later, unwilling to cause her any embarrassment with his family. Still, he continued to kiss her deep and hard. This was their first New Year's Eve kiss, and he wanted it to last.

"Well, someone needs to get a room."

Angelina stiffened in his arms at Melissa's remark, and Marc held the back of Angelina's head as he further assaulted her senses.

No escape. He would not release her, even if Melissa tried to break the spell.

But all too soon, Angelina pushed him away. Her face was flushed, whether from his kiss or her embarrassment at the woman's catty remark, he wasn't sure.

Soon they were engulfed with wishes for a happy New Year from the family. When he turned around, he saw Melissa walking out the door. Good riddance. Had she finally gotten the message she had no place in this family? *Dio*, he hoped so.

* * *

Angelina stared out at the slopes while waiting for the gondola to take her back down the mountain to the resort. Melissa's intrusion on her conversation with Damián a few minutes ago, as they'd watched Marc give Marisol ski lessons, only added to Angelina's frustration. She'd do well to remember Damián's advice to ignore Melissa, who had flounced away in a huff in her form-hugging, fur-lined Chanel ski outfit.

"She's only trying to make trouble. Marc's with you, not her."

Damián was right about that and a number of other things. She did need to talk to Marc tonight about his relationship with Melissa. The woman's cryptic remarks today emphasized that. Marc would keep his promise and tell her the truth.

Since that costume night in October when Marc had pulled off an elaborate mindfuck to show her how much he cared about her and wanted her back after he'd lied to her, Marc had stressed and promised honesty with her. Melissa seemed bent on causing trouble, whether for Angelina, Marc, or both of them, she wasn't sure.

The need to curl up in her Dom's lap and wrap her arms around him became so overwhelming that she almost marched right to the bunny slope to grab him. The man had entrenched himself in her heart in such a short time. She'd do anything to protect him from hurt or pain. She'd do anything for him…period.

Melissa's strong perfume assailed her nostrils.

Shit. Not again.

"Marco was supposed to come back here after he left the Navy. None of us ever understood what he was trying to prove by enlisting."

Angelina sighed and turned toward her. "Some brave men and women find it an honor and a privilege to serve and protect their country." Melissa rolled her eyes. It took all of the self-discipline she'd learned from Marc not to claw the bitch's eyes out. "Marc's a selfless hero in my book."

Smiles from an older couple waiting for the lift caught Melissa's attention, too, and she amended her earlier insensitive remark. "Of course he is. We're all very proud of his service."

Angelina doubted Melissa was doing more than providing lip service to show she supported the troops.

"Marc commented that he was surprised to find you at the resort. What do you do here?"

"Do?"

"You know, your career. Job."

The woman's nose went up in the air with disdain. "I assure you, I don't have to work for a living. The D'Alessios have made certain I'm taken care of after losing my Gino in Afghanistan." She reached up and brushed away a nonexistent tear, glancing at the couple again—for sympathy, no doubt.

Gino and Melissa hadn't married and there were no kids that Angelina knew about, but the family still supported her? That didn't make any sense to Angelina, but she wasn't going to try to figure out how the other half lived. Maybe they had more money than common sense.

Dio, please let me get through this weekend without pulling this woman's hair out.

Melissa's heavily mascaraed eyes narrowed as her gaze returned to Angelina. "I waited for Marc to return home, but I often wondered how his injuries might have affected his…abilities in the bedroom."

Angelina shifted her gaze to the mountain again. She could pick out Marc's form in an instant and smiled, relaxing.

Melissa filled the silence. "He was in great form just before he enlisted. I've missed his firm…hand."

"Oh, I assure you, Marc's skills in the bedroom are…" Wait! What had she said? Angelina spun toward her as Melissa's words replayed in her mind. *Before* he enlisted? She had been with Marc after Gino's death? Last night, Marc had told Angelina his relationship with her ended at the betrayal before *Gino* enlisted. Marc joined the Navy more than a year *after* Gino died. Why hadn't he mentioned continuing his relationship with Melissa?

Okay, Angie, calm down. This all happened long before he met you.

But he'd promised he would be honest with her. Once again, he'd omitted crucial facts about his past. Even though she hadn't specifically asked if he'd had anything more to do with Melissa after he'd found her with Gino, Marc still could have shared the information so she didn't have to hear it from the bitch herself.

"If I were you, I'd keep a tight rein on *our* little boy. He had quite the reputation here at Bella Montagna, providing his body and special *skills* to any woman who wanted them. I'm sure he was paid well for his time."

Marc, a gigolo?

Angelina's chest tightened, and she gripped the railing before her own common sense returned slowly. How could she trust this woman over Marc?

"Obviously, you're one to fabricate stories just to enhance your self-worth." Angelina glanced at the woman's 38Ds. "As if you need any more enhancements."

Barely able to rein in her emotions before she belted the woman, Angelina stepped back. *Breathe. Remember where you come from. Your mama didn't raise you to respond to bullies with violence.*

Where was the damned gondola?

As if her thought had conjured one up, the red, bubble-shaped gondola came into sight. When she watched Melissa prepare to get on the car, Angelina decided she would wait for the next and walked back inside the shelter. The thought of being confined in a closed-in space with that woman and to hear any more lies about Marc's past held no appeal.

Was Melissa lying about her relationship with Marc? Never mind whether he'd been a gigolo. She could accept that before she could understand why he hadn't been honest with her last night. He'd promised to answer her questions honestly, and she'd specifically asked when their relationship had ended, hadn't she?

Walking to the observation window, she watched Marc smile as he continued to instruct little Marisol, who seemed to be progressing quickly through her lessons.

Did you forget to tell me something important again, Marc?

Would she ever fully be able to trust him?

Chapter Three

Doubts about her relationship with Marc overwhelmed her by the time she arrived back at their suite. What if Melissa told the truth?

She wanted to explode in a mixture of anger and hurt. It took several waves of the room's key card before the scanner read the code and allowed her to open the door. Zeroing in on the antique, four-poster bed dominating the room and bombarding her with memories, she averted her gaze only to have it alight on the toy bag in the corner of the closet. Black spots danced in her eyes.

Breathe, cara.

At the moment, she didn't want to hear Marc's voice, real or imagined. She crawled onto the bed and curled into a ball. The lightheadedness diminished as she laid there before the burning tears started to fall.

Stop! You don't even know that he's lying!

But he'd lied to her before, leaving out very important information. She'd forgiven him, and he'd promised never to do that again. Apparently, he hadn't kept his vow.

Angelina wished she were home in Aspen Corners, in Nonna's bed, safe from hurt. She'd let her guard down with a man again, only this emotional pain was so much worse than the physical blows she'd suffered with Allen.

Even Nonna's bed had been invaded by Marc's dominant presence. Memories flooded her of how he'd so patiently shown her the way a responsible Dom should treat a sub. Those images collided with the way he'd concealed his true self from her, wearing the wolf mask that first time they'd physically met when she'd been abused at the club he co-owned. Despite her destroying the mask later, he'd never removed the internal one he hid behind.

A sob tore from her throat.

Mio Dio. She needed to get away from this room. Regroup. She reached into her pocket and pulled out her smartphone. Pressing speed dial, she waited.

"Hey, baby. Happy New Year!"

Tony's voice did little to comfort her. The silence drew out, and she sniffed to keep her nose from running.

"What's wrong?" She could hear him go on the alert. Always the big brother—well, one of the four she'd been saddled with since birth.

"I need you to come get me, Tony."

"Where are you? Are you in a safe place until I can get there?"

Angelina sighed. "This isn't that kind of rescue mission." She named the resort and started to give their room number but decided to be gone from the room before he got here. She didn't want to see Marc right now and didn't know how long he would be on the mountain giving lessons today.

"I'll be there in an hour."

"Wait!" She couldn't hang around the lobby where Marc's family would see her, so she gave Tony the name of a coffee shop she'd seen in town where she could wait for him out of the cold. After ending the call, she dragged her suitcase out of the closet, opened it on top of the bed, yanked her things from the closet and drawers, and threw them inside. She berated herself for being ten kinds of stupid for trusting Marc as she went into the bathroom to clear her things off the vanity counter. After carrying them to the bed where she dumped them without a care as to what might leak onto her clothes, Angelina zipped the case and dragged it to the door.

The bag was too heavy for her to carry downstairs. She should have bought a new one when the wheel had broken off this one, but she was too busy investing all her time and money in her business over the past year. Crap. She'd probably killed any hope of continuing her catering services in Aspen Corners after being away so long. Over the past few months, she'd put in applications at upscale restaurants all over Denver but hadn't had a bite yet. She'd just have to leave the case in the room and ask Tony to come up and get it after he arrived.

Minutes later, she exited the elevator and walked through the lobby, relieved Sandro wasn't at the front desk.

"Angelina, are you okay?"

Damn it. I really don't need to talk to anyone right now.

She blinked through her tears and turned around to see Marc's sister standing a few feet away, her brows furrowed. The young woman had been very quiet during dinner last night, and Angelina hoped to get to know her better sometime. Not now, though.

"I'm fine, Carmella. I'm just heading out for a cup of coffee."

The tear streaks on Angelina's cheeks and her red, puffy eyes had to be noticeable, but Marc's sister only quirked an eyebrow. "I could use a cup, too."

"No! I'm sorry. I wouldn't be very good company right now."

Carmella reached out to stroke Angelina's arm, and she fought hard not to pull away. They were both demonstrative Italians; the gesture didn't mean anything—just as Marc's endearments and touches hadn't meant anything. A new wave of tears filled her eyes.

Her expression growing concerned, Carmella cupped Angelina's arm above the elbow. "Come on. We have an excellent coffee shop here at the resort. My treat."

"No, thanks." She realized she was being rude but needed to escape. "I appreciate it, but my brother's coming to…meet me at the coffee shop around the corner. I really don't think…"

Her smile faded. "Does Marc know you're leaving?"

Angelina shook her head.

"Let me grab a jacket. I'll wait with you until he gets here." Before Angelina could stop her, she rounded the reception desk and ducked into the back office, returning seconds later carrying her pale-pink ski jacket.

Hooking a hand at Angelina's elbow, she guided her toward the automatic doors. Angelina didn't have any fight left and merely walked alongside her down the street in silence. She hoped Tony broke a few speed records to get here—as long as the roads were salted and clear. She'd never wanted to be away from any place more than she wanted out of Aspen.

Carmella led Angelina to a seat by the window and went to the counter to place their orders. Angelina watched the couples passing by, hand-in-hand, all smiles. The pain was too much and she turned away. A mug of frothy cappuccino was placed in front of her, which gave her something else to focus on.

After taking a sip and finding her own beverage too hot to drink, Carmella sat back and stared across the table. "Okay, what's my big brother done to upset you?"

"I'm not going to talk about it. Look, you really don't have to wait here with me."

Carmella bit her lower lip and leaned forward, touching Angelina's hand.

"Angelina, I like you. You're really good for Marc. I've never seen him so relaxed and happy. It's like he's finally found his place in the world—with you."

Tears threatened again, and Angelina lifted the mug to her mouth, primarily to break contact with Carmella's hand as well as to hide her quivering lips. She closed her eyes and inhaled the rich aroma before taking a tentative sip. Marc had lied to her again, for whatever reason. When Angelina's hands started to shake, she placed the mug back on the table before she ended up baptizing her girls with the scalding drink.

"It's complicated. And personal. I can't talk about it."

Carmella pulled out her cell phone. "I don't want you to leave upset like this. Let me call Marc and have him meet us here."

"No!" Angelina reached across the table and stayed her hand. "I don't want to see him yet."

Carmella put the phone on the table with reluctance. "Okay. But promise me you'll talk with him when you calm down. I'm sure it's just a misunderstanding."

Angelina didn't know what to say to that. She was so confused. Hurt.

Carmella brushed her hair behind her ear. "Marc didn't have it easy growing up."

I don't want to hear this.

"Second son in a competitive Italian family is not an enviable position, as I'm sure you know. Mama doted on Gino. When Marc realized there really wasn't anything expected of him here at the resort, he pretty much did as he pleased."

"That doesn't sound so rough to me."

"Kids need structure and boundaries. He pretty much ran wild. Got into some minor trouble, but that was because he had no responsibilities other than a few minor resort-related chores." Carmella took a sip of her coffee then continued. "Marc has been in love with the mountains his whole life. He'd spend days out in nature. Alone. When I was older, sometimes he took me with him. He really is in his element out there."

I know all that. "Why are you telling me this?"

Carmella took another sip. "After Gino was killed and Marc was thrust into running the resort, I watched him start to die inside. It made me sick to see him behind that desk, looking out the window at the mountains that couldn't provide comfort to him anymore. He was miserable but thought he needed to assume the responsibility of being the eldest son and fulfill Gino's role as resort manager."

Being in nature calmed Marc. He'd even managed to get Angelina out on an overnight camping trip during Indian summer. With him beside her, the wide open spaces hadn't seemed as frightening, although they'd slept inside his business manager Brian Maxwell's hunting cabin all but the first night. Feeling his arms around her as they snuggled in the sleeping bag...

No. She needed to stop thinking about being with Marc.

He lied to me. Again.

"Joining the Navy was the best thing he could have done." Clearly, Carmella was going to finish Marc's story whether Angelina wanted to listen or not. "Actually, it helped a lot of us in the family. Poor Sandro was destined to be as miserable as Marc but for the opposite reason. He loved business and running the resort, but the chances of him taking over the mantle of management were slim as long as he had an older brother in that role. It was even worse as the baby sister."

Tell me about it. "I certainly can relate to being the baby sister."

The two of them smiled at each other, and Angelina relaxed a bit.

"When Marc enlisted and put me in charge of scheduling activities and lessons, I was in heaven. Even Mama, once she got over Marc's leaving the family like that, seemed to take charge of many things she'd let go after Gino's death. She'd been so devastated to lose him. All of us were, but especially Mama."

Tears shone in the other woman's eyes, and Angelina couldn't help but reach out and squeeze her hand across the small table. "I can't imagine how hard it must have been for all of you to lose your brother. I have four, and if anything..." She couldn't even continue that unfathomable thought.

Mio Dio, she hoped Tony would take it slow on the mountain roads tonight. What if he...? Her heart pounded in her ears. She wanted to call him, tell him she was okay now and to slow down, but she didn't want him to answer the phone while he was driving either.

What a mess she'd made of things, acting part drama queen, part teenager. Why did she jump to the worst possible conclusion without even talking with Marc? If he truly had lied to her, she could deal with that later. She needed to go back to the resort and wait for Marc to come in off the slopes. He deserved a chance to explain what had happened with Melissa after Gino died, rather than have her jump to conclusions based on what a vindictive old flame had said. That woman wasn't one to be trusted. She obviously still had a thing for Marc. Who could blame her?

"Tell me about Melissa and Marc's relationship."

Carmella's eyes narrowed, and her lips tightened. "Is that what this is about? What did that money-grubbing piece of shit say to upset you?"

The vehemence in her tone took Angelina by surprise. She'd been so sweet a moment ago, but now the youngest D'Alessio appeared as though she could spit nails. Angelina was thankful the emotion wasn't aimed at her.

"I just need to know what kind of relationship she has…*had*… with Marc."

"Oh, it's definitely *had*. He hasn't had anything to do with her since before he joined the Navy."

So Melissa had told the truth then. There *had* been something between them after Gino's death. Angelina's temples throbbed as she tried to process that information. She wished she'd ordered some brandy in her cappuccino.

"In the months after Gino's funeral, Melissa kept trying to get me to help her end up back in Marc's good graces, but he wanted nothing to do with her."

Angelina relaxed a bit.

"Watching my dead brother's fiancée throwing herself at another of my brothers such a short time after Gino was buried made it clear what she was after: money. Marc isn't stupid. He saw her for what she was. But Mama seems oblivious to this day, which is so unlike her. She's a shrewd woman."

"I can't imagine that Marc would want to be in a relationship with someone his brother loved." And stole from him.

"No, but…" She took stock of her empty mug. "I think we might need refills."

Crap. Something told her this wasn't going to be a story she wanted to hear.

She peered outside and saw that the sun had set, and lights had come on to illuminate the street. Most of the shops were open late, despite the holiday, and a few other restaurants were doing a thriving business. The beautiful people came here to play and shop, especially on a holiday weekend.

Dio, Marc would never have fit in here. He hated pretentious, phony people.

People like Melissa.

Carmella placed the new drinks in front of each of them and resumed her seat, bringing Angelina's attention back to the conversation at hand.

Angelina might not discover the truth without this woman's help. "What happened between them?"

Carmella's mouth hitched up, and she sighed. "The night before Marc left to train at Naval Station Great Lakes, he announced to Mama and the family that he was leaving. Melissa was there, too. Mama has always treated her as if she and Gino had been married or something. The two of them have some odd connection that Sandro and I have never quite figured out."

Angelina wanted to know what had happened between Marc and Melissa. There were so many unanswered questions and getting Marc to talk about his past was worse than pulling teeth.

"I noticed that her presence at dinner last night made Marc very nervous."

"Because of you."

"Me?" Was Marc ashamed of her because she could never measure up to this woman from his past?

"Melissa can be a real *bitch* and has been for as long as I've known her. I think Marc was afraid Melissa would say or do something that would hurt you."

Oh, of course! Why had she thought the worst first? Probably because she hadn't forgotten the way she'd felt the first time he lied to her.

"She's been known to go for the jugular to get what she wants—and she wants Marc. Marc's inheritance, to be precise."

"But Marc lives such a simple life. She'd be bored to death with him if this glamorous lifestyle is what she thrives on."

Dio, maybe that's not the lifestyle Melissa wanted to have again with Marc. She had said she missed his firm hand. Did she want him as her Dom again, if that's what he'd been?

The past is past.

Whatever he had with Melissa happened before he was with Angelina. Marc hadn't lived like a monk before he met her. Hardly. She was certain he hadn't strayed since they'd been together, though. No, she'd never even had any inkling that he'd been unfaithful to her.

But he lied!

At least by omission. She waited for Carmella to continue.

"What happened right before he joined the Navy?"

"I only know Melissa's side of the story, and I wouldn't put much faith in that…woman's…version at all."

"Tell me anyway." She'd confirm it with Marc later. Yes, she'd come to the decision not to leave Aspen before she talked with Marc.

"Baby, are you okay?"

Angelina glanced up to find Tony approaching the table, a worried expression on his face. "Where's D'Alessio?"

Angelina flushed with embarrassment. He and Marc had appeared to get along at Christmas dinner. Hadn't they gotten beyond the whole big-brother-as-protector thing? Of course, she'd called him to be just that for her. Well, maybe not to protect her but definitely to rescue her from confronting Marc. Carmella glared up at Tony.

Hoping to defuse the situation, Angelina stood up. "Tony, I'd like you to meet Marc's *sister*, Carmella D'Alessio." Angelina glared at him.

Be polite, you big lug.

Confused, Tony studied Carmella and then Angelina. Apparently remembering the manners that had been drummed into him since he was a kid, he extended his hand. "Nice to meet you, Carmella. Tony Giardano." Their handshake ended almost before it started, but Carmella didn't mask the animosity in her expression. At least not all D'Alessios masked their feelings.

Tony's gaze lit on Angelina again. "Baby, what's going on? You sounded upset on the phone."

She really didn't want to talk about this in front of Carmella. More pressingly, she also didn't want to leave before finding Marc and talking with him.

"I'm sorry. I was upset…but it was just a misunderstanding."

Tony blinked. "Misunderstanding." He stared at her as if to say, *"You called me out on a night like this for a misunderstanding?"*

Rather than give him an explanation, Angelina reached for her mug and started clearing her place at the small table. "Yes, and I hate that I got you all the way up here for nothing. Can I get you a coffee or something for the road?" She reached down to pick up her purse.

"You aren't coming back with me?"

"No. Really, Tony, I'm sorry. I was…" *…acting like a child…* "Misinformed. It's really embarrassing, but everything's all right. I'm sure."

"You don't sound sure. Where's D'Alessio?" Out of the corner of her eye, Angelina saw Carmella stiffen. Tony must have, too, because he amended quickly, "Marc."

"He's out giving ski lessons to a friend's daughter. He'll be back soon."

Tony shifted his weight. "You sure you don't want me to stick around? Wait for him to get back off the mountain?"

Clearly Tony didn't believe she was okay. How could she convince him? She needed to talk with Marc, but she didn't need to have a testosterone-laden, overprotective big brother interfering.

Carmella cleared her mug and napkin from the table. "I'd better get back to work. Angelina, any time you need to talk, just let me know."

Tony watched Marc's sister get up to leave. "We'll walk back with you. It's getting dark."

Angelina tried to hide her smile, feeling sorry for Carmella who was now, by virtue of her feminine parts, on this overprotective Italian male's radar, too.

Carmella seemed confused before surprising her by smiling at his concern. "This is Aspen. We have a very low crime rate. I walk around alone at night all the time."

Angelina reached for Carmella's elbow and led her toward the door. "Don't even try, Carmella. We're heading back—together."

Tony remained at Angelina's side as they walked down the street, but he didn't say anything more.

"Carmella, thanks for talking me out of making a big mistake."

"What are friends for?"

Angelina hurried along, not wanting Tony to stay too late and drive home on near-deserted mountain roads.

"Mr. Giardano, I'm sorry we don't have any vacant rooms. Otherwise, I'd offer you a place to sleep tonight before heading back."

"The name's Tony, and that's okay. I'm on duty tomorrow morning at the fire station. I need to get back tonight."

"Tony, I'm so sorry I dragged you up here." *Dio*, what a mess she'd made of things for everyone. As they walked into the entrance to the lodge, Angelina said "Look, we're here, safe and sound. You need to get back on the road before it gets much darker."

After Carmella said good-bye and excused herself, Tony turned Angelina to face him, placing his hands on her upper arms. "What's going on, baby girl?"

She sighed. She really *had* acted like a baby tonight. "Tony, it's between Marc and me. We just need to talk about some things. I'm sure we'll clear everything up tonight."

"You sure?"

"Yeah, I'm sure." She pulled him down by a hand on his shoulder and kissed his cheek. "Thanks, Tony. I'm going to grow up one of these days."

He searched her eyes and smiled. "If you do that, then whose dragons can I slay?"

"I'm sure you'll find some damsel in distress in dire need of her very own knight in shining armor someday. It'll be a lot more exciting if it's not your baby sister."

"But not nearly as much fun." He tweaked her nose.

She grinned and hugged him before watching him walk back out the automatic doors and down the driveway toward where he'd parked his truck. Taking a deep breath, she turned and headed for the bank of elevators.

Would Marc be back upstairs yet? She hoped not. It would be better if she could unpack her things before he had any inkling of what she'd intended to do. Then maybe they could have a long overdue talk. Clearly she hadn't completely forgiven him for lying to her in October about who he was—or hadn't forgotten, at least—but if she wanted to have a long-term relationship with him, she needed to learn to trust him. And forgive.

Angelina waved the key card over the scanner and opened the door on the first try.

"Marco, it's about time, darling…"

The blood drained from her face as she came face-to-face with a very naked Melissa, her perfect body taunting Angelina. Even without her Spandex, her butt looked perfect. When had Marc invited her up here? Had she approached him on the slopes this afternoon?

"Oh! I thought you were Marco." She smiled, but the cold, calculating look in her eyes showed no hint of either warmth or remorse. "He told me to wait for him here when I told him you'd left."

A buzzing sounded in her ears. *How could he…? Wait a minute.* Marc would never have done that. Not in their room. No, not anywhere. This had to be another one of this bitch's lies. Angelina needed to trust Marc at least this much and call the bitch's bluff.

She pushed at the door, forcing Melissa out of the way. "Marc doesn't share anymore, Melissa. I think you'd better get dressed and get out of our room."

Melissa's jaw dropped. Wonder of wonders, the woman had been rendered speechless at last! Emboldened, Angelina continued, "If you aren't dressed and out of here in sixty seconds, I'll call security, and they can drag you down the hall in your birthday suit for all I care. Get out of our room. Now."

Angelina's stomach clenched as her heart beat wildly. She clutched her purse against her midsection, trying to still the queasiness. Standing up to this gorgeous, confident woman had catapulted her so far outside her comfort zone it wasn't funny. Melissa stared Angelina down, taking her measure. A smirk spread across the woman's lips, causing Angelina a spark of fear.

"Don't hang onto Marco expecting to inherit any of this." The woman's hand swept to encompass the room, although she clearly meant the entirety of the posh, European-style resort owned by Marc's family. "You'll be disappointed."

Angelina loved Marc for who he was, not what his family owned. She refused to rise to the woman's bait, but that didn't deter Melissa.

"It's a good thing he found another little business to get into, because this could never have been his."

Angelina had no idea what the woman was getting at but didn't care. "I'd be happy with Marc even if his family was penniless."

The woman's heavily mascaraed eyes drew together into tiny slits. "Oh, we both know they're far from penniless. However, Sandro and Carmella are the only ones who have blood rights to this place." Why was Angelina discussing Marc's inheritance and family finances with this woman? Before she could formulate a suitable response, Melissa added, "You know he's not really a D'Alessio, don't you?"

Angelina's muscles stiffened. If the woman could say something like that, maybe everything she'd said had been a lie. "Do you have no shame, spreading such lies in order to split us up? Do you honestly think he'd give you a second glance after what you did to him?"

Melissa's eyes narrowed. "Oh, not lies at all. Marco's adopted. So was Gino, who told me about it in the only letter he sent me from Afghanistan. Still, the way Mama D'Alessio doted on Gino, I thought he would be running the family business eventually. But Marco never belonged here. And he knows it."

Angelina put no credence in the woman's pronouncement but couldn't resist making it clear to Melissa what she thought of how she'd treated Marc. "Which is why you threw Marc under the bus?"

"I never—!"

"Marc told me you cheated with Gino even though Marc was the *D'Alessio* who brought you here. Did you forget which brother you were supposed to sleep with, Melissa?"

Melissa clenched her fists, but Angelina held her ground.

Don't back down from her.

"I'm sure you can understand why I have no faith in anything you tell me. Now get the *hell* out of our room."

After one very long, tense moment, Melissa turned and went to the bed where her clothes were strewn about. Angelina tried not to compare the bitch's perfect body with her own less-than-stellar one.

Marc's with you, not her.

Damián's words lifted her spirits. Marc had chosen her over Melissa and many other women from his past. Angelina stood taller as the affirmation replayed in her head, blocking out all sound until she heard the lock whirr to life and the door open. She turned to find Marc standing there, his gaze going from Angelina to the still-naked Melissa. But his immediate expression of disgust became one of concern as he focused again on Angelina. His foot inadvertently kicked her suitcase by the door as he stepped into the room, but he appeared to dismiss it without a glance and continued toward her.

"Are you okay?" His fingers brushed her left cheek, and she leaned into his hand, closing her eyes.

I am now.

Angelina opened her eyes and smiled as she gazed up at him. Why had she let her old insecurities rise to Melissa's bait?

"I'm fine now. How are you?"

Chapter Four

Marc glanced at Melissa before dismissing her again and turning back to Angelina. What the fuck had happened in here? "What's going on?"

"Melissa is about two minutes past the time she was told to be dressed and out of our room."

He glared at the nipped-and-tucked Melissa, who sped up her efforts to get her dress back on. Hoping to hurry her out even faster, he walked across the room and picked up her damned stilettos, handing them to her.

"Here. You can finish dressing in the hallway."

"Marco, she…she said some very hurtful things to me. She's not the woman for you. How can you want to be with that *sow* instead of me?"

Marc growled and took Melissa by the upper arm as he half-dragged her toward the door. "Because she's real, Melissa. Not plastic. Not fake. And she loves me for me, not for my bank account."

"I don't understand how you could even think that…"

"I wouldn't expect you to understand. Your privileges at this resort will be revoked as soon as I report this incident to Mama. If I were you, I'd start packing tonight and leave by morning."

"You have no right…"

"Make no mistake, I have *every* right."

Before he could open the door and send her into the hallway, she turned and squared her shoulders. "Oh, but that's where you're wrong, Marco. You have no rights here. You aren't even one of them."

A flashpoint of light bolted across his eyes. "What are you talking about?" What game was she playing now?

Seeming to sense an advantage, she stood taller and grew smug again. "No game. Gino told me that you both were adopted."

"Bullshit."

The smile on her lips didn't warm her cold, calculating eyes. "I still have his letter. If you don't believe me or Gino's letter, just ask your mother."

"I am not going to disrespect Mama with such a question. Now get out and stay the hell away from my family."

He opened the door and waited for her to exit.

She ignored him. "Mama isn't going to send me away, Marco. Of that I can assure you." They stared at each other a moment, neither backing down. At last, she held her nose even higher in the air, turning to leave.

Adrenaline coursed through his veins as it had when he'd arrived on the rooftop in Fallujah. Fight or flight. Why was he letting her affect him this way? Not knowing if Melissa still had a passkey, he closed and bolted the door, engaging the security lock before turning to Angelina.

"Are you okay, Marc?"

"Of course." The concern he saw on her face puzzled him. Surely Angelina didn't believe Melissa. Marc would know if he'd been adopted. Mama wouldn't lie about something like that. His earliest memories of childhood were with Mama, Papa, and Gino.

Clearly, Melissa was up to some new scheme to hang on where she wasn't wanted. Marc had confided in the woman back in college about how he'd felt growing up, never quite feeling that he fit in here. Not because he had any notion of being adopted, but because he'd wanted something different out of life than his siblings and parents had. Melissa always sensed weakness and went for the jugular to get what she wanted.

"Don't listen to her. She's trying to find a way to keep her greedy claws dug deep into my family's pockets."

Angelina nodded and came toward him. He wrapped his arms around her and held her tight against his chest. Being with her felt so right, as if he had found a home, a safe place. He relaxed for the first time since he'd found Melissa in their room and cupped Angelina's chin as he lifted her face to his, bending to kiss her.

She pushed at his chest instead. "No, Marc. We need to talk."

He tore his gaze away from her full lips but chose to ignore her words as he bent to nuzzle her neck. They hadn't touched since this morning.

She wrenched herself away and put several feet between them. "No!" She bowed her head. "I mean, not yet, anyway."

Her nipples pebbled, and he ached to take one between his teeth. "Damn your timing, pet. I missed you today." When he moved toward her, she held up her hands.

"Marc, we *need* to talk."

Talk was the last thing Marc needed right now. Undeterred, he pulled her stiff body to him, nipped her earlobe, and whispered. "Talk about what, *cara mia?* How I'm going to turn you over my knee and spank you until you scream for me as you come?"

She melted into his embrace, but he knew he'd lost her to another stray thought the instant she became rigid again. Once more, she retreated. Reaching tonight's objective of having sex with the woman he loved wasn't going to be easy if she didn't show better discipline. She'd improved in her ability to control errant thoughts in recent months as he'd continued to train her in the art of submission. What had happened to throw her off today?

Melissa. It had to be the woman who kept turning up like gum on the soles of his Guccis.

Angelina moved around the foot of the bed, placing the dominant piece of furniture between them. The sight taunted him with the need to throw her onto the mattress and drive himself inside her. *Dio*, he needed her more than ever tonight.

Merda. All he wanted to do all damned day was get back to Angelina, and now she was fixated on some lie Melissa had told her. Finding his ex naked in their room had nearly doused the fires and brought up memories best kept in the past. His gaze drifted to his gorgeous girl who made him want to—

Wait. He looked down at her luggage sitting next to the door. Something niggled at his brain. "Why is your suitcase out?"

Angelina walked toward the door. "It's not important anymore." She took the case by the handle and began dragging it into the center of the room. A broken wheel left a black mark on the floor in its wake. He needed to gift her with some new luggage.

Focus. Broken luggage wasn't the issue here. He picked up the bag to carry it back to the closet. Definitely not empty. Then he noticed her clothes weren't hanging next to his any longer.

A sense of dread threatened to overcome him. Marc set the case down and turned toward her. "You were leaving? Without me?"

Leaving me?

What the hell was going on? He'd been out on the slopes for a few hours only to come back and find his whole goddamned world turned upside down.

She took his hand and led him to the foot of the bed. "Come. Sit down."

When she started to sit first, he halted her, sat down, and pulled her into his lap where she belonged. Her dark-brown eyes looked worried and a crease formed between her brows.

He straightened his back. Enough of the games. "Tell me what's going on."

Angelina's chin quivered, making him wonder even more what the fuck was wrong. Was this about the adoption crap Melissa was spouting a few minutes ago? Was Angelina worried there was some truth to him not being a D'Alessio?

No. Forget that. Why would Angelina care one way or another? She wasn't after the D'Alessio name or fortune.

"*Cara*, Melissa lies to suit her own purposes. She's just trying to..."

She shook her head. "It's not her. Well, not Melissa's lie anyway."

Who had lied to her? "Then what?"

She bit her full lower lip to still its quivering, the lip he should have between his teeth right now. His cock stirred.

She met his gaze without blinking. "Were you a gigolo?"

Aw, shit. He did *not* want to talk about those dark days of his youth. He had no doubt where she'd heard about Master Marco. He'd shunned the title of Master at the club and elsewhere, hoping to shed all connections to his ill-spent youth.

How to respond? "A what?"

"Melissa said you used to perform...um, special services here at the resort. She hinted they were of a sexual nature. Is that true?"

Fucking Melissa strikes again.

Marc relaxed and forced a smile to his lips. "I see my reputation lives on." He brushed the hair behind her ear. When she didn't smile back, he sighed and grew serious. She needed to know all about him and what he'd been. Truth-telling time, no matter how distasteful it might be to say the words or remember that time in his life.

"It's not as sordid as Melissa made it sound." Not that it was wholesome either. Marc took a deep breath and began, "When I was seventeen, a guest at the hotel—a wealthy woman in her forties—introduced me to BDSM. I was bored, out of control really. It *wasn't* about sex." Marc needed to be clear about that from the start. "There was never sex with her or any of the women who followed. No money ever exchanged hands." Did she really think him capable of that, even all those years ago?

What about…?

Focus.

His pulse raced. Marc pulled her head against his shoulder and stroked her silky hair remembering how he enjoyed brushing it out for her some evenings. Almost as effective as a spanking to relax her.

"Over the next few years, I gained a reputation among her friends—and then their friends—for a willingness to play the Dom in their fantasies. I was more their Service Top, if you will. In-the-know female guests would call me to their rooms or cabins. I wasn't attracted to the women. I would call this my initial Dom-in-training period." He chuckled, but there was no humor in the sound. He'd been so fucked up back then. The women had given him a sense of purpose, twisted though it had been.

Angelina was so quiet he had to push her away and lift her face in order to gauge her reaction. Tears shone in her eyes. *Shit.* Had he blown it again by not telling her about this part of his past? There were many things he was ashamed of and would rather not reveal to Angelina, but…

She reached up and stroked his cheek. "They used you, Sir."

That she addressed him as if they were being formal surprised him. Perhaps she had a need to nurture him at the moment, bringing out her submissive side. Even more surprising, though, were her words. Obviously, she'd misunderstood.

"No, it wasn't like that. They didn't use me. I probably used them more than anything."

She touched her index finger to his lips to quiet him. "You were nothing more than a plaything to relieve the lack of excitement in their lives. To fill the void left from the emptiness of their loveless marriages."

Marc tried not to think about this period in his life. The only void he'd been trying to fill was the one in his own life. She made it sound as if he was a victim. Hell, he was seventeen. Lots of his friends were doing worse things sexually than he was doing with those women at that age.

"They had no interest in helping you understand your innate need to dominate. They exploited you."

Hell, in retrospect, he wasn't sure he had dominated anyone. They had topped from the bottom, getting whatever they wanted, not necessarily what they needed.

Probably not what Marc needed, either.

"I'm not sure my need to dominate was innate. It was a diversion at the time. I was bored."

She smiled. "Oh, Sir, you very much have a natural need to dominate. Karla and I talked about it a couple of months ago. You, Adam, and Damián use the lifestyle to establish control over yourselves and your lives, especially since your last deployment."

"You girls have been talking about your Doms behind their backs?"

She glanced away. "Sometimes you leave us to ourselves too long. Subs talk." She shrugged and grinned as she looked back up at him. "It helps us improve as submissives to learn to please our Doms better, so we share information."

Marc wasn't sure if she was bullshitting him and making excuses for gossiping with her friend but one thing he knew was that he'd fought a losing battle trying to get those women at the resort to allow him to take charge of the scenes the way a more experienced Dom might have done. Still, something changed in him during his time with the cougars. Afterward, he was able to stand up to Mama and choose a degree that fit his personality better. He may have even used that newfound inner strength to make his decision to join the Navy and set a new course for his life.

"I didn't truly find Domspace until I met you, pet. I just went through the motions." For Angelina, he wanted to be the best Dom he could be. After merely playacting at the role for so long, he still wasn't sure he knew what the fuck he was doing. In truth, he'd learned more about what it meant to be a responsible Dom by watching Adam and Damián in recent years.

"I hate that they took advantage of you, Marc."

Wanting to get off this topic, he stroked her cheek. "It's the past. I must say, though, I like your possessive streak."

She quirked her brow at him in question.

"The way you stood up to Melissa…sublime. Thank you for believing in me, *amore*."

She looked down at her hands, twisting them in her lap, but didn't meet his gaze. *Shit.* Something else was wrong. He waited until, in a small voice, she asked, "When did you break up with Melissa?"

Marc's heart pounded again with a vengeance. Would he ever be rid of Melissa and the memories of the past? He wished he could watch that vindictive bitch's backside beat a hasty retreat for the last time. He'd never been more ashamed of anything in his life than his last two encounters with her. Marc didn't want Angelina to know about that part of his past. But he had hurt her before by lying about how he'd met Angelina, almost losing her. Their time apart had made him miserable, even though they'd only known each other a few days at the time. He wouldn't lie to her again even if he thought a lie would be better than the truth.

He swallowed hard and cupped her chin until she met his gaze. "As I said before, anything I might have had with Melissa ended abruptly that September day. Unfortunately, that day also ended my relationship with Gino." Something flashed in her eyes and then dimmed. *Dio*, he didn't want to share this with her. He realized how important it was to have Angelina love and accept him, but how could she love the cad he'd been?

He glanced down at the floor. "While that was the end of any emotional attachment, we had two physical encounters after that. I'm ashamed to say both included sex, not just play scenes."

When Angelina tried to get off his lap, he held her tight and forced her to meet his gaze. "Wait." Her chin quivered in his fingers, breaking his heart. "Angelina, neither time meant anything to me, but…"

His chest constricted. He fought to breathe. He needed to tell her but couldn't find the words.

Trapped.

The walls from the past began closing in on him.

"No, Gino! Stop lying!"

Needing some breathing room, he twisted until he could seat Angelina on the mattress beside him and stood up. "I'm going downstairs for a while."

Marc walked toward the door needing to get the fuck away from her. He couldn't bear to see the disappointment, even revulsion, he was certain he would find in her eyes if he told her anything more. That time in his life wasn't open for reexamination.

"Marc!"

"Don't wait up. I may be late." He let the door slam and decided to take the stairs to expend some energy.

Marc needed to alleviate the crushing weight smothering him right now. He couldn't face Angelina who now knew the truth about his sleazy past. He'd revealed enough. She didn't need further tawdry details.

Downstairs in the lounge, he ran into Damián. Better to keep drinking. Maybe he could get ripped before he went back upstairs. If he was really lucky, Angelina would be asleep, and he wouldn't have to talk about the past anymore.

Not wanting to talk about Angelina or Melissa's bombshell, Marc engaged him in conversation about Savi and Marisol. Marc had enjoyed being out on the slopes today with Savi and her daughter. He'd forgotten how much he'd enjoyed giving ski lessons at his family's resort. *His* family's.

Damián mentioned that Adam and Karla were returning from their honeymoon tomorrow and invited Marc over to welcome them home. Adam had been like a big brother to Marc since Fallujah. After his falling out with Gino and his brother's untimely death, a long time passed before Marc had trusted anyone enough to confide in them. Adam always gave great advice, sometimes as a big-brother figure, sometimes as a master sergeant.

Merda, who was he kidding? There was no fucking way Marc wanted to see Adam right now. The man would probably interrogate him until he told him what the fuck was going on. Marc needed some time on the mountain alone first. He needed breathing room.

"Tell them we'll invite them over later this week. Angelina would love to cook something up. Why don't you all come over, too?"

"I'd like that, but I'll have to check with Savi."

The two finished their drinks, lost in their own thoughts for a while.

He'd come to Aspen this weekend to give Angelina a chance to meet his family, perhaps even ask her to marry him. *Was* this his family? He was surprised how much it mattered that he be a D'Alessio in more than name. If not, where did he belong?

Should he talk with Mama and Papa? Why was he so afraid to upset them—or was he more afraid to hear the truth? Something kept niggling at the edges of his mind. What if…?

No, this was ridiculous. He belonged to this family. Why else would Mama and Papa have visited him in the hospital in Germany at the height of ski season? If that didn't show he was family, nothing would.

Yet, he admitted he hadn't felt a part of the family before that. He was different from them in so many ways. Marc didn't have the business drive of Mama and Gino. Even Sandro and Carmella exhibited that trait. Marc hadn't figured out his calling until he'd enlisted in the Navy.

But had he placed distance between himself and his family, or had they?

He decided to ignore Melissa's accusations. She only wanted to cause trouble. Did she think his new girl was a gold-digger, too? This had all been about her trying to undermine Angelina's sense of security, hoping she'd leave Marc so Melissa could go after him full force again. As if he wanted anything to do with Melissa.

However, Angelina *had* recognized the family name earlier at daVinci's bar.

No! She isn't Melissa!

Talk about insecurities! Shit, he knew she had no interest in his money or his family name. She'd fallen for him as a person before she knew where he lived or about his roots. With Angelina, he felt a sense of belonging. She loved him—and not because she wanted his money, his family name, or anything else. She simply loved Marc.

"*Merda.*" Marc stood up. What the fuck was wrong with him? He ran his hand through his hair. Why did Angelina put up with his shit? Hell, he hadn't even seen to it that she ate dinner tonight. Some fucking Dom he was. "I need to go check on Angelina."

Goddamn Melissa to hell for intruding in his life again.

After determining that Damián wasn't interested in joining him and Angelina for dinner, he motioned to Karen and settled both checks.

Was the family that owned Bella Montagna really his by birth? Why did he have the feeling everything he'd known about himself his entire life would turn out to be a lie?

Did he really want to know the truth?

Chapter Five

Angelina lay curled into a ball on the humongous, empty bed. The thermostat had been set low because she and Marc liked to share body heat, but without him here, she was freezing. Lying with Marc, tangled up in his arms and legs, she'd always felt so cherished, protected...loved.

Dio, she missed him. Her heart ached.

Why was he running from her? Heck, maybe she was the one who ought to be running. What wasn't he telling her about Melissa? If the woman truly meant nothing to him any longer, he wouldn't get so emotional talking about her.

Maybe she should have let Tony take her home after all. She and Marc had a lot to work out, but they weren't going to do that in a place like this. She wanted to get back to what resembled real life and get out of this messed-up fantasy.

Funny, but she'd come here fighting her own insecurities. Marc had worked hard to get her to accept herself as beautiful, at least in his eyes. Melissa's hurtful comments about her weight didn't sting nearly as much as they would have four months ago. At dinner last night, she'd forgotten all of her insecurities. Marc's family welcomed her as if she belonged in their world, and their lives; they even seated her as the guest of honor.

Now she didn't know if Marc was even going to return to their room tonight. She'd been accepted by his family only to be rejected by him. Well, rejected was too strong a word. Neglected, maybe. But this weekend, she had discovered Marc had a few insecurities of his own. That knowledge endeared him to her even more. Marc sometimes had an arrogant Dom swagger, but at other times, he seemed like a lost little boy. He accepted her, along with her insecurities and imperfections. How could she expect him to have none? She wasn't looking for a perfect man, secure in himself all the time.

Still, Marc had been used by so many women in the past. No wonder he didn't trust her gender. Would he ever be able to let down his guard with anyone—with *her*? To think she thought *she* was the one with trust issues after what Allen had done. Clearly, if she was going to establish a lifelong commitment with Marc, they'd have to work on some of *his* issues.

"Don't wait up." His hurtful dismissal reverberated through her mind. As if she could sleep without him.

What if he didn't return tonight? If she had a clue where to find him on this monstrous property, she'd search him out, but maybe he needed to regroup and come back on his own terms.

What was he running from this time? Was it what Melissa had said? He didn't seem to give any credence to her claim that he was adopted. Then what was it? Tonight Marc had started to open up to her, only to pull the mask back in place and run from her.

Tired of shivering, she tossed the bed's coverings back and went to the thermostat near the closet to adjust the dial. Soon the hum of the heater drowned out the deadly silence.

Angelina heard the lock on the door behind her whirr to life, and her heart tripped a beat. *Marc!* Relief flooded her as she turned to watch him kick the door open with his foot while struggling with a server's tray laden with two room-service covers. The only light in the room came from the bathroom. His gaze homed in on the empty bed first, and then he scanned the room until he found her standing naked by the closet.

Angelina rushed to hold the door open and noticed the bottles of club soda and the familiar rectangular one of amaretto—the makings for an Italian tickler, her favorite cocktail. Maybe she was in store for an Italian tickler of another sort tonight, too.

He smiled at her, and for a moment, the world righted itself. Her spirits lifted.

"I raided the kitchen."

Her stomach growled at the mention of food, even though she couldn't smell anything from the tray he set on the bed.

"I'd planned to order you to strip first, but I see you've taken care of that already."

What happened to alter Marc's mood since he'd gone downstairs a couple of hours ago? Who cared? He was back with her. She walked into his embrace, loving the feel of her cheek against his shirt and his warm chest.

"I missed you, Marc."

"I wasn't gone long enough to miss, was I?"

Maybe not in chronological time, but she felt as if he'd been light years away. "You scared me. I didn't know if you'd come back at all tonight."

He grasped her upper arms and held her away, searching her face. "I'm sorry about earlier."

She thought he might explain what that was all about, but he didn't.

"It's too late to take you out for dinner, but I'm going to make sure my girl is fed at least." He pulled away and gazed down at her. "Wait here."

He was leaving her again already? She stifled a groan, watching as he disappeared into the bathroom, returning with several fluffy white towels. He spread them over the pillows and the center of the bed and went to the bar to retrieve the ice bucket.

"Don't move. I'll be right back."

"Yes, Sir."

He set the latch on the door to keep it from locking automatically and carried the bucket out for ice. Soon he returned to the room and placed the bottle of club soda in the ice bucket on the bedside stand. Why didn't he just put it in the refrigerator?

He turned to her again.

"Lie in the center of the bed. On your back."

A mixture of excitement and disappointment warred within her, but when he walked to the closet to retrieve some things from his toy bag, excitement won out. She crawled onto the bed and assumed the position he'd requested. Her Sir was back in control and taking care of her. Everything would be okay. Later, they could deal with whatever had happened earlier. Right now, it was Marc and Angelina and the rest of the world could go to...

When he brought the cuffs with chains toward her, she quirked a brow. "How can I eat if I'm in chains?"

"That's for me to worry about. Tell me your safeword."

"Red." Her heart pounded as their oh-so-familiar Safe, Sane, and Consensual dance began. *But why would she need a safeword to eat?*

"Your caution or slow-down word?"

Angelina swallowed hard to get past the pulse beating wildly in her throat. "Yellow."

"Good girl. Now, I want silence unless you need to use one of your words or I ask a direct question." He reached his hand out to her. "Give me your wrist."

She obeyed, and within minutes he'd restrained both to the headboard posts. She always loved this position, because it lifted her girls to where they looked almost perky. Marc tweaked one nipple, and it swelled to life. He liked this position, too.

Preparing to get into the right headspace, she lowered her gaze to her feet only to be surprised when he cuffed the left one and chained it to the post on the footboard. Her stomach growled, and she looked up at him. "Is there even going to be any food tonight?"

He gave her a stern look, and she remembered her place, casting her gaze downward once more.

He surprised her by responding. "My girl has been known to have a problem lying still when I play with her, so I'm just ensuring there won't be any limbs flying when she gets ticklish."

When, not if. So he was going to tickle her? Apparently, she'd underestimated how many Italian ticklers she'd be having. What did he have planned for tonight?

She watched with delight as he unscrewed the cap on the amaretto, poured a splash into a highball glass, and added a healthy amount of mixer. No ice. She wouldn't get a buzz off that small amount of liquor, but he never let her drink much while playing. She smelled wine on his breath when he'd held her but had never known him to over-imbibe. The man was a bit of a control freak.

After pouring a similarly weak drink for himself, he sat on the edge of the bed, raised his glass and said, "*Alla mia bellissima ragazza.*"

Her heart warmed at his words—his very beautiful girl. He took a sip, nodded his approval before setting his glass on the nightstand, placing a straw in the other glass, and putting it to her lips for her to taste. The bubbles in the club soda went straight to her nose.

She giggled but remembered not to speak as she sipped.

He placed her glass beside his and lifted a cover off one of the plates. Thin slices of prosciutto had been rolled around chunks of cantaloupe, one of her favorite appetizers. Beside them was a medium-sized zucchini, its stem removed.

"Open for me, pet."

Marc fed her half a dozen pieces of the wrapped cantaloupe and slowly took the edge off her hunger. He turned his attention to the tray once more and lifted the other lid off a plate of at least a dozen plump strawberries.

He held one to her mouth. "Bite it in half."

She did so and couldn't believe how fresh it tasted. Where had they found such flavorful berries this time of year? Well, she supposed no amenity was too good for the guests of a four-star resort.

Marc took the uneaten part of the berry and rubbed it over her lips, coating them in the cool juice. He bent to kiss her, flicking his tongue along her mouth as he lapped up the sweetness. She swallowed the bite of berry before opening her mouth to him and letting him plunge his warm tongue inside.

Breathing hard, he backed off. "Not so fast, pet. I want to savor our time tonight."

Angelina groaned. She'd been anticipating making love with Marc for days. Now he wanted her to wait even longer?

Marc took another berry from the plate. "Bite."

She followed his orders. At least she was getting dinner in bed.

"Ack!" She shrieked, jerking away as much as she could when he lowered the remaining half berry to her nipple and rubbed. The coldness of the fruit caused the peak to bunch and swell. He repeated the motion with her other nip and then cupped her heavy girls in his hands as he lifted one to meet his descending mouth. He flicked his tongue against the sensitive tip, and she felt it grow even larger.

Electricity zinged to her pussy and clit, and she bucked her hips toward him. Marc chuckled but ignored her lower half as he continued to lave her nipples long after the strawberry juice was gone. He bit her other nipple, and she bucked again. How much longer would he make her wait?

Wait for what? Him—or the food?

She wanted both. *Needed* both.

"Does my girl want more of her tickler?"

Which tickler did he mean? Oh, heck, she was ready for either—or both. "Yes, Sir."

He picked up the glass with the straw, and she was momentarily disappointed; then he put his mouth to the straw and sucked in. Using his finger to plug the end when he removed it from his mouth, he brought the straw toward her. She opened her mouth and nearly screamed when he released his finger to allow the cold drink to dribble onto her breast.

"*Mio Dio!* That's cold!"

The fizz from the soda made her skin tingle. Her nipple tightened again.

"You weren't given permission to speak. We'll have to work on discipline later. But here, let me warm you up."

Mio Dio, her face grew flushed as he lowered his mouth to her so his tongue could lap up the drink. She closed her eyes and gave herself over to the sensations as the warmth of his tongue and the fizziness of the drink sent electrical pulses to her clit. She hissed when more soda water dripped onto the other nipple and moaned as he sucked her hard peak into his mouth.

She reached for him, but the restraints kept her from touching him. She wanted him to hurry, touch her everywhere, and enter her pussy hard and fast, but he continued to suck on and lick her nipples.

Please, Sir. More!

He chuckled and withdrew. Had she actually spoken aloud or was he just that in tune with her thoughts? Oh, no! Maybe he'd gotten a diabolical thought about where else he could put that fizzy drink. He sat up, grinned at her, and filled the straw once more. Never removing his gaze from hers, he brought the filled straw toward her. A drop splashed on her belly, but he didn't stop there. She tried to close her legs, but they wouldn't budge.

Do. Not. *Tell. Him. No.* Trying to maintain her composure, her discipline, she closed her eyes and waited.

"Look at me."

She wrinkled her brow but complied.

"You are not to come without permission."

She groaned. He only said that when he intended to make her wait a very long time to reach her climax. The bastard.

She watched as he reached for the bottle of club soda and poured a liberal amount over her. The cold liquid fizzed over her labia and clit hood, awakening her senses.

"Dio!" She remembered her discipline but heard the bed groan as she fought the restraints. Thank God she'd adjusted the thermostat in the room. She hadn't expected to be doused in chilled club soda tonight.

Before all of the bubbles had burst, Marc crawled onto the bed, snagged a pillow from under her left arm, and ordered her to lift her hips. He crouched down and used his cold fingers to open her lower lips.

"Bellissima."

For him, she did feel beautiful. Angelina watched as he bent to her shaved mound, and his tongue lapped at any remaining liquid on her skin.

Just when she'd begun to warm up, he reached for the capped bottle lying on the bed beside him and unscrewed the top. She momentarily clenched her eyes shut until she remembered his instructions, and with a deep breath, she opened her eyes, met his gaze, and waited.

He grinned, his teeth white against his olive skin, and she felt him spread her labia open a half second before he poured the soda directly onto her clit.

Don't scream this time.

She fought to maintain control but melted as he lowered his mouth and licked the fizzy liquid from the folds of her sex. He didn't touch her clit but teased the sides of the hood until she was ready to beg for mercy.

Don't beg. Wait.

She fought for self-discipline—but she wanted to come. Now!

Marc rammed two fingers inside her pussy, and she clenched her hands, fighting for control.

"So wet for me. Perhaps my girl's pussy needs to be fed, too."

Her muscles tightened around his fingers in anticipation. She hadn't been asked a question, but she hoped her eyes expressed her need to be filled with whatever he wanted to ram inside her.

Please let it be his penis.

She heard the familiar foil wrapper.

Yes, yes, yes!

He lowered his face to her pussy once more and took her clit between his teeth, holding it while he reached up and tweaked her nipple. His hand left her. She gave in to the sensations of his mouth on her when something cold pressed against her opening.

She glanced at the tray. What happened to the zucchini?

He wouldn't.

Oh, but he would. He shoved the chilled vegetable inside her, filling her, stretching her.

"Mmmph." She couldn't call him all the names she wanted. Discipline. She'd already earned some kind of *fun*ishment for speaking before and didn't want to turn it into outright punishment, but *Gesù*, that thing was cold!

Then his warm mouth was on her clit again, and the discomfort receded as she felt the pressure of an orgasm rising. He pulled the zucchini out and rammed it back in. While the veggie was warming up, she really wanted his hot cock inside her. When was he going to give her what she needed?

His mouth left her sensitive bundle of nerves before she exploded.

"Does my girl need to come?"

Even though she was permitted to speak, she could only nod vigorously and whimper.

"Beg me for it."

"Please, Sir. Please fill me with your cock. Bring me release. I'll be your good girl. I'll do anything you ask. Just please, *please* let me come."

He groaned as if in pain, pulled out the zucchini and tossed it into the wastebasket, and crawled over her leg to stand beside the bed, never taking his eyes off her as he hurriedly removed his dress pants and black boxer briefs. His cock stood proudly erect, and her pussy muscles clenched in anticipation. He quickly donned a condom.

"I think you'll be more comfortable without these." He released the cuffs from her ankles, letting the chains clank as the cuffs hit the floor at the foot of the bed.

She expected him to release the wrist cuffs as well, but he climbed back onto the bed and stretched out on top of her. His body weight pressed her into the mattress and stretched her arms. "Wiggle your fingers." She did as he ordered. "Any numbness?" She shook her head no. "Speak loudly if you need me to remove or loosen them now, because I'm going to lose my mind as I drive my cock into your warm, tight pussy, and you may need to capture my attention."

Her breath hitched in anticipation of the visual his words created. "No, Sir. I'm ready, waiting."

Without further warning, he took his cock in hand and rubbed it against her cleft. "So wet." He pressed inside, retreated slightly, and pushed farther into her, filling the emptiness. His eyes never left hers. Pulling out a third time, he grew steely-eyed before ramming himself into her completely.

"Oh, yes!"

"Mine."

She wasn't sure if he was claiming her or her pussy, but both were his for the taking. "Yours, Sir."

A pained look crossed his face. He grimaced and rammed his cock into her again and again. She wanted to reach up and touch his face, smooth away the creases in his brow, reassure him she'd always be his, but when he reached down and pressed his finger against her clit, her focus shifted instantly.

"Please, Sir. May I come?"

"Yes, pet. Come for me."

She closed her eyes, lost in the sensations. If her complete and utter surrender didn't convince him she was his, nothing would.

*   *   *

Release came to both of them with explosiveness, and he collapsed on top of her, gasping for breath. For a moment, all was right with his world. Angelina was with him. He'd met her need to come, not to mention his own.

When the ability to function returned, he freed her from the cuffs, and they showered together. Soon he cuddled his angel with his chest and thighs pressed against her backside until her breathing told him she'd fallen asleep.

He lay awake as long as he could to keep the memories at bay...

Marc's phone jarred him awake. Sun streamed through the drapes. What time was it? He glanced over as Angelina rubbed the sleep out of her eyes. Her hair looked rumpled and her body well-loved. His cock stirred to life.

He glanced at the caller ID and sighed before answering. "Good morning, Mama." He reached out and pinched Angelina's nipple, but she slapped his hand away, pointing to the phone and rolling her eyes. He chuckled.

"I trust you and Angelina slept well last night."

"Very well." *When we finally went to sleep, anyway.*

"What did you say to Melissa last night, Marco? She's very upset."

Marc sat up against the headboard. "Mama, I found her in our room last night—" *naked*—"harassing Angelina. I'm not sure why she hasn't moved on and left this family alone. Gino died almost a decade ago."

"Marco!" Mama didn't sound happy. "How can you be so insensitive? She needs us. She loved Gino very much."

"I think she's using you. The only thing she needs is your money."

There was a long pause before she said, "There are things you don't understand, Marco."

No shit, Mama. Why don't you explain them to me?

Perhaps he didn't want to understand. If Mama wanted to wear blinders where Melissa was concerned, let her.

"I'll have a talk with Melissa about entering guest rooms without permission."

"Mama, when I come to visit with Angelina again, I'd appreciate it if you didn't invite Melissa to the family gatherings."

Angelina stroked his chest, and he turned to her. She mouthed 'thank you' and he smiled.

"Oh, Marco, are you still upset with your brother and Melissa? We can't control where our hearts lie. Why can't you let that go?"

His smile faded. This had nothing to do with Gino's heart. *Aim a little lower, Mama.*

"Look, Mama. I'm not upset with Gino anymore, and I'm happy to have Melissa out of the picture. There are some things you don't understand, too, Mama."

Things that would remain buried with Gino.

Marc ran his hand through his hair. He didn't intend to talk with Mama *ever* about his past with Melissa. The shame of what they had done after burying Gino…

"Listen, Mama, we're going to head home right after we check out this morning. Thanks for making Angelina welcome at dinner. I promise not to be a stranger so long the next time."

After saying good-bye, he ended the call and stared at the ceiling. Angelina rested her head on his chest, and he reached up to stroke her hair.

"Thank you," she whispered.

"For what?"

"For asking Mama to keep Melissa away from me when we visit again."

"I was just doing Mama a favor."

She raised her head and turned to him, quirking a brow. He grinned. "*Cara*, one thing my mother hates is drama. I imagine the fur would be flying if you and Melissa ever shared the same space again."

A slow smile warmed her face. "She does bring out my claws, doesn't she?"

"Thank you for standing up to her. It thrilled me to see you defending yourself *and* me when I found you two in here last night."

Angelina stretched out on Marc lengthwise and kissed him before rising and resting on her forearm. She stared directly into his eyes. "No one messes with my man and gets away with it."

Her fingertip traced an abstract path through the hair on his chest. She seemed lost in thought before asking, "Marc, what were you running from when you went downstairs last night?"

"I don't want to talk about it. I came back, didn't I?"

"Well, yes, but you distracted me so that I didn't remember to ask why you'd left in the first place."

He reached out to tweak her nipple, and she swatted his hand.

"Quit changing the subject. You always do that—substitute sex for having a conversation."

Because I'd rather have sex than talk about it, cara.

"What had we been talking about when I left?"

"You and Melissa."

"I don't think there's anything else that needs to be said." Marc rolled over and got up. "We should get packed. We slept late."

"I'm already packed."

The reminder that she'd nearly left him last night slammed home. Why couldn't he just tell her what had happened and be done with it? By making such a big deal about it, he would only blow things out of proportion. Sometimes just stating the truth was the best thing to do.

Why couldn't he tell her?

Shame. He had never been more ashamed of anything in his life.

"Angelina, all that happened before there was an 'us.' Suffice it to say there were those two other times, but neither of us needs to give a blow-by-blow about past relationships."

Angelina got up from the bed and walked into the bathroom without a word.

Marc ran his fingers through his hair. *Shit,* he'd handled that all wrong. The drive back to Denver was going to be a long one.

Why was hearing the details so important to her? What was he missing?

Chapter Six

"What the fuck happened while I was in South Dakota?"

A week later, Marc looked over at Adam who had dragged him out of the living room where Damián and Marisol were watching a princess something-or-other movie and into Marc's den. He could hear the girls in the kitchen working on dinner and laughing. Well, Karla and Savi were laughing. He didn't hear much laughter from Angelina. She'd been subdued since they had returned from Aspen.

"What do you mean?"

"I mean besides the fact I came home to find out I'm the grandfather of an eight-year-old." The man had a sappy grin on his face. Apparently becoming a father and a grandfather the same year met with Top's approval. But he wasn't as pleased with Marc. "The tension between you and Angelina is thick enough to cut with a Bowie. You getting ready to run again?"

Marc walked over to the bar to pour another glass of wine. Adam's bottle of water was still half full. "Again?"

"Doc, remember you've told me about your little history of running when a woman gets too close, *if* you let one close at all, which is pretty damned rare for you. Closest one I've seen before Angelina was Pamela more than a year ago."

"That was different. She was looking for something I couldn't give her." When Pamela had said she'd wanted a Total Power Exchange as a Master/slave, he'd definitely run—run like hell.

"You and Angelina are good for each other, but tonight there's been a wedge the size of Mount Evans between you. You barely even make eye contact. What the fuck happened since my wedding?"

Marc took a gulp of wine. "Nothing. We've just got a lot hitting us right now. She still hasn't been able to find a job. Family stuff. And this business of someone trying to hurt Savi and Marisol has us both concerned."

"Aren't we all? We've got Damián's apartment under surveillance twenty-four/seven."

Thankfully Marc had managed to divert Adam's attention from his and Angelina's problems. Marc didn't want to talk with Adam about what was going on in his own life.

Angelina definitely wasn't going to let him ignore the situation the way he wanted to, though. She kept trying to get him to talk about what had happened New Year's weekend, and Marc had managed to distract her with a play scene or sex most of those times, but last night she'd walked out of the bedroom and told him she'd be back when he decided to talk. She hadn't said a whole lot to him all day. Big surprise. But this dinner had been planned for days, and he couldn't very well tell his friends not to come over.

"Don't fuck it up. You need that girl, whether you realize it yet or not. I nearly lost Karla because my head was too far up my ass. I don't want to watch you screw the—"

"Dinner is served!" They turned to find Angelina standing in the doorway, glancing from Adam to Marc, resting her gaze on him a moment longer and giving him a tentative smile.

Walking over to her, Marc bent to give her a peck on the cheek. *"Grazie, amore."* He placed an arm around her shoulders, feeling grounded with her soft body next to his, and led the way to the dining room where a feast had been spread out on the table. Angelina made this monstrous house a home.

Adam was right, as usual. Marc had better not screw this up. He just didn't have a clue what the fuck his problem was lately. Why was he lashing out at Angelina? She wasn't the reason for him feeling …unsettled.

An hour later, Marc watched as Adam placed his hand around the back of Karla's neck and fingered the filigreed necklace she'd been wearing since the couple had returned from their honeymoon. Clearly she'd been collared. Karla looked at Adam, and the heat arcing between them was palpable.

Marc wanted to have Angelina look at him like that again.

Angelina served Marisol a homemade cannoli covered with powdered sugar. Seated beside Marisol, Savi focused her attention on her daughter. He'd noticed throughout the dinner that Savi seemed intimidated by Adam and rarely made eye contact with him. The man was daunting until you realized he was more bark than bite—well, mostly. Savi really didn't interact much with Damián, either. Must be hard to form a family after being apart since their child's conception.

The thought that he might have other parents out in the world some-where made him wonder what they were like. Why they hadn't been able to—or *wanted* to—keep and raise him.

Stop thinking that way. I am not adopted.

People comparing them often remarked that Marc had his mother's forehead and chin. Not as conclusive as DNA but close enough for him. And no one could deny that he and Gino were brothers or that Sandro and Carmella bore a striking resemblance to him.

Marc's gaze locked with Angelina's for a moment, and she gave him a smile that warmed a place around his heart that had grown cold again recently. Perhaps tonight they could spend some time in the playroom before they went to bed. He might let her think he planned an impact session, but he was more in the mood to hear her giggle. Definitely some sensation play was in order for his ticklish girl. He loved planning scenes for her as he continued with her training. At least when they were playing, they didn't have to deal with anything he'd rather avoid.

Karla rested her head on Adam's shoulder and smiled sleepily. Adam kissed the top of her head, placed his napkin on the table, and announced as he stood to pull out Karla's chair. "We're heading home. Still haven't caught up on our sleep from the honeymoon trip."

Somehow Marc doubted either had sleep on their minds, but his words sent everyone into a flurry of clearing the table, followed by cleaning up the kitchen. Soon, the house was quiet again. Marc walked over to Angelina as she closed the dishwasher, and he wrapped his arms around her waist from behind.

"Another fabulous meal. Thank you for all your hard work."

She turned and looked up at him, smiling. "You know I love to cook. If I can't do it for strangers in a restaurant, then I'll gladly invite our friends over every night and cook for them."

"Don't make that offer. We'll never have any time to ourselves."

She grew serious. "Marc, about last night…"

"Shhh." Marc tilted her chin up and bent to capture her lips in a tame kiss, not wanting to go too far until he could get her up into the playroom. The last thing he wanted to do right now was talk.

The kiss quickly deepened, and his tongue slipped between her lips to take possession as he pressed her backside against the island counter, trapping her with his hips. His hand grazed her shoulder, and he felt the flesh rise as he skimmed his fingers down her bare arm until he cupped her breast. He twisted her nipple through her blouse, and she hissed drawing breath from his mouth to hers. His cock stirred.

Weeks ago, as a reminder of something he'd said to her when they'd met at daVinci's bar in her hometown, he'd attached fuzzy handcuffs to a chain and placed them inside the drawer next to the stove. He slid the drawer open and retrieved them for the first time. Her body tensed at the sound of the chain. Marc smiled knowing she couldn't see him as he fastened one of the cuffs around her wrist. He retreated a bit, wiping the smile off his face when he stared down at her.

Her pupils dilated with excitement. "I thought the chain and cuff were for when you wanted to force me to slave over this stove preparing the dishes Nonna taught me to cook."

He grinned. "Sometimes slaving is more about eating than cooking."

"I couldn't touch another bite." She scowled at him. "How can you be hungry after all the food I put on the table tonight?"

"I haven't had my dessert yet."

"I distinctly remember watching you devour two cannoli."

Marc's hand roamed over her abdomen to the thigh-high skirt, and he tugged up the hem as his fingers pushed the triangle of the thong aside and delved into the cleft hiding her bare, wet pussy. She gasped as he stroked her clit and closed her eyes.

"With you, *amore*, I will never be satisfied. Hold onto me."

She placed her hands on the tops of his shoulders, and he took the waistband of her thong down and shimmied it over her hips, thighs, and calves, letting it pool at her feet before wrapping his hands around her waist. In a quick movement, he lifted her onto the granite countertop. The chain clanked but didn't stretch beyond its limits.

"Oh! I'm—"

She stopped before uttering the words he'd conditioned her to refrain from saying, whether about being too heavy or some other negative remark. Instead, she smiled. "I'm hungry, too, Marc, but we need to talk first. About last night—"

"No more talk. Lie back, and spread your legs."

Her gaze grew steely for a moment and then drifted to his chest. She ignored his command as she nibbled on her plump lower lip.

"Marc, you keep diverting my attention from talking about—"

He leaned forward and took her earlobe between his teeth, biting hard enough to distract her once more. The hiss in her breath told him he wouldn't have any trouble getting her to where he wanted her tonight. The last place that would be was to rehash what had happened in Aspen or talk about what he should do about it.

He whispered in her ear, "I said lie back. Spread your legs. Now."

She groaned in frustration, but when she began to unbutton her blouse, he grew harder.

He waited until the last button had been undone and she started to remove it. "Leave the blouse. Lie back. Don't make me tell you again."

The catch in her throat nearly made him come undone. "Marc, you know I want my after-dessert, too. Just promise me we'll talk later about—"

Marc growled. Her fingers stilled before she complied without further argument and leaned back, propping herself up on her elbows. Because the kitchen island had a serving bar for guests on the back side, her shoulder blades rested against the raised counter behind her. He couldn't leave her pressed against the granite too long. Without hesitation, he took his thumbs and opened the outer lips of her pussy, staring for a moment at her tempting clit awaiting his teeth and tongue.

Bellissima.

He drew a ragged breath. *Dio*, he needed her. Like a starving man, he lowered his mouth to her waiting treasure. The musky scent that was Angelina's essence reached him before his tongue lapped at her wet pussy.

Mine.

Never again would he share her with anyone. Thank God he'd come to his senses before he'd let things with Luke go too far. He tongued the side of her hood, and her hips jerked.

Marc pulled away. "Lie still, pet, and remain quiet. Remember your discipline."

"Yes, Sir." The breathy note in her voice made his cock strain against his pants. He wasn't sure how long he could hold out. Plans to go up to the playroom with her flew out the window. He could play with Angelina anywhere he wished, and right now, the kitchen seemed the perfect place. He lowered his head again and teased her clit outside of its hood.

Her sharp intake of breath was all the encouragement he needed, and he flicked his tongue against her before he reached up and pinched her still-clothed nipple. No time to strip her now.

*   *   *

The abrasion of blouse and bra against her nipples sent a peculiar zing up Angelina's chest to her chin. Feeling his tongue on her clit short-circuited her brain again. She knew they hadn't resolved anything. Last night they hadn't even slept in the same bed. He refused to talk with her about both Melissa and the possibility of his being adopted. Getting him to talk with his parents to find out the truth had been equally impossible.

Frustrating man. He'd been pulling away from her emotionally more each day, but in this moment, she'd settle for an explosive physical connection even if she never got him to confide his feelings to her.

They'd get over this bump in their relationship faster if he'd just open up to her more. Right now, though, she was the one opening up to him— physically, at least. The man had a way of getting her to forget everything when he was in Dom mode or when he was going down on her.

His tongue worked its magic, laving the sides of her hood, teasing her to the brink of an orgasm several times, but her mind kept drifting back to the issues facing them since Aspen. Of course, he was teasing her, too. Every time she thought she might come, he moved away from her clit to tongue her pussy hole, never letting her explode. His finger grazed her asshole, and she nearly catapulted off the counter. She loved when he touched her there. It had taken weeks of preparation to get her ready to take him anally the first time. Now it was one of her favorite positions.

"Stay here."

As if she had a choice. She giggled and took a deep breath as she watched Marc walk into the hallway. He wouldn't leave her alone and restrained more than a couple of minutes. Soon he returned with his toy bag slung over his shoulder and a sofa pillow under his arm. The man always saw to her comfort and must have known that the counter pressing against her shoulder blades was beginning to hurt, even though she hadn't complained out loud. "Your ass is mine."

"Yes, Sir, it is." What was he planning? Impact play or—

"Turn over."

Oh, yes! Please, please, please!

Marc placed the pillow on the counter behind her and helped her roll over into position, the juncture of her hips wrapped around the curved edge of the countertop.

"Hold on."

She reached up and grabbed onto the bar shelf above the counter. He unzipped the bag, and she waited, wondering what he planned for her. She didn't have long to wait.

Swat!

Impact play. Much as she loved the crop he was using, she'd hoped for something much more intimate. He continued to swat her several more times, though, and her mind began to drift into subspace. Yes. She needed this.

Cold lube trickled against her anus, and she jumped. Marc touched his finger against her asshole, and she pressed back against him, welcoming him inside. Yes! Another finger followed.

"So tight. It's been a while since you've had a plug—or me—up there. Are you going to be ready for me tonight, pet?"

"Oh, yes, Sir. Please!" She didn't attempt to hide the pleading in her voice and tried to relax her sphincter to show she wanted this. No, she *needed* him to fill her in this special way that no one else ever had. She needed to feel that connection to him again. To hear his groan when he entered her. His growl of release when he came.

Marc removed his fingers, and she heard him open a foil packet. Soon! She waited, her stomach in a knot of anticipation.

"Shit. Sorry that lube was so cold. I didn't realize."

He must have lubed the condom. "Don't apologize, just—"

His cock pressed against her anus and all coherent thought left her. He pushed past the ring of resistance slowly, but the burning had barely begun when he rammed himself into her until his hips slapped against hers.

Angelina grunted. "Umph. *Mio Dio!*"

Marc's groan told her he felt it, too. He'd never taken her so quickly this way. Maybe he needed this as much as she did. His hands stroked the sides of her butt while he waited for her to adjust to his size. When he began to pull out, she tried to hold him by tightening her ring of muscles but soon heard the sucking sound when the tip of his penis left her empty.

He reached under her and stroked her throbbing clit. "I'm not going to last long, pet. Prepare to come with me after the fourth stroke."

Stroke of what? Her mind was still fuzzy from nearly entering subspace during the spanking. Marc groaned as he thrust himself inside her asshole again.

Ah! Angelina counted. "One, Sir."

Oh, thank God, her Marc was back again. They could talk later, but having him share himself this way was enough for now. His finger stroked her faster, and she clenched around his cock as he pulled completely out again. She loved the burning each time he rammed himself into her. Somehow her ass never seemed to get used to being breached this way. Each time was as intense as the first.

Again he rammed himself into her until they both groaned at the impact. "Two, Sir."

She panted, not sure she could hold out for two more slow strokes of his penis.

"Do. Not." He gasped for air, clearly as affected as she was. "Come. Yet."

His hand shifted away from her clit, but he kept his penis buried to the hilt inside her. This would make it a little harder for her to come, which was good. She didn't have permission to come yet. She wanted to please him more tonight than ever before.

Again he pulled out. It wouldn't be long now. *Please, God, let her come on command.*

"Spread yourself wider for me."

How much more open did he expect her to get? She spread her legs a little wider, and something hard and cold pressed against her pussy. Definitely not his finger or penis. Besides, he wouldn't enter her pussy without changing the condom.

Bzzzz.

Oh, no! Not the vibe!

"This is the only way I'll ever share my girl and her body, but it feels so good having this vibrating cock pressing against me through your pussy walls, both of us filling you, taking you where you need to go."

His finger returned to her clit as he rammed himself inside her once more. Her body began to shake with the building orgasm.

"Auggghhhhhhh!" *Wait for him!* "Three, Sir."

Only three. She wasn't going to be able to hold out for him to come with her. Why didn't he see he wasn't playing fair? Frustration brought tears to her eyes. The vibe changed to a pulsating rhythm, and she gulped a lungful of air. Damn him and his remote. He was going to make her suffer before he let her come.

Sweat rolled over her temple, and she squeezed her eyes shut, trying to use her discipline to hold herself just at the precipice without going over. Marc slowly pulled out once more, but the vibe's rhythm changed again, and his finger assaulted her clit mercilessly.

"I can't wait any longer, Sir!"

Marc chuckled, the bastard. "But you will, if you know what's good for you."

She came closer and closer to the edge. She couldn't hold back. "Please, Sir! Please let me come!"

Marc's finger left her tormented clit, and he grabbed onto her hips, ramming himself in her to the hilt the fourth time. This time, he didn't pull out all the way and quickly began fucking her asshole with shorter strokes.

Temporarily lost in the sensation of incredible fullness, feeling the vibe being bumped each time he entered her, she held on to the ledge of both the countertop and her sanity.

"What. Are. You. Waiting. For?"

"Oh! Four, Sir!" He rammed her incessantly. "Come with me, Sir!" She wanted him to fully share this intensely intimate moment and not hold back as he had so many times. He'd given her permission to orgasm several strokes ago. When did he plan to let go himself? "Oh, *mio Dio*, I'm coming!" *No!* Hurry, Marc.

She lost count of his strokes, not that he intended for her to be counting them beyond the fourth one in the first place. Marc's moans grew louder as his fingers dug into her hips.

"Auuggghhhh!"

He came with her, and she let the euphoria wash over her as he collapsed against her back. The pulsations of his penis and the vibrations from her pussy continued for a very long time. They'd both needed this release so badly.

Just as the vibe's throbbing went from ecstasy to torture, it stopped abruptly. She slumped against the counter as if she'd become one with it. Marc's weight against her entire body felt delicious. He was with her again in the one way only he could be.

"Thank you, *amore*. I needed that more than you could know."

Oh, Marc. "Not nearly as much as I did. Thank you, Sir."

He sighed and stood, removing his cock and the vibe at the same time, leaving her feeling empty once more. If he'd ordered her to stand right now, she'd have been a puddle at his feet.

"Let me clean us up."

He took the roll of paper towels and wet several. The cool towel against her raw asshole soothed away the burning as he wiped the lube away. He discarded it in the trash and wet another one to clean her pussy. Being ministered to like this was another form of intimacy she had missed the past couple of weeks.

She heard Marc remove the condom and assumed he was cleaning himself off, but she hadn't a care in the world as she floated down from the heights he'd taken her to tonight. She wouldn't let this much time pass between them without connecting in this earthy, vital way again. Marc needed her as much as she needed him.

"Come, *amore*. I'm exhausted. Let's finish cleaning up in here and go to bed."

The promise of sharing a bed with him swelled her heart. He helped her down off the counter, and when her legs gave out, he lifted her into his arms. How he could carry her she had no idea but didn't want to protest. She rested her head on his shoulder and sighed.

He chuckled.

"I'll come back down after I tuck you into bed and clean off the counter."

Which bed? Please, let him take her to the one they'd shared every night since she moved in, except for last night. The thought of sleeping separately at this moment would have killed her.

When he laid her gently on the bed, she opened her eyes and saw Nonna's vanity across the room. She smiled. Everything was going to be okay. They could talk tomorrow. Tonight she just wanted to cuddle.

Chapter Seven

More than a month had passed and their relationship continued to deteriorate. Marc took the S-curve a little too fast in his Porsche 911 Carrera and forced himself to ease his foot off the accelerator. If he hadn't lingered so long at the outfitter store this morning going over the books with Brian, he and Angelina wouldn't be late for dinner with his parents. A psych officer might have said his sudden interest in accounting because he was avoiding something. Lord knows Marc had never taken much of an interest in the business end of things before.

Angelina's silence for the first hour of their drive grated on his nerves, mainly knowing he was the cause of it. They'd slept apart again last night. His patience had been at an all-time low worrying about this visit and whether Mama would include Melissa in yet another family gathering. Perhaps his nerves were frayed at the thought of bringing up Melissa's accusation to Mama and Papa.

He'd probably barked at Angelina enough this morning to warrant this silent treatment. They'd drifted a thousand miles apart in the past weeks. Why was he distancing himself from her?

Because you distance yourself from everyone.

He thought he had changed since meeting her, but apparently not. For now, he was content to leave her to her own thoughts. The expected drama at his parents' dinner party was enough to keep him on edge.

Going to Aspen together this weekend probably wasn't such a good idea after all. He'd considered coming alone, but Mama and Papa insisted he bring Angelina along to celebrate their anniversary. He wouldn't let them down. They liked Angelina a lot.

Hell, so did he.

So why was he forcing her away emotionally?

Because emotions are messy.

Sex, kink—those connections he thrived on. He could make her happy in the bedroom—or playroom or wherever—without having to share his feelings, doubts, fears.

He'd tried to put Melissa's New Year's lies behind him, but something kept niggling at the back of his mind. What if she was right and these people weren't his birth parents?

Why was he afraid to just come out and ask them? Even if they didn't give birth to him, they'd been there when it counted throughout his life. He loved them and knew they loved him, too.

Of course, that was partly why Angelina was upset with him. She'd been after him about getting the truth clarified, or at least out in the open, for the past six weeks. Why did knowing the truth seem like a much bigger deal to Angelina than to him?

The more she pushed, the farther apart they'd grown. *Merda,* when was the last time they'd had sex? Two weeks? No, it had been more than a month since he'd chained her to the kitchen stove. He just hadn't been in the mood. She'd accused him of using sex to avoid confrontation, but she seemed to be demanding more than he could give lately. Maybe she was right. The end result was that he spent more and more time at the store or hiking in the mountains—with or without clients.

But always without Angelina.

"The boys have asked us to come to Leadville next weekend. Matt's practicing for the upcoming skijoring festival."

Hanging out with her brothers only stirred up feelings he didn't understand, as he'd learned at Christmas. He hoped his noncommittal grunt made it clear he didn't want to spend a weekend with her brothers, much less watch some jackasses on skis being catapulted off a mound of snow and dragged by racing horses. There was skiing and there was horseback riding—and skijoring was an abomination of both. Just leave the two sports separate.

"Luke says he has a mustang ready to work with another rider for the festival."

"Listen, I'm not much on horseback riding."

"We don't have to ride. Luke just got a new rescue pony last night. This one's pretty banged up."

Marc hadn't seen much of Luke lately, but apparently Angelina had been keeping in touch with him. Marc trusted Luke not to cross the line from friendship to something more with Angelina, but if Marc didn't get his head on straight soon and focus more on her needs, who's to say Angelina wouldn't go trolling elsewhere?

The deepest commitment Marc might ever be able to achieve was to satisfy her body's needs. Given how badly he had performed at that lately, he wondered why she hadn't left him already.

They always do.

No, not always. He'd been the one to leave Pamela, not the other way around. Hard to tell who left whom with Melissa. He'd just been happy she was gone once he saw her true colors.

Dio, he needed a diversion. "Why don't we go out and spend some time with Luke instead of going to Matt's this weekend?" He had missed having Luke around since he'd moved out to his new place.

"Sure." The disappointment rang loud and clear in her voice.

"If you want to go to Leadville, go ahead."

Just don't expect to take me with you.

They drove on in silence once again. Thirty minutes later, he parked the car at his parents' condo. Angelina opened her own door before he reached her side of the car, but Marc took her hand to help her out of the Porsche.

Man, they were late. "I'll get our bags later." With Valentine's Day resort packages booked solid at Bella Montagna, the only place for them to stay overnight had been his parents' condo unit. That certainly might account for some of his anxiety about this trip, too. Was he leaving the bags in the car in case they decided to head back to Denver tonight instead?

Angelina nodded and took a few steps toward the lobby entrance before doing an about-face. "Oh, wait! I forgot the salad in the trunk."

As he retrieved the bowl, he couldn't help thinking that her mind must be very busy for her to have forgotten the dish she'd insisted on making for dinner, even after Marc assured her Mama's chef would have everything covered. Her dish would be the best on the table, though, without a doubt.

Inside the building, Angelina tensed as they stood waiting for the elevator. Was she remembering the last time they had come here? Surely Mama had honored his request and hadn't invited Melissa here today.

He stroked Angelina's back, and she graced him with a tentative smile. He hadn't noticed the dark circles under her eyes before. He reached up and brushed his thumb across the left smudge.

"I'm glad you're here with me." He had been anxious about this visit all week, perhaps even longer. Having Angelina with him helped relieve some of his stress.

She wrapped her arm around his waist, and her smile grew. "I love your family, Marc. I've been looking forward to this for weeks."

That made one of them.

The elevator opened onto the penthouse floor. "Marco!" He looked up to find Mama standing in the open doorway to her unit. "And Angelina! So nice to see you both could come." Mama glanced at the bowl in Angelina's arms. "What have you done? You did not need to bring anything."

"Oh, I just threw together a salad. Hope it complements the meal."

"I'm sure it will. Here, I'll take it to the kitchen." She took the bowl. "Please, come in."

Marc kissed Mama's cheeks before entering the condo he'd once called home. The place had never seemed particularly cozy. The modern furniture was stark white—well, when he wasn't trudging through after playing outside, dirtying everything up. He really hadn't fit in here, even then.

"Marco, Angelina, good to see you both."

"Happy anniversary, Papa."

Mama joined them again, and Marc and Angelina extended the well-wishes to her, as well. He noticed Papa seemed to be moving a little more slowly. The circles under his eyes were more pronounced, and his skin rather sallow. Had he been sick? He'd have a talk with Mama later to make sure everything was okay.

His parents weren't getting any younger. Maybe it was time for them to turn over even more responsibility to their younger children. They should be enjoying some of the money they'd made over the past few decades.

"Let's ask Marc." Sandro and Carmella came out of the den, and each latched onto one of Marc's arms. "Angelina, mind if we steal him for a few minutes?"

"No, go ahead."

He shrugged helplessly as his brother and sister dragged him into the den and looked back over his shoulder toward Angelina. "Have a glass of wine, *amore*. I'll be right back."

She smiled as Papa claimed her arm. "What can I get for you, *cara mia?*"

Marc watched them head over to the bar until the doorway to the den blocked her from view.

Sandro steered him toward the sofa. "We have to be quick or they'll know we're up to something."

*   *   *

Thank God Melissa wasn't here. Angelina hadn't been sure if Marc's mama would finally sever the bond with Gino's fiancée or not. Hard to know if the woman was still holding on to the fringes of the family, but she definitely wasn't at the dinner table this time.

"Angelina, if you have time before you head back to Denver tomorrow, I'd like for you to share your recipe for this pasta salad with Chef Alfonse. It's delicious. Our guests would love it."

Angelina beamed at Mama's compliment. "I'd love to. Secret's in the marinated prosciutto." She looked forward to having a chance to get a behind-the-scenes look at D'Alessio's, the resort's premier restaurant. She'd been doing some catering work, and while Marc's kitchen was a dream to work in, it wasn't the same as being in a bustling restaurant.

Marc's papa, seated beside Angelina, patted her hand. "Why some restaurant in Denver hasn't snatched you up by now is beyond comprehension."

"Thanks, Papa D'Alessio. From your mouth to God's ear."

Dinner passed with lighthearted banter between Marc and his siblings. Too bad Marc's Gramps and Karla's grandmother, Vivian, weren't here, but apparently they were on a Mediterranean cruise with some of his surviving World War II buddies.

After the table was cleared, the family proceeded into the den. Marc took Mama's arm and Papa Angelina's. Carmella and Sandro brought up the rear of the entourage, but Sandro soon took charge.

"Mama, Papa, you sit here on the sofa. We have a surprise for you."

"A surprise?" Mama truly sounded stunned. "What have you children been up to?"

Sandro picked up the remote and turned the power on the wide-screen TV. He turned to Angelina, "Hope we don't bore you too much."

Now Angelina wondered what they had planned, too.

"Mama, Papa," Sandro began, "Carmella and I have been going through the boxes of old family photos and digitizing them, so we could put them together in a slideshow."

Marc's hand in hers grew stiff, and she turned to him, seeing an expression bordering on terror in his eyes. She squeezed his hand, and he gazed at her. Her smile of assurance did nothing to change the look on his face.

What was he afraid of seeing in these photos? Or was he afraid of what he wouldn't see, such as himself as a baby?

"Everyone take a seat."

At Sandro's instruction, Angelina started toward a chair in the corner before Marc guided her to a wingback next to the sofa. He sat first and pulled her into his lap. She blushed at the intimate position, but no one was paying attention to them. Leaning in, she gave him a peck on the cheek.

"I promise not to tell a soul what secrets from your childhood are revealed in the photos."

The arm under her fingers stiffened, and he stuck his chin out. "I have no secrets."

Angelina wondered about that, especially after what Melissa had said last month. Sometimes there were things people didn't know about their pasts that could come back to bite them or family members in the ass, like her papa keeping his cancer a secret. Her mama had wanted her children to remember only that Papa had died a hero's death. But understanding why he'd sacrificed himself that day rather than allow any other SAR worker to be hurt made him even more of a hero in Angelina's eyes.

Maybe this was just what Marc needed, though. If he saw himself as part of the family, perhaps some of the insecurities Melissa had stirred would be allayed.

Angelina curled against him. How long had it been since he'd held her like this? Even if he merely sought comfort, she was glad he'd reached out to her.

The first photos showed a house in a quaint village.

"That's Brescia," Marc whispered in her ear. "My hometown."

Angelina remembered her visits to Nonna in Marsala, Sicily, and her throat grew tight. She still missed her grandmother after all these years. *"Bella."*

Mama said, "That house belonged to a dear friend of mine from secondary school."

"Sorry, Mama," Carmella interjected. "I thought that was yours and Papa's house. It was in so many of the photos we went through."

Angelina looked at Mama, who frowned and paused before explaining, "My sister Emiliana and I lived there, though at different times. Gino and Marco spent many months there. Do you remember any of that, Marco?"

He shook his head in the negative, but his body tensed. She turned back to the screen and saw an image of Mama holding a tiny baby. A woman who could be her twin rested her hand over the baby's pale-blue crocheted blanket.

"That's my Aunt Emiliana and Mama at Gino's baptism. She died young."

How sad. She looked so vibrant in the photo. Marc's voice held little emotion, but he probably only knew the woman from photos if she had died when he was very young.

There were a few more photos, all with the same three subjects. Angelina glanced over at Mama, who remained stoic. The inability to express emotion seemed to run in the family. Angelina couldn't imagine losing one of her brothers and not being a basket case whenever she heard his name or saw his photo. Her heart went out to the woman who always seemed to hold it together, much like Marc did. Maybe that was Mama's coping mechanism.

"Is that me?"

"Yes, it is, Marco."

Marc almost sounded surprised to find himself in the show. Melissa's false accusation really had rattled him. Angelina turned back to the TV to find Marc as a tiny baby with Gino looking on, a protective hand on his baby brother's head. This time his Aunt Emiliana held the baby wrapped in a pale blue shawl similar to the one Gino had been wrapped in at his baptism. A younger Mama stared at the camera, dark circles under her eyes. Such sadness in her face. The two sisters must have been very close.

Out of the corner of her eye, Angelina watched as Papa reached out and squeezed Mama's hand. Odd that they hadn't included any photos of Papa in the slideshow yet. Turning her attention to the screen again, that was soon remedied by images of a young Mama and Papa together. The two boys—*Dio,* Marc was still so young, perhaps three or four—stood straight and tall in a family portrait next to his parents in front of a plaster-covered church. Both children stared blankly toward the camera, eyes glossy and tragic, reminding Angelina of images her own papa had shown her of his family after the devastating World War. But this was the early 1980s. Italy hadn't been involved in a war then. Perhaps this was around the time Emiliana had died. Mama's face seemed to have aged more, too, in the years since Marc had been a baby in the photos.

A sense of sadness for Marc overwhelmed her, and she blinked away the tears but continued to watch the boys grow older as the show progressed. Soon a third son was born to the couple, Alessandro. Marc could be no more than five years old then.

The family was complete with the addition of baby Carmella a couple of years later. "Finally, *mia bella bambina.*"

"I'm your *only* baby girl, Mama." Carmella beamed at her mother, though.

Angelina hadn't seen much of this maternal side of Mama D'Alessio before, but the woman's love for her children—all of them—was genuine. She might be a driven businesswoman, but she probably had only wanted to provide a good life for her family. Having lived in Italy after the war must have shaken her sense of security in where her next meal would come from.

The next snapshot caused Angelina to lean closer to the TV. "Look at you, Marc, in your First Communion suit! Adorable!" She smiled and turned toward him. "You should wear a suit more often."

He pinched her butt hard, and she jumped as he leaned forward to whisper in her ear, "Bite your tongue, *amore*. I detest wearing a suit—and I'll leave the ties to you." She hoped he'd spoken quietly enough that no one had heard but held no doubts that Sandro and Mama at least were aware of Marc's kinky nature. Therefore, by association, hers as well.

The scenery changed on the screen to Aspen when Marc was now eleven or twelve. *Dio,* what a handsome boy he was even then. He and his entire family, including Gramps, posed next to a hand-carved sign touting the name Bella Montagna. The place hadn't started out as a four-star resort. Back then, it had a mom-and-pop feel to it, but the sense of old-world charm probably soon had American skiers flocking here.

"Remember how much we paid for that sign, Papa?" Mama shook her head. "Highway robbery."

Angelina smiled. The woman's business acumen was keen even then. Although they could barely afford it, she'd invested in a sign that would attract guests from far and wide to their beautiful mountain property and give the appearance of a world-class resort.

In the next few slides, Angelina's attention was riveted on the growing boy who had become the man holding her in his lap. He'd relaxed since the show had started. She stroked his arm where his rolled-up sleeve revealed the soft hair on his forearm. She'd missed touching him these past few weeks. Maybe they could get back on track once they put this weekend behind them.

As the two older boys grew into teenagers, she noticed how Gino often had his arm draped around his little brother's shoulders in a protective gesture. Angelina blinked back the tears again, saddened that they had drifted apart before Gino's death.

In his late teens, Marc more often than not was pictured alone. Lots of sports activities, with soccer and skiing being the most prevalent. There was an increasing wildness about him. His disheveled hair—sexy as hell—made her want to reach out and finger comb it into submission. He often sported the beginnings of a beard, even in his late teens, attesting to why he sometimes had to shave twice a day. His eyes exuded a defiant, careless nature, with a hint of loneliness.

He had a cocky way about him, though, as if he could control any woman he wanted. She shivered, and he wrapped his arms around her. Oddly, there were no photos of him with girlfriends, including Bitch Melissa, but Sandro and Carmella may have just kept those out knowing Angelina would be here today. A number of photos featuring Carmella and Sandro followed. The two usually stood separate from their older brothers, possibly because of the nearly five-year age difference between Marc and Sandro.

Marc grew quiet and tense when an image of Gino in his Marine portrait filled the screen. Angelina stroked his arm, knowing how hard it must be to see his brother appearing so vibrant mere months before his life had been snuffed out in an ambush far from his family's safe haven. She blinked away the tears and glanced surreptitiously at his parents, who remained stoic as they stared at the screen. Marc's Navy portrait in his dress whites was next. Angelina hadn't seen the photo before but had loved seeing him in his dress uniform at Karla and Adam's wedding a few months ago. A man in a military uniform was hot, but none could compare to *her* man in *his* uniform.

Or out of it. She stifled a giggle, but Marc pinched her as if guessing where her thoughts had roamed.

A photo of Mama and Papa D'Alessio standing outside a quaint church flashed on the screen. "Ah, Papa, our thirtieth anniversary. Wherever did you find that photo, Alessandro?"

"I have my sources, Mama." Sandro seemed pleased he'd surprised her.

To Angelina, she added, "We returned to Brescia to renew our vows and take a little time away from the resort, because we couldn't get away on Valentine's Day, the actual day. We didn't think anyone in the family even knew."

Marc's arms tightened around Angelina to the point of crushing her. "When was that?"

Mama's expression turned wary, and she evaded his gaze. "Last summer."

The tension was thick between them. Angelina turned to see a pained expression in Marc's eyes before he masked it. What had she missed?

"Your thirtieth?"

"Oh, dear. I misspoke. *Scusa.* I meant to say our thirty-seventh." Mama patted Papa's leg. "Now, who wants dessert? *Grazie, bambini,* for going to all this trouble for us. It was—"

Mama stopped speaking and faced the screen again. Angelina followed Mama's gaze and found a portrait of Marc, Sandro, and Carmella taken in this very room earlier today judging by the clothes the three were wearing.

"Oh, Papa, our children all together." Tears streamed down her cheeks, and Papa wrapped an arm around her. Angelina caught a glint of tears in Papa's eyes, as well.

Sandro turned off the power using the remote, oblivious to the emotional level of the couple on the sofa. "I have the camera set up still. Let's take a complete family portrait today while we're all here."

Angelina hated for this fascinating glimpse into Marc's past to end, but when she tried to scoot off Marc's lap, he held her tighter. "Join us in the photo. You have as much a place in the family as I do." His words held a defiance that confused her.

"I think it's up to your parents, but I'm sure they'd like one of just the immediate family." She wasn't even engaged to Marc and didn't want them to have to photoshop her out of a family portrait somewhere down the road if things didn't work out for her and Marc. As much as she didn't want the two of them to drift apart again, nothing had changed since New Year's and more often than not they were apart.

Unless perhaps the love exhibited in these photos had convinced Marc he was very much a part of this family—and loved by all of them.

Several shots were taken, both with and without Angelina, before Mama announced dessert was served. As Angelina started toward the dining room, Marc took her hand and pulled her back.

"We're leaving after dessert."

"What? I thought we were spending the night here."

"Change of plans."

"But what—"

"We're leaving, Angelina."

*　*　*

Lies.

His life had been built on a lie, and his parents had just slipped up royally in the perpetuation of that lie. Mama tried to cover her mistake, but he realized Melissa had told the truth all along. He probably should have called them outright liars to their faces, but all he wanted to do was get away without making a scene. Shit, the look on Mama's face when she realized she'd slipped up made it abundantly clear he'd been deceived all of his life.

He didn't care if they believed the story he'd told after dessert about not feeling well—a lily-white fib compared to the bigger ones he'd been fed the past thirty-four years. In truth, he felt like crap, so it wasn't a lie at all.

"Are you going to tell me what happened back there?"

The oncoming headlights blinded him temporarily, and he flashed his brights at the jerk. "There's nothing to tell."

Angelina sighed and resumed staring at the scenery out the passenger-side window, not that she could see anything this late at night. Just as well she found something out there to look at, though, because it meant she wasn't focused on trying to get him to express his feelings or open up.

He had no feelings anymore. If he'd only remembered to keep his emotions buried deep inside, perhaps he wouldn't have felt that momentary stab of pain when the deception became evident at long last.

Angelina seemed bored with the silence. "Sandro and Carmella sure put a lot of time into that slideshow."

He grunted noncommittally, hoping she'd drop the chattiness. He realized he'd seen many of the photos before but hadn't made the connection that Papa was missing from the photos until about the time Marc was four. He'd just assumed Papa had taken the photos, as he'd often done later.

Wait. Mama had been there when he and Gino were babies. But who's to say the babies in the photos were actually Marco and Gino and not someone else's babies? *Dio,* this wasn't going to be simple to figure out. Already he had a headache.

"Maybe we can get a copy of the slideshow on a thumb drive."

"I don't need any more reminders."

"What do you mean?"

"Nothing."

She looked his way. "Why can't we talk with each other anymore?"

"What do you mean? We live together—*sleep* together, for Christ's sake." *Most of the time, anyway.* He heard her intake of breath and knew he'd spoken too harshly, but he didn't want this line of questioning to follow to its logical conclusion. He knew they weren't communicating but didn't want to analyze it.

"Take now, for instance." Angelina wasn't going to let it go. "Tell me what's bothering you. Talk to me. We should be there for each other at times like these."

"There's nothing to talk about."

"What happened, then?"

"I don't even know what the hell is going on." *Who the hell I am.*

"Well, welcome to the club. How can we have a committed relationship when you won't confide in me?"

Did he trust Angelina? Could he trust any woman?

"Obviously this has to do with your family. If you won't talk with me, then perhaps you should talk it over with them."

"Drop it, Angelina. This doesn't concern you."

Merda. That hadn't come out right. He reached across the console to stroke her thigh but kept his gaze focused on the road. "I'm sorry, *cara.* Look, I'm on edge tonight. I need to think some things through."

"If that's the way it has to be for me to be a part of your life, okay. But I worry you're just afraid to tell me it's over."

He heard the hitch in her voice. *Over?* What the fuck was she talking about? The walls closed in around him.

"Nothing's over. And I'm not afraid of anything." Oh, *Dio,* but he truly was. Scared to death. Would she leave him?

Not to mention worrying about who he was. Where he came from. He needed answers but without the messy, emotional drama he'd get talking with Mama and Papa, if they would tell him the truth.

Should he even call them that anymore?

The churning in his gut worsened until Marc maneuvered the Porsche onto a roadside pull off. He gripped the steering wheel hard enough that his knuckles showed white in the dim glow from the dashboard lights.

Angelina placed her hand over his right one, and her thumb stroked his knuckles. "Talk to me, Marc. What happened back there?"

He filled his constricted lungs, hoping to calm his nerves.

Epic fail.

The words came out in a whisper. "Melissa was telling the truth."

Her thumb stopped moving.

"Marc, you need to go back and talk with your parents before making that assumption." She laid her forehead on his shoulder. "But so what if she wasn't lying? You can't run away from this forever. The not knowing is eating you alive. You know I'll be there for you, no matter what."

But running had always been so much easier. Relieved she was here with him now at least, he patted the back of her head until she leaned away and smiled her encouragement at him.

"I need to go back." He'd intended it as a question, but the words hadn't come out that way.

"I think that would be a good thing to do. Get answers to your questions rather than let your imagination run away from you."

He took a deep breath. After checking traffic, he drove onto the highway and executed a tight U-turn to head back to Aspen. Marc nodded his head toward the cell phone lying between them. He'd never equipped the vintage Porsche with hands-free capabilities. "Call Mama, and let her know we're on our way back. Tell her I need to talk with her and Papa. Tonight."

Chapter Eight

Marc held Angelina's hand as the elevator ascended to Mama's office the next morning. Papa had answered the door last night and said Mama had gone to bed early with a headache. Must be going around, because Marc's head had been pounding ever since the slideshow yesterday. After taking hours to fall asleep last night, he'd overslept this morning and missed finding Mama or Papa at the breakfast table.

Angelina squeezed his hand, and he turned toward her. Her smile helped ease some of his anxiety. "No matter what you find out, Marc, it doesn't change who you are."

He nodded, hating that his moody ass was giving her unnecessary anxiety this morning. The gods had smiled on him when they'd brought her back into his life—twice now. With Angelina, he felt as if he'd found a safe haven at long last. He just hoped he wouldn't do anything to fuck it up with her—again.

Why did he keep sabotaging his relationship with her? *Merda*, having Angelina with him this morning was a double-edged sword. She gave him a sense of calm he wouldn't otherwise feel, but he didn't want her to witness the drama about to unfold. He had no control over what would be revealed.

Angelina hadn't left him for good—yet. So far, she'd always come back. Sometimes he wondered if he was trying to get her to leave him.

The elevator doors opened into the reception area. Evelyn Begali smiled from the glass-topped desk outside the door to Mama's inner sanctum. "Marco, good to see you again!" Marc introduced Angelina to his mother's long-time executive assistant, and the three chatted about inane topics as long as he figured he could stall.

"Mrs. D'Alessio is just finishing up with someone." Evelyn cast a worried glance at the door to Mama's office and then at Angelina before turning back to Marc. "She asked to see you alone."

Angelina started to pull her hand away from his, but Marc refused to release her.

"We'll *both* be meeting with Mama this morning."

Angelina looked up at him. "Are you sure that's best, Marc? I don't mind waiting out here. This is a family matter."

Marc leaned down and whispered in her ear. "I want you with me, *cara*." He kissed her lightly on the cheek and, when he stood upright again, was relieved to see the sparkle in her eyes and the smile on her lips that had been absent so much lately. He hadn't asked her just to make her happy, though. In truth, having her there was something he *needed*. For whatever reason, though, she seemed as nervous as he. Whatever he learned today could affect them both, not that he wanted to let the news have that much control over him. He was a grown man and had been on his own since he'd joined the Navy.

Why did he dread finding out if he was adopted?

He had his family, the mountains, his friends, the club, and—best of all—Angelina. They provided him with the emotional stability he'd sought all his life.

Until last night. He'd lost control of his life in an instant.

At least he didn't have to face the truth alone.

"You're a fool! You knew the consequences!"

Mama's voice came through the door, startling Marc. He'd never heard her lose her cool before. Who was she talking to?

Evelyn pressed a button on the remote lying on her desk before she stood, and Pavarotti's exquisite tenor filled the air, blotting out the heated discussion emanating from Mama's office. "What can I get you two to drink while you wait?"

"Nothing for me, thanks." Marc turned to Angelina, who declined as well.

The door opened, and he turned as Melissa stomped out on her stilettos. The venom in her expression as she caught sight of Marc and then Angelina was lethal. To Angelina, she said, "I hope you know what you're getting into with this family."

Angelina tried to pull away from him, but he held her hand tightly as they watched Melissa storm out the door. The portal still open, Marc motioned for Angelina to precede him into the office. Mama stood at the window, staring out as a new flurry of snowflakes swirled to the ground far below. Her shoulders rose and fell sharply as she breathed, obviously still upset by her encounter with Melissa. He didn't think Mama was one to even notice the beauty of the snow. For her, snow was green—more snow equaled more skiers, which equaled more revenue.

"Good morning, Mama."

She didn't face them.

"I hope you don't mind me joining you, Mrs. D'Alessio."

At the sound of Angelina's voice, Mama did turn around. She didn't seem pleased. Then he noticed her eyes were red-rimmed. Mama had been crying? He'd only seen her cry once before, while he was recovering in the hospital in Germany after being injured at Fallujah. What had Melissa said to upset her?

One thing he knew. He wanted Angelina here for whatever discussion was about to take place. Marc squeezed Angelina's hand. "I asked her to join us, Mama. Whatever we discuss affects her, too. She's a part of my life now."

Dio, he loved his girl. He placed more trust in Angelina than he had in any other woman—ever. So why did he fall short of committing to her completely? *Merda*, he'd been close to proposing to her several times but never could. Why? She'd become a part of his life but would never be a permanent part if he didn't overcome his irrational fears and ask her to marry him.

He hoped that finding out what secret Mama had kept from him all these years would be one of the keys to unlocking his inability to commit.

Mama motioned them to the seating area. "Please, both of you, sit down." After offering them refreshments from the pots on the coffee table, she took her seat across from them. They could have been in a business meeting, rather than having a family discussion.

"Where's Papa?"

Mama averted her gaze. "He...had some errands to run."

Mama fiddled with the napkin in her lap but didn't advance the conversation. No doubt Mama knew what they were here to discuss, but he'd better make sure.

"Over New Year's weekend, Melissa said some things that I wanted to ask you about."

"Yes, I can imagine she did, based on the visits she paid to me later that weekend—and this morning."

Concerned the gold-digger might still be causing trouble for his family, he cautioned, "Mama, you need to cut her out of your life. She's looking for trouble and money, nothing more."

"Do not worry. She no longer has any hold over me."

No longer? What hold could Melissa ever have had, other than being Gino's fiancée at one time long ago? Marc's chest constricted, and Angelina reached out to stroke his thigh, reminding him to breathe.

"So what she said is true?"

Mama met his gaze at last. "What exactly did she say?"

Why did he get the feeling Mama wasn't going to divulge any more information than she had to?

"She said Gino and I were adopted."

She sighed before taking a sip of her tea. "It's complicated."

"We've got all day, Mama."

She sloshed some of the tea onto the napkin in her lap as her hand shook. He'd seldom seen his mother in any state other than total control, except for the time in Germany and again a few minutes ago after the confrontation with Melissa. Numbness enveloped him as he began shutting down his emotions, preparing himself for the worst. He looked out the window to the mountains, wishing he could be out there now. Angelina's hand stroking his arm kept him in the moment when all he wanted to do was escape.

Get a grip, man. Stay focused.

Steeling himself for whatever his mother was going to reveal, he turned his gaze back to Mama. Were he and Gino even brothers? How much of his life had been a lie?

Mama seemed a million miles away—or perhaps only as far away as the Lombardy region. Then, in a low voice, she began to tell her story.

"My younger sister, Emiliana, was my mama's favorite."

Marc had no difficulty commiserating with his mother about not being the favorite. He'd felt that way about Gino most of his life. Still did, in fact. He didn't know much about Aunt Emiliana, other than she'd died young and that she was Mama's half-sister. Gramps had gotten Marc's grandmother pregnant during the Second World War while she nursed him back to health in the winter of the Apennine-Po Valley campaign. His Mama had found Gramps, her father, when Marc was about ten, prompting the D'Alessios' move to Colorado.

During her early childhood in Italy, though, Mama had been raised by her mother and her grandmother, without the presence of a father figure, until Emiliana's father came along a few years later.

Shit, his family tree already was complicated enough, but Marc had a feeling the story was going to make it even more so before he sorted it all out.

"Emiliana married Paolo Solari when she was twenty-one." She made a face when saying the man's name as if she'd just eaten something distasteful. "He was thirty and from a wealthy *Lombardia* family."

So his aunt married well. Good for her. "What does that have to do with Gino and me?"

Mama didn't try to hide her annoyance, piercing him with a glare. "I'm telling this story, Marco. It will become clear soon. Just listen."

"*Scusa.* Please, continue."

Mama placed her cup and saucer on the coffee table and sat back, once again avoiding his gaze. "I worked as a domestic in one of the mountain lodges Paolo's family ran. I dated him a couple times before he met my sister." Resentment. Sounded as if there must have been some kind of rivalry between the sisters for this Solari guy, not unlike Marc and Gino both lusting after Melissa.

Marc decided to keep his mouth shut and let Mama tell her story the way she wanted.

"Emiliana married Paolo." Mama cleared her throat. "Not too long after, they had a little boy."

She had his full attention again. *Gino?* Sounded as though Aunt Emiliana had been pregnant already when she married. Must be something in the water in Lombardy.

"Being tied down with a baby didn't fit their busy young lifestyle." Censure crept into her voice again. "They hired my best friend to be a nanny to their son."

If she wouldn't say, he needed to ask, even though he wasn't supposed to interrupt. "Gino?"

Mama nodded but didn't look up from playing with the edge of her napkin. Angelina stroked his arm, but he didn't need comforting or grounding. He needed answers. Truth. He hung onto Mama's every word, definitely in the moment now.

She brushed a tear from the corner of her eye with the back of her hand and continued in a whisper, "You were born three years later."

Well, there he had it. He and Gino were the sons of two people he knew nothing about—the Solaris. His Aunt Emiliana—no, his *mother*—was dead, but what about his father?

"Is Paolo still living?"

Mama's fingers stilled. Her nostrils flared, but she continued to stare at the floor and nodded. "He retired and now lives in Siena."

"You've kept in touch?"

Her eyes opened wide, and she met his gaze at last. *"Mio Dio,* no!" The vehemence in her words took him by surprise. The man was her brother-in-law, but apparently there wasn't any love lost between Mama and this Paolo Solari man.

But he was also Marc's father.

"What happened to Emiliana?"

"She died young. A fast-growing cancer."

His mother rarely spoke of her sister. Papa, the man Marc had considered his birth father and papa all these years, had only told him his Aunt Emiliana—no, his *mother*—had died tragically at a young age. Cancer? Marc always assumed it had been an accident of some kind.

Dio, his head hurt trying to process all this incoming intel. Marc had seen photos of her before, including the ones in the slideshow yesterday, but had been told very little about the woman who had given him life.

Did Papa know all this? Clearly, he had to know he wasn't the father of Gino or Marc, yet he'd never treated them differently than Carmella and Sandro. Papa was solitary and non-demonstrative with all of them, but he loved his family. Marc assumed Papa was Carmella and Sandro's biological father, at least. Mama's slip yesterday that they were celebrating their thirtieth anniversary made it sound as though they married before Sandro came along.

If the photo he'd seen of Mama and Papa in front of the church with Marc and Gino had been their wedding day, then they must have married when Marc was about three and Gino six. Had Papa chosen not to be a part of this discussion today because he wasn't Marc's birth father or because Mama kept him away?

Marc was finding more questions than answers here.

"Does he know about me?"

Mama nodded and glanced at her lap again. "He let Papa and me adopt you and Gino after Emiliana's death."

A tear splashed onto her hand, and she surreptitiously tried to wipe it on the napkin. Marc was halfway across the room before realizing he needed to offer comfort to the only woman he'd ever consider his mother. He sat beside her on the settee and put his arms around her, stroking her back.

Losing a sibling, compounded with survivor's guilt, was something Marc understood all too well. That the two sisters had grown estranged before Emiliana's untimely death only made it worse. Marc missed Gino every day, even though he'd been gone ten years now. The pain and guilt never went away. He regretted the precious time he had lost before Gino deployed for the first and only time.

Realizing Mama wasn't getting any younger, Marc didn't want another falling out between himself and any other members of his family. Mama wrapped her arms around his waist and held on tightly. She hadn't hugged him like this since she and Papa had shown up in his hospital room at Ramstein back in 2004.

"I never meant to hurt you, Marco. I thought I did the right thing."

"Shhh. You did a great job raising Gino and me, Mama." He patted her back, hoping she would stop crying. His mother had always been stoic and aloof. He didn't like seeing this side of her knowing—in part—his insensitivity and questions had caused her turmoil.

"You're my child as much as Alessandro and Carmella are."

If not for her, he might not have had any mother at all. "Mama, no one else could ever be a better mother than you have been." He realized as soon as the words came out that he truly meant them and wasn't merely saying what she needed to hear. From what she'd said, Paolo wasn't cut out to be a father. He and Gino had been lucky their then-aunt and uncle had taken them away from what their lives might have been like.

Mama withdrew from him, dabbing at her eyes with her napkin before looking directly at him. "Marco, I made so many mistakes, things I regret to this day." More tears spilled from her eyes.

Please stop crying, Mama.

"That man didn't deserve to have two beautiful boys like you and Gino." She looked down at her lap. "I'm just sorry I couldn't have taken you away sooner, Marco."

Why did she keep apologizing for something that wasn't her fault?

Stop crying, Marco. They won't keep you if you're a baby.

Gino's admonishment blasted into his consciousness and nearly brought him to his knees. Marc needed no further reminders; he never cried.

A buzzing in his ears yanked him from the scene, and he found himself hiding in a cold, dark place staring into the face of...a wolf?

"...*Come out now, Marco.*" Mama? *No...*

He stood too quickly and swayed on his feet. Blood rushed through his veins, increasing the pounding in his head. Angelina wrapped her arms around his waist from behind him before he realized she'd come to stand next to him. He held on to her arms to further ground himself as he tried to draw from her support, her strength. Slowly, the room stopped spinning, but he couldn't shake the feeling that walls were closing in on him.

Trapped.

He needed to run. Now. "Mama, I need some fresh air." He turned to Angelina and handed her the Porsche keys. "Stay with Mama until Evelyn comes in. I'll have her call Papa."

She whispered, "Marc, are you okay?"

He nodded as he made his way toward the door. "I need some time to think. Meet you back at the condo." He gazed at his mother, who had stopped crying but sat immobilized on the sofa.

What the fuck was the matter with him? He should be consoling her, not running away. Unable to shake the need to flee, Marc nearly sprinted toward the door.

Escape.

"Marc, I'll meet you back at the condo!"

He nodded but didn't turn around again.

*　　*　　*

Angelina left Mama's office as soon as Evelyn came in to take over consoling Mama. The story she thought Marc feared most had been confirmed—he *had* been adopted but by an aunt and uncle, not strangers. He had been handling the news so well. What caused him to suddenly snap and run out?

Fewer than five minutes behind Marc, she wasn't sure if he'd walk around the property to get his head on straight or go directly back to his parents' penthouse condo. She knocked on the door as she tried to get her breathing under control. The moment he opened the door, the shuttered expression in his eyes told her Marc had shut down emotionally—again. His lifelong beliefs about who he was had been shattered.

There probably wasn't a damned thing she could do to ease his pain, but she could hold him, talk with him, love him. She reached out, but he sidestepped and motioned her into the foyer.

"I've packed everything. We can leave as soon as you're ready."

She glanced at their suitcase near the door. How had he done that so fast? Her gaze returned to him. "Marc, I think we should talk."

"There's nothing to talk about."

She reached out to stroke his arm, "But there is."

He wrenched his arm away from her and glared at her. "I *said* there's nothing to talk about. If you need to hit the head before we leave, do so now. Otherwise, let's shove off."

She'd learned over the months that Marc didn't revert to Navy jargon unless he was seeking to hold onto a sense of stability. Security. She wished he'd find that sense of security in her, but it hadn't happened yet.

Blinking back the tears, she turned toward the elevator. "I'm ready. Let's go home."

Maybe on the way back to Marc's place, they could talk. Or would he retreat into his head as he had so many times since New Year's? Worse yet, would he run to the mountains—away from her—where he knew she most likely wouldn't follow?

The drive back to Denver was a silent one, each lost in his or her own thoughts. Once home, Marc unloaded the car and left soon after to go downtown to the store. He said he needed to meet with Brian to discuss weekend sales figures and see what treks had been scheduled for the coming week, but he could have done all of that over the phone. Clearly he just wanted to be away from her tonight.

The house was cold, and she jacked up the thermostat on her way to the bedroom. Exhausted from the emotionally draining two days, she shivered and crawled under the duvet seeking warmth and sleep. As if she could sleep without Marc's body snuggled against her backside. Despite having to sleep without him many nights lately, she'd never gotten used to it.

Would she ever get him to face whatever it was he feared so much?

Please stop running, Marc.

Just when he'd started to open up and let her in, insisting that she be included in the meeting with Mama, he had quickly tugged the mask back over his face and made his escape. He hadn't seemed upset to hear Mama confirm he wasn't her son by birth, so what caused him to shut down? Maybe it was a delayed response to the news—emotional shock.

Angelina couldn't imagine how she'd handle discovering she wasn't the biological daughter of her Mama and Papa or learning that her brothers were half-siblings. *Mio Dio!* Carmella and Sandro weren't Marc's blood siblings at all but his cousins instead! She didn't blame Marc for going into a tailspin, but surely he knew the youngest two D'Alessios only knew him as a brother and weren't going to treat him differently once they were told the truth. Angelina doubted Carmella and Sandro had any clue about their gnarled family tree, but the four children had been raised together as siblings and always would be. Mama and Papa loved them all equally.

Oh, Marc. Come back home. I need to hold you.

If Marc continued to shut her out, they'd never break through whatever kept him running. She refused to continue to let him push her away when he was at his most vulnerable. He needed her now more than ever, even if he couldn't admit it.

She shivered and turned onto her back before scooting up and sitting flush against the headboard. Maybe if she'd brought some flannel PJs with her, she wouldn't be shivering, but Marc preferred she sleep in the nude. Not a problem when she had his body heat and hot sex to keep her warm. But the flannels she lusted for at the moment were packed away in a storage facility at Aspen Corners with most of her furniture.

As much as she wanted something more with Marc, she might have jumped into living together too soon. What did they really know about each other? Their negotiations for play scenes might have given her a false expectation of the level of trust and intimacy they had established in reality.

While she'd never been able to ditch the feeling that he wasn't being as open with her as she needed him to be, she had hoped he'd change and that this relationship would lead to something permanent.

No, she wasn't going to give up on him this easily. Marc was a good man, just going through some things he wasn't processing very well right now. They were compatible in so many ways. She would hang in there with him and try to find ways to break through those protective walls he surrounded himself with.

Why did he feel such a need to run and hide from *her*?

One thing she knew for certain—there would be no body heat, kink, or hot sex tonight. Missing Marc more than ever, she tossed the covers back and went to the closet where she pulled out one of the white silk shirts he'd worn but not yet sent to the cleaners. The bergamot and lemony scents of Armani Code assailed her. She started to put the shirt back on the hanger and choose one he hadn't worn, but with tears in her eyes she brought it to her face with both hands, inhaling deeply.

Marc, come home to me.

Tears sprang to her eyes as she swallowed past the lump in her throat. This long-sleeved, square-hemmed shirt wouldn't provide her with any warmth and barely covered her hips, but just having Marc's scent surrounding her made her feel warmer inside.

Angelina pushed her arms through the sleeves and rolled the cuffs several times to get them past her wrists. She struggled with three of the buttons covering her chest before giving up on the rest. Why couldn't men's shirts button the same way women's did?

Because nothing is ever easy when it comes to men.

She glanced at the floor of the closet and saw Marc's toy bag. On a whim, she bent down and unzipped it, spotting first the paddle he'd last used on her New Year's weekend at his family resort.

Mine.

Like the long-gone mark on her butt from that session, their relationship seemed to be vanishing quickly. Could Marc trust anybody? Well, maybe he trusted Adam, Damián, and Luke to a certain extent, but definitely not women. Okay, Grant maybe, but she was one of his Marines. A corpsman's relationship to the Marines he served with gave them an elevated status.

He most definitely didn't trust Angelina enough to build a solid foundation. Wasn't it ironic that in the beginning the problem had been her inability to trust him? She'd forgiven him for the lie by omission that had snowballed into quite a mess when they'd first met. But she hadn't forgotten it and couldn't shake the feeling he was hiding something else about his past relationship with Melissa from her.

He might not even know what he was hiding. His nightmares had been coming more often, but he hadn't shared much about any of them since the one on Christmas night. Was it something buried so deeply inside even he didn't know it was there?

Oh, they both definitely had serious trust issues. How could they begin to overcome them and move forward together? She'd learned a lot about trust through discipline while being restrained during their play scenes. Maybe she should plan a play scene that would teach Marc.

Spying the stilettos she rarely wore because Marc always worried about her hurting herself, she decided to slip into them and channel her inner

Mistress Grant, who always wore over-the-knee stiletto boots in a Domme scene. These mules would have to suffice. She wondered when Marc would…

"Bellissima."

She turned and Marc cocked his head. How long had he been standing there? His gaze captured hers and then explored the length of her body before returning to linger on her chest. When his gaze shifted to the open toy bag, he grinned and her stomach flip-flopped.

Don't even think it, Marc.

Suddenly, she knew what needed to happen. Marc needed a lesson in discipline tonight. But could she deliver as a Domme, even for one scene?

No time like the present to find out.

Chapter Nine

M arc's cock grew stiff seeing Angelina wearing his Armani shirt. She'd never looked sexier. He'd come home expecting to give some long, drawn-out explanation about why he'd been such an ass since their return from Aspen, but apparently she was in the mood for some stress relief instead. Good. He needed to expel some energy right now.

She turned and bent down to his toy bag. The silk shirt molded around her hips, and then he spied the stilettos.

"Lose the fucking shoes."

She stood and turned to him, puzzled. "They're called fuck-me shoes…"

Marc didn't know why the damned things bothered him so much but stared her down until she shrugged and kicked them off, returning them to the back of the closet where they belonged.

Angelina bent again and rummaged through the toy bag. He wondered which implement she'd choose to play with and didn't have long to wait. She turned toward him holding one of the fourteen-inch floggers in one hand and a pair of leather wrist cuffs clipped together in the other. He wondered why she hadn't chosen the pair of floggers; typically his girl preferred Florentine-style flogging. No worries. He'd make sure he met her needs in whatever way she desired.

Angelina motioned in the air with the hand holding the flogger, swishing the falls in the process. "Strip, boy."

The glass of wine he'd had downstairs after returning from the store must have affected his hearing. "Beg your pardon?"

"I. Said. Strip. *Boy.*"

Marc chuckled. She was cute, trying to exert control, but if she thought he was going to…

"Now." There was no humor in her eyes, only steely determination.

What was her game tonight? His mood tumbled like an axe off an icefall.

"Angelina, you know how I feel about you topping me from the bottom. I'll determine when or whether you need a spanking."

"Oh, I'm not topping from the bottom at all, Marc." She set the flogger's falls twirling rhythmically and stalked toward him. As she drew closer, the flying leather tips slapped against his shirt, but she continued with the rhythm. "Tonight, I plan to top. Period."

Obviously, she'd been nipping at something, and on an empty stomach, too, no doubt. He really shouldn't have left her alone with her thoughts for an entire afternoon. Marc reached out and stilled her hand's movement, but she extricated herself deftly from his grasp.

"You do not touch me without permission or instruction," she parroted perfectly the command he'd given her many times while establishing the ground rules for a scene. She didn't *seem* to be under the influence.

Enough.

"Pet, you won't enjoy the spanking you are earning nearly as much as you think you might. I'm really not in the mood…"

"Neither am I." Her chin quivered a bit before she set her lips into a straight line. She motioned with the end of the flogger toward his shirt before placing the implement over her shoulder. "I want you to show me you can trust me, Marc. I want you to strip. Now."

Trust her? He trusted her more than any woman he'd ever known. "What's this all about?"

"We're going to negotiate a role reversal tonight."

Like hell. He wouldn't relinquish control to anyone. Not even Angelina.

She held one of the cuffs toward him, the Velcro flaps open. She clearly wasn't getting the message from his glare alone.

The need to regain control took over, and he wrested the cuff from her hand, taking Angelina by surprise. The flogger fell from her shoulder to the floor.

"*I* am the Top in this relationship, Angelina. If anyone will be restrained, it will be *you*."

"Not tonight." She took a step away from him. "Marc, if you can't trust me, then we really don't *have* a relationship. Trust has to go both ways."

What the fuck was all this talk about trust? Why did she think he didn't trust her? Of course, he trusted her. She had never been unfaithful to him. She would never betray him. She would never leave him.

Would she?

The truth hit him with the force of the rebar that pierced his side on the rooftop in Fallujah. An image of Melissa standing naked in their room New Year's weekend crossed his mind. Angelina had packed her suitcase and left it by the door.

He narrowed his gaze. "New Year's Eve, when I came back to the room to find Melissa there, had she inadvertently stopped you from leaving?"

She looked away. "No. I found Melissa in the room after I came back."

So Angelina hadn't just packed a bag? She'd actually left him? What little control he thought he had in this relationship ebbed away.

Angelina continued to stare at the floor, her voice barely above a whisper. "I thought you'd been less than honest with me about your relationship with Melissa."

"Why didn't you come to me first as I asked?"

Her face shot up, a spark of fury in her eyes. "I was having an insecure moment, okay? Besides, what happened with you and other women you met before me is none of my business." She took a breath before continuing. "But I feel as if there is some big secret hanging between us that needs to be aired." She took a step toward him. "Marc, this isn't about Melissa anymore. It's about us."

"Glad to hear you say that, because I've been over Melissa for a very long time."

"Are you sure?" Was there an edge to her question? How could she be insecure about someone like Melissa? The pained look on Angelina's face reminded him he hadn't given her any details about what had happened in those last encounters with the conniving gold-digger. He hated to remember those two times, much less talk about them, but she needed to know he'd been over Melissa for a very long time.

"The two times after Gino's death were…" Unable to meet her gaze any longer, he grabbed onto the bedpost. He should face her, but the shame wouldn't let go of him. He drew a deep breath needing to get this out. Her gaze bore a hole to his soul, even though he didn't make eye contact.

Marc released the breath slowly. "When my brother was killed, I blamed myself. I thought I was the one who had driven him to join the Marines. To get killed. I was…lost without him."

Dio, how to admit what kind of man he'd been back then? "She came to me the night of Gino's funeral." Marc heard her gasp at what she must know was coming and lowered his head. He continued barely above a whisper. "I was angry, trying to reaffirm life. Perhaps I even wanted to take revenge on Gino."

No excuses, remember? You fucked up.

He shrugged and ran his hand through his hair. Angelina's breathing became more agitated. She must hate hearing what he'd done with his brother's fiancée right after burying the body. "Hell, I don't know *why* I did it! But we had sex that night. Disgusted with myself afterward, I sent her away. For good, I'd hoped."

"That bitch!"

Marc cocked his head. She was angry at Melissa, not him? Angelina walked up to him and wrapped her arms around his waist, squeezing him against her. "To take advantage of you in your time of grief…" She rested her head against his shoulder blade.

He gripped her forearms, not wanting her to let go of him or to leave him again. Marc gained strength from Angelina's support, but now he had to tell her the rest. Reluctantly, he broke the tight hold of her arms and spun around toward her. He couldn't bear looking into her face yet, so he pulled her into his arms and took a shaky breath.

"There was that other time, too." Her body stiffened, and he rubbed his hand up and down her back to relax her. Or perhaps to calm himself. Touching her was like a talisman for him. "It was the day before I enlisted, the catalyst that helped me decide to leave my family to join the Navy."

Breathe.

"Melissa showed up on my doorstep and—I took advantage of her." When Angelina tried to pull back, he held her tighter.

Don't leave me.

So many of those he loved had left him, including his own birth parents. *Wait.* Mama, Papa, Carmella, and Sandro hadn't deserted him. Ever. Gino had driven the wedge between them to end their relationship, but they would have reconciled eventually if Afghan rebels hadn't taken that opportunity away.

Thank God he had his family of choice now—Adam, Luke, and Damián. The guys would never reject him.

What about Angelina? He'd known her barely six months, and she had left him early in their relationship. But he'd screwed the pooch that time.

He continued to hold onto her like the lifeline she was, but she persisted in pushing him away and stared up at him. Smiling? Puzzled, he quirked his head.

"Marc, Melissa isn't the type of woman who relinquishes control easily, if at all. Nor would she take no for an answer. I'm sure she orchestrated the entire scene just before you enlisted. If you want to talk about someone topping from the bottom…"

Marc hadn't really thought about it before, but Melissa *was* a control freak. Probably more than himself, if possible. Thinking back, Melissa did seem to have the upper hand with him that night, from the moment he'd found her kneeling on his doorstep. She'd certainly not complained about anything he'd done to her. When he told Adam about the scene, his friend had no sympathy for her either, but Marc had been so knotted up with guilt he hadn't really listened. Still, he knew she'd been drinking. He should have remained composed that night.

He hadn't loosened the tight rein on himself since. He sure as hell never allowed another woman to play him like that again.

But Angelina wasn't just any woman; she had never used him. His emotional connection with her was stronger than he'd ever experienced. Even Pamela hadn't evoked such strong feelings. To be honest, she hadn't used him, but he may well have used her. She deserved a more authentic Dom, one confident in his ability to provide what she needed and honest up front about his limitations.

Then along came Angelina, who disrupted his safe but lonely world like a fast-moving blizzard. She was the woman for whom he'd given up all others, the woman he never wanted to lose. He'd even been jealous of her being with Luke, despite the fact Marc knew she deserved someone more stable. Someone—well, like Luke.

No. Mine.

But for how long? If he didn't put his trust in her, he was going to lose her as early as tonight. He couldn't fuck this up.

Would letting her top him fulfill some need she had? Would it prove something to her about him? If this is what she needed in order to believe he trusted her, could he do it?

Not a chance.

He started to leave but halted when she said, "Marc, how many times have I given you my submission?" She didn't wait for a response. "In doing so, I also gifted you with the highest possible degree of trust that you would never harm me and would only act in my best interests."

"And I thank you for that gift, pet, but we aren't talking about you submitting to me now."

"No, I'm asking you to trust me enough to know what you need and to allow me to give that to you. You know I won't harm you."

Of course she wouldn't, because he wouldn't give her that much authority over him. He was no submissive. "You aren't a Domme, pet."

Her gaze remained steady, unrelenting. "Maybe not, but this submissive sees her Dom is neglecting his own needs. I think surrendering your need for constant control might help you discover some things about yourself that can help you sort out what's happening in your life right now. I can't bear to watch us drift further apart."

Merda. He glanced away. One thing Angelina was right about, though— they *were* drifting apart.

"Marc, I want to show you that you can trust me as much as I can you."

He'd screwed up enough lately, pushing her away and shutting himself off. He definitely didn't want to talk about what happened at Mama's earlier today, and if this scene would distract her, he might as well humor her and see what she had planned.

"Fine, I'll submit, but there will be no talk about what happened in Mama's office today."

"Hard limit?"

"Very."

"Eyes on me, Marc."

He met her gaze, sizing her up. He recognized the moment she sensed his decision to submit in her almost imperceptible smile.

Trust her.

All she asked of him was to meet that objective. Marc drew in a deep breath and handed the cuff back to her. "Have it your way, Angelina."

Her eyes opened wider, and she sounded as if the words barely made it from her throat. "Thank you."

"I'm *bottoming* for you, *amore*. For this one night only, I will allow you to be the Top. The few times I bottomed during my training as a Dom were…uncomfortable… to put it mildly." He remembered how he'd freaked out during a paddling training session when the club first opened. He had nearly ripped the spanking bench apart in his effort to get out of the straps, steadfastly refusing to use his safeword.

Adam demonstrated ways in which he might conduct himself better in the Dominant role, helping him unlearn some bad habits he'd picked up on his own over the years. The senior partner in the club's ownership had put Marc and Damián both through their paces before allowing either of them anywhere near the unattached submissives at the club.

"I find no excitement in being dominated and certainly none in giving up control. But if by doing so I can prove to you that I trust you, I will do it for you, my pet."

She grinned and her face lit up. "How do you know you won't find it exciting, boy? You've never been dominated by me before."

"Oh, on the contrary, my love."

You have dominated my life since the moment I found you on the St. Andrew's cross at the club being abused by Sir Asshole.

Angelina cocked her head waiting for him to elaborate but soon shrugged and reached out to take the cuff from him. Any hint of a smile was long gone. "Now, boy, I believe Mistress has given you an order, and you have hesitated long enough."

He'd taught her well, apparently, the persona of the Dominant.

Marc reached up and dispensed with the buttons on his shirt quickly, enjoying the way her eyes widened. Obviously, she hadn't anticipated his cooperation. He removed his shirt and unbuckled his belt, slipping it from the waistband loops. Just as he was about to let it fall to the floor, she held her free hand out.

"I'll take that."

Surely she didn't think she would be using a belt on him. Their gazes battled for supremacy for a moment until he remembered his place in this powder-puff exchange dynamic. He sighed, extending the belt to her. She draped the flogger over her shoulder once more, doubled the belt over, and slapped it against the inside of her free hand. Her slight wince had him fighting to suppress his grin.

Angelina blushed but recovered quickly. She quirked a brow at him then swung the belt as if practicing. Would she use it on him? He'd never used one on *her* before.

After leaving him wondering for a while, she wrapped the belt around her waist with a malicious grin, cinching herself into his Armani shirt. Her ample cleavage showed above the vee, reminding him of a lady pirate. The square hem fit snugly over her hips, and he looked to see if he could catch a glimpse of her bare mound.

Merda. So fucking sexy. Marc's cock stirred to life.

"Now the pants. Fold them neatly, just like they showed you in the Navy, and place them on the chair."

He'd always been conscientious about putting his things away, even before his Navy training. He sat on the bed to remove his shoes and socks. Standing again, his gaze still on her, he unzipped his pants, removing them.

Marc placed his slacks and shirt, neatly folded, on the chair and turned to face her.

"The boxer briefs, too."

When his hard-on sprang free of the black skivvies, she licked her lips. He almost ordered her to suck him dry, but that wasn't his role tonight. Something niggled at the back of his brain, but he couldn't determine if this was a new uneasiness or just more of the same as he submitted to Angelina for the first time.

He'd better get some reward tonight after all of this. The need to bury his cock deep inside her pussy intensified. Maybe he found her little Domme performance stimulating in some way. It certainly might be the diversion he needed from his dark thoughts lately.

If she was going to play the Dominant, though, he'd make sure she did so correctly.

"I don't recall negotiating the terms of this scene."

A glimpse of uncertainty crossed her face before she regained composure. "Because we haven't gotten that far yet, boy. Don't think or anticipate; that's my job. Now, name your hard limits."

"Being topped."

She sighed. "Acting like a brat will get you nothing except punishment. *What* are your hard limits, boy?"

Admitting any weakness to her didn't sit well with him. He paused a moment, soon realizing he would have to take this seriously. The woman meant business.

She narrowed her eyelids.

"Paddling."

"Any specific implement?"

"All of them."

Welcome to the world of the Dominant, pet. Subs didn't always make things easy.

Angelina grew even more serious as she squared her shoulders and stood her ground. "How about floggers, belts, tawse?"

"Not the tawse."

She nodded. "Any soft limits?"

"None that I'm aware of."

"Extend your hands toward me."

She held one of the leather cuffs he'd used on her many times.

Wait! Marc's heart pounded erratically at the implications of surrendering control.

Angelina nuzzled his neck, placing a kiss on his pulse, and whispered, "Trust me." Her hand reached up to stroke his biceps and arms in gentle, sweeping motions.

Marc closed his eyes. "Pet, you know I trust you." So then why wouldn't he follow her command?

She stepped back. "Prove it by obeying me, boy. You know I'll keep you safe. Give me your hands."

Her withdrawal left a tight coil of anxiety in his chest. He attempted to draw air into his lungs, but they closed up tighter than when the shrapnel from the mortar round had collapsed his lung. Sweat popped out on his forehead. He swallowed hard, reminding himself that anxiety and even a little fear were normal for a submissive at this point in a scene. That must be what was going on in his head.

Trust her.

Marc presented both hands to her.

Angelina's voice dropped in timbre as she instructed him while attaching first one then the other cuff to his wrists. "Tonight, you'll address me as Mistress, Mistress A, or Ma'am. You will not speak unless I ask you a direct question. You will not touch me unless I give you permission or tell you to do so. And you will keep your eyes down unless I tell you to do otherwise. Do you understand?"

The feel of the leather cuffs on his wrists wasn't as unpleasant as he'd expected, but she hadn't restrained him yet.

He grinned as his cock tightened. She was sexy as hell exerting her authority over him. "Yes, Mistress."

"Tell me your safeword, boy."

Boy, indeed.

His gaze lowered to her chest. "Tits."

"Be serious. You know damned well it has to be something you wouldn't normally say in a scene."

"I won't need a safeword."

She sighed. "If you don't give me your safeword, now, I'll give you one to use."

Her words gave him a clue she meant business. Of course, he knew she was right to insist on one. He'd taught her well. He glanced around the room but drew a blank. Maybe because he'd never used one before and he had no intention of doing so tonight.

"Fine, boy. How about Lombardy?"

In an instant, the mention of his birthplace conjured up memories of where he'd grown up in Italy. Normally, thoughts of his homeland were pleasant but not so after Mama's revelations earlier today. Where would Angelina's scene take them tonight?

He didn't have long to wonder. His gaze roamed over her body once more, her bare legs apart and his shirt barely covering her ass. The flogger once more in her hand, he marveled at her transformation from submissive to Dominant.

She stood with her legs planted apart, shoulders back, with a Domme stare that exuded confidence. Without warning, the falls of the flogger thudded against his thigh, their ends stinging as they wrapped around his ass.

"Eyes on the floor."

He grinned at how ridiculous it felt to submit to her.

"Wipe that smirk off your face, Sir...I mean, *boy.*" Her cheeks flushed at the slip, but she quickly regained her composure.

"Twice now I've told you where your gaze should be. Don't make me repeat myself again or you will force me to plan your first punishment."

First, perhaps, but it would definitely be the last.

Appease her. "Yes, Mistress."

His cock grew rigid as he let his gaze take in her gorgeous body once more while slowly following her command.

The falls slapped his ass again. "No hesitation next time."

Apparently, she intended to go through with this preposterous role reversal. He'd agreed to the power exchange, so he needed to try and wrap his mind around his new status. A bottom.

"Yes, Mistress."

She surprised him once again when she explained without hesitation the scene she had planned.

"You will be restrained to the bed. No honor bondage, not because I don't trust you, but you need to feel the caress of the leather on your wrists and ankles, the restriction of the restraints. At all four points."

Arms *and* legs? *How long had she been preparing to top him?* It would definitely be the last time he would leave her alone to her own devices for too long. Oh, but there would be no next time for a scene like this.

His heart pounded harder, but his cock softened as blood rushed to even more vital parts of his body. Fight or flight. What was he so afraid of?

Angelina leaned in, closing the space between them and reached up to stroke his cheek and neck. She whispered, "I know this is difficult for you, but Mistress is here to take care of you. No harm will come to you in this scene. You have your safeword if you need it. Understand?"

Marc swallowed hard, reminding himself his initial responses were common for a submissive, especially a new one. He watched for signs of fight or flight in Angelina every time they played. Apparently, she knew what to do to calm his fears. Somewhat.

"Yes, Ma'am."

Angelina patted his cheek before she reached down to check the tightness of both wrist cuffs, just as he had done so many times with her.

Angelina pulled the bed covering to the bottom of the mattress. "Lie on the bed, face up." He hesitated a moment too long apparently. "Mistress is tired of repeating every command multiple times. Last warning without consequences." She flicked the falls of the leather flogger against her upturned palm a few times to make her point.

Marc grinned and met her gaze.

"What does my boy find so funny?"

"Nothing, Mistress."

"Why are you still standing here then—and where should your eyes be?"

He lowered his gaze to the floor.

"Good boy. Now, on your back."

"Yes, Mistress."

He crawled to the middle of the bed, propped a couple of pillows behind his head, and stretched out on his back. Would she straddle him? *Dio*, he hoped so. Angelina nibbled at her lower lip, her gaze fixed on his recovered erection.

"Perhaps you should cuff my ankles now," he prompted.

"Are you instructing your Mistress, boy? I'm in charge here, and it's none of your concern if I have chosen to take a moment to admire the obvious display of your excitement at my dominance over you. You would do well to remember your place, boy."

"Mistress, I assure you, seeing you wearing my shirt and nothing else does excite me, no matter which power role I'm fulfilling."

"Well, then, perhaps I need to remove the shirt."

Marc wanted nothing more than to feast his eyes on her tits. "Be my guest."

"You just addressed me without permission. I see I'm going to need something with a little more sting to it to teach you proper discipline."

She walked to the toy bag and retrieved something he couldn't see. What did she hold behind her back? At least the canes were upstairs in the playroom; otherwise, he might be in real trouble right now.

"I've counted two strokes for disobedience since my last warning."

Without further warning, she displayed the riding crop and in one motion brought it down swiftly just inches below his balls. He pulled his legs up instinctively to protect any errant blows from castrating him.

Fuck, it stung! He'd never hit her that hard with it.

Without delivering the second promised blow, she returned to the bag and came back with ankle cuffs.

"I'll decide when the time is right to deliver your remaining punishment stroke and any others you earn."

The little minx. "How much practice have you had with the crop? You came perilously close to neutering me."

Her glare reminded him to lower his gaze and shut his mouth.

Angelina sighed. "Marc, you're a lousy submissive."

"It's not as if I didn't warn you…*Mistress.*"

"Well, then. Maybe I need to step up my game and become a better Dominant."

Merda. He'd unleashed her inner Domme now. Heaven help him, because this woman did *not* hit like a girl.

*   *   *

Angelina had had enough of Marc's rebelliousness. Right now, he was just toying with being her bottom. He hadn't submitted one tiny bit. How would she build trust between them if he didn't respect her authority?

On her way back to his toy bag to gather what she'd need, Angelina thought about how much more enjoyable it was to be on the receiving end of domination, not having to worry about all of the details. She had to deal with enough of those when running her catering business, and she enjoyed letting go of responsibility when she submitted to Marc during their play scenes.

Marc would have planned this scene ahead of time to fit the occasion or her needs. Flying by the seat of her pants, she couldn't exhibit any hint of insecurity. She'd had a couple close calls already but thought she recovered well. By delivering the first of his punishment blows—harder than she'd intended to—clearly he knew to take her seriously.

Spontaneity wasn't optimal for a play scene, but Marc had rolled with the punches before, adjusting a scene to explore whatever came up. She'd do what was needed without bowing to his previous authority over her. Marc needed to relinquish that tight grip on his self-control, whether he wanted to or not. He needed to trust her to take care of him.

The execution of *this* scene was in her hands. What should she use? Angelina dug around in the leather bag, found the items she was looking for, and returned to the bed, concealing some of them for later under the sheet piled at the base of the bed. She hoped the batteries were fresh in the one, because she planned to wear it out on him tonight.

First, though, the restraints. *Oh, shoot!* Angelina sighed at having forgotten something so obvious and went back to the bag. Pulling out four chains, she fastened the end of one of the chains to the D-ring on his left wrist cuff and pulled his hand toward the carabiner she knew was hidden discreetly behind the headboard.

"How's that?" Marc moved his arm nearly a foot. "Wait. Let me hook it here." She pulled the chain taut and fastened it. He wasn't able to move more than a few inches now. Better.

Angelina walked around the bed but felt his gaze on her again. "Where are your eyes supposed to be, boy?"

"On the floor, but I can't see the floor now."

When she was his bottom in a scene, she had never been this dense at following commands. Why didn't he use a little common sense?

"Your insolence just earned you another stripe. Any further snarky remarks will earn five each. In this scene, I have made it clear several times that you are not to look directly at me unless instructed to do so. Do. You. Understand?"

"Yes, Mistress A."

Relishing the thought of wiping the smirk off his face, she waited until he settled his gaze somewhere near the foot of the bed before she continued to the other side where she attached another chain to his right wrist cuff and hooked it to the bed frame. She followed quickly with the ankle cuffs. This would hold him when the scene became more active. Marc tested his range of motion, and she watched as the smug expression left his face. Perhaps he fully understood his predicament at last.

Standing back, she admired the image of Marc stretched out before her, magnificently naked and at her mercy. A red stripe welted his thigh—*Dio*, that must hurt—serving as a reminder for him to behave. She hadn't done much to teach him discipline yet, though. He'd earned two more already, and she was certain they wouldn't be the last.

A surge of power coursed through her. Being the Dominant was heady stuff and more than a little sexy. His pecs were so taut and lickable she had to tear her gaze away to keep from indulging too soon.

His focus returned to her face, and he flexed his fingers. "I'll let you know if my hands tingle or anything else goes numb."

Angelina blinked. *Crap.* She'd forgotten to tell him to do that. *Focus. Don't let him control this scene.*

"Boy, you and I have been together long enough I shouldn't have to remind you of our safety precautions. Mistress is very disappointed. I count four times you've disobeyed me by looking directly at me. I already owe you three punishment stripes." Clearly, Marc would continue to top from the bottom unless she did something about it. "Might as well deliver those three now."

His legs jerked as if trying to protect his rigid penis. He should have thought about that before.

"Count for me, boy, and ask for the next."

The crop whistled through the air as she brought it down hard just an inch away from the first strike. She aimed to move away from his balls.

"I can't hear you."

He gritted the words out. "One, Mistress. May I have another?"

She brought the crop down again, only this time it hit the same spot as her first blow earlier. Marc fought the restraints and perspiration broke out on his upper lip. "Two. May I have another?"

Trying to go for new territory this time, she moved to the other side of the bed before delivering the third blow.

"Three, Mistress. Thank you."

He sounded anything but grateful, but he'd obeyed her. "Good boy."

Red welts raised on his thighs. She'd apply the lidocaine later.

Since he not only had trouble averting his gaze but also keeping his mouth shut, she returned to the toy bag and pulled out the new ball gag she'd found in her Christmas stocking. Marc hadn't used it on her yet, but he'd given it to her technically, so...

"You aren't putting that thing on me."

She turned to find him glaring at her. She hadn't intended to use the gag right away, but have it be a visual deterrent. Apparently, she would have to reconsider.

"You've earned five more lashes for not disciplining your eyes and five more for speaking without permission. To keep your thighs and backside from being raw by night's end and because I am a loving Dominant, I'm going to gag you." She crawled onto the mattress. "Open wide, Marc."

He glared at her, jaw clenched.

"I said, avert your eyes and open your mouth. You've earned ten more strikes. Don't continue to defy me. I need to concentrate on this scene, and you topping from the bottom is distracting."

"I'm not topping—just offering you some helpful suggestions."

Now Angelina clenched her teeth. "You have earned five more for sassing me. They will commence as soon as you put this on. Now. I said. Open wide. *Boy.* I'll give you a safe signal. Now, open."

He sobered, but his mouth remained closed.

"Eyes on me." He obeyed. "Be honest with me, Marc. What scares you about the gag?"

He remained silent for several moments. "I'm not scared."

"Your eyes disagree." Angelina understood Marc's fear of losing one of his coping mechanisms—that snarky mouth of his—but knew they'd reached a turning point in the scene. "Boy, the intent of this scene is for you to show you trust me. Therefore, as I see it, you have two choices. Either you use your safeword and we are finished with this scene, or you choose to trust me and let me continue. Which will it be?" He remained silent, defiance and fear mixed in his eyes. "That was a direct question, boy."

He glared at the ball gag for several long moments.

"I'll give you the clicker to hold for your safe signal when I apply the gag. If you click it, I'll remove the gag immediately and the scene will end, as if you'd spoken your safeword."

Chapter Ten

*T*rust me, Marc. Can't you please just trust me?

"Fine," he said grudgingly. "I'll take the gag."

Angelina tried to hide her surprise, not expecting him to relent. "Good choice, boy."

"I want the clicker in my hand before you put the gag in place."

She had no desire to terrify him, though. Something about being gagged scared him. She just wanted to get him to trust her. Maybe she could gain some ground here. "We can continue this scene without the gag, if you behave." Marc's body relaxed into the mattress. "But if you start topping or speaking out again, I *will* use it. Understand?"

"I understand, Mistress. Thank you."

Angelina smiled and leaned over to place a kiss on his lips. Maybe by backing down on the gag she'd made giant leaps in earning his trust. That he would accept something that obviously terrified him gave her hope, though.

When he kissed her back, she became momentarily distracted. *Dio*, the man knew how to make her weak in the knees.

She broke the kiss. "Mmmm. Thank you. Mistress is now very pleased with her boy."

His eyes twinkled when he smiled, but he quickly averted his gaze. To reward him, she reached down to stroke his penis before straddling him and pressing her bare pussy against his erection. He pumped his hips against her core, and she closed her eyes, moaning. She reached for the top button of her shirt and undid it. When she opened her eyes, Marc's gaze lingered on her girls waiting not-quite patiently for her to undo the next button. Well, at least he wasn't challenging her by looking her in the eye.

"Tell Mistress A what you need, boy."

He licked his lips. "I need to see Mistress's tits, so I can suck her nipples into my mouth, one at a time, until the peaks harden. Then I need to bite them until she screams for me."

Mio Dio. Her pussy muscles clenched. Well, she'd asked him a direct question and had gotten honesty in return. Drawing a deep breath, she undid another button and spread the flaps of the shirt open, tucking them around her breasts like a sling. As she leaned forward, she reached out to hold onto the headboard, dangling a breast just in front of his face like a ripe apple hanging from a tree.

"Suck Mistress's tit, boy."

When her left breast was still an inch or two from his mouth, Marc raised his head to grab her nipple between his teeth, tugging at her breast. Her clit spasmed, stimulated not merely by his sucking but also by his throbbing penis pressed against the tiny nubbin.

Marc's tongue flicked against the captured peak, and she moaned.

"Bite me, boy." His teeth bit into the engorged tip and she screamed. "Oh, *Dio*, yes! Again." He bit down harder and pulled her breast with his teeth as he laid his head back on the pillow. When her breast plopped out of his mouth, she looked down at him, and he smiled.

"Put my cock inside your pussy, pet. Now."

She almost reached down to comply but stopped and glared at him. "Who gives the orders tonight, boy?"

Marc's body grew rigid, but his cock bobbed against her hidden entrance, making her wish she could just do as he'd commanded. It was what they both wanted, but he hadn't earned that reward yet.

He turned his gaze from her chest to the mattress. "You do, Mistress. I'm sorry. Quite sorry, actually, as I'm sure you must be."

He only sounded sorry that she hadn't followed through on his command.

"What did I say about sassing your Mistress?"

His gaze went to the ball gag lying a few feet away on the bed. He paused a long, tense moment. "Do as you must, Mistress."

She didn't miss the flash of fear in his eyes nor the arrogant dare. Did he think she wouldn't do it? As his Domme, she had to follow through on any promises if she wanted him to come to trust her in the slightest. For her, the ball gag was a major annoyance, but something about it really scared Marc.

As his Domme tonight, if she could get him to trust her enough to let her do something that scared him so much, maybe they would be able to make some headway toward breaking down the barriers between them. But he had yet to relinquish control.

She silenced him with a scathing glare. "I've given you ample opportunities to behave. You were told to only speak if I ask a direct question, so you also know what you've forced me to do."

He smiled at her and relaxed again. "Your boy understands and thanks Mistress for her patience."

With a sigh, Angelina got off the bed and returned to the toy bag. She ought to just bring the whole damned bag up onto the bed but hoped this was the last thing she'd need to retrieve for this scene. How did Marc seem to know everything he'd need and have it at the ready for their scenes? Being the Dominant partner was damned hard work.

She found the clicker from a long-forgotten board game. She'd used the noisemaker as her own safe signal several times in the past and took it to him, placing it in his right hand.

"Click it, and we stop. Immediately. Do you understand you have a safe signal now?"

He paused a moment then nodded. "Yes, Mistress."

She almost expected him to click it immediately, but he held on until his knuckles turned white. Straddling his waist again, she pressed the gag against his mouth. He didn't open at first, not even a tiny bit. She wiggled her ass against his erect penis to distract him. Slowly, he opened his mouth, and she pressed the red ball against his teeth but couldn't insert it between them.

"Open wider and rest your tongue flat on the bottom of your mouth." She knew how uncomfortable it would be in short order if his tongue wasn't positioned properly. He did as she commanded, but when he began to panic, taking short, shallow breaths, she gave him time to adjust to the idea of the gag. "Deep breath." He ignored her. "Now, boy. Don't make me repeat myself."

Marc inhaled deeply through his nose. When he released the breath, the air felt warm at first and then chilled her bare, wet nipple. She wanted his mouth on her again but helping him overcome his fear of the gag was her main objective, not her own satisfaction. "Again."

What were some of the things Marc had done to help her get over her own anxieties? He touched her a lot, spoke softly to her.

"Good boy. Keep breathing through your nose." Of course, he knew how to breathe with a gag in his mouth. She just didn't want him to let the anxiety get the better of him again. She knew firsthand that remembering to breathe was the first thing to go out the window when she grew anxious. She tried to remember how Grant had handled some of her male subs, but they tended to be less intimidating than Marc.

Angelina stretched out beside him, draping her arm and leg over him. When he jerked his legs, she remembered the stripes on his thighs and removed her leg. "I know this isn't easy for you, boy, but Mistress is proud of you for trusting her." Her words of praise had the same effect on him as his often had on her. He relaxed.

"Now, we're going to proceed."

He nodded.

"That's my good boy." She straddled him again. "Lift your head." He complied without hesitation. She stroked his cheek, satisfied that he'd gotten his anxiety under control again and trusted her enough to do this. She maneuvered the ball between his teeth with little resistance this time, wrapping the strap around his head and tightening it. "How does that feel? Nod if you're doing okay." He nodded. Good. She tried not to laugh at the image of him with the gag in his mouth. His male ego would so not appreciate that.

Oh, hell, gags were messy things. Humiliation wasn't her goal tonight. "Mistress will be right back. I just need to get something for you from the bathroom."

Angelina scooted off the bed and ran to the bathroom to get a washcloth and a tube of toothpaste for later, scurrying back to him. His gaze was on the bathroom doorway waiting anxiously for her to return, but he averted his eyes immediately. Did he not trust her to return?

He obviously wasn't going to obey her either, so she walked over to the dresser drawer and opened it, retrieving the kelly-green resistance band her oldest brother Rafe had given her. He'd refused to do any more physical therapy with it on his leg after an injury during a fire call four months ago. She'd been using the stretchy latex band to build the muscles in her arms and legs.

Now it would serve as a blindfold. Having Marc continue to challenge her authority with his gaze was preventing her from maintaining Dominant authority over him.

Taking the ends of the band, she returned to the bed, ignoring his frown as she straddled his chest. "We both will enjoy this scene better if you can't see what's coming. As you know, sensations are so much more intense when one or more senses are removed." She wondered if he remembered telling her something similar when he blindfolded her in her bedroom in Aspen Corners that first time. He captured her gaze with his and held it, defiant to the end.

"You just earned five more lashes for looking at me." He tensed, but she planned to use the flogger for some of these. His skin would be raw otherwise. Amazing that, even after she'd shown him how hard she would deliver the punishment blows, he still wouldn't obey.

Stubborn, stubborn man.

Though his eyes blistered her with defiance, she stood her ground. After a tense standoff, he closed his eyes and raised his head off the pillow, allowing her to tie the blindfold around his head. The shift in authority as she removed yet another of his defense mechanisms gave her a sense of power she'd rarely felt. She adjusted it over the bridge of his nose, preventing him from being able to see what she was doing.

Trust me, baby.

Angelina stood and stared down at Marc's gorgeous, restrained body. Where to begin? First, something simple. She stood up beside the bed and picked up the deer-hide flogger. She wanted to warm his skin with the thuddy implement before setting him on fire with erotic tingling and a mixture of sting and thud with the nylon chain flogger later. Soon she'd have him begging for more. For her.

Well, not verbally begging.

She smiled.

She'd been on the receiving end of this implement many times. Marc was an expert, but he'd let her practice with it a few times and had pointed out where her technique was lacking.

Now, how many lashes had he earned? Twenty-five? Thirty? She hadn't been keeping count as he racked up the transgressions.

Taking the wrapped handle, she dragged the soft falls over his chest and abdomen, working around his penis to his thighs. He clenched his fists when they touched his welted skin but relaxed within seconds. She lifted the flogger off him and began swishing the falls in the air, coming closer and closer to his skin each time but not touching. Surely he felt the breeze the motion created and heard the sound, though. He held his body rigid, as if waiting for the first impact. But when it didn't come, he relaxed. She'd made that mistake many times, letting down her guard too soon.

Flick, flick, flick.

When she struck his sides and pecs the first time, he raised up his chest as if to meet the falls. His nips enlarged as she repeatedly struck them, light at first, then harder. He clenched his fists but seemed to be enjoying it, if his bobbing erection was any indication. Over and over, she flicked the deer-hide tips. His olive skin turned a dusty rose. Time for the nylon-chain flogger. She switched the softer flogger to her left hand and moved down his body, flicking him with the harsher falls, bypassing his balls and penis. She flicked his striped thighs, and he hissed at the impact on his now-sensitive skin.

Angelina walked around to the other side of the bed and, at first, just stroked him with the soft falls of the flogger. Then she began lashing him again. As she drew closer to his penis, it bobbed in the air, seeking contact with the leather. Precum dripped from the tip of his erection. She began to lash his balls ever so lightly at first, then harder. His hips jerked away as much as they could move, which wasn't very far. This he didn't enjoy.

"Lie still. Mistress didn't give you permission to move."

She smacked the flogger across his balls with a thud, and he jumped, groaning through the gag.

"Quiet. Mistress knows what her boy needs."

Dio, I hope so, anyway.

As she let the falls thud more heavily against his penis and balls, he hissed. Deciding to give him a rest, she brought the flogger down in an overhand motion onto his chest. He jerked his torso up when they slapped against his nipples again. Ah, so her boy wanted more play there.

"Lie still." She hoped her voice sounded firm, but it was difficult to contain her happiness at bringing him excitement. He seemed to enjoy having his nipples stimulated.

Happy to oblige, she laid the flogger on the bed and walked over to the toy bag. "I know just the thing." She rooted around a bit. "This should do the trick." She knew he couldn't see what she'd found, but anticipation was good for him. His nips were smaller than hers, but these alligator nipple clamps would exert enough pressure to make him squirm—and he'd squirm even more later on when she removed them. She wondered if her man's nips were as sensitive as hers.

Setting the clamps at his side, she straddled his hips again, wiggling her ass against his penis just for meanness—and because she could. Suddenly, her own desire rose, and she wanted him buried deep inside her. Nearly overwhelmed, she fought to tamp down her errant libido.

Not yet. *Above all, self-control.*

She giggled, remembering the line spoken by the wicked stepmother in the *Cinderella* video she and Savi had watched with Marisol the other day.

Focus, Angie. Cartoon characters have no place in a BDSM scene.

Angelina bent over Marc and licked his nipple. When she took the little nip between her teeth and tugged, he moaned. Sitting up again, she picked up a clamp and rubbed it against his swollen nipple, letting him hear the tinkle of the dangling chain. She wasn't sure if he tensed at the coldness of the metal or because he knew what was coming, but he held his entire body rigid.

"Prepare to feel the bite, boy." Without prolonging the anticipation as long as he might have with her, she clamped the first one over his nip.

He tried to pull away from the pain, groaning into the gag, but had nowhere to go. She picked up the washcloth and wiped the spittle off the corner of his mouth. The way he bit into the ball told her he hadn't anticipated that much pain.

"And again." He tensed and stopped breathing. Without further ado, she clamped the other nipple. Marc moaned again as the clamp's teeth bit into him. "Breathe, boy." She stroked his chest, making circle eights around his upper and lower pecs while avoiding the nipple clamps and the chain between them.

Angelina straddled his knees and couldn't resist bending down to place a kiss against the cleft at the head of his penis. It bobbed against her mouth, and she took just the head inside, sucked gently, and then released him with a plop. The salty precum on her tongue made her want more.

Not yet.

Dommes needed discipline, too—*self*-discipline. She nearly giggled remembering how Marc had exuded self-control until his balls were blue that first week they'd been together at the start of their D/s relationship.

What next? She wished she knew what Marc needed most from her, so she could give that to him in this scene. How did he always seem to know what *she* needed? Marc withheld orgasms from her many times, but…

Remembering how long he'd gone without coming during their first week together—four *days*—something occurred to her. What if having an orgasm was another way in which Marc kept tight control of his emotions? Did allowing himself to have an orgasm with her equate to vulnerability to him?

She grinned.

We'll see who's in control of your orgasms now, Sir...boy.

Time for some fun. Maybe she wasn't supposed to be enjoying this more than her sub, but now that he was cooperating, she was getting into what she thought might be Domme headspace quite nicely. Excitement bubbled up inside her as she slid her hand under the sheet near his left foot and pulled out the cock ring. The vibrator buzzed to life. Angelina smiled and looked up at Marc. Judging by how much stiffer his penis became, he knew what she held. He'd enjoy it, too—up to a point anyway.

"Instead of the negative reinforcement of continuing to use the lash as punishment, Mistress is going to use another method to help you remember self-discipline, so you never make the same mistakes again."

He mumbled against the gag—probably assuring her there would be no next time—but she merely grinned and crawled closer to him. She wished she had some fuck-me stiletto thigh-high boots on to give her more of a Domme appearance, but she had seen plenty of femdoms at the club wearing comfortable walking shoes. Marc couldn't see her anyway and if stiletto shoes were out, she guessed he wouldn't want her to wear stiletto boots either. So she'd remain comfortably barefoot.

Leaning back, she lubed the gel-and-plastic ring, placed it over the head of his penis, and slid it down to his balls. A quick reach under the sheet again, and she pulled out a banana-flavored condom to sheath him. Even though she wasn't ready to do anything sexual yet, preparation was good, not to mention the anticipation.

Encourage him to trust—and then make him loosen the tight reins on his self-control.

"Mistress is proud of you for trusting her with both a ball gag and a blindfold. My good boy."

He sank into the mattress, surrendering to her.

Straddling him, she took her fingernails and raked down his torso, digging a little more deeply into his skin as she drew closer to his hips. She bent over him and grabbed the chain between the nipple clamps with her teeth. Raising up slowly, she pulled on them while pressing her pussy tightly against his erection, rocking up and down on him. He moaned and bucked against her.

"Lie still." She stifled a giggle, knowing she was teasing him.

Angelina dropped the chain and trailed kisses down his abs as she scooted down the bed until she reached his hard penis. Taking him into her mouth, she wrapped her lips around him and let her teeth graze the sheathed skin. His sharp intake of breath through his nose emboldened her, and she reached for the cock ring to turn it on. The vibrations of her boy's banana-flavored cock made her mouth tingle and water at the same time. She sucked harder, knowing he wouldn't come while the ring restricted the blood flow to his penis.

After a few minutes of teasing, she thought now might be a good time to make it clear where this scene was heading. But they would need to communicate fully, so the need for the ball gag had passed. Time to release him before she forced a release from him. For what was probably his first time with a gag since he'd trained to use one, he'd done really well. She'd made her point.

Taking one leg and swinging it over his waist, she unstraddled his hips. She unsnapped the strap of the ball gag. "Open wide for me, boy."

He did so without hesitation, anxious to get rid of the thing no doubt, and let her remove the gag. Picking up the washcloth, she wiped the drool off the corners of his mouth. She'd never understood the attraction of gags and hadn't liked when Marc gagged her. It was the only really humiliating thing he subjected her to. Luckily, he didn't do it very often, but only because she'd taken to discipline much more quickly than he had today.

No sense removing the blindfold just yet. His penis throbbed against her pussy as he worked his mouth and jaws. Good, because she planned to work them some more in a few minutes. She wanted some answers, communication.

"What are you feeling, boy?"

"Relieved to be out of the gag."

"Was it as bad as you expected?"

He was silent for a moment. "Not what I expected at all."

"Didn't you train with a ball gag at some point?"

He shrugged. "I just put one on myself."

She rolled her eyes. "Not quite the same when you're at the mercy of someone restraining you, is it? Someone taking away your decision for when it could be removed?"

He shook his head.

"But why were you so afraid of it?"

His body tensed. "Who said I was afraid?"

"Marc, don't lie to your Domme. You were terrified."

"I don't know."

"Honest answers."

"That's as honest as I can be. I don't know why the thought of a gag freaked me out, but you're right, Mistress. It did."

Acknowledging that her assessment was accurate thrilled her. He was often cocky and arrogant, never wanting to admit any sign of weakness.

"Thank you, boy, for your honesty." She stroked his cheek, and he smiled.

"Mistress has something special for her boy now. She's going to torture your cock and balls a while, but you won't be permitted to come until she's ready." Now for the clincher. "When Mistress tells you to come, you will do so immediately and show her how you trust her to take care of your needs. Is that clear?"

"Very, but I can't come on command."

"Are you saying you plan to defy Mistress?"

"I'm just stating a fact Mistress might not have noticed in the past several months."

Oh, I've noticed.

Now to do something about it. "We'll proceed. You do not want to disappoint Mistress, though. The consequences may be felt long after this scene ends."

"All I can do is try."

"Try very hard, boy."

*   *   *

Cock-and-ball torture? Where the hell had she learned about that? Had she been taking lessons from Grant? Surely she wouldn't have one of Grant's male chastity belts. No way in hell would she find CBT gear in *his* toy bag. Of course, there were other ways to torture a man's cock and balls.

What the fuck did she mean by consequences beyond this scene?

Hell, submitting even for this short time was torture, but he wasn't going to permit her domination beyond tonight. He just wished she'd achieve whatever it was she needed to get out of this scene soon so they could put an end to it.

Not that the entire scene had been bad. He'd enjoyed parts of the flogging. Having Angelina's mouth on his cock always felt good. One thing he didn't want to think about was what these nipple clamps were going to feel like when she removed them.

Her hand cupped his balls, and he held his breath, waiting for whatever she intended to do to him. She squeezed them lightly, not hard enough to raise his voice an octave. Her mouth enveloped the head of his penis again, and he gave in to the exquisite sensations. Her sharp nails grazed his balls, and his hips jolted up, sending his cock further down her throat.

Sweet.

Until she pulled away. "Didn't Mistress tell you to remain still, boy?"

"Yes, ma'am. But it's hard to do when you touch me like that."

"How many times have you teased and tickled me while teaching me to discipline my body?"

True. But she'd needed long-term discipline. He wouldn't be...

She squeezed his balls more tightly.

Fuck!

"Mistress asked you a direct question."

His throat constricted, but he answered in a harsh whisper, "Yes, Mistress A. Many times, too many to count, actually. I have a new appreciation for your incredible willpower."

Her chuckle either meant she appreciated his compliment—or thought he was bull-shitting. But if the latter, one thing he'd learned tonight was that he would earn swift punishment. He waited to see what her response would be. The cock ring continued to buzz, keeping him erect. Maybe his fate was to suffer all night with a hard-on.

Better than coming on command.

Whoa! He enjoyed a good orgasm no matter who was in charge. Was he worried about letting his guard down enough to allow her to control his orgasm? He found it easier to reach orgasm with Angelina than with any woman he'd ever been with. Even if he couldn't always get there, he always made sure Angelina did.

Angelina's lips wrapped around the head of his cock again, and he fought hard not to move his hips. So she hadn't decided to call this off? Her teeth grazed his head as she pulled away, setting his own teeth on edge.

Careful there, Mistress.

She turned off the cock ring and took him deeper into her mouth. He shook with the effort to remain in control. Her finger pressed against his perineum, and he nearly escaped from his restraints.

"Please forgive me, Mistress." Perhaps she'd go easy on him if he admitted his inability to lie still.

She removed her mouth and left his cock wet, cold, and rigid. He noticed a burning where she'd touched the area over his prostate gland that grew warmer and warmer. What the fuck had she put on him?

"Want to feel something else burn, boy?"

Unable to process her words, his first inkling at what she meant came when she tugged on the chain between the clamps. He steeled himself for the release of the first one, but the cock ring buzzed to life a half second before, short-circuiting his mind. He fisted his hand at the blinding pain as the first clamp released. A whoosh of blood rushed into his nip. He hissed before masking his discomfort.

Merda. He'd forgotten how badly clamps hurt.

She bent to lave the sore nip with her tongue, dispersing the residual pain more quickly, just as he often did with her.

"Better?"

"I'm fine." His heart continued to race but not because of the clamps. He just wanted this fucking scene to end.

Sweat broke out on his upper lip, but he managed to discipline both body and mouth.

Angelina didn't remove the other clamp but tugged at the cock ring instead.

"Get ready to please Mistress, boy." She turned it off as she worked it up his cock. His perineal area burned like crazy from whatever she'd used there. She took him into her mouth once more. When her tight throat encased the head of his penis, he nearly came undone but regained control.

His cock throbbed. Close. Very close, but Mistress hadn't given him permission to come. He fought hard against the needed release.

Her hand grabbed the base of his cock like a vise, and she began pumping him.

"Please, Mistress, may I come?" *Dio*, she had him begging!

Her head rose off his cock and, in a raspy voice, commanded, "Come for me, boy. Now."

"Come for me, Marco. You will come for me—now!"

The Italian woman's grating voice threw ice on his libido, and his cock lost the urgent need to come. Suddenly, the thought of having an orgasm at her command nauseated him. His softening erection reflected his disgust.

"Let me help." She removed the second nipple clamp. As the pain ripped through his chest, he couldn't keep from pumping his hips upward against her hand. He'd had no warning she was ready to remove that clamp. He'd disobeyed her by moving but no longer cared.

He fought to keep his cock hard, yet knew it was a losing battle.

Angelina straddled him, but he'd lost his erection completely now.

"What is it you need from me?"

His chest muscles tightened, and he struggled to remove her weight by twisting his torso side to side. "Get the fuck off me."

Not waiting for her to loosen her thighs and slide off him, he managed to twist hard enough to dump her on her ass on the mattress.

He couldn't feel her any longer but knew from her voice she was next to him. "What's going on, Marc? Did I hurt you?"

He fisted his hands, fighting the chains holding him immobile, but didn't respond.

She stretched the latex blindfold over his forehead. "Your shrapnel injury. Did I hurt it?"

He blinked to clear his vision, his chest heaving as he fought for breath, but he didn't look at her. He couldn't. His initial response was to ask if she meant the emotional wound she had inflicted unknowingly, because that was the only place that hurt. "No. It's fine."

"You shut down. What's going on? Eyes on me."

He kept his gaze averted.

"I. Said. Eyes. On. Me."

He wouldn't allow her to read his emotions through his eyes, so he masked his expression before gazing at her with reluctance.

"Tell me what's going on, Marc. What do you need?"

Her words slammed into Marc's already wounded psyche like a projectile, instantly sending his heart rate through the roof as adrenaline pumped into his system. Angelina had only meant to play with him, but something—perhaps commanding him to come or asking him to convey his needs—had shut him down completely.

"That was a direct question, boy."

He fought to regain control of his breathing, which became shallow and labored as the air chilled his clammy forehead. The safeword she'd given him lay on the tip of his tongue. He wouldn't have to answer if he spoke his safeword—but doing so was a sign of weakness he couldn't reveal.

What the fuck was going on? Even the ball gag, which had just about sent him over the edge, didn't compare to the anxiety he felt now.

"Untie me."

She touched his chest but didn't reach for the cuffs. "Marc, do you want to use your safeword or are you role-playing? Say 'Lombardy' if this is for real."

The mention of his childhood home sent a bead of sweat rolling down his face and into his ear. He tried never to reveal deep emotions to anyone. Adam probably had dented Marc's protective armor once or twice with his badgering, delving into the past as he tried to figure out Marc's sometimes illogical motives and actions. But he couldn't make himself that vulnerable again—not to a woman, anyway.

Again?

Where had that thought come from? He'd had a happy childhood, well, what he remembered anyway. He had no memory of his birth parents. But who wouldn't want to grow up at a ski lodge in the Alps or in the Colorado Rockies with a family who loved him? He might not have been the favored son, but he'd been loved by Mama and Papa nonetheless.

Did his visceral response have something to do with Gino?

When they were kids, they'd been very close. Marc had worshipped his older brother until they reached their late teen years. That drifting apart was mostly Marc's fault, as he became aware he wasn't living up to his parents' expectations for him the way Gino always had. Perhaps Gino just tried harder. Marc had let his emotions get the best of him when Gino took Melissa from him. He and his brother had barely spoken after that. Marc had pushed Gino into enlisting in the Marines, only to get himself killed in Afghanistan.

Marc didn't want to think about those times. What the fuck was happening to him? Did he want to call this scene off? No. Angelina needed to know he trusted her. She needed this scene. He would continue. For her.

"Nothing's wrong. You just confused me; that's all."

Confusion creased Angelina's forehead. She tilted her head and studied his face. He didn't care if she bought his lame explanation or not. The subject of his panic attack was not open for discussion, especially because he didn't know from where it had originated.

"What is Mistress going to do with me? Her boy disobeyed yet again."

Angelina reclined beside him again, placing her arm over his chest and her leg over his hips without putting too much pressure on him, as if he'd break. She made such a lousy Domme.

Grazie, Dio.

She smiled and turned her face toward him, placing a kiss on his lips before moving away and staring into his eyes.

"Lombardy, Sir. I don't want to play anymore. If I untie you, will you just let me hold you?"

She'd used the safeword for him? Was she feeling sorry for him because he'd freaked out on her?

Keep your pity, pet. I'll never give up control to a woman, not tonight or any other night.

He fought the impulse to run, as if he could go anywhere while in four-point restraints.

Maybe Angelina was projecting her own need to be held, which he would honor as soon as he regained control. Without waiting for him to respond, she reached up and ripped the Velcro open on the right cuff followed quickly by the left. His arms didn't move much from their position at first, having been bound there so long. She bent over him and kneaded the muscles in his shoulders and upper arms until he was able to lower them.

Hold her.

He wrapped his arms around her, still struggling to fill his lungs. *Numb yourself.* He tried to shut down emotionally, but the overwhelming urge to run dominated his thoughts. It always did.

He pulled her closer as if she were a lifeline and he a drowning man.

Angelina laid her head on his chest. "Shhh." She stroked his chest.

He willed his heartbeat to slow down, not wanting to tip her off that he was still in fight-or-flight mode. As if she was too blind to notice. She wouldn't have used their safeword if she thought he could handle continuing with the scene.

He inhaled deeply, feeling the familiar hitch in his side from old adhesions. Did this have something to do with post-traumatic stress from his combat wound?

No, he didn't think so.

"Don't forget the ankle restraints."

She sat up quickly. "Sorry!" He enjoyed the view of her backside as she faced away and undid the cuffs.

Needing to reassert his control once she freed him, he sat up and wrapped his arms around her. He rolled her onto her back and rested his weight on his elbows as he stretched out on top of her. Some of his anxiety began to recede now that he was back where he belonged. He gazed down at her as she bit the corner of her lower lip. She was overthinking this. Before she let her old insecurities—

Wait. Sounded like *he* was the insecure one here.

Bullshit. He'd gotten over that years ago.

She brushed a stray lock of hair from his forehead. "Feeling better, Sir?"

"I told you, I'm fine. But you know I prefer being on top like this."

She smiled, and he relaxed a little more. The woman could ease his fears with just a smile. No woman had done that for him before. Ever.

Certainly not Mama.

Holy shit! Do *not* be thinking about your mother when you have a hot, sexy woman under you.

Too late. That thought certainly did nothing to help his struggling libido. Angelina wormed her hand between their bodies, and his cock sprang to life. He needed to focus on something he could control—like having sex with Angelina. She always knew what he needed.

"Did I give you permission to do that?" When she furrowed her brows in worry, he grinned and ground his cock against the juncture of her legs. She formed an O with her mouth before a smile lit her full lips. He relaxed even further.

Well, not everything relaxed this time, thank God.

"No, Sir. I guess I was experiencing some lingering effects of Domme headspace."

He hoped she hadn't gotten anywhere near being in the headspace he enjoyed so much with her. He'd much rather put her in subspace, where she belonged. Right now, the only thing he needed was to bury himself to the hilt inside her tight pussy. Marc bent down and kissed her, his tongue invading her sweet mouth. She held nothing back, tangling her tongue with his.

"Open for me, pet."

She raised her knees, and he rubbed the tip of his cock against her very wet cleft. Playing Domme seemed to have turned her on. Luckily, he knew other ways to engage the submissive side of her, because the last thing he wanted was for his girl to get off on dominating him.

Needing to exert his control again, he drove himself into her with one thrust.

"Oh!"

What seemed like a flash of pain was replaced by her gasp for breath. *Merda.* He'd hurt her. Then she smiled.

"Oh, yessss!" Her eyes glazed over.

"You are not to come until I give you permission."

She groaned, and his chest swelled. This sense of control was the best aphrodisiac he knew. Withdrawing almost completely, he charged home again. "Do. Not. Move." He punctuated each word with another thrust of his cock as he drove himself home.

"Please let me come, Sir!"

Again and again he pistoned into her but refused to give her the release she sought. Not yet. Control. He was in control now. *He* would decide when she came.

Her screams and panting gasps sounded as if she was on the edge of pain and his cock pulsated more. "Come, pet. Now." She screamed her orgasm loud enough for half of Denver to hear. His own release soon followed.

Home.

He cuddled with her the way she liked until he could stand the messy condom no longer, got up, and went to the bathroom to discard it and clean up. Angelina had exposed huge chinks in his emotional armor tonight.

He needed to find out who he was before he could give Angelina what she wanted most—his love. No. His trust. He needed answers but wouldn't find them in Denver.

Marc crawled back into bed and drew Angelina's sleepy body against him, his hand on her tit as he claimed his possession.

Mine.

He couldn't imagine sleeping without her. *Merda,* he couldn't imagine life without her now.

So what was keeping him from taking their relationship to the next level?

*   *   *

Angelina shivered as she watched Marc sleeping. Much more soundly than he did on most nights. After she'd hit some kind of trigger for him in their scene earlier, she'd have expected him to be restless. Tormented.

Instead he'd reclaimed authority over her with a vengeance and had laid siege to her body, giving them both incredible orgasms. He certainly hadn't let her give him one. Was controlling his own orgasms—sometimes to the point of having none for days—another way he maintained a wall around himself?

She sighed and lightly fingered a lock of his hair, careful not to wake him. Running scared. After all these months, he hadn't come close to engaging his heart and soul in this relationship. If not tonight, perhaps he never would trust her not to harm him. He went through the motions of what was expected of him as her lover and partner, but only so far before he shut down. Getting him to bottom for her tonight had hit a nerve with him and opened her eyes to some things. Marc wanted to be in control of *everything*. While she didn't mind his controlling her in the bedroom, she wasn't going to relinquish authority to him over everything in her life.

Is that what Marc wanted—needed? Why hadn't she noticed his insecurities before? Well, because Marc masked them. Hell, he'd worn a mask since the night they met. Literally then, but despite her having destroyed the actual wolf mask he used to wear at the club, he continued to conceal his inner self from her. Not just her but from his friends, as well.

Who hurt you so badly you can't open up to me, Marc?

Melissa for one, but Angelina was convinced this went back further in Marc's past. That bitch had no emotional hold on Marc from what she could see. Angelina didn't know what had happened with his last girlfriend and didn't really want to know, but history had a way of repeating itself. She didn't want to be yet another of Marc's ex-girlfriends.

Mama hinted that Marc's and Gino's birth parents hadn't been shining examples of what a little boy would need to feel safe and secure in the world. Maybe she could talk with Savi about it, once she got to know her better. Getting a therapist's perspective on how to give Marc what he needed might free him from whatever chains prevented him from experiencing life and love to the fullest.

Angelina tucked a loose tendril of hair into the curls on the top of his head and whispered, *"I can give you what you need if you'll only let me."* He grimaced but didn't awaken.

Angelina snuggled closer to him and closed her eyes. She wasn't going to get the answers she needed tonight, but she definitely needed to find out more about Marc's childhood.

An unknown number of hours later, she awoke to find the sun streaming through the drapes and blinked. Her hand reached across the mattress. Gone. Marc had gotten up early. She glanced at the open bathroom door but didn't hear any sound. Tamping down the disappointment that they wouldn't make love this morning, she tossed the covers aside and sat up, waiting for the fog to lift from her brain.

Where have you run to now, Marc?

Chapter Eleven

Angelina tried to focus on preparing the antipasti for Damián's birthday dinner party tomorrow night, but her mind kept wandering to the meeting with Mama D'Alessio ten days ago and what Marc planned to do about what they'd learned. Marc's talk with his mother left more questions than answers, and they were no closer to figuring out what had happened back then than they had been before. Each day, he shut her out further. He hadn't said a word to her about it or the pitiful scene where she'd tried to get him to relinquish control to her, hoping to get him to trust her more. Why couldn't he see she could help provide support if he'd just let her be a part of his life?

Why can't you trust me, Marc?

Instead, his mask remained firmly in place again. He insisted that nothing be said about any of this to their friends. They'd probably be as disappointed as Angelina that Marc didn't trust them with such personal information that might also help them understand or help him.

But an intimate relationship like theirs required a level of trust and sharing unlike what he might have with friends. If Marc could exclude her from something this important, what else would he deem too personal for her to be a part of? How could they have a future if he wouldn't share his life— good and bad—with her?

The chopping knife slipped, and she sliced the skin over her knuckle. "Ow!" Tears sprang to her eyes, not so much from the cut as from the release the pain gave her. She needed a good cry over the dismal future she saw with Marc.

"God, Angie! What have you done?" Karla came over and quickly took Angelina by the wrist of her injured hand, cupping her own hand beneath to catch any drops of blood.

Angelina tried to wave her away. "It's nothing. Occupational hazard."

Ignoring her, Karla dragged her over to the sink where she ran cold water on the slightly bleeding cut. "Bull. I've never seen your knife slip before."

When the water ran clear, Karla grabbed a paper towel and wrapped it around Angelina's sore finger. "Put pressure on that. Where do you keep the Band-Aids?"

After Angelina indicated the corner cabinet where they kept first-aid and over-the-counter remedies, she moved toward a bar stool at the island.

"No, Boots!" Marisol jumped down from the stool she'd been sitting on and chased the kitten through the kitchen and into the foyer, nearly toppling Angelina on her way to a chair. Her legs felt a little shaky, probably because she and Marc had been up half the night ignoring each other. She couldn't sleep without him next to her, and at two o'clock in the morning he'd finally gone to a spare bedroom leaving her to toss and turn alone.

"Angie, you look like you haven't slept in days. And not for any good reasons, either. What's going on?"

Angelina sighed. "I think I'm losing him, Karla."

"Who? Marc? That's crazy! You two are perfect for each other."

"I'd like to think so, but he keeps putting up walls, blocking me out. I don't think he wants me to stay here with him."

"Should I ask Adam to talk with him and see what's going on?"

"No!" The look of surprise on Karla's face caused Angelina to ease off. "I mean…he doesn't want anyone to know what's going on. It's personal. I shouldn't have said anything. Forget about this. Let's check on the cake." Angelina pulled away and stood, going around the island to open the oven. She tested the cake with a toothpick. "Almost."

Karla wrapped her arms around Angelina from behind and hugged her against her ever-increasing baby bump. "Adam has a way of getting these stubborn guys to see things more clearly. Maybe you can encourage Marc to open up to him."

Not wanting to discuss the problems they were having any longer, Angelina nodded. "We'll see." She prepared a place on the granite countertop to cool the cake.

"I know what 'We'll see' means, missy." Karla stroked Angelina's back. "Hon, even if he won't open up, any time you want to talk or need a shoulder to cry on, you know I'm here for you."

Angelina's throat closed off as she fought back more useless tears. She nodded. "I know. I'm sorry I can't say more, but Marc's a very private man, and this is the way he wants it."

"I don't expect you to divulge anything to me. I'll just hint to Adam that he needs to keep an eye on Marc and, if there's an opportune moment, try to get him to confide in his former Master Sergeant."

Adam never stopped caring about the Marines who had served with him, so keeping a watchful eye on Marc wouldn't violate any confidences or be out of the norm. "I think that would be a good idea."

"Besides, he already knows something's up. I can see it in the way he watches Marc when you two come to the club. If Damián hit Adam's radar as having a problem, Adam would haul him into his office by his ear." Karla laughed sharply before growing serious again. "For some reason, he tends to give Marc more time to mull things over on his own."

"Maybe I've been doing that, too. Marc might need to be pushed—or yanked by his ear." Angelina smiled at the image of her boy from their recent role reversal.

Karla shrugged one shoulder. "Never hurts to try."

"Well, actually, I did try once. It didn't work out very well." Angelina didn't elaborate. "What if I lose him, Karla?" Her throat closed up, and she blinked to try and dry her eyes.

Karla wrapped her arms more tightly around Angelina's shoulder. "You aren't going to lose him. Stop worrying!"

If only she could. But Angelina had a feeling things were coming to a head and could go either way with them. Marc's view of the world had been shaken to the core. Everything he thought he knew about himself had been snatched out from under him. She didn't care if he was a D'Alessio or a Solari or a Jones. She just wanted him to be the Marc she had come to love. She wanted to have him by her side. Always.

* * *

Marc had barely spoken to Angelina since Damián's party last night. While everyone else was around, he put on a strong game face. No, another mask. Tonight, the tension sizzled between them, but she could get no response from him. Something had changed. What?

Even getting bratty to provoke an erotic spanking, hoping the release would be good for them both, hadn't worked. He'd threatened a punishment session instead. So she had backed off and given him his space. He'd promptly gone to ground in the shower where he'd been for the past thirty minutes. His Navy days usually had him in and out in just a few minutes—unless he invited her in there with him.

He hadn't this time.

Sitting at Nonna's vanity, one of the few pieces of furniture she'd brought to Marc's house, she brushed the tangled mess from her solo shower earlier. Marc used to brush her hair at night before bedtime. *Dio,* she loved it when he did that; her scalp tingled at the memory.

But that was before.

The bathroom door opened, and Marc entered the bedroom, his hair wet from his marathon shower. He wore nothing but a towel wrapped around his waist, and her breath caught in her throat looking at his lean, hard body. They hadn't made love in…forever. He hadn't even gotten her off since the night she'd tried to top him. Intimacy between them had become almost nonexistent.

He shucked the towel, giving her a brief glimpse of his sinfully delicious body only to crawl between the sheets without a word. He opened his latest Italian murder mystery, shutting her out much as he had been doing for days.

Angelina stood and faced the bed, reaching for the top button of her blouse and working her way down slowly. If Marc would look her way, perhaps she'd be able to entice him into engaging in some make-up sex.

Only they hadn't broken up. They hadn't fought. They were stuck in limbo.

She removed the blouse and tossed it at the foot of the bed, hoping to capture his attention.

Marc turned the page and kept reading.

She reached for the clasp of her bra behind her back and released her neglected girls before she tossed that scrap of lace a little closer to where Marc lay stretched out. He didn't seem to notice. She sighed.

Maybe there was no hope for them. She certainly wouldn't continue like this, two strangers coexisting in the same house.

Angelina fought to tamp down her frustration, but she loved him too much to let him bury himself alive.

"I'm worried about you, Marc."

He looked up from his book with a vacant stare. "Why?"

In what universe could he not see he had a problem? In Marc's, where he thought he could mask all emotion and fool the world.

"I don't want to see you hurting like this."

"I'm fine. I can take care of myself."

Clearly he had no intention of allowing her to take care of him.

He set the paperback across his lap, open and face down. "Oh, before I forget, I'm leaving for Italy in the morning. I'll probably be gone before you wake up. Should only be gone a few days."

Angelina's heart banged against her chest. "Italy?" There had been no mention of his leaving the state, much less the country. No mention, either, of her going along, even though he knew her passport hadn't expired from the times she'd visited Nonna in Marsala. It wasn't as if she had a job to tie her down either. Not even a nibble at a sous chef's position.

"What's in Italy?"

Was Marc going to look up his biological father?

"Evelyn gave me the number for Solari. I'm meeting him for lunch day after tomorrow."

How long had this been in the works without him saying a word? And why did this surprise her? Needing to regroup, she turned away and faced the mirror.

Still, the thought of him going alone to confront the man who had rejected and ignored his own son wrenched Angelina's heart. Marc was vulnerable right now. That bastard could hurt him. She wanted to be there to pick up the pieces, to comfort him—if he would allow her inside his inner sanctum.

Trying to sound casual, she continued to brush her hair. "Take me with you."

"This isn't a vacation, pet. I'll take you on holiday to Italy another time."

Stunned, she turned toward him. If he'd slapped her across the cheek, he couldn't have hurt her more. She slowed her breathing to regain control, but it was a losing proposition. When he picked up his book again, Angelina slammed the brush onto the vanity. "I don't want a damned vacation to Italy! I'm trying to get the man I love to let me be a part of his life again."

Who was she kidding? She'd never been a part of his life.

His eyes widened in surprise. At least he noticed her. His gaze lowered to her bare breasts then back up to her eyes. He made her feel the only part she'd ever have in his life was that of a sexual partner. Sorry, the sex was great but not enough.

"You *are* a big part of my life, *cara*, but I don't want you going with me.

This is between him and me. You don't need to be a part of that."

The backs of her eyes stung. She spoke just above a whisper. "Too late, Marc. I'm already a part of it, whether you accept me there or not."

Marc ran his hand through his hair. "Angelina, this is something I have to do alone."

She saw the hurt in his eyes but what about her pain? They were supposed to be a couple, to share each other's ups and downs. If he was cut, she bled.

She didn't want him to get hurt while she wasn't there to make it better for him.

"Stop shutting everyone out, Marc." She came around the bed, and sat down on the mattress, reaching out to stroke his arm. When he shook her off, yet another rejection, she turned away. The dream of any future together with Marc blurred in her tears until it became impossible to see anymore.

He doesn't trust me.

She stood, dashing the sudden tears from her eyes. She'd dreaded this moment since Valentine's weekend, but it became clear to her there was no hope he'd ever change.

Angelina cleared her throat. "I don't think this is going to work."

"I won't know unless I try."

She faced him as he picked up his book again.

"I don't mean meeting your birth father, Marc. I'm talking about us. I can't love someone who is incapable of loving me back."

He laid the open book on his chest, like an armor shield over his heart. "What are you talking about? You know I love you, Angelina. I just have a lot on my mind lately. If you want to go up to the playroom," he said as he glanced at the clock on the nightstand, "we have an hour or so before I should catch some shuteye."

He'd confirmed her doubts.

Angelina swallowed past the lump in her throat. "I don't want to play or have sex. All I want is for you to trust me."

He huffed his irritation. "I trust you more than any woman I've ever known."

"That isn't saying much, is it, Marc? What woman have you ever trusted?"

She had his attention, but his own Italian temper flared. "I let you tie me to the fucking bed, Angelina. I let you put a ball gag in my mouth and a blindfold over my eyes. What more do I need to do to prove I trust you?"

A lump lodged in her throat as she pictured the little boy who had been Marc being cast aside by his birth mother. He couldn't have much of a conscious memory of those early years, but clearly the event had made quite an impression on his emotional development.

What might he have been like if that hadn't happened?

If wishes were horses...

Understanding why he couldn't trust her didn't make the knowledge any easier to accept.

Even with the scene he spoke of, he hadn't let his defenses down the way she did in a scene when she submitted fully to him. He'd continued to shut her out then, just as he was doing now.

Maybe he needed time to sort this out? But *could* he do so without help? Sometimes he could confide better in his Marine buddies. "Have you talked about what's going on with Adam?"

"No. He doesn't need to be bothered right now with all that's going on with Karla and Damián."

"Marc, it's not a bother for friends who love and care about you to want to help." Had he ever relied on anyone to give him what he needed? "I need to know where we go from here."

"Look, pet, I have a lot on my mind right now. I can't deal with you, too."

Angelina balled her fist and drew in a slow breath, initially wanting to pound on the door he'd metaphorically slammed in her face. They stared at one another in silence for a long moment, and she watched him withdraw further into himself.

She'd lost him.

Ha. Joke's on you, Angie. You never really had him.

He ran his hand through his hair. "I'm just going away a few days. Why all the drama?"

Her throat constricted, forcing her to clear it again. "Marc, I won't continue in this relationship if you won't trust me."

An expression of pain crossed his face before the mask once again fell into place. Marc sighed. "Look, it's been a hell of a day. I'm tired." He placed his book on the nightstand. "Let's get some sleep. I have an early flight to catch."

Without making some drastic modifications to his coping strategies, she held no hope he'd ever be able to change the way he dealt with life. That certainly wouldn't come overnight.

He tossed the duvet off and swung his legs over the side of the bed. "Why don't I take the spare bedroom tonight?"

His words robbed her of breath. Why had they surprised her so much? Marc had been running from her emotionally since New Year's. The physical chemistry that had been there from the moment they met had all but disappeared. The emotional chemistry had been an illusion.

"No need for you to get up, Marc." He halted, and she felt his gaze on her as she walked to the closet and pulled out her rickety suitcase.

Time for a reality check, Angie. Your fairy tale is over.

"I'll take the spare, Marc. It's too late for me to drive home tonight."

Home? She didn't have her own house anymore. The thought of moving back with Mama embarrassed her, but all she knew was that she had to get out of here.

Oddly enough, no tears formed this time. Careful not to disturb where he sat, she threw the suitcase on her side of the bed, opened it, and walked to the dresser to grab the clothing from the top drawer. She left behind some of the sexy lingerie he'd bought her. She wouldn't be needing them.

"Don't leave."

His voice seemed a million miles away. She wouldn't look at him. He'd only weaken her resolve. From the night they'd met, he would allow her to come just so close but never *too* close before he'd push her away again. Marc had worn a real mask then. Now he'd merely started wearing a figurative one.

Dio, and she once had thought *she* was the one with the trust issues.

"Look, Angelina, I just need time to process this shit."

Angelina's heart hammered to life, and her hands became ice cold. Fight or flight?

After emptying the second drawer of her jeans and a few sweaters, she had reached capacity in her case. She glanced his way. His gaze silently pleaded with her for...something. Solace? Comfort? Her nurturing instinct kicked in, and she nearly moved to hold him in her arms.

Then his expression became shuttered again. "This trip is not about you, *cara*. You know who you are, where you came from. I have to figure this out on my own."

He couldn't have been any clearer.

Her voice came out in barely a whisper. "I hope you find what you're looking for out there, Marc." She closed and zipped the case, hauling it to the floor faster than he could get to it to help.

"Are you leaving me, too, Angelina?"

She flinched. Too? If he thought she *wanted* to leave him, he was so very wrong.

"Marc, I can't stay if you continue to push me away, cast me aside. I have needs, too. And foremost is my need to meet *your* needs. That's what love is, Marc."

"No, that's what being a mother is. I never asked you to be my mother, Angelina. It seems I've had no shortage of those in my life."

She knew he was hurting, lashing out, but if he thought she wanted to be his mother they definitely had serious problems. She began dragging the case with its broken wheel toward the door before he wrenched the handle from her hand. His touch sent sparks up her arm, and she stepped back as if burned.

Marc pleaded, "I can't love you any more than I do now."

Angelina avoided eye contact. "That's what I'm afraid of, Marc. It's just not enough."

Angry that he hadn't even talked with her about the need to meet his birth father, she asked, "What's going to happen in Italy to change anything?"

"I'm going to find out who the fuck I am." The torment in his voice reverberated around the room.

Hating to hear the pain in his voice and watch him hurting like this, she wrapped her arms around his waist. He held himself rigid, not embracing her in return.

No more excuses, Angie.

"Per favore, cara, I just need some time alone. Time to think."

She let go of him physically, even though she knew she wouldn't be able to let go emotionally for a very long time. He would always be the love of her life, whether he wanted to be or not. "I'll always love you, Marc, but I won't live this way. I hope you find the answers."

Marc extricated her hands from his waist and pushed her away by her upper arms. "Listen, I'll call you when I get back. We'll talk more then."

"Don't call unless you're ready to make some changes, Marc." She opened the door. "I'll carry the case downstairs in the morning."

Walking down the hallway to one of the guest bedrooms, her legs felt weighed down with chains. He'd once put her in culinary bondage. Many times he'd restrained her. Those times, he'd always released her. This time, though, he'd shackled her *heart* in chains she'd never be able to break, and then he'd tossed away the key.

Ironically, he'd helped her regain some of her self-confidence in the months she'd been with him, which only helped her not to backtrack now. She crawled naked into the lonely, queen-sized bed and hugged the pillow. Still no tears. Maybe she'd cried them all out before she'd lost hope.

After a night spent tossing in the half-empty bed, she listened as Marc shut the door to the house and fired up his Porsche. He really was leaving without saying good-bye. She tossed the blanket aside and got up.

What now?

As her brother Tony would say, it was time to fish or cut bait. Frustrated at falling for the wrong man yet again and with no clue where she could go, she walked down the hallway toward the bedroom to retrieve her suitcase, but it was gone.

On her way downstairs to the kitchen for coffee, she found the bag sitting near the door leading to the garage. He'd carried it down for her, as if he couldn't get her out of here fast enough. A part of her wished he'd have at least fought to keep her. If she didn't know better, she thought he'd almost expected her to leave.

On the counter, she found a note stuck to her purse: "Be back in a week." What happened to a few days, which he'd told her last night?

He must not think she'd leave. Or he expected her to be back by the time he returned.

Sorry, Marc. You're going to have to run to *me this time.*

She carried her first mug of coffee to the living room. It was too early to call friends or family, so she clicked the remote and her comfort movie began showing on the screen. Maybe Luc Teyssier and Kate could show her that sometimes the girl did get the guy and her perfect little stone cottage with a happily-ever-after ending.

Okay, maybe her dream home was more a cabin in the woods—not the wilderness, though! She needed the assurance civilization was close by. She looked around the living room. This house had no charm or character. How did a "chintz sofa and ornate Italian iron bed" kind of gal come to be living in a bachelor pad?

Maybe she was a mismatch to Marc's life, too.

Her attention once again on the screen, she watched Kate dressed in an adorable sailor-style boatneck top sitting on a beach chair on the Côte d'Azur trying to make her boyfriend jealous by flaunting her pretend-boyfriend Luc.

Angelina realized that through most of *French Kiss*, Kate chased after her unfaithful loser of a boyfriend who had gone to France for a medical convention and immediately fell for another woman. A beautiful woman with a sexy body.

A woman like Melissa.

Stop it, Angie.

Marc hadn't run off to Europe to be with another woman. Once again, he had gone off alone, shutting out everyone who loved him on some quest for an unattainable dream. Sadly, Marc had rejected her offer of love, family, and a sense of belonging. He might never be able to see what was right in front of his face all along—not only with her, but with the D'Alessio family. *His* family.

An hour later, a call to her former landlady told her what she'd expected—the house in Aspen Corners was under a six-month lease until mid-April. Marc would be gone a few days, so there was no rush leaving today, but the thought of staying in this lonely house held no appeal.

Usually Marc ran to the Fourteeners in the Rockies for solace and escape. She supposed the Alps and Apennines would provide comfort for him now. He probably could never love any woman as much as he loved the mountains. Once upon a time, he'd told her they had made him realize how much he wanted Angelina to be a part of his life. He'd fought to win her over back then.

Well, somehow she didn't think he'd interpret the message from the Italian mountains the same way. They held too many secrets. He didn't have anyone there to help translate if he got his signals crossed with all the emotional baggage he was lugging around.

Already the familiar tugging at her heartstrings had begun. She wouldn't stay away if Marc gave any indication of being ready to deal with their relationship head on. Maybe her leaving would be the catalyst he needed to change, if he truly loved her the way he said he did.

After cleaning up the kitchen, she put the mugs away and spotted one Luke had left behind a few months ago. She'd enlist the help of someone else who loved Marc. Guys had a different kind of bond with each other. Of course, Marc could seek help from Adam, but he intimidated Angelina too much, so she'd rather call Luke.

Luke had moved from Denver last December onto a small spread in Fairchance near Aspen Corners where he'd been pursuing his latest passion—training rescued and abused mustangs for SAR work. She realized Luke also liked to play his cards close to the vest. They hadn't even known Luke had been working on a house there for the last half of the year until he'd moved in after Thanksgiving.

Men.

Wait. Would going to Luke just cause more trouble? In *French Kiss*, Kate's boyfriend Charlie became jealous when he saw Kate was interested in someone else. Would Marc think she was trying to manipulate him as Kate had done? *Dio*, he already had enough trust issues.

Then again, staying with Luke might bring Marc's inability to trust to a head. Luke was her friend now, too. If Marc couldn't trust them both not to betray his trust, then she wouldn't be able to try and work on reconciliation with him. Jealousy sent Allen Martin off the deep end last fall. Better to find out now if Marc would have such issues. He always claimed her as his. Would he trust her?

Hanging out at Luke's would be safer, too. She didn't want Rafe or Tony to see her back in Aspen Corners, in case she was able to resolve things with Marc. They'd finally started to accept Marc over the past few months but would automatically blame him for her unhappiness in a breakup.

Angelina hated that word. She wasn't ready to give up on Marc D'Alessio, but the fewer overprotective brothers there were trying to keep her from being hurt, the better.

Why couldn't she have fallen for the much less complicated Luke? He was easygoing, well-adjusted, and stable. Instead, her heart had been captured by a sexy, unattainable Italian.

Realizing she was too tired to attempt to drive right away, she decided to think a while longer about her options before calling Luke. She returned to the living room and rewound the DVD to one of her favorite parts—the train ride where Luc first realized he was falling for Kate when she fell asleep on the bench seat. Luc kissed her. So romantic.

Angelina missed Marc so much already. She curled up on the sofa and pressed the power button off. So tired. What if Marc never figured out that she was his perfect Kate?

Oh, Marc…

She awoke with a start, and a glance at her watch told her it was after noon. Her stomach growled, so she went into the kitchen to eat some leftovers from Damián's party. A call to Luke got his answering machine. She told him she'd be stopping by later today; she didn't say she might be staying a while. Of course, if he didn't think it was a good idea, she could go to Mama's.

Upstairs in what once had been their bedroom, she gathered more things in grocery bags and packed the toiletries in the bathroom. She retrieved a few things from the closet as well, but didn't take the outfits that reminded her too much of her time with Marc.

Glancing around the bedroom she and Marc had shared since October, a pounding between her eyes warned of an oncoming headache. She'd better get on the road before it became unbearable.

Would Marc ever be able to commit to anything more than the happy-for-now so popular in her erotic romance novels? Those fantasy endings where great sex led characters to believe there was a stronger foundation than there actually was?

Marc, I hope you find the answers you need in Italy. Or better yet, that you'll come home with your heart open and ready to receive my love.

Chapter Twelve

Angelina rolled over in bed and saw the sun streaming through the slit between the heavy blue and brown drapes that may have begun life as Indian blankets. Good grief! She tossed the ivory chenille bedspread aside and swung her legs over the side of the mattress. How long had she slept? After a few misses, she managed to maneuver her feet into her slippers. The floorboards at Luke's ranch house were cold when she'd prepared for bed last night, and she was sure they hadn't gotten any warmer this morning. She pulled the drapes open and saw the snow-covered ground awash in midmorning sunlight.

Rubbing the sleep from her eyes, Angelina padded over to the dresser to grab her toiletries bag. In the light of day, she noticed for the first time the framed sketch Cassie had drawn at the hospital when Adam had been recovering from the cougar attack. The smiling woman in the image had an angelic face surrounded by a halo of wildly curly hair. She held a tiny baby in her arms. Luke had said it was his wife Maggie and that she'd been pregnant when she'd died on Mount Evans with Papa. She liked to think her papa was up there in heaven, too, watching over Luke's family as well as the Giardano brood down here.

Her glance strayed to the hand-carved wooden frame, and upon closer inspection she saw two gold wedding bands inset at the lower right-hand corner, the smaller one fitting inside the other. She recognized the larger one as the ring Luke had been wearing when she'd first met him in Rico's bar. He must have made this frame himself. She saw intricately carved leaves and flowers on the face of the frame, wondering at the significance of the objects he'd chosen to carve in a tribute to his wife and baby. So much love and attention to detail.

Angelina's eyes stung. He must have been devastated to lose them so tragically. Angelina pictured her father insisting on going down alone to rescue the injured woman, knowing his time on earth would be cut short anyway by cancer and not wanting any of the other SAR professionals to be taken away from their families if the snowpack gave way. Pride in Papa's selfless heroics almost outweighed the loss of having him with her a few more months.

Hearing the protesting whinny of a horse coming from the direction of the new barn on the other side of the corral, Angelina turned and headed toward the kitchen to find it deserted. She'd intended to get up early enough to make Luke breakfast, but the mug and egg-encrusted plate in the sink told her Luke had taken care of himself. Some guest chef she was. Part of the deal when she'd asked him to let her hide out—er, stay—here a while was that she'd prepare him gourmet meals.

Not that Luke had demanded anything in return for giving her a safe place to land. He'd welcomed her with open arms and no strings attached.

Surely Marc would come to his senses and realize she only wanted to help him face whatever tormented him from the past. She couldn't help but wonder where he was and what he was doing. Had he found his father yet? If so, how had the meeting gone?

After toasting a couple of pieces of the sourdough bread Luke had made in his bread machine, she downed half a cup of coffee and returned to the bedroom to dress in jeans and a T-shirt. She slipped into one of Luke's flannel shirts for an extra layer, not planning to be outside long. Five minutes later, shivering from the cold despite the added shirt, she entered the horse barn in search of Luke. It was warm inside the building, once she got out of the wind.

Someone was singing. Luke?

I rescued you,
you rescued me

She crept toward a stall at the opposite end of the barn and peeked inside to find Luke leaning against the wall opposite a brown and white mustang. He strummed a guitar and seemed totally uninterested in the horse, which eyed him cautiously from more than half a double stall away. The poor thing had gouges in its flank, and part of its right ear had been torn off. The abuse these animals had suffered was criminal. Thank God someone rescued them, and Luke had then been able to give them a place to further heal and regain their strength and spirit. She didn't know how many he'd been able to take in so far. She'd seen six in the corral last night, but with a heart as big as his, she guessed he'd always have room for one more rescue.

Heck, he even had room for a rescue of the human variety—her.

But singing to them? Angelina stifled a giggle, not wanting to disturb the scene. She had no idea Luke could sing—and so well—much less that he sang to his horses.

The mare moved closer to Luke with infinitesimally small steps. What the heck? She'd heard of horse whispering, but horse serenading?

Inch by inch, Luke seemed to be coaxing the animal toward him as he sang Paul Brandt's *I Do*. Finally, the horse was only a foot or so away from the blue feed bucket hanging on the wall next to Luke when she dipped her nose inside. Luke continued to sing as if the horse wasn't there at all.

Amazing.

"That's my girl."

Luke's soft-spoken words jarred Angelina until she realized he was speaking to the horse. She nearly giggled again but was mesmerized as he slowly laid the acoustic guitar down, propped it against the wall, and reached out to stroke the horse's neck. The skittish creature stopped eating and backed away again. "There, now. You're safe with me. I'm not gonna hurt ya, darlin'."

He continued to speak in his soft drawl and tears welled in Angelina's eyes as she watched these two in their version of a slow-motion Texas two-step.

She missed Marc even more. He'd always assuaged her anxieties and insecurities much like Luke was doing with this gentle giant of a horse. What if Marc didn't come to realize they belonged together? What if he didn't want to face the past? What if the two of them had no future with each other?

What if he never stopped being such a stubborn ass?

Not wanting to intrude on Luke's time, she began to back away until he looked her way and motioned for her to wait. Careful not to touch the horse, he picked up his guitar and eased toward the stall door. The mustang must be spooked by sudden movements. Poor thing.

After latching the door behind him, he turned to her and smiled. "Good morning, baby girl. Sleep well?"

"Like a...well, a baby." She grinned then peeked around him at the battered horse. "It's beautiful how you connect with these abused horses." She glanced down at the guitar.

"If you tell Marc I serenade my skittish girls, I'll be the one wearing your butt out with a paddle next time."

She gave him a half-hearted smile. "No worries there. He hasn't been in a talkative mood for a while." Not with her anyway.

Luke wrapped his arm around her and hugged her. She breathed in the strong scent of leather and missed Marc even more.

Luke whispered in her ear. "Don't you worry, Angel. He may be slow at figuring things out, but he isn't going to let the best thing in his life slip away."

She wished she could believe him but would rather focus on something else. Putting an end to the much-needed hug, she nodded toward the stall he'd just left. "What's her story?"

Luke's smoky-gray eyes darkened. "O'Keeffe came here two weeks ago. It'll take months to erase some of the effects of the physical abuse she's been through and even longer for the emotional wounds to heal. Her former owners crushed her spirit. She's afraid of her own shadow now."

"How can anyone be so cruel?"

"Search me. I'm just glad the mustang rescuers found out about her and got her out of that situation. It's not too late to turn things around for her. It may be years before I can ride her and use her for search-and-rescue operations, but right now, I'm just content getting her to eat with me standing close by. We've made a helluva lot of progress in a short time."

Angelina reached up and tugged at his denim shirt collar to bring his face closer to hers, giving him a peck on the cheek.

"What's that for, darlin'?"

"I thought you were just out here hiding from something or working on your furniture and play equipment, but it's a good thing you're doing, Luke. You have a way with skittish fillies."

He laughed. "Well, the four-legged variety maybe."

She wondered what he meant as they walked out of the barn and squinted in the bright sunlight reflecting off the snow-covered ground. He and Marc had certainly taken good care of her shaky spirit the night Allen attacked her in her home. Luke draped a protective arm over her shoulders as they ambled toward the house in companionable silence.

Was he dating someone? She hoped so.

Luke needed to find someone to love again soon. His wife had been dead a long time. He deserved to find someone else. Lord knows the man had a lot to offer someone special.

There'd been a brief time when Angelina thought she and Luke might be a possibility, until a certain Italian Dom took her into her bedroom and showed her where her heart, mind, and body belonged.

She blinked back the sting of tears, refusing to let any more spill over thoughts of Marc. He was a good man, too. She hoped Luke was right and that he'd figure out what was going on soon so they could get back together.

Gunmetal gray clouds appeared to be dumping snow on Cassie's cabin at Iron Horse Peak right about now. Not that she would mind. Cassie preferred her isolated existence to being with people. Angelina had no doubt she was well-stocked and able to outlast any amount of snowfall.

Just before they entered the house, a sudden thought occurred to her. "How'd O'Keeffe get her name?"

Luke paused, holding the door open for her before turning his attention to the same mountain peak. She saw a longing in his expression she hadn't noticed before.

"She reminded me of someone."

Interesting. Angelina smiled. Well, if ever there was a skittish filly for Luke to love and help to heal, it would be Cassie. He certainly was a rescuer at heart. Maybe Angelina could help bring the two of them together. He might also help the reclusive artist reconnect with her long-buried playful side. Karla said she used to be fun-loving and carefree. Luke didn't take himself or anything seriously. He was also a rock-solid man with a firm but gentle hand and a big heart. Perfect to help Cassie recover the parts of herself she'd lost.

*   *   *

Luke took Angel's elbow and guided her up the steps and inside the house, feeling a shiver course through her. Why had she come outside wearing nothing but a flannel shirt and jeans? He wasn't dressed much warmer, but he was used to the strong winds whipping down from the mountain pass.

He glanced once more up at Iron Horse before following Angel inside. He'd tried a couple of times since Adam's cougar attack to get Cassie to notice he existed, but she seemed hell-bent for leather on running from him as far and as fast as she could. Once at Adam's, she'd opened up a bit about her love of art, which at least gave them some common ground. He'd even gone to see one of her art exhibits in Denver, but she'd nearly had a panic attack when he walked in, as if she thought he was stalking her or something. That's when he'd decided he'd better just steer clear of Cassie Lôpez, dream or no dream.

Maggie, you sure know how to send a guy on an impossible mission.

While he'd noticed the beautiful woman sitting across the waiting room at the hospital, it hadn't been an appropriate place to hit on her. When his wife delivered a message loud and clear that Cassie was the angel she'd promised in a dream, he looked a little closer at the Peruvian recluse.

Not that he needed his dead wife's help finding dates and not that he'd heard from Maggie, even in a dream, since the hospital. He just hadn't been interested in women until recently. Cassie had some serious issues when it came to men, judging by the response he'd gotten from her when he went to her gallery opening. At the moment, he had his hands full trying to get his mustang rescues to trust him.

No, he didn't need a woman in his life to complicate matters. He'd done just fine since he'd lost Maggie. Although it sure was nice having Angel around. He watched her warming her hands by the fire he'd laid in the Buck Stove this morning. Last night, she'd prepared a feast. He never could understand how she could take the same ingredients he cooked with and turn them into such mouthwatering dishes.

What the hell was Marc's problem? Luke hadn't seen much of his friend since he'd moved out here, but if anyone could break through Marc's barriers, Angel was the one. Finding out they were having problems pissed him off. Maybe he needed to have a talk with the big lug. Might help if he knew a little more about the problem.

Angel turned around to warm her backside. "Where'd you learn to play guitar?"

"An elective at UT. Maggie was taking the class, and I wanted to make a move on her." He grinned, remembering how the woman who later agreed to be his wife had warmed up to his serenading her on dates—clothing optional.

At least Angel hadn't found him singing in the nude.

He sat on the couch and motioned to her. "Come here, darlin'. We need to have a talk."

She came to him without reluctance. Why couldn't Cassie be more like Angel? Trusting. Open.

He gave himself a mental headshake. He needed to forget about Cassie. Maggie was just plain wrong about her being the one he needed—unless

Maggie thought it was Cassie who needed him? Damn. How could he turn away from her if there was something he could do to help her get over her fear of men? He was pretty laid-back and non-threatening. He thought so, anyway. Cassie apparently begged to differ.

Angel sat beside him and leaned her head on his shoulder, and he wrapped his arm around her. "Now, tell ol' Luke what happened to bring you out here last night?"

She sighed and paused for a while before responding. "Marc and I have been, well, having some problems. I can't really go into what's going on, but there's something from his past he's not facing."

"Does it have to do with Gino's death?"

"Not directly, but I'm sure that hasn't helped any. It's definitely something to do with his childhood and his family, especially his parents. I don't want to divulge anything more, but until he faces the past, he's stuck. *We're* stuck."

"Want me to talk to him?"

"Anything could help, I guess."

Luke chuckled. "Thanks for the vote of confidence."

Angel retreated, and he saw the anguish in her eyes, which made him regret teasing her.

She blinked away the tears that filled her eyes. Damn. Not tears. He hated seeing a woman cry.

"Marc is so stubborn and totally shut down emotionally. He won't let me in." She sniffled. "I had to leave. I couldn't stand to watch him in so much pain while he refused to let me help."

"Lie down." Luke guided her to stretch out on the couch, her feet in his lap. He pulled her boots off. "Darlin', you can't make someone face something they don't want to face. They have to want to do it themselves."

He kneaded the soles of her feet, and she moaned as she closed her eyes and let him minister to her. Marc would have probably turned her over his lap and whaled the tar out of her butt until she released her anxiety, but that was neither Luke's style nor his place. When he sent Angel back to Marc, he didn't want his buddy to think anything improper had gone on between them. Luke's romantic interest in the woman ended before it had started, really.

Marc and Angel were meant for each other. Didn't take a message from Maggie in a dream or a sketch on a piece of paper to prove that.

Quit thinking about Cassie.

He pushed at a knot in the ball of her foot, and she winced. He decided to probe the knot, and Angel, a little further. "What do you plan to do, darlin'?"

She stared at him as he continued to work on the stress she was holding in her feet. "Do? Ouch!"

He grinned but didn't let up on that tender spot. "Yeah, *do*. Marc's stubborn. And proud. Hell, you know what Italian men are like."

She snorted.

"You also know he's not going to make the first move to get you two back together again."

Angel tried to yank away from him, but he wasn't finished with her yet and firmed his grip on her dainty foot. She squared her shoulders. "He did try to win me back once."

Luke assumed she meant the costume-party night at the Masters at Arms Club where Marc, Luke, and Adam had helped pull a mindfuck on Angel. Luke had enjoyed the hell out of getting the woman to submit to him, even if only for a few minutes before Luke had to pass her back to his buddy where she belonged.

He ran his finger down the sole of her foot and she recoiled. Ticklish? "Why weren't you ticklish a few minutes ago?"

"Mind over matter."

He cocked his head and waited.

"Marc has been training me to control my response to being tickled. If I know what's coming—or can at least see what's happening—it's easy. I knew what you planned to do, so I steeled my body to keep from becoming a giggling mess when you rubbed my foot."

"But you did jump back eventually."

"Lost my train of thought. I was remembering that costume night at the club."

"Maybe it's time for a little more mind over matter. Maybe this time *you'll* need to make the first move, baby girl."

She raised her chin higher. "Luke, I'm pretty darned stubborn, too. Until I know he's going to deal with this issue, I'm not going to do a thing."

Luke laughed. "*Two* stubborn Italians."

She rolled her eyes and looked away, then grinned sheepishly when she glanced back at him. "*Dio,* help us both."

"Ask nicely before you go to bed tonight. I'm sure He will."

Worry returned to her big brown eyes. "You think so?"

"Reasonably certain, if He agrees it's what's best for you two. I want to see you two together, too. You were made for each other."

Her chin quivered before she shored up her defenses and put up a good front. "I'm sorry I've put you out of your bed."

"No worries. I spent the night out in the barn with O'Keeffe. She needs to get used to sleeping with me if we're going to be doing rescue and other close work over long hours, or even days. I think being out there all night helped me get as far as I did with her this morning."

Angel smiled. "I'm glad you've found yourself out here. You weren't meant to be cooped up in a Denver townhouse. And giving these poor horses a place to recover and regroup, not unlike what you're doing for me, is… Well, you're a gentle soul with a big heart, Luke. Your parents sure raised you right."

Luke glanced away. "I think buying this spread is the first thing my old man approved of me doing since I played football in college." Luke had been a bitter disappointment to his dad, that's for damned sure. The man had wanted an athletic son, but Luke had been more interested in photography, art, woodworking, and girls. He'd learned carpentry to gain his dad's respect, which was how he'd met Marc and the others at the club. But his heart wasn't in building cabinets. He preferred working on unique play-scene equipment for the club and other custom-carved furniture, including a bed he was working on in his workshop right now. If his dad saw him carving whimsical creatures into the headboard of a perfectly functional bed, he'd shake his head and walk away.

Angel's cool fingers reached out to stroke his cheek, bringing him back to the present. "*I'm* proud of you, Luke. Although I could have done without you making that 'MINE' paddle for Marc."

He grinned. "See? The big lug knows what he wants—he knows what's his. He just needs a little time to get his head on straight." Now for changing the subject. "While you're waiting, darlin', the way to *this* man's big ol' heart is through his stomach. What's for dinner?"

"That's a good eight hours away. I'll surprise you."

"No, darlin'. Where I come from, dinner's the midday meal, followed by supper at night. I need something to tide me over for my workout with Cassatt and Picasso this afternoon in the corral. I aim to be on the back of either the mare or that gelding before I come in tonight."

Angel swung her feet off his lap, enthusiasm showing in her eyes at the prospect of doing what she loved most. "Well, I checked your pantry last night to take stock. Pretty basic, but I think I can find something to tide you over 'til *supper*." She padded across the braided rug to the hardwood floor. He was keeping the house warmer than he normally would because he didn't want Angel to get cold.

She turned her head toward him as she continued to walk away. "Give me thirty minutes to rustle up some grub." Her wink made him smile.

Marc, you're an ass if you let this woman get away.

Chapter Thirteen

Marc sat in a corner of the hotel restaurant, watching as each male patron entered. None seemed to be searching for anyone they didn't know. He glanced at Gino's Breitling on his wrist. Marc had worn it since he'd met Staff Sergeant Anderson at Adam's wedding. He hadn't wanted that tangible a reminder of Gino before, but he'd forgiven his brother and begun to make peace with his loss that day. Being here in Tuscany, the neighboring province to his native Lombardy, he'd thought a lot about his brother this morning while expending some nervous energy walking around Siena.

The man was late. Figured. About thirty-four years late, to be exact, not that Marc wanted any kind of father-son relationship with him after all of these years.

Granted, he was in Italy where time had very little meaning. He'd grown up in a family obsessed with punctuality, not to mention his Navy training.

He just needed to know where he came from. He'd spent much of his early years feeling as if he didn't belong. Perhaps this man could provide the missing clues to his identity. His past.

He'd stopped in at a jeweler's this morning in search of something special for Angelina, thinking a Lady Breitling would be nice. Her watch was the most unreliable thing ever assembled.

Angelina hadn't been far from his thoughts, either. Everywhere he went he wished he could be sharing the sights with her. So why hadn't he brought her here with him?

Would she be waiting when he arrived home? He hoped so but couldn't blame her if she'd bailed. He'd treated her badly. Problem was he didn't have a clue why he'd refused to let her get any closer. What was he so afraid of happening?

Her leaving him.

Well, how's that working for you?

Another ten minutes passed. Apparently, meeting his son wasn't high on Paolo Solari's list of priorities today, if Marc had been even a second thought for him. Marc began to feel like a fool for having contacted the man. He'd never even managed to speak with him over the phone. A house servant had finally returned Marc's call this morning and relayed messages between the two men to arrange this meeting location. Did Solari intend to show up or had he just given a time and place to get Marc off the phone?

Did he even remember he had a son? Shit, two sons. Marc had been three when his mother died and Gino three years older. In several decades one could forget a lot of things, but his own sons? Marc couldn't fathom that.

A tall man in a white silk suit entered the room and commanded every ounce of attention in the very air around him. Exuding confidence, not a strand of his silvering hair straying onto his tanned forehead, the man's gaze didn't scan the room. Instead, he gave a female server the once over, eliciting from her a blush and a smile. Taking the response as an invitation, he went up to her, bent down to whisper in her ear, and pinched her ass. She giggled and jotted something on a piece of paper, handing it to him.

He was old enough to be her grandfather. Marc felt a tightening in his gut. No doubt this man was Marc's father—birth father. Suddenly, the thought of conversing with him made Marc want to run out the back door, mainly to avoid the feeling of looking at himself in the mirror twenty or thirty years from now. Until Angelina had come into his life, Marc had an early history of treating women as his personal *smörgåsbord*, just as this man seemed to do.

Chip off the old block.

Until Angelina had changed him.

Before he could bail out on this train wreck in the making, as if in slow motion, the older man scanned the room and zeroed in on him. Fighting the urge to flee, Marc heard Angelina's voice. *Keep breathing.* The time for running was over. He needed to face his past if he was going to avoid a similar fate for his future. He couldn't move forward with Angelina until he knew who he was, good or bad.

While he would have hated for Angelina to see the man whose sperm had contributed to making him, he wished Angelina was here with him. He needed her steady presence and the comforting touch of her hand. She would have given him much-needed courage right now to face this man from the past who ambled toward Marc's table.

"Marco Solari?"

The name jarred him for a moment, but he recovered and stood, automatically extending his hand and trying not to flinch as the man shook it. Firm grip. Eye contact. "Marc D'Alessio." He'd never carry *this* man's name.

"Of course. Good-looking young man. *Tutto tuo padre.*"

Even though Marc thought the same thing when he'd first seen Solari, he detested being compared in any way to the man who had spawned him. He hoped the similarities ended at the facial features. Motioning for Solari to be seated, Marc resumed his own seat.

They ordered drinks and dinner before staring silently at each other a moment, both at a loss for words. After an awkward period of time passed, Marc broke the silence. "So I take it you knew I'd come looking for you one day."

Solari shrugged. "I figured you'd have a healthy curiosity and might wonder about your origins someday. Though it took you longer than I expected."

Marc ignored the censure in his voice. "I didn't really know about you until recently." *And now I wish I'd never heard about you.*

An arched brow told him he'd surprised the man. Solari nodded. "I guess you were a bit young when your mother took you back. She always regretted giving you to her sister to raise."

His words confused Marc. He still couldn't wrap his mind around the fact that his mother was his aunt. "What do you mean?"

"Well, times were different then. Here in Italy, it was frowned upon for a single girl to turn up pregnant."

Marc grew even more confused. "I thought you and Emiliana married before Gino was born."

"Indeed. I'm talking about *your* mother. Your grandmother had encountered the stigma and shame of carrying an American Marine's *bastardo* after the Second World War. When Natalia got pregnant, your grandmother forced her to give you to Emiliana to raise with our son, Gino."

Marc's heart began to pound. Hearing Paolo call Mama—Natalia—a bastard bothered Marc, but more upsetting was hearing a radically different story from the one Mama had told him. Who had lied? Or had he just gotten this increasingly complicated story confused?

"Maybe it would help if you started at the beginning."

The server who had probably slipped Solari her number or address earlier came to the table and brushed her hip against his father's arm, distracting the man from the conversation. After setting plates of antipasti in front of them, she winked at Marc and walked away. Marc turned his attention back to his father.

No, Solari. Papa was the only father Marc had ever or would ever know.

"You were saying."

"Well, I'm sure Natalia filled you in on most of this. She and I slept together once—our hormones got away from us, I suppose—but that indiscretion resulted in you."

Mama had said she'd dated this man before her sister had married him, but he insinuated something had transpired between Mama and her brother-in-law years later. The knot in Marc's stomach made it impossible for him to eat, and he set his fork beside his plate.

"Terminating a pregnancy back then was unheard of here, so your mother went to live with an old schoolmate for the duration of her pregnancy while Emiliana pretended to be pregnant when in public." He popped a kalamata olive into his mouth and leaned forward. "My wife detested being pregnant, real or make-believe, so that was not a happy time in our marriage."

Marc couldn't help but feel the man was blaming him for that inconvenience in his life when Marc had had nothing to do with the choices of three screwed-up adults.

Solari leaned back in his chair and took a sip of wine. "Seven months later, you were born and came to live in my household."

The cold way he described his beginnings rankled Marc. Love hadn't been part of the equation. He was merely a problem to be passed off to another couple.

At least one person in that household had cared about him at one time, anyway. "Gino is my half-brother then." Well, according to this man's account.

"Yes. He doted on you. There was no chance of him having a brother any other way. Emiliana had quit fulfilling her wifely duties to me by that point."

Judging by the man's roving eye, no doubt he hadn't lacked for female companionship. For all Marc knew, any number of half-siblings could be running around Italy with his father's genes.

"You know Gino was killed in Afghanistan."

Without emotion, Solari nodded. "*Sì.* Natalia sent me a telegram. Sad business that war."

The man hadn't bothered to show up at his son's funeral. That was even more sad, although Gino had never mentioned this man, so perhaps he'd also considered Papa to be his only real father.

Marc took a long, slow draw from his pinot bianco before nailing his father with his gaze once more. "Tell me more about Gino as a boy."

Solari shrugged. "I didn't really have a lot to do with either of you growing up."

Big surprise.

"I suppose Gino was a typical boy. I do remember how protective he was of you when…well, especially when Emiliana became ill."

An image of a frail woman in a bed flashed and faded as quickly as it had come to mind but not before Marc felt the urge to flee.

"*Marco, andiamo alla nostra tana!*" Gino's boyish voice, calling out to him to go to their lair, sounded loud in his ears, as if he could turn and find his brother standing next to him again. Sweat broke out on his upper lip as adrenaline rushed through him. Marc gripped the stem of his glass and attempted to regain control of his emotions.

Good boy. Keep breathing.

Hearing Angelina's grounding words helped calm him. After taking another sip of wine, he decided he needed to know more if he was ever going to understand his past. "Tell me what happened to Emiliana."

The man waved off the question. "Jealousy. Insecurity. She was a mess even before she got cancer. Emotionally unstable. I left her for good a few months before she died."

You must be very proud of yourself.

The image of the woman lying on the bed must have been Emiliana. That this man would abandon his dying wife and two small sons spoke volumes to his character—or lack thereof.

"Gino found her. He was only about six. They found you hours later in that rat's nest hiding place in the woods behind the house. I doubt you remember much about that night."

Jumbled images from his childhood, but who knew which had happened that night and if any of them were even real. Might be dreams. Rat's nest didn't sound right. Marc had no memory of a favorite hiding place.

Dio, poor Gino. He'd been the one to find their mama lying dead. The backs of his eyes burned as he lifted his glass, drained it, and refilled both glasses from the bottle left at the table. Gino hadn't deserved to be cast aside by Marc over some gold-digger opportunist like Melissa. He also hadn't deserved to die on that mountainside in Afghanistan. Marc couldn't remedy any of that. He just needed to—

"Your mother was nothing like Emiliana." Solari's smile made Marc uncomfortable but pulled him back into the conversation with slight relief. He didn't want to think about Gino right now, for some reason.

"Natalia had a passion for life. She was strong, willful. Much more difficult to break."

Marc didn't understand the last statement but remained silent to let the man continue uninterrupted.

"Of course, our affair only complicated things between the sisters. There never had been much love lost between the two of them."

Affair? When the man didn't seem intent on continuing, Marc knew he needed more information.

"You had an affair with your sister-in-law?"

Solari waved his hand in the air. "More of a one-night thing. Imagine our surprise when you were the result of one lousy lay."

Blood pounded in his ears. He had no intention of discussing Mama's affair—or one-night stand, which sounded more accurate—with this philanderer who had fathered him.

Did Papa know Marc might be her son and not her nephew? Curiosity nearly won out, but he decided he didn't want to confront Mama about any of this. Not yet, anyway. He needed time to sort it out and determine what questions he wanted to ask. Then he'd talk with Mama. Later.

Would she be any more honest with him the next time? Marc wanted answers. He needed to find out who the fuck he was. But an equal part of him wanted to put off the confrontation he expected. He'd never liked drama.

When Solari began paying more attention to the server than the conversation with his biological son, Marc asked for the check without any offer from Paolo to pay.

"You know, I'm not opposed to sharing." Marc thought he was talking about the bill but realized the man's gaze focused again on the server. "That one might be more than one man can handle."

Marc thought he was going to lose his meal. He pulled the bills out of his wallet, not wanting to wait for a credit card to be processed. "I've got some things I need to attend to." *Like getting as far away from my past as possible, namely you.*

"Give my regards to Natalia. Tell her I never forgot her."

Somehow Marc knew he wouldn't be extending the man's greetings to Mama, not anytime soon at least.

With more questions than answers, Marc said good-bye and headed outside. The late-winter air was chilly but the sun bright and warm. He needed to walk, to think, to breathe. Leaving the side street, he headed toward the *Piazza del Campo*. The pleasure of being back in his homeland for the first time in twenty-some years, albeit only as close as nearby Tuscany, had been dampened by meeting the man who had fathered him.

He entered the *Campo* and a flock of startled pigeons took flight, distracting him. He watched two of the birds alight on a sculpture perched high on a pedestal above the plaza. The bronze-looking sculpture showed two babies suckling at the tits of a wolf. Sweat broke out on Marc's forehead. Why did the statue send a chill down his spine? He'd never been to Siena before, but of course, he was familiar with the story depicted by the sculpture. Every Italian schoolboy learned the tale of Romulus and Remus being rescued by the she-wolf. But he hadn't thought about the story since primary school. And that story was about the founding of Rome, not Siena.

Images of a child's costume mask flashed across his mind before being replaced by the wolf mask he once wore at the Masters at Arms Club, the one someone stole four months ago. Why anyone would want to steal something like that was beyond him, but he hadn't really missed it. Why he'd chosen to wear a wolf's mask when Mama had asked him to be discreet while at the club was beyond him.

The child's mask flashed again before his eyes.

Marc shook off the eerie feeling the sculpture gave him and continued through the *Campo* on his way to his hotel. He needed to see if he could catch an earlier flight home. Remaining in Italy even another day held no appeal. He wanted to get back to Angelina.

What would he tell her about the man who had fathered him? He'd prefer to forget this meeting had ever happened.

Dio, he needed to hold Angelina.

* * *

Marc opened the garage door and saw that her car was gone. Maybe she'd gone over to Karla's. The two had become good friends. He'd texted her to let her know his plane had landed and asked if she'd like to have dinner out. No response.

He needed to talk with her about Siena. Marc placed his keys on the granite countertop and surveyed the kitchen. Spotless, not that unusual. Even the leftovers from Damián's birthday party had been removed from the fridge.

The silence within the house threatened to envelop him as he walked toward the foyer. Too quiet. He took the stairs two at a time and went straight to their bedroom. Inside, he found the bed made, his latest mystery on the nightstand, but no sign of Angelina's e-reader. Crossing the room, his heart pounding, he opened the closet. Only her red dress with the keyhole in the back hung there, the one she'd worn at daVinci's the night she'd come back into his life. Did she want to taunt him with it, or just rid herself of the memory of him and that night?

Everything else was gone.

Angelina was gone.

He was alone.

Again.

He couldn't believe she'd actually left him. She'd threatened to do so, but he hadn't expected her to follow through.

Or had he?

Marc turned back toward the vanity and saw a card propped against a photo of him and Angelina taken at Adam's wedding. Trying to keep calm, he walked across the room and picked up the card. He opened the tucked-in flap and pulled out the small flowery card. Marc stared at the columbines on the card's face a moment, afraid to open it and see what she'd written. He set the card down again.

Maybe if he didn't read it, none of this would be real. Angelina would still be here. Perhaps this was just a dream, and he'd awaken with Angelina by his side.

He looked at the card again. No, this was more like a nightmare that had started more than two months ago. He glanced at the bed.

The room began to close in on him.

Trapped.

Funny, but in the past, he'd gotten that feeling when a woman got too close. Now the prospect of being without one very special woman left him feeling suffocated.

Needing to get out of this room where they'd shared so many special times, he exited and headed back to the kitchen, pulling a bottle of pinot bianco from the wine rack and placing it in the chiller. His hands automatically reached for two wine glasses from the cabinet before he remembered he was alone.

Again.

Wait. She'd left her beloved Nonna's vanity. No way would she leave that and not plan to come back. The image of the flowers on the card had been branded on his mind. He poured a glass of wine and returned to the bedroom, needing to know what she'd said. Picking up the card once more, Marc walked over to the bed. He set the glass on the nightstand, sat on the edge of the mattress, and stared at the front of the card a little longer.

Open it.

He lifted the glass to his lips and drained it before finally opening the card. Angelina's neatly printed words filled the entire inside of the card. He began to read:

Marc,

I love you more than life itself, but if you can't let me be a part of your life, it won't be good for either of us. I need to know that you want—no, need*—me by your side, in good times and, well, times like now.*

She'd drawn two lines under the word need.

I hope one day you will be able to shed whatever pain from the past holds you hostage. Call me if you ever decide to let me share your heart and your life.

Yours,
Angelina

Marc blinked as the words blurred. He picked up his glass, needing a drink, and realized he'd already emptied it. Leaving the card on top of his book on the nightstand, he carried the glass back to the kitchen and refilled it before he picked up the bottle to carry into the living room.

Once more, this enormous house closed in on him like a mausoleum. Angelina had brightened it up with her presence, but she was gone. From the sound of that letter, she wouldn't be back until he got his shit together.

If she could wait that long.

Perhaps he should have taken her with him to Tuscany, but that mess was between him and his father. No, Solari. The only man who would be honored with the name father was Marc's *real* father, Papa. That man in Tuscany had done nothing but donate some of his sperm. Still, Marc hadn't wanted to involve Angelina in something that private—and potentially volatile. He'd had no idea what he'd find in Italy.

Nothing had changed.

Realization dawned. Therein lay the problem. How many times while in Siena had he wished Angelina had been with him? He'd included her in the discussion with Mama, and she'd helped him remain grounded—up to a point. Unfortunately, his own stubborn pride and need for privacy had kept him from having her with him—both in Italy and now in their home. No, his home. She'd left. She wanted no part of being here with him.

He was thankful she hadn't met the bastard who had fathered him, though. Would she have seen traits of Marc in Solari? Marc preferred to think there were no similarities between them other than those requiring a microscope to detect, but what if he was destined to be like his sperm donor—lecherous and lonely, looking for his next lay and never finding a woman he could share himself with?

A woman like Angelina.

He took another gulp of the wine and picked up the remote to turn on the DVD player to finish a movie he'd started watching last week, some blockbuster action flick that would take his mind off Angelina.

Instead, he found himself on a high-speed train barreling through southern France with the couple in Angelina's favorite film, *French Kiss.* He'd always balked at watching the sappy chick flick with her unless she cuddled up next to him watching while he read and relaxed.

In this scene, the callous Frenchman Luc was rummaging in the leather handbag being used as a pillow on the train by the sleeping Meg Ryan character. Her hair was too short. Too blond. Not long, lush, and dark like Angelina's. But when the sleeping woman reached out and drew the Frenchman into a kiss, Marc felt his balls tighten as he remembered the feel of Angelina's lips against his. He took another sip of wine to banish that memory.

The actor deepened the kiss. No amount of wine would help Marc forget kissing Angelina. He remembered that first kiss when she, too, slept. Well, sleep wasn't the right word. Angelina had tried to kiss him while in subspace the first night he met her, but he withdrew from her even then. Why couldn't he stop pulling away?

As he reached to press the remote's power button, the kiss ended, and Meg Ryan's character rolled over, her back to the Frenchman, leaving him as confounded as Marc felt so many times while trying to process what Angelina did to him emotionally. The man on the screen had been run over by a slip of a girl who had barreled into his life and changed everything. Forever.

Just as Angelina had done in Marc's life.

Not wanting to see anything more, he turned off the television. A burning ache targeted his heart in a way he'd never experienced before, a pain worse than having cement rebar pierce his lung in Fallujah. Ignoring the wineglass, he drained the remaining wine straight from the bottle. He wanted the pain to go away. He wanted to be numb again.

Returning to the kitchen, he pulled another bottle from the rack but didn't bother chilling it this time. Just before popping the cork, he pushed the bottle away and went into the living room to the cocktail cart to pour an amaretto neat.

Carrying the glass in one hand and the bottle in the other, he climbed the stairs to the bedroom. Who the fuck was he kidding? He couldn't sleep in that bed tonight without Angelina. Perhaps never again.

Marc crossed the room and opened the door to the tower. He and Angelina hadn't played in here since Christmas night. He flipped on the light switch and surveyed the pristine equipment. They preferred to play in the bedroom. The living room. The kitchen. The club.

Dio, he realized the playroom might be the place least touched by Angelina's memory. Good. He stripped, pulled the comforter back, and crawled in between the sheets.

Escape. Sleep.

Perchance to dream.

Dear God, don't let her be waiting for him in his dreams. The thought of waking to find he'd only dreamt about her would be more than he could take right now.

The walls were closing in around him.

Trapped.

He shut his eyelids, only to be accosted immediately by his sweet angel's smiling face. He opened his eyes and stared at the ceiling a moment. There would be no escape in sleep tonight. He reached to pick up his mystery, hoping Guido Guerrieri could distract him before he realized the latest Carofiglio novel was on the nightstand in their bedroom. *His* bedroom. Tossing the comforter back, he went down to retrieve it, keeping his gaze away from the lonely bed, and returned to the playroom bed. He opened the book to Chapter Two. After rereading the same paragraph three times, he resigned himself to the fact that he wasn't going to be able to escape inside these pages as he usually did. This would be one very long, sleepless night.

The first of many if he didn't go after Angelina.

But what had changed? He certainly hadn't. Maybe she was right, and he should let her go.

The stabbing pain to his chest led to a burning in his eyes. He was just drunk enough to cry. But no tears came. *Dio*, he'd fucked up everything.

An indeterminate number of hours later, he awoke with a jolt. He glanced at his Breitling. Oh-two-forty. Marc picked up his cell and hit Angelina's number in recent activity.

Merda. He ended the call before it was too late. Calling her in the dark of night wouldn't endear him to her.

He rolled over onto his side. No adventure treks scheduled at his outfitter store this week, but the call of the mountains was stronger than it had been in a long time. He set about planning an escape to the mountains first thing in the morning. He'd find peace there. Angelina hadn't been on any long treks with him, although she'd gone with him on a couple of camping trips before the weather set in for the winter. He knew the wilderness still frightened her.

She accused in her note that he hadn't let her inside his heart, but hadn't he shared his beloved mountains with her? The mountains were as close to him as any lover had ever been. How could she say he hadn't included her in his personal life?

Didn't she know he loved her as much as he did his mountains?

So why was he rotting away in this mansion in the city? Because Gramps had gifted him with this mausoleum after Marc had been discharged from the Navy. Marc didn't want to hurt the man's feelings.

At least with Angelina it had begun to feel more like a home.

Merda, he would feel at home anywhere on earth as long as she was beside him.

I need you, mio angelo.

He clenched his fist. *No.* He didn't *need* anyone.

Gino's voice haunted his thoughts. Marc translated from the Italian. *Stop crying. They won't keep you if you're a baby. Don't let them see you're weak.*

When had Gino spoken those words? Once again, he sounded like a kid in Marc's mind. Marc closed his eyes. He didn't want to think about Gino right now. He'd gotten closure when he'd talked with Adam and even more at Adam's wedding when he'd met Staff Sergeant Anderson, the Marine whose life Gino had saved in Afghanistan.

He'd forgiven Gino for what he'd done with Melissa, hadn't he? In reality, nothing could be done about the way Gino had left things between them before being killed in combat. They'd burned that bridge.

Marc rolled over and closed his eyes. Perhaps it wasn't too late to resolve issues with Angelina, but that would mean going to her and begging her to take him back. He had no clue what he was going to do without her, but he sure as hell knew he wouldn't go crawling to her like some big-ass baby asking for another chance. She had to want to come back on her own.

Don't let them see you're weak.

If she couldn't accept him the way he was, they had no future together.

Besides, he'd been left behind before and survived.

Dio, but those other women hadn't battered down his defenses the way Angelina had. He should have stuck to his guns that night at her house. Why did he lower his guard and let her walk away with his heart?

Chapter Fourteen

Adam helped Karla undress and wrap the flimsy paper gown around her body, which was growing bigger and more beautiful every day. If someone had told him even six months ago he'd be looking forward to becoming a father within a year—and have the hots for a very pregnant wife—he'd have called them drunk or fucking deranged. He'd given up on that dream long ago with Joni.

Until this slip of a girl he now helped on to the gyno table came crashing into his life. She awakened long-dormant feelings—and dreams—like that of becoming a father to a tiny baby.

"I'm so nervous."

Me, too, hon.

He needed to be strong for her, though. "Nothing to be nervous about, Kitten. Doctor Palmer said a few days ago everything's going well. All the labs are good, heartbeat's strong. She said it's good that you can feel the baby moving around now."

"Yeah, but why do you think she was so insistent on us doing the ultrasound so quickly when before she'd been okay with us not even having one—? Oh!" Karla grabbed her belly.

Adam leaned closer but had no fucking clue what to do to help. "What's wrong?"

She smiled at him. "Relax. I just felt the baby move. Felt like butterflies, or my ka-thunk moments."

Adam shook his head. Karla and her ka-thunks. He still had no idea what she was talking about but guessed it either made her want to puke or gave her the feeling she'd lost her stomach as if driving too fast over country roads.

The door opened, and Doctor Palmer entered. She wore a white lab coat and four-inch heels. How the woman could walk in those things all day confounded him.

"How are we doing?"

Karla faced her and smiled. "Fine. A little nervous." She bit her lower lip but added hastily, "Excited, though!"

"You should be. Seeing your baby on the monitor for the first time, well, the only moment better is when I place the baby on your chest at the delivery. I can even give you some first photos today for your baby's album. Now, no guarantees we'll get the baby at the right angle today, but if we do, are you still wanting to keep the sex of the baby secret?"

Karla turned to Adam and smiled. They'd already talked about this. He nodded and she faced the obstetrician. "Absolutely. We want to be surprised. Our nursery won't be done in traditional colors anyway, and we like the mystery of not knowing."

"Not a problem. I doubt you'll be able to tell without some training at reading these things anyway. Sure you wouldn't prefer the 3D scan? Lots of parents love having them as a keepsake."

Karla shook her head and Adam agreed. "We don't want to know the sex and the only reason we're even doing this scan is because you insisted." Karla bit her lip. "Are you looking for something in particular?"

As the doctor lifted the gown and squirted lube all over her belly, she began to explain why they were here. "You measured a little bigger than anticipated the other day. Could be any number of things—an error in the conception date, unusual growth, multiples. I just want to have a look, take some measurements, and find out why."

Adam's hand began to shake at the rapid-fire, confusing information coming at them. He took Karla's hand in his to reassure her, but her returning squeeze helped him a little, too. His heart pounded so loudly he doubted he'd be able to hear their baby's heartbeat over the racket.

They'd originally planned not to have a sonogram because of the possible risks to the baby, but when Doctor Palmer insisted based on Karla's prenatal checkup a few days ago, they'd been worrying ever since. Despite her trying to keep them calm, he was convinced something was wrong.

The pregnancy book he and Karla read from every night said the baby had reached the age of viability, although Adam didn't know how anything that tiny could survive if born this prematurely. Given their genetic history—between Adam's first child being stillborn and Karla's mom having had two miscarriages—he and Karla couldn't avoid the risk now.

From the first time he'd heard the swoosh-swoosh of their baby's heartbeat in January, this kid had a grip on his heart tighter than any Shibari tie he could rig. If anything happened…

Adam stared at the screen on the monitor. Soon they would see their baby for the first time—God, let everything be okay. Not that they'd terminate if the baby was less than perfect. They'd decided that already, too. But they prayed their baby would have no added hurdles. Life was fucking hard enough as it was.

He bent down to kiss Karla and felt the trembling in her lips. The familiar swooshing of the heartbeat filled his ears, and both turned in unison to the monitor.

What looked like a baby's head came on the monitor. Adam swallowed hard.

"Breathe, Sir," she whispered.

"I will if you will."

They watched in silent wonder a moment as the doctor took measurements and photos.

"Look, Adam! The baby's sucking its thumb! Isn't that right, Doctor Palmer?"

When the doctor didn't answer, Adam shifted his gaze and the worried expression on her face caused him to forget to breathe again. She peered closer at the screen and slid the wand a few inches across Karla's abdomen.

Adam gripped Karla's hand tighter, but a quick glance at her showed Karla wasn't aware there might be a problem. She was enthralled with the fascinating miracle they were watching, and he turned back to the monitor. The baby's head had flipped completely around, surprising him. He relaxed a little. That kind of rapid movement had to be a good sign.

"Karla and Adam, this certainly isn't what I expected given that I've seen you twice already."

Karla's hand squeezed his in a death grip, and he leaned down to whisper, "I've got you." She turned to him with a pleading expression on her face, as if he could control anything. So fucking helpless. What was wrong with their baby?

"I said I wouldn't tell you the sex, but I do have to tell you that you're having multiples."

"Mul—" Adam stopped to clear his throat. "Multiple whats?" he whispered hoarsely.

The doctor smiled and turned to them. "Babies. You're having twins!"

Holy fuck. Adam was certain the expression of terror on Karla's face was mirrored on his own. He turned back to the monitor a half-second after Karla did, but neither relaxed his or her hold on each other's hands.

"Here's Baby One's face." Sure enough, he could make out eyes and a tiny fist pressed against what must be the baby's mouth. "That's the one sucking its thumb."

Holy shit. How did a baby know how to do that already?

Tears blurred his vision and he blinked rapidly until he could see again.

"I'll snap a photo for the baby albums. You might need to get another book for Baby Two if you already started one."

Two babies.

Hell, Karla had been recording her pregnancy journey in the baby's book since the honeymoon. Now she'd need two books. Two cribs. Two car seats. Two strollers—no, he'd seen tandem ones of those. Adam couldn't find words to string together in a coherent thought to take in this news.

Doctor Palmer maneuvered the wand through the lube slathered across Karla's belly. "Do twins run in either of your families?" Before either could answer, she added, "Oh, here's Baby Montague Two."

Adam couldn't make out anything. Damned screen was blurry again. "It's pronounced *Mon*-tag."

"Oh, my apologies!"

He didn't know why correcting the pronunciation of his surname was important at a time like this, but it was. Only there would be two babies carrying his name, not just the one.

"My maternal great-great-grandparents had two sets of twins." A portrait of Kate Gannon and Johnny Montague hanging in his family's Black Hills cabin had fascinated Adam as a boy. When he ran away from home, he chose their name as his new one. Why the sudden interest in his heritage, he didn't know. Maybe because he'd just found out he was having twins to add to his family tree. Seeing that first baby's head on the screen had brought home pretty fucking fast that he was going to be passing on his name—and taking on a shitload of responsibility.

The doctor finished up, giving Karla the photo strips and a new prescription for iron pills along with instructions to take her vitamins at night if she experienced extreme nausea. Doctor Palmer left them alone for her to dress, asking them to meet in her office when ready.

"Adam…"

He glanced in Karla's direction, and her expression took his breath again a third time. Tears shimmered in her eyes before her face swam in front of him.

"Why are you crying, Kitten?" His voice sounded hoarse.

"Twins, Adam. Are we ready for this?"

I'll be fucked if I know. I'm not sure I was ready for one yet.

However, Karla didn't need to hear that right now.

"What are you saying, Kitten? You don't think we can handle two tiny babies? Hell, we have four months to get ready."

Her eyes opened wider. "You mean you're okay with having two at once?"

"Hon, I don't think we have a choice." He grinned. "But I learned a long time ago nothing was going to be ordinary or predictable with you."

She sank into the table with relief, and her face glowed even more than it had all these months. Then her face became worried and her chin quivered. "We don't even have a place to live yet."

"Don't you worry. We'll find a new agent and start looking at a new place every day until we find one." Fuck, though, she was right to worry. They hadn't had any luck finding a suitable house they could afford yet. But he would shut down the club and turn that place into a home if need be, not that he wanted to raise a family in the middle of the city.

Aw, shit, now he was crying, too. Maybe if he ignored the tears, she wouldn't notice.

Karla reached up and brushed his cheek with her thumb, leaving a cold wetness in her wake and a shocked look on her face. "You know I love you, Adam…" Sounded like a *but* coming so he waited, not sure what she was going to say. She smiled. "…but I haven't been able to envision you as a hands-on, diaper-changing dad—not right away at least."

Me either.

He sat up straighter to defend his potential for having—or learning—parenting skills. "How hard can it be with those disposable diapers? At least I won't poke them with pins. Besides, we can do anything we put our minds to. Hell, there are two of us, too."

He helped Karla up, and she dressed as quickly as she could. "Sounds like your sperm are responsible for this. We don't have any twins in my family."

"No point laying the blame—"

"Who said anything about blame? I think having twins will be amazing. I'm going to treat them as individuals, though. No wearing the same clothes, even if they are the same sex."

How did she already have them popped out and wearing clothes? Adam still couldn't wrap his head around how he would be able to provide everything needed for two babies.

Where the hell were they going to live? They hadn't found any two-bedroom houses they liked in their price range, but did they need to be looking for a three-bedroom now? Of course, when the babies were little, sharing a room would be good for them. Help them bond, not that twins needed any help bonding from what little he knew. He needed to find some training manuals on raising twins just as soon as he got Karla home. They only had four months to figure this out.

Suddenly, the thought of having twins scared the shit out of him.

*   *   *

After more than two weeks at Luke's isolated ranch, Angelina more than needed to hang out with her gal pals in Denver, so she jumped at the chance when Karla called to say that Savi needed someone to watch Marisol in order for Damián to take Savi to the club. Apparently, he'd had a breakthrough with her a week ago, and without divulging any information Karla said he didn't want to impede their progress. Angelina made the two-hour drive to Damián's in record time.

Anxious much, Angie?

Did she hope to see Marc while here for the weekend? She hadn't heard a word from him since he'd returned from Italy, and she'd been too stubborn to return his text then, thinking he needed a little more time to suffer.

Who's suffering now?

She wanted to know how the meeting with his father had gone. From what Karla had said on the phone, he hadn't been at the club for weeks. Maybe she should ask Adam to check on him, if he hadn't already. What the hell had happened in Italy?

Angelina and Savi sat down to share a cup of tea at her kitchen table while waiting for Karla to join them. She and Adam had gone house-hunting again. They decided recently they needed something bigger than originally planned, although the way Karla made it sound, their budget was stretched pretty thin already on Adam's pension and his cut of the money brought in from club memberships, sales, and the stipend they paid him to run the Masters at Arms.

Angelina glanced down at her watch. Darn. Stopped again. As she smacked it a couple of times, she peeked at the one over the stove. Marisol wouldn't be picked up from school for another hour.

Savi hadn't shared anything about her experience at the club, so Angelina didn't pry. What happened at the club was private, and she respected Savi's privacy. Angelina didn't really know her all that well yet, but apparently she confided in Karla, so at least there was someone she could talk with besides Damián. Sometimes you just needed to talk with another woman, especially when trying to sort out these Doms and their issues.

Angelina wished she could confide in someone about what had caused her and Marc to break up. Well, maybe they hadn't totally broken up yet…

Oh, who was she trying to kid? He'd texted a message inviting her to dinner as if nothing had even happened. How could there be any hope of reconciliation if the man remained entrenched in denial?

The sudden knock at the door caused Savi to jump and then hold her breath. Fear. Who was she afraid of? Angelina remembered the woman's meltdown on Christmas morning and reached out to pat her hand. "I'll get it. I'm sure it's just Karla."

A moment later, after a peek through the peephole confirmed it, Angelina opened the door wide and held out her arms. Karla walked into them.

"I've missed you so much, Angie! You two have to work this out and come back home soon!"

The two hugged tightly. Angelina nearly gave in to tears. Instead, she managed to put a lid on the raw emotions threatening to overflow. "I've missed you, too, sweetie." She'd ignore the part about working it out. That ball was in her stubborn Italian's court right now.

Karla pulled away and scowled at Angelina. "Good Lord, woman! How much weight have you lost?"

She didn't realize she'd lost enough for it to be noticeable, and she certainly could stand to lose a few pounds, but she'd left her appetite behind with Marc. If Luke didn't make her eat when they shared a meal once a day, she'd have lost even more.

Most days, Luke was busy with his horses and furniture making. She'd lined up some new catering jobs, not realizing until then how much she'd missed her clients and her business. A local restaurant was letting her use their refrigerator and freezer during the off-season until she could get back into her house in Aspen Corners. She also pitched in mucking stalls and refilling water and feed containers to help repay Luke for giving her a safe place to land.

In an effort to deflect the conversation away from her problems, Angelina patted Karla's expanding belly. "Probably about as much as you've gained. Karla, you look absolutely radiant."

Karla's blue eyes flashed. "Well, I'd be a whole lot more radiant if Adam would stop trying to wrap me in cotton balls to keep me safe. We haven't had sex in weeks. How will I ever survive this deprivation until six weeks after the baby is born?"

Angelina took Karla's hand, needing that connection to her friend more than ever, and led her toward the kitchen table indicating a chair. "Sit. Has he said why he's refusing to have sex?"

"Oh, I know why. It's just not a logical reason."

Angelina didn't want to pry, but Karla looked at her and then Savi, who had been preparing another pot of water for the three of them to enjoy some herbal teas. Karla shared, "Adam and his first wife lost their only baby at birth."

Savi turned toward Karla, her hand shaking so badly she had to place the empty mug she'd just taken from the cupboard down on the counter with a thud. "How awful. I can't imagine what I'd have done if anything happened to Mari."

Angelina stroked Karla's arm. "You have to admit that would mess with anyone's head."

"I know, but Adam's not being rational about it. He thinks he did something while having too-rough sex with Joni that caused the baby's umbilical cord to wrap around their son's neck, but Doctor Palmer explained to him again this morning that it was just a freak occurrence. She said babies turn somersaults all the time without anything going wrong and without it having anything to do with sexual activity." Karla's face suddenly grew concerned, and she stroked her belly. Angelina stroked her arm, not realizing how much women had to worry about when pregnant.

"But he's blamed himself ever since, and nothing either of us says has changed his mind. He's the most stubborn—"

"He's afraid of losing you or the baby."

Savi's soft-spoken words captured both Angelina's and Karla's attention.

At a dinner party at Marc's after Adam and Karla had come home from their honeymoon, Savi had been intimidated by Adam. Apparently, going to the club last week had changed her opinion of him if she was now defending him.

"Karla, the man lost his first wife to cancer, and before that, his baby died. I think we can understand how worried he might be that he could lose someone else he loves."

Karla stroked her protruding belly and sniffed loudly. "Okay, I'm being a brat. I'll concede there's a perfectly logical reason for him to feel the way he does." She met Savi's gaze again with tear-filled eyes. "But I have needs! He's opened up this whole new world to me, and now I can't even get him to touch me."

Angelina thought she must be exaggerating. "Not even gently?"

Karla grinned a bit sheepishly. "Okay, I'm also being overly dramatic. Occupational hazard. Yes, he'll touch me." Karla closed her eyes and smiled. "He strokes my belly in a long, sweeping motion when he cradles me against him, and he talks to them—*us*."

Angelina ignored the pang of jealousy as she watched Karla's face transform. The love of her life. A baby on the way. Karla had it all.

Still, Angelina couldn't quite picture the big Marine in question talking to his baby in the womb that way. Would Angelina ever experience that scene with Marc? She cleared the knot in her throat. "That sounds really sweet to me."

Karla opened her eyes and gazed at Angelina. "Oh, it *is*, and I love it. But it only turns me on even more and makes me want him to touch me in other places. As soon as he realizes I'm getting into it, he stops as if I'm going to break or explode or something, and he pushes me away. Man, how I wish he'd let me explode again. I'm so frustrated I could—"

Savi spoke up again. "Karla, be patient with him." The other women turned their attention to her. "It sounds as if he has some guilt and abandonment issues. You aren't going to be able to reason with him. His perceptions of the situation are based on what are, to him, very valid reasons. They are just different from yours."

Savi had been a social worker before she'd fled to Colorado last December. The mention of abandonment issues brought home something Angelina had read about online while learning about the lingering emotional baggage sometimes experienced by adults who had been adopted. She so wanted to ask questions and find out how she might be able to reach out to Marc during his identity crisis, but—

The teapot whistled. Angelina rose and helped pour tea, carrying two of the mugs to the table while Savi brought her own. The three of them sat in silence and doctored their mugs with sugar; Savi added cream to hers.

Perhaps Savi could help Angelina understand Marc's issues without her having to reveal why she wanted to know. She'd seen some of the symptoms of abandonment in herself as well, stemming from the loss of her father almost eight years ago.

"Savi, how would fear of abandonment stemming from a childhood event affect an adult?"

"It's often worse for someone who suffered a traumatic abandonment incident at a young age."

Marc had lost his mother and been adopted at the age of three. "What if he was too young to even remember what happened?"

"Even pre-cognitive children form impressions of their environment that can haunt them later." Savi's gaze grew distant a moment before she refocused. "Any traumatic loss of a loved one can lead to recurring problems later in life until the person deals with that loss and works through it. Incidents with being abandoned again as adults can trigger those suppressed or forgotten feelings, even if they don't consciously remember the original abandonment or understand why they feel the way they do."

That certainly seemed to be the case with Marc. "How might someone with a fear of abandonment react?"

Savi stirred her tea slowly, weighing her words. "Often, they've come to expect everyone in their life will abandon them. They may even jump the gun to avoid the inevitable break-up. It's easier to accept they weren't the victim of another abandonment if they leave the other person first."

Karla's eyes opened wider. "Or they do things to drive the other person away, shut them out, to keep from being hurt again!"

Savi nodded. "The expectation of being abandoned again becomes a self-fulfilling prophecy."

Before Angelina said something too personal about Marc, Karla chimed in again. "Adam was sixteen when his father was killed. Could that have triggered him to have issues at a later age?"

"Possibly. His later losses of the baby and eventually of Joni just reinforced that sense of losing the people he loved. He probably experienced a sense of being out of control. I'm not saying this happened, mind you. I haven't spoken with him enough to know, but he may even have gone into survival mode, cutting himself off from others emotionally."

Karla nodded and grinned. "He tried to, at least. I managed to batter down his defenses, but it took a very long time."

"Not surprising. At the very least, he's going to do all he can to make sure that the people he loves will survive whatever may come their way. That's a daunting responsibility."

"He's a Marine. He feels that responsibility to all of us in his newly formed 'family' every day."

"Right. He isn't going to jeopardize your health and safety, no matter what. Often they can go from survival mode to hyper-controlling, not realizing there are things beyond his control."

Karla snorted. "You try telling him he isn't in control." Her eyes widened. "Dear Lord! I didn't realize how deep-seated this could be. I have my work cut out for me, don't I?"

When her face broke out in another grin, Angelina had little doubt Karla would bring Adam to his knees before this baby was born.

At the moment, though, Angelina wanted to direct the conversation more to Marc's issues without revealing whom she was asking about. She wouldn't break her promise to keep Marc's past a secret until he was ready to tell their friends. She'd just have to ask questions that appeared to relate to herself.

"I lost my papa when I was seventeen. I never really thought about that leading to later relationship problems—" Something suddenly became clearer to her, too. "I always avoided attachments with men, letting my brothers keep most of them away. When I finally trusted one enough to enter into a more intimate relationship with me, he shattered that trust and abused me." She didn't want to think about Allen Martin either. With Marc, though, maybe she'd fallen too quickly. Did the kink dynamic lower her defenses or otherwise get her involved with him too soon? Or had her leaving Marc been more of a self-preservation tactic, seeing as how he had been distancing himself from her all these months? Had she just wanted to beat him to the *finish* line of this relationship?

Dio, which one of them was messed up the most by the losses of loved ones? But Angelina, for one, didn't want to keep repeating this cycle. "What might help ease that fear of abandonment?"

"Developing a sense of trust."

She laughed, but the sound was bitter even to her ears. "Well, let's not start out with anything too easy."

Savi gave her a sympathetic smile. "I know. I struggle with the same problem, albeit for a different reason."

So many women at the club seemed to have issues with past abuse. Karla and Grant were the exceptions, as far as she knew.

Without a doubt, Marc didn't trust Angelina. She'd inadvertently played right into his negative expectations by leaving him, the very thing he feared most. Maybe that's why he hadn't called or reached out to her since that one text. At the time, she'd thought leaving him might be the wake-up call he needed, but instead she may have succeeded in causing Marc to distance himself further to avoid more pain and hurt.

She'd only managed to meet Marc's very low expectations.

Savi's voice drew her back to the conversation at hand. "Karla, I suggest you talk with Adam. Express your needs to him in a non-threatening way."

Karla smiled. "You mean I can't grab his cock and demand that he service his horny wife—*Now*?"

Angelina grinned until she watched the color drain from Savi's face before she picked up her mug to take a sip. Savi set the mug down again. "No. That wouldn't be very helpful."

Karla reached out and touched Savi's hand, but the woman pulled back. "Sorry, Savi. I was just kidding. Or maybe not. I'd love to get that close to his...*him* again." She grinned. No, clearly Adam didn't stand a chance.

Savi regained her composure. "When you talk with him, try to identify his needs, Karla. If you can get him to go back to any of the major losses in his life, have him tell you what might have helped him then."

She wrinkled her forehead. "I don't think he wants to talk about those times in his life."

"Well, if he doesn't let it out—or recognize that it has had such an impact on him—he's going to have trouble getting beyond having those distorted perceptions that are holding you both back from having the intimacy you need."

Angelina felt lightheaded. She'd messed everything up with Marc. Rather than try to understand his needs, she'd tried to force him to meet hers. How could she undo the damage now?

"Angie, are you okay?"

Angelina looked up at Karla and nodded. She forced herself to smile, hoping she masked some of her inner turmoil. Great. Now *she* was the one wearing the mask.

She turned to Savi. "How do you get someone to remember something buried too deep?"

Savi scrutinized her for a moment. "Well, some have tried regression therapy, hypnosis, and other techniques. I'm not sure there's empirical evidence showing that those things work, but there have been some who reported individual successes." When Savi looked at her, Angelina was sure that sharp counselor's mind could see right through her cover.

Angelina wished she could go to the club tonight to talk with Marc again, but she'd promised to watch Marisol so that Savi could have another session with Damián. The difference in Savi today from when she'd first met her on Christmas morning was astounding. Savi had a spark in her eyes that hadn't been there earlier.

Angelina remembered her own first sessions exploring this kink lifestyle with Marc. He'd definitely lit a flame inside her, too. Images of her being chained to the center post as he flogged her left an aching emptiness inside that no one would ever fill.

No one except Marc.

She closed the door on those memories. Too painful.

Savi needed her time with Damián at the club tonight more than Angelina needed to try and patch things up with Marc. Besides, she knew where to find Marc any time she wanted him. Clearly, this analysis approach wasn't something she would try to do on her own, though. What if she failed and only hurt Marc even more?

Chapter Fifteen

Marc swung the ice axe above his head and heard it sink into the ice with a satisfying ka-thud before he maneuvered to the next ledges. His shoulders ached and his biceps strained as he pulled himself up the frozen face of Lodgepole Falls. The sharp crampons on his boots sank into the ice below him, helping him gain traction on the slippery surface. Sweat broke out on his forehead with his efforts. While he'd been out here on the mountain nearly three weeks, using his store manager's hunting cabin as base camp, he hadn't challenged himself this hard during the entire trek.

The sun was warmer today than he'd expected, but the temperatures were still cold enough, despite the fact that it was mid-March already. Escaping as far as he could into nature where no one could invade his thoughts or physical space, he had chosen this particular site based on his experience with it and his ability—even in these late-season, thinner ice conditions. He'd also chosen to climb solo. No partner, no rope; pushing his own limits.

Probably not the wisest move he'd made lately either. He hadn't been climbing all winter, and his muscles weren't at peak conditioning. He'd feel the consequences tonight for sure. Not to mention he was having a damned hard time focusing on this climb and not on what—or rather whom—he was running from.

At least the hero ice made it easy for him to look capable of doing something right. Every placement sank into the soft ice on the first swing.

But some fucking hero he was. He couldn't save himself, much less win the girl.

The exertion of reaching the next foothold blotted out all thoughts but those needed to ensure his safety.

Almost. Adam had texted him over the weekend saying Angelina was visiting Denver.

She'd left him weeks ago. Packed up and moved out. Okay, so she'd said she'd be gone when he got back from Italy, but he hadn't believed she'd do it.

What the *fuck* had happened to his controlled, orderly life?

No amount of soul-searching these past few weeks had helped him sort this out. Normally, the mountains held all of the answers, but they were sadistically silent this time.

When he met Angelina last fall and she moved in with him, he knew he'd found the only woman he would ever be able to love. But the love he had to offer hadn't been enough for her. Just when he thought he'd gotten his shit together, a couple of weekends with his family in Aspen turned his life upside down. Now Angelina was gone.

Hell, could he even say the people in Aspen were his family? He had no clue who he was, where he came from. His life was full of secrets and lies, not unlike the ones he'd perpetrated on Angelina and even Pamela. Neither had deserved that, but maybe that's all he knew. As long as the lies were told with good intentions, they wouldn't hurt anyone.

But that was yet another lie he told himself. Both women had been hurt by him.

He kicked into the ice to plant the front points of his crampons and then stood on them before swinging the axe again. Missed. *Merda.* He'd been climbing nearly an hour and already was exhausted. His muscles strained as he fought to land the axe on the next try.

He hadn't climbed with wrist-attached tools for years, because they gave him the screaming barfies, a feeling somewhere between wanting to scream and wanting to barf at the same time when he lost circulation to his hands because of the straps.

He grinned. Not unlike the pain he felt when Angelina had topped him and removed that first nipple clamp. No wonder she didn't like those things. But she'd taken the pain for him many times, so he'd sucked it up for her.

He swung the axe again. Got it. Now the other one. *Ka-thud.* Success on the first attempt! He pulled himself up, the steel points on the toes of his boots easily sinking into the plastic-like ice. The temperatures and sunlight had warmed up the ice enough to make climbing a breeze. Not that brittle ice he encountered on colder days.

Sweat trickled down his back as he continued to strain muscles he'd neglected for months. Maybe describing ice climbing as a breeze wasn't the right term.

He hadn't been gone more than a few days at a time since Angelina had moved in. He hadn't wanted to be away from her that long. Now she was gone, and he'd been out here for weeks. He took a moment to let the raw beauty surround and envelop him. The wind whistled through the spruce and fir trees below in the valley between the peaks. A hawk screeched overhead. He spotted it, despite the glare of the sun, soaring on air currents as it sought its next meal.

Women weren't like the mountains he loved. These rocky slopes were predictable, constant. Okay, not really, but they were a helluva lot more stable than the women in his life had been. Maybe more stable than any of the people in his life had *ever* been.

Out here, away from people, Marc felt at peace. From what Solari had said, he'd been running to nature for comfort and solace his whole life.

So why couldn't he find either today?

Thoughts of his biological father brought on memories of Gino. Even though Siena wasn't the same as their birthplace in Brescia, he'd been haunted by dreams of Gino ever since he'd returned from Italy. Disjointed images of Gino. Always the big brother, good and bad. They'd fought, as brothers often do, especially just before Gino enlisted, but Marc was surprised that more of the memories he'd been flooded with lately were of a Gino he'd forgotten about since that time. The Gino who had always tried to guide and protect him. In the absence of a healthy paternal role model in their early years, Gino had assumed that role. Despite being only three years older, Gino had taught the young Marco a lot about life and how to build character.

"Don't let them see you cry."

"I didn't, Gino."

Ka-thud. Now more than halfway up the face of the falls, he groaned as he pulled himself up a few more feet.

He'd fought his whole life to keep his emotions hidden away. He thought being strong meant never losing that iron-tight grip on his self-control. But how much control did he really have?

Marc stretched and swung the axe again. His foot slipped on the wet ice, but he quickly regained his hold by sinking the steel points into a new patch. Enough had slipped away from him lately. He wouldn't let a fucking frozen waterfall get the best of him.

Gino's words continued to bombard Marc as though his brother were right there with him. His voice was older now, perhaps during Gino's college years. Marco became a bit of a wild child. He'd always chosen nature over his classroom studies, and when it came time to choose a college program, he'd been lost. One thing he knew for certain, he wouldn't be following Gino on the MBA route.

"Set your goal and then map out a strategy to get there. Just break it into smaller components. What is it you like to do?"

"Hike. Camp. Ski."

Gino tolerated the outdoors more than enjoyed them. In a resort community, the things Marc loved were a commodity to be bought, sold, and marketed by Gino and his family.

Surprisingly, instead of telling Marco he needed to be more mature and responsible, Gino smiled.

"Then get a degree in recreational studies. You need to find a calling in life that is fulfilling for you. One you can enjoy. Otherwise, you'll just wind up resentful, bitter, and unhappy."

Marc stopped and looked over his shoulder at the mountains and valleys stretching behind him for miles. He hadn't remembered that conversation until now. Gino had accurately described how Marc felt the time he'd been forced to help run the resort in his brother's absence after Gino joined the Marines.

Before that, though, Gino helped steer Marc toward the degree he had earned. How had he forgotten that? The view blurred, and he blinked until it cleared again.

His gut knotted as he remembered those months after Gino's death when he had tried to fill his brother's shoes, knowing Gino wouldn't be back at the desk ever again. *Dio,* but he'd been so fucking miserable. He could never replace Gino.

But he didn't need to. Gino had never demanded it of him. Even his parents hadn't stopped loving him when he'd left home to join the Navy. Sure, Mama had been bitter at first, but she and Papa had shown up to sit by his hospital bed in Germany when he'd been injured. It became clear to him then that she'd been worried about his safety, not about the bottom line at the resort.

Ka-thud.

Almost there. *Focus, man.*

But if Gino had cared so deeply about Marc's welfare, why had he turned around and stabbed him in the back by stealing his girl away, even if it had turned out to be one of the best things to happen in Marc's life? He shuddered to think what life with Melissa would be like.

His mind flashed back to the moment he'd found Gino screwing Melissa. Marc had blocked out the visual memory for years, focusing instead on the fight that ensued afterward and the distance it created between the brothers—a chasm that would never be bridged. Something didn't mesh with the memory he'd had all this time, but he couldn't put his finger on it.

"Mr. and Mrs. D'Alessio, we regret to inform you..."

Mama's scream in anger and grief ricocheted through his head. When she'd been given the news Gino had been killed in Afghanistan, she'd clung to Papa a moment before beating her fist against her husband. Neither had shed any tears that day, but Marc hadn't either. In fact, he had yet to cry over the loss of his brother.

"Don't let them see you cry."

Papa had thanked the uniformed Marine and the Navy chaplain for fulfilling their duty and coming to tell them about Gino's fate.

Mama and Papa might not have cried, but they had taken the news of Gino's loss as hard as any biological parent would. Marc had seen that haunted look in their eyes when they came to visit him in the hospital in Germany, too.

Clearly, it hadn't mattered to Papa that Gino and Marc weren't his sons by birth. He and Mama had raised them almost their entire lives. Marc had never thought about becoming a parent before but knew he could learn to love, protect, and nurture an adopted child as much as one he'd helped make himself.

Why was it so hard for him to believe his parents could do the same? Why was the notion of being adopted so difficult for him to accept? Would it change who he was?

Perhaps he'd never figured out who he was in the first place. He'd run to the Navy hoping to find himself. He thought he had, but recent events had shown him he had no clue what he was even searching for.

Pulling himself up by the embedded axes, Marc listened in disbelief as the right one popped out and ripped from its purchase. *Merda.* He watched the axe hurtling toward him and grabbed for it with his gloved hand and missed. Hanging precariously by the one embedded axe, he hoped it wouldn't give way as well.

The loose axe came to the end of the bungee leash attached to his harness and bounced a few times off the wall of ice before he pulled it back to him. Climbing with one axe would have been more of a challenge than he wanted right now. Good thing he hadn't thrown caution to the wind and left the axes untethered.

Climbing alone today had pushed the boundaries of safety enough. A climber much more expert than Marc had been killed not too long ago after making a simple mistake, and he'd even had a partner climbing with him. Marc needed to focus.

Swinging the axe again, he continued to climb a few more meters, hypervigilant to make sure he didn't screw up. He wasn't about to switch to wrist straps now, though. He'd just be more careful. He took a deep breath, waiting for the adrenaline surge to hit. When it did, he grabbed the other axe and planted his crampons into the ice for a safe hold.

The stillness of the day wrapped around him as he continued to climb. Peace surrounded him. Maybe this was where he needed to be—away from everyone, alone on the mountain.

His inability to come to terms with his past might have cost him Angelina. Hell, no *might* about it. She left him without a single attempt to initiate reconciliation. She'd also made it clear she wouldn't return unless Marc made her a part of his life.

What kind of life did he have without her in it?

But how could he be the man she deserved—needed—if he didn't even know who he was?

Remembering to climb, now only ten meters from the crest, he swung the axe in his right hand once more and pulled himself up.

Crack. The stillness exploded again, and he looked up to see a chunk of ice the size of a toaster oven hurtling toward him. Too fast for him to react in time, the ice made a thudding impact against his chest, robbing him of breath. Memories of the mortar attack in Fallujah sent him into full-blown panic mode. His heart raced as his body fell backwards at the impact, but he maintained his toehold as he gripped the still-embedded axe.

He attempted to fill his lungs. No luck.

Oh, fuck. Please, not another pneumo.

At least he hadn't been knocked off his boots and down the icefall. He clipped himself into the only tool at hand, a nylon sling girth, attaching it to the clip-in point at the base of his axe with a carabiner, which freed up one hand. Hoping to relieve some of the pressure on his chest, Marc twisted and let the chunk of ice fall off of him. The searing pain in his ribs and chest from the simple movement gave him something else to worry about. Had he cracked a rib? If so, he ran the risk of puncturing his lung, if it wasn't already deflated.

Shit.

He reached for two ice screws from his bag. This ascent was over. He needed to get off this ice before any more chunks came hurtling toward him. While his head was protected with his helmet, obviously other parts of his body remained vulnerable.

He'd ended his climb far short of the goal, but he had no control over that.

Much like his life.

Taking advantage of yet another adrenaline rush, Marc slammed two screws into the ice to create an anchor and attached a carabiner to each. He reached for a bundle of rope from his pack and clipped it onto the carabiners.

Putting himself into a slow, painful rappel, he fought hard to keep his body from bumping along the face of the ice. About halfway down, he dangled in midair a few moments while catching his breath, bracing himself against the wall of ice with gloves and boots as best he could. Pain radiated from his chest, more pain than he'd experienced since Iraq, and the thought of the motion of planting the front points into the ice caused sweat to break out on his upper lip. He grimaced. He needed to get down off this frozen waterfall to assess the damage to his chest and lungs.

Breathe, man.

The last thing he needed was to lose his focus—again. He'd blundered today in more ways than one, including not informing anyone of his ice-climbing itinerary. He had his satellite phone with him, though. He'd been involved in enough search-and-rescue missions that had rapidly become recovery operations for people who hadn't taken that basic precaution.

When he reached the base of the fall, Marc didn't bother to recover his rope or other tools. He held his side to keep the aching ribs from being jostled as he inched his way to a nearby boulder. The effort to walk only a few meters drained him. Sagging against the rock, he removed his gloves and then the pack. He dropped them to the ground beside him, and his chest burned from the exertion.

Marc opened the zipper of his jacket and pulled the black T-shirt from the waistband of his pants. He gasped when his wrist rubbed against the sore rib. He gingerly palpated the area with his cold fingertips. No apparent break. No blood—not externally anyway. He still wasn't sure how stable that third rib was and didn't want to chance packing his gear and driving.

Marc sighed and reached into the side pocket of his pack to pull out his sat phone. Damn, he hated to call, but Luke was the closest to this location with Fairchance only thirty minutes away. He'd rather have Luke know what a fool he'd been than anyone else. If he put out a distress 911 call, word definitely would get back to his squad in Denver. Bad enough he had to call Luke.

He chose Luke's number from his contacts list and waited, trying to catch a full breath. Memories of his collapsed lung assailed him, but this didn't feel that bad. Perhaps he hadn't reinjured his lung. He hoped not, anyway.

Luke answered after two rings. "About damned time." Luke's voice had an edge to it that confused Marc. Okay, so he hadn't called his friend in nearly two months. Luke had been easier to shut out lately than his friends in Denver, because Luke had moved two hours away and they were no longer working together on the same SAR squad.

Now it was Marc who needed rescuing—in more ways than one.

"I screwed up."

"I'll say. And I have one gorgeous Angel here who would have to agree with us."

His chest contracted, making him wonder if maybe he *had* aggravated the old injury. Angelina had gone to Luke's?

Marc tried to tamp down the feelings of jealousy that assaulted him. Why had she gone to Luke, instead of just heading back to her family in nearby Aspen Corners? Of course, she'd given up her rental house there soon after moving in with Marc, but her mom and two brothers lived there. Any of them would have taken her in.

Had she rekindled something with Luke?

No. Don't think like that. The two of them were just friends. Luke wouldn't betray him the way his own brother had.

Would he?

"How is she?"

"Other than waiting around here for weeks until you got your act together, she's fine."

Okay, he deserved that. *Wait!* She was waiting for him? That sounded like there was still hope. But he didn't want her to see him like this.

"Can you get away for a couple hours without telling her where you're headed?"

"Sure. Angel's busy in the kitchen fixing dinner. You know that'll take hours. She's happier next to a stove than anywhere—except maybe with you, you big ass."

Some of the fear and pressure receded, causing him to notice the pain in his chest again. He could trust Luke with his life—and had on occasion during dangerous rescue missions. He also trusted Angelina, even if she didn't think so. He ought to be grateful to his friend for giving his girl a place to stay.

Shit, could he still consider Angelina his girl if she'd moved out on him and they hadn't spoken to each other since last month?

He wasn't ready to deal with the reasons why she'd left him right now. He wasn't any closer to finding answers to so many questions about his past and who he was than he had been before she walked out.

Dio, he missed her. But he didn't want her to see him like this.

"Look, I'm in a bit of a predicament."

"What the hell have you done? If you did anything to hurt Angel—" The censure in Luke's voice surprised him, more pronounced than at the beginning of this conversation. He knew the man had feelings for Angelina and wouldn't want to see her hurt, but hell, Marc didn't want to hurt her either.

"No, it's nothing like that. I've just had a minor accident."

"Damn it, man. Why didn't you say so? Where are you?" He heard a rustling at the other end. Luke was probably gathering up his gear.

"Base of Lodgepole Falls. Hang on for the coordinates." Marc pulled the phone away from his face and looked at the screen. He read off his GPS location to Luke. "Got it?"

"I know exactly where you are. I'll be there in forty tops, depending on road conditions. Top-rope?"

"No top rope."

"Damn, Marc. What were you thinking?"

Problem was he wasn't thinking very clearly lately. But he didn't need Luke giving him a lecture right now. He knew he'd fucked up. "Hey, just take your time busting my ass. I'll hang around until you get here." He looked up at the falls he hadn't been able to conquer today.

"Any injuries?"

"Sore rib, tight chest, but I don't think there's a pneumo."

"I'm on my way."

*　　*　　*

"What happened? Where's Marc?"

Angelina had overheard enough of the conversation to know Luke was talking with Marc—and that he was in some kind of trouble.

"Don't worry about a thing, darlin'." Luke grabbed his sheepskin jacket and Stetson on his way to the door. "I'll be back in a couple of hours."

"Luke, stop! Is he okay?"

Luke twisted the doorknob and opened the door, tossing back over his shoulder, "Pride's hurt worse than anything. He slipped on some ice. He just needs a little help getting up again...or maybe down."

Angelina knew from the way he'd reacted on the phone it was more serious than he was letting on. Was Marc lying on the cold ground with a broken ankle or leg or something? What did Luke mean by getting him down? Maybe he'd been climbing and was hurt on a ledge or something. Her imagination ran away from her like Marc's Porsche hurtling around the mountain curves.

She didn't want to remain calm. Damn it, she wanted to make sure Marc was okay.

"I'm going with you." She removed her chef's apron and tossed it on a dining-room chair as she ran across the room, grabbing her coat off the hook by the door where she'd hung it this morning after helping Luke clean stalls.

Luke closed the door again and took the coat from her hands. His face grew serious. "Angel, you're not going with me. Call it a macho guy thing, but his ego isn't going to want to have you seeing him in the predicament he's put himself into. If you want to run over and play nursemaid to him later, I'll take you to him myself. But not until he's back on solid footing. 'Til then, you're staying here to keep working on that fabulous supper I smell cooking. I'm going to be hungry when I get back. Maybe I can even talk the big lug into joining us."

She blinked away the tears of frustration, clenching her fists to keep from yanking her coat away and following him, if need be, to wherever Marc was waiting.

But Marc needed help, might even be hurt. Clearly, Luke wasn't going to back down. She yanked the coat away from him and returned it to the hook.

"Hurry! Go take care of him." If she couldn't be the one, she wanted someone he trusted to be there for him.

Luke reached out and stroked her cheek. "You know I will. But he's gonna be all right. This might just be the attitude adjustment he needs. I'll let him know how badly you wanted to come with me. How much you care."

"Wait!" Angelina rushed into the kitchen to bag some biscotti she'd baked last night and ran back into the living room. "Here. Take him these."

Luke added the bag to his pack. With a peck on the cheek, he reopened the door to a blast of cold air and slammed it resoundingly. He was gone.

Anxiety took a firm hold of her. She could do nothing but wait.

And make cannoli—Marc's favorite. She returned to the kitchen, grabbing her apron on the way, and started pulling out the ingredients from the fridge and pantry. Luke's kitchen was much better stocked now than it had been when she'd arrived.

The howling of the wind picked up outside, and she tried to tune it out by singing some of Papa's favorite Dean Martin classics. When she heard the howl of a wolf or coyote in the distance, she dropped the spoon and looked out at the pitch-black night. Her man was out there at the mercy of whatever might happen across his path.

"Please, Luke, hurry. He needs you."

*   *   *

The phone disconnected, and Marc closed his eyes. Images of Angelina in the French maid's uniform he'd asked Adam to buy for her last October invaded his mind for some reason. Maybe it was Luke's mention of her being in the kitchen cooking. A vision of her chained to the stove in their kitchen back in Denver sent his cock to throbbing, which only caused his chest to ache even worse.

He really had been an ass where Angelina was concerned. She'd done nothing but try to help him face the truth and come to terms with the past. In return, he'd done nothing but run—from both her and the past.

He was going to lose her forever if he didn't do something about it. About her.

But could he stop running? He'd always managed to keep the drama and emotion around him at least an arm's length away, but since Angelina had left, he'd been fucking miserable. Even if she wanted him to deal with things he'd rather run from, his whole world had collapsed when she was no longer in it. He couldn't eat, sleep, or work.

He couldn't even climb a fucking icefall.

Marc watched the sun sink behind Iron Horse Peak and pulled his jacket closer around him. Without its rays, the temperature would drop like an anchor.

The sound of boots trudging through the once-again crunchy ice alerted him that Luke probably had shown up. Marc watched where the trail opened up to the area at the base of the falls and waited. Having his friend come to his rescue didn't sit well with him.

Luke rounded the bend and zeroed in on Marc's location immediately. He gave him a slow grin.

"You're a sight for sore eyes."

Marc stood taller, hoping to alleviate any concern Luke might have for his well-being, but the movement exacerbated the pain in his rib, making it smart even more. He smiled, refusing to let on. The sooner he got back to Brian's cabin, the better.

Luke set his pack on the ground and unzipped it. "When's the last time you ate?"

Merda. He hadn't even thought about eating since breakfast. "Not too long ago."

Luke pulled out a zippered bag and opened it. "Well, I'll bet whatever it was didn't taste as good as these."

The smell of almond biscotti he knew had been made by Angelina's own hands caused a lump to form in his throat that would make eating them next to impossible.

"She made them last night. Damned good."

Last night. So she'd made them for Luke. Well, of course she hadn't known Marc would be calling on Luke for help, but the thought of her making her special dishes for someone else just rotted his gut.

"Open your jacket." Marc unzipped the jacket again and pulled up his T-shirt. Luke whistled through his teeth. "Hell, man. You're going to be black and blue for a few days." Luke gently probed at the place where the edge of the ice chunk had impacted Marc's rib. It took all of the strength he had left not to pull away.

"Probably need to head to the ER in Breckenridge and get that x-rayed to be sure it's not broken."

"No need. Even if it is, you know all they'll do is tell me to take it easy for a while until it mends. But I think it's just bruised."

Luke scrutinized him a moment. "Coughing up any blood?"

"No."

"Take a deep breath."

Marc complied, remembering the time he'd given Damián similar instructions over the phone to help determine if Savi had suffered broken ribs from the beating she'd gotten before showing up at Damián's a couple weeks before Christmas. She'd driven halfway across the country with a cracked rib. Marc felt a little foolish to have had to call Luke out here for a minor injury.

"Mind telling me what the hell you were doing climbing alone out here?"

"Needed to think."

"You've had plenty of time for thinking. Isn't it about time you started *doing* something to straighten out the mess you've made of things with Angel?"

Marc didn't need his friend pointing out his shortcomings. "I didn't call you out here to play matchmaker. Just help me pack up my gear, and get me back to the cabin.

Luke shrugged. "Suit yourself. But she's not going to wait around forever for you to get your head on straight."

Was Luke still interested in Angelina? Why had she gone to him and not her mom's or brothers' homes?

Luke walked over to the falls and reeled in the dangling rope Marc had used to rappel down. "You're going to lose more than a coupla sixty-five-dollar ice screws if you don't swallow your pride and talk to her. I've found her to be a good listener. And she's smart as a whip."

Was that just an expression or had Luke and Angelina been doing play scenes together? The man had been working with Damián to perfect his butterfly kisses with the single-tail bullwhip since, well, before Savi had shown up.

Merda, what was he worrying about? Luke was one of his closest friends. He trusted him to keep things casual and not make moves on Marc's girl. Besides Angelina and Luke had played at the club before when Marc was out on a trek with clients. But those times, Marc had always given his submissive permission to play.

His girl? His submissive? Since when? He'd blown it with her the night he'd shut her out of his decision to go to Italy, shut her out of his life. He didn't like replaying the conversation from that night in his head either, but he'd been insensitive and rude. That's no way to treat someone you want to be your girl.

The thought of her out there playing with Luke or anyone else wasn't an image he welcomed.

Angelina was his.

At least he hoped she'd agree to be his again. She wasn't going to wait forever for him to get his head on straight.

Dio, he missed her, but he hurt like hell right now and needed to be at his best before he faced her again. The last thing he wanted was for her to see him any weaker than he must already look.

"I'm going to rest up tonight at Brian's. I'm sure I can get there on my own steam, but I'll call if I have any problems."

"You sure? I can drive you up there, and we can come back tomorrow for the Explorer."

"No, I'm fine. I promise I'll get in touch with Angelina as soon as I get back to Denver. I'd like these bruises to heal before I see her."

"You worried about your bruised chest or your bruised ego?"

Marc shrugged. "Maybe both."

Angelina meant everything to him—but how could he go to her if he couldn't commit to her one hundred percent? Whatever had happened all those years ago to cause him to avoid long-term attachments with women still hung over him. If he didn't figure out the reason and face it, how was he ever going to be able to make things right with Angelina?

When he got back to Denver, he knew what he needed to do. If anyone could get the answers out of him, Adam could. Time to come clean with his friend and face whatever it was he was harboring deep inside.

Adam would be the perfect one for digging that deep. Besides, he trusted him more than he would a psych officer at the VA. Adam would have his six, no matter what was revealed.

*   *   *

The cannoli had cooled and were ready to be filled when, true to his word, Luke returned to the house about two hours later.

Alone. She'd hoped Marc would be with him.

Luke must have read her disappointment. "Sorry, Angel. He said he couldn't face you yet."

"Couldn't *face* me?" Before she let her temper flare any further, she took a slow, deep breath. First, she needed to make sure he was okay. "How is he?"

"His chest will be smarting for a while. And his ego."

"*Mio Dio!* Where is he? The hospital?" Memories of her father's fatal injury suffered on Mount Evans overwhelmed her. "Was he alone?"

Luke nodded. "He was climbing Lodgepole Falls and had a run-in with a block of ice."

Angelina's heart stopped for a moment. She didn't want him to die out there alone. Why had he taken such a chance?

Luke stroked her cheek. "Stop worrying, honey. He's fine. I followed him back to the cabin on Iron Horse Peak where he's been staying the last couple weeks."

"Alone? He's up on a twelve-thousand-foot mountain alone and hurt?"

Luke patted her arm and grinned. "Yes, very much alone, unless you count some of the ghosts he seems to be running from." She thought she heard him mutter, "jackass" before he continued. "Angel, you two are meant for each other, if you'd both just quit being so stubborn and talk to each other."

Angelina raised her chin. "My number hasn't changed." Did she sound like a petulant brat? Tough. She wasn't going to try to rekindle what they had before. Obviously, their relationship didn't have what it took to stand the test of time.

Luke shook his head and chuckled. "Don't worry about him. He has his satellite phone and a well-stocked pantry. May be a little sore in the morning, but he's survived a lot worse."

Indeed he had. Severely injured in Iraq. Losing his brother in Afghanistan. Heck, losing his birth mother at a young age, too. Savi had said the other day that losses later in life were amplified for those who had been abandoned in childhood. Whether Marc understood it or not, he still needed to face and heal from losing his birth parents.

The urge to go to him and wrap her arms around him was so great she shook with the effort to keep from grabbing her coat and keys and heading to Brian's hunting cabin. He'd taken her there a couple of times, knowing she preferred the comforts of a solid structure over sleeping in a tent when they spent time in the great outdoors. The wilderness no longer scared her, though, when Marc was beside her. But she wasn't sure she could find the isolated cabin on her own.

"Come here." Luke wrapped his arms around her and gave her a tight squeeze. His arms felt good, but they weren't Marc's.

Marc was a proud man. She already knew that about him, but Luke said she might need to be the one to reach out to him. If she did, perhaps he'd come around to trusting her sooner, and they could have a hope in hell of sharing a life together.

"Luke, you're right. I think I'm ready to go to him. I can't keep pretending life can go on without him, because it can't. He may be stubborn and have all kinds of problems, but he's mine and I want him back in my life."

Luke grasped her upper arms and gently pushed her away so he could gaze into her eyes. He smiled.

"Why don't you wait and go to Denver tomorrow? He said he's heading home in the afternoon. Give him one more night of miserable aloneness to seal the deal, but I think he came to some kind of realization out on that mountain. He's as ready as you are to have you home with him."

One more night without Marc. She could survive that.

Barely.

Chapter Sixteen

The Marines' Hymn sounded on his phone the afternoon after Luke had hauled his ass off Lodgepole Falls, jarring Marc from his thoughts on the drive home from Brian's cabin. Adam. He'd left the man a message this morning saying he needed to talk but had said he'd call again when he got home tonight. Marc took the call without hesitation. Adam wouldn't call to shoot the shit.

"Get to Damián's ASAP. Savi and Marisol are in some kind of danger."

"On my way."

Merda. Good thing he was nearly home already. He took the next exit ramp and headed downtown. Still, it took him twenty-five minutes to navigate rush-hour traffic. Every time he hit the brake, the seatbelt pressed against his bruised chest, reminding him of his accident while ice climbing.

He rolled into the parking lot at Damián's building and found Adam's Silverado, Grant's Jeep, and Damián's Harley parked haphazardly around the foot of the staircase. Marc parked the Carrera equally askew and winced at the pain in his chest as he took the stairs two at a time, entering the open door to the apartment.

Hearing familiar voices in the bedroom, he followed the sound and relaxed when he saw Marisol in Damián's arms. Thank God. Damián spoke to his eight-year-old daughter with a quiet firmness while the little girl held on to him tightly. They were okay. What the hell had happened?

"You did well, my little warrior." He kissed her on the cheek before setting her on her feet and turning to face Marc.

"Sorry it took me so long." He looked around the bedroom. No sign of Savi.

Damián looked at him, seething rage barely contained in his buddy's eyes. "They have Savi."

Fuck.

Marc didn't know what to say and watched Damián hunker down in front of Marisol. "Uncle Marc is gonna take you over to Karla's house. I might be gone awhile, but she'll take good care of you."

Marisol wrapped her arms around her daddy's neck, begging to go with him. He hugged her back but remained resolute as he promised to bring her maman home.

Breaking her tight grip on him, Damián extended her hand to Marc. "Take good care of her."

"You know I will. I'll rejoin you as soon as I can." Marc turned to Marisol and tried to lighten his voice. "*Bambolina*, how would you like to take a ride in my sports car?"

Her fierce expression made it clear she wanted nothing to do with her Uncle Marc right now. Obeying her father's firm instruction, though, she took his hand, and Marc propelled her toward the door into the living room. Her gaze remained steadfastly on her daddy until she could no longer see him.

Marc squeezed her tiny hand as they descended the stairs. "Wait here, *cara*." He went to Savi's car and retrieved the booster seat from the backseat. Soon he had her buckled in and on the road to Adam and Karla's. "Don't worry. We'll get your maman home safely to you."

"Maman needs me."

"I know, but your daddy doesn't want to have to worry about you, too. It's better if he knows you're safe with Grammy Karla."

The little girl was silent most of the rest of the way to the house. As he parked beside Karla's Hummer, Marisol turned to him. "Do you think Maman is going to be okay?" Her little chin quivered as she tightened her lips and tried to maintain a strong front. Most kids would have been bawling by this point but not Damián's little warrior.

He cupped her chin. "She has the Marines on her side. No one is going to let anything bad happen to her. You just hang in there, and we'll have you back with your maman as soon as we can. Stay strong for her."

Marisol nodded and unbuckled her belt. "I will. You better hurry. Daddy needs to go."

Karla rushed down the steps to the passenger door and opened it before Marc could get out. She bent to look inside at Marc over Marisol's head, the fear in her eyes evident.

"Don't worry, *cara*. We'll get her back. And I'll make sure Adam's back here again, too, as soon as he can be."

She nodded, but he didn't miss the tears filling her eyes before she turned away. "Thanks, Marc." Her voice had grown husky, forcing her to clear her throat before continuing. "Come on, munchkin. Let's go make some chocolate cupcakes. Auntie Angie is coming over."

Angelina? He needed to talk with her, work things out. *Dio,* he'd give anything to see her, hold her. But that would have to wait now.

Marc waited until they were safely inside, watching Karla waddle a bit more than she had the last time he'd seen her. *Dio,* that had been nearly a month ago. He couldn't believe she had until July to deliver that baby. Nearly four months to go, unless she went past her due date.

Marc shifted into gear—mentally and physically—and exited Adam's driveway. Before he'd taken his gaze off them, Karla had placed a protective hand on Marisol's shoulder. Marc hoped nothing went wrong on this rescue mission. If Adam didn't arrive home safely, or if anything happened to Savi or Damián...

Now that he didn't have Marisol in the car, he gunned the engine as he sped across town to Mac's clinic. He'd need medical supplies in case Savi or anyone else was injured.

Pulling into the parking lot, he saw his friend's beat-up station wagon. This was the clinic's half-day, but Mac worked late, as usual. The man seriously could use more staff but refused to spend his limited funds on anything other than medical equipment and supplies. Marc and several other board members donated what they could, but healthcare didn't come cheap, especially when Mac gave most of it away free or at cost.

Knowing Mac would be in his office filling out patient charts and calling in today's prescriptions, Marc went to the back door and knocked. He stared up at the security camera. Mac kept his narcotics under lock and key, only dispensing them on rare occasions, and posted signs saying there were no narcotics on the premises to prevent would-be thieves from targeting the clinic. Hence the security. But Marc knew there were some here—and that he'd need them.

The heavy steel door swung open. Mac waved him inside. "What brings you out tonight, man?"

"The woman I brought to see you just before Christmas has been kidnapped. We're going after her, but I don't want to go in unprepared. Can you get me some gear?"

"Hell, yeah. Follow me."

The sandy-haired doctor led him down the hallway to the dispensary. Inside, he grabbed a black satchel and filled it with bottles of sterile saline, four-by-fours, and a few more items. Moving a stack of gauze-filled boxes out of the way, he revealed a safe and turned the knob back and forth until it opened.

"I'm going to give you two narcotics and half a dozen syringes. As I recall, she's not one to admit she needs painkillers, but before you administer anything, make sure she was lying about allergies. I doubt she's allergic to everything like she tried to convince us, but I don't want you exacerbating her problems if she does have a known allergy."

Marc nodded. Like Mac, he was certain Savi had claimed allergies because she hadn't wanted to be under the influence of anything that might cause her to lose control that night. She might not be able to take whatever the perps dished out this time, though. *Merda,* the last time she'd encountered these shitheads they'd broken her rib, and she'd managed to drive for two days before seeking treatment.

After checking Savi's chart, Mac jotted down some notes and handed a sheet from his prescription pad to Marc. "Call or text me if you need help calculating the dosage. My patient chart only shows her weight as of three months ago, so this is a rough estimate of what she might weigh now, give or take."

Marc folded the paper and tucked it inside the front pocket of his jeans. "I appreciate this."

"Just return whatever you don't need and make a note of what you do use and on whom. I need to account for it."

"No problem."

Marc sprinted down the hallway with the full bag in hand and exited the building. After texting Damián he was on his way back, he drove back to the apartment building and saw Grant and Adam stowing their gear in the back of an unfamiliar SUV. He pulled alongside it and transferred the medical kit.

"Whoa!" Grant took a step away from him.

"Sorry." He wished he'd been able to stop by the house to take a shower and change clothes, but time had been of the essence. Brian's cabin was primitive to begin with and then the hot-water heater had gone out, so he'd skipped showering the last week.

But they'd already fallen at least three hours behind the men who had abducted Savi. No time for showers.

Damián came down the stairs, holding onto the handrail. The strap of Damián's seabag dug into his shoulder. The strain in the man's eyes was evident, but he didn't hesitate. "Let's roll."

Marc thought back to those terrifying hours when Angelina had been taken by Allen Martin. He'd imagined all kinds of things that *bastardo* could have been doing to her. Thank God none of that had happened, and she'd managed to overpower and hogtie the asshole. He hoped Savi would be as lucky or that they'd get to her in time.

The four of them piled into the SUV with Grant behind the wheel. In the front passenger seat, Adam opened his laptop and checked the coordinates. "They're on 70 heading west. Not too far ahead of us actually. They must have stopped somewhere."

After Grant asked how they were able to track her, Marc looked over at Damián, whose expression was devoid of emotion except for the clenching of his jaw. He kept his eyes on the road ahead. Silent and pissed. Marc explained to Grant that he'd put a GPS chip in a necklace Damián had given Savi for Christmas. The chip he'd put in Angelina's bag had helped them zero in on her whereabouts, so when he'd learned Savi and Marisol had been in danger of being taken, he'd suggested the same to Damián. Clearly Damián had expected this kind of trouble all along. What had happened to the surveillance Adam and Damián had worked out for the apartment, he wondered?

Marc hoped they wouldn't trash Savi's necklace like Allen Martin had the GPS chip in Angelina's backpack.

Still, the news they hadn't gotten too far didn't sound good either. They would have had more opportunity to hurt Savi if they stopped than if they continued driving.

Taking turns at the wheel, shifting drivers every three hours, they made good time and closed the gap to barely ninety minutes. Still not good enough. Apparently, there was more than one person sharing the driving in the vehicle with Savi, too.

Marc's turn came as they refueled and stocked up on food just over the Nevada border in Mesquite. They lost fewer than ten minutes before getting back on the road. Savi—or her GPS necklace at least—was headed toward Las Vegas. More than likely to Southern California from there, where her attacker had first caught up with her before she'd fled to Damián's apartment in December.

Before they entered California, Damián filled them in on what he knew about Savi's father. The story of her ordeal made Marc sick. How could any father do such despicable things to anyone, much less his own daughter? And the man's business partner didn't sound like any prize to humanity either. The woman had been through hell and still managed to keep her sanity and raise such a well-adjusted daughter. Damián was a lucky man.

Marc should count his blessings that he'd grown up in a happy home. Hell, he hadn't been abused. Mama had always treated him and Gino like her own. If Melissa hadn't said anything about the adoption, Marc never would have suspected a thing. Nor cared.

Still, he couldn't lose that niggling feeling someone was withholding something from him, based on the revelations he'd gotten from Solari on his trip to Italy last month. That's probably what bothered him more than the fact that he'd been adopted. When he returned to Colorado, he needed to seek out Mama and the answers she was withholding about his past.

A day and a half after the abduction, in the wee hours of morning, they arrived in Rancho Santa Fe, the exclusive community on a hill outside Damián's hometown of Solana Beach. The GPS coordinates had stalled here an hour ago. One fucking hour. A long time for Savi to be alone with her abductors. If he hadn't lost valuable time because he'd had to go to Mac for supplies…

They'd blasted through the gate with minimal delay. Good thing some Cobra helicopters on maneuvers from a SoCal base had ventured over the area to provide a counterbalance to the noise of the blast at just the right time.

Grant set up her communications equipment inside the once-again closed gate as Adam and Damián donned ski masks and headed for the house. They didn't trust Marc's rusty shooting skills, so he was ordered to wait with Grant until they neutralized any combatants. They'd need him later to assess and treat Savi. He hadn't been in corpsman mode for almost eight years, but it felt good.

Still, he hoped he wouldn't be in over his head medically. His weaponry skills weren't the only ones he'd let go by the wayside after he was discharged. He hoped he'd at least be able to provide the triage and initial treatment necessary to stabilize her enough for the trip to the medical facility.

"You've been awfully quiet, Doc."

Marc glanced over at Grant. Her leg shook with nervous energy. She probably wished she could have gone in with Adam and Damián, but they made it clear her expertise on this mission was communications. No engagement with the enemy, just as her activities in the recon unit in Fallujah had been restricted—well, until the SNAFU situation on that rooftop.

Marc cleared his throat. "Just thinking. Hope they get to her before any real harm is done."

"You and me both. Sounds like she's seen her share and then some."

"Yeah. I had no idea. She's a helluva strong woman."

Grant averted her gaze and fiddled with a setting on her gear. "Most people have no clue what someone else has been through as long as they put up a solid front."

Marc realized how very little he knew about Grant. She'd been assigned to the same Marine ground unit he had been because of her communications expertise. He knew nothing about her life before that and not much after, to be honest. She'd shown up at the club a little over a year ago but hadn't talked much about the years in between Fallujah and the club.

No time like the present to catch up, until they were needed for this current mission.

"What did you do after your enlistment ended?"

"Contracting."

"Government?"

She grinned. "Not quite."

Hell, she'd been in Black Ops?

"Communications work, of course. I was stationed in Iraq—Ramadi and Fallujah mostly."

"I was glad to be out of there, although I didn't like leaving my unit behind. How could you stand going back?"

"Had a score to settle."

"Did you?"

She grinned at him. "Fuck, yeah."

When it became obvious she wasn't going to elaborate, he decided to prod. "What type of score?"

She seemed to weigh her words a moment too long, making him think she wouldn't go on, but then she surprised him. "Took care of the bastards who attacked our unit on that rooftop."

Merda. "Seriously? Do Adam and Damián know?"

"Top suspected as much and got it out of me during a weak moment. I haven't told Damián." She held her hand over her headpiece, placing it closer against her ear, then shook off whatever she'd heard. She grew serious. "Things went south not long after that. I'd rather forget about it."

Marc knew forgetting wasn't an option for most of them but didn't push her for details. He'd never had a strong desire for revenge. It wouldn't have changed the outcome. Still, knowing that the insurgents who had killed Sergeant Miller and maimed Damián were no longer breathing the same air on the planet, much less enjoying their lives and families in that shithole or anywhere else in the world made Marc feel a little better.

"Thanks." The word sounded lame but came from his heart.

"Don't mention it. After you guys kept me wrapped in so many protective layers on my tour, it felt good to be able to put my Marine training to use. Black Ops gave me that opportunity—well, up to a point."

He heard the bitterness in her tone but approaching footsteps dragged their attention to Damián and Adam running down the driveway, returning their focus to the mission at hand. No sign of Savi. Marc's gaze zeroed in on the flecks of blood on Damián's armor-plated vest but Adam assured him no one had been injured—yet.

Thank God, but then where the fuck was Savi?

Soon they had hiked back to the SUV and were headed to the Yucca Valley. Marc remembered receiving some of his combat training at Twentynine Palms. The area was desolate. Isolated. He hoped the coordinates would take them right to her. If not, they might never find her in that godforsaken place.

Marc decided to get some shuteye before taking his turn behind the wheel again. He needed to be as sharp as possible when they arrived on scene, because there was no telling what kind of trouble they were walking into. At the very least, he'd have Savi to patch up, but all of them would be targets when they went in to rescue her. He couldn't let his buddies down again. Why hadn't he kept up his rifleman skills or at least trained with a sidearm? Not to mention furthering his medical training. His medical knowledge was basic, just what he needed to meet federal and state standards for SAR professionals.

Within minutes of arriving at their staging site on the backside of Bear Mountain, the four reconnoitered the perimeter and had subdued the only visible guards. His recon training with the Corps came back in an instant as

Damián spelled out the next phase of the mission. Marc would cover the front entrance, Grant the road away from the isolated cabin. Adam and Damián would enter the cabin first to locate Savi.

Dio, don't let them be too late.

When the four of them split up, Marc followed instructions and waited for the agreed-upon signal before he moved closer to the cabin.

The signal came soon after, indicating Damián and Adam had gotten inside. Marc low-crawled to within a hundred feet of the front of the cabin to await further instructions. The perimeter security at this place had been surprisingly light. Marc prayed they didn't walk into a can of worms inside the cabin.

A woman's high-pitched scream split the still desert air. *Merda*. Savi. Marc's heart drummed loudly, and he itched to move closer to the front door but had his orders not to enter until he received the signal. It wouldn't help if he was shot or wounded himself. Still, he struggled with his impatience to get to her and begin assessing her condition so he could provide her with some much-needed relief from the pain. If only—

The report of a sidearm popped. *Dio*, don't let it be his friends. The long seconds of waiting for the go-ahead to enter stretched out like an eternity, but he was ready to charge in when Adam finally sent him the all-clear signal.

Marc kicked the flimsy door in and made his way to the voices and moans he heard at the back of the rustic structure. He followed the sound of voices and entered an open doorway to find Adam and Damián removing the restraints from Savi, who lay bloodied and draped over an ottoman. Her back, ass, and legs had been torn to shreds with a whip. His gaze strayed to the floor where a riveted flogger lay, blood dripping from the points. *Gesù*. Marc's anger boiled to the surface when a movement out of the corner of his eye diverted his attention to where an old man raised a small weapon in the direction of his friends. Marc drew his own sidearm and took aim at the man's chest.

The sound of the shot split the air, and the small pistol flew from the man's hand. *Shit*. He'd missed the bastard by a long shot, but at least the man didn't have a weapon any longer. Marc hurried across the room to retrieve the weapon and placed it in his medical gear. Might need it as evidence later on.

Damián complimented him on his marksmanship, but Marc hated that he hadn't taken the *bastardo* down when he'd had the chance.

"Out of practice. I was aiming for his chest."

Moments later, Marc tuned out the old man whining about his superficial injury as Adam hauled the bastard's sorry ass out of the room. Returning his focus to Savi's wounds, he tried to distance his emotions from the scene the way he'd been able to in Fallujah.

Epic fail.

His chest tightened, and he felt as if his own skin had been laid bare by the steel points embedded in the flogger. In Fallujah, he'd been able to shut down his emotions without a problem. Just do his job. Even when he'd failed to save Sergeant Miller, he had never let emotions get in the way of focusing on helping someone else who needed his skills.

The Marines hadn't trained him to shut down his emotions. They'd just helped refine the mechanism he'd had in place all his life.

Savi's screams earlier had torn through him like an ice axe through his heart.

Focus. Don't lose your focus.

Not that he was having any success with shutting down his emotions now. Whether he'd just been out of combat too long or he'd never had to deal with wounds on a defenseless woman's fragile body before, seeing the loose, bloodied flesh in slashes across Savi's back made him want to beat the shit out of the man who had done this to her.

Get a grip. You have a job to do.

Savi didn't move as he worked on her back. Was she conscious? Her eyes were closed. Being unconscious would make it easier on her, but he needed to gauge whether she'd gone shocky.

Marc began removing supplies from the bag. "Savi, can you hear me?"

She nodded but kept her eyes shut. Marc took her blood pressure and checked her pupils and respirations. He turned to Damián. "She's not in shock." Not clinically, anyway, but her rapid pulse told him she was in emotional shock. Who wouldn't be? He needed to help control her pain so he could work on her, which no doubt would cause even more pain at first. He turned to her once more. "*Cara*, tell me the truth this time. Any allergies to pain meds?"

Savi shook her head. "No."

"Fentanyl?"

"None."

"How much do you weigh?"

"Getting closer to one-ten with how much Damián makes me eat."

Marc filled the syringe and injected the powerful narcotic into Savi's hip. Unable to wait for the medication to fully take effect, he poured the sterile saline over the gashes and welts from her back to the backs of her thighs. Savi hissed as the water made contact with the deeper cuts. Even though she hadn't lost a lot of blood, he knew the solution would help clean the cuts without causing further damage to her body. He wet a four-by-four with more saline and tried to clean the more superficial wounds while he waited for her to surrender to the medication.

She hissed at the touch of the gauze against her raw skin and tensed, fighting against the pain.

Damián stroked her cheek and tried to soothe her. "You're safe."

Marc applied the antibiotic cream to the less serious cuts and bandaged the two deepest ones. Savi hissed again at the contact against her ravaged skin, twisting Marc's gut. He didn't want to cause her any more pain, but the threat of infection in this hellhole was too great to delay.

"Sorry, *cara*. Almost done."

Savi nodded. He was glad she'd remained conscious, so he could be sure she hadn't slipped into shock.

Damián continued to talk to her, stroking the back of her head. "Don't fight it anymore. Go to your safe place now."

A sob tore from her. "I tried not to scream, but I couldn't hold it back in the end."

Marc couldn't imagine what had gone through Damián's head when he'd heard her, though her screams had led them to her faster.

Savi's body slumped. Good. The meds were working. Marc checked her pulse again. Strong. He heard what sounded like the SUV pull up outside.

Marc put some of the supplies back in the bag. They were moving to Plan B. "Damián, we're going to need to call for air transport. Savi's not going to be able to stand the SUV ride on those rugged back roads."

"Savannah. Her name is Savannah."

Marc nodded and patted Savi—Savannah—on the calf, trying to avoid her injuries and bandages. He radioed Grant to place the call to Palm Springs. The sooner she was at the trauma center, the better it would be. Marc could only do so much in the field, much like when he'd patched up his Marines in Iraq, just enough to get them to the next facility down the line. The civilian EMTs might not assess this as warranting air transport, but he knew Grant would make sure someone responded, even if she had to call in someone from nearby Twentynine Stumps, as he and his Marines called the desolate place. Savannah might not be one of his tough Marines, but she'd certainly gone through more than even some of them had.

Without warning, Savannah began flailing her arms, struggling to get off the ottoman. She wasn't letting the meds do their job. Still had too much fight in her. Damián placed his hand on the back of her head. "No, *bebé*. Lie still. Do not move."

Once more she sank down, limp.

Marc continued to assess the damage and applied ointment to the cuts on her back. When he reached for more four-by-fours, the sharp pain in his chest made him wince and reminded him to be careful how he moved. The tendons were sore still from the accident on Lodgepole Falls the other day.

"What's wrong? You injured, too?" Never could get anything past Adam.

"Had a little accident before we came to California. It's nothing."

"Aw, fuck." Adam patted Marc's arm and pointed to Damián's bloodied pants leg. *Merda.* Adam went around the ottoman and knelt beside Damián, tugging the pant leg out of his boot. "You stay still, too, son. We need to pack this wound." Damián's calf above the prosthesis had a bloody hole in it.

"Fuck, son."

Marc grabbed the medical bag and joined Adam. Damián tried to wave him away. "I'm fine, Doc. You need to work on Savannah."

"She's stable. I want to give that ointment a chance to work before I put bandages on the rest of the cuts."

Savannah gasped. "Damián, you've been shot!"

"Just a flesh wound."

She tried to rise off the ottoman. "You're bleeding. Oh, God! What have I done to you?"

Damián opened his mouth before his head began to sway as his eyes rolled into his head. Worried he'd pass out, Marc reached for him, but Damián fought his way back, staring up at Adam. "I am not leaving here until justice is done. Go back, and keep an eye on him."

Both of the men behind Savannah's abduction had been caught, and Marc couldn't imagine either getting away without severe repercussions. Their accomplices and the guards were immobilized. Still, Adam assured Damián that Grant had Savannah's father under control. He wouldn't be going anywhere but jail.

"Damián!" Once again, Savannah fought to get closer to him.

As Damián pushed her down and admonished her to be still, Adam ordered both of them to stand down. Savannah complied first, lowering her chest to the ottoman but keeping Damián's face within her line of sight. Damián slumped onto the floor face up. He gasped for breath, which worried Marc. Damián closed his eyes, but they shot open again a moment later when Marc poured the sterile saline over his calf. Damián gritted his teeth. "How bad, Doc?"

He'd asked something very similar when Marc had treated his wounds in Fallujah. At least this time he didn't have to gloss over the truth or hide anything.

"Through-and-through wound, fleshy part of your calf." Marc injected the skin around the entry wound to numb it. "Blood loss is minimal. I don't think you'll have any long-term problems. We'll fly you to the trauma center with Savannah."

Damián reached out and grabbed Doc's arm. "*My* mission…isn't…over."

Adam squeezed Damián's shoulder. "Son, this mission just changed. It's over."

Damián glared at Adam, unwilling to back down in spite of his injury. "Not leaving…until I've finished…what I came…to do."

Adam growled and looked ready to head slap Damián, but instead he looked at Marc. "Can you do something to counter the reaction to the blood loss?"

"I can hook up an IV and do a quick infusion of Ringer's; it's a temporary blood replacement."

"Plain English."

Marc grinned. "Yeah, I can help."

"Do it, Doc."

Marc went to work as Adam tried to find out what Damián's mission entailed.

"This is between me and the motherfucker who hurt my girl."

Adam got in Damián's face in true Master Sergeant fashion. "You aren't completing this mission. Not without me, anyway."

Marc heard the whoop-whoop of the chopper blades. Time to get these two the medical attention they needed. He hoped he'd bought Damián some time before the man passed out so that he could get whatever satisfaction he deemed more important than his own health.

Damián grabbed Adam's sleeve. "Get me out of here before they come in. They'll have to report a gunshot wound, and I'm not going anywhere until I've taken care of business." After he kissed Savannah and assured her he'd see her soon, Adam and Marc carried him to the room where Savannah's father was bound and gagged. Then Marc headed back to meet the EMTs from the flight crew.

The medical crew rushed into the room moments later. Grant must have assured them the scene was secure. Marc shared his assessment of her condition but watched as they confirmed it by performing many of the same actions. He admired them for not letting their emotions get in the way and hoped he hadn't done anything to jeopardize Savannah's recovery.

Watching them load and take off, he wondered what it would be like to be an EMT. He'd never wanted to be cooped up in a hospital setting, but these guys—and women—experienced things much as he had as a Navy Corpsman. He'd never felt more fulfilled than when he'd been with his Marines. Maybe he'd look into what it would take to train to be an EMT when he got his life back on track.

After they'd left, Adam had ordered Grant to report to Karla and Angelina that all was under control and to book flights to California. Marc felt at loose ends. Grant told him they'd also been ordered out of here, so they set out for Palm Springs where they'd keep watch over Savannah until Damián and Adam finished whatever it was they needed to do.

Marc envied the bond Adam and Damián had formed since Fallujah. Adam hadn't assumed the parental role with Marc, probably because Marc hadn't let him get that close, but he'd sure as hell given him advice over the years. Hell, even a head slap or two when needed. With Marc, Adam had picked up where Gino had left off. A protective big brother.

But he was more a father figure to Damián. Maybe parental love had nothing to do with genetic bonds but more with who raised you. Solari would never be a father to Marc. Gino, though only a few years older, had been the first to guide him in his early years. Then Papa, who had provided a steady influence over the man Marc had grown to be. He'd been Marc's prime example of how a gentle, loving man treated his woman and raised a family.

Dio, Marc wished he could hold Angelina right now. Would she even want to have anything to do with him after he'd avoided her for so long? Why couldn't he get his head on straight when it came to her? To his past?

First, though, he needed answers and wondered how many of them were buried deep inside him. Whatever happened in his childhood had affected his life, on a subconscious level at least. But Gino was no longer here to answer his questions. And Papa, well, Marc couldn't talk to Papa about this identity crisis either. He was ashamed to tell the man who raised him as his own that he'd felt the need to seek out Solari, the man who was nothing more than a sperm donor to Marc.

Grant glanced over at Marc. "You're awfully quiet, Doc."

Doc. Funny how they all reverted to his nickname from deployment so easily. This certainly had been a combat mission.

"Just thinking. Hell of a mess."

"We've been through worse. They survived."

Thank God. "Duly noted."

Marc remembered how Angelina had been abused by Allen Martin—not nearly to this extent but enough that she'd had emotional scars from the ordeal.

Why were some men such fucking assholes?

There had been a time he'd thought he'd lost her to death. Damián had just been to hell and back thinking he might lose Savannah, too. Marc didn't want to lose Angelina. He needed to get her back, but how?

That self-protective wedge he'd inserted into every adult relationship with a woman since Melissa and his tendency to run rather than face confrontation had caused Angelina to walk away from him. And he hadn't done a damned thing about it. Was there still time to save their relationship? Maybe it wasn't too late.

But first he had to sort out what to say and do. He couldn't go straight to her and talk things out, because there was too much he didn't understand about himself even now.

Before they'd left the cabin, Adam had smiled slightly and nodded, as if telling him he'd done well. That simple acknowledgement had warmed a cold place inside him. The man was the closest family he had since the Navy, even though Marc had kept him and everyone else at an emotional distance.

He needed someone like Adam to pull out those secrets his mind had harbored all these decades. Adam wouldn't pull any punches or be gentle and polite about it, like Papa would.

Yes, he needed to talk to Adam. After they all got back to Denver and things settled down, he'd make sure that happened. Adam had almost lost Karla, but somehow managed to win her back. He'd know what to do.

Chapter Seventeen

ngelina jumped when Karla's phone played the chorus to "She's a Maneater."

The worry on Karla's face as she reached for the phone was tempered slightly by her muttering, "I need to change that ringtone." She slid her finger across the screen and held the phone to her ear, fear evident in her eyes as her other hand reached for Angelina's. "Hi, Grant. Is everyone okay?"

Grant, not Adam. Did that mean...? No, she wouldn't go there. Angelina squeezed Karla's hand in support. *Dio,* please let them all be okay. *Papa, watch over them.*

When Karla slumped against the back of the glider chair, Angelina's heart sank. She held her breath, waiting.

Karla asked, "How bad is she hurt?"

Fear clawed at Angelina's throat. But she'd said hurt. Savi was hurt, which sounded as though they'd found her alive.

Karla didn't give anything away until she suddenly sat forward in the chair and made eye contact with Angelina. "Damián's been shot?"

Oh, God, no! What about Marc? And Adam? Grant must be okay if she was calling. Knowing the men, they'd kept her away from most of the danger.

Hearing only half the conversation was driving her insane. "Put her on speaker, Karla!"

Angelina turned toward the doorway and saw that the door to Marisol's bedroom remained closed while she took a nap. The poor little girl had been having nightmares and screaming for her maman and daddy for two nights in a row. She needed her sleep.

"Sorry, Angie." Karla put the phone on speaker, and Grant's voice came through as if through a tunnel.

"Doc says it's a through-and-through. Not even serious enough for him to get airlifted out with Savannah."

Doc. Marc must be okay then, but she hated hearing one of the guys had been wounded.

"Where was he shot?" Angelina asked.

"In the calf, just above the prosthesis."

Karla drew a deep breath before she could speak. "Will he lose any more of his leg?"

Angelina heard Marc ask Grant for the phone. She hadn't heard him in such a long time that she froze, unable to breathe or speak.

"Damián's fine. He won't lose any more of his leg if he gets it looked at soon, and I'll make sure he does pronto. He and Adam need to finish up the mission first."

"You mean it's not over yet?" The worry in Karla's voice must have caused the baby to kick because she pulled her hand away from Angelina's and rubbed the top of her belly.

"Don't worry. They're in no danger. We found Savannah, and the men who kidnapped her have been…detained. Just a little clean-up to do, that's all."

Angelina wanted to say something to him, but no words would come.

Karla spoke for them both. "Thank goodness. Let Savi know we're thinking about her and tell her Marisol is okay."

"Roger that. She's been airlifted to a Palm Springs trauma unit. We'll let you know what we find when we get there, but most of her wounds are superficial. I'm more worried about her mental state than anything else."

Karla continued. "She's strong. She's already survived so much. I know she'll pull through."

"Look, our signal is getting weaker."

Karla added quickly, "Wait, Marc! Is Adam okay?"

"He's fine. Listen, Karla, Adam wants you to check with Doctor Palmer and make sure it's okay for you to fly out with Marisol tomorrow. He said you might be on restrictions. I hope everything's okay."

What was going on? Why was she being restricted this early in her pregnancy? Karla didn't make eye contact with Angelina. "No, Marc, everything's fine. But I'll make sure."

"If not, then one of us will fly back to get her. The sooner Savannah is reunited…Marisol…quicker…heal."

"You're breaking up, Marc."

"…call…later…" And the call ended.

Neither Marc nor Adam had included Angelina in that invitation to go to California. Why would they? She was just a friend, not family like Karla or even Savi. Maybe Marc wasn't even aware she was sitting here beside Karla.

Why hadn't she been able to say something to him? She'd had her chance to talk with him but had blown it.

Thank God he was okay.

She melted against the wingback chair as Karla set the phone on the table between them. A shuffling sound behind her caused them both to turn. Marisol stood in the doorway, her chin quivering with emotion. "Is Maman going to die?"

Poor thing! How much had she heard? Angelina was able to get up and go to her faster than Karla could, and she wrapped the little girl in a tight hug. "Your maman is safe now. The doctors and nurses are going to fix her right up. She wants you and Grammy Karla to fly out tomorrow so you can see her when she's ready for visitors."

Marisol broke into sobs and held on tightly to Angelina. These were the first tears she'd shed since this ordeal had begun, other than when her defenses were down in the middle of the night. She'd kept up such a brave front, despite having witnessed her mother being kidnapped. Not to mention the little girl had nearly been taken as well.

"Come, honey, let's sit and talk." Angelina didn't know what she'd say but wanted to put the little girl's mind at rest any way she could.

Angelina stroked her hair and held her against her chest. "Shhhh. Uncle Marc took really good care of your maman, and now she's at a hospital where lots more people are going to make sure she's all better, so she can come home."

"Which home?"

Angelina didn't know what Savi planned to do after this, whether she'd stay here in Denver near Damián or go back to her home in Solana Beach now that the threat against them seemed to be gone. "Home will be wherever you are." That seemed safe enough.

"What about Daddy?"

Oh, she didn't need to be having this conversation, although she and Marisol had gotten to know each other during the times she babysat while Savi and Damián went to the club.

Karla rescued her from saying the wrong thing. "Your daddy and maman both love you very much and will talk about all this when you see them. But first we need to do some packing."

Marisol sniffled and picked at a decorative button on the sleeve of Angelina's shirt. "The bad men shot my daddy?"

Karla nodded. "Yes, but he's going to be all right, munchkin."

"You asked Tía Grant if he would lose his leg."

Angelina spoke up this time. "Uncle Marc said your daddy wouldn't lose any more of his leg, honey. It wasn't a bad wound."

"More?"

"More what?"

"You said more of his leg. My Daddy has two legs, like me."

Oh, dear God. Marisol didn't know? How could she not know after all these months of living with Damián? And how was Angelina supposed to respond?

Once again, Karla came through for her.

"That's something for Maman and Daddy to talk with you about, too. I promise I'll let them know. They can tell you about what happened to Daddy when he was in the war with Grampa Adam, but he's going to be okay."

"Maman gave me a book about a soldier who got his leg cut off after bad people in the war hurt him. Is Daddy's leg cut off?"

Marisol wasn't going to be deterred. Apparently, Savi had been preparing her for the time they would tell her about the amputation, but it wasn't Angelina's or Karla's place to reveal something so personal. That needed to come from the little girl's parents.

"Why don't you find that book for Grammy Karla so we can read it on the plane?"

"I left it at Daddy's 'partment."

Karla stood and reached for Marisol's hand. "Then we'll go there and pack anything you want to take on the trip. But first, I think we need to fix some supper. Grammy Karla and her baby are hungry, and I'll bet you and Aunt Angie are, too."

Angelina knew Karla would need to give Damián a heads up before Marisol bombarded him with questions. Angelina berated herself for not paying more attention to her surroundings, so they'd have known when Marisol was standing at Karla's open bedroom door.

She still couldn't believe Damián hadn't told his daughter he'd lost his foot in Iraq. How did he hide it from her all this time?

* * *

After days spent at Savannah's bedside, Damián thought she might heal faster if she got to see their daughter. He also needed a shower and to change the dressing on his wound. He walked into Rosa's house and heard Marisol's squeals followed by José's shouts for mercy in the back of the house. He hoped his little warrior princess wasn't in the process of annihilating the kid.

He walked into the family room and found Marisol had her older cousin in a hammerlock.

"Marisol, let José go!"

"Daddy!" She released her grip and ran across the room to Damián. "I missed you so much!"

"Looks like you've been too busy to miss me."

"Oh, we were just playing. Right, José?"

The ten-year-old rubbed his shoulder to ease the cramp he must have gotten from having his arm twisted behind his back so far. "It's okay, Tío Damo. She was just showing me some moves Tía Grant taught her."

"Daddy, how's Maman? Does she want to see me yet?"

Damián sat on the couch and lifted her into his lap. "*Mi muñequita*, you know Maman has missed you like crazy. She's just been really tired, and I wanted her to rest, but I'm going to let you see her a little bit tonight."

"Damián, you're back!" He looked up to see Karla in the doorway. "I need to speak with you about something." He was too exhausted to get up again, wanting nothing more than to hold his daughter. He'd missed her so much.

"Can it wait until later, Karla?"

Her gaze went from him to Marisol as if not wanting to talk in front of his little girl.

"Well…"

"Grammy Karla, Daddy's going to take me to see Maman. Can you help me pick out something pretty to wear? Maybe my new shirt!"

"Sure, munchkin." Karla cast a worried glance his way but took Marisol's hand and walked toward whichever room she'd been sleeping in. Probably sharing with his niece, Teresa.

Relieved he didn't have to face one more damned thing, Damián scrubbed his face with his hand. An exhaustion like he'd never felt before descended on him. When's the last time he'd slept more than an hour at a time? Not since Savannah had been kidnapped almost a week ago.

A tiny hand rubbed his arm. "It's going to be okay, Tío Damo." He opened his eyes to see José looking up at him with a worried look on his face. He'd forgotten all about him. Damián didn't like to worry his family with his problems. His nephew and niece had had to grow up too fast as it was. He wanted to shelter them from any more of the ugliness in the world. Their bastard of a father had already shown them enough of that.

"I'm fine, José. Just tired. Thanks for playing with Marisol. She missed playing with her friends while in Colorado where she's been stuck with grownups all the time."

"I like her. I'm glad you found her."

Damián smiled. "So am I, kiddo." It was more like they had found him. He couldn't imagine what life without Marisol and Savannah would be like, and right now he didn't want to think about how close he'd come to losing them both. He rubbed the soreness out of his calf, careful not to touch the wound.

"Does your leg hurt?"

"Not as much anymore."

"I don't mean your stump but where you got shot rescuing Tía Savannah."

"That's what I meant. My stump stopped hurting a long time ago." Unless he aggravated it.

"Then it's true, Daddy? Your foot got cut off?"

Damián looked up to see Marisol standing in the doorway wearing a hot pink shirt with sparkles splashed all over it. *Madre de Dios.* Apparently, she'd heard about it before. Karla stood behind her, an apologetic look on her face.

He wasn't prepared to talk with Marisol about this right now but couldn't ignore her question either. No more hiding who he was.

"Why did you tell José but not me?" Judging by her quivering lower lip, she seemed more upset about the slight of not being told first than the fact her daddy was missing his foot.

"Aw, come here, baby doll." After she was settled on his lap again, he took a deep breath. How to begin? "You know I lived with José for a long time before I even knew you."

"But I lived with you a long time this year, too."

Shiiittttttt.

How to confess to her he was ashamed of his weakness? To admit that he didn't want his daughter to be ashamed of him, too?

"I'll leave you all alone." Karla slipped away.

Damián had no clue what to say. He should have fucking planned this talk, knowing it would come sooner or later. But tonight wasn't about him. How did he think Marisol felt, learning her daddy was a cripple?

"Marisol, I didn't tell you because I wanted to wait and be sure you were ready to find out I'm not like other daddies."

"How did your foot get cut off? Did it hurt?"

Now how to sugarcoat it for her innocent ears?

José chimed in before he could form a response. "The doctors cut your foot off when you're asleep, so you don't feel it."

Damián grinned. "That's true, José. It did hurt when I got wounded, but Tío Marc was there and he helped take care of me." He realized he'd lapsed into the Spanish term for uncle. Must be being in Rosa's house in the old neighborhood or something. "Then I went to surgery, and I don't remember much until I woke up in Germany."

"Were you asleep a long time, Daddy?"

Not long enough. Damián remembered those dark days for months afterward when he'd wanted nothing more than to have died in combat. His eyes burned from a lack of sleep.

Begin at the beginning.

"Way back when you were a tiny baby, I was serving with my Marine buddies in Iraq."

"Lots of my friends at San Miguel's have dads who are Marines. And Chuy's mom is in the Navy."

Not surprising given that Marisol lived in Solana Beach—situated between naval bases in San Diego and the Marine one at Camp Pendleton. Well, she used to live there. Since December, she'd lived with him in Denver, and he hoped they planned to stay there. Everything was still up in the air until Savannah healed from the trauma of her beating and they could talk about their future together.

"Was it an IED?"

How the hell did someone eight years old know about Improvised Explosive Devices? Apparently he wasn't telling the story fast enough to stay ahead of her questions.

"No, *bebé*, my unit was on a rooftop trying to find some of the bad guys, but they found us first, and I lost my foot in a hand-grenade explosion."

"Did it hurt?"

Like a motherfucker.

"Yeah, but I don't remember much about it. Doc—Tío Marc—helped keep me alive."

"Was he a doctor?"

"No, but we called him Doc, because he was trained to patch up any Marines who got hurt. He tried to keep us alive until we could get to see the real doctors."

"Like a medic."

He wasn't sure how she knew about medics, either, but he nodded. He supposed growing up near so many military installations. She must be exposed to a lot more knowledge of combat than the average American kid was these days. Or maybe some of her friends had told her about these things.

Back to his story. "But the doctors couldn't save my foot, so they decided it was best that I learn to live without it."

Damián remembered back to that time when he had decided living was the last thing he wanted to do. Now, holding his precious daughter on his lap, he cringed to think how close he'd come to ending it all. Marc and Adam had rescued him at Balboa during the darkest moment of his life and kept him going for months until he could start living again, which he really didn't do until Savannah and Marisol came into his life last December like gangbusters. If he'd killed himself, he never would have gotten to meet his beautiful daughter nor reunite with the love of his life.

"Can I see your foot, Daddy?"

He had nothing to hide anymore. Damián stretched his leg out and pulled up the trouser leg to reveal his biker boots. He reached down to unzip the one covering his prosthesis and expelled a lung full of pent-up air. He knew why the nerves. What if she wasn't ready to see his stump?

After removing the shoe, he pulled off the stump sock and waited for her to take it in. She didn't reach to touch him the way Savannah had. Good thing. He didn't want her to get that close to it.

Marisol stroked his sleeve but didn't take her eye off the stump. Her usually strong voice came out in a whisper as she said, "Amputeddy says you'll still be my daddy."

Who? "Amputeddy?"

"Maman got me some books about Amputeddy. He lost his leg and got a new one. And his friend Brandon Bear's daddy lost his arm in the war."

Damián should have known Savannah would have been preparing Marisol for the time when he'd be ready to reveal his true self to his little girl. He blinked away the burning in his eyes, this time knowing it was tears and not a lack of sleep. *Dios*, let him get through this day without fucking bawling like a baby in front of his little girl. He didn't deserve to have Savannah but was so glad she was back in his life.

He pulled Marisol closer and hugged her. "You know I'll always be your daddy, baby princess." Maybe knowing what she already understood would help him determine what else she needed to know about his amputation. "What else did you learn from Amputeddy?"

"That you'll still love me even if you can't do things like go skiing with me on Tío Marc's snowy mountain."

Wait a minute there. "Would you like me to go skiing with you someday?"

"It's not important. We can do other stuff together." He didn't miss the disappointment in her voice as she played with the zipper pull on his Harley jacket, not making eye contact. Clearly, skiing had become important to her since Marc had given Marisol her first lesson New Year's weekend in Aspen. Seemed like a million years ago.

Damián knew what he needed to do—order a blade prosthesis, socket, and liners, and then get out on the slopes with his daughter the next chance they got. Of course, Marc would have to give him some lessons, too. He'd never been on skis before, even when he had two feet.

"What if I told you I could learn to ski, too?"

"Really?" Her eyes lit up as a smile stretched across her face. "When can we go again? I can show you what I know already."

Damián laughed at her enthusiasm. She didn't sound like she'd be ashamed to have him there on the slopes with her at all, rather than sitting on the bench playing it safe as he'd done the last time. "Well, we may have to wait until fall for the snow to be deep enough."

Some of the light went out of her eyes. Then she looked down at his stump again. For a long time, she remained silent, and he wondered what she was thinking. Finally, she tugged at the hairs on his chin to get him to look her in the eye. "Daddy, will you still be able to carry me?" Her little chin quivered, and he pulled her closer, wrapping his arms around her.

"I think so, *bebé*. I won't be able to do that on long walks or anything, but I can lift your mommy for short distances, so I think I'll be able to carry you for many years to come."

"I'll just stay little so you can always carry me." She sounded so resolute, as if making such a pronouncement would make it so.

Damián laughed. "No, that's not going to work. I want to watch you grow up into a beautiful woman. But the blade I'm going to get will make it easier for me to do more active things, and I will keep working on my strength training and do the best I can to keep up with you."

"My teacher says that's all we should do—the best we can."

"She's right, *mi muñequita.* Do you have any other questions?"

Without hesitation she asked, "When do I get to see Maman?"

Chapter Eighteen

A month had passed since Savi's—*Savannah's*—rescue. Marc drew a deep breath and rang the doorbell. Would she even be home? He probably should have called first but was afraid she'd just tell him to take a hike. Off a very high mountain cliff.

"Yes?"

Her voice sounded wary. *Good girl for being careful.*

"It's Marc D'Alessio. I need to talk with you." He wondered if she'd even remember him. As the silence dragged out for several tense moments, he knew she did.

"I don't think there's anything more to say."

"Oh, there's a helluva lot to be said. Starting with an apology—*my* apology."

Another pause, and then she buzzed him through. He took the stairs two at a time to the third floor and knocked on her door. His heart pounded, probably not from the mild exertion of climbing the stairs. What was he going to say to her? Could he undo any of the damage he'd caused without—

The door opened, and Pamela stood there wearing a long, baggy sweater and jeans rather than her usual power suit. Her strawberry-blonde hair was pulled into a ponytail, not perfectly coifed as before. She'd lost weight, even in her face. The wary expression in her eyes told him he had his work cut out for him.

She stepped aside and waved him in. After offering him a glass of his favorite wine—they'd always shared a love of pinot bianco—they sat across from each other, he on the sofa and she in a French provincial chair with her left foot tucked under her knee.

They talked a bit about their jobs and social lives as if they'd never parted. But Pamela soon got him to focus.

"So, Marc, just why did you come here?"

Pamela had never been one to beat around the bush. "I just need to set some things right. Understand some things about myself better. I've screwed up a lot, including with you. Now I've met someone and just don't want to make the same mistakes."

Pain flashed in her eyes. *Merda.* He realized how selfish he'd been to come here. He'd made it all about him, not what Pamela needed.

"Pamela, I owe you an explanation for why I ran last year."

"I think you made it very clear. I pushed too hard. I should have been happy to settle for what you could give without stirring the pot."

Marc glanced away and ran his hands through his hair. He needed to unfuck this.

Force of will helped him return her gaze. "Pamela, you weren't the one at fault. You should never settle. Your needs are just as important as your Dom's, even more so." He glanced down. "But it wasn't you, Pamela. It was me. I'm sorry I left without much explanation, but I don't think I could have explained what sent me running until I realized some things recently."

Losing Angelina had brought a lot of things into focus, even though he still didn't fully understand his behavior.

Pamela didn't acknowledge that she'd heard him, but he couldn't look at her. *Dio*, he'd never meant to hurt her. She deserved respect and some man's undying love. He hoped she'd find what she needed someday.

"Listen, I'm just starting to figure out some things about myself and my past, and I've come to see now how badly I handled our parting. I seem to have a history of doing this and you didn't deserve to have no explanation." He ran his hand through his hair. "I'm still trying to learn how to be a Dom. I ran scared at the thought of being any woman's Master, of having that much control over anyone. Hell, I barely have control over myself anymore."

"It wasn't about control, Marc. For me, being submissive is about serving someone I choose to give authority to. At one time, I thought that could be you." She shrugged. "Most people don't have a clue about those of us needing the Master/slave dynamic. There are so many negative connotations. But I know what I want."

When he could speak again, all he could say was, "You always were direct, assertive. I admired that about you."

She glanced away. "I accepted you as my Dom at first, but it wasn't until I talked with Patti at the club that I figured out what was missing for me in our relationship. You and I came at M/s from two different perspectives.

Her explaining that need to serve someone twenty-four/seven—to give up authority over everything, not just in the bedroom or club—just clicked for me. Unfortunately, we'd already gotten too far along a different path. Then, when I tried to renegotiate our dynamic, I freaked you out." She grinned. "In a bad way."

He relaxed. "I don't guess most of us go into this lifestyle knowing what the hell we want, only that there's something missing." For him, that something had taken him a long time to discover. "You would not have been happy with me in the long run if a Master/slave relationship is what you needed. As your Dom, I would not have been able to let you settle for less."

"How did you get into the lifestyle, Marc?"

Marc thought back to his introduction to BDSM. "Unlike most Doms who just know innately they have a need to dominate, I was thrust into the Scene by a guest at my parents' resort. She wanted a Dom, and I guess I looked vulnerable enough to be coerced into meeting her needs."

"How old were you?"

"Seventeen."

"Jesus, Marc, you weren't even legal."

What he'd done sounded pretty sordid. "There was never any sex with any of them."

"You mean there were others?"

Marc nodded. He'd lost count. "I got a reputation over the next few years. Most were midlife-crisis, bored wives whose husbands sent them to the resort for weeks or months and ignored them."

"That explains a lot."

He looked at her. "What do you mean?"

"I don't think you've ever really thought about what you need in a power exchange, Marc. Whether it's to be a Dom, a switch, a sub, or vanilla. You were forced into meeting other people's needs before you'd even matured enough to know what you wanted or needed. Didn't these cougars provide your training?"

"Not all of it. I worked with a number of Masters, including Adam, over the years." He realized that had mostly been about learning techniques, though. He'd never really talked about what it meant to be a Dom. He wouldn't even entertain the thought of anything else. He was a Dom. Giving up control to another person freaked him out in the worst way.

"I think when you can't meet the needs—or demands—of the women you're with, you run. Or distance yourself from them so that they leave you."

There weren't many women he'd allowed beyond the superficial level, but something she said seemed to ring true.

"You sound like a shrink."

She grinned. "Psychology major in college. That makes my advice worth about five cents at Lucy Van Pelt's sidewalk clinic." She sobered. "Your needs, Marc, are a lot more complicated than you let on. I think you need to look at your issues with those cougars for starters. Then maybe look at your relationship with your mother."

He hadn't said anything about Mama or his past. He definitely hadn't come here to be put on Freud's couch and psychoanalyzed. She'd never even met his mother. "I have no clue what you're talking about."

"You used to have nightmares, Marc. You talked in your sleep—even screamed sometimes. You yelled at your mother and your big brother, begging them for something you were very upset about. I'm not sure which one has you the most tied up in knots—Mama or Gino."

Marc had no clue what she was talking about until he remembered waking to the dream Christmas night. Angelina had said the same things. Many other nights, he remembered waking in a cold sweat with Pamela comforting him for reasons he didn't understand.

Marc drained his glass and stood. "Listen, I'm not sure how we got off topic. I just stopped by to apologize if I'd hurt you and to make sure you're okay."

She untucked her foot and placed it flat on the floor as she leaned forward, staring up at him. "Marc, you need to forgive yourself and move on. I can't say any magic words to make it all better. Whatever has been eating you—and don't think I didn't see it in you back then—is something you have to overcome. That vulnerability was one of the things that endeared you to me, but you have some serious wounds buried deep inside that need to be healed. You brought out the service submissive in me. I wanted to serve you and help ease your pain—maybe even discover its root cause."

"I don't need anyone's pity."

She stood and met him face-to-face. "I wasn't offering pity, Marc, then or now. I was offering comfort. Healing. That's what you need most."

He wasn't sure what kind of vibe he was sending out to make her think that about him, but he didn't want to delve any further into his issues today. He needed to go for a hike or something to expend some pent-up energy.

"Pamela, you're welcome at the club anytime. Patti and Grant asked about you for a long while."

Pamela smiled. "How's Grant doing? Still dominating a bunch of pantywaists?"

Marc grinned. "She does tend to attract weak malesubs. Not sure why."

She grew serious. "Because she hasn't come to terms with her past either. She doesn't understand that the strong submissives have much more to offer than the doormats. Right now, she prefers the power trip of topping men—any men."

Marc hadn't really analyzed his Marine buddies' motives in the lifestyle any more than his own. Maybe he wasn't the only Dominant at the club trying to figure out what he—or she—wanted.

No, *needed.*

"Come to one of our monthly munches. You may find someone in the kink community who's looking for what you have to give."

"Marc, I don't need you to help me find partners."

"I know, but I feel a certain responsibility toward you."

"That ended when we ended our D/s relationship. You don't owe me anything."

They stared at each other without speaking several moments. "I hope you find the Master you deserve someday, Pamela."

He moved to leave, and then at the open doorway, he turned toward her. "You have a lot to offer any Master or Dom, *cara.* Don't settle for anything less than what you need and want in a relationship."

"Don't let her get away, Marc, whoever she is. If she's got you doing this much soul-searching, she must be something special."

"She is." Which is why he was scared shitless he'd fuck it up even worse with Angelina if he didn't figure out what his problem was. Was he ready to talk with her yet?

No, he needed to have a talk with someone else first.

*　　*　　*

"What do you need, Doc?"

Marc looked across Adam's desk and shifted in his seat. He always felt like a grunt trainee when facing his retired Master Sergeant across this massive desk.

"I have no clue." Why had he come here? He'd lain awake the past several nights trying to sort out things for himself. Earlier this week, he'd come home to discover Angelina had removed Nonna's vanity and some smaller things she'd left behind. She was gone. He'd found no sleep and no resolution to his problem.

Except in one area.

"Have you and Karla found a place to live yet?"

"No. The market's got plenty of houses, but most exceed our budget. We keep scaling back in what our basic needs will be, but now we have to look at school systems and make sure the neighborhood is safe for kids. Sure was easier when I could just find a big-ass house in a neighborhood going through a renaissance and fix it up. We just don't have time for that. Baby will be here in about two months and I won't raise kids in a kink club."

"How would you like to raise your family in a house like mine?"

"Focus, Doc. That's way beyond our price range, and we aren't moving in with you."

Marc grinned. "I've talked with Gramps. He understands it's way more house than a bachelor needs."

"You so sure you and Angelina won't get back together and want to start a family of your own? I can see a lot of little D'Alessios running around that place in no time."

Marc had never really thought about having kids so he didn't share the same vision. Hell, he and Angelina weren't even together anymore. "No, I'm not too keen on living in the city. I need someplace in the mountains."

"That I can see."

"Anyway, Gramps couldn't think of anyone else he wanted living here more than you and your family. He respects the hell out of you for your service to the same branch of the military he served in and for being there with Gino and then me when we, well, you know…"

Karla's grandmother was pretty happy about it too when Gramps told her.

Adam and Karla would make that house into the home it should have been all along. Adam narrowed his eyelids. "I don't need anyone giving me a house. I do have my pension—and my pride."

"No!" Marc held up his hand to halt Adam's thoughts and words. "I fully intend to sell you the house. Just name your price. Hell, I'm going to need to find another place. I just don't need to sell it at market value. I didn't put any money into it. So consider what you can afford, and it's yours."

Adam cleared his throat. "Karla loves that place. The view of the city, the playroom that's private enough we can still fool around at home without worrying about the kids finding our toy room. Hell, she even loves that kitchen. Might get her to spend a little more time there." He grinned and drummed his fingers on the desktop. "We could take one of the rooms, soundproof it, and give her a studio to work on her music. Being close to the baby will make it easier for her to pursue that without feeling guilty she's spending too much time away from home."

"Sounds like the perfect place for you, Adam."

"Yeah, it does. Let me talk with Karla and get her okay first. Then I'll make you an offer. Our Realtor can draw up the papers to make it all legal, if you're sure."

"I'm sure. I already feel like a huge weight has been lifted off my shoulders." He did, too. That house had been like an albatross around his neck since the day he'd moved there. The only time it had seemed like a home was when Angelina was with him.

"You've solved one of my biggest problems, Doc. Now what can I do for you? Seems you've been spinning your wheels lately. Got your issues figured out?"

Could anyone get at the root of Marc's issues? Marc didn't even know what the problem was anymore. His conversation with Pamela had only left him more confused. What he feared most—losing Angelina—had happened, and he'd been paralyzed rather than going after her.

"When did you know you were a Dom?"

"Eleven or twelve, I guess. Playing with one of the girls in my class after school in her family's garage. Tied her up. Good thing her parents thought we were playing cowboys and Indians or I'd have been arrested for the thoughts and feelings going through my mind and body that day."

Marc smiled but didn't have any such memories of his own coming of age. By then, he was content to spend more time alone in the woods than hanging out with girls. Was he a Dom? At the moment, he didn't even care. There was more to his relationship with Angelina than kink. That was just for fun.

Suddenly he knew what he wanted. Maybe Adam would know how to get there.

"I need her back, but I don't have the first clue how to do it. Karla left you once. How'd you get her back?"

The pain in his friend's eyes was difficult to witness as Adam appeared to wander back to that time not so long ago. Marc turned away until Adam began to speak. He'd feel the same if he didn't get his girl back.

"I didn't have a clue what I was going to do when I found she'd left. I just knew at gut level I had to go after her. I roamed around this place all night and couldn't stand to be without her another minute."

Marc hadn't even contacted Angelina after she'd left months ago. "I blew the chance. I guess I just expected her to come back to me. Now I know that's not going to happen unless I act."

"You're two of the most stubborn people I've ever met."

Marc shrugged but didn't smile. "It's in the genes." He'd never wanted to get involved with an Italian woman, but now he couldn't imagine going on without this one by his side.

Would she even want him anymore? Somehow the thought of her rejection scared him even worse than continuing to live without her. At least then he'd still have the fantasy of the possibility of her returning.

What did Angelina want? Had she moved on emotionally as well as physically? "Has she played at the club lately?"

"You know the rules about confidentiality at the club."

Adam wasn't going to divulge whether she'd played with any other Doms or even if she'd stopped by for a drink to hang out with the other submissives. Again, the fantasy of believing she hadn't come to Denver for anything more than babysitting Marisol made it easier for him to imagine Angelina had been as miserable as he had been these past two months.

"Ball's in your court, Doc. Women don't come with instruction manuals. I had no five-part frag order in place last November. Just one objective—bring Karla home with me where she belonged. You have to do the best you can with what you know. Get those boots on the ground, and deal with whatever comes at you as it happens. I learned a long time ago that you can't plan for every contingency, especially not when you're dealing with women. They're wired differently."

"I'll say." Even so, Marc wasn't sure he could just charge after Angelina with no clear plan. What if he failed? He might not get yet another chance to make it right.

Adam became lost in thought a moment before continuing. "A lot happened at Karla's folks' place last Thanksgiving weekend that I had no control over. Things eventually fell into place, even though there wasn't time to process and sort out everything." Adam's gaze returned to Marc. "My bottom-line objective was all that mattered. The other stuff we'll deal with when we have to or have time, but Karla's back by my side, we have a baby on the way, and we have our whole lives ahead of us to work on those issues and any others we'll have to face somewhere down the road."

Adam reached for a bottle of water and took a swig. "What is it you want out of life? Out of a relationship with Angelina? Once you figure that out, then go after her."

"I don't even know where she is."

"Well, tomorrow night she'll be at Damián's. He's planned a pretty intense mindfuck for Savannah. Angelina's watching Marisol overnight. You might want to be a part of this scene, though. We're going to need all hands on deck to get through to *that* stubborn but wounded submissive."

"Count me in on the scene." Marc listened intently as Adam laid out the plan for where Victor and Patti, Adam and Karla, and Marc would reinforce the redirected message Damián wanted to get through to Savannah. Sounded intense. He hoped it wouldn't backfire on Damián.

"If all goes as planned, Damián and Savannah will be staying the night at the club, and Karla and I are headed back to the hotel suite where we spent our wedding night."

Late the next evening, long after Damián and Savannah's mindfuck had ended and the two were ensconced in one of the private bedrooms upstairs processing the scene, Marc walked into the dungeon to clean up as he'd promised. Wiping down the St. Andrew's cross Luke had made, he reflected on the powerful scene's ending. Savannah's tear-drenched eye mask tore at his gut when he walked into the room, but once the truth had been revealed to her, she'd been transformed almost instantaneously.

Seeing his friends come together in that way—to help a member of the family welcome another into the fold—moved him but also showed him what he was missing. The others all had their girls with them. He'd been the one standing alone, less a part of the scene than he might have been with Angelina beside him.

Had Adam invited him to participate in that scene to show him what he was missing?

Marc put away the cleaning supplies and walked back upstairs. Heading out the kitchen door into the night, he knew what needed to be done.

About damned time.

Chapter Nineteen

Adam waited for the bellman to open the door to the honeymoon suite. When Karla would have followed the man with the luggage cart inside the room, Adam placed his hand firmly on her arm and held her back. After tipping the man, Adam bent to lift his beautiful wife into his arms.

"Adam!"

Karla's giggle made him hard instantly. *Fuck*. Maybe he hadn't thought this through. He had every intention of getting her off tonight any number of times after depriving her for so long in his own selfish effort to keep himself from becoming aroused. Clearly, though, he was fighting a losing battle. All he could think about all day and night was having sex with Karla.

Not even sex the way he wanted—rough, raw, and fast. That wasn't on the agenda until after the babies were born. But at least he could see to it one of them was satisfied before this night was over. He also could pamper her. Love her.

Dear God, but he loved her. If anything happened to her or their babies…he wouldn't survive another loss of someone he loved. Not an option. He remained riddled with guilt over the loss of his son, despite Joni's and now Karla's doctors saying it had nothing to do with their having had rough sex in the seventh month of her pregnancy. He'd go to his own grave knowing he'd caused his baby's death.

At least now he wasn't a horny young man ready to deploy without any sense of self-control.

No, he was a horny *old* man. Tonight, he'd do well to remember the discipline he'd learned during twenty-five years in the Corps.

He set Karla on her feet again, and she molded herself to his body. *Fuck*. The way his body responded, maybe he hadn't evolved so far from that horny young man after all. Just the look and feel of Karla's body made his cock even harder. Being back in this room where they'd spent their wedding night conjured up too many carnal memories.

Damián had better appreciate Adam and Karla for vacating their own house so his surrogate son could have some time alone with Savannah tonight. He hoped Damián could break down more of Savannah's walls. They'd certainly made a lot of progress in the dungeon tonight with the slut scene.

Karla placed a peck on his cheek and went to lift her suitcase onto the bed. "Kitten, put that down!"

She sighed, and he easily wrested the bag from her and plopped it onto the bed himself. "Adam, why do you keep treating me like an invalid? I'm pregnant, not terminally ill or something."

"You know how I feel about you overdoing it. And don't be insubordinate."

"Yes, Sir." She rolled her eyes and then grinned in a most insolent way. He needed to continue to work on her lack of discipline, but gently. He didn't want to risk doing anything to hurt her or the babies.

She unzipped the case and pulled out some filmy, white clothing and wadded it into a ball, keeping her body at an angle so he couldn't see what she carried toward the bathroom. "I'll be right back. Make yourself comfortable, Sir."

He took the suitcase off the bed and set it on the luggage rack, noticing the bottle of sparkling grape juice chilling in the ice bucket. He'd also had the hotel stock the refrigerator earlier this afternoon with a number of items he planned to feed his bride of almost five months tonight. He remembered verbatim the invitation he'd sent her for this get-away evening.

Baby Tiger,

My beast needs to feed tonight. Wear your most demure harem outfit, and I will escape with you to a private oasis where we can enjoy a night of indulgence and romance.

Your sultan

The scene he'd planned for tonight was about indulging in food more than sex. He shed his shirt, shoes, jeans, and skivvies and pulled out the robe and sultan's headgear he wore when they made use of the Arabian Nights theme room at the club. He wished he could see her in one of her sexy red belly-dancing outfits tonight, but all that gyrating couldn't be good for the babies—or him—so he'd forbidden her to wear those the last couple months. As long as she covered as much skin as possible, including that belly where his two tiny babies resided at the moment, he should be okay.

Adam would do nothing to jeopardize this pregnancy. Already he felt closer to these unborn babies than he had to his first, primarily because he was present for Karla's pregnancy. With Joni's, he'd been training for a mission in the early months and then deployed at the end. They'd wanted a child more than anything, but he had been so focused on doing his job during that deployment he'd felt separated from all that was going on back home. Joni had gone through the last stages of pregnancy and the horrific stillbirth on her own, like she'd had to face so many other things without him.

Hearing Joni's voice on one of the tapes she'd left him talking about the regret she felt at not being able to give him a son had caused him to break down and bawl like a baby himself for the son he'd never know. The pain in Joni's voice—a pain she hadn't expressed to him while alive—was like hearing the news for the first time. He really hadn't allowed himself to process the loss at the time it happened, not unlike the way he'd compartmentalized his loss of Joni to cancer many years later.

This pregnancy was different. He'd been with Karla ever since they realized she was pregnant last Thanksgiving weekend. Since then, he'd done a lot of thinking about what it meant to be a father.

Sharing Karla's pregnancy had opened him up to a vulnerability he rarely permitted himself to feel. He had so little control over the lives growing inside her body, which scared the living hell out of him. Helplessness wasn't something he handled well.

God, just let these babies be born and live healthy lives. He didn't have a preference for sons or daughters, but being able to nurture and love two tiny babies he'd helped create with Karla was something he wanted more than anything on earth. He also wanted to live long enough to raise and guide them into adulthood over the next couple of decades.

He'd told her once he wanted six kids, but in truth, he didn't think he could go through another pregnancy with her. Hell, Karla hadn't even delivered these babies, and he was already thinking about the next four. If they had two healthy babies, he'd die a happy man.

He couldn't wait to tell her about Marc's house—soon to be *their* house. Making do on a Marine's pension and income from the club wouldn't have let them even afford the outbuildings of a property like that. He'd checked the taxes and, while hefty, knowing his wife and kids would be in a safe place was worth it. The house would be as safe as he could make it, and that knowledge relieved some of the anxiety he'd carried since finding out he and Karla were about to become par—

Karla hummed a Middle Eastern tune to herself as she opened the bathroom door. Time to get into sultan headspace. Using a remote, he dimmed the lights in the room. Maybe if he didn't look at her, he'd make it through the night without losing control.

Music that conjured up thoughts of Scheherazade spilled from her smartphone, and he turned to watch her undulate toward him.

Fuck. Fuck. Fuck!

She disobeyed him completely! This belly-dancing outfit might be white and pure-looking, but it was nothing but wisps of sheer scarves over her hips and a beaded bra. Her belly was covered only by strands of pearl-like beads.

Clusterfucking-A!

Karla's more voluptuous breasts nearly spilled from the top of the bra cups. Adam wet his lips.

Dear God, he wanted her.

Her hips swayed as she clanged the tiny cymbals on her thumbs and middle fingers. Her eyes had been heavily made up. Even though she wore a half-veil across her lower face, her lips shown ruby red through the gossamer material. His dick throbbed, standing in a full salute. He ought to take her over his knee for torturing him like this. Or perhaps torture her in return with delayed orgasms.

No, he might hurt the babies. He needed to remember them tonight, first and foremost. He felt his hard-on relax a bit. Good.

Karla definitely would need to be punished for pulling this stunt on him tonight, though. She'd been taught enough discipline to know he wouldn't tolerate disobedience. His instructions had been explicit—hadn't they? He probably should have ordered her to wear a burka, covering her body from head to toe. Only one problem—Karla was sexy no matter what she wore. He ground his back teeth together. God had better help him get through this night. She already tempted him beyond all thought and reason.

Maybe if he deprived her of the orgasm he'd planned for her he might get her attention and make her behave. Hell, why couldn't she see he was looking out for her and the twins? Why couldn't she just…

Karla continued to gyrate her hips, sending the beads and bangles on the hips of her harem pants into a frenzy of motion. He couldn't take his eyes off of her protruding belly and shimmying hips. He wanted to grab her by her waist and pull her toward him but held back. She removed the finger cymbals and placed them on the nightstand before unhooking one side of the face scarf and then the other. She twirled the scarf in the air and trapped him by the back of the head, pulling him toward her. Rather than direct his face to hers for a kiss, she lowered it to her cleavage.

Adam groaned and resisted the gentle pressure the scarf applied to his head. "Karla—"

"No talking."

He growled. "Don't forget your place, Baby Tiger."

"Oh, I won't, Sir. My place is to please my sultan with my body and to fulfill all of his needs. That's all I intend to do tonight."

"Tonight is not about you fulfilling my needs, Kitten, but me fulfilling yours."

"Ah, then we're on the same page, Your Excellency. I *need* this."

Ignoring his growl of disapproval, she let the scarf fall loose around his neck and reached behind to her back, unhooking her bra. He couldn't help himself. He watched as she lowered the heavily decorated bra, dripping with the strands of beads that had covered her swollen belly, revealing her luscious tits. Breasts, damn it. Her nipples and areolas had turned a dark brown during her pregnancy, sexier than ever. Her breasts were larger, too, as her body prepared to nurse the twins.

Feeding their babies. Fuck, in a few months, they would suckle at those very breasts. He needed to stop thinking about his baser desires and focus on the purpose her breasts would serve in the near future.

Keep your hands—and mouth—off them, old man.

Besides, she'd said they were super-sensitive these days, though whenever she'd reminded him of that, she seemed to be asking him to suck, bite, or clamp them. The woman hadn't let up in her attempts to lower his resolve the past couple of months.

When she cupped her tits and offered them to him, he nearly came in his robe. He reached out and brushed her hands away, stroking the soft flesh of her belly as she moaned, bringing his attention back to her face. It had been torture limiting himself when touching her body. Her tongue darted across her upper lip, and his dick throbbed even more. He reached up and brushed the pads of his thumbs across her swollen nipples, and she sucked in a sharp breath. Afraid he'd hurt her, he let go, but she only took his hands and returned them to her breasts.

"Please, Sir. I need you to touch me." Her voice cracked with emotion.

The Dom in him felt torn between his need to protect her and his need to provide for her needs. The pleading in her voice was his undoing, and he lowered his mouth to take one protruding nipple in his mouth.

Gentle. Just be gentle.

"Bite me, Sir."

Okay, maybe just a nibble. Not enough to hurt her. He sucked harder and grazed his teeth across her nipple. She grabbed his head and held it to her so he couldn't move away, as if he'd wanted to. He needed to be nowhere else. He sucked at her tit like a starving man.

Fuck! Adam pulled away. He'd been sucking on the tit—breast, damn it. They're breasts now—the same breasts his newborn children would be using to gain strength and nourishment. With a groan, he scooped her into his arms and placed her gently in the middle of the bed.

Time for him to take care of the mother of his child—*children*—and stop letting his raging hormones get the better of him. He went to the desk and poured two glasses of juice, and then he opened the fridge and pulled out the first course—grapes.

He placed the plate and the two glasses on the nightstand, glancing at Karla sprawled seductively on the bed. The scarves parted enough for him to get a glimpse of her smoothly shaved pussy.

Dear God, what was he thinking?

Control, man. You're the Dom here. Don't let her manipulate you.

Remembering the scene he'd planned for tonight, he stretched out beside her and picked up the plate from the nightstand. He looked for a place to rest it. Normally, that would be her belly, but his babies had swollen that part of her body so much that the plate would tip over, sending the grapes onto the bed. Instead, he laid the plate in the center of her chest. Karla hissed as the cold glass made contact with her nipple. Good thinking. With them hidden from view, he wouldn't be distracted by her gorgeously full tits.

Breasts!

Picking up a large bunch of grapes, he held it to her mouth. "Open for me, Kitten."

Her legs opened, and he looked down at her gossamer-covered knees.

Don't let her control this scene.

He growled before delivering a stern warning first with his eyes. "Don't think I won't punish you, Baby Tiger." Her pupils dilated. "And by punish I mean that I can shut this night down faster than you can blink, and I'll roll over and go to sleep in this huge-ass bed without touching you again."

Her eyes narrowed. "You wouldn't."

"Don't tempt me."

Karla scrunched her brows together in a cute pout before a slow smile crept over her lips. Somehow he knew he ought to be worried, but she looked so fucking beautiful he couldn't think straight.

"Open." He cleared his throat from a voice grown gravelly with desire. "Now."

Like a little bird, she opened her red lips and waited for him to remember the grapes in his hand and why he wanted her mouth open. All he could think of was driving his dick as far down her throat as she could take him, but he hadn't done that in the past couple of months either. She'd probably gag on him the way she used to in the beginning of their relationship.

When she stared at the grapes, he remembered what the fuck he was supposed to be doing and lowered the bunch to her mouth. Karla yanked one away and held it between her teeth. Slowly she pressed her teeth into the soft yet firm flesh, and his dick jumped. She smiled, clearly having felt him against her thigh. He wanted to feel her teeth on his dick so badly he had to push himself away to avoid all contact with her flesh. Karla bit into the grape, and the juice trickled down her chin.

Fuck. How could she make eating a grape so goddamned sexy?

Karla chewed with great deliberateness, her gaze never leaving his face until she swallowed and looked at the remaining grapes in the bunch. He pinched off another and held it out to her. "Open." Maybe if he placed it deep into her mouth she wouldn't make him think about…

Aw, fuck. Don't think about putting anything deep into her mouth.

His hands didn't get the message, though. He didn't have to tell her to open. She was ready for him.

His dick throbbed. The goal tonight was to take care of Karla, give her the nurturing she'd been asking for. He wasn't going to let his little head overrule his big head.

Adam reached for another grape.

"Peel one for your sultan."

She latched onto the stem end and began stripping away the layers of the white grape's skin with her teeth. Again, all he could picture was her teeth grazing his dick. After what seemed like an eternity, she finished but took the peeled grape between her teeth and held it for him. As he bent down to take it from her, she bit it in half, and he gladly shared it with her. After both had swallowed, he took her mouth with his and drove his tongue inside her sweet warmth.

Don't think about driving anything else into her mouth.

He pulled back and looked at the plate of grapes again. God, why'd he choose such a big bunch? What else could he pull out of the fridge to feed to her without sending his dick into overdrive?

Forget the whipped cream. He didn't want to think about licking frothy cream off her breasts, not to mention her pussy lips. He drew a ragged breath and held the bunch above her mouth. The point of her tongue reached out, and she lifted her head to latch onto one. Rather than pull it free of the vine, she wrapped her lips around it as her gaze locked with his. Then she sucked, nearly causing him to explode all over the bed.

Fuck, fuck, fuck!

Maybe Doctor Palmer was right. He wouldn't hurt her or the twins if he slathered a little whipped cream onto her nipples. Taking the plate off her chest and setting it on the bed beside her, he got off the bed and went back to the fridge. He started to reach for another plate to scoop out some of Angelina's homemade creamy topping but decided cold and straight from the bowl would stimulate Karla more. Her nipples were hypersensitive now. She deserved a little discomfort after all the pain and suffering she was putting him through tonight.

He returned to her side and dipped his finger into the bowl scooping up a large dollop of whipped cream and transferring it to her left nipple and areola. She hissed at the coldness, then smiled, and closed her eyes.

Damn if she wasn't even more turned on—and turning him on.

Bending over her, he let his tongue lap at the quickly melting cream, surprised at how quickly it had been warmed by her body. He was careful to avoid the sensitive peak, rising up like a snow-covered Mount Evans. She pressed her chest upward toward his mouth.

Adam licked at her areola, uncovering it one fraction of an inch at a time. Her moan nearly stripped away his resolve to go slowly, gently. All he wanted to do was slam his hard dick into her in the worst way. Instead, reining in his libido, he took her swollen, waiting nipple between his lips and suckled.

Don't think about your babies doing this in a few months, old man.

Separating the sexy woman he'd fallen in love with from the mother of his unborn children was nearly impossible. What was that expression? Something about a woman being a lady outside the bedroom and a slut for her man inside the bedroom. Despite the scene earlier tonight at the club for Savannah, Adam didn't really get off on calling Karla his slut. But he didn't mind her behaving like one—for him alone, in private.

He took her peak between his teeth and bit.

"Oh, yes!"

Fuck. He'd forgotten himself.

He pulled away to assess her eyes. "Sorry, hon. I'll try to be more gentle."

Did she just growl? "You ass, I don't want gentle. I want my sultan to give me what I need. You know I like it rough, Your Excellency."

"Remember your place, Baby Tiger."

She rolled her eyes.

"Rough sex isn't going to happen, Karla, no matter how bratty you get. I won't risk hurting you or the babies."

Karla's gaze spit fire. "Doctor Palmer said we have nothing to worry about. As long as I'm comfortable with it and we make some concessions for my enormous belly, we can do anything we did before. And I'm *very* comfortable with the way we had sex before, Adam." She paused a moment. "Please!"

Her pleading tone and seemingly rational argument nearly undid his resolve, but he shored up his reserves and held firm. Very firm. God, his dick was going to explode.

He took her nipple between his teeth again but forced himself to tug more gently. Her moan told him he was meeting her needs well enough, and he continued. He alternated between sucking and nipping at her flesh. Then he pulled back, lathered a dollop of cream onto her other tit, and went down on her again.

Breasts. Nipples. Quit calling them tits!

And stop thinking about going down on her.

Karla squirmed on the bed and grabbed his head to pull it closer to her body. No, that wouldn't do. Leaning back, he looked around on the bed and found her face scarf. Taking both of her hands in one of his, he tied them just above the wrists with the scarf, secure but not too tight. Silk scarves weren't the safest thing to use, but he hadn't planned on restraining her to the bed tonight.

Clearly, she needed restraints, though, or they'd never make it through the scene. *He* wouldn't, for damned sure. He raised her bound hands and secured them to the notch in the center of the headboard.

Her breasts jutted up, even more inviting than before. Her smile told him she was enjoying the hell out of this position, too.

"Tell me if your arms get tired or tingly."

"Always, Sir. But I'm fine. Very fine."

Unable to resist her tied up for him like this, he commanded, "Open for me."

Karla opened her mouth and closed her eyes.

"Not your mouth this time, Kitten."

*   *   *

Ka-thunk!

She opened her eyes and met his gaze. "Thank you, Sir. I thought you'd never ask."

She spread her legs for him.

Karla's heart beat wildly. He was going to make love to her for the first time in months. She was certain of it. Lately he hadn't even gotten her off using his hand or vibes. She missed having him inside her most of all. Lying here, arms stretched and tied above her head, she waited, watching as his head came down on her swollen nipple again.

His sucking motion sent electrical impulses throughout her body, most of them zeroing in on her pussy. Oh dear Lord, if he pulled back this time, she'd die. She needed this. She needed him. She'd missed this intimacy. God, she'd missed him so much. Even though he'd barely left her side, the lack of physical contact and the emotional distance it caused between them was wearing on her nerves.

His finger and thumb pinched her other nipple before he slowly began to trail kisses and gentle nips at the flesh between her breasts. In agonizingly slow motion, he moved lower. She waited. Soon.

He pulled away and glanced up at her. "Breathe, Kitten."

"Yes, Sir," she said on a whisper before filling her lungs.

"Good girl." His head descended on her once more, and she felt his tongue circle her now protruding belly button.

"Oh, yes!" She'd never thought of a navel as being sensual, but dear God, she nearly came from his gentle ministrations. Maybe she didn't have to have it rough all the time, although she still wanted it that way *some* of the time.

Scooting from beside her down the bed, he placed his head between her thighs and just stared at her. She squirmed. The crotchless harem pants left nothing to the imagination. Adam's intense stare made her nervous. Hopefully she hadn't changed there, as well. Becoming used to her pregnant body had been a challenge. At least she didn't think he was repulsed by her yet. She hadn't been sure what he would think when she put on her belly-dancing outfit and came out of the bathroom, but he seemed to be enjoying their time together. Maybe even a bit turned on by her enormous body again. It had been forever since he'd done more than cuddle in bed with her.

Thank you, Damián, for giving us tonight.

Just when she thought she'd scream if he didn't say or do something, Adam traced his finger over her mons and slit as if petting her pussy. "I've missed my sweet kitty."

She felt herself growing wetter. Her voice came out in a whisper. "Your kitty has missed you, too, Sir."

He looked up at her. "If I do anything that hurts, you'd better tell me ASAP, or I'll not touch you again until these kids are three years old."

Jesus! Three *years*? Was he serious? Even three months was killing her. Her words came out as a husky whisper. "Yes, Sir. I will."

Oh, please touch me. Make love to me, Adam.

His head lowered as he spread the filmy scarves and pantaloons aside, baring her completely to his gaze. "So fucking beautiful." His head lowered to the flesh above her pubic bone where his teeth nipped, leaving love bites in a trail growing closer and closer to her outer lips but not spreading them to reveal the core of her need. She tilted her pelvis toward him, but he pulled away.

"Lie still unless I give you permission to move."

Ka-thunk!

Discipline. Even though they hadn't had sex lately, they had definitely been working on her learning to discipline her body and mind during a scene. She hadn't quite managed to tame her sometimes-Domme personality completely but didn't want him to grow weary of her constant defiance, so she'd put those urges on a back burner. She was content to be his submissive, if that's what he wanted and needed. Someday perhaps she'd turn the tables on him again, but they had the rest of their lives together. Dear God, she hoped that would be an eternity.

When Adam's tongue traced the line of her closed slit, she nearly came up off the bed but willed her hips to remain plastered to the mattress.

Lie still for him.

He kissed her just above her clit hood. "Good girl."

Her chest swelled with pride at his praise, and her hands clenched the taut scarf above her head. He'd tied her loosely knowing she wasn't going to try to get away while tightly enough to remind her she was under his control. As if she had any desire to escape.

Her nipples grew rock hard as her excitement built. Adam took his thumbs and parted her lips, exposing her hood to the cool air. The muscles in the pit of her pelvis tightened, anticipating his next move. He blew on her clit at the same time he rammed two fingers inside her pussy. Not expecting this double assault on her senses, her hips bucked upward before she could stop them.

"Tsk-tsk. We're going to have to do something about that, aren't we?"

"I'm trying, Sir. But it's been too long!"

"Well, it's going to be even longer now."

"No! Don't stop! Please, Adam! I mean, Your Excellency! I need this!"

He just chuckled as he got off the bed and went to the fridge. How could he possibly think about food or drink at a time like this?

Concealing the object from the fridge, he then went to the suitcase and pulled out a tight bundle of black straps. Was he going to slap her with it? What the hell was it?

"Doctor Palmer said you might need some help supporting your legs. Since we aren't in one of the club's playrooms with a sling handy, I'm going to cheat a bit and use this."

He began to undo the Velcro straps until he revealed a long nylon contraption with cuffs at the ends. "Lift your head." She followed his command, and he placed the center portion of the thing behind her neck. "Lie back down and get comfortable. How are your arms?"

"Fine, Sir." Okay, not fine. She felt a cramp in her shoulder. "Maybe they're a little tired of this position." If she didn't tell him about any discomfort and he discovered it later, he might never play with her again until the twins *were* three years old. Or maybe thirty.

A worried expression crossed his face and he immediately loosened the scarf from the headboard. His strong hands kneaded the muscles in her shoulders until she moaned. Having him touching her in any way felt so good.

"Place your hands beside your head and hold onto the pillow. Do *not* let go unless I tell you to."

She followed his command. "Yes, my sultan."

He grinned at her. "Don't you ever forget it, Baby Tiger."

He then released the Velcro on one cuff and opened it. He stared at her harem pants a moment. "Raise your hips." He unfastened the beaded waistband and lowered the only thing standing between her and Adam. *About damned time.*

He returned to place the soft cuff around the middle of her thigh, then proceeded to do the same on her other leg.

He pulled the straps near the side of her head and her legs went up into the air. *Wow!*

"How's that? How does your lower back feel?"

There was absolutely no pressure on her lower back. The contraption made her feel as if she could fly. "Fine, Sir. Quite wonderful, in fact."

He smiled. "Remind me to thank Angelina later. She picked it up for me at some sex-toy party."

That Angie had been trying to find ways to get Adam to make love with her just made her realize all the more how blessed she was to have that woman in her life. She just wished Marc would get his head out of his ass and realize how much he needed her in *his* life before she gave up on him and found someone else.

But she couldn't worry about them now. Tonight was about her getting Adam's head out of *his* ass. Again.

"If you feel any discomfort or cramping and don't tell me about it, this will be our last scene for a very long time. Understood?"

"I understand, Sir. Really, but this is so comfortable I could stay like this all night." She hoped they'd be able to play all night, even though they had a long drive to Aspen Corners tomorrow afternoon.

"You'll stay as long as I say you will—and I'm not sure comfortable is the end goal here."

Adam reached toward something on the nightstand. It must have been whatever he'd pulled from the fridge earlier, because he began to trace her lower lips with the cold, pointy object. He stretched out on the bed and trailed hot kisses to warm the places left cold by whatever he was playing with. His tongue stroked the side of her clit hood as he rammed the object into her pussy.

Remain still, Kitty!

How? She wanted to move. The object didn't hurt, didn't even fill her the way Adam's cock would, but feeling something there after so long felt heavenly. Her body adjusted to the coldness, or perhaps the object just warmed to her core temperature. When he began to move it in and out, causing a slight friction against her walls, she clenched the feather-stuffed pillow as she held on for dear life.

More.

With the fingers of his free hand, Adam spread the apex of her lips apart, and his mouth descended on her clit hood again. This time, rather than gently kissing or licking her, he bit down.

Karla jerked. "Oh, dear God!"

"Control yourself, Kitten."

She gasped for air. "Yes, Sir." But how could she when he was bombarding her senses like this?

"You don't come until I tell you to come. Understood?"

"Y-yes, Sir." God help her, she hoped he wouldn't make her wait too long. She wasn't sure she could hold out more than a few minutes. But she didn't want him to go on another bent of many months—or years!—where he'd ignore the needs he'd awakened inside her, so she'd better behave.

He chuckled in the most diabolical way, and then she heard a click just seconds before her pussy pulsed to life. Oh, damn. Not a vibrator! She'd hoped it was a carrot or something.

"Hang on, Baby Tiger."

She couldn't hang on much longer but tightened her grip on the pillow anyway. He began his assault on her clit hood again, nibbling, biting, sucking, all the while the vibe in her pussy alternated rhythm in a most unpredictable pattern, which only drove her more insane. She drew a ragged breath and struggled for control. This felt so fucking good.

Watch your language.

Yes, Sir.

Control. Adam spread her folds even more and drew her clit straight into his waiting mouth. He sucked—hard.

Hold your hips still.

Control.

His tongue flicked at her swollen clit, and tears came to her eyes as she fought against the sensations rolling through her. Her body began to shake uncontrollably. How much longer? When he rested his chin on the vibrator protruding from her pussy, it hit that delicious bundle of nerves at her G spot. Her hips bucked as his tongue became even more wicked.

Jesus!

He pulled back. "What part of remaining still don't you understand, Baby Tiger?"

"I'm sorry, Your Excellency. It's just that…" Where had all the oxygen gone? "I've missed you so much. I'll try to control my body better."

"You're going to feel so much more if you lie still and let *me* control where you're touched and stimulated."

Adam only wanted to make this better for her. *Feel.* He wanted her to stop thinking, stop talking, stop moving, stop everything, and just *feel*—and yet he didn't want her to come? How could she give in to his attack and not explode?

Control. He'd been teaching her to control her body's responses for months. To empty her mind of stray thoughts and focus only on her body. More specifically, what he was doing to her body. Among other things, teaching her to come on his command. God, she wished he'd command her to come right now. She couldn't hold out much longer.

The vibe increased its speed at the same time his teeth bit into the swollen flesh of her clit. He pulled his head back, taking her clit with him. She met his gaze over her swollen belly.

Lie still. Don't move. This is a test.

She had to pass if she wanted to play again anytime soon. Karla willed her hips to remain still. Focus only on his touch.

He released her clit. "Very good girl. You've learned a lot, little Kitten."

She took a deep breath, a smile on her face. Adam averted his gaze, lowered his head once more, and pulled out the vibe before ramming it back inside. Though disappointed that he wasn't going to ram her with his penis, she wasn't going to complain at the moment. She had a job to do. She needed to show she'd learned the self-discipline he'd been teaching. Dear God, she hoped to be permitted to come soon—screaming for her beloved sultan.

He continued to piston her pussy with the vibe. Then he withdrew it and placed it against her anus. Oh, no. She loved anal play, even more so now that her pussy seemed to be off limits for anything but his fingers or small vibes. The vibrator went into her opening easily before stopping at the ring of muscles. "Bear down, Kitten."

She did as he'd trained her to do, and the vibe went a little further. She wasn't sure if it was lubed by her pussy juices or if he'd used something earlier, but there was no resistance. His mouth descended on her clit once more.

The vibe pulsed at erratic speeds as his tongue flicked against her clit. When his fingers plunged inside her pussy, tears came to her eyes as she trembled, fighting the urge to come. She held on while he assaulted her senses on three fronts. The man didn't play fair.

Do not scream, Kitty. Do not come. And most definitely do not beg.

Sweat broke out on her upper lip and forehead as her body shook more violently. She couldn't hold out much longer. *Please, Sir, let me come!*

She didn't know if she'd said the words aloud or not but nearly sobbed with relief when she heard him speak his next words.

"You've been a very good slave girl. Now for your reward I want you to come—loudly. Don't hold anything back from your sultan, Baby Tiger." He lowered his mouth to her clit again as he rammed three fingers into her pussy. The anal vibe ramped up to yet another speed.

Convulsions tore through her, and she moaned as he ripped the orgasm from her body. "Yes, Master Adam! I mean, Your Excellency! Oh, shit! Yesssss!" She bucked against his tongue, his fingers, the vibe. "Yes! There! Don't stop!"

The orgasm continued to roll through her body for what seemed like forever—but as the sensations ebbed, she realized it had been oh, too short. Her belly tightened as she bucked against the restraints, both real and imaginary. After an endless ride, she breathed in and out for several minutes until her body began to relax.

"Fuck, Karla. Your belly's hard as a rock. Did I hurt you? Are the babies okay?"

Dear Lord, let me survive this man's worrying until these babies are born. Somehow she knew he'd just worry more after the twins arrived, though.

"Adam, it's perfectly normal for my uterus to get hard when I come." Her womb was just the size of a watermelon now, so it was more noticeable to him. She wouldn't tell him how often she'd masturbated these last frustrating months just to try and maintain her sanity during this "no sex" dry spell. She and her Hitachi would be seeing a lot more of each other before she would get Adam to stop freaking out about everything related to sex.

He stroked her belly, which remained hard for at least ten minutes. That was the most incredible orgasm she'd had in months. Maybe forever. Her body relaxed into the mattress. She wanted to reach down and stroke his hair, touch him, but hadn't been given permission to move her hands yet.

As he removed the thigh cuffs on the harness, she asked, "May I move my hands, Sir?"

The worry on his face caused her to sigh. "Of course. Are they hurting? Numb?"

"No. I just need to touch you."

His body relaxed, and he nodded. Karla reached down to guide him up to join her on the pillow, and then she chose to snuggle against his chest instead. Her hand stroked his nips, inside the sultan's robe. The man didn't have an ounce of flab, even after being retired from the Corps for years. His pecs were like satin on steel. Unable to resist, she propped herself up on her elbow and pulled the robe open to reveal the object of her ministrations. His nip was hard when she pinched it and grew even harder between her thumb and middle finger. Glancing down his body, she saw that wasn't the only thing that was hard.

Forming her plan of retaliatory attack, she bent over him and took his rock-hard nipple into her mouth, sucking gently. His hand went to the back of her head and held her there. God, she loved when he took control of her head. Needing no encouragement, she flicked her tongue against the peak.

"That feels so fucking good, Kitten."

She smiled before nipping at him gently with her teeth. His hips jolted. She enjoyed when he lost control, and his using the F-bomb in addition to the unexpected body movements were a clear indication he'd missed her as much as she'd missed him—and his censors were off. It didn't happen often enough but gave her hope of one day having rough sex with him again before she became a grandmother. Oh, too late for that. Marisol's arrival soon after the wedding made that a reality already.

Damn it, I want it rough, Sir!

If Adam didn't have such a tight rein on himself at all times, she'd be sitting astride him right now but knew from past attempts that would shut the scene down immediately and win her a couple of swats on the butt with his belt. She really didn't like the belt, so she'd behave. More or less.

Karla pinched his other nip a few times until it became swollen, too, and then glided her hand across his six-pack abs to the sexy valley leading the way to any number of carnal delights.

She didn't stop, continuing to stroke his skin as she neared his lower abdomen. His hips made an imperceptible movement, and his cock nodded its approval. She licked her lips. Unable to resist, she straddled him, facing away, and lowered her lips to his cock. Salty precum greeted her, and she greedily took him inside her mouth.

Her large belly rested lightly on his abdomen, pinning him down. She knew he'd will himself to lie still so as not to jar the babies. She smiled when she felt his fingers playing with her pussy lips.

"This position isn't going to work, Kitten. Your Dom wants his mouth on that pussy he owns."

She giggled, and his cock bobbed out of her mouth. "Your pussy is quite satisfied and can wait, Your Excellency. Right now, your slave girl has work to do elsewhere."

"Who's in charge here?" He inserted his fingers into her tight and very wet pussy.

"Oh, you are, of course, Sir!" She giggled. His cock bobbed again, and she took him inside her mouth once more. He groaned and tilted his hips slightly to give her easier access. He wanted her to be in charge at the moment, even if he wouldn't admit it out loud.

"I'm enjoying the view, Kitten."

She wiggled her ass at him and clenched her vaginal muscles around his fingers, causing him to emit a low growl. Her pussy grew wetter for him. Frustrated that he wasn't filling her with something a lot bigger than his fingers, her mouth took him deeper. He hissed and grabbed her hips. Oh, god. She needed him inside her.

Turning as quickly as she could with her lumbering body, she faced him and lowered her pussy over his cock until her pelvis rested on his.

"Karla—" His expression of displeasure and growl of warning nearly caused her to obey, but it felt so good to have him close to being inside her again.

"Sir, I can't stand it anymore! You've teased me mercilessly. I need you to fill my emptiness. Please don't deny me this, Your Excellency. Your weak and humble servant needs to feel your hard cock inside her. Now, Sir."

She impaled herself on him and couldn't move as the fullness of Adam overwhelmed her. It had been so long. She closed her eyes, unable to take the censure in his eyes. Something so right couldn't be wrong. Lifting herself up, holding her belly with both arms to cradle the precious cargo inside, she pulled away and dropped herself onto him again, savoring the friction of his cock rubbing against her neglected portal.

"Karla, stop! You'll hurt the babies!"

She shook her head. "The babies are fine. *I'm* fine. Please." She pleaded, near tears. "Don't stop."

"I haven't started anything; you have."

True enough. He wasn't moving at all. How could he just lie there like that?

Because he didn't want her. She'd grown as big as a whale, and her body would only get bigger as the months of this pregnancy went on.

Tears of frustration slid down her cheeks. She didn't want him to see her cry. *Damn these fucking hormones.*

"And, no, I won't watch my language!"

"What language?"

She rolled away from him, curling into a ball on the other side of the enormous bed. Wracking sobs soon overtook her. Clearly this wasn't about his concern for their babies. He just didn't find her sexually attractive anymore.

Adam's strong fingers caressed her arm before he pulled her hair away from her neck and leaned over to whisper in her ear, "Are you okay, Kitten? Did I hurt you?"

"Only my feelings."

"Stop crying." He stroked the back of her head and softened his tone. "You know I can't stand it when you cry." She brushed his hand away. "Let's just cuddle tonight. I don't need to get off."

Exactly what she didn't need to hear. Another flood of tears poured out. Adam loved having sex. He thrived on rough sex. He just didn't want to have it with her. When he pressed his hard body against her backside, she tried to scoot away, but he hauled her back against him by grabbing onto her thigh. His hard penis pressed against her butt crack. Maybe he'd changed his mind. Maybe he'd make love to her.

But all too soon his hand splayed over the babies and wrapped her in his warmth. "There. Doesn't that feel better? Let's just get some sleep. We have a long drive ahead of us tomorrow."

His rejection crushed her, but she didn't even try to talk to him about it. The thought of driving down to see Cassie held no appeal anymore, but they had promised to follow Angelina home. Snow was predicted tonight and tomorrow, and Adam worried about her getting through the mountain passes, but she'd insisted on this long overdue visit with her friend. Who knew when she'd get there again?

July and this delivery couldn't get here soon enough. She was ready to begin the motherhood stage—and to get her body back in shape so she could be the wife Adam needed.

But what about her needs? When she'd accepted his offer to be his sub and had been collared by him during their honeymoon, perhaps she hadn't fully understood what she was agreeing to. Despite being at the club for months, the role of Dom and sub had been very private to each couple she'd observed and not information she was privy to as the club's entertainer.

One thing she'd discovered from hearing Angelina talk about her regrets in her relationship problems with Marc was that communication was a two-way street. Clearly, Adam wasn't very good at negotiating or communicating either. He got off on Master Sergeant headspace rather than Master Adam headspace. Damn it, she wasn't one of his Marines, even though she was feeling more like his subordinate than his submissive. As she'd grown stronger in her understanding of this lifestyle, she'd hoped to take a more active role as Adam's sub.

Despite her decision to let it drop, she couldn't resist. "Isn't a good Dom supposed to see to the needs of his sub?"

"Of course. That's a Dom's main responsibility. Didn't I just give you an orgasm?"

"Yes. Thank you, Sir." She kept her back to him, happy she didn't have to meet his gaze. "But when you collared me, you promised to help me learn and grow as your submissive. To *negotiate* with me."

His body tensed. "What are you getting at?"

"I want you to be my Dom."

"I *am* your Dom."

"I want you to be a Dom like you would be a Dom to another sub at the club."

"What the fuck does that mean? What we have is much more special than anything I could have with any other sub in the world, much less at the club."

That sounded encouraging, at least. "Thank you, Sir." Her heart pounded at the thought of calling him on where his mastery of her was lacking, but she wouldn't back down now. "But we haven't really negotiated for months. You just dictate what's what and never ask me what I want."

"Being your Dom isn't about giving you what you want. We agreed Christmas morning to negotiate until we knew each other's needs. I know your hard limits. I've learned to read your body language, so I've learned what you enjoy and what your needs are from observing you."

She drew a deep breath. "No, you haven't—unless you're totally blind. You're projecting *your* needs onto me." Maybe she'd been hanging around Savannah too long with the psychobabble.

She rolled onto her back, forcing him to move toward the middle of the bed. The confusion and hurt in his eyes gave her pause, but she needed to get this out. And he needed to hear it. "Adam, stop assuming you know what I need. Ask me. Listen to me. You're not my Master Sergeant. You're not clairvoyant. You're my Dom. I think it's time for some new negotiations." In reality, they'd never negotiated much of anything. His intense gaze became too much for her, and she averted her gaze.

Adam forced her to look at him by lifting her chin. "Kitten, what's really going on here?" He stroked her arm and drew her closer. "Talk to me. What's troubling you."

When her chin began to shake, she pulled back and turned onto her side again, away from him. He hadn't asked her to express her feelings in so long that she wasn't prepared to now.

He swatted her butt, not nearly hard enough to excite her and definitely not the way he used to spank her when she displeased him. He didn't care anymore.

"That question wasn't a suggestion for you to answer or not, Kitten. Answer me. Now. What's going on?"

She tried to grin but failed miserably. In a quiet voice, she asked, "Do you still find me attractive?"

Adam ground his pelvis against her butt, and she felt his erection. "Does that answer your question?" Yes, in true Adam fashion. But getting an erection was a natural reaction from his body, not the willing response of his mind finding her sexy anymore.

"Sir, why can't you see that I'm aching for you to take me the way you used to?"

His body stiffened—not the way she liked—and he pulled away. "Kitten, we've talked about that. You know why I'm not going to have rough sex until after you've gotten the go-ahead from Doc Palmer—after the babies arrive."

"But Doctor Palmer said there was no reason we couldn't enjoy an active sex life, just like before."

"I doubt Doctor Palmer knows just how *active* our sex life was." He reached around her and pinched her nipple. Karla hissed at the unexpected pain. "See? Your body has changed. You aren't into pain. I'd hurt you. I'm meeting your needs as they exist today, seven months into your pregnancy. This has nothing to do with whether I find you sexy or not. One of my main roles as your Dom and as your husband is to make sure you're protected and safe."

So he *didn't* find her sexy anymore? Or did protecting her from herself trump both of their libidos? His words served only to confuse her more. "You always have protected me, Adam, and made me feel safe, ever since I was sixteen." She swallowed past the lump in her throat but wasn't going to back down now. "Adam, I need something different now, too. I need to know you desire me physically, even if I look like a beached whale." Lying on her side like this, taking up more than her share of the king-sized bed, just made it even more apparent. "I want to please you, and I know you are just as frustrated as I am with this ridiculous freeze on sex."

She rolled onto her back once more and faced him. "I need this, Adam. I have these raging hormones right now that have made me hornier than ever. I even talked with Sage at the club, and she felt the same way at this stage in both of her pregnancies. She has two perfectly healthy children now. I know having such strong sexual urges doesn't make a bit of sense, because our bodies aren't trying to procreate. But it is what it is."

Adam sighed, and she could almost see the wheels turning in his head. After a very long time, he finally spoke. "When do you see Doctor Palmer again?"

She tried not to get her hopes up. "Not until after Damián's wedding."

"Let me talk with her, and we'll see what we can do safely."

His "let's wait and see" attitude sounded like a perfect parental non-response and definitely wasn't the "let's do it" Karla had hoped for.

She knew there must be fire in her eyes, but she'd had it. With lumbering movements, she pushed herself up to a seated position and leaned against the headboard, crossing her arms, which rested on the top of her swollen belly. One of the babies kicked her, and she lifted her arm off of the little darling, not wanting to disturb its sleep. "Don't treat me like a child, Adam. I understand why this scares you, after what happened with your son, but Doctor Palmer assured me that was a fluke, an accident, and had nothing to do with you and Joni having rough sex. You know I'd never do anything selfish that would jeopardize the health and well-being of our babies."

"I never said you were being selfish."

"No, but it was implied."

"Not intentionally. Just hold out another month until I have a talk with the Doc."

"Making me wait another whole month to have sex the way I want it isn't fair, Adam."

He pinched her nose. "Anticipation is good for you."

"But I've been anticipating for months and am on my last nerve! Besides, anticipation only works if I know I'm going to receive my reward for being patient eventually. Can you promise that we'll have sex the way I need it after Doctor Palmer gives the go-ahead?"

"*If* she gives the go-ahead."

Karla had no doubt the obstetrician would agree to it, because Karla had been very open about what type of relationship she and Adam enjoyed, both the rough sex and the D/s part. Trying to hide the man's dominant nature wasn't going to happen. Karla already pitied those poor labor and delivery nurses who had the misfortune of being on duty the day or night she went into labor. The man would drive them insane as he tried to cope with her going through the pain-filled experience of giving birth.

Still, she wanted a more firm commitment from the man. "So you agree to abide by what Doctor Palmer says?"

Adam already looked a little worried but nodded. "She's the boss when it comes to this pregnancy. Whatever she says goes."

She smiled. "I'm going to hold you to that, Sir, even if I have to jump your bones myself to get what I need."

Chapter Twenty

Angelina took another sip of her margarita, feeling the frozen blend slide down her throat. Karla and Cassie were deep in conversation at her table, talking about music, art, and Adam, but Angelina couldn't stay focused. Karla had mainly followed her home from Denver so she could see Cassie. Adam wouldn't let her make the trip alone or go anywhere near Cassie's isolated cabin southwest of Denver.

Despite the ten inches of snow piled onto the previously melting snow mass last night, Cassie had been able to maneuver her way off her mountain-top refuge. The two best friends had a whole season of events to catch up on, a separation caused in part by Cassie's reclusive nature and Adam's not allowing Karla to visit her on the mountain any longer.

Angelina was content to sit back and let them catch up. She hadn't been in a social mood in a long while. Adam and Luke had helped move her things from Marc's house back to her newly re-leased bungalow a week ago. The Marc chapter—*chapters*, really—in her book of love had closed with a resounding thud. She'd been content to just lay low there, unpacking and settling back in, except for her trip to Denver a couple days ago to babysit Marisol. *Dio*, she loved that little girl and hoped Savannah and Damián had gotten the cathartic healing needed to move on with their lives. Karla teared up just talking about the generalities of the scene. But the smiles on their faces when they got home this morning were well worth it. She hoped this meant they were well on their way to healing from their recent ordeal.

Having nothing fresh on hand to prepare any kind of decent meal for her friends, she'd called her high-school friend Rico and asked if they could hang out here at daVinci's on this blustery Tuesday afternoon.

Angelina glanced around the room. Rico was behind the bar taking inventory of his liquor bottles. Three pizza boxes sat open at the other end of the bar, their contents all but polished off. Rico had kept the Closed sign on the front door so the party would remain private until the bar's regular opening time of four o'clock.

Some party. The friendly neighborhood bar held so many bittersweet memories for Angelina that everywhere she looked she pictured Marc. No one mentioned his name to her face, but she knew they were just trying to keep her spirits up.

Moving the last of her things out of his house had been more painful than she'd expected, even though she hadn't lived with Marc for almost two months. Before she'd arranged for a U-Haul, she'd had Brian assure her Marc would be gone all day. She didn't want to confront him or, worse yet, succumb to his powers of persuasion and wind up in bed with him. Their relationship had ended as quickly as it had started, because they'd never been able to move from their potent sexual attraction to a much more satisfying emotional one.

Adam stood at the bar talking with Luke. Suddenly, Angelina wanted answers. She excused herself from the table with Karla and Cassie and walked over to the men but didn't interrupt their conversation. She stood a few feet away, waiting to be acknowledged. Soon, the two stopped talking about the training of Luke's newest rescued wild mustang long enough to turn toward her.

Although Adam intimidated the crap out of her, she addressed him anyway. "I'm sorry to interrupt, but when you have a minute, I wanted to ask you something."

Adam looked at Luke, who nodded before grinning at her and excusing himself. "What is it, hon?"

Adam called everyone hon. Her face warmed under his intense stare, but she regained her focus in an instant. She hadn't been able to find even a few minutes to ask him before but could stand the suspense no longer. "How is he?"

Adam raised his eyebrows. "He?"

The man wasn't dense, so he must want her to say his name aloud. "Marc. How's he doing?"

"Oh, him."

Angelina glared at Adam. He stared back at her in silence. Was there a twinkle of humor in his eyes? Did he find her groveling for some word of Marc's well-being amusing? She'd given up on him answering her when he motioned for her to move toward the corner of the bar, leading to the poolroom. He stopped at the last booth—not just any booth, but the same one Angelina, Marc, and Luke had shared the night she'd met them here in late September. That was the night she'd *thought* she was meeting Marc for the first time, anyway.

Had she ever really met the real Marc D'Alessio?

Angelina scooted to the middle of the bench that had been occupied by Luke that night so long ago. Maybe sitting here would make the memories of sharing the opposite bench with Marc less intense.

Hardly. She could see Marc as if he, rather than Adam, were sitting across from her. She could almost feel Marc's hand on her shoulder as he shielded her from Allen in such a protective way that night. Her eyes stung at the memory. How had they grown so far apart after having shared so much these past months?

And how could she still miss him when he wanted nothing to do with her? She'd thought he might call after he got back from California. Luke said he'd come to some kind of epiphany after his accident on the ice just before he'd left with the team to rescue Savannah. So where was he? It had been a month since the rescue.

Maybe epiphanies were only for the characters in her romance novels.

"What did you need to know, Angelina?"

She brought her focus back to the moment and blinked. "Is he taking care of himself?"

Does he need me anymore?

"Not from what little I've seen of him lately. Spends too fuc…damned much time alone up in the mountains."

Still? Marc escaped to the mountains when he needed to think. From what she'd heard from Luke, he'd been doing that for months, with or without clients from his outfitter/adventure business. Hadn't he figured out yet he wasn't going to solve his issues about his murky past by hiding out in the mountains?

Did he ever think about what he wanted to do about Angelina while he was out there?

"You want to vocalize any of those questions running through that pretty little head, hon?"

Oh, she'd forgotten about Adam! "Sorry. I'm out of shape when it comes to mental discipline these days."

"You need a Dom. He'll teach you to focus fast enough."

"I *had* one. I don't think I'll ever want another." She blinked rapidly, trying to stop the flow of tears. "What did he tell you about what happened with us?"

"Not much. I have a feeling there's a lot he hasn't figured out for himself—or maybe just a lot of stuff he doesn't *want* to figure out."

"He learned a long time ago to repress, suppress, and otherwise hide behind a mask."

Adam raised his eyebrows as if this was some kind of revelation. Or was he simply surprised at her perception of the situation? He narrowed his gaze on her, making her squirm on the hard wooden seat.

"What are you doing about getting your Dom back?"

"Doing?"

"I hear you left him, not the other way around."

Angelina's heart pounded as her Italian blood began to simmer. Adam knew more than he was letting on, but she had a feeling he didn't know the reasons behind her leaving. She'd promised not to divulge Marc's secrets but he shouldn't come across as a victim needing sympathy either.

"I might have left him physically, but he left me emotionally months before. He never let me in."

Adam stared at her for a long time before taking a swig from his bottle of water.

She and Marc should have been able to confide in each other. Why hadn't he been able to open up to her? Instead, he'd just closed himself off until there was no hope. She thought giving him a wake-up call by leaving would get his attention and make him see that running from her, even mentally, wasn't going to fly, but he'd let her go without even a phone call to see how she was.

Well, he *had* texted when he got back from Italy. She just hadn't been ready to forgive him yet, so she hadn't replied.

Damn it, more than two months had passed since they'd talked with Mama without any progress in sorting out his past. How long did he plan to go without doing anything?

"I'm not going to let him keep running, Adam."

She almost thought she detected a crinkling of his eyes, but he didn't smile. "How do you plan to stop him?"

Angelina had no clue. Heck, she'd just moved out on him for good. Why did she want to find some way to win him back? And how did she intend to do it? *Dio,* how could she be such a loser to hang onto a man who couldn't commit? They'd both spent so much time avoiding each other.

She leaned forward. "I'm going to go to Denver and haul his ass down off the mountain, for one thing."

Adam did smile this time.

Emboldened that he didn't say she was overstepping her place, she added, "Running never solved anything."

"That's for damned sure."

He agreed with her. She might need him as an ally, so this was good. She knew he loved Marc, too. In fact, Marc and Adam had a lot in common. Both of them were lost little boys inside strong men's bodies. Adam's mother told her at the wedding about how hard Adam ran from the emotional baggage of his past for most of his life. Well, Angelina wasn't going to let Marc run for thirty-something years. He'd run long enough.

Suddenly, Angelina realized she'd been running, too. Rather than stay and insist Marc deal with his past and their future, she'd walked away from him. No, ran. And she'd regretted it every day since, as if she'd lost a part of her own heart. Her strong, stubborn Italian heritage had led her to choose being miserable instead of just going back to him and forcing him out of his mental isolation.

So now what?

Perhaps she needed to form a plan of attack...er, action. She'd already tried the full-on attack when she'd topped him, up to a point. She needed a new strategy.

She leaned toward Adam. "I know you and Karla are house hunting. If you'd like someone to stay at the club, I'd be happy to until Marc and I get this worked out." Staying here in Aspen Corners when her heart was in Denver wasn't going to work.

"We just moved you down here."

"I made a mistake."

"Well, I appreciate the offer to keep an eye on things at the club, but Grant's already agreed to come into the partnership of the club as a co-owner and she'll move in when Karla and I move out."

"Oh." *Darn.* Without a job, she couldn't afford her own place in Denver.

"But there's Karla's old room, not to mention the one you stayed in before. I'm sure Grant wouldn't mind the company."

She smiled. He was throwing her a life preserver, which he wouldn't do if he didn't think she was right for Marc. She realized he and the others here hadn't written her off when she'd left Marc. They counted her as a friend as well, which warmed her heart.

"That'll work for me. And I'll be happy to prepare bar food for club members to earn my keep, too."

"You don't need to earn anything except maybe the trust of a man who doesn't trust easily. But I won't discourage you from cooking anytime you want. Maybe you could give Karla some more lessons. We've had steak Florentine more times than I can count since you taught her how to make it. Good grub, but I need something besides that and her tuna and broccoli casseroles."

"That would be perfect, Adam! Thank you!"

He grew serious again. "I'd also appreciate it if you could just provide some diversions for Karla in the coming months. She needs someone to keep her…busy." Adam made a sour face and, from what she'd overhead from Karla earlier about Adam's oh-so-doomed plan to abstain from having rough sex, Angelina could imagine what was bugging him.

Soon reality hit. She couldn't move in to the club. She just signed a six-month lease and had no steady income except for catering jobs.

A knock at the bar's front door jarred her thoughts before she could explain the situation to Adam. Someone passing by probably thought he could get in before the bar's regular hours. She brought her focus back to the conversation quickly. She needed to practice on maintaining her focus if she was going to have a chance winning Marc back.

Adam turned toward the bar and nodded at someone. Now who had the focusing problem? Karla must be there.

Adam turned back toward Angelina. "Back to Marc."

The strains of Dean Martin's rendition of *Return to Me* poured from the jukebox. Angelina's mind returned to the night she'd danced to another of Papa's favorite old tunes on the jukebox in this bar, held in Marc's embrace. Tears filled her eyes. She once again wished she hadn't given Rico Papa's record collection. Only now they reminded her of the loss of Marc, too, not just of Papa.

What was Marc doing now? He never seemed to be around their mutual friends when she was, so she assumed someone was making sure they didn't bump into each other. Awkward. At least she could still be friends with Karla, Luke, and the others she'd met through Marc. She looked up at Adam.

"Does he ever ask about me?"

"That's between Marc and me, but I don't plan to share this conversation with him, either."

"Fair enough." Adam wouldn't break a confidence. Of course, Marc knew she'd always been a little intimidated by Adam. She had a feeling he intimidated Marc somewhat as well. She doubted Marc would ask Karla, but maybe he'd ask Luke, especially after he learned she'd spent weeks at his place.

Dio, she missed Marc. What if they never could patch things up? Would he ever fully trust her? Could he trust anyone? She looked at Adam.

"How did he come to trust you?"

Adam brought his gaze back and zeroed in on her. Her heart thumped under his scrutiny. "In combat, you either trust the people you're with or you get killed. Many weeks of training during boot camp broke him of any notion he could fend for himself over there. The Corps breaks down that streak of independence most recruits start out with. Later, during his training as a roper at Pendleton—"

"Roper?"

"That's what we call the recon Marines in training because—well, never mind." He waved the thought away. "Anyway, he learned he had to rely on the members of his team, and they would need to have each other's backs when our boots hit the ground."

"How can I ever make him see that I have his back? That I don't want to harm him?"

"Time."

"But we've run out of time. He doesn't want me."

"I wouldn't be so sure about that. You two just need to talk and work this out."

Adam glanced up just as a warm hand cupped her upper arm, and a chill ran down her spine.

"Dance with me, *tesoro mio?*"

My treasure?

Marc! Her heartbeat pounded into her throat. She looked at Adam who just grinned.

In slow motion, she turned her face upward and found Marc standing beside the booth, several days' growth of beard on his face, hair disheveled— and sexier than she'd ever seen him before.

"Marc?"

"In the flesh. Come, pet." He held out his hand to her.

Adam cleared his throat. "I was beginning to think you weren't going to get here, Doc."

"There are some avalanche warnings out, so I tried to find a safer route. It took longer."

So Adam had asked him to come—or at the very least knew he might come. She wished Marc had chosen to come here of his own accord; of course, he wouldn't have known to find her here if Adam hadn't told him.

She took Marc's hand, and he guided her out of the booth and onto the dance floor. She'd missed his touch. She'd missed him, period. He cupped her chin and tilted her head back. Electricity ricocheted throughout her body, especially where the sides of his fingers touched her chin and neck.

"You look so beautiful, *mio angelo.*"

Walking into his arms again, she felt as if the world had suddenly righted itself after months of being off kilter.

Safe, protected...

No, wait! She pulled a few inches away. How could she just melt into his arms like this? Nothing had been resolved. He'd shut her out for months. She steeled her resolve. "We need to talk."

"Yes, but first, I need to hold you. What we need to do right now is dance."

Angelina saw pain and something that looked like fear in his moss-green eyes and decided the time to talk could come later. She pulled him into her arms, wanting to comfort him and tell him everything was going to be all right—but she had thought that before and things hadn't turned out so well.

"You feel so good, *cara.*" They danced for several songs, content to say nothing.

After a while, Marc's hand glided up and down her back before creeping under her untucked blouse. He touched her bare lower back, sending a shiver up her spine. "You've lost weight."

His accusation making weight loss sound like a bad thing made her smile. Even though she hadn't intentionally tried to lose weight, she had dropped about fifteen pounds since she'd left Marc. But she could stand to lose a few pounds.

"I haven't been very hungry lately."

He grunted and pinched her ass. If she still lived with him and was under his training as a submissive, that grunt would have meant he planned to remedy the situation later—both by hand-feeding her in the kitchen and flogging her in the playroom so she wouldn't neglect her body's needs. Of course, his grunt meant nothing this time. Just an automatic response.

"Do I need to put you in culinary bondage and make you eat every dish your nonna in Marsala taught you to make? You know, this can be arranged quite easily. The equipment is still at my house."

Her heart raced at the thought of being restrained by him again. She wanted to be in any kind of bondage with Marc again.

Stop it!

She admonished herself for being weaker even than Marc when it came to her desire for sex and submission. She needed to fight this urge to kneel at his feet. If anyone needed to be tethered to an appliance, it was Marc—to keep him from running from her. She wouldn't let him use her body and send her away again. For Marc, their relationship always had been about the physical. She needed more than that. She needed an emotional bond that couldn't be broken.

His hand crept further up her back, and she felt her breasts freed of their bonds with a deft flick of the bra's clasp. She tried to pull away, but he held on tightly. "Let me touch you. I missed you so much, pet." His hands reached between their bodies to cup her breast.

"Marc, stop. We aren't ready…" The catch of anticipation in her voice made her protest sound lame even to her ears. When he pinched her nipple, her hips jolted into his body, and she pressed against his erection.

But nothing had been resolved! Sex was a bad idea.

She pushed him away and looked up at him. "I can't think when you're touching me like that."

He grinned. "I don't want you to think."

His charm wasn't going to work this time. He'd played her body like this too many times, getting her to back down or forget what she'd wanted to say. Steering her focus away from the issue at hand. She needed to get him off this dance floor and turned to present her backside to him.

"Rehook my bra."

Marc sighed. "You used to be so easy to distract. Where did you learn to be so focused?"

From you.

But she felt anything but focused now. Her nerves were raw, her mind scattered.

His hands slipped under her shirt again, and he took his sweet time fumbling with the hook of her bra, spending a lot of time rubbing the valley of her spine. Tingles coursed down her back to her pussy. He was touching her the way he used to when he prepared her for a play scene. Warming her up.

Angelina put several feet between them and turned around, not caring that her girls were still loose. "I'll be back and then we're going to talk." She marched into the ladies room and rehooked her bra, checked her makeup, and took several deep breaths.

Adam had vacated what was becoming "their" booth, and she slid into the spot where he had been sitting earlier but not far enough in to invite Marc to join her. She tried to ignore the disappointment in his eyes.

"Now, Marc, we're going to talk. No more touching. Except maybe hands—no further than the wrists."

He sighed again. "You've gotten a little bossy. I told you there would be no encore for Mistress A."

Despite his words, Angelina saw a smile flicker across his lips before he obeyed and kept his hands off her. She smiled back at him.

Before she could find the words to begin, Rico placed what looked like her favorite white zin in front of her and a glass of white wine in front of Marc.

She looked up and smiled. "Thanks, Rico."

"Don't thank me, babe. Just doing my job. Marc ordered them."

She looked back at Marc. "Well, then, thank you."

This was her second drink, so she'd better go easy on it. She needed to keep her wits about her in case something came of this reunion later.

After Rico returned to the bar, Marc's expression became serious. "I'm sorry."

She blinked rapidly, hoping to stave off the tears.

Do. Not. Cry.

Not in front of him, anyway. He already had too much power over her.

"You didn't deserve the way I treated you, Angelina. None of this had anything to do with you."

His words stung. *Nothing to do with her?* They were stuck in the same place as before. "Marc, when are you going to learn that when you hurt, I hurt? I thought you wanted me to share your life with you, but…" She picked up her glass and took a gulp of the fruity wine, searching for courage, then gazed across the table at him again. "What I didn't deserve was to be shut out. If we're going to have any kind of relationship, we can't keep secrets from each other. We need to support each other—in good times and bad."

Marc glanced down at her hand on the table. Had the familiar wedding vows sent him into retreat?

"I fucked up."

Angelina nodded. "That's an understatement."

What did Marc want from her—from life? When he didn't say anything, she leaned forward. "What are you going to do about what your mama told you?"

He met her gaze. Fear again. "I'm not sure."

Two months to think about this on his own, and he didn't have any answers yet? "Have you talked with her since February?"

He looked away again. No, she didn't think so. Marc didn't confront people about important issues.

"We've talked but not about that."

What was his motto? KISS—Keep it Superficial, Sweetie. Or something like that.

She could see where his avoidance tactics came from. Marc's whole family was the same way. How could his mother talk with him since that emotional breakdown in her office and *not* mention the enormous elephant standing in the room? The D'Alessios suppressed, repressed, and denied anything too painful. Mama had secrets she hadn't revealed. Marc might even have discovered things from his biological father in Italy that Mama could confirm or deny.

But only if he'd *talk* with her!

"Do you even want to find out what happened back then, Marc?"

He shrugged. "I don't know."

He'd been almost cocky before, supremely sure of himself. Now he was in full retreat. The world of illusion Marc had so carefully created for himself disappeared in the glare of reality.

* * *

Marc sipped his pinot bianco. Why did he act like a fucking teenager around Angelina? When he'd been with Pamela, he'd managed to have a mature, adult conversation. With Angelina, he thought with his little head. Sex wasn't going to win her back. He set the glass down and reached across the table to take her hand, pulling back when he remembered she'd said no touching.

Talk to her. Don't blow this.

Angelina met him the rest of the way and squeezed his hand. "I said hands were okay."

She'd changed since she'd left. She'd gained a lot of confidence—without him. Or maybe because of him. She'd walked out on him, after all. But he'd shut her out for weeks—nearly two months, actually—before she'd finally given up on him. Coming home last week to find every remaining trace of her gone had been the wake-up call he needed. As long as her nonna's furniture had been in his house, he expected her to come back to him.

Okay, he'd been an ass when she'd first left and pretended to himself he welcomed the time alone.

Until the mission to rescue Savannah. Seeing Damián's girl beaten and abused had stirred up all the protective feelings he'd had for Angelina after the abuse she'd suffered at the hands of Martin. He hadn't been able to get back to Colorado fast enough to check on Angelina but still hadn't mustered the nerve to call her directly.

What if she was happier without him? Tonight, she showed no signs of a desire to rekindle their relationship or that she even needed him.

Marc downed the rest of his wine in two gulps. She'd thrived without him. More beautiful than ever. Out with her friends. Hell, his friends. *Their* friends.

Perhaps he needed her more than she needed him.

She blinked, her chin quivering. "Is there any hope for us being able to talk with each other, Marc? This silence is killing me."

Merda.

Sometimes he felt safer inside his own head. He should be able to communicate better, especially as her Dom. He ran his thumb through the condensation on his wine glass, avoiding eye contact. "Perhaps you deserve someone better."

She leaned against the back of the booth, and he felt the withdrawal of her hand like a knife stab to his gut. "I never wanted anyone else, Marc. I only want you to stop running from me."

Marc still couldn't look her in the eye. "I don't even know who the fuck I am. I can't be your Dom until I get my head on straight again."

"Then just be my man. My friend. I can live without kink, but I've been miserable trying to live without you. Maybe this time we can start more slowly and build on what we both need."

He glanced up. She'd been miserable, too? Whenever he'd asked about her, she'd been busy doing something with their friends, not moping over what had been lost between them.

But they had yet to resolve the main reason he'd backed away from her. "You don't even know who I am."

"I know all I need to know."

"Well, then *I* still need to know who I am. I've spent months trying to come to terms with what I might discover, and it still scares the shit out of me to face the past."

"Marc, finding out who your parents are or what happened when you were a little boy isn't going to change who *you* are today. You're a good man. A friend to so many who love you and choose to have you in their lives. A hero—you've saved lives both in Iraq and in your SAR work. Heck, you even saved me at the club and went after me on Mount Evans when you knew I was in danger." Angelina reached out once more to grasp his hand, and he made eye contact again. "And you're the only man I want to be with—ever."

Marc blinked, dumbfounded to hear she wanted him, despite how he'd fucked up so badly. Angelina was no needy doormat. She was beautiful, intelligent, and could have anyone she wanted, but she wanted him, flaws and all.

Never afraid to speak her mind or let him know when he was being an ass, she'd head slapped him more than once when he screwed up, same as Adam. Except in the middle of a D/s scene. At those times—well, except for the Mistress A one—Angelina had been beautifully submissive. He loved all facets of her.

He loved *her*. Period.

So how was he going to unfuck this?

"Why don't we go over to your place and talk?"

"Is talk a euphemism for something more sexual?"

He grinned. "Well, our bodies are very expressive, as well, *amore mio*." What he wouldn't give to make love to her again tonight.

"I can't make myself that vulnerable to you, Marc. Talk, yes. Sex, no."

Two words he didn't want to hear in conjunction with each other. No sex. He'd missed her. When they pushed all the bullshit aside, their bodies knew how to communicate with each another.

He'd better be very sure of the limits tonight, more so than in any kink scene they'd negotiated. "State your limits, pet."

She blinked in surprise before a flicker of a smile spread across her full lips. "Talking is okay. Cuddling—with clothes on. That's okay." She grew serious again. "We have so much to sort out. We haven't resolved anything since I left in February, because we haven't *talked* since I left. The big question is what's changed since then?"

He thought a moment. What had changed? He still had no answers. Still hadn't spoken with his parents. Hadn't found answers in talking with Pamela—only more questions. Hell, Pamela had just stirred up his insecurities about being the Dom Angelina needed and deserved.

"Savannah. What she went through. What *Damián* went through trying to get to her before it was too late." He squeezed her hand. "The thought of losing you terrifies me."

Angelina brushed her thumb over his knuckles. "Marc, the only threat against me is sitting in jail now and has been for half a year."

"I have a need to protect you from hurts, big and small. I worry about you."

"I don't need or want a bodyguard, Marc. There has to be more to our relationship than that."

Realization dawned slowly. "I know losing you to another attack is improbable. Instead, I've come very close to losing you forever—and for no reason other than my own inability to…" He couldn't even find the words to explain.

"Communicate?"

How ironic. He nodded his agreement. He needed to express his reasons for wanting them back together. "I am more in control when I'm with you."

"Still not a reason for us to get back together."

He was screwing this up. How could he convey what he needed her to understand? He ran his hand through his hair. "Just before the mission to rescue Savannah, I had planned to meet with you."

"That was more than a month ago."

The unspoken *What took you so long?* hung in the air. What, indeed? He scrubbed his face. "I guess I wound up with more questions than answers after that mission."

"Then what brought you here tonight?"

"You."

"That's not what I meant."

Angelina's tone of voice had changed. She wasn't going to let him evade her questions anymore. Well, good for her. She deserved straight answers.

"While I had your nonna's furniture, I assumed you'd come back any day."

"Yet in the two months since I left, you only contacted me once."

"You didn't respond to that text."

She held her chin higher. "I was still upset about you going to Italy without telling me until the night before. With you shutting me out of such an important and difficult time."

At least she was talking with him again, even if she remained pissed about that asinine trip to Italy. He'd better not blow this chance at reconciliation. "I called Adam the other night to see if he'd heard anything after you moved your things out of our house." He hoped to conjure up some shared memory of what they had once shared.

"You checked up on me?" She didn't ask the question as an accusation for him meddling in her affairs but more as if she'd been pleasantly surprised he'd bothered.

He reached across the table to take her hand and brushed her knuckles with the pad of his thumb. "I never stopped worrying about you, caring what you were doing."

"No one told me you'd been asking. I thought..." Her voice cracked.

"I didn't always have to ask. I observed what was going on with Damián and Savannah. I knew you were taking care of Marisol. I'm glad you weren't abandoned by our mutual friends."

"I owe you a lot for sharing your friends with me. They've been wonderful through this...separation period."

He didn't want to hear that word either, but at least she didn't call it a break-up. "After talking with Luke last month, I knew what I wanted—you. I just didn't know how to go about bringing you home again and being the man you deserve." He wasn't sure he should admit this but needed to be honest. "The man you needed."

She paused long enough to make him worry. "I don't think we should rush things this time, Marc. Maybe that was our problem before—we moved too fast, before we'd really established trust."

"You know I trust you—"

"No, I don't, Marc. You talk about being the man I need and deserve, well, unless you start sharing your life with me and stop shutting me out when things get difficult or emotional, how can I possibly know that?"

He pulled his hand back. Why had he come here in the first place?

He remembered.

"Adam mentioned you'd be here tonight. Since this is where it started for us, more or less, I thought it might be a place where we could get back on track. Rekindle some memories of happier times."

"Marc, are you ready to accept me into your life? It all boils down to your answer to that question."

Chapter Twenty-One

Luke watched Marc lead Angelina off the dance floor and back to their booth. A lot had happened since the last time the three of them had been here. He hoped those two reconciled tonight. He was tired of watching people he cared about being so damned stubborn and throwing away a chance at happiness. They belonged together. Anyone with eyes could see that. What if the unthinkable happened and one of them was ripped out of the other person's life? Luke learned the hard way that you couldn't count on tomorrow. Grab the gusto while you could.

Adam stood next to him describing a Shibari scene he wanted to work on with Luke's help after Karla had their baby—something involving roping two submissives together. Sounded interesting, but all Luke could think about was Cassie Lôpez being the second demo model. His gaze strayed to the woman seated near Karla across the barroom. The girls had been deep in conversation the whole afternoon. He'd wanted to spend some time with Cassie, who'd been haunting his dreams lately, but apparently she and Karla had a lot of catching up to do.

He had no idea if Cassie had a submissive bone in her body, but from the way the woman closed herself off from everyone except her friend Karla, he didn't think he'd ever find out.

"Grab your beer, Luke. Time we break up that hen party over there. They've had more than enough time to roast my nuts over the fire by now."

Luke grinned at Adam. *Hell, yeah.* He picked up the long neck and followed Adam to the table where Karla and Cassie sat.

"Mind if we join you girls?" Adam set his bottle of water on the table without waiting for a response.

Cassie blinked before glaring at Adam and sitting back in her chair as far away from him as possible. She was more skittish than the mustang he'd spent the last month trying to train for SAR work—and just as worth working with to get past her fears. When Cassie zeroed in on Adam's hand stroking Karla's cheek, Luke didn't miss the instantaneous look of longing in her big, brown eyes before she masked it. He didn't know what she feared a man would do to her, but one thing Luke had in spades was patience and a gentle hand.

Adam sat down next to Karla at the square table while Luke took a seat with Adam and Cassie on either side. The girl scooted her chair closer to Karla in retreat.

Hearing Karla mention her baby had just kicked splashed cold water on his mood. Maggie hadn't been far enough along for them to feel their baby's kick. In some ways, that made it easier to pretend their baby hadn't been real. Well, until Cassie drew that sketch of Maggie holding his baby up in heaven and gave it to him at the hospital while they were all holed up in the waiting room waiting for news about Adam's condition.

Luke didn't want to think about all he'd lost that day in the mountains nearly eight years ago this month. He also didn't want to think about Maggie at the moment.

"So Cassie, what are you working on now?"

She looked up at him as if she'd just realized he was there, which didn't do a lot for his ego, and then she sputtered on a swig of what looked like a margarita.

"You okay, darlin'?"

Luke leaned forward to pat her hand, but she snatched it back as she coughed to clear her windpipe. He didn't try to get too close, but when she regained control of her breathing, they talked about her plans for fiber art. The girl made it clear she didn't want him coming anywhere near her or her alpacas.

Fine. Might as well enjoy himself. Watching Cassie scowl at him all afternoon wasn't going to cut it. He shifted his focus to Adam. "How about a round of pool? You and Karla taking on Cassie and me?"

Adam smiled. "Sounds good to me."

Luke turned back to Cassie only to find the blood had drained from her face. Now what had he said? She had a glazed look in her eyes, and her hand shook. *Damn.* He stood and went to her, trying to bring her back to the present with a firm arm around her back. He placed his hand on her quivering arm.

Karla reached out for her friend's other hand and squeezed it. "Deep breath, honey. You're safe."

Safe? What else would she be? Had Luke missed something?

Karla directed her next comment to Luke. "No, thanks. We don't play pool."

When Adam tried to remind her they had just played pool recently, she argued her belly was too big, but Luke didn't take his eyes off Cassie. She looked terrified.

Abruptly, she pushed the chair back and stood, announcing her departure. "It'll be dark soon."

With the threat of avalanches, especially in the passes like the one near Cassie's cabin, Luke grew worried and pulled out his phone. "Let me check my app before you head out."

"No, really! I'll be fine." She assured him she wasn't one to rely on anyone for anything, but a quick glance at the app told him the roads up that way were clear—as of last reports, anyway. Things could change in the blink of an eye this time of year with all the new, wet snow. "Why don't I follow you home, darlin'?"

"No!" The sheer panic in her eyes surprised him, even though she tried to convince him she'd be fine. What the hell kind of guy did she think he was?

Someone had hurt her. Bad. Just like the abused horses he rescued, she needed a kind word and a gentle touch. He hated seeing someone with so much of her spirit broken. Luke wasn't looking for forever-after love again. That came along once in a lifetime. But hell, after spending time with Angelina lately, he would sure enjoy a woman's company again. He and Cassie shared a love of art. If nothing else, perhaps they could be artist friends. He didn't really hang out with local artists much. She only lived thirty minutes from him, high up on that lonesome mountain.

One of these days, he'd find a way to breach her defenses.

Right now, though, he wasn't going to let her go up that mountain on her own without making sure she made it home safely. Adam helped Karla to her feet, and she and Cassie said their good-byes with a long hug. Another glimpse of longing crossed Cassie's face bordering on something painful as she embraced her friend.

He gave Cassie a few minutes' head start before letting Adam know he'd make sure she got home safely. Marc and Angelina hadn't come up for air since they'd become ensconced in that back booth. The look on Angelina's face didn't bode well for them, but he still hoped they would give their relationship another chance. Hell, one thing for sure, both were miserable apart.

Luke said good-bye, grabbed his sheepskin coat, and donned his Stetson. Walking out the door, he bowed his head against a brutal gust of wind. Once he was certain Cassie had made it home safely, he'd head back down the mountain to his ranch about ten miles away. At least he was making some headway with his skittish fillies there.

No reason to follow Cassie so closely that she'd make him, because he knew where she lived. Soon, though, he had her Tahoe in sight. Maybe he was a little more anxious than he thought. He eased off the accelerator and followed her up the mountain at a safer distance, watching as the taillights of her vehicle made a left turn at the pass. He navigated the same turn two minutes later and opted to switch to the truck's running lights so as not to frighten her. Some of the ruts in the road were bone jarring. Maybe he could have the lane to her cabin graded for her early this summer. Of course, she probably knew how to avoid the ruts with her eyes closed. He was driving half blind in the evening dusk.

Her taillights disappeared around the bend, and he sped up a little to make sure he had the cabin in sight before she got out of the Tahoe and heard his engine. He didn't want her getting spooked—again. Then he'd head home himself. Not the night to be out in the passes like this.

A glimpse of the sketch of Maggie and their baby flashed across his mind. He hadn't seen or dreamt of Maggie since last fall and felt a little guilty that he'd barely noticed she wasn't part of his daily life anymore. He'd thought of her every day for seven years but lately had been so busy with the horses, a pipedream he and Maggie had once shared that they hadn't had the time or finances to pursue. Until he'd learned about Picasso, he hadn't really thought he would get into this sideline either, but couldn't let the horse that had saved so many lives be taken to the slaughterhouse.

New orders for furniture were coming in all the time now, too. Maybe his mind had been too busy to be quiet and let her talk to him. Or maybe she'd said her good-byes when she'd inspired Cassie to draw that sketch, and she'd moved on.

"Maggie, darlin', I hope you found whatever it was you kept searchin' for."

The ominous crack breached the still air leaving no doubt what had happened. A mountainside of snow roared toward him. He floored the accelerator, and his head jerked back as the truck shot forward. He hoped he was moving away from rather than into the avalanche—and that he wasn't hurtling off the side of the damned mountain. Hell. Maybe following Cassie up here without headlights wasn't the smartest move he'd ever made.

Luke turned on the low beams and saw the bend in the road half a football field ahead as the roar grew louder. Sounded like the worst of it was behind him, so he must be moving in the right direction. "Come on, Betsy. Give it all to me."

The snow pack crushed against the bed of the truck, and Luke lost control, veering off the rough grade as if in slow motion. He flashed back to the sound he heard when another avalanche took Maggie from him. Sweat broke out on his forehead, and his heart thudded to an abrupt stop.

Was he dead already? Would anyone find his body? He hadn't promised anyone he'd check in when he returned home from Cassie's mountain.

Had Cassie made it past the tumbling snow pack? She must have. He hadn't seen her taillights even when he gunned the engine. She was safe. God, he hoped so at least.

The avalanche shoved his truck off the roadway as if it were a diecast toy. How far down the mountain would the snowpack carry him? A second later, as if the mountain answered his question, his body slammed against the door, his head hurtling toward the window as the truck came to an abrupt stop against something. A tree maybe.

His head banged against the glass, and Luke heard the window shatter before everything went black.

*   *   *

"Luke, open your eyes!"

Cassie heard him moan. *Thank you, goddess.* At least he wasn't dead.

Karla's frantic phone call had sent Cassie outside searching for Luke. She'd never expected to find him up here, certain her friend had been mistaken that he would follow her home. What possessed him to do that? He had to have been up to no good. He'd also shown up at the gallery reception last winter. Was he stalking her?

Maybe not, if he'd told Karla and Adam of his plans. Stalkers didn't do that, as far as she knew.

"Hell, woman. Let me sleep. No more dreams, damn it."

Dream? Freaking nightmare, more like it.

She struggled to pull him out of the truck. The dried blood on his temple indicated a scalp wound of some sort; he might even have a concussion. He was lucky he hadn't been killed. What was she going to do if he needed more medical attention than she could offer up here? The avalanche would keep the road blocked for days if not weeks. There was no easy way off this mountain other than the road or backcountry hiking. Normally, being snowed in didn't bother her, but she'd never been sick or injured before with no way out. Nor stuck here with a wounded man.

Damn fool. She fought to support his weight, but he was practically dead on his feet. No, don't think about him being dead. She didn't wish that on him. Still, the fact that he had followed her home didn't sit well with her. She didn't get any particular creep vibe from him, no more so than any other man. Maybe even a little less than most men. He didn't push her, and she liked talking with a fellow artist who could understand her world a little better than most of her acquaintances. But knowing he'd followed her home put her on edge.

What was she going to do with him when she got him to her cabin? No man had ever invaded her sanctuary, well, except for Eduardo. But she trusted her brother with her life. He'd saved her once before.

A chill ran down her spine.

"What are you doing out here, Luke?" she muttered, straining under his weight. Looking up at the hill in front of her, she wondered how she'd ever get him up to the roadway.

"Makin' sure you got home safe."

She hadn't expected him to answer but was relieved he was at least lucid. A shiver wracked his body, and he pulled her closer. The breath left her body, and she placed a hand on his chest to keep him at as much of a distance as possible. Not that she could keep from touching him. He was all over her. She needed some space.

"You'll need to help me here, Luke. I can't lift you up the hillside."

"No worries." He released her body and wobbled on his feet before crouching to pull himself up the slope. Maybe he wasn't too badly injured. She helped him along by placing her hands on his backside before realizing touching his butt wasn't the safest move she'd ever made. She let go and watched him crawl the remaining few feet on his own. Scrambling up the crest of the bank, she found Luke standing with his head pressed against the roof of her Tahoe. He must be exhausted.

"Here, Luke, let's get you inside."

She figured he might feel more comfortable stretching out in the back seat, but he had other ideas and opened the front door, crawling inside. He grinned a dopey smile at her before she shut the door. Resting his head against the window, he closed his eyes.

"Please don't pass out on me, Luke. I need to get you inside to warm up."

What on earth was she going to do with him once she got him inside? She had a twin bed and a tiny cabin. Her studio took up more than half of the floor space, because that's where she spent most of her time. The thought of any man other than Eduardo invading her space made her stomach queasy. Sure, Luke would be easy to fight off now, but what would happen when he regained his strength?

How long was he going to be here?

She might have to use the self-defense skills she'd learned while in college with Karla before this nightmare ended.

Cassie got behind the wheel and put the SUV in reverse, careful to follow the dimly lit roadway back to the cabin, but there wasn't enough room to turn around without the risk of sending them hurtling down the hillside. Luke groaned each time she hit a rut. She'd planned to have the annual grading done once the permafrost heaving was over.

"I'm sorry."

Luke grunted. She glanced over at him and saw he leaned heavily against the window. At least he wasn't pressing against the cut he'd gotten from hitting the driver's side window in his truck. She hated to see any living thing in pain, even a man.

Luke had never done anything to hurt her, either. She needed to stop assuming every male on two legs was out to harm her the way her ex-boyfriend and his drunken friends had during that college break in Peru.

Cassie shuddered and closed the lid on the memories of that horrific ordeal. At the cabin, she put the gearshift in park and exited the vehicle. Before she could get to his door Luke opened it, and she watched in horror as he started to tumble out.

"Luke!" She charged underneath him to break his fall, but the man's weight came down on her full force. She flashed back to the scene in the Andean bar for an instant before she regained her equilibrium.

You aren't in that place.

Never again. With strength that could only have come from an adrenaline rush, she shoved him back toward the cab of the truck.

"Sorry, darlin'."

"I'm not your darling. Now, put your arm around my shoulder, and let me get you inside the cabin before you hurt yourself even more."

"Yessss, mmmma'am."

"Don't you pass out on me."

Luke grunted but leaned more heavily against her. She needed to get him into bed before he fell. Briefly releasing her hold on his belly, she reached for the doorknob, wrenched the cabin door, and returned her hand to his abs to steady him. She propelled him forward with an arm around his lower back and waist. The man was as cold and chiseled as a marble statue.

Shivers wracked his body telling her she needed to get him warm and soon.

"Just a little bit farther, Luke." She steered him through the tiny living room toward her bedroom before remembering there wasn't a fireplace in there to keep him warm. However, his long frame wouldn't fit on her loveseat, so she'd have to tuck him into bed and find some other way to raise the heat level in the bedroom.

She lifted the alpaca-fiber blanket that covered the doorway to the bedroom and felt a blast of cold air. Normally, she preferred to sleep in a cold room under lots of handwoven blankets, but she'd never had hypothermia before.

Her brother had, though. She remembered the winter he had been injured while backpacking with the family. Papá had stripped both of them and had given his own body's warmth to his son until the wracking shivers had stopped.

Cassie shivered, and not because of the temperature in the room or Luke's chilled body.

I can never do that.

Another shudder even more intense than the earlier ones went through him. Goddess, she was going to have to do something to warm him up. A hot-water bottle? Heating pad? Maybe the space heater?

"Why me, Luke?" Why did he follow her home and get himself into this predicament?

"My dream."

Again, her question had been rhetorical, but at least she knew he was still semi-conscious.

"What dream?"

"You were in…my dream."

"I'm nobody's dream, Luke. You're delirious."

He chuckled, giving her a squeeze on her upper arm that prompted her to release him like a hot potato. He swayed on his feet until she sighed and caught him. He gripped her arm as she guided him onto the bed before he fell back onto the mattress. His grip remained on her arms, though, and she toppled onto his chest. The breath whooshed from her lungs, and his grunt of pain soon turned to a murmur of appreciation that sent chills up her spine as he wrapped his arms around her.

"Let go, Luke." She ground out the words, hoping to convey how close he was to losing a part of his anatomy he probably fancied.

Another wracking shiver coursed through his body, and he held on even tighter, nearly smothering her. Involuntarily, she reminded herself. He wasn't making a pass. Still, she fought to escape the confines of his arms, trying to control her breathing before going into a full-blown panic.

"I…said…let *go* of me." She tried to yank herself away.

"Yes, ma'am." His arms slackened and his head lolled to the side.

"Don't you dare go to sleep, Luke! Do you hear me?" She raised her voice, "I need you to stay awake."

He moaned, but his eyes remained closed.

Cassie needed to call for help. She had no idea how to handle someone with a probable concussion and hypothermia. Going to the blanket chest in the corner, she pulled out several more heavy wool covers, because he had fallen onto the ones she used herself. She spread them over his body before running to the living room to call her friend.

"Kitty! I have him. He's hurt but alive."

She heard her friend muffle the receiver to announce, "Adam, Luke's alive!" Then her voice came through more clearly. "How badly is he hurt, Cassie?"

"Concussion, I think. Hypothermia for sure. He needs medical help, but the road's blocked."

"Let me have Marc talk with you. He'll know what to do."

Cassie didn't want to *do* anything; she just wanted someone to come and take this giant of a man off her hands.

"Listen, he'll call you back on his phone. Let's hang up."

With reluctance, she said good-bye and carried the phone into the bedroom where Luke lay sprawled on her bed, shivering uncontrollably now. She knew there wasn't anyone else around to do this. Luke could die without treatment, and she didn't want that karma marring her soul's journey.

She hurried into the kitchen to get the space heater. At least this would raise the temperature in the room a little bit faster. The phone buzzed just as she turned on the heater and pointed it toward Luke on the bed.

"Cassie, this is Marc. Tell me what's going on."

After filling him in on how she'd found him and the visible injuries, she added, "I think he might have a concussion."

"First I need you to help me evaluate his condition."

He walked her through several things to check, and she reported that his pupils both contracted normally in the light and he had a steady pulse. "He's shivering non-stop now, Marc."

"A concussion isn't my biggest worry. I need you to keep him from falling into a deep sleep, though. The main concern is warming him up fast. First, get him out of those clothes. They're probably wet and leaching what little warmth he has left in his body's core."

Strip off his clothes? She didn't want to even consider that notion. She was an artist, not a nurse. But in actuality, she simply didn't want to deal with touching or seeing him that intimately. She remembered the camping experience with her father and brother.

Skin to skin.

Bare skin to bare skin.

Why me, goddess?

Dharma or karma, it didn't matter. She did not need this on her soul's chart.

Care for him.

She sighed. "Let me put you on speaker phone, Marc." After doing so, she set the phone down, tossed the blankets aside, and went to work unbuttoning Luke's shirt. His coat must have been on the seat in the truck. The sleeves of his denim shirt were cold and wet from his climb up the embankment. She could only imagine how wet his jeans must be.

Why me?

"How are you doing, *cara?*"

Trying not to freak out about the very real possibility of having a naked man in my bed in a few minutes.

"I'm...getting him out of these...wet clothes."

"Luke!" A woman's voice came over the speakerphone. Angelina. "You do whatever Cassie says, you hear me? I'll kick your ass if you don't."

Luke smiled, but didn't open his eyes. "'K, Angel."

At least he was still halfway aware of his surroundings. That had to be a good sign. He grimaced as another shudder coursed through him. She needed to hurry.

"I need you to sit up, Luke. We need to get this wet shirt off you."

Another grin, and he opened his eyes. She felt his wicked leer.

Don't even think it, mister.

She helped him sit up and stripped away his shirt, leaving his chest bare. He had little to no hair on his chest. Several scars made her wonder how he'd gotten them, but she averted her gaze. Easing him back onto the pillow, she unbuckled his belt and tugged it from the loops, tossing it aside. She undid the button at the waistband and unzipped his fly without looking at what she might reveal underneath. Turning her head, she worked the jeans over his tight butt. Repositioning herself at the foot of the bed, she tugged off his boots and then followed with the cold, wet jeans.

Thankfully he wore boxers. No way was she removing those. Warming up his chest and extremities was more her concern, not his...

"When you get everything off, you'll need to strip, too, and crawl under the covers with him."

She wasn't surprised by Marc's command, she just didn't welcome hearing her greatest fear put into words. Relieved to see Luke's eyes had closed again, she removed her clothes quickly but kept her bra and panties on as symbolic protection at least. She grabbed the cell phone.

"Okay. I'm going to disconnect now. I'll call you back if anything changes for the worse."

Marc told her the signs to look for to indicate a worsening of his condition, but said helicopters wouldn't be able to come in to airlift him out for days, not if the blizzard conditions predicted for tonight came about. No surprise there. More bad luck.

Cassie ended the call before stretching out beside Luke. The blankets had been dampened by his clothes, so she got up and maneuvered the top one from under him, rolling his body back and forth until she tossed the wet wool onto the floor.

His body temperature was frigid and she couldn't suppress a shudder of her own. Pulling several heavy blankets over them both, she curled up beside this near-naked man who had invaded her sanctuary.

When black spots clouded her vision, she realized she'd stopped breathing. Drawing slow, ragged breaths helped clear her mind and vision, but the thought of lying next to him, touching her body against the length of him, sent her mind into the depths of hell.

Cassie struggled to keep the memories from overwhelming her. At least she wasn't underneath him.

Luke wrapped his arms around her and pulled her closer. She pushed him away instinctively before realizing she needed to get closer if she was going to do him any good. Why couldn't he just lie still and keep his hands off her? The urge to squirm out of her skin almost overtook her, and she fought to fill her lungs to keep the panic at bay.

"Baby girl, it feels good to hold you like this."

He was delirious again. She was nobody's baby girl and never would be.

"Luke, this is Cassie Lôpez. You're in my cabin. You had an accident. The snow ledge gave way and…"

"Avalanche." He stiffened and opened his eyes, trying to focus on her face. His smoky gray eyes had a haunted look. "You okay, Cassie?" His calloused hand cupped her cheek, and she drew away.

"I'm fine." Physically, at least. Her mental state was in shambles right now, though. He knew who he was with at least. She liked it better when he was thinking about someone else.

"Good. I'll keep you safe. Promise."

His other arm gripped her more tightly for a moment until his eyes closed and his head lolled to the side. The hand touching her dropped to the mattress where she hoped it would stay. He grimaced as another chill convulsed his body, and she forced herself to press her body against his, trying to infuse him with her warmth at the same time she felt as if the lifeblood was being leached from her own body.

Cassie's heart thudded as she fought down the bile threatening to rise at touching a man again, especially in such a compromising position.

His baby girl might be safe, but Cassie wasn't. Not as long as this man was in her cabin—not to mention her bed.

With her.

"You had better get well fast, Lucas Denton," she whispered. "I want you out of here as soon as possible."

Chapter Twenty-Two

Marc updated his friends on how it sounded like Luke was doing and turned to Adam. "Why don't you head back to Denver before it gets much later? They're predicting some nasty weather in the passes tonight. We can't do anything for Luke until the weather cooperates."

"No way." Adam placed his arm around Karla securing her against his side. "Roads are too dangerous and someone needs to keep an eye on things out at Luke's place. Karla and I will bunk down there tonight."

Angelina reached out to touch Karla's arm. "That'll mean a lot to him. He loves those horses so much. I'll call my brothers; Rafe and Tony can take over tomorrow until Luke gets back home."

Two Giardano brothers lived within a dozen miles of Luke's and knew their way around a stable. "Good thinking, *cara*."

The mood at daVinci's bar disintegrated quickly, and Adam and Karla reached for their coats. Marc wasn't ready to leave yet. Nothing had been resolved about where they'd go from here, not even for tonight.

The thought of parting again left him feeling cast adrift.

Marc turned to Angelina. Moments ago, he'd watched the stress leave her body when she heard Luke respond to her command to be a good patient. Now he noticed an almost imperceptible shaking in her arms and pulled her to his chest.

"He's going to be okay, *cara*. He's out of the elements, and it sounds as though Cassie is going to take good care of him." He tried to convince himself of that, anyway. Luke was lucky to have survived the avalanche but wasn't out of the woods yet.

"Poor Cassie."

Luke was the one injured. He pulled away and met her gaze. "What do you mean?"

She evaded his gaze. "I can't reveal a confidence, but it's going to be really hard for her to do what you've just asked of her."

All Marc had done was ask Cassie to take care of his friend. With the likelihood of hypothermia, sure, she needed to get skin to skin with him and warm him up. Big deal. Anyone with a sense of compassion for another human, no matter how prudish, would do whatever it took to save his life, even if that meant going beyond their comfort level. Marc began to worry he might need to get up the mountain tonight—somehow—to help Luke. He wasn't going to leave his friend with someone he couldn't trust to get the job done.

"Will she take care of him?"

Angelina looked at him. "Oh, no doubt! She can't stand to see any living creature suffer, even if that creature is a full-grown man. If she said she'd take care of him, she will. It's just...not going to be easy."

Marc wasn't convinced he could trust Cassie. "There's no way we can safely get anyone up there to get him out until the weather clears in the passes. But if he's in imminent danger... Are you sure he's—?"

Angelina rested her hand on his chest. "Stop worrying until we know more." She leaned her head against his shoulder, and he wrapped his arms around her. *Dio*, it felt sublime to be holding her again.

Angelina cared a lot about Luke. They both did. He'd never really thought anything had happened when she'd gone to Luke's after leaving Marc's house in Denver, but there had always been a part of him that questioned the arrangement. Hell, his own flesh-and-blood brother had screwed the woman he'd once planned to marry. But whenever he saw Angelina and Luke since she'd become Marc's girl, Luke displayed only big-brother affection.

Despite the fact he and Luke were about the same age, Luke sometimes behaved like a brother to Marc, too, closer even than Marc had been with Gino in the end. Of course, Gino's life had been cut short before Marc had had a chance to grow up.

If he'd ever grown up.

"Marc, I know we have a lot we need to talk about, and I know we need to resolve those issues before we become intimate with each other again." Angelina's words brought him out of his musings. He prepared himself for her to send him on his way soon. "But I don't want to be alone tonight."

Wait! That didn't sound like the brush-off he'd been expecting.

"Why don't we go over to my place? We'll be more comfortable while we wait for news from Cassie." She pulled away and gazed up at him. "But we're *just* going to talk. If we sleep, it won't be together. Or we'll be fully clothed. Do you understand?"

"Loud and clear." At this point, sitting up all night with her and talking sounded like the best date they'd ever had. He remembered the marathon sensation-play scene with her the night he and Luke had been invited over for dinner last fall after meeting up with her again at daVinci's.

Come to think of it, they hadn't really dated much. Perhaps they should have done more of that and gotten to know each other better before he'd asked her to move in with him. But he'd known from the moment he'd rescued her at the club she would haunt him if she wasn't by his side for the rest of his life.

Now how could he keep her there?

Ten minutes later, they walked into her living room.

"Sit down, Marc. Let me pour you a glass of wine."

"Coffee might be a better choice. Remember, we're going to be up all night. Talking." He knew she didn't need the reminder. He did.

"Good thinking. I'll start a pot."

While Angelina worked in the kitchen, he walked over to the stereo to choose some music. Italian singers Laura Pausini and Elisa were well represented, but it was Mary Chapin Carpenter's *Time*Sex*Love** CD on the top that caught his eye. He glanced at the playlist and saw *King of Love*. His mind flashed back to the time Angelina had surrendered herself on the sofa nearby. So not what he wanted to listen to right now. Despite spending so much time steering her in Luke's direction, thoughts of her being with anyone but himself churned Marc's gut.

She'd tried to give him the time and space he needed to figure out his shit. But how much patience could one woman have? Would she wait until he figured out what held him back from claiming her as his own?

That constant sense of being trapped, he supposed. Angelina must have sensed it. She hadn't pushed him to commit to anything. Would they ever be able to resume their relationship where they left off—or better yet, move forward into something more solid and permanent?

Next on the stack was Andrea Bocelli's *Romanza*. Much better. He loaded the CD and surveyed the room. She'd only been back in this bungalow a week but had already made it look more like a home than his place felt after living there for years. The only time he'd been happy in his Denver house was when she was with him.

He glanced under the table near the window. Well, almost everything had been put back in place. Her nonna's sewing basket wasn't on the floor where it once was. Not that he would need to be scavenging for playthings tonight. A play scene was not in the cards.

Marc sat down on the peony-print sofa, and Angelina returned a few moments later. "Here you go."

He reached up to take the mug from her and took a sip. Strong, hot, and black. Perfect. He watched her take a tentative sip from her own mug.

"Both of us don't have to stay up. Why don't you enjoy a glass of your white zin, and let me chug *caffè?*"

"No, I won't be able to sleep anyway. I'm too worried about Luke."

Their plans to talk about their relationship tonight would be overshadowed by worry about how Luke was doing. If he didn't get another report in the next hour or so, he'd check in with Cassie.

Angelina sat down at the far end of the sofa and tucked her left foot under her right thigh. He wished she wore a skirt and not jeans. No, he needed to rein in any thoughts of enjoying her body tonight. The prime objective tonight was to talk.

"But I don't mind sharing."

Sharing? He glanced back up at her. What had he missed? Again, flashes of her spread open for Luke invaded his mind. "Beg your pardon?"

"It's just easier to share the same drink, so I made an entire pot."

"Ah, coffee!"

"What did you think I…Oh!" A flush crept into Angelina's cheeks.

He grinned. "Nothing to worry about, *amore.* I do not plan to share you ever again."

"That night with Luke was so out of character for me. I'm glad it didn't go any further. Luke's like a brother to me now. It would be… awkward, to say the least, to face him if we'd done anything more."

Hearing her words relieved any lingering doubts he might have had about the time she'd spent with Luke recently.

I trust them both.

Good thing, because if he couldn't trust Angelina with one of his best friends, then he'd never be the man she needed. Jealousy would shatter any trust they might build.

He raised the mug to his mouth and took another gulp as the music wafted around them. He didn't know how to begin talking about what needed saying. The topic of his origins wasn't easy for him to talk about.

"What happened when you went to Italy, if you don't mind sharing? Did you find your birth father?"

"Sperm donor, more accurately. I come from rather inglorious paternal stock."

She tilted her head, waiting for him to elaborate, but the last person he wanted to talk about was Solari.

"Did you learn anything more about what happened back then?"

He nodded. As much as he wanted to change the subject, he knew she was testing him to see if he'd share even the more sordid and painful parts of his life.

"He did drop a bit of a bombshell. I don't know if he's telling the truth, but he said Mama actually gave birth to me, but that he and Emiliana raised me because of the stigma of illegitimacy."

"*Mio Dio*, Marc! That's not a bombshell, it's an H-bomb. What if what he says is true? Why haven't you asked Mama?"

Marc's blasé attitude about the whole sordid mess flared into anger. "How exactly would you suggest I phrase the question, Angelina? 'So, Mama, any truth to the rumor that you slept with your brother-in-law and that I'm the resulting love child?'"

Angelina set her mug on the coffee table and scooted closer to the middle of the sofa and placed a hand on his knee.

"I'm sorry, Marc. But you know I'm right. This is something that needs to be discussed. You don't know whose story is the truth, and it's eating you alive."

He ran his hand through his hair. "No, *bella*, the only thing that's eating me alive is that we're discussing this when we could find something much more interesting to talk about—or do." The opening strains of *Por Amor* burst from the speakers. "Let's dance."

Angelina pulled away, retreating to the far end of the sofa again. The hurt on her face was evident, but at least he could breathe again. "I'm not sure that would be a good idea."

Merda. This isn't the way he envisioned tonight going. He was making the same fucking mistake as before, shutting her out. But why did she have to push so hard on the issue of talking to Mama?

"Why not? I need the diversion."

She scrutinized him a long moment, making him uncomfortable. Suddenly, she rose from the sofa and held out her hand to him. "Okay. Let's dance then."

He stood and walked around the coffee table to join her. There wasn't much of an area for dancing, but he didn't care. The main thing was having her in his arms again, however brief that time might be.

They swayed to the music a moment. "Thanks for staying with me tonight. After what happened to Luke, I wouldn't want any of you on the roads heading back to Denver."

Good. A safe topic they could agree upon. "The main roads probably are fine."

"Well, I'm glad I don't have to worry about you."

"You'd have worried, even after the shit I've been?"

She rested her head on his shoulder. "This is what someone does when they love a person. There isn't any logic to it."

She still loved him?

What did she need to hear from him?

They danced into the next track, until she pulled away slightly to look up at him. "You've grown awfully quiet. What are you thinking?"

"That's a loaded question…" *that I do not wish to answer.*

"I wouldn't ask if I didn't want to know. I don't like it when you shut me out, Marc. I'm trying to learn to let it bother me less. I hope and pray some day you will come to trust me enough to share your thoughts. That you'll allow me to be a part of the major decisions in your life. Maybe even let me try to meet some of your emotional needs."

With relative certainty, he believed she would never harm him—not intentionally anyway. But lowering his defenses invited too many risks for him to take.

"What if I can't?"

She paused for so long, he began to worry that there would be conditions placed on how long she'd give him. No woman waited forever for a man to get his head on straight.

"I have faith in you. One day, you'll realize I am not one of the people who shattered your ability to trust." She traced his jawline with her index finger. "I will work hard every day to earn your trust."

Her words blazed like a beacon shining through the dark cave he'd lived in these past couple months… No. More like forever.

She pulled him closer. "While we're waiting for news about Luke tonight, I want us to figure out what derailed us, so we can fix it and get back on track. Tell me what you *need*, Marc."

His throat tightened as he heard her urgent plea. He didn't need a woman to fulfill his needs. That would create an obligation on his part; obligation left one vulnerable. What if he failed—again? He wouldn't allow himself to show weakness to her or any other woman. Besides, focusing on satisfying her needs usually resulted in keeping her from demanding anything deeper from him.

Angelina waited no longer for him to respond to her declaration. "All I know is that I'm miserable when we're apart."

"Me too, *amore*. I've missed holding you like this." That much he could admit truthfully. Her words gave him hope that she would give him time, and he relaxed a little more. "I thought I'd lost you forever, *cara*."

"We still haven't resolved anything. You know I want what's best for you. So even if you don't want me to point out things that make you uncomfortable, I will continue to do so."

"Tonight, let's just be together in this moment and leave the past where it belongs. We can't do anything about that, but we do have some control over the future." When she opened her mouth to speak, he pressed two fingers on her lips. "Shhh. No more talking. Let's just dance."

She sighed and pressed her cheek against his chest, tracing a finger down his jawbone to his chin. "I think what you need, Marc, is to be held. Cuddled. To be loved by a woman who doesn't want you to give her anything but your presence."

He took her upper arms and pushed her away. "I don't *need* anyone, pet. My role in life is to provide for the needs of others. To fulfill *your* needs. To make *you* happy fulfills my needs."

Marc needed to reassert his authority over her. To regain control. "Strip."

The sadness and disappointment in her shimmering brown eyes tugged at his heart. "Marc—" She cleared her throat. "I love you. Nothing you do or say will ever destroy that love, even now when you're so clueless you drive me insane." She stepped away from him. "What I need right now, though, is some space. Good night."

Without a backward glance, she turned and walked down the hallway. He waited a few minutes for her to change her mind and return, but she didn't.

She'd walked away from him yet again. Only she wouldn't leave her own house, would she?

The only way he knew how to express his feelings for a woman was to make love to her. *Merda,* how else would he be able to...

Wait. They hadn't had sex the first night they'd shared that bed in the other room. Feelings of extreme vulnerability assailed him that night as well. Lost and confused. Despite that, he'd never felt a closer connection with any woman before—or since.

Not wanting to have them part like this, he followed her through the open bedroom door and heard her blowing her nose in the bathroom. She hadn't closed that door either, so he entered the closet and stood in the doorway of the bathroom, watching as she plucked two more tissues from a box and dabbed at her eyes and cheeks.

He'd hurt her. Again. He fought the urge to wrap her in his arms and comfort her, but he needed distance, too. Being together tonight had been a mistake.

"What were you expecting to happen, *cara*? Some great breakthrough into figuring out the enigma that is Marc D'Alessio? Well, good luck with that. I've been trying for months—no, *years!* Give up. He's a lost cause."

"Marc, you're worth the time, even when you're being an ass. I wish you could let go of the pain from the past, so we can get to the bottom of whatever is eating away at you." She wrapped her arms around his waist, but he broke free.

Trapped.

Unable to formulate a response she'd want to hear, he turned and left the room, walking into the kitchen where he pulled a bottle of her rot-gut white zinfandel off the wine rack. He opened several drawers before finding the one with the corkscrew in it then remembered that Angelina's wines rarely contained corks. He rolled his eyes. Marc was the one who kept things tightly corked. Picking up the bottle, he twisted off the cap and poured himself a glassful.

His phone vibrated in his pants, reminding him of Luke's situation. *Merda,* he couldn't lose himself in *vino* tonight. Already he'd forgotten about Luke once. Glancing at the phone, he recognized the number as the one Karla had given him for Cassie earlier.

"Yes?"

"Just wanted to give you an update, as requested." Cassie's voice had an edge to it; she didn't want to have to talk with him. But she *had* called, which was something.

"Luke is sleeping. He's been in and out of sleep the last couple hours. When he wakes up, I understand most of what he's saying."

"Good. How's his body temperature?"

"Warmer. He's not shivering as violently but still does sometimes. Should I try to feed him anything the next time he wakes?"

"Don't worry about food tonight. He ate before he left the bar. Keep him hydrated. Water tonight and try some unsalted soup or something light tomorrow."

"I'll start a pot now." She paused before adding, "Thanks, Marc."

"Thank *you*, Cassie. You're doing a great job. All Luke's friends appreciate you."

When she said nothing more, he said good-bye and ended the call. He drew a deep breath and let it out slowly.

"Sounds like he's better, doesn't it, Marc?" He turned to see Angelina in the doorway. The worry in her voice made him open his arms and she walked into them. "Is it a problem if he's sleeping too much?"

"It's a good sign that he's not shivering as much and sounds like he's resting but not unconscious."

"Cassie's handling this better than I expected."

"I'm not as worried now, that's for sure."

He held on to her, not wanting to break contact and start rehashing his past or their issues. He knew she wanted him to lower his defenses and seek answers about his childhood. Could she accept him without resolving those issues? Would she let him continue to run from his past provided he wasn't running from her any longer?

Weariness crept into his bones. He wouldn't find answers tonight. "Why don't we get some sleep? I don't expect to hear from Cassie again until morning. We don't know what's ahead over the next few days."

Angelina nodded but didn't let go.

"I'll take the sofa."

"Marc…"

She paused so long, he prompted her to continue. "Yes, *amore?*"

"Having even two walls separating us is too much for me right now. I don't want to sleep alone tonight."

She wanted to sleep with him? Operative word being *sleep*. She'd made that very clear and he would honor her limits. *Dio*, but he wished it could be different. Sexually, they were compatible. Even during sex—*especially* during sex—he could keep an emotional distance. Cuddling? Lying next to each other and falling asleep—that made him too vulnerable.

But she needed him tonight. He pulled away and reached out his hand. "Let's go to bed."

* * *

Marc's hand in hers gave Angelina a sense of security she'd missed. They walked down the hallway toward the place where she'd first started to explore submission with him, hesitating inside the doorway as she looked at the bed. She couldn't keep at bay the memory of holding onto Nonna's headboard in honor bondage as she fought so hard to please him and do as he'd instructed. Her pussy grew wet just thinking about that scene.

She nibbled her lower lip. "Maybe this isn't such a good idea."

"You're in control, *cara*."

She glanced at the bed and then back at him, tamping down her rampant desire and nodding. "We'll just cuddle." She knew they'd already established that, but needed to remind herself. It was going to be a long night.

"You know you can trust me, *amore*."

"I know I can, Marc. It's me I'm worried about at the moment." She grinned and reached up to undo the buttons on her blouse.

Marc brushed her hands aside, leaving her skin tingling. "Do not remove your clothing."

She lowered her head in instant submission, but he lifted her chin until she met his gaze.

"No, *cara*, you are not submitting to me tonight."

Hurt by his rejection of her gift of submission, she took a step back.

"I'm not a masochist, *amore*. Seeing your beautiful body naked and not being able to make love to you is hard enough, but having you in submission as well will be torture of the worst kind."

"Oh!" She grinned in relief. "I'll just go in the bathroom and change into a nightgown."

"Sounds perfect, *cara*."

"I'll wear the flannel one."

She didn't miss the disappointment in his eyes. "I'll wear my boxer briefs."

Angelina's heart fluttered at his words, her mind instantly flashing to the countless times she'd helped him remove them herself. Sometimes with her teeth. Her face flushed at the memory.

Control yourself.

She intended to maintain her resolve. Cuddling. *Only* cuddling. She walked over to the dresser and pulled out one of her gowns, tossing it over her shoulder as she walked toward the bathroom.

If they hadn't become sexual so fast last fall, maybe they could have built a stronger foundation that would have weathered the avalanche of revelations and trust issues they'd been bombarded with this winter. Marc's solitary quest for answers—shutting her out—hadn't helped.

Why wouldn't he talk with Mama, the very person who would know what had happened back then? Clearly he wasn't ready to face whatever he'd been running from his entire life.

Had he truly come to grips with anything in her absence? Not likely. All she knew was that she wanted him to include her in this journey of self-discovery, to lean on her when times got rough, and to celebrate when things worked out. She wanted it all. They had no problems with their sexual connection. The kink was good, too. Now how to make the rest of their relationship work?

Marc was far from ready for any kind of long-term commitment. Would he ever be able to commit? Savannah's words about how hard it was for someone with early childhood abandonment issues to form relationships caused her to doubt whether loving him was going to be enough.

How long could she continue to wait for him? She wouldn't turn twenty-six for a few more months, so her biological clock wasn't ticking too loudly yet, but she did want to have a family someday.

And she wanted those children to be Marc's, not some random sperm donor she had yet to meet. The thought of being with anyone but Marc was out of the question. She wouldn't give up on him yet. He was worth it—even if that meant she'd have to wait a very long time.

For several minutes after she'd done everything she could to prepare herself for bed, she stared at the bathroom door. Could she stay strong for him tonight? What had possessed her to think she could cuddle up next to Marc and not want more?

I can't hide in here all night.

Drawing a deep breath, she steeled her shoulders and prepared to face the alpha wolf waiting in her den, er, bedroom.

Her wolf needed nurturing, and she was just the she-wolf to do it. Steeling herself, Angelina opened the door and walked through the closet into the bedroom.

Marc didn't play fair. He'd removed his shirt and dress pants. Yes, his black boxer briefs remained on, but his rigid cock left nothing to her long-deprived imagination. Avoiding staring at his erection, she focused instead on his pecs, specifically at the sprinkling of hair between them that she'd missed running her fingers through for so long.

Why did the man have to wear form-fitting, sexy-as-sin black boxer briefs? Averting her gaze, she made a bee-line for the bed. "Bathroom's all yours."

"I'll only be a minute."

"Take your time. There's a new toothbrush in the upper right-hand drawer of the vanity."

"*Grazie.*"

She pulled the quilt, blankets, and top sheet back. Sleeping alone, she'd burrowed under all the layers, but if she would be sleeping next to Marc tonight wearing this heavy gown to boot, she didn't need any more heat. After separating the quilt and folding it at the bottom of the bed, she climbed in and reached to turn off the bedside lamp before he returned.

Please let me be half asleep before he joins me.

Scooting to the opposite side of the bed, she pulled the covers up to her neck and waited. The shower started. *Don't think of him being naked in your bathroom, Angie.*

What did she hope to accomplish by cuddling with him tonight? Somehow the nurturing thoughts had deserted her. Would he make himself vulnerable to her, or take his usual tack and attempt to distract her by trying to melt off her panties again? As if he had to try all that hard.

Stay strong for him, Angie.

The last thing they needed was to complicate matters further by having sex tonight. The water shut off, and her heart rate tripled.

Breathe.

She closed her eyes. Would he buy that she'd fallen asleep while waiting for him? Hardly.

Don't let him know you're a nervous wreck.

So much rested on tonight. Angelina turned around to face the door to her closet and waited. This house was so small compared to Marc's. His mansion was more modern, had a kitchen to die for, and sported enough square footage to house the entire US Olympic ski team. But she'd missed the intimate times they'd shared in her cozy little house before she'd moved in with him last October. He seemed more relaxed here, too.

Marc opened the bathroom door, and she watched as a wall of steam billowed through the doorway. He entered the room, and she saw he wore a towel tucked in at his waist. *Dio*, help her. She knew Marc liked to sleep in the nude and usually insisted she do the same, but they had a deal. And she wasn't submitting to him tonight.

"You'd better have briefs on under that towel." Or was he just trying to hide his erection? No, he hadn't seemed worried about that earlier.

He grinned. "I didn't bring a change of clothes, so I washed them out in the sink. No worries, though. I'll keep this towel on. It's dry."

He lifted the sheet and blankets and crawled between them. Just how long did he expect the end of that towel to remain tucked into the makeshift waistband while he moved around in the bed? Marc had never been one to sleep calmly. The man was all arms and legs when he slept.

Angelina reminded herself that tonight wasn't about allowing Marc to put the moves on her. He'd always used sex as a diversion whenever she'd gotten too close, but not tonight. If she wanted his needs to be met, she'd have to remain steadfast. Focused. For both of them.

She'd gone for months without sex. What was one more night?

Only she hadn't had Marc's hot body as temptation before, except in her dreams.

Focus on his needs.

Angelina tucked her arm under his and around his waist. Her hand automatically went to his butt cheek before she moved it up to his back.

Don't touch his butt!

Marc placed a kiss on her forehead and drew her closer, despite her attempts at resisting. "You smell so good. I've missed holding you like this, too."

"I'm not sure this is a good idea after all."

"We're only going to cuddle."

"Is that what this is?"

He grinned. "Seems so to me, unless you grab my ass again."

"I didn't grab…"

His hand stroked down her arm and then homed in on her breast, tweaking her nipple. "Tit for tat."

She smacked his hand. "No, Marc! Behave!"

Marc pulled his hand away.

Angelina stroked the stubble on his cheek and traced a path down his jaw and neck. "What do you need from me tonight?"

His eyes grew shuttered. Should she push, or let it go for another day? If she just let him retreat, they'd have gotten no closer to resolving their issues.

"Tell me, Marc. I can't read your mind."

He had said the same to her so many times. Maybe hearing the words thrown back at him would drive home the fact that he'd rarely shared his needs or innermost thoughts with her.

When she reached out to touch his cheek again, he grabbed her wrist and stilled her progress. For a long moment, they simply stared at one another, before he released her and reclined onto his back looking up at the ceiling.

"I envy what you have with your family, *cara*."

She sat up and looked down at him, raising her eyebrows in surprise. "What do you mean? You have a wonderful family that loves you very much."

"Yes, I know, but there have been too many lies, secrets. Too much trust has been shattered. I don't even know who my family is anymore. You, however, know where you came from. You have had a lifetime to build trust in the people around you. I've been betrayed too many times. I lost that ability to trust at a very young age. It's very difficult for me…"

"Who have you accepted as your mother, Marc?"

He turned to her, puzzled. "Mama is the only person I'll ever think of as being my mother."

"You believe her, then?"

He idly traced a pattern on her shoulder, causing her errant nipples to swell, but his gaze remained on her face.

"I don't know what to believe. I still don't understand why she didn't tell me the truth when she adopted me. Gino knew."

"You were just a little boy then, lost and confused. The woman you thought to be your mother had died suddenly. Besides, society was so different back then. You know how traditional those small Italian villages could be. Still are. She didn't want to have you treated badly by other children because of a mistake she'd made with the wrong man."

"There was no reason for her to continue to lie about having given birth to me after we left Brescia. I was eleven. No one in America would have cared."

Angelina wondered about that, too. "Maybe she was worried what Gramps would think. She'd just found him and I'm sure wanted to make a good impression on her father."

"You're forgetting that Gramps fathered Mama illegitimately while my grandmother cared for him in her home after he was wounded in the Po Valley Campaign. He wouldn't have thrown stones."

"There's a double standard for men and women, Marc, and it was even worse back then."

He nodded. "I guess so."

They stared at each other in silence for a while before she broke into his thoughts. "Have you told her how you feel yet?"

He glanced away, and the motion of his fingers on her collarbone stopped. She reached up and stroked his forehead, letting her fingertip trail over his temple and cheek. "I think she can help heal that wounded little boy inside you better than anyone else."

He grabbed her hand again as his gaze zeroed in on her, ferocity in his green eyes. "I'm a grown man. The past can't be changed. I have to accept what happened and move on."

"How's that worked for you so far?"

"Touché." He glanced away. "I'll admit, I have no clue what to say to her."

"Saying that you understand might be a good start. That you forgive her for not being honest with you."

"But I *don't* understand. Far from it."

He didn't say whether he could forgive Mama, but Angelina didn't think he'd gotten there yet. Maybe she could help him process the feelings a little bit.

"Okay, you say you accept that she's your mother, because you've known no other your entire life. I think she needs to hear that from you."

He sighed and cupped her cheek with his warm hand. She fought the urge to turn her face toward his palm and kiss him. Every ounce of her being wanted to nurture and cuddle him, but he didn't need coddling. He needed prodding.

Once more, his gaze became shuttered. "Let's get some sleep. I'll check in with Cassie in the morning and see how Luke is doing."

He'd slammed the door shut, but for a few moments beforehand, he'd left it open just enough to shine some light on his thoughts and insecurities.

"Good night, Marc."

She pushed his shoulder, guiding him onto his back and placing her head on his right pec. Marc wrapped his arm around her and stroked her hair.

Her eyelids grew heavy.

Home.

*   *   *

Angelina's head grew heavier and he knew she'd fallen into a deep sleep. The dark circles under her eyes and the weight loss were testament to how hard she'd taken these past couple of months. Conversely, he'd gained weight during her absence by eating out too much. He'd missed her fabulous, healthy meals.

Hell, he'd missed everything about her. Quiet times like these when he could just hold her. Watching her dress to go out—or undress when they came home. Sharing a meal with her. Could they sort this mess out and get back together?

How would she feel about living with him again, especially if it wasn't in the Denver house with a kitchen that was any chef's wet dream?

Don't think about wet dreams right now.

Still, she loved that kitchen. It was her favorite room, unless they were playing somewhere else in the house. They'd practically lived either in the kitchen or the bedroom when they were together with occasional visits to the playroom. But he'd never needed a well-equipped playroom to play.

He still needed to ask Adam and Karla what their final decision was on buying the house from him. He'd planned to check with Adam earlier this evening, but then all hell had broken loose with Luke's accident.

Living in Denver once fed that place in his soul that had been disconnected when he'd returned from Iraq. Adam once encouraged him to find some cause that made him feel needed, and he'd latched onto search-and-rescue work. Not to mention the Masters at Arms Club, but it was more the connection with his Marine friends that fed his soul. But Damián and Adam had new families now.

Had he ruined any chance of having Angelina in his life again? He'd tried to share some of himself with her a few minutes ago, but how much would be enough to satisfy her? Even if she agreed to be with him again, he didn't want to be cooped up in the city.

Angelina moaned and wrapped her arm across his abdomen. Memories of the first night he'd spent in this bed holding Angelina in his arms seeped into his consciousness. He had thought he would have only the one night with her and still wasted much of that night and following week trying to figure out how he could get her interested in Luke instead. He'd known from experience no woman would be satisfied with the little he had to offer.

Mine.

He held her tighter. The thought of anyone else touching his girl made him ill. He cherished the months she'd been with him. His outlook on women had changed drastically since they'd met. Before, he'd trusted no woman and had kept even his male friends at arm's length emotionally. He'd lowered the walls a little bit since Angelina entered his life but had never totally opened himself up. A year ago, he wouldn't have been able to imagine trusting a woman as much as he did this one.

What made her different? She was Italian. He didn't understand his aversion to Italian women, one he'd had long before Melissa had come into his life during college. Allowing himself to become vulnerable to Angelina had shaken him to the core. The time she'd topped him had been nothing compared to coming to her at Rico's place tonight with his heart on his sleeve. She could have crushed him, told him to take a hike.

Instead, she opened her home to him once more.

Angelina wouldn't take any guff off of anyone. Her father and older brothers had helped prepare her well for the assholes of the world—including him.

Angelina moaned again, and he reached up to stroke the creases from her forehead.

"You're safe, *amore*. Sleep now."

Soon she relaxed against him again. Feeling the weight of her head on his chest gave him a sense of peace he hadn't felt in a long time. He wished they could return to the time before New Year's. Everything had been going so well then.

Or had it? Perhaps that had been yet another illusion. His inability to fully trust Angelina would have become an issue at some point. Here he thought he was trying to win her trust when all along he was the trust-deficient one.

He glanced around her bedroom. He'd grown up in a resort condo unit—a glorified hotel suite, really. Before Angelina had made the Denver house feel more like a home, he hadn't paid attention to the difference between his home with Angelina and the one he'd grown up in back in Aspen. In those few months, she had made a number of changes, but Angelina's house here in Aspen Corners reminded him of the one he remembered from his childhood in Italy. Cozy. Intimate. Perfect for a couple or a family starting out.

Or a woman living alone. Angelina hadn't said anything about wanting him to move in. He'd better not start making too many plans. He hadn't won his girl back yet.

Marc rested his chin on her head and closed his eyes. So much of his life remained unsettled.

*   *   *

"*No, Zietta Natalia!*"

Angelina jolted awake when something forcefully pushed her away.

Marc screamed in Italian. "I don't want to come out!"

She raised herself up from Marc's chest, leaning on her elbow, and gazed down at his contorted features in the early-morning light. It took a moment for her to remember why he was here in her bed.

In her best Mistress A voice, she commanded, "Marc. Wake up." He blinked awake instantly this time and stared at her in confusion. "You had a bad dream." Again.

"Sorry. Didn't mean to wake you."

She shook her head. "Want to talk about it?"

"Not particularly."

"You called out in Italian to your mama—only you called her Auntie Natalia."

He shoved her head off his chest and onto the pillow. "Drop it, Angelina. I said I don't want to talk about it."

"Marc, I hurt when you hurt. How can I help you?" Her thumb moved back up to stroke his bottom lip, hoping to coax them to open and speak.

"I don't need you—your help."

She yanked her hand back as if he'd bitten it.

He reached up to tuck a strand of hair behind her ear. "*Cara*, you know I would do anything for you—"

She shook her head. "Then talk to me. I'm not asking you to do anything *for* me other than to stop shutting me out."

"I know what you're asking, *amore*, but it's not something I can give."

"Why can't you talk to me the way you did earlier tonight?" His shuttered expression told her that wasn't going to happen. "What is it you need from me, Marc?"

"I need nothing from you!"

She didn't try to mask the pain those words caused her. She'd asked for honesty, hadn't she? She saw the bitter truth in his response. For whatever reason, he was incapable of letting himself be vulnerable with her, probably with any woman.

Angelina got up from bed and pulled her robe on as if it were a suit of armor. "Let me tell you what you need, Marc."

"What is that?" Was it fear she saw in his eyes?

Why couldn't you trust me, Marc?

Suddenly everything came into focus for her. "You need to leave. I can't be in a relationship with someone who doesn't need me. Who doesn't even trust me."

He didn't fight to save their relationship, if they'd ever really had one. He dressed and walked toward the door. Tears burned her eyes.

Please leave before you see me cry.

"I'm sorry I can't give you what you need, *cara*."

"Can't or won't?"

He shrugged.

"You unleashed the submissive in me, Marc, in this very room. If I am not permitted to serve your needs, I am left with nothing."

Marc held onto the bedroom doorknob for a long moment. Could he hear what she tried to express? Would it make any difference?

He straightened his shoulders and opened the door. She watched him leave through a blur of tears knowing he wouldn't come back again.

She'd gambled her heart—and lost.

Chapter Twenty-Three

"When the *fuck* are you going to figure out why the hell you keep screwing things up with that girl?"

"I'm trying, Adam."

"Sure could've fooled me."

Marc scrubbed his hand over his face. He'd barely slept in days. Exhaustion made it impossible for him to think anymore. "I know. You're right, but I'm stuck. That's why I came to you."

"What do you think I can do?"

He hadn't really come here for empathy, but thought Adam would understand. Hell, the man had driven his own girl away to Chicago, a helluva lot further than where Angelina had run. But Adam had managed to win Karla back.

"You know me better than anyone." Marc really had let very few people close enough for any kind of glimpse inside him. Adam had been there in the field hospital in Fallujah when he'd been doped up and at his weakest. He had been one of the few to even temporarily breach his defenses. Between the lack of sleep for more than a week trying to figure out how to get Angelina back and worrying about Luke the last couple of days, he'd reached the end of his rope.

"Losing Angelina the first time was like losing a part of my soul." He cleared his throat. "Worse than the aftermath of what happened to us on that rooftop in Fallujah. Worse than losing Gino, because I'd lost him six months before he actually got killed."

Marc's eyes filled, and he looked away before Adam could pounce on that sign of weakness. He would not break down in front of Adam. He took a moment to regain control by drawing several deep breaths.

"I expected her to come back any day. We're right in so many ways. The sex is fantastic, she enjoys the hell out of the kink, and I've given her the kitchen of her dreams. What more could I give her?"

Adam raised his eyebrows briefly, but remained silent. Okay, that hadn't come out right, but Marc decided to keep going. "She said she wanted me to open up and let her in. I've never opened myself up more to any other woman. Never wanted to. Giving anyone that much control scares me shitless. I guess I couldn't give her what she needed."

Silence. After a few awkward moments, Marc continued. "Anyway, she didn't come running back, as I'd expected. Instead, she went to Luke for comfort and shelter."

"Anything going on between them?"

Marc shook his head. "No. Other than one time last fall where the three of us got pretty intense, they're practically brother and sister."

"You're sure she isn't trolling for your replacement?"

"Hell, no! You saw how it was with us at daVinci's bar. There's still something between us."

"So what are you doing here in my office two hours away from her instead of sitting down with her and talking this out?"

Marc sighed. "I shut down on her again yesterday morning. She basically told me not to come back until I decide that I want a real relationship." Marc leaned forward, leaning on the arms of the chair. "Adam, I don't fucking know what that looks like. What's wrong with me? I'm going to lose her if I don't figure it out soon."

Adam smiled, which threw Marc off-kilter even more. What did he find so fucking funny?

"What do you plan to do about it?"

"That's why I came to you. I don't have the first clue where to start to unfuck this."

"I'm no fucking head shrinker. Why haven't you talked to someone all these months who's trained in that department instead of hiding out in the mountains? You could have been facing this head on for weeks, if not months."

"It's too easy to run away from a psychO's couch."

"A what?"

"Sorry, psych officer. I forget the Navy and the Marines have their own jargon." Where was he? "Besides, Angelina isn't going to wait forever. I've made her wait long enough. I want you to do whatever it takes to break down these barriers holding me back. I know you won't pull any punches. I trust you to do what needs to be done."

"You won't get an argument from me there. Just hearing you say you trust me enough to yank a knot in your ass and get you to face your demons is news to me. I never thought you trusted yourself, much less me or anyone else."

Marc hated hearing those words, but realized Adam spoke the truth. Maybe that lack of trust and security is what kept him from having as close a relationship as Adam had with Damián. His master sergeant didn't ride Marc's ass as hard as he did Damián's either. Something Marc often envied was their father-son relationship.

"Look, I need some kind of mindfuck or something like the one Damián pulled with Savannah the other day. I swear there's just some kind of mental block that keeps me from relating to people on anything more than a superficial level. I'm not only keeping women at a distance, but you guys, as well." Marc drew a deep breath after delivering his heartfelt spiel. He needed to get beyond whatever was holding him back. In a ragged whisper, he begged, "You have to help me get her back."

"I can't."

Adam's outright refusal to help took Marc by surprise. He found no words to form a response.

Adam walked around his desk to tower over Marc and placed his hands on his hips. "You're the only one who can win her back. I might be able to help you get to the bottom of what's going on in your head, but the truth might be more than you want to face."

"I'll do anything you say at this point."

"You sure about that?"

"Absolutely."

"You willing to try an interrogation scene?"

Interrogation scenes could be effective in getting at triggers and buried memories. He'd seen Adam and Grant perform them in the club before. Some had caused him to remember his SERE Course training in the Navy where he'd been taught to survive, evade, resist, and escape. If captured or lost behind enemy lines, the tactics taught him what to do if tortured in order to maintain some measure of self-worth. Truth was that no one could hold out forever. The best one could hope to accomplish was to hold on to their dignity and avoid giving in completely.

Could his training help him if the enemy he faced was his own subconscious mind? The training had been so intense, he'd been given R&R leave afterward to recover. Most of the BDSM interrogations he'd seen, while intense, lasted only a few hours at most, and usually resulted in the subject confessing which playing card was being concealed from the interrogator. How could that be enough?

"Do you think we're going to get anywhere with the typical club scene?"

"Can't say. If I feel the need to employ SERE Course tactics, are you willing to subject yourself to that level of intensity? This isn't the Corps. You have a choice this time."

Hell, no, he wasn't sure. But deep down, he didn't have a choice either. No doubt in his mind it would take something along those lines to get him to break down the barriers he had painstakingly erected with years of practice. Perhaps he'd break before Adam had to take it to the SERE extreme of sleep-deprivation psychosis and torture. He hoped so. The short- and long-term effects of such manipulation weren't anything he wanted to mess with. But if he did nothing, he was doomed to spend the rest of his life floundering much as he had been all year—perhaps most of his life, if he ever admitted to himself how empty it had been until Angelina had come along.

"It might be my only chance of finding out what has me so twisted up inside."

"I want to hear the words of consent before we go any further."

Marc paused to make sure he wanted to go through anything like that again. The prize at the other end would be being able to make a commitment to Angelina—if he didn't wind up in the psych ward at the VA.

"I want you to do whatever it takes. If that means SERE training revisited, then so be it."

Adam nodded, giving no visual cues as to what he thought about the idea. The scene wouldn't be easy for him either. It was one thing to break the enemy and quite another to do the same to a friend.

"I appreciate that you're willing to do this."

"I'm not making any promises it's going to help." Adam reached for a legal pad and pen. "First, though, we need to set some ground rules. Any triggers I need to be aware of?"

Marc thought back to an aversion he'd had for a very long time, but couldn't explain. "Stilettos."

"Wasn't planning on wearing any. What else?"

Marc would have laughed if he weren't so nervous.

"I'm sure I've got a mixed bag of crap from childhood, adolescence, even adulthood that may churn up and need to be addressed."

"What types of implements would you place on the hard-limit list?"

Did Adam plan to use them if Marc identified them? Didn't matter. Marc had to answer honestly. "Paddles."

"Hard or soft?"

"Hard." *Very* hard. Marc didn't mind using them, and Angelina sure loved them, but he hadn't let her use one on him. She'd honored his limits.

"What else?"

"Not too crazy about ball gags."

Angelina had used one on him, and he hadn't totally freaked out. "Soft, but leaning toward hard, if that makes sense."

Adam nodded. "Blindfolds?"

"No known issue. But you need to push me to the limit if I'm going to get past whatever is holding me back."

"I didn't say I planned to avoid your triggers or limits. I just need to know what they are, if possible."

Merda. What did Adam plan to do with him? Marc's heart rate ramped up.

"Doc, if you had to guess the root of your problem, what would it be?"

"Women."

"Wanna be a little more specific?"

"Italian women."

"And yet you're doing all this to win back a certain Italian woman?"

Marc shrugged. "I'm an enigma."

"Wrapped in a fucking riddle." Adam tapped the pen against the pad.

Marc grinned, even though there was nothing humorous about his situation.

"Could this have anything to do with the girl Gino stole from you? Damián mentioned some Italian bitch—sorry, *woman*—giving Angelina a hard time when you took her to your family's resort for New Year's."

"No need to apologize. And, yes, Melissa is Italian, but my aversion must have started before her. Not sure why I wasn't the one running that time. Maybe I never really surrendered enough of myself for it to be anything more than physical. What can I say? I was young and horny; it was more of a grudge fuck than anything meaningful."

Adam nodded his understanding. "Who else do I need to consider? Have any issues with your mother?"

"Don't we all?"

"Anything specific about *your* mother?" Adam clearly didn't want to discuss issues with his own mother.

How to explain the situation, well, as far as he could even understand it himself? "I'm not sure Mama *is* my mother."

"Come again?"

"I think she's my aunt and later adopted Gino and me after my birth mother died suddenly when I was three. But Mama could be lying about that, too."

"Jesus, Marc, you sure you don't want to set up an appointment with a shrink at the VA? Why don't you just talk with your mother—aunt, whatever the fuck she is."

Marc shook his head no. "She's the only mother I've ever known, or can remember at least. I've had a conversation with her about my origins, but I am certain she skirted the truth. I've also flown to Italy and talked with my biological father. He's a pompous ass and a womanizer. If not for Angelina, I probably would have wound up being just like him twenty-five years from now. I guess blood is thicker than water."

"You're not pompous. And, as far as I've seen, you've only been with one woman at a time. Might have been joined by another Dom on occasion to fulfill some sub's fantasy for a scene, but there still was only one woman at a time."

Maybe he wasn't as fucked up as he thought. "I guess I've just gone through too many of them over the years. I could never commit to any of them."

"Maybe none of the others was right for you."

"Possibly. But Angelina's the one. I want to share the rest of my life with her." *But I'm going to lose her if I don't get my shit together.* Marc blinked at the stinging in his eyes.

Adam nodded. "What else do you know about your past that might be relevant?"

"Solari—my sperm-donor father—said he and Mama, my adopted ma-ma, had an affair that resulted in my birth."

"This is sounding like a fucking soap opera. Is he credible?"

Marc ran a hand through his hair. "How the hell should I know? I can't trust anyone."

"No small wonder, but why do you put your faith in an ass you hardly know when you've known your mother your entire life, or close to it? Blood has nothing to do with who your family is. Joni's mom taught me more about good parenting than my own parents did. Surely you can see that Mrs. D'Alessio *is* more your mother than anyone who gave you up for adoption."

Marc avoided eye contact. "There's something she isn't telling me. For all I know, she gave birth to me. So why won't she just tell me that? Why should it be a secret thirty-four years later?"

"Since when does a parent have to tell her kids everything?"

He wasn't getting anywhere with Adam. How could he make him understand the way he felt?

Adam leaned forward and propped his elbows on the desk. "What are you expecting me to get out of you if you aren't able to remember on your own?"

"Find out what the hell I'm blocking out. I need answers."

Adam thought for a long time and came to some sort of decision. He rested his hip on the edge of the desk. "Marc, I know how hard it is to sort out shit from the past. Last year, I started having flashbacks about how my dad died. Hell, I was convinced I'd murdered him myself."

Holy shit. Marc had no idea the man's father had even been murdered. He didn't really know a lot about Adam's past. The man didn't talk much about anything like that.

"How did you know you didn't do it?"

"That's the thing, if left to my own repressed memories that had started bubbling up for some damned reason, maybe because my defenses were down after the cougar attack, I'd have gone to my grave thinking that's what happened. I was ready to go to the authorities in Minneapolis and turn myself in when Karla, with Grant's interference, located my mother."

Marc couldn't tell if he was happy about the women interfering in his past, but he had seemed proud to have his mother at his wedding.

"That's when I found out what really happened. There was a time I didn't ever want to face her again, but she held the key to so much information I never would have discovered poking around my head. I still don't remember that night with any clarity. Our minds will fight to the death to keep us from seeing some things."

"You think there's something that fucked up in my head?"

Adam reached out and squeezed Marc's shoulder but didn't respond.

Marc thought he'd break down then and there. He'd closed himself off from everyone for months. Just having that simple human contact did something to him. His eyes filled with tears, but no fucking way would he cry, even if he did hover on the edge of exhaustion.

Marc leaned back in the seat, breaking contact, and Adam returned to his seat behind the desk. Perhaps they both needed the desk as a buffer. Marc breathed a little easier again.

"If your real mother died when you were three, your mind had no way of processing reality at that age. Being abandoned by your mother that young would fuck up any kid. Doesn't take a fucking magician to figure that one out."

"How can it be repressed if I know it happened?"

"You said yourself you didn't know about another mother until recently. It's information you have lying on the surface now, but until you can face that moment of ultimate separation head on, you'll remain that little boy who's afraid to love again for fear of losing another person in his life."

Marc narrowed his gaze before he looked away, scowling. This conversation had gotten deeper than anything he and Adam had ever discussed.

Adam leaned his elbows on the desktop. "You know as well as I do nothing we try is going to guarantee any accuracy in retrieving long-buried memories. With both types of interrogations, those in the club and ones using SERE School tactics, you get more reliable results if the subject is at least aware on a conscious level of the information the interrogator is trying to obtain. Mindfucks are most effective on someone who isn't expecting one."

"I feel like the information is right there, I just can't retrieve it. I wasn't so young that I'd have zero memory of it. My biological father dropped a few hints about what happened."

"May *I* talk with your parents?"

"Which ones?"

"As far as I'm concerned, your real ones—Mama and Papa D'Alessio. They're the only parents you've known most of your life."

Marc wasn't sure why Adam talking with them bothered him. He didn't want them to know how fucked-up he was about his past. They'd tried their best and, if not for Melissa dropping the bombshell about him being adopted, he'd probably have gone to his grave believing they were his biological parents. According to Solari, one of them was.

"I don't want to appear ungrateful for all they've done for me. Somehow digging into the past seems disloyal. I'm not sure I want them to know what's going on."

"Soft limit then."

Soft? Well, he had said he wasn't sure, rather than give Adam an adamant "No."

Adam leaned back in his swivel chair and rubbed the back of his neck. "How about talking to Angelina?"

As long as Adam kept her out of the scene. Marc would be in an extremely vulnerable state if Adam went anywhere near SERE training techniques. Did he want her to see him that way? Yet, wasn't that the fucking problem? If he couldn't let her in on something this crucial, how would he be able to give himself to her in a serious, life-long commitment?

No, he didn't want her there. "She may be able to fill in some of the blanks to help jar my memory, but use her as a last resort." Why was he being such a chickenshit?

"What does she know so far?"

Marc explained what they'd learned from the conversation back in February, after the anniversary dinner, and what Marc had told her the other night about the visit with his father. "I'm sure she doesn't know anything more."

"Haven't you talked with Angelina about this since daVinci's?"

"No. We aren't talking again."

"You sleep together the night of Luke's accident?"

"Yeah—we *slept*. No sex." He'd honored her limits, just hadn't been able to give her what she needed, other than that tiny glimpse into the inner workings of his soul.

"Good. You two need to figure out some shit before you jump into bed again."

Adam had never given Marc dating advice before. Perhaps he should have come to him sooner. Marc had blown any chance of reconciliation because of his boundless insecurities when he shut down on her again.

"Speaking of Luke, heard anything from Cassie?"

"Sounds as though he's out of the woods medically. Not sure when we'll get him down off the mountain, though. Angelina's brothers are helping with the horses out at his ranch."

Adam shook his head. "They were damned lucky. That avalanche could have killed them both. Thank God I didn't let Karla go up there for a visit."

If anything happened to Karla or the baby…Marc didn't think Adam would survive. He'd suffered so many losses already. This time, his overprotectiveness paid off and Karla had been safe. The man had been hypervigilant all these months worrying about every potential threat to his pregnant wife's health and safety. Being responsible for others took a lot out of a person.

Yet, Marc knew he'd be the same way in Adam's shoes. The thought of seeing Angelina carrying his baby warmed something deep inside him and was something he hoped to experience one day with her.

"I need Angelina in my life, but I can't go back to her unless I know who the fuck I am and get past this block that's keeping me from being able to commit myself to her completely."

Adam nodded. "Anyone off-limits for being an active participant in this scene?"

Marc thought for a while. *Angelina.*

"What was that thought?"

Observant man. He had to be if he was going to get Marc through this scene successfully.

"Just wondering if Angelina has to be involved other than feeding you some information up front."

"Can't say until we get started. She on your hard limits list?"

Was she? Did it matter if she was? Marc had no idea if Adam planned to honor or push him on his limits. The goal of this scene was all about reuniting with her and working out their problems that seemed insurmountable. Would seeing him in such a weakened state make that outcome more or less likely? Making himself vulnerable to her would be one of the hardest things he'd ever done, but wasn't that the reason she'd left—twice—because he wouldn't let down his guard or let her get that close? Having her there might not be a bad thing.

Marc sighed. "Soft limit. If you can do it without her, I'd prefer that, but if you think she can help, I don't want to tie your hands."

"Speaking of which, any types of restraints on the hard-limit list?"

Angelina had restrained him when she tried to top him, and he hadn't freaked out. "Don't think so."

"Do I need to uphold the Geneva Convention and avoid torture tactics?"

Marc's heart pounded with a new ferocity. Torture? Just what did Adam have in mind? He wasn't planning on a military interrogation scene where

Marc would be considered the enemy.

Trust him.

Marc called his bluff. "Do whatever you need to do."

The grin on Adam's face didn't bode well for him. "What's your biggest fear?"

Fear? "Losing Angelina."

"Deeper than that. Something that's been with you longer—maybe your whole fucking life."

Marc thought, but drew a blank.

"What makes you break out in a cold sweat?"

As if on cue, his skin became clammy.

"Yeah, that's the one. Tell me."

"Feeling trapped."

"Like in a hole?"

Marc shook his head. "Not exactly. I don't know how to explain it. Trapped. Cooped up. Unable to breathe. Smothered."

"Alone?"

Marc's throat closed off and he croaked, "Yes. Well, I think so, anyway."

Adam scrutinized him a while longer across the desk and then noted something on the pad. He leaned forward on his elbows, staring at Marc. "Just to clarify, you're giving me full control without restrictions. Any hard limits are mere suggestions. You're giving up your use of a safeword. That's the only way this will have a chance of working. While you trust me to do no harm, there are some inherent risks in doing what I have in mind. I can't predict or control all outcomes. You going to allow me to proceed and relinquish your safeword?"

Marc's chest ached from either holding his breath or from the pounding of his heartbeat. If he allowed himself to safeword, it would give him an easy out again, enabling him to continue to run from whatever had kept him in fear mode his whole life.

Marc cleared his throat. "I am giving you full control in the scene. No restrictions. No hard limits. No safeword. I'm aware of the inherent risks, but I want you to proceed as you see fit. Do whatever it takes." He paused a moment before adding, "I'd prefer not to have an audience unless absolutely necessary. Just you and me."

"Are you already trying to control the parameters of my scene, Marc?"

Marc felt a moment's dread, but he really did need to turn himself over completely to Adam in order for this to work.

With no small amount of trepidation, he responded, "No, Top. You do what you have to do."

"Let's finish this discussion in the interrogation room. Grant's got a video camera set up there. I want to tape your consent before we start. No doubt some of those I'd ask to participate in the scene will balk before they'll join me unless they see you giving full consent. I'll also want you to sign a statement of consent for the RACK conditions and giving up your safeword, in case I need further proof I didn't go batshit crazy on you."

He'd never participated in a Risk Aware Consensual Kink scene before, as Top or bottom, but knew Adam would need to cover his own ass at list among the kink community in case something went terribly wrong. "That's fine."

They walked upstairs to theme room four and Marc entered wondering if this is where Adam would conduct the scene, as well.

The red light flickered, but Adam quickly grabbed Marc's attention.

"Give a statement about what you've asked me to do."

Marc repeated much of what they'd talked about in Adam's office.

Adam added, "Once the scene starts, safeword or not, you *will* tell me immediately if there's any numbness in extremities or muscle cramps so I can determine if they warrant a change of position or tactics."

Marc nodded.

"This is a video, Doc. The proper response is 'I understand, Top.'"

"I understand, Top."

"You're aware I won't be telling you anything about what I'm planning to do ahead of time or during this scene."

"Yes, Top."

Marc couldn't know which tactics were real and which were mind games once they began. He'd have to believe it was all real as Adam took him through the scene and broke him down to a level psychologically, somewhere beyond losing his ego and full-on sleep-deprived psychosis, where Adam could pick at those buried memories.

"I need to get my life back, Adam…" he turned to the camera, "…and whoever else is watching this." He focused on Adam again. "I need to know why the hell I keep screwing things up with Angelina. I need to know what happened to make me like this. Simply hearing it from Mama won't cut it. There have been too many lies. I need to experience those early feelings again. It's no different than what Damián does with his bottoms, only I need catharsis of a different kind."

"Well, if it will help get your head out of your ass, then you've got my full support. I'll close the club down for a week when we do this and send out e-mail notices to members so they can plan accordingly."

A week? What the hell had he just committed himself to? How long did Adam think he'd need? Marc had figured on two days tops. Perhaps Adam was including aftercare in that assessment, the time he would need to process whatever happened during the scene. Unless Adam expected him to need time to reintegrate after a full mental break. Hell, that would take *more* than a week.

Marc hoped this worked.

"Just remember, Doc, you've agreed to a RACK scene. I won't stop when you hit the emotional wall that's blocking you. There's every possibility of you experiencing an emotional breakdown that can't be mended. You sure you want to go through with this?"

This definitely wasn't going to be a military interrogation adhering to the Geneva Convention bans on torture either. In a RACK scene, Marc would be broken down, mentally and physically. If his mind wasn't able to reintegrate, he might lose Angelina anyway. He might even lose the ability to function physically and not be able to relate to her in the only way he knew how—sexually and as her Dom.

But if he didn't try, he would lose her anyway—not to mention his very soul. "I have no choice. I can't keep running."

Adam proceeded to get him to repeat that he'd forego a safeword, as well as the Geneva Convention, and agree to whatever Adam decided he needed in the scene.

"Consider it done." Adam stood and walked around the desk to shut off the camera. "Oh, and on your way home, hit the surplus or thrift store for clothes you won't mind losing. Wear them when you come over for the scene. Don't want to mess up any of those high-priced civvies of yours."

Marc swallowed hard as he rose from the chair. He didn't know what Adam had planned but had no choice but to comply.

"I'm going to ask you again before we start to ensure your willingness to proceed, so if you have any second thoughts, or even fourth or fifth ones, you'll be given one more time to opt out. After that, your ass is mine."

"I understand and appreciate that, but I won't be backing down."

"I'll still ask."

Lord, don't let me chicken out.

"Any blackout dates you can't do, Marc?"

Marc pulled out his phone and pulled up the calendar app. "Let me check and see if I can find a few free days in a row." Things were slowing down at the outfitter store with the snowmelt and instability of the remaining snow and ice. "The remainder of this week looks pretty clear, actually."

"We'll probably need two full weeks before you'll be able to work again—inside the store, at least. You won't be in any shape for a nature trek for about a month."

The man hadn't been kidding. He might lose a few clients in the process if he couldn't find other outdoor enthusiasts to lead any already-booked treks but to hell with clients. Angelina was all that mattered.

"I understand." Both stood, and Marc reached out to shake Adam's hand. "I appreciate this."

"Don't thank me yet. This isn't exactly something someone wants to do to a friend."

Again, Marc felt a moment of dread. He remembered SERE resistance training but wasn't sure which tactics Adam expected to employ.

"I'll work on the plan tonight and let you know tomorrow by text what your instructions are."

Marc started toward the door. "Oh, Doc." He turned back toward Adam. "Karla's ecstatic about the possibility of buying your house. She loves that place. Thanks for the offer."

If Adam could make things right for Marc and get him back with Angelina long-term, he'd sign over the deed to him without a penny changing hands, not that Adam would accept such a gift.

Dio, Marc hoped the house would be a better fit for them than it had been for him.

"My pleasure. We'll talk about closing sometime after all the dust settles from this scene."

Adam chuckled. "Why not wait until after Damián's wedding? You may not be capable of signing legal papers for a while."

Marc swallowed hard. He would *not* back down no matter how frightening Adam made it sound.

Chapter Twenty-Four

The text from Adam came early the next morning. Marc had waited up all night. *"If u still want to go thru with this, b at Club at 1530 hrs today. Kitchen entrance."*

Marc had packed an overnight bag in case he needed toiletries or a change of clothes. He figured he'd either be nude or wearing the thrift-store clothes he had on now, even if he was there two full weeks. Not knowing what Adam had planned set his nerves on edge, but he had no intention of backing out now.

After rattling around in his lonely mausoleum for hours, he headed downtown a little early and grabbed some fast food on his way to the club. Probably should have eaten something healthier, but he was anxious for this process to start—and end.

He entered the kitchen as Karla carried a plate of what looked like her peanut-butter brownies over to Adam, who was seated at the table wearing the same mock Desert MARPAT uniform he'd worn on the mission to rescue Savannah. Marc recognized it by a few stains of blood spatter that hadn't come clean.

This time, Marc needed the rescuing. There might even be more blood spatter added to Adam's digitals—his.

"Marc!" She nearly ran across the room after placing the plate on the table and wrapped her arms around him.

"Smells good, *cara.*" He gave her a kiss on the cheek.

"Are you sure you want to do this?"

Marc was surprised Adam had told Karla about the upcoming scene. "My mind's made up. It's something I need to do."

"I'd hate to put you out of your home, but it's the sweetest thing any-one's ever done for us, and I can't tell you how excited I am. We'd about given up hope of ever finding anything."

The house! She was talking about selling them his house, not the upcoming scene Adam had planned. It pleased him to know that, without a doubt, he'd done one thing right. "That house needs the pitter-patter of little feet and your beautiful voice singing in the hallways."

"Well, that kitchen is going to go to waste, unless Angie—" Karla's face flushed, and she looked away. "Help yourself to brownies. At least I know how the oven works here! There's way more of them than Adam needs to eat."

Marc held one up to her first. "How about you? A chef should always sample her dishes." Angelina had taught him that. And a lot of other things.

Karla patted her well-rounded stomach. "I've gained enough weight as it is. No empty calories for me."

Adam still hadn't acknowledged his arrival, so he munched on a brownie and watched as Adam continued to read the newspaper. The man seemed in no hurry to get the scene started. Marc glanced at the clock over the stove and saw he was twenty minutes early. Might as well take a seat at the table while he waited. But first he pulled out a chair for Karla. "Here, sit."

"Oh, I'm fine. I'm just going to clean up my mess."

Marc took the seat himself. His heart pounded in anticipation. Adam turned the page of the paper in silence. "The Twins don't look like they'll go the distance."

Twins?

"Adam!"

Adam glanced dumbfounded at Karla; then Marc's attention strayed to her belly. "The *Minnesota* Twins, Kitten."

"Oh!"

Karla flushed and turned toward the sink where she continued washing the dishes.

Marc wouldn't have expected Karla to give a rat's ass what a Minnesota team was expected to do, given her roots were in Chicago which had no shortage of professional baseball teams, but he had no interest in talking baseball or any other sport at the moment. He made a noncommittal grunt. Adam apparently remained loyal to the local boys of summer from his childhood home.

Anxious to get going on the scene, Marc said, "I'm ready to start anytime you are, Adam."

Adam glared at him. "What time did I tell you to be here?"

Merda. He didn't want to piss Adam off just before putting himself into the man's hands for the intense scene to come. "Fifteen-thirty, Top." Adam's demeanor told Marc he needed to take a subordinate stance with his Marine Corps Master Sergeant now. All too soon he would be referring to him as a Top of a different sort.

"And what time is it now?"

Marc glanced at his watch. "Fifteen-seventeen."

"You still going through with this scene?"

"Yes. All systems go."

"Well, if you want to work with me, you're going to follow orders to the T. Do I make myself clear?"

Shit. Marc nearly stood at attention. "Loud and clear, Top."

Adam returned his gaze to the sports page. After a few more minutes, Marc reached for another brownie. They were damned good. "Did you ask me for permission to have that brownie?"

Adam's question threw him off guard. "No, but Karla offered…"

Adam stood so abruptly his chair hit the backs of his knees and toppled over with a crack. Karla turned and pressed her back against the counter, her eyes wide at the transformation in her husband. Marc had seen Adam in master sergeant mode before, mostly during those early days of Marc's recon training with the other ropers at Pendleton. This must be new to Karla, though.

"This scene began the minute you gave me the all go, devil dog. From this point on, you don't eat, drink, piss, or shit without permission. Do you understand?"

"Yes, Top." Marc dropped the uneaten brownie back on the plate and stood at attention.

"Haul your ass down the hall to the head and take a piss, empty your bowels, and do whatever else you need to. Might be the last time you take advantage of the porcelain facilities for at least the next week. Then I want your ass in the dungeon, standing at attention, and waiting to spill your sorry guts by the time I get down there."

Karla gasped, and Marc glanced at where she stood transfixed, staring at Adam. Her respirations had increased, not unlike Marc's, but for her there was more excitement than fear as the cause.

"Leave your watch and other jewelry on the table. Empty your pockets of anything metallic. Remove your shoes and socks up here, too. Karla will stow everything until you need it again."

What did Adam have planned? The man wasn't into electrical play. Violet wands were Damián's and Grant's area of expertise. Of course, he remembered the use of Tasers in SERE school resistance training. Any one of his Marines would be proficient in the use of those tactics. Marc had no clue who would be brought into this scene. He'd given Adam *carte blanche*.

What the fuck was he getting into?

Marc leaned down to pick up his overnight bag.

"Drop it. You won't be needing anything in that bag. I'll decide what you need until this scene is over."

Marc followed orders, leaving the bag in the kitchen and hitting the head before taking the stairway to the dungeon. When he walked into the room, he noticed a number of changes. A straight-back wooden chair from the kitchen had been set up behind a utilitarian wooden table about two-thirds of the way across the dungeon, both similar to one from an episode of *NCIS*. Marc listened for Adam to approach while surveying more of the dungeon. A work lamp, its bulb caged in wire, hung above the chair, reminiscent of something from one of his spy novels. Marc trusted Adam to do what needed to be done, but the level of authenticity surprised him.

Footsteps. Marc moved to…

"I told you to stand at attention."

Too late. "Yes, Top." He stood straight and still, waiting.

Adam walked over to the table and uncovered a tray of implements— leather tawse, steel-gauge needles, a wire brush, dragon-tongue bullwhip, rope, and a black cloth. Adam ran his finger over several of the more menacing items, picking up the needle and holding it to the light. Did he know needles couldn't be used if exposed to…

"On your fucking knees, grunt." Without giving him time to move, Adam kicked the backs of his knees and he collapsed into the position. "Eyes on the floor."

Not sure where to put his hands, he kept them at his side.

"Hands behind your back, wrists crossed."

Marc's lungs constricted as Adam worked the rope onto his arms just above the wrists. Without conscious thought, he began to strain against the rope.

"Move another fucking muscle, and you'll wish you hadn't."

Marc clenched his fists but willed his body to remain still and accept the restraints even though every nerve in his body lay poised on the edge of fight-or-flight response. After Adam tied off the end, he hauled Marc up by the ropes at his wrists and would have wrenched his arms out of their sockets if Marc hadn't scrambled to get his feet underneath him fast enough.

"Sit."

Marc walked toward the chair and sat down.

"Did I tell you you'd earned the right to sit in a chair?"

"No, Top." Marc stood and surveyed his options. The only other place to sit was on the floor, and he did so, first going to his knees and trying not to fall over with his hands restrained behind his back.

"Get your ass on the chair."

Fuck. Getting up would be harder than getting down here. Why didn't he make up his mind? Once on his feet again, he waited for further instructions to clarify which position Adam wanted him in on the chair, afraid to make the same mistake twice.

"Sit, facing forward."

Marc got up and sat in the chair as instructed. The light bulb above him shined in his eyes, but only briefly. Adam dangled a gag in front of Marc, and fear rose again in his throat.

"Breathe, Marc." Angelina's voice helped calm him.

"Last chance to back out. Do you consent to give me free rein as to what this scene requires?"

Marc still had a choice. Adam obviously meant business. What lay ahead scared Marc shitless, and he could choose to end it now. "Yes, Top. I give unconditional consent."

"You're aware of the risks, including full-on psychosis, hallucinations, torture, and physical conditions intended to make you face your phobias and triggers head on?"

Marc drew a deep breath. *I'm doing this for you,* amore. *I have no choice.*

"I fully understand the risks. I fully consent."

He also did this for himself, if he wanted to be honest. He'd been running long enough. Time to reclaim his past and start living his life.

"You've given up use of a safeword. Is that correct?"

"Yes, Top. I have given up my safeword."

"If you have any numbness to extremities, muscle cramps, you name it—report those to me ASAP. I'll determine if you're just trying to weasel out of facing something or if a change of position is needed. Understood?"

"Yes, Top. I understand."

"Evade the questions of any of your interrogators, and there will be consequences."

"I understand, Top." Who else would be involved in this scene? He remembered the sting of the crop and nylon flogger when he hadn't been truthful to Angelina. Adam's punishments would be so much worse.

After a long moment's pause, Adam reached up and turned out the light, but the bulb had been burned onto Marc's retinas where it continued to shine yellow and bright, its cage visible still for several seconds as his eyes adjusted to the darkness of the windowless cellar room. Adam placed a blindfold over Marc's eyes. With one sense deprived, he became more aware of sounds in the room. A clock ticked somewhere, growing louder and louder. He hadn't noticed one being in the dungeon before, certainly not a few minutes ago.

Something heavy scraped across the floor and into position nearby. Marc wondered what it could be but knew better than to speak without permission. He didn't have to be told there would be ramifications to that breach of basic protocol. He'd been a Dom long enough, not to mention a grunt serving under Adam. He'd also submitted to Angelina once and his mouth had gotten him in a lot of trouble.

Adam's suede combat boots barely made a sound on the floor. The silence dragged out for an unknown amount of time.

Without warning, Adam ripped the blindfold off Marc's face and hauled him out of the chair by the collar of his shirt. Once on his feet, he shoved him across the floor until Marc's chest rammed against the wall. Adam's voice roared in his ears, his mouth mere inches away.

Adam spoke in a calm, commanding voice. "Your ass is mine now, grunt. You will do as you're told until I release you from this scene. You will answer my questions, every fucking one of them, with total honesty. You under-stand?"

"Yes, Top."

"I'm not your master sergeant anymore. You will refer to me as Sir. We're in a fucking BDSM dungeon in a fucking RACK scene, not on some military base where I have to comply with the Geneva Convention or the Uniform Code of Military Justice. You got that?"

"Yes, Sir." It sounded strange to Marc to call him sir. Adam wouldn't stand for any of his Marines to do so, nor his Navy Corpsman. But Marc had better get used to it pronto.

Adam loosened his grip and stepped away. Marc remained in place breathing hard and deep, well on his way to hyperventilating before he employed meditation techniques to try and calm his nerves. Adam slipped a black hood over Marc's head. He'd seen them used in scenes to totally block out a submissive's sight. They'd also been used in SERE resistance training.

And at Abu Ghraib prison.

"Take one step back, and then get on the balls of your feet." Marc complied. "Lean forward, and press your nose against the wall. Stay there until I tell you otherwise."

Marc moved into position quickly, feeling off balance from the get-go. Silence. Time crawled by, as far as he could tell. How long had he been in this position? A cramp seized his calf, but by lowering his heel and stretching out his calf muscle, he eased the pain away.

Where the fuck had Adam gone?

Click-click-click-zzzzt!

Marc's forehead slammed against the brick wall, crushing his nose as pain radiated from his side. *Dio*, Adam had zapped him with a stun gun or Taser.

"What the fuck, Adam?"

"What did you say?" Adam stood to his left, judging by the direction of his voice.

Marc pushed himself away from the wall and tried to resume a normal breathing pattern.

"Sorry, Sir. I just didn't expect that."

"Good. Now why didn't you tell me you had a leg cramp?"

Adam shot him full of electricity for not reporting a fucking leg cramp? *Shit*. Marc's heart beat double time.

"I took care of it myself, Sir."

Adam hit him with another jolt of electricity to his side, and Marc screamed in pain as his knees nearly buckled.

"Since when is a chickenshit like you able to take care of himself? You were given a simple order to tell me when you have a cramp, numbness, anything like that, and you couldn't even do that. It's *my* job to assess your condition. If you withhold information, you're going to get hurt—unintentionally—and piss me off. Got that?"

"Yes, Sir. I understand." He still didn't comprehend the need for extreme force, though, just for working out a problem on his own. Marc had been taking care of himself a long time. He didn't need to have someone baby him.

"Back in position." Adam yanked him slightly sideways. Disoriented, Marc stood a moment trying to determine where the wall was in relation to his face.

Click-zzzzt!

Marc jumped away from the sound before he realized Adam hadn't hit him with it this time. With his hands tied behind his back, he couldn't reach out and feel for the wall. He had to trust that Adam had placed him where he needed to be. Slowly, he leaned forward. Just when he thought he was going to topple forward onto his face, his forehead made contact with the wall. He quickly adjusted his position so only his nose touched.

His muscles ached from the stun gun. Surely Adam hadn't gotten access to a Taser. It wasn't an Air Taser for sure. Maintaining the stress position became harder now. The only thing breaking the silence was the ticking of the clock. Marc didn't know if hours had passed or mere minutes. He hadn't heard Adam move or even breathe for a while and didn't know if he had stayed in the room. Responsible Tops never left restrained bottoms in a room alone—ever—so Marc trusted that Adam was still with him.

"At ease."

Relief at hearing Adam's voice again washed over Marc as he relaxed, lowered his heels to the floor, and stood upright. He flexed his legs at the knees, trying to get the feeling back in them.

"Did I give you permission to move your legs, grunt?"

Marc straightened his legs and stood still. "No, Sir."

"You always this slow to follow commands?"

"No, Sir. I'll do better, Sir."

"It's my job to see that you do." Adam paused before adding, "Maybe we need to make you a little less comfortable." Adam stood behind him now and began cutting through the rope, not worrying about saving it for a future scene.

Once freed, Marc waited for instructions before massaging his sore arms and shoulders. Permission didn't come.

"Strip."

It's just Adam.

He removed his outer shirt and khakis then his undershirt. Standing in his boxer briefs, he hoped Adam would be satisfied and not demand the full monty.

"What part of strip don't you understand, you devil dog?"

Being naked definitely would increase his anxiety level and vulnerability. Marc sighed and shucked them off. He wasn't sure what Adam wanted him to do next, so he waited. After what felt like maybe twenty minutes, Adam grabbed his forearm and pulled him backward. Marc fought to remain standing, having no idea where Adam was taking him until he felt something pressing against the backs of his knees.

"Sit!"

Marc hoped there was a seat behind him as he eased down. When his naked ass slapped against a cold, hard surface, he breathed a sigh of relief. Even if this was part of a mindfuck and not an actual chair at all, at least he hadn't wound up sprawled in a heap on the ground.

Adam tied his ankles to what must be the legs. He jerked Marc's arms behind his back, and Marc's fingers latched onto the slats in the back. Definitely a chair. Adam soon had him restrained so that he couldn't move.

"What's your name?"

"Marc D'Alessio."

"You sure about that?"

Marc thought a moment. Sitting here, stripped naked, he wasn't sure about anything anymore. "I think I might have been born Marco Solari, Sir."

"Where were you born?"

"Milan, Italy. In Lombardy, Sir."

"You sure?"

Slap!

Marc paused a moment too long, and Adam slapped him on his thigh with what felt and sounded like a tawse. He didn't like that implement. Wouldn't even use it on Angelina when she'd asked him. Without a warm-up, the hard leather strips stung like the dickens, but Marc wasn't going to give Adam the satisfaction of knowing that.

"I asked you a question, grunt."

"Yes, Sir! It's what my birth certificate says."

"You've been sold a bill of goods. You were born in Brescia, same as Gino."

Certainly possible. It wasn't all that far from Milan. Marc certainly had been told other lies surrounding his origins. What's one more? Or had Mama and Papa had more than his name changed on his updated birth certificate after the adoption?

Wait. How did Adam know where he was born? Had he gotten access to

Marc's and Gino's military records? How? Through Grant's connections, no doubt. She'd tracked down Adam's mother.

"That's where we lived when we were kids, before we emigrated."

Slap!

What the fuck did he do to deserve that one?

"You don't open your fucking mouth unless I ask you a direct question. Got that, chickenshit?"

"Yes, Sir."

"What's your mother's name?"

"Natal—no, *Emiliana*. Emiliana Zirilli Solari."

"What makes you so sure?"

"I'm sure of nothing. Mama, my adopted mother, told me so."

"You believe her?"

Marc didn't know if she'd told the truth or not. "Not sure, Sir."

"Any siblings?"

"Yes, Sir—Gino is my full brother. Then I have two cousins, Alessandro and Carmella, who I was raised with in my adopted family. They've been my brother and sister...until this year."

"Who changed that status?"

"Melissa told me I was adopted."

"What's that got to do with your relationship with Alessandro and Carmella?"

Nothing. "I guess I just put distance between us. I didn't feel like I belonged in their family anymore, Sir."

"What kind of relationship did you have with Gino growing up?"

"Typical brothers. Played hard. Fought hard."

"Fought over a woman."

"Biggest mistake of my life."

Slap!

"I didn't ask a question, and I don't want you making observations with that fucked-up mindset of yours. Just answer direct questions. Got that?"

"Yes, Sir."

"So you let some conniving bitch come between you and your brother?"

Shame washed over him. "Yes, Sir. I did."

"What do you plan to do about it?"

Do? What the fuck can I do? Gino died more than a decade ago.

"Nothing I can do. It's too late."

"What's the worst thing you ever did to your brother?"

Marc drew a blank. "I can't think of anything, Sir."

The tawse stung his ass. "Try again."

Marc was the one wronged. Gino's the one who had fucked Marc's girlfriend, not the other way around. What did Adam want to hear him say? Why was he focusing on Gino? Marc's problem was women, not Gino.

"I'm going to leave you here a while to think about how you're going to solve the problem with your brother."

What the fuck was he talking about? Hell, Adam had retrieved the body after Gino had been killed in an ambush in Afghanistan. How could he expect Marc to do anything about fixing that relationship? He'd come here to deal with the issues revolving around Angelina, not Gino.

The clock ticked loudly. Marc heard the door to the dungeon open and close. Gone. SSC rules didn't apply in this scene where safe and sane weren't guaranteed or even expected.

Tick-tock. Tick-tock.

Marc thought back to that early September day in 2001 when he'd brought Melissa home with him from college to meet his family. He'd left her alone at his apartment and returned to find her naked and on top of Gino, fucking him.

Marc's blood began to boil as he found himself back in that bedroom. His big brother had deliberately gone after the woman Marc intended to marry.

"Gino, get the fuck out of here!"

Marc launched himself across the room at them, and Melissa scrambled to the opposite side of the bed.

"She's mine, you bastard!" Marc straddled Gino and began pummeling his brother's face until Gino heaved his body upward, knocking Marc to his ass on the floor. Gino had always been bigger, stronger. Marc had more of a skier's wiry body.

While Marc had bulked up some later while training with the Marines, he probably never would have been able to take his brother down.

But he'd never seen Gino alive again after that morning when Marc had severed all ties.

Gino, why'd you have to be such a fucking bastard?

His brother had everything—their parents' love, the career he wanted. He could have had any girl in Aspen with their family's money and his good looks. Okay, neither of them had done a lot of dating because the resort kept them so damned busy. Marc had spent less time with his nose in a textbook than Gino and more time instructing female guests in the techniques of skiing, hiking, and submission.

Most of the women seeking BDSM training were older, not to mention married.

Marc didn't want to think about those days anymore. He couldn't change anything about his past or his life with Gino.

Tick-tock. Tick-tock.

Time passed slowly, as far as Marc could tell. He didn't know what time it was or how long he'd sat here thinking.

Having had so little sleep the past week, he let his head drop back and decided to catch some sleep while he could.

"Who the fuck told you you could sleep, grunt? You think you're back at your family's resort?"

Marc sat up straighter. Adam hadn't left him. He'd seen Marc dozing off fast enough. Almost too late, he realized Adam had asked a direct question. His response time had slowed. "No one, T—Sir." He'd almost slipped and called Adam Top.

"You're not going to sleep until we get to the bottom of every fucking thing you need to figure out to get your sorry life back on track."

So they would be using SERE resistance tactics. Sleep deprivation. Hell, he was halfway there already. Should speed things up.

Adam didn't say anything more. Marc listened for movement but didn't hear anything. He got the impression Adam was staring at him. Waiting for him to slip up or nod off.

Tick-tock. Tick-tock.

Time. Nothing but time on his hands. Marc had been ordered to figure out how to unfuck the problem with Gino, so he'd better damn well focus. But on what?

His mind wandered to an unfamiliar kitchen, yet he felt at home there. Terracotta tiles on the floor, a weathered table that would seat only two comfortably, four including children. On it sat a Mediterranean blue ceramic bowl filled with pears and plump red grapes. The smells of coffee, garlic or onions, and rosemary permeated his senses. His stomach growled. How long had it been since he'd last eaten? The fast-food lunch on his way to meet Adam had worn off. How long had he been here? Surely only a few hours.

Gino's voice as a young boy, speaking Italian, filtered into his consciousness, calling out to Marc from beyond the grave. *"Marco, andiamo alla nostra tana!"* Marc hadn't thought of the lair in what seemed like a lifetime. Tears stung his eyes.

They'd been happy as kids back in Lombardy. No worries. He missed his homeland sometimes, although he loved Colorado and being an American.

Marc heard his own voice speaking his native Italian. *"Go play with Gino?"*

The pretty lady he didn't recognize dried her hands on her apron. "Put on your coats first! It's still May, you know."

Wait! What was the woman's name? *Dio*, he hadn't thought of her in forever. She babysat for Gino and him. As best he could remember, he and Gino had spent a lot of time there as young children.

Gino helped him put on his coat, and they ran out the kitchen door into the yard. "Let's take our rifles in case we find enemies." Gino led him to the place at the back corner of the yard where they kept their secret weapons stash. He handed Marco one of the tree branches they pretended with, and the two squeezed through a hole in the fence, soon to scamper off to their favorite place to play.

"Drink this."

Marc came back to the present with a jolt, feeling a tug on the hood as Adam uncovered his mouth. He pressed something cold and hard against Marc's lips, which opened to accept what turned out to be water. *Dio*, he was thirsty. He gulped it down, not caring that some trickled down his chin to his chest. He quickly drained the contents of the bottle but wanted more.

"Stand up."

Marc stood, surprised the ropes had been removed from his arms and legs. When had Adam done that? Had he been sleeping? Adam allowed that?

Marc's legs shook with the effort of holding his body upright. How long had he been sitting in the chair? Adam had gone relatively silent after asking questions about Marc's past. How much time had passed while he'd gotten lost in memories of Gino and their childhood?

"Here's your chance to piss in the bucket, if you have to go."

Adam led Marc several steps to what he assumed was the bucket he'd seen when he surveyed the dungeon after he'd first come down here. Adam grabbed Marc's cock like a garden hose. It took him a long while, but Marc finally heard the stream of piss hitting the bottom of the bucket.

Adam knew what had to be done to break him—humiliation and demoralization would play a part in it, for sure. Marc would gladly forego food and water if it would help him reach the breaking point faster, not that Adam had offered him anything to eat. Food he could live without, but he'd been given the bare minimum of water he'd need to survive without having his kidneys shut down.

No way did he see how this scene was going to accomplish anything Marc wanted to uncover. He trusted Adam too much to suspend belief and see him as a heartless inquisitor. Besides, how was he supposed to dig up answers if Adam asked so few questions? He'd spent a lifetime burying shit like that memory of Gino and their lair.

A lair? Who called their childhood hideout a lair? He wondered what it had looked like and regretted that Adam had disturbed the memory before he'd seen it again with his mind's eye.

Gone. Again.

Adam said nothing. Marc stood, waiting. What if the scene was over? Would Adam give up on him? No! They hadn't gotten anywhere! Disappointment flooded his senses that another attempt at getting to the root of his problems had failed.

"Arms in front."

Adrenaline pumped through his veins instantly. This scene wasn't over! Marc extended his arms in front of him, anxious to continue. His shoulders ached from having been in the same unnatural position for however long. He shook them out before presenting them to Adam. At least, he assumed Adam stood in front of him. That's where his voice had come from on the last command. The room was still pitch black, his hood firmly in place.

Adam wrapped something around Marc's left wrist and pulled tight. A cuff. Adam easily slipped his finger between Marc's skin and the padded leather. Not too tight. He then cuffed the right wrist. A raspy noise and jerking motion with his hands told him Adam was threading rope through the D-rings.

"Lift your arms."

Marc did so and soon found himself restrained from the ceiling, an eye-bolt, he supposed. Adam adjusted the ropes until only Marc's toes made contact with the floor. The strain on his arms hurt more, because this was the opposite of how his arms had been restrained so far.

Silence. No more questions. No commands.

Tick-tock. Tick-tock.

Even the clock became white noise after a while. The quiet left Marc sinking slowly into his own dark thoughts. Only this time, memories of Gino with Melissa clouded his mind.

"She's not worth this, Marc. Why don't you think with your head for once, you asshole?"

Gino slammed him against the wall and restrained Marc's arms above his head.

Somehow, Marc managed to shake him off, or perhaps Gino released him. Marc surveyed the scene in the bedroom, his chest heaving as he gasped for air. Where had Melissa gone? After what he'd just seen, did he care? Marc grabbed his jacket and left Gino behind. If he wanted her so badly, then he could have her. Fuck them both!

Marc's head nodded, and he jerked back into his stance.

Slap!

The sting of the tawse across his bare ass stung momentarily, but he soon grew too tired to care. Definitely a tawse, though. He'd felt it before. When?

How long had he been hanging in this position? Sleep wasn't advisable if he wanted to keep from hanging by his wrists, so he fought to stay awake and try to keep his legs steady.

Adam made no sound at all. Was he even there? Surely, he was. Adam wouldn't abandon him, not like so many others had done in his life. His birth parents. Melissa. Gino.

Angelina.

His chest ached at the thought that she'd walked away like all the rest.

Marc tried to adjust his position but had very little wiggle room. Surely Adam would cut him down soon. How long would he have to remain in this position? He fought the urge to call out to his friend, not wanting to mess with the scene. Adam would interact with him when the time was right. He knew how to break a man in an interrogation.

Tick-tock. Tick-tock.

Crack!

The sting of something on his shoulder dissipated more slowly than that from the tawse. *Merda*, it stung. Marc fought his restraints, shifting on his toes again to relieve the strain on his shoulders.

Adam! It took a while, but Marc's mind registered he was no longer alone. The sense of relief washing over him made the sting in his shoulders more bearable for a moment. Adam hadn't left or, if he had, he'd returned. How long had Marc slept before Adam had woken him so abruptly? His arms ached from hanging.

"Enjoy your nap?"

He was told to answer truthfully. "Yes, Sir."

"Good, because that'll be the last one you'll have for a while. Time for some music."

Adam placed a headset over his ears. The padded headphones masked some of the ambient noise in the room. Marc waited, unsure what music his master sergeant had chosen. He expected loud and obnoxious if they were using sleep-deprivation tactics. Marc preferred Italian opera or…

The first chords of the "music" blasted forth. Way too loud. A demonic voice screamed into his ear. Who could possibly deem this music?

Tangled in a web of reversed lies
and my reflection is the one that's on my side.

Marc's nerves, already on edge from a lack of sleep and time/space disorientation, screamed, too. One cacophonous "song" bled into the next. Damián had to have done this. Did that mean Adam had told him about the scene? Was he one of the interrogators Adam referred to earlier? The man was into serious metal music. This crap made Marc's jaws ache. How could anyone call this shit music?

Marc couldn't always tell when one track ended and another began but needed to keep his focus. He guessed there had been eight or nine of them. If each lasted three or four minutes, he'd been listening for twenty-five to thirty-five minutes. Focusing on the number of songs could help him keep track of time. Not that he had any idea how much time had passed already. He needed to keep his mind occupied.

Focus.

Time—and the noise—droned on without a break. Eleven. Twelve. Thirteen tracks.

I am a dominant gene—live as I die

Was he a Dominant? He didn't have a clue.

Slap!

The tawse stung his thigh, jerking Marc awake. How the hell had he fallen asleep with that god-awful crap blaring in his ears? Marc couldn't think about the present, much less the past. Fuck. He'd lost count of the number of tracks. How long had he slept this time? Was Adam waking him immediately or letting him rest some to skew his ability to judge the passage of time?

I can bury the hatchet and let some shit go
But I got too many grudges to hold!

He'd never let go of one grudge. Awfully hard to bury the hatchet with someone who didn't exist anymore.

Gino, why did you betray me?

Slap!

Fuck, that hurt! Same spot on his thigh, still sore from the last slap. Did that mean he hadn't remained awake very long? He'd never played with a tawse and had no idea how long the sting lasted. Yet it was oddly familiar.

He needed to stay awake. He hadn't even been down here all that long—had he? Hell, he had no fucking clue what time—or day—it was anymore. Every time Marc's head nodded and he dozed off, Adam slapped his ass or thigh with the tawse and woke him. He also couldn't control his yawns, although moving his jaw was difficult under the tight hood.

Tired. Bone tired. After a hellacious week of very little sleep, being further deprived of rest while having his senses bombarded by this incessant noise left his body and mind screaming for escape.

No way out. He'd given Adam complete authority—no, control. Adam didn't remove the headphones to speak to him. Instead, he just kept waking him with the tawse. At least he assumed Adam was doing it. He needed to sleep, though, and if this went beyond eighteen hours or so, Adam would have to bring Damián or Grant from the club to wield the implement in order for Adam to take breaks.

Marc hadn't been smacked by the tawse for such a long time, he wondered if Adam was still here.

Sleep is overrated.

How many times had he heard Adam say that? So perhaps he hadn't taken a sleep break. As a Navy Corpsman, he'd seen Marines appear awake who no longer responded to wakeful stimuli. Micro-sleeps lasted mere seconds. Had he zoned out in one of those?

What if Adam had left him here alone, though? Marc didn't want to be left alone down here.

His mouth was dry, but no one had offered another drink since the first one however long ago. *Auuuggghhhhh.* A cramp in his right calf had him screaming in pain, but he couldn't put enough pressure on it to relieve it. Would Adam come to his aid or leave him dangling from the ceiling?

"Leg cramp, Sir!"

A tug on the rope above him and Marc felt himself start to fall before his back was slammed against the wall. He'd been cut down. Adam hadn't left him! Wrists still cuffed, arms aching at yet another change in position, he stood as Adam massaged the cramp in his calf away. He gritted his teeth as Adam's hands caused more pain than comfort at first, but slowly the cramp eased.

Adam, or whoever it was, broke contact, and Marc continued to lean against the wall, uncertain his legs would hold him without the crutch. The hood lifted off his lower face, and a cold, hard plastic bottle pressed against his lips. He opened wide to gulp down the precious water. When no more poured from the bottle, his tongue reached out to lick the lip of the bottle for any remaining drops. *Dio*, he wanted more!

Marc waited as the minutes—or hours?—ticked away.

The headset continued to blare into his ears. If Adam said anything, Marc couldn't hear. No one touched him any further.

Abandoned. Again.

Where did that thought come from? Adam wouldn't abandon him. Even if he had to leave, Marc was merely alone, not *abandoned*. He had spent time alone many times. Sometimes he preferred that to being with people.

Until Angelina.

Why did he feel so much more insecure now at the thought of being left alone?

His mind flashed back to another time when he'd felt alone. His whole world had been blown apart...along with his big brother.

The casket had remained closed at the funeral-home visitation. Gino's body had been too mangled by the mortar for the mortician to even try to make him look like he once had. Mama insisted on holding onto her memories of him alive.

Numb. Marc felt numb. He stood apart in the corner, observing as Sandro comforted Mama while Carmella, her face streaked with tears, accepted the condolences of the many people standing in line. Melissa, dressed in a tight black cocktail dress, was being fussed over by some of her friends from college. She took to being the near-widow like a hand to a glove, but did she really love Gino the way he deserved? Hell, they hardly knew each other.

Except for business interactions, his family had left him alone since they'd returned to Aspen following Gino's funeral. Did Mama and Papa blame Marc for Gino enlisting in the Marines—blame him for getting the favored son killed?

No, that wasn't logical. Gino had enlisted because their adopted country had been attacked.

Marc's gaze returned to his former girlfriend. Melissa. Why he'd ever thought he wanted to spend the rest of his life with her, he didn't understand anymore.

Comparing her to Angelina, well, there *was* no comparison. How had he and Gino both been so blind?

The first volley of the twenty-one gun salute jolted Marc's senses and brought him back to Fort Logan where Gino had been laid to rest. Row upon row of military-issue tombstones covered the hillside. Snow blanketed the ground, except where Marc and his family stood preparing to say their final good-bye to the once-vibrant Gino D'Alessio.

Rage filled him at the fucking waste.

"Why did you leave me behind, Gino? You promised…"

The words reverberated in his head, but he didn't think he uttered a sound aloud. If he screamed, Adam would punish him…

He couldn't hear himself think anymore. He didn't have permission to speak. Adam was watching, listening, protecting.

Wasn't he? Wanting some kind of confirmation he wasn't alone, even if it meant painful punishment, Marc screamed, "Adam! Where the fuck are you?"

No response. Adam was gone.

Fear clawed at Marc, but he refused to give it a foothold. Adam would be back. Maybe he'd gone to the head.

Marc remembered waking up in Fallujah with Adam watching over him from across the room. His master sergeant told Marc all about Gino, the Marine. Gino, the hero.

He couldn't blame Adam for abandoning him. Unlike his big brother, Marc had failed at all attempts to play the hero. Angelina had been beaten senseless by Sir Asshole because Marc had been late to arrive at the club for his dungeon monitor duties. Sergeant Miller had bled out before Marc could reach him. No, wait. There was nothing he could have done for Miller. He'd been dead before Marc had answered the "Corpsman Up!" call.

But Damián lost his foot in the same attack. Could a more experienced corpsman have saved it? In those days, training was accelerated to get as many corpsmen into the field as possible, with the country fighting combat in two active arenas.

The headphones continued to blare the fucking music into his ears. How long did Adam plan to keep that shit up? This bombardment of his senses wasn't going to achieve anything but give him a migraine.

The floor was cold, and a shiver coursed through his body. How had he gotten to the floor? Oh, yeah. Adam had cut him down. How long ago had that been? His muscles ached from shivering and his jaw from clenching his teeth. No relief. Every muscle in his body screamed for release. The incessant noise filled his ears, and his mind ached as much as the other parts of his body.

Honestly, somehow it always seems that I'm dreaming of
something I can never be

Manwhore.

Anger boiled beneath the surface. "Turn this fucking shit off!" Marc's voice came in loud and clear through the headset. He hoped Adam heard him. Exhausted. He needed sleep. He didn't want to continue with this fucking scene anymore.

Marc shouted, "What the fuck are you waiting for, Adam?" Nothing. "Interrogate me!" Silence. "This is a fucking waste of time!"

So he'd remembered a couple of scenes from the past; how were those memories going to win Angelina back?

Screwin' may be the only way that I can truly be free.

Marc ached to make love with Angelina again. He felt his cock grow rigid with thoughts of her sexy body restrained for him to pleasure her. The image faded, along with his hard-on.

He waited for Adam to turn off the music. Even to have Adam slap him with the tawse—at least that was human contact. He wanted this scene to be over.

Nothing.

Marc sagged against the floor in defeat. What did it matter if Adam stayed or not? The only person he wanted to speak to would never hear him again. His face was cold and wet. Tears.

"Stop crying…"

"Gino? Is that you?"

Silence.

Gino, you were supposed to protect me. Why did you abandon me?

Chapter Twenty-Five

*G*ino, *home from college for the winter break, nabbed Marc as he crossed the lobby after a hard day on the slopes.*

"Mrs. Giovanni in the Presidential Suite wants you to help her with something, Marco."

Gino had sent him up there. Had he known just what kind of help she wanted? Had she really asked for him or had Gino turned her down already?

Marc walked into the suite when she opened the door after the first knock. The middle-aged woman had been staying at the hotel every ski season for years. Marc and his family provided individualized attention to their regulars, and Mrs. Giovanni was certainly a regular.

"How may I help you, ma'am?"

"You've grown into a handsome young man, Marco." She sipped at her amber-colored cocktail on the rocks. "I watched you giving ski lessons today. You're very much in control there."

"Thank you, ma'am." He still had no clue what she wanted with him but had an uneasy feeling. He wanted to leave the room, but he'd just been lectured by Mama for not pulling his weight at the resort. She complained that he'd spent too much time in the mountains hiking or skiing alone, without clients. If one of their guests needed something, he'd been ordered to assist.

"What is it I can do for you, ma'am?"

"Do you sometimes feel like you have no control over anything in your life?"

All the time.

He simply nodded.

"How would you like to learn to take control whenever you want it, Marco?" Her gaze roamed over him from head to boots before settling on his groin. "To take control of your body?"

"I beg your pardon?"

The old lady was creeping him out. When she slinked toward him, her gaze locked with his in steely determination, like that of a predator about to pounce on helpless prey. Although he didn't think himself helpless, he couldn't fight one of the resort's frequent patrons. He fought the urge to run.

Her stilettos click-clicked on the parquet floor.

Her gaze never left his.

"I want to show you how to take charge of a woman. Of me."

At seventeen, busy at the resort and school, Marco hadn't had much time for girls. They made him nervous. He never seemed to say or do the right thing when he was around them. Most weren't interested in the outdoor activities he loved.

Mrs. Giovanni reached up and traced her cold finger, damp from holding the cocktail, down his cheek to his lower lip. He felt his cock start to grow in his pants.

"Take control of me, Marco. Make me submit to your will. Let me show you where your potential lies as a man."

Marco took a step back. "N-no, thanks, Mrs. Giovanni. It's my job to make sure you're satisfied during your stay here. You aren't supposed to do anything for me."

She grinned, and his heart pounded. "True." She took him by the shirt. "Then come into the bedroom. There's something I need you to do for me."

Realization dawned. He wasn't so naïve he couldn't tell she was seducing him. All his friends at school were making out with girlfriends. He wanted to find out what the big deal was and maybe learn how to do it right if he ever had a girlfriend of his own.

No, this went way beyond what his parents expected of him as far as servicing the guests. And she was old enough to be his mother. He dug in his feet and stood stock-still. "No, Mrs. Giovanni. If you need me to lift or carry something, give a ski lesson, take you hiking in the backcountry, I'm at your service. Otherwise…"

She slapped him. "What on earth do you think I was asking?" The change in her demeanor made him wonder how he'd misread her. "My boy, get out before I tell Mrs. D'Alessio what horrible things you accused me of!"

Cheek stinging, fearing he'd fail meeting Mama's expectations yet again, Marco faltered. "I'm sorry. I misunderstood. What is it you need?"

She glared at him a long moment and then smiled, making him uneasy again. "I assure you it's perfectly innocent. I have no intention of removing my clothes, and you'll remain fully clothed, as well. I just need you to help me learn discipline."

"The resort has trainers who can help you come up with a workout program that's right for you."

"I want help learning to discipline my mind as well as my body."

He'd learned about self-discipline and mind over matter in school. The subject fascinated him. He had even learned to control his breathing and heart rate using meditation techniques. Perhaps he could share some of what he'd learned with Mrs. Giovanni.

As Marco followed her to one of the suite's bedrooms, he wondered why they couldn't work on this in the living room.

Slap!

Marc jerked awake again as something slapped across his ass. The head-phones were yanked off his head, but the ringing in his ears continued even after the music stopped.

"I can see you need a lesson in discipline if you're going to stay awake as you've been ordered."

While he'd been sure a man had spoken, an image of Mrs. Giovanni slapping his face set Marc's heart pounding harder. He hadn't thought about that woman in years. He thought he'd put the memory of her to rest somewhere so deep it could never resurface. The woman had spent the next several months indoctrinating him into the ways of being a Dominant.

Angelina had asked if he had been a gigolo. Too nice a word for it.

More accurate would be manwhore, sans sex.

"Tell me where you are." The male's voice sounded as if it came through a long tunnel yet comforted Marc in some way.

"The resort my parents own in Aspen."

"What's going on?"

Marc couldn't talk about this with a stranger. He didn't even want to think about that time in his life again.

"Deep breath. Now." A firm hand rubbed the strained muscles in Marc's nape.

Marc drew as deep a breath as he could, but his heart continued to race.

"Who are you with?" The voice wasn't harsh the way it had been before. He cared.

"Mrs. Giovanni."

"Does she work at the resort?"

"No, she's one of the guests. A regular. Very rich."

"How old are you?"

"Seventeen."

"She the one who introduced you to the world of kink?"

How could this man know about that? Marc had never told anyone. No, he had told someone once about these older women who had so much power over him.

Had he spoken the secret aloud? He thought he'd been asleep and dreaming. Was he hallucinating? Hell, he didn't know what was real anymore.

"What did she have you do?"

"I'm not talking about this anymore with you." *I don't want to remember.*

Smack!

Something slapped against his ass again, the sting worse than ever. "You answer me now or I'll beat it out of your hide."

"Paddling, sir!" *Master Sergeant Montague!* The name that went with that voice was Adam, but somehow Marc knew he shouldn't have called him sir.

"She had you paddle her?"

"No, Top."

"Breathe." Marc followed the order. "Again." Adam paused until he'd complied. "So she paddled you."

"Yes, Top. With her hairbrush at first. Then a tawse." Why did Master Sergeant Montague want to know about his kink?

"Did you like it?"

"Hell, no! She restrained and gagged me, so I wouldn't scream too loudly and tip off any of the staff."

"That the only time you've been gagged?"

He had to think a moment. "No. Angelina did it, too." Angelina. He rescued her at the Masters at Arms Club. No wait. She was his girl. Adam was a member of the club, too. Not his master sergeant any longer.

"She tops you?" The surprise in Adam's voice couldn't be missed.

The pause stretched out longer than was comfortable. "I let her top me *once.* Didn't like that either."

"Probably not. You're a Dom, not a switch or sub."

"How do you know?"

"What makes you ask?"

"I never felt like a Dominant until—" There she was again.

"Until what?"

"Mrs. Giovanni. That first time I figured out I didn't want to be the bottom, but then she gave me the paddle, and she bent over the bed. I walloped her good to pay her back. She didn't scream. Cried a little, but mostly she just took it. Afterward, she stood up, smiled in this weird way, and told me to leave. I thought she'd tell Mama what I'd done, but the next afternoon, she sent for me again."

"And...?"

"Taught me how to use a riding crop that time."

"How did it make you feel, topping her?"

"Empty. Dirty." There, he'd said it. "I didn't get into it at all. Didn't feel like a Dominant, just a...patsy."

A Domwhore.

"You've gotten there eventually, haven't you?"

"Yeah, but it didn't happen for a very long time." He'd been used by so many women—the cougars at the resort, Melissa, Pamel—no wait. Pamela hadn't used him. They'd just needed to move in different directions.

"How is it with Angelina?"

"Best ever. She brings out the Dom in me, and I achieve Domspace regularly with her."

"Why do you think that's so?"

Marc thought a moment. "She needs me. Respects me."

Doesn't use me.

"What was that thought?"

How had Adam picked up on his errant thought? Of course, he was a Dom and well-schooled in reading body language and facial features. Marc shouldn't have tried to evade truthfully answering the question.

"She doesn't use me."

"Maybe you've just been with the wrong women. Most Doms need an emotional connection with their subs—something more than impact play and showing off their latest set of kink skills."

Not a direct question, so Marc just thought about what Adam had said for a moment. He'd gone on to play Top for any number of women at the resort after his induction into the lifestyle. He'd even gotten to enjoy himself with some of them after a while, but any time he thought about Mrs. Giovanni, he felt only one thing—dirty.

Without warning, Adam hauled him up on his feet again, but, when his knees buckled, Adam held him until he became steady. "Remain on your fucking feet!" Adam confused him. One minute he cared, the next he treated him like shit. Marc locked his knees and fought to remain upright.

"Time for you to take another piss."

Mortified at having Adam treat him like a child, Marc cringed when only a few drops hit the bucket. Probably getting dehydrated, but asking for water wouldn't help speed up this scene. Adam would meet his needs, not his wants.

"You done?"

Marc nodded.

"Fine, but next time you can piss on the floor if that's the best you can do. I'm not giving you any special favors if you don't appreciate all I'm doing for you."

Marc's face burned with shame. He'd never felt so exposed. Not since he'd been in Mrs. Giovanni's suite.

Adam yanked him by his arms several steps again, probably back to where he'd been a few minutes ago, and unclipped the wrist cuffs.

"Drink this." Adam handed him a bottle of water and lifted the hood up over Marc's mouth and nose. Marc fought the urge to rip the hood the rest of the way off, now that his hands were free. But that would only anger Adam.

Marc's hand shook as he brought the cold liquid to his lips and devoured it. By the weight of the bottle, he guessed it was only half filled. Barely enough to keep his kidneys functioning. When he finished the contents, he crushed the plastic bottle and handed it back to Adam, who pulled Marc's hands behind his back again. Marc gritted his teeth to keep from screaming at the counter strain on already aching shoulder sockets and muscles.

"Step up, one foot on each box." Adam helped guide him onto two wobbly boxes. "Bend your fucking knees and lean forward. Pretend you're leaning over the john to puke your guts out. You might just feel like puking after drinking that water."

Marc assumed the position he thought Adam wanted and fought to find his balance. His legs began shaking almost immediately, making the unstable boxes do the same, but he managed to regain his footing, such as it was.

Adam won't harm you.

Several tugs of the wrist cuffs, and they were clipped behind his back. Adam ran rope through them again. Probably using some sort of pulley to stretch his arms behind him, he nearly yanked Marc's arms to the breaking point. Another fucking Abu Ghraib stress position. Sweat soaked his hood in a matter of minutes.

Adam is doing this for my own good. I trust him.

He no more than had that thought when a knock at the door made him jump. "Adam! Open the door!"

Karla?

"What are you doing down here, Kitten?" Adam's voice receded. The door opened. "I told you not to—good God, Karla! What have you done to your hand?"

"I was trying to fix dinner. The knife slipped. I think I'm going to pass out, Adam. Oh!"

"Fuck! Lean on me, Kitten. How long has it been bleeding like that?"

"Ten minutes. I tried to stop it by holding it under cold water." She hiccupped through her sobs. "I applied pressure. I can't make it stop bleeding."

Sounded like a deep tissue wound. "Cut me down, Adam. Let me have a look."

"I'm scared, Adam. What if something happens to the—"

"Come on. I'm getting you to the hospital."

"What about Marc?"

"He's not going anywhere."

Marc heard the shuffle of footsteps followed by a deafening silence.

"Untie me, Adam!"

No response.

"Adam! Karla!"

The silence dragged on interminably. They'd left him here. Marc began to shift from one leg to the other to relieve the stress. The boxes shook so badly, he decided he'd better stand as still as possible. If he fell off of either of them, he'd pull his fucking arms out of their sockets.

How could Adam just leave him tied and alone like this? How long would it have taken the man to cut him down before he'd taken Karla to the hospital? Adam would never have left a sub alone and vulnerable like this.

All bets were off when it came to anything happening to Karla. Adam couldn't see reason when worrying about her or the baby.

The strain on Marc's arms forced him to unbend his knees, but when he tried to straighten his back somewhat, the movement set the boxes shaking violently. He resumed his original position.

Did anyone other than Adam and Karla know he was down here? As time stretched out into what seemed like hours, Marc lost control of his bladder. Piss ran down his legs. He didn't care anymore. No one could see him.

His body began to shake uncontrollably. So tired. He wanted to sleep, but how could he do so without inflicting major injury on his arms?

The one person he'd trusted to always have his back had abandoned him. *"I'll take care of you."*

Marc jerked awake at the sound of that voice. "Gino? You came back?"

"I told you I'd always take care of you. What the fuck kind of trouble have you gotten yourself into this time?"

Marc ignored the question. "I thought you were dead."

"Nah. Taken prisoner. I escaped."

A prisoner of war? Why had Adam lied to him when he'd described the scenario of Gino's death in detail? He'd said he even went in to recover Gino's body.

Adam lied. Everyone did.

"Cut these ropes. Let me down."

"I can't." Did Marc detect a Spanish accent in Gino?

"Why the fuck not?"

"Top will string me up by the balls if I mess with what he's trying to do here."

"He's not even here. He left me!"

"You sure about that?"

How could he be certain of anything anymore? But all indications were that Adam had taken Karla to the ER. "I'm sure."

"He's my master sergeant, too, and was long before you ever knew him. I won't disobey Top. That man went through hell for his Marines in our...my recon unit. You don't even know the half of it."

Marc had seen the old shrapnel scars on Adam's back when he treated Adam on the scene of the cougar attack. Marc had a decent idea of what Adam had suffered for his Marines.

Wait! Hadn't those injuries happened during the mission that killed Gino? But Gino was here saying he'd escaped, too. His head hurt trying to sort out truth from lies.

"Take off this hood, Gino. I want to see you."

"No, you don't."

"Why not?"

"I'm pretty messed up. Besides, you heard what I said about Top's orders."

Fine. Marc would talk with him then. Maybe he could work out whatever Adam had wanted him to earlier.

"You going to come home?"

"Can't."

Marc's anger flared. "Why the fuck not? You know how much they miss you."

"Can't, but you have no excuse for staying away. Why the fuck are you cutting them off? They love you."

"Not like they loved—love—you."

"Bullshit. They loved us both equally."

"Yeah, whatever you say."

Gino paused a while before adding, "I'm sorry about Melissa, Marc."

"Doesn't matter." She really didn't matter. "Wait 'til you meet my new girl, Angelina. I'm going to marry her someday."

Silence.

Would Gino make a move on Angelina, too? "Touch her and I'll break your fucking face."

Mine.

"Hear me, Gino? I mean it."

No response.

He was gone? Marc's eyes filled with tears and he shouted, "Don't fucking leave me again. You promised!"

His body jerked as he caught himself before he fell off the boxes.

Bzzzt.

"Fuck!" Marc jerked awake smelling burning flesh. Had Adam zapped him again with the stun gun? He'd fallen asleep. Had he been dreaming? Hallucinating, more like it. Gino alive? Impossible. While he'd give anything to have his brother back to be able to apologize for the way they'd parted that last time, he knew in his heart he was dead. His mind was playing tricks on him. Sleep deprived psychosis.

Why hadn't Marc told him he was sorry just a few minutes ago? God-damn it! He'd had his chance in that exchange with him, whether real or a figment of his imagination. Instead, Gino had been the one to apologize for screwing Melissa.

"I'm sorry, Gino!" He knew no one was there but screamed out anyway. "I was wrong! I always expected you to come back. You promised you'd never leave me."

Silence.

Tears dripped off his nose. What day was it? Would anyone be in the house to be able to hear him? Was it a club night? Did Adam close the entire club or just the dungeon area?

What if club members were looking at him now? He'd asked Adam not to allow spectators. But Adam was in control or had been before he left him alone down here.

How could Adam fucking leave someone alone and restrained in a position like this? Even if he did have to get Karla help stat, he could have at least called someone to take over the scene.

He must have. Surely they were there watching over him now. "Damián! Grant! Somebody get me the fuck out of here!"

No response.

Panic clawed at his chest. Marc twisted his fingers in an effort to reach the buckles on the wrist cuffs. Handcuffs would be easier to get out of. Or Velcro closures. He needed to find a way to get down from here. "This scene is over, Adam! Red! You hear me? I'm putting an end to this fucking scene!"

Silence.

"Can anybody goddamned hear me? Dungeon monitors, do your fucking jobs!"

Not that he'd always done his job as a DM. Marc remembered back to when he'd been the DM Supervisor charged with protecting the submissives in the club and making sure the scenes being played out were safe and consensual.

Angelina's screams that night cut him to the core even to this day. She'd been left at the hands of a poser Dom who had beaten her beyond her limits all because Marc had been late to his post.

Some protector he was.

"*Amore*, I'm so sorry. I failed you, too." Shame washed over him. "I left you with Sir Asshole too long. My fault."

Exhausted, his legs began to shake with the effort to remain on the boxes. How long had he been left here? Abandoned. Gino could have cut him down.

But Adam leaving him alone cut even deeper. He'd trusted Adam to take care of him in this scene. But hadn't Marc instructed him to involve as few people as possible? Maybe if he'd trusted his other friends, someone might have been here to step in when Adam left to take care of Karla's injury.

Why hadn't he cut Marc down? Hell, Marc could have treated her and stabilized the wound in minutes. Adam knew he had emergency medical training but had panicked. His paralyzing fear that something would happen to Karla or the baby was…

But Adam had suffered both those losses in the past. No wonder he didn't trust Marc to take care of Karla. Adam expected Marc to fuck up, just like that other time...

"*Bambino mio!*" If his hands had been freed, Marc would have covered his ears. He didn't want to hear her voice ever again. Block it out. "*Water! Marco, bring Mama water!*"

Marc's throat burned as a racking sob tore from deep inside.

"Fuck you, Gino! Fuck you, too, Adam!" *Leave me. I don't care.* "I don't need any of you! Do you fucking hear me? I don't need you! Rot in hell, for all I care!"

He gasped for air as his lungs constricted. The hood was wet with tears.

"Bambino mio! *I need you!*"

"Mama, I'm sorry. I failed you." He drew another ragged breath. "All my fault." The crushing weight on his heart threatened to consume him. "I let you die."

Chapter Twenty-Six

"**B**ingo. Now we're getting somewhere." Adam watched the monitor as they moved into hour fifty-four.

Adam squeezed Damián's shoulder. "Convinced him you were Gino."

Damián shrugged. "Flubbed up once saying *our* recon unit, but his head's so fucked up, I don't think he noticed.

"You did a great job on the music selections, too. I'm not sure I'd have been able to hold it together for more than two days listening to that shit the way Doc did. You'd have had to lock me up after about thirty minutes."

"I don't know why you two think it's so fucking awful," Damián said. "I find metal music relaxing."

Adam shook his head and turned to watch Marc struggle against his restraints.

That's it, Doc. Exhaust yourself.

If Marc had already reached the mild psychosis phase, this interrogation might go quicker than Adam had predicted. Of course, Marc showed up Friday looking as if he'd had little to no sleep the last couple nights, which probably helped speed him toward the breaking point.

Adam continued, "Where'd you get that stun gun?"

"Made it myself. It's great for a mindfuck like this."

"Remind me never to volunteer to do a demo with you using it."

Damián grinned. They watched silently a few minutes before Damián interjected, "Before I forget, Savannah, Marisol, and I are flying out to California Friday. Already got our tickets. Do you think you're going to need me here that long?"

"No problem. Looks like he'll be in aftercare no later than Wednesday. Hope so, anyway. That's Karla's birthday. Grant's coming in tomorrow morning for the duration, including the week we'll probably need for aftercare."

Adam had never done a scene this edgy or drawn out, not for someone he cared about anyway. All three of them had been through SERE resistance training, but had been on the receiving end then, not dishing out the torture.

Marc stopped fighting but hadn't fallen asleep yet, as far as Adam could judge from the strain in his forearm flexors.

"What's taking you all to SoCal again so soon? It's too early for any court appearances against those neutered scumbags." Dishing out torture to shitheads like Savannah's father and Lyle? Well, that had been pure, unadulterated pleasure.

"Nothing like that. Just a marriage prep talk with Father Martine."

Adam had never had a church wedding so hadn't had any preparation classes. Maybe he could have used some—both times. Karla was none too happy with him lately. Knowing she carried not one but two little Montagues just strengthened his resolve even more. He would let nothing jeopardize the health and safety of his family.

"Sounds good," Adam said. Savannah wasn't strong enough to face her abusers yet. He kept his eye on Marc for any signs of danger. While the rope was rigged to give way if Marc fell off the boxes, he still could get a nasty head injury if he hit the boxes instead of the mattresses surrounding them. "Son, you make sure I'm in the front row for those hearings whenever the DA lets you know they've been scheduled. I'm going to make sure those shitheads remember everything we promised them if they try to skirt justice."

Damián nodded. "I'll be right there with you." He paused before adding, "I'm taking Savannah on base Saturday to visit some of the recon unit members. Another deployment coming up."

"Tell them *Semper Fi* from me." Adam watched Marc's head nod. "How's Savannah doing?" The rescue had only been five weeks ago.

"Surprisingly well. The slut mindfuck worked better than expected."

"Judging by the headboard you broke, I'd say so."

Damián grinned. "Thanks for helping me plan parts of that scene. Hardest one I've ever had to do."

"Redirecting those messages from fucking abusers sometimes takes extreme measures." Adam wasn't sure he'd ever rid himself of the tapes in his own head, although reuniting with his mother last year had helped him heal some of the hurts and correct some of the bad information he'd stored away. "Keep an eye on her. Survivors of childhood shit have had a lifetime to learn to mask things so as not to worry those around them." He ought to know.

Was that what was going on with Marc? Some kind of abuse from his past? "Never know when a trigger will hit."

"Don't have to tell me. She's still having a lot of nightmares from the abduction, mostly worrying about Marisol's safety even though she protected her from harm. Hopefully those will decrease the further we get away from the incident."

Marc's head rolled forward, and his body relaxed, straining his biceps. "You're on, son."

Damián nodded and picked up the leather tawse. Marc didn't flinch or correct himself as Damián approached. Must be in a micro-sleep if not REM. Damián aimed for his ass.

Slap!

"Fuck, Adam!"

Adam grinned and waited to see if Damián would announce his presence in the scene.

Marc's body tensed and began shaking as he nearly toppled off the boxes.

"Wrong, my friend. Not Adam. Your worst nightmare. You know what I can do to that soft body of yours."

Marc's body tensed. He had to be squirming at hearing Damián's voice. Adam grinned. Marc wouldn't let his guard down for a while now. He found his balance on the boxes again before Damián returned to the observation area in the weight room.

Adam shook his head. "I must be slipping, because I didn't get so much as a *Merda* out of the man last time I hit him with the tawse."

Damián grinned back at him and shrugged. "You're not the sadist around here."

"Looks like you have things under control. I'm going to go catch a few hours of shut-eye. Grant's due at 0700 hours. We need to mess with his head and straighten out some shit for memories that have him stuck."

Hearing a woman's voice might just do the trick.

* * *

Marco ran from the house and across the backyard. He had to get away. From what, he couldn't remember.

He only knew he needed to run. The briars grew thicker and scraped his legs, but he didn't slow down. Gino would have kept him on the path, but Gino wasn't here this time.

A few yards ahead, he saw his destination. Safety. He dropped onto his knees and crawled the last few feet under the canopy of brush and sticks until he'd entered the safety of his lair.

He labored to catch a deep breath. The rustle of leaves drew his attention to the entrance of the lair. No!

Hiss. Whack!

The whistling sound of air being dispersed around an unknown impact implement wasn't enough to fully jar him from the memory, but the sting of what felt like a cane across the tops of his thighs jolted Marc back to the present.

"Tell me where you are, boy."

Grant? What the fuck was she doing in here? Maybe he was hallucinating again. She scared him as much as Damián did.

Adam had cut Marc down what seemed like a couple of hours ago and had tied him to a chair. He'd also removed the hood. The caged light bulb glared from above, casting the room in shadows with Marc enveloped by the spotlight. He'd only closed his eyes for a moment to get some relief. He hadn't been sleeping, but his head must have lolled to tip her off. Adam allowed him to rest his eyes every now and then, or maybe he just wasn't keeping watch over him twenty-four/seven.

Not Grant. She appeared to be in charge now.

Where had Adam gone this time? Probably off sleeping in a nice warm bed with Karla curled up beside him. At least he'd come back down here to check on Marc after he'd gotten back from the hospital.

Marc opened his eyes. Grant leaned over him, her face mere inches from his. He smelled her patchouli scent. "Answer me, boy."

She was dressed in black fatigues, her hands encased in leather gloves. He closed his eyes. *"Sono nel bosco."*

"Speak English."

"Yes, S—" How was he supposed to address her? He'd almost slipped and called her Sir.

"You answer to me as Mistress, boy."

"Yes, Mistress." He couldn't keep his eyes open.

Hiss. Whack!

Fuck!

"You do *not* fall asleep on my watch and make me look negligent in the eyes of my master sergeant. Do. You. Hear. Me?" To punctuate each of her last words, she slapped him with the cane on the same part of his thigh where she'd already slapped him twice before to wake him up, stinging before his skin began to burn.

"I'm going to enjoy playing with you and making sure we get to the bottom of every fucking thing you need to figure out to get your sorry life back on track."

Sounded like both Tops would be using SERE resistance tactics.

"Now, tell me where you were just now in that screwed-up head of yours."

"In the woods."

"How old are you?"

"Three."

"Who's with you?"

"No one. I'm alone. It's dark." He shivered, partly because he was naked but more so because of the memory of the scene he'd just witnessed. "I'm cold." Perhaps she'd bring him a blanket. Mistress Angelina would have. Hell, he would have if his submissive was cold.

"Why are you outside alone at that age?" But not Mistress Grant.

As the memory of the dream or whatever it was washed over him again, Marc's breathing became labored.

She grabbed his chin. "Eyes on me, boy." He looked at her scowling at him. "Take a deep breath. Now."

Not wanting her to become upset with him for misbehaving, he did so.

"Tell me why you were out in the woods alone at night?"

"It's not nighttime. Just dark in the lair."

"The lair?"

Marc nodded. "I was in the old wolf's lair where Gino and I played."

"Where's Gino?"

"Don't know. Probably at Mrs. Mil—I can't remember her name, but the lair was the only safe place I could escape to."

"How were you connected to the lady you can't remember the name of?"

Marc tried to remember if she was any relation. "A neighbor, I think. Or maybe a friend of Mama's. She used to watch us a lot after…"

Mistress Grant waited for him to continue before prompting, "After what?"

He shook his head. He didn't want to remember that time.

Hiss! Whack!

"I asked you a direct question, boy. I expect an answer. *Now.*"

Marc stared at her, defiantly refusing to answer.

Hiss! Whack!

Shit! He looked down and watched the new stripe appear on his thighs about an inch away from where the first ones landed and already half as red.

"After Mama got sick."

Grant patted his cheek. "Good boy. Now why did you have to escape to your lair?"

Hiss! Whack!

He refused to look at his thighs but knew she'd hit him in the same place. He screamed, "Because she's dead!"

"Who's dead?"

Marc glared at Grant, not wanting to talk about this any further. When she raised the cane to strike again, he ground out between gritted teeth, "None of your *fucking* business."

Something flashed in Grant's eyes before her lips broke into a slow, deliberate smile. "You think not?" She released him from the restraints and pulled him out of the chair and onto his feet in a matter of seconds. His body wavered a few times before becoming steady. "I've just been waiting for an excuse to do this. Adam told me you'd be responsive to a good paddling."

So Adam had briefed her on his earlier revelation. He'd betrayed him. Again.

She dragged him into the dark area outside the circle of light.

"Fuck Adam—and fuck you, too!" Marc struggled to get away, but his hands remained cuffed together behind his back, rendering him helpless.

"On your knees." When he refused, he heard the whistle of the cane again. The stinging implement hit the backs of his knees and his legs gave way. He fell onto the cushioned kneelers of one of Luke's spanking benches, similar to one in his playroom at home. Marc renewed his efforts to get away from her.

No way in hell was Grant going to spank him like some naughty boy.

Or some manwhore to be used by another bitch.

Marc put the full force of his weakened body into a charge for her abdomen, targeting her web belt, but she sidestepped and easily deflected him by bringing her clasped hands down in the center of his left shoulder. *Merda!* Marc went to his knees feeling as if he'd been hit with a sledgehammer.

Grant's voice remained calm as she walked behind him. "You are so going to regret that move, boy. But I won't." She yanked him into place on the kneelers, then slammed his face against the leather bench. She delivered her whispered promise right next to his ear. "You just earned ten more blows on top of the twenty I'd already planned."

"Bring it, bitch."

"Flattery will get you nowhere, *boy*."

Grant wrapped the waist strap around him and cinched it tightly. She left his wrists cuffed together behind his back. When she tried to apply the first of the thigh straps to restrain his legs, he kicked out.

"We're up to forty. You like to test the boundaries, don't you, boy?"

"I'm fucking tired of you calling me *boy*, lady. I'm a Dominant, just like you."

Grant laughed. "You sure about that?"

Marc wasn't sure of anything anymore. Her words left him feeling further betrayed. Had Adam told her about his self-doubts?

His thoughts distracted him long enough for her to cinch his other thigh into the restraints without resistance. Helpless. He detested being helpless, especially with a woman in control.

No, this was no ordinary woman. She was an Amazon in top physical condition. After the Marines, she'd joined Black Ops. Later, she'd trained as a Domme under Gunnar Larson, the man who also taught Damián the ways of sadism and throwing a whip. She'd learned some vicious means of controlling men twice her size.

His junk was at her mercy for the foreseeable future.

Marc struggled to wriggle out of the bonds but stopped when he realized his efforts only succeeded in exhausting him. He needed to conserve his energy to attempt an escape when she finally released these straps. No woman would ever make him feel helpless again. He wouldn't give Grant that satisfaction either.

"Maybe I can help you develop an appreciation for the paddle. It's one of my favorite toys."

Marc stared at her, trying not to let her intimidate him with her calculating smile. Still, he was in no position to continue to defy her. "Mine, too. *Mistress*."

Grant laughed. "But I'll bet you prefer being on my side of the paddle, don't you?" Out of the corner of his eye, he watched her walk over to the table where Adam had laid out a number of implements. But she ignored the paddle Adam had placed there instead opening her own toy bag. When she turned, he saw she'd retrieved a wooden paddle into which she'd driven rounded-top upholstery tacks, causing the surface to be uneven in order to inflict greater pain. He'd seen her reduce bigger men to tears with that thing. The surface was only about two inches wide, which would heighten the pain. Judging by the muscle tone in her abs and her arms, Marc knew she wouldn't hit like a girl.

She returned to his side and surprised him by rubbing the paddle over the backs of his thighs. She used the smooth side of the paddle until she flipped it to run the raised tacks over the tawse welts on his ass. She warmed him up with a number of light taps to bring the blood to the surface and prepare him. Marc's fists clenched in rage and humiliation as his cock began to stir to life.

Grant laughed again. "Does my boy like that?"

"No, Mistress. Anyone touching my ass like that could get a rise out of my cock."

"How about when I touch it like this?"

Whack!

Marc growled, but the impact ended any chance of arousal. A masochist he was not.

He gritted his teeth and spat out, "Bring it."

She gave a menacing chuckle before delivering four more swats in rapid succession, alternating between two spots, one on each cheek. She seemed to be using the smooth side of the paddle, but the stinging on his already raw skin grew worse with each swat.

Her scratchy-gloved hand stroked over his burning skin, further irritating the marked areas. She smacked him with her hand, the rivets or whatever digging farther into his skin.

She delivered the next twenty-five swats with the smooth side of the paddle, as well.

Anger boiled up. "Fuck you!"

"Now, boy. I see we haven't broken you of that nasty defiant habit yet, have we?"

Before the paddle even hit, he knew she'd flipped it over to the tack side. *Gesù. Fuck! Fuck! Fuck!*

The sting hadn't begun to dissipate before she landed another blow.

Marc fought his bonds. "I'd rip your fucking head off and shit down your neck if I wasn't restrained!"

The bitch did nothing but smile. "Silly malesub. Think you're a match for Mistress Grant?"

"I'm *not* a sub."

Whack!

Rather than alternate cheeks, she landed this blow on the same spot as the last, and it took Marc longer to regain his senses. He wasn't sure he could speak without betraying how much pain he was in. How many had that been? Was she even counting? *Merda,* could he handle any more like that one?

"You've had two more added because you can't fucking police your mouth, sailor boy."

Raking her gloved fingertips over his sore ass and up his back, she leaned toward his ear and whispered, "Tell me who else paddled you, boy."

Marc refused to answer.

Whack!

She put her mouth up to his ear. "Tell. Me. Who was the first to paddle you?"

Marc remained silent.

Whack!

"I've got all fucking day. You've earned ten more." Again, she rubbed the raw skin on his ass before stroking more gently up his back to his neck. Maybe it just felt gentler because the skin on his back hadn't been pummeled.

His focus concentrated on the burning in his ass.

Whack!

"I can't *hear* you, sailor. Who was it?"

"Fuck off."

"If you can't obey and speak to me properly, I might as well remove your ability to talk and give you more time to think about obeying and answering my fucking questions. Open."

He kept his mouth closed tightly until she pressed the joints of his jaw causing him to lose control of his muscles. His mouth opened and she rammed the ball gag inside with ease, strapping it snugly around his head.

"How does that feel, Marco?"

Why was Grant calling him by his childhood name?

Damn you, Adam, for unleashing this bitch on me and giving her just enough ammo to take me back to that night.

The next two blows on the same spot elicited an uncontrolled scream into the gag. Sweat ran down his forehead to the side of his face, but he'd lost the ability to fight any longer.

"Does it make that cock of yours hard?"

No! Mrs. Giovanni's voice shattered through his psyche.

His screamed obscenities were lost in the ball gag. She dragged her nails down his back and onto his inflamed ass. He hissed as he drew a breath and tried to hold it as she ventured further down to his balls and squeezed them. His cock sprang to life under him. He hoped and prayed she couldn't see it. His face grew as red as his ass must be.

She reached under him and grabbed his erect cock. Her chuckle made him boil with impotent anger.

"My own Italian stallion. If only my husband were hung half as big as you. You're going to be God's gift to women for the rest of your life."

Marco didn't want to be any woman's gift.

Whack! Whack!

Why was his cock so hard, throbbing?

She continued to paddle him with her carved wooden hairbrush. "Come for me, Marco. You will come for me now!"

His cock exploded onto her bedspread. He'd fucking come! Of course, it didn't take much at his age to get an erection, but he felt mortified nonetheless.

Anger seethed beneath the surface. If he ever got the chance, he would let Mrs. Giovanni feel the bite of that hairbrush. He would show her no mercy. But he fucking wouldn't make her come. She'd probably like that way too much…

*   *   *

Hour sixty-six. Adam stood next to Grant trying to determine what to try next. Adam hadn't counted on Marc regressing to a time he didn't speak English. When Grant removed the ball gag, they'd had difficulty understanding what was going on in Marc's head.

Grant adjusted some knobs on the surveillance equipment. "My training focused more on Arabic and Farsi, Top. We need Angelina in here. She'll be able to communicate with him in his native tongue."

"No way we're bringing in anyone who didn't train at SERE School. Let's move him, then give him some water."

He and Grant removed Marc from the spanking horse, and Grant helped Marc down his daily eight-ounce allotment of water. Together, they laid him on a mattress in the back of the room. She applied ointment to his welts to help ease the pain. Grant had followed his orders perfectly and had taken him back to the memory with Mrs. Giovanni in record time. Adam knew a woman's voice would succeed much better than his own.

But what the hell had happened at the end of that triggered memory? Marc had reverted to Italian gibberish in a small boy's voice. The past two hours had been under Grant's control. Marc didn't take well to women having authority over him.

A litany of Italian shouts spewed from his mouth, and Adam watched Marc thrash around on the mattress.

Had they managed to get Marc to a point where he'd be able to remember some of what had blocked him and wreaked havoc in his relationships with women?

As they returned to the weight room, Grant said, "I can call her. Just say the word. You're in charge, of course."

Marc let loose with another string of words Adam couldn't decipher.

Adam scrubbed his face. He wished he'd never started this fucking scene. Watching Marc go through so much shit, even if Adam didn't understand what was happening, and not being able to provide Marc with anything that would help him resolve the demons from his past made Adam feel as if they'd only made it to the edge of the abyss.

"*No, mamma!*"

Those words he understood even with the accent, but Marc added more Italian and lost him again. What the hell had she done—and which mama was he remembering?

"Call her."

Grant nodded and left the dungeon.

"She's gone." The lost tone in Marc's words led Adam to return to him. He hunkered down next to Marc's face. "Who's gone?"

The word barely came out in a whisper. "Mama. I didn't help her, and she went away forever."

The flashback crashed through his defenses. Adam saw his father lying in a pool of blood. His mother lay next to the body and told Adam to run. He'd left her lying there paralyzed.

This isn't your scene. Adam shook off the memory. He needed to regain his focus on Marc.

Adam's attention returned, but his heart raced until he was able to put a lid on those feelings from his own past. He'd made peace with all that.

"What were you supposed to do to help her?" Had Marc's mother abused him?

"Get her some water."

"How would not having a drink of water kill her?"

"It did! Mama needed water because…" Marc's voice trailed off.

Adam waited and watched Marc's eyelids flutter rapidly as images of the past bombarded him in his trancelike state. Nothing made sense to Adam yet. He needed to dig further. At least Marc spoke in English now.

"Tell me what happened."

Marc's brows furrowed. "You won't understand."

"Try me. What's going on?"

Marc became silent, but the expressions flitting across his face told Adam the movie of his past continued to play out. Tears trickled down his cheeks unheeded, not that Marc could have wiped them away if he'd wanted to. His hands remained tied.

"Tell me who is with you now."

"No one. I'm alone. In my safe place." He paused a moment before adding, "She's dead. My fault." Marc screamed in anguish, a sound filled with so much pain, Adam felt it in his gut.

"Slow, deep breaths." Adam wasn't sure if he was instructing Marc or himself.

"*Mio Dio*, no! What have you done to him?"

Marc gasped for air and struggled against the ropes as Adam turned to see Angelina rushing toward them. How'd she gotten here so soon? She had to have been waiting upstairs. Who had let her know what was going on? Karla?

Adam wasn't ready for her to enter the scene. He needed to brief her first. When she knelt beside Marc and reached out to him, Adam motioned for her not to touch him. Tears streamed down her cheeks. He needed for her to regain composure, to have some assurance she'd maintain her focus and control before he let her participate in this interrogation. There had been too many distractions already. They were so close.

He hiked his thumb in the direction of the doorway. She stared at him with defiance before standing, glancing once more at Marc, and starting toward the entrance.

Adam left Marc, who calmed down after his initial response to hearing Angelina's voice. When Adam caught up to her, he grabbed her upper arm and steered her out of the dungeon and into the weight room.

"Sit."

She looked around and sat down on the bench press nearby. He placed his hands on his hips and towered over her. His dominant stance had the desired effect. Some of the anger left her expression, and she waited for him to speak.

"Interfere in my scene again, and I'll make sure you don't come back into this club again while I'm in charge. Understand me?"

Her eyes opened wide, but she nodded, hugging her hands to her waist for self-comfort.

Adam went to the camera monitoring equipment and queued up the video Marc had taped before entering into this. "Watch this."

He watched her expressions as she viewed Marc's statement giving up all rights and safeguards as he turned himself over completely to Adam. He switched off the video and went back to the live feed from the dungeon.

After assuring himself that Marc was still huddled on the mattress, probably sleeping, Adam turned back to Angelina. "Grant called you down here because we need someone who can speak Italian to help decipher what's going on in case he lapses into his early childhood memories again."

Angelina nodded. "What has he revealed so far?"

Adam filled her in on what he knew about Mrs. Giovanni, Gino, and now his confusion about his mothers. "I'm trying to get at something he just remembered. Has to do with his mother's death."

"So he thinks of Emiliana as his mother."

"Which one is she?"

"Mama's sister. She raised him until Mama and Papa adopted him and Gino after her death."

"Seems to blame himself. How'd she die?"

"Cancer, I think."

"Why would he blame himself for killing her?"

Angelina seemed as confused as he was and shook her head without answering.

"I need to get back in there, but if you join me, you'd better not speak unless spoken to. I want you to only speak to me, not Marc, unless I tell you otherwise. And if you so much as touch him and bring him out of the scene, I'm going to string you up in the great room and let every member of this club have a crack at your butt with their implement of choice. Do you understand me?"

"Yes, Sir."

Adam started back to the dungeon and motioned for her to follow. He hunkered down again next to Marc and Angelina knelt in submission across from him on Marc's other side. She kept her hands clenched on her thighs, though, indicating she was anything but relaxed or submissive. Maybe she was just afraid those hands would accidentally get her hauled out of here for good.

Good girl, for obeying.

He turned his attention back to his subject. "What happened to your mama?"

Marc shook his head. "I don't want to see that anymore." His breathing became agitated again, and he turned from his side to his stomach, facing toward the silent Angelina.

"No, Gino! Don't make me!" He fought the restraints. Was he still in his childhood, or had he moved forward in time? He spoke English, so probably the latter.

"What's going on?"

Tears streamed down Marc's cheeks. Angelina reached out to him but pulled back when Adam glared at her. They were close to something, but comforting him now would break that connection. The time for aftercare would come later. That's when Angelina would be able to do the most to help.

Marc needed to remain agitated and be forced to face whatever had happened that he'd kept buried his entire life.

"Mama woke up."

"Does your mama know you're there?"

"No. I'm hiding in the closet."

"I'll be good. Don't lock me in there, Mommy!" Adam realized those words sprang from his own memories and shook with the effort not to be pulled back into the nightmares of his own childhood. Why was he having so much trouble keeping his past buried deeply in the past?

He regained his focus in an instant. "What do you see? Or hear?"

"Gino's calling for me. He's crying."

"Does he find you?"

"No. Nobody can find me. I'm invisible. Hiding in my lair."

"I thought you were in the closet."

Marc's brows furrowed in confusion. "That's right. I'm in a closet."

Adam hoped he wasn't changing the past and leading Marc to remember his life events differently.

Marc lapsed into Italian. "Zietta Natalia?" Marc paused, his lips quivering. "*No, non voglio andarci!*"

Adam looked to Angelina for a translation. "What did he say?"

"He's talking to his Auntie Natalia—Mama D'Alessio—telling her he doesn't want to go somewhere with her."

"Ask him in Italian where she wants him to go."

Angelina did so and then translated for Adam. "Church. Gino told him he has to tell Mama good-bye, because he won't ever get to see her again." Tears shimmered in her eyes, but she fought the trembling of her chin. He admired the effort it took for her to hold it together for Marc.

"Have him move forward in time. Did he go to the funeral?"

Before Angelina could translate, Marc answered, the word came out in barely a whisper. "No."

"Why not?"

He reverted to English. "Scared. She didn't look like Mama anymore. Gino said she looked shriveled up. My fault."

Angelina asked something in Italian, providing Adam with the translation. "Why is that your fault?"

Again she translated Marc's response: "He said she wanted water. He didn't bring it to her. He was mad at her for a punishment he'd gotten."

Marc mumbled in English, "Gino would have gotten some water for her, but he was at school."

No way in hell did Adam believe Marc had been left alone in the house with a dying mother. "Who is taking care of you while your Mama's sick?"

Marc furrowed his brows. "Mama's friend, but she can't come."

"Why not?"

Marc's lower lip quivered. "My fault."

Clearly he was still stuck on whatever he thought he'd done to hurt his mama.

Adam knew they were on the brink of something big, but what? Hell, he had no fucking clue what was going on in Marc's head, truth be told. Was the death of his first mother the trauma that had kept him running from commitment? Certainly fit. But why did he blame himself?

This scene would work a lot better if he didn't have to have every question and answer translated. He hiked a thumb at Angelina and stood, expecting her to follow him.

Chapter Twenty-Seven

A ngelina stood and followed Adam, clenching her fists at her sides to keep from strangling him. "I followed your orders." *Mostly.* "That is *my* man in there and I'm not leaving him. Period."

Adam glared at her. "Don't you forget that I'm in charge of this scene, and I'll do whatever I think needs to be done."

She wanted to bite his head off, but knew he had Marc's best interests at heart, too. She backed off—for now. "Let me have a conversation with him in Italian—without the subtitles. It's jarring to have to translate everything for you."

She would follow Adam's plan, but he'd damned well better listen to what she had to say. "I not only know the language, but I know what his mama told him. I don't think he's spoken with her again since then to change that story." He scrutinized her a long moment. With each passing second, she feared he'd boot her out.

"You sure you know what you're getting into?"

He wasn't saying no. Angelina nodded and nearly smiled when she saw the big, tough Marine visibly relax along with her. Normally, Adam didn't give her or any of the subs in the club credit for being strong enough to handle things, although there had been a few moments when Angelina had first entered this room that she'd wanted to run away as fast as she could.

Adam nodded and delivered his orders in rapid succession. "Get your tears under control. Be strong and firm with him. Don't touch him, or you'll pull him out of the memories. The more they continue to bombard him, the harder it will be for him to run. Ask a mix of both open ended and targeted questions."

"Yes, Sir."

Satisfied she'd obey, he extended his hand in Marc's direction, in effect turning over control of the scene to Angelina. For the moment.

Dio, let me find the right questions. I need to help Marc find release.

She walked back to where Marc lay on the floor, his body rigid and turned once more on his side, legs curled up in a fetal position. Angelina stretched out next to him but didn't touch.

"Bambino mio." She attempted her best Northern Italian accent and spoke in a voice more firm and sure than her own.

Marc's body grew stiff. His breathing stopped. *"Mamma?"*

She fought the urge to brush a lock of hair from his forehead. *Don't touch him or Adam will yank you out of this dungeon.*

She continued to speak in the dialect of Marc's childhood. *"Sí, bambino mio.* Why are you hiding from me?"

Marc grimaced as if in pain, and his chin quivered. His voice sounded like a child's. *"Scusa, mamma.* I didn't mean to disobey you."

"Remind me. What did you do?"

"Lots of things, but mostly you wanted a glass of water." He choked on a sob. "I'm sorry I can't be good like Gino, Mama. He wouldn't have let you die."

His words threw her. "What is this talk of letting me die?"

"You needed me. I disobeyed. Again."

The anguish and regret in Marc's voice broke her heart. It took every ounce of discipline she possessed not to reach out and comfort him. "Nonsense. You are my precious baby boy."

He paused for several moments as if to mull that over. A peaceful look came over his face. Perhaps she'd gotten through to him.

*   *   *

Mrs. Giovanni set the hairbrush down on the bed. Marco stood and went to the bathroom to clean himself up.

"Marco, why did you disobey me?"

The voice he heard wasn't Mrs. Giovanni's. She sounded like Mama—almost but not exactly. Had she witnessed his shame?

Wait. That wasn't the voice of the mama who had raised him and ran the family resort.

Marco found himself in a darkened bedroom. The bed was empty. Mama was gone...

"I must punish you."

Marco turned to find Mama in her nightgown, dark circles under her eyes. She wasn't dead! But she should be in bed.

"I do this only because I love you and want you to grow up to be a good boy and a good man someday, even if I won't be here to see that happen." She walked over to her vanity and picked up her hairbrush. She used to let him brush her long hair with it, but she'd lost her hair. Gino said it was because she was sick. This was one of those times when she planned to paddle him with the hairbrush, though.

She sat on the bed and motioned him over. Tears streamed down his face. He didn't like being punished. He already held his hands over his bottom. *"Scusa, mamma. I'll be good from now on."*

Again, she crooked her finger. *"I'm going to help you remember to be better next time."*

He shook his head. Like a big baby, he started to cry. *"I'm sorry, Mama. I'll be good!"*

"Marco, don't make me call Papa. You know he would hurt you much more than I will."

Papa's whippings always hurt more than Mama's. But he hadn't been home in a long time. Not since Mama got sick and came to live with Mama's friend. Marco forced one foot in front of the other and crossed the room to stand by her. Mama patted her lap and helped position him across her thighs.

"Tell Mama what you did wrong."

"I left my toys on the floor, and Mrs. Milanesi tripped and got hurt."

"Haven't I reminded you time and time again that someone could get hurt if you didn't clean up after yourself?"

"Sí, mamma. Scusami."

"Saying you're sorry this time isn't going to make Mrs. Milanesi's sprained ankle any better. But perhaps if you feel some pain yourself, you can understand better how she feels."

He didn't have to wait long for the first blow. He prepared to scream before he realized, surprisingly, it didn't hurt nearly as much as he'd expected from earlier whippings she'd given him. Maybe Mama's illness made her arm weaker, too. But after the fourth blow, he yelled like a baby. She kept spanking him far longer than he'd ever remembered being spanked before. Mama was very upset with him.

Finally, the punishment ended, and Mama helped him onto his feet again.

"Now, go wash your face. And bring Mama a glass of water."

Marco squirmed off her lap and ran to the bathroom. He scrubbed the tears off his face and dropped his pants to look at the red marks on his bottom. Marco hadn't hurt Mrs. Milanesi on purpose, but Mama had made these marks on purpose.

"Bambino mio! *Bring me a glass of water!*"

"No, mamma! *I hate you!*"

Marco ran out of the bathroom and down the hallway to the kitchen. Mrs. Milanesi sat at the kitchen table, her ankle propped up on a chair and a bowl of flat beans in her lap as she snapped them for dinner. Tears streamed down her face, too.

"I'm sorry, little one. I know you didn't mean for me to get hurt."

He refused to make eye contact with her. Marco didn't blame her for his whipping but didn't want to talk to her right now either. He was ashamed at being such a bad boy. If only he could be more like Gino. They loved him better. He ran out the back door.

"Don't forget your coat, Marco!"

He wished this lady were his mother. He wouldn't go back to Mama. Ever. He was going to run away...

Marco flipped on the bathroom light and stared at his face in the mirror—his seventeen-year-old face. His ass still burned from the paddling Mrs. Giovanni had given him.

"Marco, stop hiding in there! Be a man and come back in here."

How was he supposed to be a man when she'd just paddled him like a disobedient child?

Marco needed to get out of this guest suite and get away from the woman in the bedroom. Run away...

* * *

Angelina had hoped her words a little while ago would help Marc feel less guilty about one or both of his mothers, but he'd only grown more agitated.

Emiliana must have loved him if he had so many regrets over failing her. Good. Children shouldn't suffer because of the sins of the parents. She would have hated that Emiliana had blamed Marco because his father couldn't keep it in his pants or his mother couldn't say no to her brother-in-law.

Marc opened his eyes, but she could tell he wasn't actually looking at her as Angelina. "Mama, may I ask you something?"

"Of course, *cara*."

"Gino said my real mama isn't dead like his. Is that true?"

Angelina gasped before regaining some composure. Gino had told him that at such a young age? Could she blame him, though? Gino was only six when his mother died. He wouldn't have been able to process such a profound loss any more than Marc had been. Marc had blocked out that memory all these years, until Melissa had opened a can of worms New Year's weekend.

What should she say? Angelina didn't know the truth about his birth any more than Marc did. She needed to keep her words vague enough not to skew his beliefs if and when the truth ever came to light.

"Marco, you are a gift from God to me and Papa. So is Gino. I love you both equally." She hoped he'd tip her off as to which of his mamas he was speaking with now and that her vague response would satisfy him.

Marc remained silent before his face broke out in a sweet smile. "I love you, too, Mama."

His entire body relaxed into the mattress. Angelina's did as well, albeit on the hard floor next to the foul-smelling mattress. Perhaps he could put the demons to rest now and sleep. Again, the urge to wrap him in her arms was so great she shook with the effort to obey Adam's order not to touch him.

"No!" Without warning, Marc's body stiffened before he began to wriggle away from her. "I heard her. She talked to me, Gino! She's not dead. She's just sleeping!"

Damn. He'd heard her as Emiliana, not Natalia. What now?

Marc's eyes remained closed, but his eyelids darted as if in REM sleep. "Get Papa!"

She spoke to him in Italian. "Marco? Can you hear me?"

He responded in his native tongue, as well. "*Mamma?* Gino keeps saying you're dead. Tell him I'm not lying."

Her talking with him as the mama he lost was messing with the way the memories were playing out in his head. She prayed she wasn't doing any psychological damage by continuing this scene as the first mama he'd ever known. "Tell me what is happening, Marco."

"Gino found me in my lair and made me come home. He keeps saying you're dead. But you aren't. He lied. Gino isn't *always* the good one."

Marc's head turned as if someone had entered the scene in his head. "No, Gino! Stop lying!"

"What did Gino say?" Gino's voice seemed to come through loud and clear in Marc's head. She wished she knew what he was saying.

"He said Papa left us, too." What? Angelina wanted to explode with fury. What kind of bastard would leave a dying wife with two young boys, much less abandon the boys after her death?

Marc's labored breathing and leg movements indicated to Angelina he was running. Again. After a while, he shrank into the mattress, his back to her. He fisted his hands. Slowly, his breathing returned to normal.

"Where are you now, Marco?"

"Hiding." He gasped for breath. "In my lair."

He confused her jumping between hiding in the closet and hiding in the woods. Both seemed to be his safe places as the memories played out in his head. Angelina stroked his forehead. "There, there. You're safe now."

Too late, she remembered Adam's dictate. She looked over at Adam and saw he looked ready to send her packing, but she no longer cared and turned away, ignoring him. Marc was alone and afraid and needed human contact right now. "Marco, I must leave you now and go to heaven. But I'll always watch over you."

"*No, mamma!* Don't leave me again! I don't want you to be dead anymore! I'm sorry I wanted Mrs. Milanesi to be my mama."

Oh, Dio. She closed her eyes and absorbed some of the pain and guilt Marc had felt as a little boy. She opened her eyes again to find tears streaming down his anguished face.

He whispered, "It hurts. I don't want to remember. I'm sorry I made you go away, Mama."

"I was sick, Marco. There was nothing you could do to save me or keep me here. It wasn't your fault."

The veins in his neck bulged as he fought against unseen resistance. "No, Gino! I won't go back there!"

Angelina stroked his hair. "What's happening, Marco? Where are you?"

He began sobbing uncontrollably. "No! Leave me alone!" He pulled away from her and rocked his body to comfort himself as he fought some unseen entity. "Let me go! I don't want to go!"

She reached out to touch his arm, but Adam intercepted her hand before she could make contact again. He jerked his head toward the door. She brushed Adam's hand away and glared at him, vehemently shaking her head. With a thump to her chest, she declared her intention to remain in control of this scene for the foreseeable future. Pulling away, she took a deep breath and regained her composure. Standing up to this intimidating man rattled her to the core. But she wouldn't let him continue this scene without her.

Kneeling beside Marc but not touching him, she continued. "Marc...*Marco*, who tried to take you away from your hiding place?"

Silence.

"Who are you with, Marco?"

His voice sounded small, weak. "Zietta Natalia, please make Mama wake up."

He was with Mama D'Alessio now. Time to change voices. "I know you want her to wake up, Marco, but she went to heaven to be with God and all His saints."

Marc shook his head.

"She was very sick. Her body couldn't fight any longer."

"I should have helped her fight. She needed me. I was bad. I left her alone."

"Marco, what is Zietta Natalia saying?"

"She wants to take me and Gino to live with her. She says we'll be her little boys forever." He paused and cocked his head listening to voices heard only to him. "You can't love me. I'm bad!"

Again Marc's head turned as his attention was grabbed by some new player on the stage in his head. "Gino? Am I in trouble?"

Adam stepped forward. "No, Marco. You did nothing wrong."

Tears stung Angelina's eyes that Adam had stepped into the role of Gino.

When Marc spoke again, he wrinkled his brow and his voice was that of an adult again. "I never stopped loving you, Gino. I forgave you, but it was too late. I wish I'd been able to tell you I was sorry before…"

Adam cleared his throat. "You have nothing to apologize for. None of this was your fault. We were both just young and stupid to fight over a girl like that. But I needed to be in Kandahar to bring something good out of a great big mess."

"Saving Staff Sergeant Anderson?"

"Yeah."

"You may have died a hero, Gino, but you were my hero my whole life." Tears fell from his closed eyes.

Adam squeezed Marc's shoulder. "You got that hero thing down, too, little brother, after what you did for Damián and your Marines in Fallujah."

Marc shook his head in the negative but didn't say anything. After a moment, Adam took his hand away.

"Gino, I wore your mask just like you said. No one ever knew…"

She brought her fingertips to her lips to still their shaking. *Gino* was the one who made Marc wear a mask all these years? Why? Angelina's heart went out to her man.

He looked confused for a moment. "…except for Angelina. She's too smart for us both."

She grinned through her tears at his words.

"You'd like her, Gino." His expression grew fierce. "But if you ever try to take her away, I'll kill you."

Angelina was taken aback by the vehemence in his words, but knew it was just *machismo* speaking.

He continued with intense emotion. "We both wore the mask, didn't we? Neither of us was one."

One what? What were the boys trying to mask? Marc's body slumped, and his head lolled to the side. Adam reached for something that looked like a stun gun, but she held her hand out to him and shook her head.

"He's done, Adam. It's over."

Adam stared at her a long moment, sizing her up, and finally he nodded.

For the first time in months, Marc's face was free of worry. She'd accomplished what she'd set out to do. Now to get out before Marc knew she'd been here.

Angelina got to her feet and started to walk away but ran into Adam's solid chest. Before she could step around him, he wrapped his arm around her back, and propelled her from the room into the weight room. No sooner had she crossed the threshold, knowing Marc wouldn't hear her, she gave in to the torrent of tears she'd been trying to shore up since she'd entered the dungeon and found Marc filthy, restrained, and helpless.

Adam handed her a clean towel from a stack in the corner and she wiped the tears from her face and eyes. She couldn't make eye contact. "Will he remember any of this?"

"Doctor McKenzie says even if he doesn't remember the specific scenes that played out down here and in his head, he'll remember the feelings and possibly some of the memories we triggered."

"I don't know what he was seeing, but I don't want him to wonder about the past anymore. He needs to be at peace." Angelina pulled away. "I'm going home now. He needs to do some thinking about us, too. I don't want him to make any decisions in a vulnerable state like this."

"I think you two have a lot of talking you need to do. You need to stay and be a part of his aftercare."

She shook her head. "Marc doesn't like to show me any sign of weakness. He'll be too vulnerable when he comes out of the effects of the interrogation. As it is, he probably won't remember I was here. He thinks he was talking with his mama and his aunt. But if he wants me, he knows where to find me."

Adam held her upper arm lightly, keeping her from leaving. "You were right, Angelina."

He'd just admitted she was right about something? Had the earth tilted on its axis? "About?"

"About coming into the interrogation as his mother. About touching him. You've done an incredible job of helping solve some of the mystery that is Marc's past."

"I still don't have a clue who is his aunt and who is his birth mama. *Dio*, it's so confusing. I only shared some of what I knew about his past. One thing I know, though, is that Mama D'Alessio wants to have her son back—maybe even to really *have* him for the first time as her own. They're going to have to work out some things."

Angelina wanted Marc to put this behind him and move on—with her, she hoped—but dredging up more of the past might lead to more hurt for him.

She shrugged. "I love that man more than the air I breathe. I just want him to find what he's searching for."

The urge to run to him and throw herself into his arms was difficult to fight, but she'd only confuse and upset him. She needed to get away before she lost it. "Have him call me when he's ready to talk."

Angelina turned away without waiting for a response. Suddenly feeling as if she bore the weight of the world on her back, she left the dungeon hoping she'd never have to come back down here again. Unless it was to play with Marc. *Dio*, she'd go anywhere that man asked her, do anything he wanted—if only he'd let her back into his life again.

But she wouldn't beg him.

Marc needed to figure out what to do from this point on his own. She hoped he was willing to work on their relationship. Surely he would, once he wasn't so lost and confused.

*   *   *

Adam watched Marc toss around on the rack as his psyche tried to process more of the shit that had just gone down the past five days.

RACK. Hell, this had gone beyond RACK even.

Fuck. Adam rarely got involved doing scenes mined with so many fucking boobytraps. Mindfucks were one thing, but he'd not only fucked over Marc's mind but had put his body through hell as well.

"Why'd you have to be so hard to break, Doc?"

Once they'd gotten into the scene, there had been no turning back. He just hoped Marc would find some kind of closure after all the hell he'd been through. He'd barely been lucid the first thirty-six hours of aftercare. Sleeping mostly.

"Don't fucking leave me again, Gino!"

Marc's arm struck the bed beside him. Time to talk out some of this shit.

"Doc! Open your eyes."

Marc furrowed his brows at Adam's order, but his grunt training won out and he obeyed his master sergeant. Blinking several times, he soon focused on Adam's face.

"Where am I?"

"One of the private bedrooms at the club. What were you just dreaming about?"

He thought a moment. Adam saw the flash of pain in his eyes when realization dawned.

"Gino. He was talking to me." Marc's eyes filled with tears.

Fuck. Marc wouldn't want Adam witnessing the waterworks, but Marc's filters had been annihilated. His voice grew raspy. "He told me he wasn't dead. I believed him. So real. I wanted to ask him to forgive me, but he left before I could. Again."

"Forgive you for what?"

Marc didn't answer for a while and then shrugged. "I guess for being so pissed at him over Melissa."

"Sounds like he ought to be the one apologizing for that business. 'Bros before hoes.'"

Marc rolled onto his side taking the sheet with him. He curled his legs up to his chest practically assuming the fetal position. "She wasn't worth losing my brother over."

"Hindsight's twenty-twenty, Doc. You just relived the same pain you felt as the drama unfolded back then. Pretty intense for what, a twenty-two-year-old?"

"Twenty-three."

"Fuck. You didn't know shit about women at that age."

Marc grinned. "Still don't." He wrinkled his brows together again.

Adam ran his hand through his short-cropped hair. "Listen, we're going to need a debriefing about all this over the next several days as you continue to process what happened."

Marc nodded.

"Friends don't use SERE School resistance tactics on their friends. I need to know if we're okay with each other after what I put you through."

Marc cocked his head. "You did what I asked you to do. Why wouldn't we be okay?"

Adam felt a weight lift off his shoulders. "I will say you were a damned hard nut to crack. A simple BDSM interrogation scene wouldn't have worked."

"I agree." He remained silent for a moment. "I don't know if what I remember ever happened or not."

"Flashbacks and memories are going to hit you in small blasts for a while, especially the next week. Just be prepared. Don't worry too much about what's real. Memories are fluid and pretty unreliable as far as truth goes; just look at eyewitness accounts. The important thing is what you take away from the process. You need to focus on the feelings wrapped around those memories."

He thought some more before hiding a yawn. "I hope it's worth it. I'd hate to have put you through this for nothing."

"You aren't getting rid of me yet. The aftercare period is probably more important than the scene itself. Grant's here, too. Damián's getting ready to head to California to prepare for the wedding, but he also contributed to the scene."

"I don't remember Damián much, but definitely Grant." The expression on his face made it clear he didn't remember her fondly. Adam grinned. "I never knew when I was hallucinating and when it was real."

"They weren't the only ones there. Remember anyone else?"

He thought a bit and his eyes opened wider. "Karla! How's her hand? Why the fuck didn't you let me take a look at it?"

Adam grinned. "Mind game. She's fine. I just needed you to think something had gone wrong. Only way you'd believe I'd abandoned you while restrained was if I lost my head because I thought Karla was hurt."

"Shit, Adam. I thought..." Marc didn't finish the thought.

"Remember anyone else?"

*   *   *

Angelina?

Marc didn't say her name, though. No doubt he'd conjured up memories of her. Wishful thinking. The whole scene had been for her—rather for him to be able to break down barriers that were keeping him away from her. But Adam wouldn't have allowed her into the room to see the state he was in if even half of what he remembered about the scene was true. She wouldn't have understood.

He grinned. More than likely, she'd have strung Adam up by the balls for hurting her man.

Her man.

"What's so fucking funny?"

Marc almost didn't say, but spoke anyway. "Just had this image of what would have happened if Angelina had found me strung up in the dungeon. She'd have strung you up by the balls, I think, for hurting me."

"Don't be so sure she didn't."

The smile faded from Marc's face. "You mean she was there? When? What did she see?"

His face burned with shame that she'd seen him in that state. Why didn't he remember her?

"We needed someone to talk to you in Italian once you regressed to your younger years in Italy. She knew about the scene already somehow. My guess is Karla tipped her off. How she stayed upstairs until we called her down shows some damned fine discipline."

His girl. He'd helped a little with that maybe, but she had been strong from the get-go.

"I didn't think she'd be able to add anything to a SERE scene, but that girl has your six. Thinks on her feet, too. Oh, and she definitely would have strung me up by my junk if I had tried to keep her away from you."

Dio, what had she seen and heard? Would she still want to be his girl? Had Marc learned anything from the scene that would help him straighten things out with Angelina?

Marc remembered Mama's talking with him at some point. "Please tell me you didn't have Mama down there, too."

Adam grinned. "No, that would have been Angelina. She's quite good at mimicking voices. She also did the voice of Gino's mama and maybe some others, too."

Marc relaxed a little. At least Mama hadn't witnessed him humiliated and broken.

Never show them your weaknesses.

Marc tried to replay more of the scene, but a pounding headache and the need for sleep made it difficult to concentrate. "Lots of people were there who are gone forever. Gino. Aunt Emiliana." He knew they weren't real, but in his mind they'd been very real again for a short time. "There was a woman who took care of Gino and me. Mrs. Mila…" He shook his head. "I can't remember now."

"Others?"

Unable to fight back another yawn, Marc covered his mouth.

"That's enough for now. You get some more rest. Someone will be with you at all times until we release you from this scene."

Marc nodded and closed his eyes.

"I just had a thought, though, given how many times you were talking to Gino."

"What's that?"

"We'll be out near Pendleton for Damián's wedding Memorial Day Weekend. How would you feel about getting together with some of the Marines who served in the unit with Gino?"

Blood pounded in Marc's head and he opened his eyes again. He hadn't realized how far he was from forgiving Gino until this interrogation scene. What could talking with a bunch of strangers do to resolve his issues with a long-dead brother?

"I'm not sure."

"Think about it. You know how you grunts talk in the barracks and during down time. You wondered once after you were injured in that shithole whether he'd been a good Marine or if he'd even wanted to be one. I know he was a damned fine Marine from the perspective of being his master sergeant, but I think hearing what his peers thought of him might help you put things in perspective with his memory."

Marc's eyelids grew heavy again. He didn't want to think about that right now.

Too tired.

"I'll think about it."

"Fair enough. Get some sleep."

Chapter Twenty-Eight

"Where is he?" Angelina glared at Karla the moment she walked into the kitchen. She needed to get to Marc. Where had Adam taken him after that nightmare of an interrogation scene ended? She needed to save him from himself. How could he have agreed to something so risky and detrimental to his health? Angelina had been battling a mixture of sorrow, frustration, and rage ever since she'd called Karla an hour ago to check on him only to have her friend let slip that he'd barely started to come around two days after the scene ended. Why hadn't anyone called her?

Because you abandoned him again when he needed you most.

"Don't make me tear this place apart looking for him, Karla, because I will."

"Angie, I wasn't even supposed to tell you as much as I did. Adam said you didn't want to be involved in the aftercare. That Marc wouldn't want you to see him like this."

She swallowed hard. "It's too damned late for that. Marc involved me when he invited me into his life last fall, letting me in as far as he could. How was I supposed to know why he couldn't open himself up any further? I just thought he was being a stubborn Italian male."

Angelina's frustration melted into a simmering anger. "He's not going to shut me out again. Adam asked me originally to be there for the aftercare. I had no idea it would take this long. Think how you would feel if that was Adam and someone was keeping you away from him."

Karla started toward her, but Angelina took a step back. "Look, Angie, I had no idea what those two had cooked up before this scene started and never could have imagined anyone would willingly go through what Marc agreed to do, but he made the choice to take the scene far beyond the edge of safe and sane. He was risk-aware. This has been terribly hard on Adam, too.

He loves Marc like a brother."

"He has a strange way of showing it."

Anger flashed in Karla's eyes. She clenched her jaw before taking a deep breath. "You don't want to go there, Angie. You haven't seen how tormented Adam is about this. Last night, he leaped up from lying next to me in bed, jumped over me, and landed on the floor on the opposite side of the bed." Her hand went to her belly and her voice cracked with emotion. "If he'd landed on me and the…baby." Karla shuddered. "Now he says he won't sleep with me starting tonight for fear of hurting us. I know this interrogation scene churned up something in him…"

For the first time, Angelina noticed the dark circles under Karla's eyes. That Adam cared enough about Marc to have nightmares made her finally open her eyes and let her anger dissipate. This added stress couldn't be good for Karla or her baby. Everyone had to be totally exhausted from the havoc this scene had unleashed in their small community. They were a family, and this nightmarish scene had affected each one in some way. Time to regroup.

"Karla, I'm sorry." She blinked back tears. "I'm out of line." She glanced away and noticed a bouquet of a dozen long-stemmed roses on the counter and a box from a jewelry store next to it. Angelina thought the garishly hot-pink color of the roses a strange choice, but didn't say anything. The roses were just the thing she needed to defuse more of her anger. Karla's birthday was today! "Oh, God! I completely forgot!"

Karla waved her hand away. "It's not important. Adam always sends me flowers. That he remembered my birthday with all that's going on now floored me." Tears sparkled in her eyes. "He's not as tough as you all seem to think."

She walked over to her friend and hugged her from the side, avoiding her protruding belly. "Karla, I'm not angry at you. Or Adam. I know everyone is trying to do what Marc asked for in that damned video consent. Just tell me where he is."

Karla waited so long to respond that Angelina stepped back. After a silent exchange, Karla's gaze strayed toward the hallway.

Surely they didn't still have him in the dungeon, although the hallway also led to the upstairs. She expected him to be in a comfortable bed now. "I'll knock on every door upstairs and down until I find him."

Her friend sighed and leaned her hip against the counter. "Adam took him up to the room at the opposite end of the hall from our bedroom.

Doctor Mac ran IV fluids the first twenty-four hours to stabilize him. We couldn't take him to a hospital or they'd have hauled half of us to jail on charges of torture, unlawful imprisonment, and abuse."

No goddamned kidding.

"Marc's mostly slept today, but Adam and Grant have kept watch over him in shifts twenty-four/seven, and Doctor Mac will check on him again after the clinic closes tonight. He's never been alone."

At least they'd gotten that part right. "Thanks—now go sit down before you drop. You look exhausted, too."

"Angie—I'm so sorry I played any part in this, but I had no idea the scope of what they'd planned."

Angelina nodded but couldn't take time to discuss it further. Marc needed her. She rushed down the hallway to the stairwell and took them two at a time. She and Marc had played upstairs in this very bedroom once after watching an intense fireplay scene in one of the theme rooms downstairs.

Steeling herself for the battle she knew would be coming, Angelina knocked quietly on the door. She didn't want to wake Marc if he still slept. His body needed all of the rest it could get after the ordeal it had been through.

The door opened about a foot, and Adam blocked her from entering or looking into the room.

"I need to see him."

Rather than let her inside, Adam opened the door just wide enough to step through into the hallway, forcing her to take a couple of steps back. He closed the door behind him. She noticed he hadn't shaved in days and didn't look as if he'd been getting much sleep.

"Adam, if you think you can keep me out of there—"

"Quiet."

Adam used to intimidate the hell out of her, but no more. She wouldn't allow him to keep them separated. Marc needed her.

"Tell me how he is. Is he going to come out of this okay?"

Adam scrutinized her so intensely she almost took another step back but willed her body not to submit to him. He might be a Dom, but he wasn't *her* Dom. No, he'd just broken *her* Dom and reduced him to an almost infantile state.

"Everything's going as expected."

Angelina's hands flew up as she spoke, unable to keep her emotions under control, but she kept her voice at a harsh whisper. "How can you say that? Has he come out of it? Is the old Marc back yet?"

Adam pointed a finger at her as if she were a petulant child. "You listen to me…" Again she fought hard against the urge to back away.

Stand your ground; Marc needs you.

"…Marc chose to do this the way we did it, no holds barred, because he wanted to be able to come to you afterward without any barriers. We only did what he asked us to do."

Was Adam trying to convince her or himself?

I will not cry.

But she did and hated every tear that rolled down her face. Her nose clogged, and she had to force her words out of a constricted throat. "I never wanted him to do anything like that for me. I would never have asked such a thing."

Mio Dio, *what have I done to him?*

Marc loved her in his way. She thought pushing him to prove it by letting her into his life completely would get him to move forward from where he'd gotten stuck. In the process, she'd nearly destroyed him.

"Adam, I need to make this right. Why won't you let me see him?"

"I didn't say you can't see him, but you need to be aware of the situation before I let you go in there."

Angelina nodded, a mixture of fear and anxiety overwhelming her. She wiped the tears off her face and stood taller. She needed to be strong for Marc, now more than ever.

"He's only started coming out of it today. Grant and I have helped him process some of the triggers when they hit, but it's probably going to get a lot more intense before he's fully reintegrated."

She nodded, wishing Adam would finish his spiel quickly so she could go and be with the man she loved more than her own life. That Marc had done this to himself to win her back broke her heart—and pissed her off.

"I never wanted to break him. I just wanted him to trust me."

"You didn't have to ask him, hon. He'd have gone through much worse if need be. He loves you that much."

Her chin shook, but she gritted her teeth to regain control.

Adam looked away before seeming to come to a decision. He nailed her with his Dom stare. God, she hated when the Doms used such unfair tactics with submissives.

"This isn't about you, Angelina. He might have gone into it for you initially, but what he achieved in that interrogation scene was nothing short of catharsis. He needed to remember those events his mind had blocked out for decades. His coping strategies—like running from close relationships with women or pushing people away before they could abandon him—served no purpose other than keeping him distant and alone." Adam glanced away. "Whether the memories conjured up in the dungeon are real or imagined, they're a part of his psyche now." He seemed to have regrets about that, but added, "This aftercare phase is crucial to help reintegrate him into the adult Marc *wants* to be."

"Is he still lost in his memories of childhood?"

"Sometimes, but that's not unheard of this early into aftercare after such a long scene. He'll be hit with triggers for days, maybe weeks. They will jump around to different points in his life at random, depending on what reminders or dreams he has."

"It's already been two days!"

Adam glared at her. "Keep your voice down and your emotions in check if you want to get past me into that room, girl. Deep breath. Now."

"I want to be with him. I can help."

"Don't make me repeat myself."

Angelina fought the urge to shove him aside and get to Marc, but didn't want to have Adam kick her out. She took as deep a breath as her anger would allow.

"Better. Listen, it may be several more days before he reintegrates fully. He might not even know who you are some of the time."

"He'll know in his heart by the way I plan to love and nurture him."

"I hope so." How could she convince Adam Marc needed her? "Right now, he's going back and forth between the period before he joined the Navy and when his first mother died. He talks to Gino a lot, too."

Her hand flew to her mouth. Poor Marc. The need to hold him grew even stronger. She pressed her fingertips against her lips to keep them from shaking. *Control yourself.* She needed to prove to Adam she'd be strong for Marc. She took a deep, steadying breath and squared her shoulders.

Adam assessed her a moment before giving a slight nod. "Be strong for him. Remember, you're his submissive. You hold the power in your dynamic, and it's up to you how you choose to use that power."

His words made her even more nervous. "What do you want me to do?"

A few minutes ago, she was ready to batter down the door, if need be. Now she was terrified to go in there. She was so out of her element. If she did anything to make it any worse for Marc...

"I think a little TLC might be in order. Just take care of him."

I can do this.

"Feed him, bathe him, hold him—hell, sing him lullabies, for all I care."

Despite their separation, she wanted nothing more than to take care of her former Dom. This she could handle without a doubt.

"I'm sorry for charging in here like this, Adam."

Adam smiled. "Hon, if you hadn't been in full-on mama bear mode, I wouldn't be about to let you pass through that doorway. He needs someone like you to fight for him right now. I think he's tired of seeing me every time he wakes up."

For the first time since she'd seen Marc in the dungeon, she smiled back as relief washed over her.

I can do this.

"Now, I'm going to leave you two alone. If you need anything, there's a baby monitor on the nightstand. Just turn it on and call out. Grant's sleeping down the hall, and we each have a receiver, so one or both of us will be here before you can blink."

She nodded and looked toward the closed bedroom door.

"Can I order you some Chinese? It's Karla's birthday, and she needs a little aftercare, too, after all this. We're staying in, though, in case Marc needs us."

Angelina shook her head. The thought of food turned her stomach. "Go to Karla. I don't think I helped her stress level any. I was so upset—" Angelina took his arm and indicated for him to head for the stairs. "Hurry. She's in the kitchen."

Without another word, Adam rushed down the stairs.

I'm sorry I took my anger out on you, Karla.

She'd make it up to Karla later. Right now, she had to focus her entire being on Marc. Angelina steeled herself and grabbed the door handle. Adam said days of aftercare could be expected, but none of this was normal to Angelina.

Deep breath, cara. Marc's voice in her mind reassured her.

"Yes, Sir," she whispered.

The door creaked as she opened it wider. Her gaze zeroed in on Marc immediately, curled in an almost fetal position on the bed. He had kicked off his covers and wore nothing but a T-shirt and boxer briefs. He hugged one of the pillows in the curve of his body. When she reached the bed, she slipped off her shoes, reached out, and tugged the pillow out of his grip with a bit of a struggle and a moan from him. She slipped between the covers to wrap him in her arms as tightly as she could with his arms and legs separating their bodies.

"I've got you, Marc." She stroked his hair. "I'm going to take care of you."

She prayed he wouldn't be so far regressed that he wouldn't remember her.

Marc's body remained rigid for a long time until he placed his hand on her shoulder and slowly pushed her away.

Oh, Marc, don't reject me again.

Once she was flat on her back and could go no further, though, he moved closer to her and laid his head on her chest, wrapping his arm over her waist as he uncurled his legs. His hair smelled sour from stale sweat, but nothing mattered except feeling his weight on her, his arm holding her in his embrace—even if he didn't know who she was. Some of her anxiety dissipated.

"Shhhh, I'll protect you."

*   *   *

"My Mama's dead. You still have yours."

Marco shook his head at Gino's words. He didn't understand. Maybe Gino didn't think Marco deserved to call her Mama anymore after what he'd done. All his fault. If Marco had gotten her the glass of water, he could have saved her.

But Mama made him mad. He ran away to hide from her, but his lair wasn't comforting when he was alone. Cold, dark, cramped.

Trapped.

He couldn't breathe.

"You have to come out now, Marco."

Leaving the lair was even scarier than hiding here. He shook his head harder. Seeing Mama again scared him even more. He couldn't look at her without feeling shame.

"Give me your hand, Marco."

Wait. That wasn't Gino. How had Zia Natalia found his hideout? "Leave me alone."

"Gino is in the kitchen with the ladies from the church. You need to be strong for him."

Marco loved his brother. If Gino needed him…

He reached out to accept her hand.

"You know I will never let anything happen to you two, don't you?"

Marco didn't know anything anymore. His world had turned crazy.

"Would you like to come live with me?"

Zia Natalia only had a tiny apartment. "Where would we sleep?"

She laughed a little bit. "I'll do whatever it takes to make a good home for you both. Don't you worry."

A few moments later, they walked into the kitchen, and Marco was overwhelmed by the grownups he barely knew all fussing over the table and counters filled with food as Mrs. Milanesi directed new arrivals as to where to put their dishes. He looked at her swollen ankle, still propped up on a chair, and guilt at causing her injury made him want to run and hide again.

He didn't see Gino anywhere.

Zia Natalia gripped his hand harder, and he looked up to see what had upset her. She seemed scared. When he followed her gaze, he saw Papa. Where had Papa been all this time? He had left them a long time ago. If he'd been here, could he have saved Mama? He laughed with one of the pretty ladies from church. Why wasn't he sad about Mama dying like everyone else was?

"Shhhh, I'll protect you."

Mamma?

He recognized her voice and turned toward the hallway. He walked into the bedroom where she lay sleeping. Not dead. Gino had lied. Why would he do that? Marco crawled onto the bed and laid his head on her chest. He felt her heart beating against his cheek. Her hand stroked his hair. He felt safe again for the first time since Mama had taken to the bed and Papa had left them.

At last, Marco escaped in sleep, feeling safe at last.

A soft, cool hand touched his neck, waking him.

"Why is it you Doms think you can control everything?" she whispered.

Angelina? She'd come back to him?

"When are you going to see you're human, just like the rest of us?"

Marc raised his head from her chest and stared into her eyes. "I don't know that I ever controlled anything, pet. Maybe that's what scares me the most about letting you in."

The sadness in her eyes made him wish it could be otherwise, but even more frightening was the thought of letting her into his heart, only to lose her. Like Mama. Could he do that?

Too exhausted to hold up his head any longer, he rested it once more on her chest and hugged her tighter.

He slept.

*　　*　　*

"Gino, get the fuck out of here!"

Sometime in the middle of the night, Angelina had to duck when Marc's fist sailed toward her face as he thrashed in his sleep.

"Marc, wake up! You're dreaming!"

Doctor McKenzie had checked him over earlier and proclaimed Marc to be doing remarkably well. He'd advised her to watch for depression, though, warning that triggers would continue to bombard him for days. She didn't want to have to call him back here this late if one of them got hurt. Besides, it was one thing hearing him talking in a little boy's voice to his Aunt Natalia and Gino earlier, but whatever was unfolding in his head now was from an older Marc. Man, was he pissed!

"She's mine, you bastard!"

Melissa again? Good God, she didn't want to share any part of Marc fighting over the Queen Bitch of the Universe, even in a dream.

"Marc, you're dreaming. Wake up. Now!"

"Stay out of this, Melissa."

Whoa! Careful who you call Melissa, if you know what's good for you.

She grabbed his shoulder to try and wake him. His arm sailed out, impacting her side and sending her flying off the bed. She quickly realized she'd hurt nothing but her ego. Her brothers had taught her to anticipate a punch like that, making her embarrassed she hadn't reacted faster. But they'd also shown her how to fall with minimal damage. She stood up and watched as he flailed his arms and legs in some silent battle with Gino.

Remembering the setup of this bedroom, she went to the closet and pulled out a package of thick rope. Hemp, a little scratchy, but she needed to subdue him before he hurt someone, namely her. Remembering the way she'd hogtied Allen Martin with the technique she'd learned in Marc's playroom and some techniques Luke had taught her since, she had Marc flipped onto his stomach and roped into a hogtie in under thirty seconds. He fought against the restraints, but in the absence of a toy bag with cuffs and other restraints, this was the best she could do.

"You bastard! You fucked my girl! I never want to see you again!"

Seriously? All this drama for a woman like Melissa? Now he was pissing her off, though she knew this was a much younger Marc rehashing something that happened long before he'd met her.

Trying to emulate Melissa's accent, she said, "Marco, darling, calm down." His struggles stilled for a moment before he raged and punched at the air again.

"You have everything. Why did you have to take her, too?" His body was bathed in sweat at his exertions.

Oh, Marc. She so didn't deserve either of you.

She used some of the inflections Melissa had used in her voice. "Marco, you're too wild-spirited. I need someone stable like Gino who can support me. But I've enjoyed being with you these past…" Angelina had no idea if they'd dated months or years, so she let her words fade away. Her heart told her Gino loved his little brother. He'd merely taken one for Team Marco when it came to Bitch Melissa.

A knock at the door drew her attention away from Marc. She made sure he'd stopped struggling before she left him for a moment. Before she reached the door, it opened and Adam stepped in. His gaze settled immediately on Marc's hogtied form on the bed, and his brows lifted before he turned his attention to her. She'd been yelling at Adam yesterday for mistreating Marc, and now she'd subdued and incapacitated him herself.

He remained silent a long moment, and then he smiled. "You seem to have everything under control."

"Um, he got a little rough and—"

"Don't apologize. I came up to check on you more than him. He's still having some pretty violent dreams?"

Angelina fought the urge to rub her left breast and side where Marc's fist had impacted with her and sent her sprawling earlier, so she gave a nod instead. "I have four brothers."

"I haven't forgotten how you took care of yourself on the mountain last fall." She would have thought the trauma of his subsequent cougar attack would have wiped away Adam's memories. He reached out and unknowingly patted her sore arm. She winced and pulled away. His gaze narrowed. "You're hurt. Let me see."

She shook her head and took a step back. "It's nothing. He's given me worse bruises when we've played."

Or during a nightmare.

She grinned, hoping to lighten the moment. No way was she removing her sweater to reveal to Adam the bruises he'd left.

"You weren't warmed up for this—and it wasn't play."

"I'm fine, Adam. Now, was there something you needed?"

He scrutinized her a moment and finally shook his head. "Karla and I will be bringing up some lunch soon. I'll ask her to check them out."

She rolled her eyes. Dio, *save me from overprotective Doms.*

"He's sleeping calmly now. Let me call you when I think he's awake enough to eat."

"I wasn't talking about feeding him but you. You haven't eaten in at least six hours. I need you to keep up your strength."

Something warmed in the pit of her stomach. Okay, sometimes she did enjoy the fact that Marc and his friends watched over all of the submissives in their community.

"Thanks, Adam." She found herself crooking her finger at him to bend toward her. The man was a couple of inches taller than Marc's six feet. He leaned over, tilting his ear toward her mouth, expecting her to whisper something. Instead, she pecked him on his whiskery cheek, breathing in his clean, woodsy smell.

The man stood straight again appearing flummoxed. "What was that for?"

"For taking such good care of all of us, Adam."

He shook his head and waved away her words.

"Deny it all you will, but I'm glad to be a part of your family."

"You've earned your place here. I'd given up on Marc ever dealing head-on with whatever was in his past. He hadn't been able to identify and move past it until you came into his life."

"He opened up a whole new world to me when he found me down-stairs."

But she still had no idea what kind of future they would have together. She'd hoped Marc would see they were right for each other, once he came out of this. After all he'd done to try and win her back, she had no doubt at all Marc had made a commitment to her, ring or no ring.

"Cara?"

Angelina turned to find a groggy-eyed Marc staring at her. Her stomach flipped a somersault. Did he recognize her or was he still talking to Melissa?

He took in his surroundings with a confused look on his face and then stared at her as if he didn't know who she was, which upset her. What if they couldn't bring back the Marc she loved? What if he was lost in a past where he thought he was still dating Bitch Melissa and wanting to marry her?

His eyes opened wider. "What are we doing in here, pet? I hope I didn't miss anything important."

Angelina relaxed and smiled, returning to the bed. She heard the door click closed behind her, already having forgotten about Adam.

"I'm sure there will be time to make many more memories in here together." She crawled between the sheets and faced him. "How are you feeling?"

"Like I've been run over by a Humvee—several times in quick succession."

She smiled. "That's more or less what happened. Adam, Damián, and Grant, maybe me even, all had a hand in making you feel that way."

"You think you could get me out of this hogtie? Who is responsible for trussing me up?"

Angelina grinned. "Well, Sir, you taught your submissive well."

He shook his head as she grabbed the safety scissors and cut the ropes. "What do you remember about the scene?"

"Adam and a bunch of crazy-ass dreams—maybe hallucinations is a better word." He grew pensive. "Mama told me the truth. I did have another mama. She died when I was three."

"What specifically do you remember about her?" His body grew tense, and she rubbed his arm until he relaxed again.

"I know the woman must have been my whole world at three, but I don't feel a connection with her the way I do Mama."

Hearing him call Mama D'Alessio his mother pleased her. "She really does love you and Gino like her own children."

"Hell, she might be my birth mother, as Solari said, but even if she isn't, she'll always be Mama to me."

"When you're feeling better, we should go talk with her. I have a feeling she still has answers to some of your questions. I hope you'll be able to forgive her someday for not telling you the truth."

He pulled away and quirked a brow at her. "I'm not sure there's anything to forgive. She did the best she could."

"My, you really did do some soul-searching this past week."

"I just have one question."

"What's that?"

"Who the hell beat my ass? Mistress A didn't make a reappearance, did she?"

Angelina suppressed a giggle. "I assure you I had nothing to do with hitting you in that scene."

*   *   *

Midmorning, Angelina led Marc down the hall to the shower in the bathroom attached to Karla's old bedroom. She let the water turn to hot as she reached for the hem of his tee to undress him.

"I can undress myself, *amore*."

"I know you can, but I have a strong need to take care of my man right now. So please indulge me."

He grinned. His face had the look of someone haunted, but a spark of life had returned to his eyes.

Adam had left Marc's overnight case containing clean clothes and toiletries in the room next door, where Angelina had been taken after being beaten by Allen late last summer. Apparently, Luke was making repairs to the bed in Karla's room.

"You'll feel better after a shower." Not to mention getting into a bed with clean linens.

All of this had happened because she'd wanted him to open up and let her be a part of his life. Could she ever forgive herself for kicking him out of her house the morning after Luke's accident?

Angelina, however, wanted nothing more than to take care of Marc. She stripped down herself so she could get into the shower with him. "Here we go, baby." She took his hand and led him into the stall. This would be one of the tamest showers they'd ever taken together. Once inside, the hot spray warmed her skin, but Marc's remained cold for several minutes. He'd been through such an intense ordeal.

She lathered the shower sponge and scrubbed his shoulders, chest, and back. They'd probably bathed him right after the scene ended, but it couldn't have been more than a hosing down judging by some of the crystallized sweat and grime on his body.

When he turned around, she saw the bruises and welts on his butt and muttered under her breath, "Hasn't anyone around here heard of a freaking safeword?"

Marc grabbed her hand and turned back to face her, his expression fierce. "No safeword. Couldn't take the chance. I've run too many times."

Of course, she'd been forced to watch the video of Marc consenting to this insanity. Was he even in his right mind when that video was made?

She took the bottle of shampoo and poured a generous amount into her cupped hand. "Bend toward me." Being a nursemaid hadn't been something she'd ever aspired to, but Marc brought out her nurturing instincts. If anyone needed to feel the loving touch of a woman, it was this wounded man.

But what she wanted more was to be his lover again. Maybe even his wife someday. The mother of his children. She'd never felt her biological clock ticking so loudly as now, perhaps because she was in Mama-Bear mode, as Adam put it.

Marc leaned forward as she'd instructed, holding onto her girls for balance and causing her to break into a grin. He held one nipple to his lips and sucked. She hissed in surprise and swatted his arm, giggling in relief at having him returning to his old self.

As the shampoo washed down her body, he pulled away, probably to keep the soap out of his mouth. She scrubbed his hair and scalp. "Keep your eyes closed, baby." After rinsing his hair, she took the bar of soap and lathered up the sponge again before washing his lower half. She was extra gentle with the welts, but the way he tensed his butt cheeks told her she was hurting him. He'd never marked her that hard and, knowing her tolerance for pain was extremely low, never would have. Tears burned her eyes, but she couldn't undo what had happened.

She turned off the water. After toweling him off, he took the towel and did the same for her, paying special attention to her breasts. She smiled and took the towel from him when her nipples became too sensitive. "That's good, Marc. Thank you."

He smiled and bent down to kiss her lips. He wrapped his arms around her to pull her closer, and she hissed when he pressed against the bruise on her breast. Marc pulled away.

"What's wrong?"

"Nothing. Just a little bruise."

He turned her sideways and lifted her arm. He growled. "Who did this to you?"

The protective Marc she loved was back.

"It was an accident. I forgot to duck." Pushing him away, she drew a ragged breath. "Let's go to bed."

"I asked you a question." He stared at her with such intensity, her stomach dropped.

"You had a nightmare sometime in the middle of the night. I assure you I'm fine. Only hurts when someone touches it."

"I hurt you?"

"You didn't know what you were doing."

Regret filled his eyes. "I'm so sorry. Perhaps it would be better if you slept alone."

Angelina placed her hands on her hips and, Dom or no Dom, let him have it. "Marc D'Alessio, if you think you can get rid of me again that easily, you have another think coming."

"I just don't want to hurt you a—"

"I. Said. It. Was. An. Accident. Normally, I'd have evaded the punch, but I wasn't fully awake. Now, let's go back to bed."

He measured her words a while longer before he smiled slightly. "Thought you'd never ask, *cara*."

He reached for her hand. Retrieving guest robes from the hooks behind the door, she helped him slip into one and put on the other before leading him through Karla's old bedroom and into the hall to the room where they'd be sleeping now. The only time she'd slept here, she'd been taken care of by Marc first and then Karla. Today, she planned to continue to take care of Marc's needs. Adam and Karla were across the hall if anything became more than she could handle, but after that one outburst, he'd been extremely gentle with her.

Choosing to sleep skin to skin, she removed his robe and slipped out of her own, turned back the coverlet and sheet on the sleigh bed, and crawled in. She beckoned for him to join her. He did so without hesitation and pulled her against him.

"Thank you for staying with me, *amore*. I like having you take care of me much more than Adam and Grant."

"I should hope so!"

They lay entwined in each other's arms, her cheek against his chest, his chin on her head holding her close. When he reached to cup her breast, she slapped his hand. "Cuddling only."

"You know how badly that plan went for us last time."

She swallowed past the lump in her throat. "I'm so sorry I sent you away that morning. If I'd known you'd concoct something as insane as that interrogation scene—"

"Enough. It's over. Bottom line is that it made me face what was holding me back. We might not be together now if I hadn't taken that risk."

"Have you remembered anything else you'd like to talk about?"

He shook his head. "I don't want to talk with you about that stuff right now."

Angelina tamped down her disappointment. Were they back where they'd been before, with him shutting her out? Maybe all this anguish had been a waste of time.

"I'd rather think about the future than the past. I've missed you so much, Angelina." He stroked her hair. "Promise you won't leave me again. I'm going to try really hard not to shut you out."

She leaned away and propped herself up on her elbow to study his face. Tears shone in his eyes, and she couldn't keep them from forming in her own. Even if Marc never completely opened himself up to her, life without him was not an option. She bent to kiss him gently on the lips before moving his head to her chest so he wouldn't see her tears.

"I'm here, Marc. I'll always be here for you."

He wrapped an arm around her waist and pulled her closer. "*Buonanotte, amore.*"

In a very short time, his breathing became steady and shallow. She didn't blame him for being exhausted, even though he'd slept for much of the past three days now. Her man was returning to her in small ways.

"Sweet dreams, my love." She hoped he wouldn't be plagued by any more bad dreams or triggers today. His mind and body needed comfort and peace.

Angelina stroked his hair, still wet from the shower, and hummed a lullaby. It had been so long since she'd heard *Ninna Nanna* sung to her. Mama had sung it in English.

> *Lullaby to a sailor,*
> *You are my beautiful sea*
> *Sometimes so nice and calm*
> *Sometimes just like a storm.*

But your mind is not free.
Please do not forget
That among the moon and the stars,
I am waiting for you with open arms

She hoped he would find peaceful sleep in her arms today. Soon enough, they would have to discuss where to go from here. Both seemed to want to be together, which was the main thing. They could work out what the future beyond that entailed later.

He groaned, and Angelina held him closer, hoping to keep the ghosts away. Right now, she wanted him to rest.

Tears burned her eyes, and she let them fall at last. Marc was safe again in her arms.

Chapter Twenty-Nine

Marc squeezed Angelina's hand as the elevator ascended to Mama and Papa's penthouse condo. He wasn't sure what information he would come away with this time, but the memories stirred up last week needed to be placed into some context he could use to make sense of his past.

"I'm proud of you, Marc."

He glanced down at her and smiled. "For finally facing my mama?"

She grinned. "No, for being courageous enough to confront the past head-on the way you did. A lot of people would just keep muddling through and not try to change behaviors that weren't working for them. That you were willing to face your fears and go through so much to break down the walls blocking you from a better life is just…one of the reasons I love you."

Marc wasn't sure any of his newfound revelations would change how he behaved, but… "One thing I do know is I never would have gone through that if you hadn't held my feet to the fire—or shown me you wouldn't put up with my shit." She had encouraged him to find the truth all along, but he hadn't been ready to deal with it until now. Thank God he had her standing beside him for today's meeting with Mama.

The elevator doors opened, and he motioned for her to precede him out of the car. They knocked and Carmella opened the door, greeting them with hugs and kisses. Marc had expected to see Mama, maybe Papa, but not his sister.

"So great to see you both again!" She waved them in. "Can I get you something to drink?"

"No, thanks. We just had lunch." Belatedly, Marc realized he shouldn't answer for Angelina and turned toward her. "Sorry. Did you want something?"

She beamed at him. "No, I'm fine. Better than fine. Thanks for asking."

Marc wasn't sure why Angelina was smiling so broadly or why she thanked him instead of Carmella for the offered refreshments, but he hoped her face would light up like that again and often. He bent to give her a kiss on the lips.

"Mama and Papa are being very hush-hush. Do you know what the family meeting is all about?"

Family meeting? Marc just wanted to have a private conversation with his parents. He wondered why Mama had told them to meet at home rather than in her office.

Placing his hand at the small of Angelina's back, he guided her ahead of him. Surprisingly less nervous than he had been in February when they had come here, he knew nothing Mama could say would be so devastating it would send him into another tailspin. He already knew most of what had happened and was coming to terms with the past, slowly.

Papa stood by the window with his arm around Mama's waist. Sandro sat on the sofa going through an old photo album. Everyone turned to face them at once. Angelina looked up at him, worry on her face. Marc no longer knew what to expect. He had no control.

Mama motioned them to join Sandro in the seating area, but Marc had some unfinished business to take care of first. He walked over to his parents and wrapped Mama in a hug.

She surprised him by holding onto him tightly and whispering, "I'm so glad you came back to me, Marco."

"Mama, I'm sorry for being such a sh—...such an ungrateful son. I know you've always loved me and taken care of me, even when you didn't have to. Thank you for adopting Gino and me."

She pulled away, tears in her eyes and a quizzical look on her face. "I could never have walked away from you two boys." She motioned them to the seating area. "We can talk more about those days. I promise to be as forthright as I can to help you put the pieces together."

"I'd like that very much, Mama."

"But first there are some things I need to say to you all." Her hand swept the room. "Things that should have been said long ago. Now, please sit, everyone."

Before following Mama's directive, Marc gave Papa a rare hug, too. This was the first time he'd seen the man since learning he wasn't Marc and Gino's birth father. "I love you, too, Papa. Thank you for being the best papa any kid could want. That includes grown kids, too." Blood or not, this man had raised him and given Marc his roots and wings. When Marc pulled away, he could have sworn the stoic man had tears in his eyes. Good, because Marc certainly did. Sometimes being Italian had its perks. No one thought you any less a man if you shed a few tears when faced with real emotion. Part of what had been unleashed in that interrogation scene and in the aftercare that followed was that Marc no longer denied his emotions. He expressed them.

Express, not repress.

The line from Angelina's favorite movie made him smile.

Angelina gave each of his parents a hug, too, before walking over to the settee and greeting his siblings across the coffee table. Marc followed and hugged them as well before taking a seat beside Angelina. Mama took the wingback, and Papa sat on the arm of her chair, his arm around Mama's shoulders. She appeared to be trembling with emotion.

Marc had intended to come in with both barrels loaded with questions, but instinct told him he needed to listen first. Mama had invited everyone here for a reason. After a long silence, Papa patted her back as if signaling her. Marc had wondered if her marriage to Papa had been one of convenience to achieve the goal of adopting him and Gino. No matter how their relationship began, though, they certainly had grown to love each other over their decades together.

"Thank you for being here today," Mama began. "This gathering is long overdue." Her chin quivered, and she pressed her lips together until she regained her composure. "I never wanted to hurt any of you."

She stared pointedly at Marc, and he nodded his understanding.

"I hope what I have to say won't upset anyone any more than I already have, but I have lived with this for a very long time and need to be honest with you about some things."

She paused, wringing her hands, no longer making eye contact with anyone.

Marc hated to see her so emotional but knew this probably was something she needed to get out. "Mama, take your time."

She nodded and smiled her appreciation to him, drawing in a deep breath. "You know about Gramps and my mama meeting during the Second World War. I was born from that…meeting." Mama didn't talk about sex. Marc grinned. "My mother then married my stepfather after the war ended, and they had my sister, Emiliana. She and I weren't particularly close growing up. Perhaps we might have been one day, but she died young, making that forever impossible."

Angelina reached across the settee and took Marc's hand. Like him, she probably was thinking about Marc and Gino and how their relationship had disintegrated in youth, something they had had no chance to rectify later.

"My sister married Paolo Solari. He owned a resort I worked at..." Mama's breathing became more rapid and shallow, and she stopped speaking.

Papa stroked her back. "Take your time, *amore*. Breathe."

She did as he instructed. "Paolo and Emiliana were Gino's parents." Marc was about to remind her of his birth to them as well but remembered what Paolo had said about Marc's origins. At the moment, Mama was busy dealing with Carmella's realization Gino was her cousin rather than her brother by birth.

"He loved you and Sandro just as much as he did Marco. To him, you were his brother and sister, just as sure as if you shared the same parents."

With tears streaming down her face, Mama turned her gaze to Marc as if in slow motion. He blocked out everything and everyone in the room except her, knowing her next words would provide him with one of the answers he'd come here seeking today.

"Paolo is your father, as well, Marco. But Emiliana is not your mother." She drew another deep breath. "I am. I gave birth to you three years after Gino was born."

Papa's voice commanded his attention. "Before you jump to conclusions, son, hear Mama out."

Marc nodded. No worries about remaining silent, because he wasn't able to form any words at the moment even if he'd wanted to.

"It's important that... I mean to say..." She drew another breath and composed herself. "Paolo Solari is not a good man."

Marc found his voice at last. "You don't have to tell me, Mama. I met him in February."

She drew in a sharp breath and raised her eyebrows in shock. "You what?"

Marc hadn't intended to drop the revelation without warning, but it was too late now. "I flew to Italy in late February, because I needed to meet the man you told me had...fathered me." Marc turned to Papa. "He is in no way someone I would ever consider to be my father. I'll always be grateful to you, Papa, for assuming that role when you married Mama."

Mama said, "I wish you'd told me before you'd decided to do that, Marco." Marc turned his attention once more to Mama. "That man isn't fit to be in your presence. He didn't earn the right to be around either of you boys." Her chin shook with emotion. "When he walked out on Emiliana, I was relieved that I could finally be with my sister again after a long absence. We didn't have many months left."

Her words led Marc to wonder if the man had abused him or Gino, but none of Marc's memories during the interrogation or the aftermath hinted at anything like that. Solari was negligent, a womanizer, and an asswipe. He dished out discipline more harshly than Emiliana, but lots of parents believed in corporal punishment. Yes, the man would remain a solid piece of shit in Marc's mind, but Mama hinted at something worse. What?

When Mama didn't continue, Marc prompted, "I don't understand, Mama. What did he do?"

She looked up at Papa and whispered, "I can't do this."

"Yes, you can. Remember, you did nothing wrong. You were a victim."

Zia Natalia gripped his hand harder, and he looked up to see what had upset her. She seemed scared. When he followed her gaze, he saw Papa.

"Your real mama isn't dead like mine is."

The memories hit him like a sledgehammer to the chest. Realization dawned at almost the same instant she spoke.

"Paolo forced me."

"*Mio Dio!*" Angelina's whispered words of shock registered as if from far away. She stroked Marc's leg, grounding him in the moment when he wanted to escape. *Run.*

Somehow the thought he had been a love child made his beginnings a little less sordid. To have been born as the result of a rape, a violent act against his mother, was too disgusting to consider.

With sudden clarity, he realized Gino had known they had different mothers, if the words his brother had spoken had been truthful in one of the dreams, hallucinations, or whatever he'd been bombarded with during the interrogation. Gino had said Marco still had his real mama while Gino's had died. At six, Marc hoped Gino hadn't known about the rape, but clearly he had been informed early on that he and Marc had different mothers. Did he remember at the age of three Marc coming into his family?

"Marc." He turned toward Angelina's voice. "Breathe. This has no bearing on who you are. That happened before you were even conceived."

Her words seeped into his consciousness by slow degrees.

"Angelina's right, Marco." Mama's voice drew his attention again.

He turned toward her but had no words to express what he felt. Sorrow for his mother. Anger at his father—no, his sperm donor. The man was not a father in any way, shape, or form.

"When I learned I carried you inside my body, I so desperately wanted you, even if you had been the product of… I never expected to find love or a husband or to have children of my own. That wasn't my fate, or so I thought. I envied my sister with her precious little boy, Gino, but I was an old maid of thirty-two. I was convinced this might be my only chance at motherhood. Besides, terminating the pregnancy was unheard of, no matter the circumstances."

Mama choked on a sob, and Marc stood to go to her, perching on the other arm of the chair. He placed his arms around her, and Papa pulled away to allow him closer contact.

"Oh, Marco, my mother insisted that Emiliana take you to raise along with her son. She didn't want the stigma of a daughter having a child out of wedlock. My mama knew how painful that road would be and wanted to protect me and you both."

Marc patted Mama's back and let her cry. She'd kept her pain locked away a very long time. Tears burned Marc's eyes. They truly were mother and son if his own tendency to bury his inner hurts was any indication. He glanced over Mama's head at Angelina, who had tears streaming down her face as well, and smiled.

"The hardest thing I've ever had to do was hand you over to my sister just hours after your birth, knowing I wouldn't see much of you because I could not bear to be anywhere near that man she had married."

Marc tried to process this new information. Mama didn't seem to be withholding anything today, so he had no doubt she told the truth. Who would make up a story like this?

"I never knew if she treated you well or resented you after finding out you were Paolo's. I did not tell her the circumstances, which of course only led to further estrangement between us."

"Mama, recently I remembered some things from my time with Emiliana, and I assure you she loved me, too. She didn't take out any anger on me that I can recall." Sure, he'd been spanked for disobeying, but he'd deserved it after hurting his babysitter because of his carelessness.

"That makes me feel better, Marco. I never knew for certain but could not ask." Mama pulled away and looked into his eyes. Her eyelashes had clumped together with her tears, but she had stopped crying. "You didn't deserve anything but to be loved. You have always been such a beautiful spirit, so wild and free. I envied you that. I've spent my whole life doing what's expected of me and letting my dreams be relegated to someday in the future when I retire."

Mama admired his wildness? His inability to stay in one place and follow through on his obligations and commitments? He'd always thought she wanted him to be more like Gino.

A loud sniffle from Carmella reminded him of his siblings. They both looked as if they'd been poleaxed, comforting each other as they watched the drama unfold.

"Carmella and Sandro, count your blessings that you had two wonderful parents. I know I speak for Gino, too, when I say thank you for sharing them with us. You will always be considered my sister and brother and to hell with that shit about being half-siblings." He turned to Mama. "*Scusa, mamma.*" Returning his gaze to his siblings, he added, "I've lost one brother and don't intend to lose any other sibling over something that inconsequential. Our bond was formed the day each of you was born and nothing will change that as far as I'm concerned."

When Carmella stood and stretched out her arms, Marc rose and stepped into them, giving her a tight hug. "Thanks, Marc. I'm more than a little shell-shocked but I couldn't bear the thought of you being anything but my big brother. I love you."

After breaking away from their hug, he went to Sandro, who managed to hold himself together despite appearing on the verge of tears. Marc hugged him, too, and whispered, "You know too much for me to ever consider you anything but a pesky little brother." Sandro barked a laugh but held onto Marc a little tighter, refusing to let him go for a long moment, hiding his face in Marc's shoulder. Marc gave him time to compose himself before breaking the embrace. Sandro could worry about *machismo*. Marc no longer cared. Marc's girl encouraged him to express emotions, rather than repress them. A few tears didn't make him weak at all.

Gino, just goes to show you didn't get everything right.

Mama interrupted their moment. "Marco, you questioned why Melissa continued to be invited to family gatherings long after Gino's death."

395

Marc's gaze went to Angelina. Seeing her on edge at the mention of Melissa's name, he sat beside her, wrapped his arm around her and drew her against his side. She rested her head on his shoulder as they waited for Mama to continue. A peace descended over him having her by his side.

"Gino wrote her a letter from Afghanistan saying you both had been adopted. I'm uncertain why he chose to do that."

So Melissa hadn't lied. "I'd like to see the letter sometime, Mama."

She wrung her hands in her lap. "I'm sorry, Marco, but she has the letter. After Gino's death, she showed it to me long enough to convince me it was real and to blackmail money from me, threatening to tell you that you were adopted if I didn't do as she demanded."

Angelina stiffened beside him, and he thought he heard her mutter "that bitch" under her breath.

A sob tore from Mama's throat. "I couldn't face having to tell any of you about what had happened to me when I'd just buried one son. I didn't want to lose another. I wanted us to continue as we had been." Papa handed her a tissue, and she blew her nose and sat up straighter. "Imagine my surprise when you came to me in February telling me she'd told you anyway. She and I had heated words, and I cut her off immediately."

Marc remembered the exchange he and Angelina had overheard while waiting to talk with Mama the day after the anniversary party before Melissa had left in a huff.

"My sources tell me she's returned to Omaha to be with her family." Mama must be keeping tabs on Melissa to keep her from going after her loved ones again.

Good for you, Mama.

Sandro chimed in. "To mooch off them, no doubt." Mama smiled at her youngest son.

Marc marveled at Melissa's stupidity. If she'd kept her mouth shut, she'd probably still be extorting money from the D'Alessios. But her need to take Angelina down a peg or two had been her undoing.

Marc took Angelina's chin and raised it until her gaze met his. "Thank you for putting her in her place on New Year's. Knowing you had the courage and strength to stand up to her and give her the put-down she deserved made me proud to call you..." He leaned close to her ear and whispered, "My submissive."

Angelina wrapped her hand around his neck and pulled him down to her mouth to whisper, "You are such a good man, Marc."

Before he could respond, Mama cleared her throat and pulled his attention away from Angelina.

"This brings me to the rest of what I need to say to you today." Marc wasn't sure how much more she could have to reveal. "Papa and I," she glanced up at Papa and smiled before turning her gaze to Marc's siblings, "have decided to retire at the end of the fiscal year on the first of July. Sandro and Carmella, you have shown us these past years that you are more than capable of running the resort and our staff efficiently. This business is for those younger than we are."

"Wow, Mama," Sandro said. His little brother looked more surprised by this revelation than all the others today.

Once more, her attention turned to Papa. "We've booked a Mediterranean cruise for mid-July and plan to take several extensive trips each year now that we won't be tied down to the resort." She spoke to Sandro and Carmella again. "I assure you we will not micromanage. As long as we can have our condo as a home base, we probably won't even be in your hair."

Carmella grinned and wiped the tears from her eyes. "You know this will always be your home, Mama and Papa. Thank you for entrusting all your hard work into our hands. We won't let you down."

Papa cleared his throat and added, "I'm going to hold Mama to the lack of micromanaging part." Everyone laughed, cutting some of the tension. "Now, if you'll excuse us, I'm taking her to dinner in Vail. Marco and Angelina, please pardon our lack of hospitality, but I'm sure you young folks have a lot to plot and plan, and we'd just be in the way. Marco, maybe you can teach your sister and brother not to take work so seriously, too. I don't want them to put off living as long as Mama and I have."

Marc stared dumbfounded, floored at Papa's words. Despite all that had happened this year, he had never felt more accepted by his family than today.

All because of the amazing woman at his side. What did he plan to do to make sure she never left that place?

* * *

At the outskirts of Denver, Marc steered the Porsche off I-70 and south onto Highway 470. "We're taking a detour. There's someone I want to introduce you to."

Angelina marveled at the further change in Marc since leaving his parents nearly three hours ago. Everything unfolded so quickly, as if Mama and everyone had just been waiting for the chance to expose all the secrets and lies to the light. Catharsis.

"Marc, I can understand now how lying didn't seem like a problem to you when we met. I don't see how your family kept all the various versions of the truth straight. Your life was built on one lie after another."

"I had the best of intentions. I never meant to hurt you in any way."

"No, I'm not trying to rehash anything. That's water under the bridge. I'm just making an observation. Your family's lies were laced with good intentions, too, but look at all the pain they brought you and Mama especially. Honesty is so much healthier."

"No argument there."

They drove on several miles in silence. The snow-covered peaks made her think of Luke. With all that had happened in the past few days, she had barely given a thought to him. The last time she'd spoken with Cassie, she sounded at the end of her rope. If they didn't get Luke down from there soon... But he didn't sound as if he should be moved too quickly, even if they could get through the snowpack to reach him.

She looked out the window at passing countryside she didn't recognize. Curiosity got the better of her. "Who did you say you're taking me to meet?"

"I didn't say." She glanced at him, but he didn't smile. "You'll guess before we arrive, if I don't chicken out. Observe your surroundings, pet."

When he exited onto Highway 285, a route she sometimes took between Denver and Aspen Corners, the scenery became a little more familiar, but she had no clue where he was taking her. He exited onto Sheridan and still she didn't know...and then she saw the first rows of white military tombstones. Tears came to her eyes, and she pressed her finger against suddenly trembling lips.

Gino.

Dio. He was taking her to meet his brother. Marc, had never mentioned to her he'd visited here since she'd met him. She glanced over at him.

His knuckles were white on the steering wheel. "I think it's time I had a long overdue talk with Gino about some things." Marc cleared his throat. "I haven't been out here since we buried him, so we'll have to stop by the office for help locating his grave."

Angelina reached out and stroked his forearm, causing him to release one hand from the wheel to grip her hand. She felt him trembling and squeezed him tighter.

Half an hour later, with their map in hand, Angelina navigated Marc through the cemetery to the place marked with an X. Her heart beat so loudly, he had to hear.

"I think it's that row," she told him, pointing. Marc pulled the Porsche as far to the right as he could and turned off the ignition. He sat and stared at the rows of tombstones for a few moments. "Would you like me to give you a moment alone?"

Marc paused and then said, "If you don't mind..."

Angelina had no clue what Marc was going through. She'd never be able to stand at the grave of one of her brothers—ever.

"No, I changed my mind. I would like you to be with me, if you think you can."

That he wanted her there warmed her heart. "You know I'll do whatever you need me to do, Marc."

Please, God, let me be strong for him.

He sighed heavily and opened the door. She waited for him to come around to her door, trying to collect her thoughts and shore up her courage. The crumpled map fell to the floor. From here on, they would walk until they found Gino's final resting place.

When the door opened, he reached in. "Watch your step. There are some slippery spots."

Clasping her hand, Marc led her down the row. She knew from having memorized the map they would have to walk about halfway down the hill before they needed to start scanning tombstones for names. She scoured the names and dates, seeing some of the more recent and familiar combat zones named—Gulf War, Iraq, Desert Storm, Operation Enduring Freedom, Afghanistan. How devastating for so many families who lost loved ones. A deep sorrow came over Angelina knowing how profoundly the loss of one Marine had affected Marc's family.

Her mind became numb to so much death and devastation until Marc's hand halted her steps. She focused on the stone to his left. No recognition. Not his. Then the next one...

Gino Z. D'Alessio

PFC US Marine Corps

Afghanistan

Purple Heart
October 5, 1974
February 24, 2002

Angelina remembered seeing the memorial tattooed to Adam's back after he'd been attacked by the cougar. Gino's name had been etched into Adam's back. The young man's loss had been felt beyond his family. She blessed herself and said a silent prayer for Gino's soul to find rest and peace in God's perpetual light. Marc had a death grip on her hand, but she merely held on. He remained silent. She hated to intrude on his moment of reflection, so she continued to stare at the grave. Gino had died on Damián's birthday. She wondered if one of the reasons things had come to a head that night was that Marc was remembering the loss of his beloved big brother.

Marc released a sound somewhere between a gasp and a sob before he dropped to his knees onto Gino's grave.

"I'm so sorry, Gino. Please forgive me."

Angelina knelt beside him, feeling the cold wet ground seep through her tights and not caring. She wrapped her arms around Marc, holding him as he sobbed for his brother. Tears fell down her cheeks, chilled by the cold wind that whipped up the hillside all of the sudden.

"Shhh. He's forgiven you, Marc. Big brothers understand."

Racking sobs poured out of him. "That's it. Let go, Marc. I have you." She cried for Marc; no one should have to bury a sibling. She cried for Gino; the man had died saving lives, sacrificing his own so a fellow Marine could return home to his wife and baby.

Sometime later, Marc reached out to touch the stone. His fingers traced the letters of Gino's name, taking special care to slow down over the surname they shared.

"He didn't have a drop of Mama or Papa's blood and yet proudly took their name, knowing full well he was adopted his whole life." Marc paused a moment before continuing. "If I needed any more proof that blood didn't matter, all I had to do was look at the way Gramps, Mama, Papa—hell, the entire D'Alessio family—treated Gino as one of their own. Papa did the same with me from the earliest memories I have. Until New Year's, I had no inkling Papa wasn't my birth father. But Papa loved Gino and me no less than he loved his own biological children."

Angelina listened as more of the pieces came together for Marc.

"I've spent months trying to figure out if I'm a D'Alessio or a Solari—figuring out who the hell I was." He sank back on the heels of his shoes, breaking contact with the stone and resting his hand on his thigh. Angelina stroked his arm, hoping to coax him to share more without intruding on his grief.

Marc turned to Angelina. "At Christmas, your family showed me what it's like to be from a close-knit, demonstrative family. I envied you and your brothers the connection you have. Despite some tensions, the love you have for each other came through loud and clear."

Angelina nodded. "I wouldn't trade my brothers for anyone, even though there are times when I have to keep my distance from them; otherwise, they'll smother me alive."

Marc's gaze returned to the stone. "There was a time when I didn't even claim that I knew Gino, much less that we were brothers. I was so angry." Tears poured unheeded down his cheeks again. Thank God he was finally able to express emotion over his loss. Angelina had no doubt he'd stood on this spot back in 2002 and watched as his brother was laid to rest with a mixture of remorse and hatred for what Gino had done with Melissa.

"But so many things are clearer to me now. We might not have been the kind of brothers who hugged a lot, but he always protected and loved me, probably since the time I invaded his family out of nowhere."

Angelina smiled. "Somehow I think having you as a brother did Gino a lot of good."

Marc remained silent a moment. "Do you really think he forgave me for shutting him out for the rest of his life?"

Angelina nodded. "I'm sure Gino learned very quickly what was important in life when he joined the Marines and deployed to Afghanistan. I have no doubt the two of you would have figured out what Melissa was really after given time."

"He was in-country only a short while, a line replacement for some casualties in Adam's unit. Despite that, Adam said he served honorably and with distinction. He died a hero. Remember Staff Sergeant Anderson?"

"Yes, I met him and his family at Karla's wedding. Gino saved his life."

Marc nodded and stared at the tombstone in silence.

"Marc, I think what's most important is that you eventually come to forgive yourself."

He closed his eyes. "I don't think I can."

"Your responses to what happened back then were normal for a young man not terribly experienced with women."

Marc sighed.

"We all make mistakes, Marc, especially when we're young. Gino and you would have shared a bottle of wine toasting your good fortune at having gotten rid of her."

Marc almost laughed at the image. She was happy she could help him picture what that reunion might have been like. "Most of us have time to remedy our misjudgments. You and Gino didn't have that luxury, but until you make peace with him and accept the fact that he just made a stupid mistake, I don't think you are going to find peace within yourself."

Marc didn't say anything. She hoped her words would convey to him the need to forgive and move on.

A blast of wind hit them, and Marc stood and helped her up, pulling her closer when she began shivering. She hadn't dressed for this visit, but thanked God Marc had brought her here.

"I need to get you back in the car, but first..." He paused a moment and cleared his throat. "Gino Zirilli D'Alessio, this is long overdue, but I'd like you to meet my girl, Angelina Cristina Giardano."

She'd wondered what the Z stood for. Zirilli. The maiden name of two complicated sisters who had mothered two equally complicated brothers, Marco and Gino.

"It's a great honor to meet you, Gino. Thank you for getting your brother off the hook of that b...*creature* Melissa. I can't tell you how much I personally appreciate you for rescuing him from her clutches, so he would be ready for me when we met."

Marc turned toward her, and she looked up at him. "Thank you. I needed that kick in the ass right about now."

"I know." She batted her eyelashes at him.

"Brat."

"Always. *Your* brat. Don't you ever forget it."

For the first time since they'd come here, Marc grinned. "I'm not sure I could ever have prepared for you. Angelina, you came charging into my life like gangbusters. I'll never be the same—thank God."

Chapter Thirty

Damián's heart pounded as he paced across the floor for the tenth time before glancing at the wall clock over the arched doorway.

Marc chuckled. "Two minutes since the last time you looked. Stop worrying. Savannah's not going to leave you standing at the altar."

"I know that."

"Then why are you so nervous?"

Who the hell knew? He certainly had no hesitation about marrying Savannah. The two of them were perfect for each other. He couldn't believe at this very moment she was standing on the other side of San Miguel's Church, preparing to walk down the aisle and into his life—forever.

How'd he ever come to deserve someone like her—or Marisol?

He shot his gaze to the case on the bench across the room, and his heart pounded harder. Why was he so fucking nervous? She'd seen his stump. She'd accept his decision to do this, probably would ask what the fuck had taken him so long to get there. But that was for later, at the reception.

His polished dress shoe pinched his foot, but he wanted a formal Marine wedding. The Corps had saved his life in a lot of ways. He'd enlisted as a lost kid with no direction in his life and come out a man forever changed by the events in Fallujah. The men and women he served with had saved him, too, when he'd thought life was no longer worth living. Many of them were a part of his family now.

"You all right, man?"

Damián glanced up at Marc and nodded. For the first time in years, he did feel all right and knew what he had to do. He sat on the bench and reached for the case, opening its lid. Inside lay his new prosthetic blade. He'd planned to wear it for dancing at the reception. The thing hurt like hell if he had to stand still on it for long periods. But on this very special occasion, he had a point to prove—to both Savannah and Marisol. No more hiding and pretending. He'd only been hiding from himself. Savannah, his daughter, and his friends loved and accepted him just the way he was. He needed to accept himself, too. His body would never be whole or perfect again. He had to live with some limitations.

Today, he wasn't just binding himself before God to his beautiful Savannah, he would be deepening the bond with his beautiful daughter, also. When he asked Savannah and Marisol to make him a permanent part of their lives, he wanted to do so honestly. No more pretending. No more secrets.

Damián removed the more realistic-looking prosthetic that had enabled him to mask his disability pretty well since he'd been fitted for it in Denver all those years ago. He pulled the new blade out of the case and drew up the leg of his dress blues. Soon, he was adjusting it to the perfect fit.

Just the way his girls were a perfect fit in his life. *Mierda*, they *were* his life. His very blessed life.

He stood up and tested his weight by bouncing on it a couple of times, as he'd done in the physical therapist's office at the VA where he'd picked it up last week. All week, he'd been trying to decide when he should wear it, but something always held him back.

Checking the clock again—twenty minutes before the ceremony would begin—he turned to Marc, one of his *padrinos de boda* and his best man, who had tears in his eyes.

Fuck that shit. Maybe he shouldn't do this.

"'Bout damned time."

"Don't fuck me up today. I'm not going to bawl like a baby in front of Savannah and Marisol."

Marc grinned. "Nothing wrong with a man showing emotion. I can make you an honorary Italian today if you want."

Fuck. Damián felt the tears burning the backs of his eyes. No way in hell would he shed them. "Thanks for standing beside me, Doc. I wouldn't be here if you hadn't stuck by me after Fallujah until you finally got through to me…"

"I think Adam's the one who finally got through that thick skull of yours."

Damián shook his head. "Dad wouldn't have known I was having adjustment problems if you hadn't called him out to Balboa."

Marc opened his mouth as if to argue but smiled instead. "I think we all rescued each other—well, at least to the point of survival mode—it took each of our girls coming into our lives to finish straightening out our shit."

Damián grinned. "That it did. When are you and Angelina going to make it official?"

Marc shrugged. "I'm working on it."

Before he could admonish his friend not to waste too much more time, the scent of cinnamon wafted to him and Damián glanced up at Marc. "Do you smell that?"

"What? Did you forget your deodorant?"

Damián would have told Marc to fuck off but couldn't form any words as his throat closed off. He reached down to twist his pinky ring and remembered too late it had been removed to be resized for Savannah's tiny finger. She would be the third Orlando bride to wear it. The ring had been worn by Damián since *Mamá* died, but he knew she would be pleased to see his father's family legacy passed down to another generation. Until recently, he'd never pictured having a wife of his own—and *never* imagined it would be his beloved Savannah.

A tear splashed onto his hand.

I'm gonna make you proud, Mamá. You, too, Papá. I'm going to give my family all the love you showed me growing up.

* * *

Anita Gonzales pinned the blusher veil to the mantilla on Savannah's head. "How does that feel, sweetie?"

"Right. So very right." Everything about this day felt so perfect. She and Damián would be forever bound today, not that anything could tear them apart, with or without this ceremony.

They had chosen to use the Mexican wedding tradition of having *padrinos* and *madrinas*, patrons of various symbols of support and guidance for the newlyweds, mainly because so many people wanted to contribute to their lives in this way.

Anita had been a mother to her since she was nineteen and now was becoming a mother figure for Damián, too. Both had lost their own mothers way too young.

"Maman, listen to how my dress sounds when I swish like this." She looked down at Mari who did half turns back and forth, setting the crinolines and taffeta to rustling. The translucent blue of the gown reminded Savannah of the butterflies that had visited her at the beach cave two weeks ago.

405

"Maman, I hope you're with me today."

Breaking with tradition, Mari's dress wasn't a miniature replica of Savannah's. She wanted her daughter to be her own person and hoped her life wouldn't be marred by hate or negativity.

Savannah heard the music filtering through the closed door to the vestibule. Time to line up for the processional. She took Mari by the hand as Karla picked up the basket of rose petals and handed them to the little girl.

She surveyed the scene through her opaque blusher veil. Karla's protruding belly gave Savannah a moment's pang of regret for dragging the woman from Denver to Eden Gardens for a wedding so close to her due date. She'd tried to let Karla off the hook from joining Adam as their *Madrina y Padrino de Lazo*, the godparents who would carry the rope-like rosary beads to wrap around the bride and her groom to symbolize their unity and commitment. But her new sister-friend insisted on making the drive here after her obstetrician ruled out air travel. She and Adam had taken the leisurely drive over four days, twice as long as usual, with lots of stops along the way.

Savannah's commitment to marriage with Damián could only be made in their home church—the place that had given her so much comfort and solace when she'd thought there was no sanctuary left in this world.

She realized, though, her sanctuary had now shifted to wherever Damián was, including their new home in Denver. He provided all of the love and protection a woman could ever want or need. But this had been his home church, too, and Savannah knew he would feel closer to his parents if they held the ceremony here.

Her adult bridal party wore black taffeta with translucent, blue satin accent bows. The tea-length, off-the-rack dresses could be worn at other occasions by the girls, making them a more practical choice. She'd hate for them to spend too much on dresses only to be worn one day. And she knew of many better uses for her unexpected inheritance from Maman.

Damián's sister Rosa Espinosa, her *Madrina de Ramo*, took her son José's hands and positioned them palms upward. "Now, remember how we practiced?" The boy nodded, his gaze intent on the pillow embroidered with the two rings representative of the ones Marc would present to be exchanged between Savannah and her groom.

Angelina, the *Madrina de Copas*, walked toward the arched door, opened it, and peeked outside. She nodded and then turned back to the party in the dressing room. "Ready, girls?"

Savannah smiled. "More than ever."

"Hey, I'm not a girl!"

"Oh, sorry, José," Angelina said. "You most certainly are not! You're quite the gentleman. How would you like to hold the door for everyone?"

Puffing out his chest, he crossed the room and propped the door open with his body.

She couldn't believe she was part of such a large extended family now, when for so long it had only been her and Mari. Well, Anita and Father Martine, too. Since she'd come here seeking refuge, they'd been her family.

Karla guided Mari to exit first, followed by Rosa who carried a simple but elegant bouquet of red roses and Angelina with the wine goblets. Savannah lifted the hem of her ivory satin gown and walked through the doorway only to find her field of vision filled by Adam in his dress blues, his cover tucked under an arm. He walked toward Karla, drawing her attention to his sword. To think, Savannah Gentry would be making her way through that archway in an hour or so and into the Marine Corps family.

Adam's smile faded, making Savannah worry about Karla. While he spoke softly, his voice carried the short distance. "How are you doing, Kitten? I know this is a difficult day for you."

Savannah had learned at breakfast this was the anniversary of her brother's death, but Karla smiled bravely up at her solicitous husband.

"Stop worrying, Adam. I'm fine. I wouldn't have missed this wedding for the world. You know what it took to get me here—you even had to buy us a new vehicle, not that we aren't going to be needing it soon." Her hand stroked her belly. "Besides, I'm replacing bad memories with good ones."

Savannah hoped so. What an amazing woman to call her friend and now sister.

Adam bent to peck Karla on the cheek, his hand covering the one propped against her belly, and he whispered something in her ear that made Karla giggle. In her hand, she carried the ropelike double rosary for the *lazo* ceremony.

Adam grinned and turned his attention to Savannah. He gave her a huge smile. "You look beautiful, hon."

She beamed at his words. Not so long ago, she'd have negated the praise in her mind or cringed at the thought of any man looking at her face or body in appreciation. Not on her wedding day. Today, she truly felt beautiful.

The dress was simple but elegant. She couldn't see spending a thousand dollars on a wedding gown. Luckily she'd fallen in love with this ivory dress the moment she'd tried it on, and it had cost only a few hundred dollars for the *madrina* in her church family who had offered to sponsor her dress. The black-lace applique over the bodice and the single shoulder strap reminded her that, despite her dark past, she would now be united with Damián until death parted them.

But the location of the applique also reminded her of the Chinese dragon tat on Damián's chest and over his shoulder. Dear lord, but she loved that tat, especially when he flexed his pec at her. Her face grew warm.

Finding her focus again, Savannah walked over to Angelina and noticed the shimmer of tears in her eyes. Savannah almost lost the shaky hold she had on her own emotions.

Angelina hugged her. "Sorry, I always cry at weddings."

"I'm sure I'll be shedding a few tears before the ceremony is over." Savannah hadn't been able to express emotion for so long. No way would she bottle up those feelings today. Savannah placed a kiss on Angelina's cheek and whispered, "Marc will come around soon. I've already noticed a major change in his demeanor."

Angelina nodded. "We'd better not keep that lucky man of *yours* waiting too long, though."

Savannah had heard hints about the extremes Marc had gone to in a risk-aware scene at the club recently. She understood a person having trust issues, but could she ever give up her safeword or long list of limits the way Marc had? Damián promised to continue to whittle away at the list as he helped her face—and slay—her dragons. And her fears.

As the music slowed, Father Martine turned to Savannah and winked. "Ready, little one?"

She nodded and smiled. "Thank you, Father, for everything, including putting out the call to local Marine officers to form the arch after the ceremony."

He nodded. "I wanted the best for the young girl I shepherded for so long. Your parish family will miss you." She hated the thought of leaving her sanctuary, but she and Damián would find a new place to nurture their faith—in Denver.

Father Martine's demeanor became serious again as he prepared himself.

The groomsmen lined up first—each in dress uniform. She'd asked all of her groomsmen to wear their military dress uniforms. Three branches of service were represented in the wedding party, and she was so proud to count so many honorable heroes as friends and protectors now.

Marc in his Navy whites was first. Just before he entered the church, he glanced back at Angelina. The smile he gave her would have melted gold. He carried hers and Damián's precious wedding rings. This man had helped save her beloved's life and would always hold a place of importance in their hearts.

Next went Damián's friend and mentor Gunnar Larsen, his long blond hair pulled into a neatly combed queue reaching halfway down the back of his Army dress blues. With Gunnar's imposing height and frame, high cheekbones, and piercing blue eyes, he had intimidated the hell out of Savannah when they'd first met at the man's private dungeon a few hours west of Denver. But once she'd engaged him in conversation a few times, his respect and love for Damián helped her to warm up to him. Gunnar, as *Padrino de Arras*, carried two tulle bags of gold coins. She and Damián had adopted the new tradition of sharing the financial responsibility of supporting each other and their family.

Grant, a Marine like Damián, also wore her dress blues with her blonde hair pulled in a tight bun at the nape of her neck. Whether Grant considered herself the last of the *padrinos* or the first of the *madrinas*, Savannah wasn't certain. Nor did she care, as long as Grant was here to make the family complete. As *Madrina/Padrina de Cojines*, she carried the embroidered velvet pillow Savannah and Damián would kneel on during part of the Mass.

Damián's niece, Teresa, carried Savannah's mother's French prayer book and red-crystal rosary. If not for Teresa's tragic rape, would Savannah ever have found Damián again? Moments ago, out of the corner of her eye, Savannah had spotted Teresa playing with Mari using her daughter's ever-present sticker book. Savannah marveled at how the human psyche healed. At least Teresa had gone into therapy early, in part thanks to Damián, to help keep the negative and hurtful scripts at bay that might make life even more difficult and lonely for her later. Moving to Colorado this summer would give her a fresh start, too, away from insensitive people who didn't understand and treated her differently since the news had come out.

Teresa's mother Rosa stepped into line carrying a small bouquet of red roses. Savannah knew tradition called for presenting flowers to the Virgin of Guadalupe, but her mind and heart were set. This was her special day and Damián would approve when the time came.

Angelina carried two ornate glass wine goblets and blushed at Marc.

Savannah wondered how much longer she would have to wait to start planning her own wedding. If only they would realize how perfect they were for each other! Still, Marc had been transformed recently by whatever had happened in the dungeon.

Karla joined the line next, carrying the double rosary *lazo*. Seeing her belly swollen with hers and Adam's baby and a loving husband beside her in the journey toward motherhood gave Savannah a pang of regret for not having Damián in her life during her own pregnancy. But he had taken to being a daddy without batting an eye.

She couldn't help but notice Karla's eyes looking so sad at the moment. Savannah walked over to her and gave her a hug. "Thanks for being here for us on this day. You're such a strong woman."

"Thank you for asking me to be in your wedding. This is my first Hispanic wedding, and I love the symbolism. So beautiful and so much meaning. I'm so happy to have you in my family now." Karla opened her arms and gave Savannah time to walk into them. Hugging was becoming easier all the time, especially with Karla.

Right now, Karla most likely wanted to be off her feet. Savannah remembered those last weeks and how uncomfortable she was. Time to proceed before the woman collapsed.

"We'd better get started, Karla."

Savannah turned to Anita who pressed a kiss to her cheek. "I'm so happy for you, Savi...Savannah. Not sure I'll get used to calling you that, but watching you walk down the aisle in a few minutes is going to be the most beautiful thing I've seen since my own daughter married three years ago."

Anita picked up two lit taper candles and took her place in the line where, in a moment, Damián would join her and escort her to her place of honor in the front of the church. As Savannah and Damián's *Madrina de Velación*, she would continue to provide a guiding light to them throughout their married life.

José and Marisol were shown where to stand at the end of the procession, leaving space for Father Martine and the altar boys to precede them. Mari instructed her older cousin one last time on the proper way to hold the ring pillow. Poor José.

The organ began to play the processional and Adam patted Karla's belly, as if she were a talisman, before he walked across the vestibule to stand beside Savannah. "I believe you wanted to remain hidden from Damián until you walk down the aisle. So now would be a good time for us to vamoose."

Her heart pounded at the thought of seeing Damián standing so proudly in his uniform. She grinned and nodded before turning to re-enter her dressing room. Adam kept an eye on the progress of the wedding party through the cracked doorway.

Her bouquet lay on the table, and she picked it up. Tears formed in her eyes again as she thought about Maman and how much she would have wanted to be here today. In her heart, she knew Maman watched over her, but...

"Ready, hon?"

She lifted a tissue from the dispenser and dabbed at her eyes.

"So very ready." She bit her lower lip. "I just hope I...I won't be a disappointment to him."

Adam laughed as he left his watch at the doorway and came toward her. "I can't imagine anything you could do to wipe the smile off his face that he wore at breakfast. He's got quite the wedding night planned for you two."

Savannah blushed. Barely a month ago, Adam's sexual innuendo would have made her cringe, but the promise of having Damián make love to her tonight—and on a daily basis, if his promises were any indication—only made her long for him even more. She hoped she wouldn't shut down on him, but if she did, Damián knew how to work through her triggers with patience and persistence. Now that she'd begun to embrace her inner Princess Slut—only for Damián—she looked forward to exploring more of her long-dormant sexuality with him. There would be days when she couldn't be the lover he deserved, but she'd always try her hardest to be the best wife she could.

As the opening strains of Pachelbel's *Canon in D* began, tears came to Savannah's eyes again. Thank goodness she'd left the mascara and eyeliner off today. The piece was her mother's favorite and one way she could help ensure Maman's presence. Savannah was even more certain now Maman would witness from heaven the marriage of her only daughter to the man of her dreams.

"I think he's waiting for you, Savannah."

Adam brushed away a tear with the pad of his thumb, and she smiled. "Not nearly as anxiously as I've waited for him. Please take me to join the other half of my heart."

Adam smiled as he took the hand not holding her bouquet and tucked it into the crook of his arm. "Love to."

He held the door of the dressing room for her and soon the two stepped through the doorway into the sanctuary. Her gaze zeroed in immediately on Damián standing proudly in his Marine dress blues. Pride and love swelled inside her. So handsome.

Mine.

"Breathe, hon. Now."

"Yes, sir."

Adam took the first step forward, and she remembered how to place one foot in front of the other, holding on to the strong arm under her hand for fear of stumbling. Her eyes never left Damián's as she inched closer to the man she'd spend the rest of her life with.

No fear. No doubts.

All mine.

Savannah couldn't see Mari and José walking down the aisle in front of Father Martine, but a couple of giggles and *awwws* from the congregation made her certain they'd done something adorable. She couldn't wait to see the video and photos later. A member of her church family was a photographer and offered to be her *padrino* of such today. She'd lost so many memories of good times past by shutting off her mind. Savannah hated the thought of losing a single wedding memory, but Damián had taught her so much about living in the moment that she didn't think she would miss very much.

At the first pew, Adam stopped and Savannah nearly groaned at being kept from Damián's side a moment longer.

Their love, tested by time and circumstance, was even stronger now, but she prayed they had many, many decades ahead to be together.

Father Martine asked, "Who gives this woman in marriage?"

Adam's booming voice clearly announced, "Anita and I do." The two would serve as their godparents today and for the future, as they had done for so long to each of them individually in the past.

Adam turned to her and lifted her blusher veil. "Proud to have you join my family, Savannah," he whispered. "We've all been waiting for you a long time." He gave her a gentle hug, as if afraid to get tangled in her mantilla, before standing tall again.

Savannah had never known a father's love before, but Adam had shown her in such a short time the powerful love he had for her and Damián.

She blinked to stop the flow of tears before realizing she had nothing to be ashamed of or any reason to hide them. She let them trail down her cheeks. Damián smiled his approval, and she melted inside before looking up at Adam. She motioned for him to bend closer to her and pressed a kiss on his evening-stubbled cheek. "Thank you, Ad...Dad." She might as well get used to referring to him the way Damián did.

Anita sniffled, and Savannah broke loose from Adam's arm a moment to walk the few feet forward to hug her long-time champion and friend.

"Thanks for getting me to this moment, Anita," she whispered.

"You did that all by yourself, sweetie. I was just there to help you focus on what was important when things got a little mucked up."

Savannah swallowed past the lump in her throat, handed Anita her bouquet, and took a deep breath before turning to Damián once more. Surrounded by their family and friends, she was ready to take this monumental leap into the arms of her man. Damián took a step forward at the same time she did, and they quickly closed the gap between them. Adam stepped back, and Damián took her by the elbow and leaned forward. "My princess has never looked more beautiful."

"And my knight, my *prince*, my protector never more dashing."

Father Martine cleared his throat, and they turned their attention to him as he proceeded with the Mass. At the conclusion of his homily, he offered a blessing on their union. He then said, "In a moment, our lives can change. Damián and Savannah, there is a special way you are together that's unlike the way you've ever been with anyone else. You've crossed many bridges to be here today, overcome many obstacles. Each bridge you have crossed has only made your love stronger."

Savannah glanced at Mari who stared in awe at her parents, as if they'd just stepped from the pages of *Sleeping Beauty*. Savannah truly felt like Damián's awakened princess today.

Rosa placed an arm around Mari's shoulder and beamed a smile at Savannah, too.

After her beloved priest concluded the Catholic Rite of Marriage, he announced that the bride and the groom would share their own words of commitment. Savannah and Damián turned toward one another. Marc handed the rings to Father Martine. Savannah hoped she would remember the words she'd written to bind herself to Damián for life. She'd kept them simple and short, knowing how nervous she would be, but each word came from the heart.

Damián cleared his throat as he reached for something under his coat. "I was afraid I might leave something out. I hope you won't mind if I refer to my written copy as a backup, just in case."

Savannah shook her head, honored that he would take the time to write vows just for her. She blinked rapidly.

*   *   *

Damián pulled the worn piece of Marisol's lined school paper from between his belt and the waistband of his trousers, unfolding it for the umpteenth time in the past few days.

He took her petite hand in his and held it, giving her a gentle squeeze as he tried to steady his own hand. Why was he so nervous? This was the best day of his life. When he looked into her eyes, he nearly lost every single word he'd been trying to memorize for the past week.

Focus, man.

Suddenly, he made a decision and refolded the paper, tucking it back inside his belt. These words needed to be spoken from the heart. If they weren't vows he could remember today, then how would he remember to live up to them later?

He took her hand and slipped the ring over the tip of her finger, stopping just before the second knuckle.

"With this ring, Savannah,
I vow to always be with you
from this day forward.
My heart will be your shelter.
My arms will be your home.
My life will be dedicated
to bringing a smile to your lips
and joyful tears to your eyes.
May God bless you always,
as He has blessed me by reuniting us.
May we always find the words to communicate
through all of life's surprises—

good and bad, happy and sad, easy and difficult.

May you feel the depth of my love,

knowing you are truly the woman I was meant to love

for the rest of my life.

May you always see your innocence and fire—

the reflection of your inner beauty—through my eyes."

Damián drew a shaky breath as he pressed the ring over her first knuckle. He looked into her Pacific-blue eyes, swimming with the most beautiful, heartfelt tears he'd ever seen, and smiled.

"*Savita*, I give you my heart forever.

I have nothing of greater value to offer.

I promise I will do my best always

to be the man you need and deserve.

I promise to love what I know about you,

to trust what I do not yet know,

and to respect you in all knowledge to come.

Through all of our years together

and in all that life may bring us,

I promise to continue to encourage, guide,

and challenge you to try new things,

and I hope you will trust that I will never harm you."

Damián seated the ring snugly on her finger and smiled as he claimed his bride as his own.

"I feel so honored and pleased to call you *mi princesa*.

I will love, honor, and cherish you and the gift of your love forever."

Hearing a loud sniffle behind Savannah, he turned to see Marisol, tears streaming from her eyes and an expression of magical awe on his *muñequita's* face. A wreath of tiny roses sat atop her long black hair, and she wore a beautiful poofy, long blue dress. She looked down at the blade sticking out from his trouser leg and smiled approval at her embellishments, he supposed. He motioned for her to join them and then took the hands of both of his girls as he added:

> "I also promise to be the best father I can be to Marisol
> and any other children we may be blessed with.
> May our family always feel the sense of joy we feel today.
> I thank God every day for you both.
> Thank you for allowing me inside your lives and hearts.
> I love you both from the depths of my soul."

Savannah took the ring from Father Martine and placed it against the tip of Damián's ring finger. He felt her hand shaking—or was it his? He smiled his encouragement, and she relaxed.

> "Damián, I know in my heart
> you will continue to be my faithful friend.
> On this special day and in the presence of
> our relatives and friends,
> I give to you my sacred promise that
> I will always be with you to support you,
> in times of sickness and in times of health,
> in times of joy and in times of sorrow.
> "I promise to love you completely each and every moment,
> to console and comfort you during difficult times,
> to laugh with you and to grieve with you,
> to share with you life's simplest and most enduring pleasures,
> to be truthful and honest with you,
> and to cherish and mirror your patient guidance and love."

* * *

Focus, Savannah.

She took a breath and gazed down at Mari, who had remained beside them as they continued to exchange their vows, before turning to Damián once more.

"I promise to be the best mother I can be to Mari and our future children
and to work beside you to keep our family strong.

I promise to slay any dragon foolish enough to mess with my family."

She paused and grinned at him, remembering their shared fairy tale in the cave at Laguna Beach before growing serious again.

"And I vow to replace each bad memory
with a hundred happy ones.
From this day forward, Damián,
I give you my hand, my heart, and my love."

Her voice cracked as she finished. Thank God she'd made it through the vows before being overcome with emotion. Savannah blinked away the tears as she seated the simple, vintage Mexican-silver band on his brown finger. She'd found it in an antique store and hoped it carried a happy story like the one attached to the ring she now wore on her finger. Seeing the pale band of skin on his pinky finger where the ring had been worn since she'd known him would take some getting used to.

A tear splashed onto his finger, and she lifted his hand to her mouth, pressing her lips against the ring she'd given him to seal her vows and kiss away the tear. Later, she'd show him the inscription when they were alone.

Semper Fi, mi amor.

Anita came toward the couple carrying the two lit candles, handing one each to the bride and the groom. As Savannah and Damián walked toward the altar where the unity candle sat, Savannah stopped and turned around, gesturing for Mari to join her and Damián to help them light the candle that would unite their family as one. She glanced over at him as they blew out the candles representing the end of their lives apart. Their flame would now burn brightly as one family.

Back in their places, Father Martine continued the ceremony, "At this time, Savannah and Damián would like to symbolize their union with a Mexican wedding tradition called the *lazo*, or lasso, ceremony. The lasso of the double rosary symbolizes the inseparable nature of the newly married couple."

Savannah had watched brides and grooms being lassoed before this altar many times, but the symbolism had never included the context in which she now found herself being lassoed to Damián. Karla and Adam looped the giant rosary first around Damián's shoulders and then, completing the figure eight, over Savannah's head and shoulder. When their wrists were attached to the *lazo*, Savannah flashed back momentarily to the first time she'd allowed Damián to restrain her with rope. Adam and Karla had been there, too. She fought to stay in the moment, not wanting to miss anything.

"Damián and Savannah, this loop is symbolic of your love and will bind you together every day of the rest of your lives. Remember the holiness necessary to preserve your new family can only be achieved by mutual sacrifice and love."

Teresa came forward as Father Martine concluded the *lazo* ceremony and presented him with the prayer book and the rosary. Father blessed the gifts and gave them to Damián, reminding him that he was now the spiritual leader of his family.

Father Martine motioned, and Gunnar came forward to present both Damián and Savannah with a bag she knew held thirteen gold coins. "At this time, we will perform another traditional custom called *Las Arras*." He explained the ancient origins of the custom, but she and Damián had agreed to modernize the tradition. "Each bag holds thirteen coins, one for each month and one to give to charity. In exchanging these coins, Damián and Savannah will pledge '*Lo mio es tuyo y lo tuyo es mio*'—'What is mine is yours and what is yours is mine.' I bless these coins knowing they are also symbolic of the unlimited good the universe has in store for this loving couple— unlimited love, joy, peace, and prosperity. I accept this for Damián and Savannah, and so it is. Amen." They exchanged the coin bags, the coins making a tinkling sound for all to hear.

Adam and Karla removed the *lazo* and handed it to Savannah as a memento of her becoming the mistress of Damián's heart. Forever she would cherish this visible symbol of the promises they made today.

Savannah turned to Rosa, who extended the small bouquet of six red roses. Savannah said to Damián, "Someone else needs to be honored for getting me here today. Please join me?" He smiled and nodded, taking her hand and giving it a little squeeze. As the couple departed toward the side of the church, Karla began her angelic rendition of *Ave Maria*.

For you, Maman.

They made their way to the side altar and to the statue of the Madonna that had drawn her into this sanctuary—in both senses of the word—all

418

those years ago, both as a child beside her mother one special Christmas Eve and again exactly twelve years later as a pregnant and scared young woman. Savannah placed the bouquet at the base of this statue of Mother and Son.

"Thank you, *mi Madonna*, the symbol of both mother and child, for your oversight and guidance. Please let Maman know how happy I am and that all is well." Tears blurred her vision.

"*Savita*, are you okay?" Damián's voice beside her drew her attention, but she couldn't meet his gaze yet. When she finally turned toward him, her gaze still downcast, she saw for the first time he wore a blade rather than the shoe prosthesis. She glanced up at him, "When...?"

"Today. It was time."

"Oh, Damián, I'm so proud of you!"

"While you were hiding from me in that room in the back, Marisol already started decorating it for me."

Curious, Savannah bent down and looked more closely at the bow of the blade to find two butterflies with blue translucent wings and black tips. They reminded her of the two she'd seen at the cave a few weeks ago that she was convinced represented a sign her maman was together in the hereafter with the man her father killed for trying to rescue mother and daughter.

Thank you for letting me know you're here, too, Maman.

Damián and Savannah returned to their places in front of Father Martine, so he could continue the liturgy. At the offering, Adam and Karla walked toward the back of the church with Marc and Angelina to collect the gifts of bread, water, and wine. Angelina carried the two engraved goblets that would be used during Communion.

At the conclusion of the liturgy, Father Martine addressed those gathered to witness their special day. "This circle of love is now complete." Father Martine blessed their union and motioned for them to stand and face each other. She looked up into her beloved's warm brown eyes. "Savannah and Damián have agreed to love one another with all of their hearts, to be one another's only intimate companion, and each other's inspiration. It may seem like only yesterday that they started their lives together and allowed this incredible love to bloom, and yet they know why they were meant to be here today. Though life may not always be as perfect as it is at this moment, Damián and Savannah vow always to keep their love as pure as it is today, promising to be there in laughter and tears, sickness and health, comfort and fears, in poverty and wealth until the end of eternity."

Father Martine paused as Damián brushed a tear from her cheek. "In the presence of these witnesses, and in the name of the Father, the Son, and the Holy Spirit, and by the power vested in me by the State of California, I now pronounce you husband and wife. You may kiss your bride."

Without hesitation, Damián leaned forward and wrapped her in the protection of his arms. As his mouth lowered to hers, she closed her eyes. He surprised her by taking hold of her head and blowing his breath into her mouth before sucking their co-mingled breaths back into his. He didn't take it so far as he had the first time they'd done a breath-play exchange, but when he plunged his tongue deep into her mouth, her bag of coins fell to their feet. He chuckled and pulled her against him.

Someone cleared his throat—it sounded like Adam—but Damián continued to lay claim to her mouth. She regretted when he pulled away, but the promise in his eyes of what was to come later tonight let her know this was just a taste of many delights awaiting her.

Father Martine chuckled before he announced to those present in the church, "Ladies and gentlemen, *señoras y señores,* may I be the first to present Mr. and Mrs. Damián Orlando."

The congregation applauded as the recessional *Ode to Joy* played on the newly repaired pipe organ in the loft. Recognizing the organist's hand, she didn't need to turn to see that Anita had left her place here in the wedding party. She smiled, knowing her dear friend brought forth the beautiful music that filled the church.

Memories of huddling in a corner of the choir loft, seeking a place to hide and sleep after escaping the horrors of her childhood, brought Savannah full circle. Being able to donate some of Maman's money to bring joyful music to the church once more warmed her heart.

"Shall we, my lady?" Damián crooked his arm for her and placed his hand over hers as he led her to the vestibule. They entered into a small chamber she'd never been in before where Father Martine had asked them to wait so they could sign the certificate and make everything legal.

"I can't get my fill of you, *savita.*" Damián crushed her against the wall, pressing his mouth to hers once more.

A male chuckle brought them back to the present some time later. "You two really need to get a room—but not until after your reception is over. Your *madrinas y padrinos* have worked long and hard to make everything special for you."

She blushed and turned to Father Martine, whose eyes exuded happiness. "Let me be the second to kiss the bride." He came to her and kissed her on both cheeks. "I'm so happy for you, little one. Seeing you so happy gives my heart great joy. As I remember back to this day, I will be able to counsel others who think there is no longer any hope for them. You two offer an amazing testament to others for your courage and persistence to survive all obstacles. I hope you won't hide that light under a bushel."

He then turned to Damián and shook his hand. "Take good care of her, or you'll have me and many others to answer to."

"I'd take a bullet for this woman, *Padre.*"

Savannah cleared the frog from her throat. "You already did, Damián."

They signed the nuptial papers and the state's paperwork before following Father Martine into the vestibule where the wedding party remained, waiting to take photos. Then they would all proceed to the church hall for the reception.

How truly blessed was she?

Chapter Thirty-One

Marc had never been more nervous in his life—not so much because of what he was about to do but of how Angelina would respond.

He breathed a heavy sigh, expending some nervousness. He and Angelina would leave in an hour for the special date he'd spent all week planning. For her, though, he wanted everything to be a surprise.

One lesson he'd learned from their separation was not to leave Angelina out of the equation when making important decisions, but sometimes he enjoyed keeping his girl guessing. However, they *had* discussed plans to move into her place in Aspen Corners after Damián's wedding; he just hadn't told her how long after that would be. First, he needed to do something he'd put off way too long.

She'd moved back to his Denver house temporarily after he'd left Adam's, in part to continue to be there for the fallout of the interrogation scene three weeks ago. He glanced around the bedroom. On the first of June, he would sign the deed to this house over to Adam and Karla. Marc and Angelina had been packing boxes the last two weeks, but most of his furniture would stay here or go into storage. Very few pieces were his or Angelina's style and even fewer would fit into her tiny rental house.

Tonight—well, tomorrow, depending on how one viewed it—he hoped to be making plans for the rest of their lives. He patted his pocket to make sure he had everything he needed, not that he hadn't performed that check a dozen times already.

Dio, don't let me get cold feet again.

The shower door opened and closed. She'd return to the bedroom soon, so Marc went to the dresser and pulled out the red satin sash he'd first put on her that night in her house when he thought he'd only have one night with her. Now he hoped there would be many more nights together—the remainder of their days. Could he win her over by blowing her expectations out of the water? Or would his need to lay more ghosts to rest in the coming days ruin the moment?

Angelina entered the bedroom with one towel wrapped around her body as she dried her hair with another. She spotted the sash in Marc's hand. Her smile caused his heart to rev up, not to mention his cock. So beautiful when she smiled. Beautiful on the inside, too. How did he get so lucky to find someone willing to put up with his shit?

"I thought you said we were going out."

"We are."

She glanced at the sash again, and her hand stilled in drying her hair before she lowered the towel and met his gaze.

"Wear something sexy but romantic. I'm taking you to a new Italian restaurant."

"Blindfolded?"

"Not only blindfolded, but I'll be blocking your sense of hearing, as well."

Her breath hitched. Apparently, the idea of a public scene and escalated sensory deprivation excited her. Fascinating woman. She would certainly keep him on his toes planning innovative play scenes for decades to come.

If he should be so blessed.

Marc took the brush and ran it through her long, silky hair. Sometimes she counted the strokes—much as she would during a spanking—but today she seemed lost in the sensation. They hadn't had sex since she'd moved back into the house, partly because of his recent ordeal and partly because he didn't want things to become physical before they resolved some issues. They had continued to cuddle and he made sure her body's needs were met.

Surprisingly, though, he'd found that touching her in non-sexual ways, even doing something as mundane as brushing her hair, only heightened his desire for her. He'd been working out in the weight room at the club. Soon he would stoke the fires again.

She pivoted and stilled his hand, holding onto the towel that hid her body from him. "You have no idea how sensual it is to have someone mess with your hair." He shrugged, surprised she'd felt something, too. When she reached for her makeup bag, he stayed her hand.

"No makeup. You're beautiful without it."

She quirked a brow, but he didn't explain further. She never overdid her makeup, always using just enough to enhance her natural beauty. But she'd be sleeping in it tonight and wouldn't appreciate the way her mascara would smear after having the blindfold on for so long. Besides, she *was* beautiful without it.

She rose and walked over to open the top drawer of the dresser. He'd made sure only her sexiest lingerie was there.

"You won't be needing a bra or panties—just the garter belt and silk stockings."

She glanced at him over her shoulder. "My, you've planned everything down to the last detail."

"I've planned as far as I can without your input. The time will come during our date when you will have to determine how this scene ultimately plays out."

She grinned. "Planning to push my boundaries tonight?"

I'm definitely going to be pushing the boundaries for one of us.

Angelina smiled as she passed him on the way to the closet. When she opened the door, she stared before turning to him once more. "What happened to the rest of my clothes?"

"Oh, I sent them to the cleaners for you."

"But they were already clean."

He shrugged. "*Scusa.* My mistake."

From the near-empty closet, she removed the red dress with the keyhole in the back that she'd worn at Rico's bar the night she'd come back into his life—the first time.

"I've lost some weight. Do you think this will still look good on me?

Anything—or nothing at all—would enhance his girl's beauty. "One way to find out."

She smiled and carried the dress into the bathroom, not bothering to close the door. He watched her drop the towel, showing she still maintained the curves he loved. She'd shaved her mound for him. Soon he would reward her obedience.

With regret, he watched as she slipped the knit dress over her head, covering her sexy curves from his view. After adjusting the skirt over her hips, she stepped back into the bedroom. Their gazes met before his broke away to roam slowly down her body, lingering at her bust and hips. When his gaze returned to her face with great reluctance, he grinned.

"*Perfetto.*"

"Why do I get the feeling you just undressed me with your eyes?"

He shrugged and grinned. "I am Italian. We know how to appreciate the female body."

Angelina drew her brows together, but she smiled and continued to dress as instructed.

When he emptied her things out of the closet, he had made sure this was the only dress suitable for a romantic date. The rest of her clothes had been packed into one of the new pieces of luggage sitting in the back of Grant's Jeep. She would be chauffeuring them partway today. Then, Gunnar Larson would take over, along with Patrick Gallagher, Adam's brother. He hoped Patrick and Gunnar would be on time. At Damián's wedding, Marc mentioned what he wanted to do, and Gunnar overheard him then offered to provide the couple with transportation. Adam immediately picked up his phone and called his brother to enlist his help. All their transportation needs had been arranged.

Ready, she walked across the room to stand before him and pivoted around to present her back to him. He couldn't resist stroking her back through the sexy keyhole. She relaxed against his hand at first and then pressed her body against him.

"I love the gift of your sweet submission."

"Are you sure we have to go out, Sir?" Her breathy voice made him hard.

Marc chuckled. "Yes, we most definitely must go out. I promised my girl a fine Italian dinner, and she's not going to get it by my hand."

"Oh, but your hands deliver decadent food for the soul, Sir."

He placed a kiss at the side of her neck and smiled when she nearly came out of her skin. He loved her ticklishness. With reluctance, he lifted the sash and tied it snugly around her head.

Grabbing a white, lacy shawl from the closet, he wrapped it around her shoulders and placed a kiss on her neck. Her heavier coat was in the car, if needed.

"Trust me to protect you and keep you safe, pet?"

"You always have, Sir. You know I do."

He found it hard to breathe for a moment and then picked up the headset from the dresser. She would wear this until they reached their table at the restaurant. He'd queued up Andrea Bocelli's *Romanza* CD.

Perfetto.

"This will help me deliver my surprise to you. I like keeping you in suspense."

"I hear anticipation is good for subbies."

"It is, indeed." He placed the noise-canceling headset over her ears. He'd already adjusted the volume to a comfortable level but loud enough for him to be certain she wouldn't hear any noise from the outside.

Time for them to embark on this next phase in their lives. At least, he hoped that would be the end result tomorrow.

*   *   *

Angelina's excitement grew as she tried to guess what Marc had planned. It seemed a little early to dress for dinner, but she obeyed, happy to have her Dom back.

Marc would never harm her, and she hoped he would continue to rely on her more each day to meet his needs, as well. Having him actually needing her physically and emotionally these last few weeks had cemented their relationship in many ways, building a stronger foundation than they'd had before.

But she needed to give Marc time. After so many people throughout his life had betrayed or abandoned him, even though the ones who loved him had done so without intent or malice, no wonder the man had trust issues.

She hoped one day that wounded little boy's spirit would heal and the man she loved so intensely would allow her into his life—and his heart. To trust her not to harm him would take time, perhaps a lifetime. Being a part of Marc's life, however small a part she was, would be enough. For now. They were young. She hoped they would continue to have time on their side, but both had suffered great losses and knew how fragile life could be.

Connecting on an emotional level the way they had been lately gave her hope they could move forward and make a life together for themselves. She'd just need to employ a lot of patience. He still had so much to sort out about his past, especially with his brother, Gino.

Angelina could wait. They had decided to take things slowly this time around. They'd moved too quickly before and hadn't taken time to build a foundation strong enough to withstand the first major crisis to come their way.

Marc wrapped his arm around her back and guided her forward. When they reached what she assumed to be the stairs, he lifted her into his arms.

"I'm too heavy! Put me down! I can walk if you'll just lead me!"

She felt the rumble of his voice—or perhaps it was a growl—and he pinched her butt hard, indicating she was out of line. He'd just been through an ordeal that caused him to lose a lot of weight, not to mention put a dent in his stamina. She'd even been afraid to make love with him, wanting him to regain his strength first, and had said no every time he tried to initiate sex since they'd moved back to his house after the interrogation.

Angelina wrapped her arms around his neck, hoping to relieve some of her weight from his arms. Even though she'd lost fifteen pounds over the last few months, she still was no lightweight.

Of course, Marc had never complained about her weight. He even said he enjoyed her extra padding, especially on her hips when he was spanking her or holding onto her love handles while ramming his cock inside her from behind. Her pussy grew wet in anticipation of whatever he had planned. If he could carry her around like this, he damned well wasn't going to break if she jumped his...bones later.

She giggled and nuzzled the scruff on his neck. Marc's distinctive scent—lemon, bergamot, and, well, Marc—made her hungry, but not for food.

So he'd planned dinner at a new Italian restaurant? It was only midafternoon. She wondered what the rush was all about. And what about afterward? Would there be a play scene in her future tonight? Heck, with the sensory deprivation she was under already, a play scene was indeed under way and her body ready. This meal must just be a part of it. He loved to feed her, especially when she didn't know what she'd be eating. He often said he was impressed by her ability to analyze the ingredients, usually naming the dish itself.

Marc put her on her feet again and ushered her into a vehicle. Definitely not the Porsche. Much higher and roomier. Rather than Marc getting behind the driver's seat, he nudged her to scoot over and soon had her buckled in, pulling her against his body where she snuggled against his shoulder for the ride. The vibration of the engine and friction of their thighs touching as they set off toward the restaurant heightened her awareness of the sexy, hard body next to her.

Which restaurant had he chosen? She'd dined at practically every one in Denver and had even applied for a chef or sous chef position at most of the finer ones, especially the ones with unexciting menus. She knew she could improve the cuisine in any restaurant if only someone would give her the opportunity.

Maybe God knew she wouldn't be living in Denver for long, which is why she didn't get any job offers. Soon, she would reopen her catering business in Aspen Corners, but Marc promised to help her find a business manager so she could spend more time doing the part she loved—cooking!

The strains of *Por Amor* filtered into her consciousness. It was a personal favorite of Marc's, and she listened closely to the lyrics, translating them into her native English as best she could.

> *For love,*
> *have you ever done anything*
> *only for love?*
> *Have you ever defied the wind and*
> *cried out,*
> *divided the heart itself…*

Oh, had she ever. Leaving Marc three months ago certainly had divided her heart. If he could shut her out of something as important as flying to Italy to meet his birth father, what else would he hide from her? Angelina had always been honest with and faithful to Marc. Perhaps in time he would come to trust her and commit to a more permanent future with her. If only…

After hearing what kind of man Solari was, though, she'd thanked Marc for not taking her to meet him. She shuddered, and Marc pulled a fleece throw over her arms and lap.

Once she'd thought *Por Amor* told of an unrequited love, but listening to the words from Marc's perspective, she wondered if it might not have been more about his feelings for his mother—*mothers*. Deep down, had he known his childhood had been a lie?

> *And you have to say now*
> *how much of yourself you have*
> *committed,*
> *how much you have believed*
> *in this lie…*

It could even have something to do with his estrangement from Gino. Complicated song for a complicated man.

The vehicle lurched to a stop, and the motor cut. Soon Marc unbuckled her and ushered her out. They walked a fair distance with the wind whipping at the ends of her loose hair before he put her hands on two handrails and tapped the back of her left thigh, indicating she should lift her leg. Steps. She climbed them with Marc's hand at the small of her back to keep her from falling backward. She didn't remember any restaurants that had a stairway to them. This must be a new place.

When she reached the top of the stairway, he halted her. She detected no smells that would hint at her being at an Italian restaurant. If anything, she smelled…jet fuel?

Marc indicated she should veer to the right, and she did so. He eased her into a very comfortable chair—leather, mmmm—and buckled her in.

So they were on an airplane? How had they gotten through security so easily—and wouldn't someone have questioned why she was blindfolded?

Minutes later, the sensation of charging down a runway left no doubt that they were flying somewhere. Wow. What on earth did he have planned for tonight? And where? Perhaps a large city. That didn't sound like his style, but he'd told her he made an annual trip to New York City to enjoy an Italian opera at the Metropolitan. He hadn't taken the trip, as far as she knew, since they'd met, although she couldn't account for what he'd done during their three-month separation.

Thank God they were back together. He'd surprised her by saying he wanted to live with her in Aspen Corners at least until her lease was up—if she'd have him. They'd made some wonderful memories there. She just hoped he wouldn't feel claustrophobic in her one-bedroom, single-story bungalow after having the run of an enormous house.

She had no idea how much time had passed when something cold pressed against her lips, and she opened her mouth. A tap under her chin told her to bite. *Mmmm.* Strawberry dipped in white chocolate. Why was he feeding her if they were going to be eating soon? Who cared? She hadn't eaten since breakfast, and the combination of two of her favorite flavors excited her taste buds. He followed with warm prosciutto wrapped asparagus spears and a sip of white zinfandel. He encouraged her to try some of his classier wines but respected her preference for the fruitier ones. A girl on a budget couldn't afford classy wines, especially not when she was building up a business.

Her next bite tasted like a cream puff that she gobbled down quickly.

Marc's tongue brushed against her lips, probably capturing some of the whipped cream she'd missed, and she opened for him. He deepened the kiss, his tongue invading her mouth. *Mmmm.* The best thing to cross her lips all day.

When he grabbed her hair, tilting her head back to plunge even farther into her mouth, heat pooled in her pelvis. She suddenly wondered what the other passengers must be thinking. But the stairway to the plane hadn't been more than a dozen steps. Didn't commercial flights use gangways? Were they on a private plane? If so, the ride was incredibly smooth. Good grief. What if it was a *jet*?

Where would Marc have found a jet?

Marc unclipped her seatbelt. She licked her lips, wanting to keep his essence with her even longer. He dragged her from the seat by both arms until she stood pressed against him, and he kissed her again. His hands roamed over her ass, tugging her against his erection.

Mio Dio! Was she about to join the Mile High Club? She blushed. What would Mama say if she ever found out?

Angelina gave a mental shrug. She was an adult. And she wanted Marc to make love to her wherever he wanted after having waited so long for him. Besides, Mama liked Marc. Eventually her overbearing brothers would come around to see he was the right man for her, even if he didn't meet their impossibly high standards.

A pinch on her butt cheek told her she wasn't focusing her mind where it should be.

She reached out and stroked Marc's back in long, sweeping motions before her hand inched closer and closer to his sexy ass. How he managed to keep his butt in such great shape escaped her. Hers was soft and jiggly; he had buns of steel. *Dio*, she loved touching him there. She dragged her fingernails over his cheeks and imagined the hiss she knew he made, even though it was drowned out by the headset. She knew her man's responses, and her imagination filled in the gaps.

Why was he still depriving her of sight and sound? He had to know she'd guessed where she was.

Marc nibbled the side of her neck. Aroused rather than feeling ticklish, she nearly melted into a puddle at his feet. His hand reached inside the keyhole of her dress, bringing back memories of the first time they'd danced. She heard the strains of *Return to Me* in her headset instead of *Volare*, and they began to slow dance as they'd done before in Rico's bar—not the chaste way Papa had taught her in high school either.

Angelina didn't expect so much room in the plane's aisle, but Marc's movements led her to imagine a wide expanse. But how could he have commandeered a jet?

Anticipation and curiosity nearly got the best of her. The song's sad lyrics had Dean Martin asking for forgiveness. Marc had played it at Rico's when he'd come back to her before Luke's accident. Before the interrogation scene. Did he ever regret shutting her out again that night? At least now they both understood more about why he did so, but she hated that it took such extreme measures to get him there.

Nothing is ever easy with you, Marc.

She needed to stop focusing on the dark days of their recent past and stay in this moment, dancing with the man she loved thousands of feet in the air. She'd missed him so much all these months and didn't want to squander a single second worrying about their past or future. If they never managed a forever kind of love for themselves, at least she'd have another special memory to tuck away and hold on to, forever. And he was her Dom again.

Marc, when will you see that I am yours completely?

He removed the padded headphones and whispered, "*Bella*, I've missed you so."

Had she spoken aloud? She didn't think so. She held him closer. "I've missed you, too...Sir." She assumed she was to address him as her Dom, given she was being deprived of two senses and in the middle of what seemed like an elaborately planned scene.

Marc's hand smacked her butt through the knit dress, and her breath hitched.

"What did I do?"

He chuckled. "Nothing. I've just missed that response, as well, *amore*."

Amore. If only she could be his forever love this time.

Dio, *stop reaching for the moon, Angelina.*

She needed to take this relationship one day at a time.

Marc placed the headset over her ears again, and she was lost in the lyrics of her favorite Mary Chapin Carpenter song as they continued to dance. His hands stroked her, but he didn't touch her where she wanted him most. Oh, the similarities between Marc and *The King of Love*.

Still when he calls your name
you have to answer

He broke contact with her body and lifted her arms above her head, slipping her dress over her head. Finally! Too late, she remembered they were on a plane.

"Marc!" She reached to cover her bare girls, and he swatted her hands away. Who else could see them? At the very least there was a pilot and probably a co-pilot. "What if the pilot comes back here?"

Of course, she couldn't hear his response, if any, because of the headphones. Gently but insistently, he guided her backward and down onto a seat. Reaching out to her side, she realized it was a sofa or bench of some sort, rather than the leather bucket seat she'd been in before.

She reminded herself they weren't on a public plane. Marc removed the headset. "We're only halfway to our destination. I thought you might need a little more to eat to curb your appetite until dinner."

This must be the slowest jet around. She had no concept of time, but it seemed they'd been on here for at least four hours, maybe longer. A nonstop commercial flight would get them to New York City faster than that, wouldn't it?

Or was this a mindfuck? Were they flying around in circles just to confuse her? Not unlike the dizzying circles she'd navigated in this relationship to get to this point.

"Would you care to eat something before we sleep? I can microwave something."

Why spoil dinner with airplane food? "I thought we're supposed to have dinner at a new Italian restaurant tonight."

"We'll dine there tomorrow. It's a little...out of the way."

Where *was* this place?

"No, thanks. I'm not hungry anymore." Not for food, anyway. Would they make love again at long last?

The sofa began to vibrate, and the back reclined to form what her mind's eye pictured as a bed in the sleeper car of a train. He stretched out beside her and pulled a light blanket over them. He'd removed his clothing as well at some point. Obviously sleep wasn't on the agenda. She smiled.

Mile High Club, here I come!

His finger and thumb teased her nipple to a hard peak, and she wiggled her butt against his erection. Now she was wide-awake for another reason. But soon his hand stopped its motions. She no longer felt his cock against her ass. A moment later, his hand fell away from her breast. When his breathing became steady, she realized he'd fallen asleep.

Angelina sighed. He still hadn't fully recovered from the ordeal he'd been through almost a month ago, and they'd only flown back from Southern California yesterday. She settled her backside against him, content to snuggle. His arm surrounding her made her feel safe.

Why he'd had her dress for a date only to fall asleep puzzled her. How could she possibly sleep so early in the evening? Thank goodness he'd instructed her not to wear makeup or she'd look like a raccoon.

The whisper of the jet engines hurtling them to their mysterious destination continued to hum. Her eyelids drooped…

"Marc…" A deep voice intruded into her sleep and made her jump.

"We've been given clearance to land, and we're about thirty minutes out. Prepare for landing and buckle up."

Angelina wondered who flew the plane. His voice sounded oddly familiar, but she didn't know any pilots.

"Let's get dressed, *amore*."

Marc helped her up from their bed. "Lift your arms." She did as he instructed, and he pulled the dress down her arms and over her head before adjusting it. He placed the headphones on her again.

Angelina groaned. "Marc, please! Not again!"

In response to her whining, she earned a swat to her butt, but he gave her a brief kiss before leading her back to her seat and buckling her in.

*   *   *

Marc dressed for dinner after he buckled Angelina into her seat. Before doing the same, he nibbled her neck once more. She tasted so good. How could he have fallen asleep when he'd planned to have sex with her on the jet? He hoped he didn't embarrass himself like that again during this four-day trip. Some Italian lover he was.

When he pulled away, she smiled at him so sweetly, he realized she must have understood. He fought the urge to remove the blindfold, so he could look into her eyes again to be certain. Nerves frayed, he took a deep breath, feeling the familiar hitch in his side from adhesions. He needed to remember to breathe more evenly.

What if he hadn't gotten any closer to being able to trust a woman than he had been when his sense of security had been shattered as a child?

But Angelina wasn't like any woman he'd ever known. She was honest, giving...*trusting*. And she seemed to genuinely love him—not because his name was D'Alessio or because his family had money or because he owned a successful business. No, she loved him just because he was Marc—

"Final call. Prepare for landing, Marc." Patrick's voice brought him back to the moment.

He buckled himself into the seat next to Angelina and reached for her hand. Marc turned away, glancing out the window as he watched the landscape zip by the window. Snow-covered Alps gave way to orchards and vineyards, cattle grazing, old stone farmhouses, elaborate villas, and more and more houses as Milan grew closer.

Home. But it no longer felt like home to him. He'd spent the first eleven years of his life in this region and expected to feel a sense of belonging, but it eluded him. Would that feeling return when he reached his childhood village?

Perhaps he didn't belong anywhere.

Angelina squeezed his hand as if she sensed his tension. He turned toward her, and she smiled in his general direction, her sight and hearing still closed off. The jet landed smoothly and taxied across the tarmac before it came to a stop. Marc unbuckled their seatbelts and, still holding her hand, helped her up from the seat.

He didn't want to spoil the surprise, so he collected their things while Patrick smoothed things over with customs by showing passports and papers. Once the okay came through, he guided Angelina to the exit, thanking Gunnar for everything and making arrangements for the return flight in a few days. He preceded Angelina down the stairs, never releasing her right hand but letting her hold onto the railing with her left for an added sense of security. He'd be there to catch her if she tripped. Marc would never allow his precious angel to be harmed if he could help it.

At customs, they still managed to get flagged despite Patrick's efforts, and Marc had a dickens of a time making the agent understand Angelina wasn't being kidnapped. Frustrated and ready to be on their way, he pulled the headset away from her left ear. "*Amore*, there's a gentleman standing here who wants to know if you're being kidnapped. Would you please explain, in Italian, what your current predicament is?" Marc hoped this wouldn't spoil his surprise completely.

She quirked a brow but said in impeccable Italian, "*Signore*, this man is the love of my life and he is taking me on a romantic date to a new Italian restaurant, but it's a surprise, hence the headphones and blindfold." Her smile would have melted anyone's heart and certainly succeeded in doing so with both Marc and the customs agent.

Italy…truly the land of lovers.

Marc intended to keep these Latin lovers away from his girl. He returned the headphone to her ear and guided her to the Ferrari rental parked outside the gate. After both were enfolded into the leather interior, he glanced over to watch her cute little nose sniffing the air. Her nipples bunched. The woman truly loved the smell of leather. He grinned as he pulled away from the lot and headed out of the city. They wouldn't spend a lot of time in Milan, although he did want to share some of the cultural sights of the province of Brescia with her during their time here.

First, though, the dinner he'd promised. It was early afternoon here, but she must be starving given the eight-hour time difference, not to mention spending twelve hours in the air. He hated that he was depriving her of seeing the scenery, but he would show her around soon. Besides, they'd see the same scenery when they returned to the airport four days from now.

The really spectacular scenery was yet to come, at least as far as he remembered, although it was too early in the year for the grape vines to be leafed out. But the snow-capped mountains and glacial lake would make up for their absence. Alpine flowers would be in full bloom when he took her hiking on the Maddalena. Angelina loved flowers.

"I'm dying to know where you're taking me for dinner."

He didn't respond, knowing she wouldn't hear him anyway. He just reached over and squeezed her thigh. When she opened her legs to him, he chuckled. *Dio*, he loved this responsive woman. He'd never met anyone who had been able to keep up with him sexually until her.

But he wanted more than a sexual relationship with her.

Could he expect to find what Adam and Karla or Damián and Savannah had found with each other? Why the hell not? The only thing holding him back was himself.

You can be the man she deserves.

He placed both hands on the steering wheel and maneuvered around a sharp curve as he continued toward their destination—and the rest of their lives together.

He hoped.

*   *   *

Angelina still had no clue where they were. She'd thought they were headed to New York. Or maybe California. Had he heard about a place while they were there for the wedding? But after speaking with someone in Italian, she became convinced they'd traveled all the way to Italy. The flight had taken so long that they had slept at some point. Her growling stomach told her it had been more than six hours.

But Italy?

Would he bring her all this way for dinner? What about passports? Well, she still had a valid one that she'd used to travel to Sicily to visit Nonna.

But not in a private jet. Marc was no jet setter, even if his family might be able to afford it. She was letting her imagination run away with her.

The smell of leather in the sports car kicked her libido into high gear. She hoped there would be a night at a hotel as part of this date. Her body swayed as he navigated the car around a number of curves. The breeze she'd felt when they'd deplaned reminded her of the Rockies in late spring.

After at least half an hour, he brought the car to a stop and cut the engine. Her heart beat wildly. Soon he'd remove the blindfold and headphones and reveal where he'd taken her on this amazing date. Wherever it was, she knew it would be romantic. Marc loved to excite her senses with food and wine, almost as much as he enjoyed sharing his favorite places in nature with her.

Heck, she'd go camping with him in a heartbeat now so they wouldn't have to be apart.

She assumed Marc opened her door when a strong hand reached for her elbow, helping her out of the low-riding car. When he wrapped his arms around her and planted a kiss on her lips, he left no doubt because she smelled his Armani Code cologne. She returned his embrace and opened her mouth to him before remembering they were in the midst of an elaborate play scene, and she shouldn't touch without permission. He didn't swat her hand away or chastise her the way he once might have.

Instead of guiding her to their destination, he picked her up and carried her. "Marc! Put me down!"

He pinched her thigh hard enough to leave a bruise. Would she ever learn not to argue with him when he decided to carry her?

436

The scent of rosemary, garlic, and lemon wafted to her nostrils. Her mouth watered as her stomach churned to life in what would have been an embarrassing grumble if she could hear. Marc most certainly must have heard it, though.

Okay, she was going to gain five pounds just from smelling such delectable aromas. Wherever he'd taken her for dinner, the man certainly had great taste.

She'd reward him richly later, wherever they wound up spending the night, even if it was on the flight home. But wouldn't the pilot have to sleep after such a long flight?

Marc lowered her legs to the floor, continuing to support her back until she became steady on her feet. He removed the headphones first, and violin music wafted to her ears. Puccini's *O Mio Babbino Caro* from Nonna's opera collection. The only reason she recognized it was that this rendition sung by Maria Callas had been Nonna's favorite. The aria transported Angelina back to her grandmother's kitchen in Sicily.

I will not cry and ruin this moment.

She blinked her eyes rapidly, thankful for the blindfold. The lyrics made her ache for Papa and miss him in an intense way.

Oh, my dear papa,
I love him, he is handsome, handsome.
I want to go to Porta Rossa
To buy the ring!

She wished Papa could have lived long enough to meet Marc. He would have approved of him as a potential husband, protector, and provider without a doubt.

What was she thinking?

Stay in this incredible moment, Angie, on this fabulously romantic dinner date.

No doubt soon she would enjoy an evening she would remember for all time. She loved this place already. A special dinner in a special restaurant chosen by her very special man.

Marc tugged at the knot in the blindfold and removed it at last. She blinked a few times as her eyes adjusted to the dim light in the restaurant.

He brushed his thumb on her cheek. "Are you all right?"

She never could hide her tears from the man. Not quite ready to speak, she nodded briskly. After gauging her response for an intense moment, he seemed satisfied and folded and tucked the sash away in his suit-coat pocket. He'd dressed formally, except for the missing tie. The man wore his clothes so well, both casual and formal.

Tearing her gaze away from him, she glanced around the restaurant. No one seemed to be paying them any mind, thank goodness, regardless of the fact he'd brought her here blindfolded with huge headphones covering her ears. Maybe they thought he just wanted to surprise his lady love, which he had.

The restaurant had no windows, but it must be late. White linens and deep pink cyclamen adorned each candlelit table. Fan-shaped napkins were tucked inside each bone china soup bowl at the place settings. Elegance personified.

Angelina turned to Marc again and smiled. "It's beautiful! How did you ever find it?"

He placed the headphones on the extra seat beside him. "A man doesn't reveal all of his secrets, *bella.*"

A man like Marc revealed very few of them, actually.

He pulled a violin-backed chair away from a table set for two. There were several groups dining family style nearby, sharing bowls of delicious-looking dishes. Their classic European clothing reminded her of summers with her grandmother in Sicily.

For the first time, Angelina noticed no one else spoke English.

Mio Dio, he really had brought her to Italy! She glanced at him, but he seemed more intent on sampling the bottle of wine the server had brought to the table. The two also conversed in Italian.

She decided to let him do the big reveal in his own time. As she surveyed the restaurant, she wished there was one like it in Colorado. She'd give anything to work in the kitchen of a place like this.

Where were they specifically, though? Tuscany? Lombardy?

Marc nodded to the server, who then poured a glass of wine for each of them. She expected to be given a menu to peruse, but again in perfect Italian, Marc asked for the specialties of the house. She loved hearing him lapse into his native language. Nothing sexier.

He'd ordered for them both a specialty popular in the region where he'd grown up. Marc glanced at her, lifted his glass, and held it up in a toast, prompting her to pick up her glass as well. Continuing to speak Italian, he said, "To new beginnings."

They clinked glasses, and she took a sip expecting dry wine and schooling her expression so as not to make a face. Surprisingly, it was semi-dry and fruitier than Marc usually preferred.

"Delizioso!" She took a bigger sip.

"Go easy on that, *amore*. You need to get some food in your stomach first."

"Sì, Signore."

The atmosphere seemed to be bringing out her inner Italian, as well. She stifled a giggle and took another tinier sip.

The waiter brought the *antipasto misto* out, and they filled their small plates with meats, stalks of fresh fennel, and marinated black olives. She dipped a stalk of fennel into the plate of herbed olive oil and took a bite. The oil must have been a first pressing and straight from the grove's private reserve stock.

"Too bad we don't have a place like this closer to home."

Marc smiled enigmatically. She planned to enjoy this meal with him to the fullest and see if she could get him to confess where they were. That he'd go to this much effort to take her to Italy warmed her heart, even though she hadn't wanted to come here for a vacation alone. She'd wanted to be with him as he faced his birth father—his past.

Don't think about that; it's over and done. Life offered up these special times rarely, and for many, they flitted by without being noticed. She planned to enjoy it to the fullest.

She picked up a piece of bread, dipped it in the oil, and stretched her arm across the table until she placed it against his mouth. He opened for her and bit the crusty bread in half before she pulled her arm back and plopped the remainder into her mouth. Marc reciprocated by placing an olive in her mouth. The sensual nature of feeding each other totally turned her on.

A saffron-flavored *risotto* was served *primo*—she couldn't help but lapse into Italian with such authentic food—and was followed by the rich veal dish, *ossobuco in bianco*. She wondered if the chef would share the recipe with her. She tried to identify the ingredients. Definitely lemon, garlic, parsley—and did she detect cinnamon? Intriguing.

"Have you determined the recipe yet?"

Angelina smiled sheepishly. "Sorry. Hazard of the trade. I can't eat anything without trying to figure out how to make it myself."

"Why don't we ask if the chef will permit you to tour the kitchen?"

Angelina's mouth dropped. "Do you think they would give me just a quick a peek inside?" To be inside an authentic kitchen in the mother country—nirvana! The times she'd come to Sicily she'd been a teen and spent most of her time in Nonna's kitchen.

"Once they learn what a talented chef you are in your own right, they'll be asking you to share recipes for some of your specialties."

Despite his supportive, but encouraging teasing, she couldn't help but salivate over the possibility of touring the kitchen. Then she remembered they were here on a date. She needed to focus on Marc, not her own selfish wants.

"How are things going at the store?"

Marc shrugged. "Brian keeps things going, with or without me. I do expect to see an increase in bookings as the weather continues to improve. We're between seasons now." Marc speared a piece of the veal and extended the fork to her mouth. "Open."

She lost herself in his green eyes as he fed her. She closed her eyes and savored the tender meat, chewing slowly before swallowing.

"I see this dish excites you."

"You know food can be better than sex for me, Marc—and sometimes combining the two is best of all."

Marc swallowed hard. "Are you throwing down some kind of gauntlet, pet?"

She grinned. "Could be."

"Perhaps you've gone too long without sex."

"Yes, I have been neglected lately. What do you plan to do about it?"

A cloud passed over his face. "About falling asleep on the flight…"

Realizing she'd wounded his ego, she reached across the table and touched his hand. "You were put through hell less than a month ago, spent a week in aftercare, and between packing the house and going to the wedding, you haven't really been taking it easy like Doctor McKenzie ordered. I think I'm amazed you aren't a zombie at this point." She squeezed his hand. "But if you play your cards right, I'll let you make up for lost time tonight."

He grinned. "*Grazie.*" But soon he grew serious again. After a pause, he said, "It's just that, as your Dom, it was my responsibility to meet *your* needs."

She brushed the pad of her thumb across his knuckles. "Marc, sometimes the Dom needs to remember the submissive's major need in the dynamic, which is to serve her Dom and to take care of *his* needs."

He didn't say anything but picked up a slice of bread and broke off a piece before placing it against her lips. He had a major problem with letting her know he even had needs. Was he trying to silence her by keeping her mouth full? He pressed harder against her lips until she opened to let him put the bread inside her mouth.

"Marc—" Once she opened her mouth, he placed the bread inside.

"Be a good girl. Don't talk with your mouth full. Chew."

She glared at him but did as he told her. The focaccia was to die for, and she took her time enjoying it. They had such a long way to go in learning to communicate with each other, but she hoped they still had lots of time to improve.

He grew serious and reached into his pocket. Her heart stopped beating. Was he going to…? His hand stilled a moment before he pulled it back out. Empty.

Silly girl.

What was the matter with her? The romantic ambiance of this place was making her daft. He probably just wanted to make sure he'd put her sash away in his pocket. Still, who could blame her for thinking something was up? He'd gone to such extremes to take her out for this to be merely about dinner.

When his gaze met hers again, she saw pain, reminding her of the haunted look he bore in the days following the interrogation. Angelina reached across the table. "What is it, Marc?"

The longer he stared at her in silence, the more worried she became. Something was wrong.

Marc grabbed her hand and held it firmly between his. "*Amore*, I have a confession I must make before we go any further."

No, don't you dare spoil this moment, Marc!

Improved communication had its place; this wasn't that place! She wanted to remain immersed in this perfect fantasy, leaving their troubles behind them. Hadn't he toasted their future only moments ago? She reminded herself he wouldn't go to all this trouble only to break up. So why did she feel she was hurtling along on the downhill side of a roller coaster?

"I must be honest with you about some things from my past, things I'm just beginning to understand myself."

Wait! Marc wanted to divulge some of his secrets? Now *this* had been a fantasy of hers for a long while. She washed down the piece of bread with a gulp of wine.

"Before you say anything more, Marc, just know that nothing you say will change how I feel about you. But I'm honored you trust me enough to share whatever it is that's on your mind."

He didn't smile. Dread seeped back into her bones. What on earth did he need to divulge?

"The interrogation brought up some things I buried a very long time ago. Buried out of shame and disgust, no doubt." Marc looked down at their clasped hands and drew a deep breath. His hand shook, and Angelina squeezed it tightly.

"I used to be a poser Dom. The cougars at the resort referred to me as Master Marco." He paused before meeting her gaze again. "I won't lie to you. There was a time when the title went to my head. But after training under Adam before we opened the club, I knew I was a master at nothing."

She felt as if she were peering into his soul. Her heart ached at the insecurity she saw there. How could he think he wasn't a Dom? He certainly had no problem dominating her.

"Even now, I'm not sure I can be the Dom you need."

She'd held her words back long enough, holding up her hand to halt any argument. "Marc, don't you dare try to shut me up. I hate those bitches— and, no I'm not sorry for calling them that—who took advantage of a trusting, vulnerable young man. Makes me wish they were here right now so I could pull out every hair on their heads—and then I'd start on their short hairs."

She paused long enough to take a deep breath and relax her hand's grip, which must have removed all circulation from his. Taking another deep, calming breath, she reached up to stroke his cheek. "Marc, your past with those women has nothing to do with you being a Dom, authentic or otherwise. You were a natural Dominant without even being aware of it. Oh, I've watched you lately trying to catch yourself from going all Dominant on me twenty-four/seven—asking what my preference might be for something or including me in decisions involving both of us in a significant way. That's fine. We don't have or want a Total Power Exchange. And, while I appreciate you seeking my input, look at what you did tonight. You ordered wine and dinner for me knowing what I would enjoy and wanting to share a special dish from your homeland." She pointed to what was left of the veal dish. "And I know this is a favorite dish in Lombardy, because I've been paying careful attention to the cuisine of this…*that* region so I can learn to make those dishes for you."

Once she got started, there was no stopping her. "Look at how you took command of me on this date. The blindfold, the headphones, those were just props. *You* were the one exerting your authority over me, causing that excitement I feel only under your hand. The Dominant in you took charge of me from the time I stepped out of the shower today…yesterday, oh whatever day it was."

She glanced around, realizing she was speaking rather loudly, but no one seemed the least bit interested in her passionate conversation with Marc, because they all seemed to be having heated discussions of their own. God love expressive Italians.

She turned her attention to Marc once more. "No matter how either of us became interested in kink, all that matters is that we find what works for us. We set our own limits, our own preferences. I'm not comparing you to any other Doms—as if I could—and you shouldn't compare me to any other submissives."

Marc's lips curved into a tentative smile. "I assure you, no other sub comes even close to comparing to you." He lifted her hand to his lips and placed a kiss on her palm, all but melting her panties. "I thank you for bringing out the natural Dom in me, because I know what I feel with you is my first taste of dominance. Exerting authority over you excites me and makes me work harder at being a more competent Dom."

Angelina leaned forward and whispered, "You're making me wet, Sir." The look of longing on his face made her smile and relish the power she had over him, as well. She couldn't wait to get to wherever he planned for them to sleep tonight. "Just know that I place myself in your hands knowing and trusting you will keep me safe and see to my needs. Trust requires nurturing and maintenance, but you know you…"

Marc held up a hand and paused her words. "You showed me you have my back by standing up to Adam and seeing to my needs during and after the interrogation."

"How did you know—?"

"Adam told me during aftercare. As you know, I don't trust women easily—but you are in a class by yourself." He leaned closer, and she did the same. "Just don't expect me ever to bottom for you again. I'm the Dom in this relationship." He leaned back in his chair. "I plan to continue to grow into being the best Dom I can be for you as we come to know each other better."

"You are the only man I would ever consider to be my Dom."

Marc's moss-green eyes shone brightly in the candlelight. She couldn't tell if she'd convinced him yet, but as soon as they left here…

After they declined dessert—she couldn't eat another bite—the server set the check on the table. They sat back in their seats, both breathing a little more heavily. She hoped they were headed somewhere she could express how much this man meant to her.

Marc pulled out his wallet and placed his credit card on the tray. She glanced at the bill, hoping to glean some information about the name or location of the restaurant, but Marc slid the card over the header, blocking the information from view.

"Why so secretive? I thought you were all about revealing secrets today."

"Your Dom will let you know when you need to know. Anticipation is good for you."

She smiled. "I like the sound of that 'your Dom.'"

"Maybe you should get used to it." He smiled, more relaxed than he'd been most of the meal. After settling the bill, Marc pushed his chair back, picked up the headphones, and stood. "Come, let's walk off some of this dinner before we head to our ho…go home."

Angelina smiled at his near slip-up. "Sounds perfect."

He scooted her chair back, slipped her hand into his, and led her toward the entrance. Thank goodness he didn't pull out the sash again. She was anxious to get a first glimpse of wherever he had brought her.

When he opened the door, a chilly breeze whipped inside, and she folded her arms over her chest against the cold.

"Wait here."

Marc exited the restaurant, closing the door behind him. She looked around the foyer and remembered the promise to ask about having a peek inside the kitchen, but Marc must have been distracted by their conversation and forgotten.

The door opened again, and he came inside carrying her shawl. She turned around and let him wrap it around her. He enfolded her in his arms, pressed her against his hard body, and placed a kiss on her neck. Now she had chill bumps for a different reason.

"Thank you, Sir. This is just what I needed."

Marc gave her a mysterious smile. "Am I not supposed to anticipate my girl's needs? Now, let's walk."

He took her hand in his, and they left the restaurant. The brightness of the day surprised her until she remembered where she was. When Angelina stumbled on the uneven brick sidewalk, Marc grabbed her around the waist to keep her from falling face forward. He kept his arm there and pulled her closer, just where she wanted to be.

"Tell me where you are, *bella*."

Knowing he wasn't asking her to ground herself in the moment for a scene, she glanced at the mostly two-story stucco buildings painted in yellows and tans and trimmed in stone. She still wasn't certain if they were in Tuscany or Lombardy, until she spied a traffic sign ahead. *Milano, 82 Km.* Angelina halted.

"Lombardy?"

He grinned broadly. "*Sì.* Welcome to the *comune* of Brescia, *amore*, my homeland."

Marc had brought her to his hometown to show her where he'd grown up? Now this was significant. That he'd trust her enough to share the experience meant a lot to her.

"Tell me, when did you realize you were in Italy at least?"

"Well, that was a very long flight, but when you had me speaking to someone in Italian..."

Marc sighed. "I hated that he spoiled my surprise but figured that would tip you off."

"Why did you...I mean, I love that you did...but how did you...?" Would she ever be able to string together a lucid question?

"I needed to explore more of my past after the interrogation. I needed some answers. This time, I wanted you beside me. I regretted so many times you weren't with me in February, even though your voice often coached me to breathe and relax. But I'd much rather have you here in the flesh this time."

Angelina wrapped her arms around him and laid her head on his chest. "Thank you, Sir, for including me. I told you before I didn't want an Italian vacation, but only to be with you and help you deal with whatever you found."

"Well, this time, you'll get a bit of both. Our pilots have taken a few days off—Gunnar said something about a delivery he needed to make in Pakistan for some Afghan region near the border."

"Gunnar! I *knew* I recognized that voice!" Her jaw dropped in a delayed response. "You mean the border with Afghanistan?"

"I had the same reaction, but apparently he does regular drops for some humanitarian organization he keeps supplied. He hooked up with them while deployed with the Army a few years back."

Marc reached out and brushed a lock of hair off her forehead. "Anyway, we have almost four days before we fly home, and I have every intention of giving you the two-cent tour of my homeland."

His eyes grew shuttered. "I must warn you, though, I'm also here to uncover more of my past, perhaps even reveal more secrets."

She wrapped her arm around his neck and drew him closer to her face before planting a kiss on his whiskered cheek. "I'm here. We can face whatever it is together."

"Come. There's a place I want to explore with you." His *'with you'* won her over. They walked on, hand in hand, until he paused at a corner and glanced around. "This way," he decided, and they turned toward the left. She wondered what he was searching for.

"Wait!" She halted him. "I need to call Mama! She'll wonder where I've disappeared to if I don't show up for that long."

"No worries. I spoke with Rafe. He will inform her of your whereabouts."

Her eyes opened wider. "You and Rafe are talking again?" Her brothers had pitched a fit when she moved back in with Marc, blaming him for nearly breaking her heart and letting her know in no uncertain terms they would take care of him if he hurt her again. "How'd that come about?"

"I just called and asked to speak with him about a matter of great importance."

When he didn't elaborate but continued to walk down the residential street, leaving her to wonder what it might be. Marc probably just wanted to smooth the waters with her brothers before moving into her house next week. They'd be seeing a lot of him in the future so having them at least on speaking terms would ease some of the tension—and testosterone-induced posturing.

A block later, he made another turn. The farther they walked, the tighter he gripped her hand. His steps became more sure, and then he halted. She noticed his puzzled expression and then followed his gaze to a small house with a tiny porch.

"It's not as I remember it."

"What is this place?"

He took a deep breath. "This is where Gino and I took refuge many, many times. In my mind, it was such an enormous house."

Angelina remembered the slideshow at the anniversary party for his parents. This was the house Mama's friend lived in.

Before she could say anything, he walked inside the open gate and guided her up the stairs to the door. He knocked and waited.

Angelina whispered, "Are you sure we won't be bothering them?"

He shrugged. "I'm sure whoever lives here will understand. I need to see something."

"Surely nothing inside will be familiar after all these years."

"I just have this feeling there's something in this house that holds a key for me."

Dio, she hoped so. This seemed important to him. She didn't want to see him disappointed. Angelina gave his hand a comforting squeeze, which he returned. She forced herself to relax against him hoping he would take comfort from her.

The door opened to reveal a wizened old woman dressed in a black dress with a white shawl. The old woman ignored Angelina but scrutinized Marc more closely. "Marco?"

Marc seemed to take forever to respond, but he spoke in her language when he did.

"How did you know, Mrs. Milanesi?"

Angelina gasped, remembering the name from the interrogation scene as someone he'd expressed guilt over injuring by leaving his toys on the floor.

She stepped back and motioned them inside. "Come in out of the cold. We'll talk."

Chapter Thirty-Two

Marc remembered her instantly, whether it was the delicious aromas emanating from her kitchen or the sound of her voice. Her sweet smile transformed her into a much younger-looking woman, more like the face he remembered. She had always smiled, well almost always. He hadn't expected her to be alive, much less living in the same house.

With tears shimmering in her already rheumy eyes, Mrs. Milanesi reached up with both hands. Marc bent to kiss her on both cheeks. When she motioned again for them to enter, Marc hesitated, unable to take that first step. Angelina squeezed his arm and whispered, "I'm here, Marc. We can do this together."

He glanced down at the woman he'd grown to love more than life itself and breathed deeply. Patting the hand on his forearm, he smiled. *"Grazie."*

Going from bright sunlight into the darkened room, he blinked while waiting for the past to slowly come into focus. He introduced Mrs. Milanesi to Angelina and they kissed European style as Marc scanned the room for anything he might recognize.

Like so much of his past, what he remembered of Mrs. Milanesi came from what Gino had told him rather than actual memories, except for those bubbling up since the interrogation scene. Gino often referred to her as Mrs. M or their babysitter. She had been the subject of many a tale from Gino as he tried to paint a picture of a happy childhood for the brothers amidst all the drama and pain surrounding them during those early years. By the time they'd emigrated, though, Gino spoke of her rarely.

Angelina made small talk in her formal Italian while the older woman used her Brescian dialect, but they seemed to understand each other. Trying to regroup, Marc glanced around the room. Surprisingly, not a lot had changed. Yes, the furnishings had been modernized, but the religious pictures on the walls were familiar in some strange way. He and Gino hadn't spent a lot of time in the parlor, though.

Then his gaze lit on her tea table filled with photos of her husband and children at various ages over the years. Two photos dominated the surface— the ones of Marc and Gino in their military portraits. Puzzled, he turned to Mrs. Milanesi. "How…?" He couldn't speak past the frog in his throat and pointed to the photos.

"Sit. We talk."

Had Gino kept in touch with her before he was killed? No, he couldn't have sent Marc's portrait. Once they were seated, he and Angelina on the divan and Mrs. Milanesi in an armchair closer to Marc, the woman began.

"Natalia sent me a long letter with the photos."

So it had been *Mama*. He'd have to thank her, once again, for opening doors and paving the way for him to gain access to this place. He needed to make peace with Gino and this place held secrets they'd shared. Marc was certain of it.

"I hadn't heard from her in so long." She extended her hands, joints swollen with arthritis. "It is hard for me to hold a pen…" She shrugged and smiled wistfully. "Truthfully, it was painful for me to think of you boys being so far away." Her gaze strayed to Gino's photo. "So sorry to hear…"

Marc glanced down at his lap, and Angelina reached over to squeeze the tops of his clasped hands, giving him the strength to face her. "He was a fine U.S. Marine." He cleared his throat which had suddenly grown tight.

A tear meandered between the wrinkles on her cheek. An uncomfortable tightness filled his chest. His eyes burned, but he fought to regain control before he pulled away from Angelina to go to the woman's side. He wrapped her in his arms and comforted her but soon felt Angelina's arms around him, as well.

"*Scusa*. I thought I had cried all my tears after receiving Natalia's letter."

Marc and Angelina resumed their seats on the divan. "What did Mama say?"

An enigmatic smile crossed her lips. "She told me that you were just learning about…what happened back then. That you might show up here asking questions." Mama knew him so well. He hadn't told her about his intention to come here, and he thought he'd been discreet a few weeks ago when he'd asked about this house. Mama had recalled the street name instantly, probably from having rediscovered the address so recently.

Marc had wanted to see if his memories coincided with reality, though.

He'd had no trouble finding this house. The neighborhood's butcher shop had been next door to the restaurant where they'd just dined. Young Marc and Gino had helped the woman carry packages home so many times.

Needing some distance from talk of Gino for a moment, he asked about her husband.

"Mr. Milanesi passed seven years ago."

"I'm so sorry." Marc truly had no memory of the man but knew this woman had spent her life loving and caring for him and so many others, including Gino and Marco. Marc surmised she'd been so taken by the boys because she and her husband hadn't been blessed with any children of their own. She had taken in the boys and their first mother when they had nowhere else to go after Solari deserted them. She'd also provided refuge for Mama when pregnant with Marco.

But the photos surrounding the ones of Marc and Gino told otherwise about her life after the D'Alessios moved to America. "Tell me about your children."

The next quarter hour was spent with her picking up each photo and telling of her two daughters, a son-in-law, and her one granddaughter.

She cleared her throat. "Let me show you a room you will be more familiar with."

The house was a tiny bungalow, much like Angelina's. Was this why he felt so comfortable in Angelina's house, as if he'd come home at last?

Marc expected her to take them to the bedroom, the room he needed to see most, but she led them to her kitchen instead.

Walking into the room, the smells that had been faint at the front door now bombarded him with memories. Anise cookies cooling on an oven rack and garlic from a pot of rich stew bubbling on the stove.

Marc's chest tightened.

Angelina squeezed his hand and whispered, "Breathe."

He smiled down at her, knowing he had made the right decision bringing his angel here to help him confront the ghosts from the past, especially the wizened woman who wasn't a ghost at all.

The tables had turned on this relationship, with Angelina once again taking care of his needs. Before the interrogation, that thought would have upset him. Now, having her beside him as he dug into the past gave him a sense of comfort he hadn't found when confronting his sperm donor in Siena a couple of months ago.

"*Grazie, tesoro mio.*"

Her smile radiated warmth and caring. Squeezing her hand, he returned his focus once more to the room. The burnished-red tile floors were exactly the same as he remembered, but an enamel-topped table for six sat against the wall where the old wooden one once stood. He and Gino had played toy soldiers under the wooden one while Mrs. Milanesi prepared dinner. An overwhelming sense of Gino's presence assaulted him, as if a glance under the table would find his big brother kneeling as he prepared to attack Marc's fortress castle.

Unable to help himself, needing to face his fear, he hunkered down and peered underneath.

"*Gino! Marco! Where have you two boys gotten to? Hurry! Paolo expects us for dinner at the hotel at half past.*"

Aunt Emiliana's voice carried him back to the past.

Stilettos and silk stockings were all Marco saw from under the table. She always called their father Paolo. He didn't like to be called Papa. Gino motioned for Marco to remain quiet, not wanting Mama to take them away from Mrs. Milanesi's. They were happier here. She cooked better, too.

The kind woman assured Mama she wouldn't mind having them spend the night again.

Mama sighed. "Perhaps it's best. Paolo has not been in a very good mood lately." She thanked Mrs. Milanesi, and her heels clicked on the tile until she reached the parlor rug. The front door soon slammed. Gino and Marco smiled at each other.

Mrs. Milanesi bent down and made eye contact with first one brother then the other. She smiled as if they had a secret. Well, they did. "Go wash up. Dinner will be ready as soon as Mr. Milanesi gets home from the factory."

Not wanting to disappoint her—or to give her an excuse to send them away—they crawled out from under the table and ran down the hallway to do as she told them.

"And you, Marc?"

Instantly returned to the present, he looked up to find Angelina and Mrs. Milanesi staring at him as if waiting for him to do or say something.

"*Scusa?*"

"She asked if we'd like something to drink."

"Nothing for me, *grazie.*"

"Do you remember all the wars you two boys fought under there?"

"Yes, I do. I think we must have staged battles all over your house." Had their childhood activities led them both to volunteer to fight in the military?

"Why don't you young people make yourself comfortable in the parlor again? I'll be there as soon as I add potatoes to my stew."

He and Angelina left the kitchen, even though Marc was reluctant to put the memories of Gino behind. He hadn't found that nebulous something he expected to find here. As they returned to the parlor, he glanced down the hallway to the back bedrooms. Would she offer a tour of the rest of the house?

After they were seated again, images of Gino and a young Marco playing childhood games here bombarded him. Smiles. They were almost always laughing, even when their rivalry tried to get the best of them.

Flashbacks of the fight in the bedroom of his Aspen apartment where he'd found Gino and Melissa having sex obliterated the happier ones. He tried turning his head to escape the painful images only to be confronted by Gino's portrait. He couldn't keep away the memories of a naked Melissa straddling Gino's chest.

Wait a minute!

He'd never focused before on anything beyond their body positions, but clear as day, he saw that Gino wasn't naked. His dress pants weren't even unzipped. In fact, the expression on his brother's face was the opposite of what he'd expect from someone in the throes of having hot sex; he appeared annoyed by the woman on top of him.

What the fuck?

They weren't having sex at all. Gino looked at Marc almost with a sense of relief. An "about time you showed up" expression.

"Why, Gino?"

"I'm here, Marc." Angelina stroked his arm, yanking him away from the scene in his head.

Going to Gino's grave had brought the finality of his brother's death home to Marc, but being back in Mrs. Milanesi's home restored the vitality of Gino's memory. Marc had focused all these years on Gino being dead without thinking about his brother's love for life.

Angelina rubbed his back in comforting strokes. She'd been beside him through so much of this intense journey into the past—the interrogation, aftercare, talking with his family, visiting Gino's grave. The woman had been his rock. No doubt in his mind she would be there for him whenever he needed her. Why hadn't he been able to allow her to get close before now?

Trust. He needed to know he could rely on her to have his back. Adam had told him most of the details of what she'd done during the interrogation scene—and of how Angelina had shown up in mama-bear mode ready to take care of him. She would put his needs and his best interests ahead of her own, even when he didn't want her to do such a thing.

However, he'd made a decision in the aftermath of the interrogation not to continue to wallow in the pain and sorrow of his past. Perhaps that was one of the reasons he'd declined Adam's offer to gather a group of Gino's buddies to talk about Gino at Camp Pendleton the weekend of Damián's wedding.

Even so, Marc practically heard Gino telling him to "man up" and face the fear.

He drew her tightly to his side and held on, at first as if afraid she, too, would leave him. He recognized that was just the abandoned little boy inside him.

Angelina wanted to be with him.

Angelina wanted him.

"Gino was such a good big brother to you, Marco. Always so protective." Marc stood as Mrs. Milanesi came into the parlor again. "When Natalia took you to America, I didn't see you again—until today."

Marc nodded. The young Marco had felt the loss of this woman in his life almost more keenly than that of the woman he once thought was his mother.

"She didn't have it easy. Such a tragedy."

He wasn't sure which particular tragic woman Mrs. Milanesi referred to but assumed she meant Emiliana. Angelina snuggled against his shoulder, and he wrapped his arm around her, needing her to be closer. He waited for Mrs. Milanesi to continue without prompting but hoped to learn more about that incident, as well.

"Natalia and I were schoolgirls together." Ah, so she wanted to speak of Mama instead. Maybe he would learn more about her girlhood. "She was so full of life then. So much fun." A scowl came over her face. "Paolo was such bad news. Born with too much money. Spoiled. He thought he had the right to sleep with any woman he wanted." The man hadn't changed any over the years from what Marc observed in Siena. This also meshed with the story Mama had told. Marc wasn't sure he wanted to hear again what Solari had done to Mama, but there was no polite way to stop her.

"But she hated the way he treated Emiliana. She didn't want him to continue to hurt her sister, so Natalia tried to get Emiliana to leave him many times. Unfortunately, Emiliana was too enamored of what his money could buy. She was young, immature, and wanting to party—until she got sick."

Beyond those newly recovered memories of around the time she died, he didn't remember much about her, except she dressed for fancy parties and often wore stilettos. The sound of them grated on his nerves to this day, but he'd never understood why until now. Perhaps the reminder of another mama was too much for his mind to grasp.

"When he noticed Natalia beginning to get Emiliana to see the reality of her situation, I think Paolo decided to punish Natalia. He took what he wanted."

The blood rushed through his head and pounded in his ears. She must know about the rape.

"Natalia couldn't stop him, but such things weren't reported to the authorities back then for fear of bringing shame to the girl and her family. Men will be men, after all."

Marc closed his eyes as a wave of nausea ripped through him. Was she excusing rape or just explaining the society in which she lived? The woman's words replayed in his head an unknown number of times before he could focus again.

"Natalia was devastated afterward. I brought her here to heal."

Angelina's hand began stroking his back in sweeping motions. "Your mama's okay now. Breathe, Marc."

At her prodding, he did so but couldn't relieve the suffocating tightness in his chest while thinking of what Mama had been through. That she could even stand to look at Marc confounded him.

"You were born in this very house. Natalia's mama thought Emiliana would do better raising you than Natalia, an unmarried girl. Her mother put a lot of pressure on her. So we kept Natalia's condition a secret from most in town. Emiliana pretended toward the latter months to be expecting another child of her own. I think she knew who had fathered Natalia's baby but am not certain she ever realized under what circumstances. It left the sisters…estranged."

What a living hell for Mama. No wonder she shut down emotionally.

"Marc." He turned toward Angelina's voice as if she called from far away. "You and Mama D'Alessio hold no guilt or shame in how you were conceived. Paolo Solari is the only guilty party."

Mama hadn't expressed any regret or animosity toward Marc. Perhaps he needed to accept himself as the man he'd grown to be and not let the past consume him. The muscles in Marc's back constricted, but her steady, reassuring hand relaxed him again.

Angelina interrupted his thoughts again. "Mrs. Milanesi, what can you tell us about Emiliana's death?"

Marc had intended to ask the question himself but couldn't concentrate. The older woman wrung her hands a moment, avoiding eye contact. "She had a fast-moving cancer. From diagnosis until her passing...mere months. Paolo couldn't be bothered playing nursemaid to a sick wife—or caring for his boys." She made a face as if she'd just bitten off something bitter. "She had no place to go, so I invited her and you boys to live here with me and my husband." Her voice cracked, and she continued in a whisper. "I tried to bring some stability to your lives." She looked at Marc. "You took it so very hard."

Marc didn't want to feel that pain again but surprised himself by asking, "May I see the room where she died?"

"If you wish. It is where my granddaughter stays when she visits now, so I am afraid it looks nothing like you will remember."

"That's fine, Mrs. Milanesi. I just wish to see the room."

"Are you sure about this, Marc?"

He stared at Angelina a long while before smiling with determination. "I'm sure. This is something I need to do. I think that room might hold the key to remembering something important."

Marc rose and helped Mrs. Milanesi to stand. She held on to his arm so tightly he couldn't let go if he wanted to, and he half-guided her toward the hallway. He knew where they were headed. Angelina fell into step behind them. He wanted her to stay close to him, but the older woman seemed to lean more heavily on his arm the closer they got to the door at the end of the hall. Or was he gripping her arm so tightly that he was pulling her down the hall?

Maybe a bit of both.

Dread descended over Marc as they walked down the hallway. The ghosts of Gino and Emiliana clawed at him as he drew closer to the bedroom at the end of the hall. The door was closed, and the light receded the further they progressed.

Stop crying.

Gino's admonishment blasted into his consciousness and nearly brought him to a halt. Until the aftercare following the interrogation, Marc would never have cried. Somehow that barrier was gone now.

They won't keep you if you're a baby.

Holy shit. He'd spent a lifetime trying to show his strength to those around him without knowing why that had been a personal imperative for him. He had fought his entire life to be independent, to not need anyone else. Had followed his own path, most of the time alone. Had bowed to no man or woman, not since he'd joined the Navy, anyway. Well, there was Adam, but that was different; Adam was Marc's superior.

Don't let them see your weaknesses.

Marc had given up his power to no one. Perhaps that's why surrendering his heart to Angelina had been so difficult. He'd followed Gino's advice since boyhood. His family had accepted him. They had never turned away from him, even when he tried to distance himself from them.

But the reason they'd given him a home—and their love—had nothing to do with the fact that he had put up a strong front. They actually loved him for who he was. Did Gino ever figure that out for himself? God, Marc hoped so.

Mrs. Milanesi paused at the door. Keys rattled as she extracted a key chain from her pocket. "My granddaughter is a very private young lady. She asks that I keep her room locked when she isn't here, except to clean. But I think she'll understand when I explain to her why I had to open the door this time."

Marc had no interest in disturbing the young girl's things and hoped she would forgive her nonna this transgression. The door creaked open, and his gaze went first to the twin bed. In his mind's eye, the pink-and-yellow coverlet flashed alternately in strobe-light fashion with a hunter green one from the larger bed that had been here in Marc's childhood. His mind transformed the present into the past as he stepped inside the room, which also appeared to be so much smaller than the one in his mind's eye.

Size wasn't the only difference. Marc remembered something more pungent than the flowery scent that assailed him now. He recalled the smell of lemons—and death. Sweat broke out on his forehead. Today, the room was filled with stuffed animals, posters of actor Raoul Bova and of Zero Assoluto, the boy band his sister Carmella loved.

Marc's gaze ricocheted off the bed and settled on the closet door, very much the same as the one he remembered; its cold metal doorknobs were now a burnished brass after years of use. The rope-rosette pattern had fascinated him as a boy. He'd stared at it for hours, almost as if in a trance.

"You don't have to go in there, Marc."

He tore his gaze away from the knobs to stare down at Angelina, taking a moment to shift his focus back to the present. The look of concern on her face melted his heart even more. He'd made the right decision to include her in this exploration into his past.

"I have to, *amore*. If I don't, I'll always wonder."

She furrowed her brows but nodded and squeezed his hand. Steeling himself once more, he turned back toward the closet. This had been one of their favorite places. Until...

He saw things so clearly now that hadn't even broken loose during the interrogation.

He remembered one of the dreams that had haunted him in recent months—fighting against Gino, both of them in the military. Clearly, he'd been remembering this time when they'd pretended to fight battles against each other, vying for supremacy. Gino called it playing Romulus and Remus, but Marc didn't like the comparison. Romulus had killed his brother, Remus.

He paused before asking, "Do you mind if I look inside?"

"Of course not, Marco. I doubt if you will see anything you remember, though. Francesca loves clothes—and shoes." The woman looked away sheepishly. "I'm afraid I spoil her a bit, but I had my children late in life and didn't expect to live to experience the joy of being a nonna."

"You were another mother to Gino and me." Marc blinked. He didn't know what compelled him to say that, but once the words came out, he realized how true they were. He'd had no shortage of mother figures as a boy. *"Grazie."*

Tears brimmed in her eyes. He absently stroked her arm in a comforting gesture before turning back to the closet door. He needed to complete this mission. Gaining access to this house and that closet was one of the main reasons he'd been drawn back to Italy so soon. The memories flitting forth in his consciousness since the interrogation proved to him this was very much where many of his issues began.

He'd found the house so quickly, as if his mind knew exactly where to go. Or perhaps Gino had led the way.

So why were his feet firmly glued to the ground and his eyes staring blankly at the closed closet door? His mind flashed to a time when Gino had taken refuge here. Apparently Marc wasn't the only one who had hidden in this closet. This new scene from the past crashed in on his mind's eye with dizzying speed.

Marco called out to Gino but heard no response. Gino had to be hiding in the closet. Why didn't he answer? The voices in the kitchen became heated. Someone argued. Why would they be yelling? Zietta Natalia screamed, "My sister is dead!"

No, Mamma was sleeping. Not dead.

Wait. This was later. He was older.

Marco walked over to the closet, always one of his and Gino's favorite hiding places, after their wolf's lair. When he reached out to open the door, he looked down and noticed he wore his Sunday suit.

"You in there, Gino?" The inside of the closet was dark. Maybe Gino hadn't come in here after all.

Marco heard a sniffle and a rustling in the corner. Gino was in here! Marco got down on his hands and knees, hoping Zietta Natalia wouldn't be upset if he got his pants dirty. He crawled inside anyway. Gino needed him.

"Go away, Marco. I don't want to see anyone today."

A gentle but firm hand on his back pulled him back into the moment. "I'm here, Marc. You won't have to face this alone."

Marc realized he was on hands and knees just outside the closet. He reached up and gripped Angelina's hand as if she was all that kept him from falling into a deep, dark abyss. When she smiled, he relaxed his hold—every so slightly.

"Come inside with me, *amore?*"

She gave him a tremulous smile and nodded. Why hadn't he realized before that having this brave woman at his side only made him stronger? She slipped off her shoes and went onto all fours beside him. Turning back around, he crawled closer to the door. When he reached it, he froze again. Somehow he knew touching that doorknob would be his undoing.

"Would you like for me to open it?"

Relief flooded him. *"Sì. Grazie."*

He'd reverted to the language of his boyhood, feeling he was back inside the body of that three-year-old who had hidden in this closet to block out the scary world outside. This place didn't feel like a refuge to him anymore. Could he put himself back in there? Did he want to?

Angelina reached out and turned the knob. Slowly, she pulled the door toward them. He had to side crawl in order for the door to swing wide enough. It came to rest against the wall.

"Why don't I go in first, Marc?"

He nodded, his vision bombarded by the sight of dozens of brightly-colored clothes, but they soon blurred and faded away.

Gino sat huddled in the corner. Crying. Gino never cried. Both were dressed in black suits, white shirts, and neckties. Marco stared at the scuffs on Gino's shoes.

Gino carried something furry in his hand. "Here. You need this."

Marco took the thing and saw it was a wolf's mask. The gray fur around the eyes was soft when he petted it. He looked up at Gino. "What's this for? It's not All Saint's Eve."

"No, of course not. Mrs. Milanesi gave it to me because we play so much in our wolf's lair. You need to use it to fool them. It won't help me."

"Fool who?"

Gino sighed. "Our new mama just got married." Marco wasn't sure what a wolf's mask had to do with that—and why did Gino still call her their new mama? This mama, who used to be Zietta Natalia, had been taking care of them since their real mama went away. Marco didn't know how long ago that was. It was harder and harder to remember their first mama anymore. He had only been three when she died. Marco understood now that death meant she would never come back. But Zia Natalia really was the only mama Marco remembered. Gino kept the memory of their first mother alive by talking about her.

"We need to be on our best behavior now, even more than when it was just Zia Natalia and us. We don't know if this man wants other people's kids or not."

"What will wearing the wolf mask do?"

"I was studying in school about Romulus and Remus. They were abandoned by their real mama and then a she-wolf found them and took care of them."

"Mama isn't a wolf."

Gino rolled his eyes. "No, but it's like she's the she-wolf in the story. She took care of us both. But she didn't have a papa wolf around to make decisions for her. We have to pretend to be like Papa D'Alessio wants us to be or he'll talk Mama into sending us away."

Gino was worried about being rejected—first by Mama and now their new papa.

All of the sudden he had Marco worried, too. "But I like our new papa. He brings me candy."

"Well, he's just trying to get Mama to like him. I don't trust him. You have to be careful who you trust, Marco. Not everyone will take care of you." Then Gino turned around and began carving something into the wall.

"G for Gino." Gino scratched out the letter with a paring knife from the kitchen. *"M for Marco."*

Marco didn't know why Gino wanted to mess up Mrs. Milanesi's wall. He hoped they wouldn't get in trouble for it.

Then Gino carved another letter underneath the G. This time, an R. He didn't explain what it meant. After carving "&R," too, he turned to Marco.

"R&R is for Romulus and Remus."

Marco nodded, even though he had no clue what it meant. Gino was smarter than he was, too. He needed to listen to his big brother.

"We played Romulus and Remus, the twins who fought over whose hill would be where the city would be built, but..." Gino grew silent and stared at him intensely for a moment. *"Don't worry, Marco. I will always look out for you."*

Gino always kept him safe.

A painful keening sound filled his ears.

"Let it out, Marc."

Jarred back to the present, Marc found himself huddled in the corner of a dark space. Curled against him, her arms around his waist, sat Angelina. She hadn't let him come in here alone to face his ghosts.

To face Gino.

Guilt at how he'd treated his brother in his last months nearly ripped him a new one. Marc's chest ached to the point of exploding.

"Dio, I miss him so much." The pain hurt more today than it had when he'd heard the news of Gino's death. Tears streamed down his face.

"That's it. Let out all that pain you've buried for so long."

He'd spent a decade telling himself Gino was a shithead who had betrayed him. Somehow that made the pain of losing him in Afghanistan easier to bear. Since Angelina had come into his life and he'd lowered some of his barriers, all these memories he'd kept under lock and key in the recesses of his mind kept blasting away at him. He hadn't remembered his brother at all the way he truly had been—only as some caricature he'd created to keep from owning up to how badly he must have hurt Gino by his rejection.

There wasn't a damned thing he could do to unfuck that now, either. A million visits to his brother's grave would never erase those last months.

"He died thinking I'd abandoned him. *Merda,* I *had* abandoned him."

"I think he understood, Marc. He loved you so much."

She didn't know what he'd remembered, and he wasn't ready to put it into words or even sure he ever would be able to do so. "Where's Mrs.

Milanesi?"

"She went to make us some tea."

"The woman must think I'm a nutcase." He sat huddled nearly in the fetal position in her granddaughter's closet. Maybe he *had* finally lost it. The breakdown in the interrogation scene had only opened a crack into his broken psyche.

"I think she knew you'd need some time alone with your memories. Do you want to talk about them?"

Marc shook his head, an automatic reflex born of decades of being in survival mode and closed off emotionally. He'd worn Gino's damned mask his entire life.

Merda, he didn't want to wear it any longer. He needed to share what he'd just remembered with someone he trusted. Angelina might even be able to help him sort out what to do now.

"He promised he would never leave me."

"Gino?"

Marc nodded.

"I know he wouldn't have left you if he could have helped it, Marc."

A ragged sound of anguish filled the tight space, and Angelina hugged him more tightly.

"But I'm the one who deserted him. I lost my best friend that September day because of Melissa. I drove him to his death."

She pulled away and framed his cheeks with her hands, turning him to face her. "Marc, listen to me. Gino chose to defend and protect his country, a mission he had prepared for by protecting and defending his little brother his whole life. He loved you so much, but he loved his country, too. His dying wasn't your fault."

Adam had assured Marc once that Gino loved being a Marine. Marc had tarnished his brother's memory all because he'd misinterpreted Gino's motives with Melissa. Why had it taken Marc so long to remember and accept the truth about Gino?

"He didn't screw Melissa."

"What?"

"In the parlor a few minutes ago, I remembered something. Gino had his clothes on. She was the only one naked. When I walked in on them, he gave me a look like 'it's about time.' All I saw was Melissa—naked and on top of him. In my rage, I blotted out all the details."

How many other things over the years had he misinterpreted through some faulty lens skewed by a history of abandonment and betrayal?

"Marc, you know he understood your anger. Big brothers expect their younger siblings to screw up. You thought your big brother, your best friend, was sleeping with that b—with your girlfriend." Her body tensed, and he rubbed her arm reassuringly. He hated reminding her of his relationship with Melissa.

"I think Gino probably even welcomed your extreme anger, so you wouldn't go back to her when you figured out he'd tricked you."

He shuddered to think what life might have been like for him if he'd married Melissa. Gino most definitely had helped him dodge the bullet with Melissa's name on it. No doubt in his mind Gino had proposed to Melissa just to make sure Marc didn't get into trouble until Gino returned from his deployment. Removing the competition made it safe for Marc.

Grazie, *Gino.*

He'd probably told her about the adoption hoping she'd see neither brother was going to have easy pickings to a fortune, although Melissa must have seen how Mama and Papa treated all of their children equally, blood or not.

Angelina stroked his cheek as she continued. "I know he expected to come home from Afghanistan and for you two to work this out, but…"

He thought about that a long while. "Do you really think so?"

"I have four overprotective big brothers. I *know* so, without a doubt." She leaned her head on his upper arm. A comfortable silence ensued, and they simply held onto each other. "I wish I could have met him to thank him for being such a good brother to you. And we mustn't forget that, if it wasn't for him, you could be married to Melissa now. Where would that leave me— and you?" She grinned up at him.

God, he loved this woman. "Perish the thought. I'm sure we'd have divorced by now, and she'd be living off whatever divorce settlement she would have gotten out of me and my family."

Angelina smiled. "Marc, if Gino was even one-tenth the man you are, he must have been very special indeed."

"No, he was more like ten times the man I'll ever be. I wish you could have known him, too, *amore.* I know he'd have approved of you. There's never been anyone more perfect for me." Her chin shook with emotion as tears spilled down her cheeks, glistening in the light from the bedroom.

After the soul-searching he'd done over the past few months, not to mention today's flashbacks, there was no longer any doubt in his mind that Gino had only taken Melissa away from him to protect his naïve, horny little brother from the Italian gold-digger. Marc hadn't been experienced enough with women back then to see Melissa's selfish motives—or to think beyond his cock. But his big brother sure had.

"I must have seemed like such a fucking moron to him."

Angelina patted his chest. "I'm sure Rafe has thought the same thing about each of his younger siblings at one time or another, including me. That comes naturally to big brothers. You should have heard the earful I got from Rafe about moving back in with you."

Oh, he'd heard it, all right. Marc hoped the talk he'd had with Rafe the day before flying to Italy convinced her brother Marc intended to do the right thing by Angelina and propose. Despite carrying the ring since Christmas, Marc only recently realized he wanted her brother's blessing before he proposed, even if the man was slightly younger than Marc. He remained the father figure in Angelina's life.

"Gino loved you so much, Marc."

Marc recalled the flashback. "Remember the mask I used to wear at the club?" Angelina stopped breathing a moment. She'd never liked the thing. "I just remembered why I wore it—Gino gave me one like it as a kid."

Her hand stilled. "What did you say?"

Marc recounted the story about why Gino had given him the mask back on the day Mama and Papa married.

"Oh, Marc! I'm so sorry."

"Nothing for you to be sorry about." She grew so still he wasn't sure she still breathed. "It's okay. Breathe, *cara*." He held her closer, uncertain if he wanted to comfort her or needed comforting himself. "In truth, I'm glad the mask disappeared. After you came along, I wanted to stop trying to hide who I am."

After long moment without a response from her, he pulled away and tilted Angelina's face up to his. "What's wrong?"

She nibbled on her lower lip, making him hard. So not appropriate in Mrs. Milanesi's closet.

"Marc, I did it."

"Did what?" Being so close to her made it difficult to focus.

She swallowed hard. "I took your mask. I destroyed it."

He didn't understand what she was saying. "Why would you do that?"

She averted her gaze, but he took her chin and forced her to look at him. "Why, *cara?*"

Seconds ticked away before she answered. He leaned closer to hear her whispered response better. "You hid behind that mask, Marc."

"I only wore it at the club."

"I'm not talking about the wolf's mask. I mean in your everyday life. You always kept some vital part of yourself hidden away—from me, from the guys, from your family. I was so frustrated that, when Karla and Cassie invited me to their cleansing ceremony on Adam's deck—"

"Their what?"

Despite the darkness, he knew she scowled at him from her tone of voice. "Please, let me finish. This is hard enough." She took a deep breath. "*Mio Dio*, I can't believe I destroyed something that reminded you of Gino."

Marc fought a grin. After all, the mask wasn't actually a gift from his brother, just symbolic. Marc didn't even know what had happened to the mask Gino had shown him. But he wasn't ready to let her off the hook yet for destroying something of his without permission. "Go on. The ceremony…"

"Well, each of us brought something that symbolized what was causing us anxiety in our lives, and as part of the ritual, we were supposed to tell why we chose that object, and then destroy or discard it."

"And you did?"

She nodded. "I'm sorry, Marc."

The tears streaming down her face caused an ache in his heart. He reached up and brushed them away with his free hand.

"Stop crying."

She hiccupped.

Dio, he loved this woman. "Stop. Crying. Now."

When he thought she'd regained enough composure to hear him, he continued. "I don't want you ever to regret caring so much about me that you would remove something from my life that was bad for me. *Merda*, you saw something in that mask my friends ignored or let me get away with—and you did something about it. Hiding behind a mask wasn't healthy. I convinced everyone else—even myself—I wore it so as not to be recognized by Mama's circle of friends, but in truth, I only used it to hide from myself. Subconsciously, I tried to do as Gino instructed me all those years ago. I wore the mask to fit in where I didn't think I belonged."

"What do you mean? You're one of the club's owners. You couldn't belong more if you tried."

"Yeah, but I never saw myself as an authentic Dom. I primarily went into the venture with them, because I had nowhere I wanted to call home after my Navy discharge. But I had too much shit in my closet to ever be able to fully embrace the lifestyle and enter into an honest, open relationship."

And no wonder Pamela sent him running when she announced she wanted a twenty-four/seven Master. At least when he limited himself to topping at the club, he only had to role-play for a short time. He frequently needed to escape from having to be "on" while playing with submissives.

"You bring those characteristics out in me naturally. I'm not playing a part with you. With you, my heart is in it for the first time."

She stroked his sleeve. "I still regret violating your trust by taking something of yours and destroying it without permission."

Funny. While he probably should see this as a violation of trust, her destroying the mask only served to make him trust her more. "Angelina, you had my six. You looked out for me. Adam told me about how you took charge of the interrogation scene at one point, too."

"I just wanted to help you. You looked awful and so alone in the dungeon."

During that scene, she'd taken on the personas of his two mamas so well he didn't know when he was talking with her and when he'd been lost in a hallucination. He didn't care. His perceptions of the truth needed some serious overhauling.

Angelina had seen him at his worst, his most vulnerable. That she sat here beside him now told him she was the woman he wanted by his side the rest of his life.

He'd finally arrived at where he could make her that same promise. One thing he'd learned from Gino was not to take one single moment of his life for granted. Life made no promises. Gave no guarantees.

Pulling away from her, he looked into her eyes. "It's time for us to go home."

She grinned. "I thought you said the pilots wouldn't be back for days."

"*Merda.* I've gotten sidetracked. I guess I'm going to have to show you my homeland first. I'm just anxious to go home—with you." Well, to their temporary home in Aspen Corners until they figured out where they wanted to live. He'd changed his mind so many times since New Year's about where to ask her to be his wife.

"Just promise me there is a hotel bed in this deal somewhere."

"But of course—in a villa overlooking a glacier lake." On the flight over, he'd decided the balcony of their hotel suite overlooking the lake and the beautiful Alps would be the perfect place to propose.

"Wow. You know how to show a girl a good time." She grinned.

He bent to kiss her, losing himself in the sensation before remembering he was making out in Mrs. Milanesi's granddaughter's closet. He pulled away from Angelina.

"After you." He watched her crawl out and got on all fours to follow her when something caught his eye. He pushed the clothing aside to illuminate the spot better. Carved into the wall of the back of the closet was *G&M* above the letters *R&R*. The R&R had a big X over the letters.

Marc's mind's eye flashed back to when he watched Gino carve that big X over the letters R&R.

Gino turned to Marc and must have seen he was once again clueless.

"Gino and Marco are not *Romulus and Remus." Gino waited for him to say something, but Marco didn't know what he wanted him to say.*

Gino sighed. "In class today, I learned that Romulus killed his brother Remus. We are not Romulus and Remus. Neither of us would ever do anything to hurt the other. We have a pact to watch over each other—forever."

"Marc, are you coming out?"

Marc whispered. "I'm sorry, Gino. I didn't uphold my end of the deal."

*   *   *

"Are you closer to finding any answers, Marco?"

Marc set his teacup down and looked across the table at Mrs. Milanesi. Angelina sat beside him in the kitchen where he'd spent so many happy times.

"Yes, I did. I never thought I'd ever open all the doors to my past, and maybe there are still others closed off to me, but I came to Italy in search of my brother. And I found him in your closet." He grinned, hearing how ridiculous that sounded.

"My granddaughter used to play in that closet, too, before she filled it with shoes." Mrs. Milanesi took a sip of her tea before her eyes opened wide. "Perhaps you can provide us with an answer, too."

"Anything I can do, I will. You've been so hospitable to us, arriving unannounced."

"Pah. Natalia announced you; she just didn't give me an exact date and time for your arrival." The woman grinned. "I've missed her so. Your quest has rekindled our friendship. She indicated she might be able to visit again this summer while on a cruise. I hope she does."

"I'm certain she will." Marc waited for her to ask her question, but she seemed lost in memories of the past now. "You said something about wanting an answer to something."

"Oh, yes! Inside the closet, there were some initials carved. Of course, I know G and M is for Gino and Marco, but for decades I've tried to understand who R&R could be. You were too young to have girlfriends."

Marc smiled. "Would you believe Romulus and Remus?" She tilted her head in confusion. "Gino was applying what he learned in school to fit with our ever-changing situation. He drew parallels to Romulus and Remus with how we had been abandoned by our parents and taken in by the she-wolf."

Her hand began to rattle the teacup in its saucer, and she let it go as if burned, moving her hand to her mouth.

Angelina reached out to her. "Are you all right, Mrs. Milanesi? Can I get you something?"

She shook her head and waved Angelina away. After a moment, she spoke. "Gino was fascinated with wolves. Both of you were. Of course, there probably haven't been any wolves in Brescia for decades, but you two played in an old lair near here. Dark, smelly place, but I guess somehow you found comfort there because of that story maybe." She shrugged. "Not important. But... I'll be right back." She left the room.

Marc looked at Angelina who seemed just as puzzled as he. Moments later, she came back carrying something wrapped in faded tissue paper rumpled with age, or perhaps from being wrapped and unwrapped many times.

She peeled back the layers, and Marc caught a glimpse of fur. His heart pounded double time. Slowly, she removed the mask from the paper, transporting Marc back to that scene in the closet. But before he could be lost once more in the past, Mrs. Milanesi spoke. "Before you left for America, Gino gave this back to me."

Marc couldn't understand why his brother had returned the gift to the woman who had given it to him.

"He told me he didn't need to wear the mask anymore. I didn't know what he meant at first; then he told me your new mama and papa loved and accepted you both just the way you were."

The burning in his chest made it difficult to speak.

She continued. "Gino told me Italy would always be his first home but that the United States of America would be his new forever one, and that one day he would serve in the Marine Corps just like Natalia's papa. I suppose she'd begun to tell him about his grandfather before your family moved to live near him."

Angelina's hand stroked his back, keeping him grounded. "Breathe, Marc."

He drew a ragged breath.

Apparently there was more. "Gino said he would fit in as an American just as he'd fit in with his new parents, but that he would always have one foot in each place."

Gino had been fourteen when they emigrated, but rather than feel he had to choose one homeland over the other, he'd found a way to embrace them both. No doubt if he'd stayed here, he'd have served the Italian military proudly, but he'd heard the tales of Gramps' bravery and eventually gave all to his adopted country and the Marine Corps. Had this vow at a young age helped him make the decision so quickly after 9/11 to answer the call?

Truly, Gino's love for his new homeland began long before he stepped foot upon American soil. Marc hadn't been the catalyst that had sent Gino off to Afghanistan and his death.

Mrs. Milanesi pushed the mask across the table toward him. "Would you like to have this as a keepsake of your brother?"

Marc stared at the mask, remembering the day his brother had tried to give it to him, but Marc hadn't understood the need for it then. Somehow, he'd started wearing a symbolic one later, convincing himself all this time it had been Mama who insisted he hide behind a mask at the club. Now he was no longer certain Mama had asked him to at all. She'd probably only asked him to be discreet and some memory bubbled up from the recesses of his mind reminding him of another time he'd had to pretend to be something other than himself.

He smiled at her but didn't touch the mask. "No, I'd rather you keep it. It belongs here with you."

Marc had no intention of donning a mask ever again.

He turned to Angelina and saw tears streaming down her face, but the smile she wore conveyed her love, support, and acceptance.

"Gino would be so proud of the man you've become."

He smiled.

Suddenly he knew where he would ask her to marry him—well, more or less.

*   *   *

Angelina stared out the window of the jet soon after takeoff from Milan. She brushed away a tear. The last four days had been more wonderful than anything she might have imagined. A deep sense of loss overwhelmed her as they left Lombardy behind. She turned to Marc to see if he was equally melancholy to leave his homeland again.

He fidgeted with something in his pocket, but seemed more nervous than sad. She brushed his thigh. "Thank you for showing me Lombardy through your eyes."

"It's so different from what I remember. Hard to call it home anymore."

"You haven't lived here since you were eleven. Colorado has been your home much longer."

"I know, but I've never quite accepted that as home either. Unlike Gino, I don't feel as if I have either foot on the ground." He grinned and shrugged.

"You'd be lucky after all you've been through lately if you didn't feel the ground moving under both feet. You've been shaken to your very roots. But you do have a solid foundation and you'll keep working on all the things we've been talking about the past few days."

Marc had promised they'd come back to visit someday, and she looked forward to that day but also wanted to get home and start building a future with Marc. "Thank you for letting me be part of your journey to make peace with Gino."

His eyes grew shuttered. "I wish we could have found the old lair. The city probably cleaned it up for sanitation reasons long ago."

"You'll always have the memories of it. And of Gino." She turned away. Leaving the place where Gino had come to life for her caused an ache in her heart. "He seems so much more real to me after you showed me the streets where you two played *bocce*, the church where Mama and Papa D'Alessio married, the school you attended. Watching those beautiful children in the schoolyard, I almost pictured you both playing among them."

"I'd lost all those memories for so long. My brother came back to life for me here, too."

She squeezed his hand. "I know a lot more walls have crumbled during this trip."

Best of all, he'd found more closure from events in his past. Sitting in that closet at Mrs. Milanesi's with him, hearing the anguish in his voice as he talked with and about Gino, and seeing the tears pouring down his cheeks had broken her heart. He'd kept so much pent up inside, and no doubt he'd be assailed by many more memories in the days and weeks to come as more pieces of his past bubbled up from his subconscious. But now he had a better context for understanding them. And he also had a number of people who could answer questions as they arose—Mama, Papa, and even Mrs. Milanesi, who was going to accept his phone calls to come even though she thought international rates were much too expensive.

Marc and Angelina had gone through so much during this short visit, forging this new bond in steel.

Marc reached out and squeezed her hand. "Okay, *amore?*"

She nodded but didn't let him see her tears. He'd think she was unhappy, but surely he knew by now she cried to express happiness, frustration, sadness, any emotion she felt in her heart. She was Italian, after all.

Angelina cleared her throat. "Thank you for bringing me with you, Marc." The mountains spread out below stretched all the way to the horizon, their white peaks piercing the sky.

Marc unbuckled his seatbelt seconds after the seatbelt sign turned off. He reached down to release her belt, too, and took her hand to help her up. He brushed the tears off of her cheek.

"Why the tears, *amore?*"

She shrugged and grinned sheepishly. "I assure you they're happy tears."

"As they should be. I'm sorry I caused you so many unhappy tears this year, though. I hope you will find it in your heart to forgive me."

She wrapped her arms around him and pulled him close. "After what you went through in that interrogation scene all so we could have a future, I will forgive anything. You showed me how much I meant to you by agreeing to go through that torture—literally." She shuddered. "I thought I might not get back the Marc I loved after they broke you, but instead I got all of the best parts back and many new aspects of you I never dreamed were tucked away inside. You definitely were worth the wait—and the work." She stroked his cheek.

He held her close, caressing her back. After a time, they put some space between themselves and gazed at each other. A light shone in his green eyes that had been dimmed for so long. Many ghosts from the past had been put to rest since the scene at the club, including many on this trip.

"Come. Let's stretch out by the fire." He took her hand and led her to a fake fur rug on the floor before he lit the gas fireplace.

"I can't believe you can light a fire on a plane—well, jet."

He reached for the skirt of her dress and began pulling it up.

Angelina glanced toward the cockpit door. "Are you certain Gunnar and Patrick won't come back here? I'm even more nervous now that I know who's flying the plane. What if they need to use the bathroom?"

"They have their own lavatory up front, but I assure you they know they are not welcome back here for the next ten or eleven hours."

"Gunnar's so…well, intimidating."

Marc grinned. "Sadists generally are."

"He's a sadist?"

"Taught Damián and Grant all they know."

"Grant, too?"

"I can assure you, Grant fits the description of sadist quite well."

"Do you remember much about her part in the scene?"

"Enough to know I wouldn't want to be her submissive."

"You don't want to be anyone's submissive."

"Very true." He stroked her arms, causing chill bumps to rise in the path of his fingers. "However, even if Gunnar or Patrick ventured back here, you have nothing to be ashamed of with your beautiful body."

The familiar dropping of her stomach made her voice sound raspy, too, as her train of thought derailed. "I remember Patrick from Adam's wedding. Such a gentleman. I love how he takes care of his mother."

"Much more a gentleman than I, because I intend to have my wicked way with your body nonstop over the next few hours."

Her clit throbbed at the promise. "You guys have formed an amazing family, you know."

Marc nodded. "I should have realized long ago I'd already been adopted—by Adam and the Masters at Arms Club family. Adam's quite the collector of lost souls. We share so much more than ownership of a kink club." He looked away a moment and sighed. "Luke's a big part of my family, too."

"I can't wait to get back and call to check up on him. I haven't gotten an update since we left for California. So much has happened so quickly."

"We'll see him soon, *cara*." She nodded. "My family keeps growing. I've been a very lucky man. Having you beside me now makes me the luckiest one around."

Still uncertain about how private they would be, she continued to hold down her dress to keep him from removing it. "Why don't we let the cabin warm up a little bit first?"

"Ah, the lady wants to be warmed up? That can be arranged."

Her breath caught in her throat. She loved having her playful Marc back. When he glanced down at her chest, her nipples peaked, and she lifted her arms to let him remove one more barrier separating them.

Angelina reached up to undo the buttons of Marc's white shirt. He squeezed her bare nipples, and she hissed. Despite the romance of being in Italy, with all the new emotions churned up every day, most nights they'd been content to hold each other and talk about his and Gino's childhood and later years.

Not that Marc had neglected giving her an amazing orgasm with his tongue last night. To relax her, he'd said. She giggled at the memory.

"I am trying to seduce my beautiful, sexy woman and am finding her giggles quite distracting. I haven't even started touching your ticklish spots. What's so funny?"

"I assure you, that giggle was because of a special memory you gave me of our time in Brescia."

Time to return the favor. She slid the shirt down his arms, and his fingers and thumb broke contact with her nipples for a moment. Together, they shucked his shoes, socks, pants, and boxer briefs.

After Marc settled onto the rug, she joined him, resting her cheek on his chest. Her hand roamed down across his abs to the curls below. His erect penis bobbed against her hand, and she wrapped her fingers around it.

Marc moaned. "Feels so good."

Once upon a time, he'd have had her on her back pleasuring her by this point. She smiled. He'd become much more responsive to her meeting his needs on this trip. Letting go of his penis, she knelt and placed a kiss on his lips before trailing kisses to his pecs, flicking her tongue over his nips.

She bit one playfully, earning her a slap on the butt, and smiled as she licked her way down his abs to his penis. His hand now stroked her butt cheek, as if to rub out the sting. Knowing how much he enjoyed the view when she went down on him, she straddled him as she took him deep inside her mouth.

She groaned, wanting more but also wanting to meet his needs. His hips bucked up, and his cock bumped against the back of her throat. Relaxing her muscles, she eased him deep into her throat and breathed through her nose the way he'd taught her to avoid the panic of a gag reflex. His fingers opened her lower lips, and his tongue flicked against her clit hood. She wasn't going to last long, unless he forced her to wait.

Please don't torture me, Sir.

They weren't in high protocol so she wouldn't have to ask to come, as if she could. Marc's tongue flicked harder, faster. She nearly came undone but wanted to wait and come with him. She pumped up and down on his penis until her lips felt his cum working its way up the shaft.

The power of his impending orgasm distracted him a moment, and his lips left her. "Oh, pet, that feels so good!" He shot his cum deep into her throat, groaning his release. "*Merda!* So hot!"

He rammed two fingers into her pussy, curling them around to her G-spot.

"Oh, yes! There, Sir!"

She moaned as she continued to milk him while he prepared her for a takeoff of her own. His tongue flicked against her hard clit and she ground herself against his face. She pulled away from his penis and screamed her own release through her raw throat as he took her over the edge.

"*Mio Dio!* Yesssss!"

*   *   *

Hours later, and another orgasm behind each of them, Marc tossed back the sheet he'd covered them with. "I'm going to get dressed."

"But we're only halfway home. What's the rush?"

He shook his head. "You're insatiable, pet."

The time was almost right, but he wouldn't do this naked. She might someday tell their children how Papa proposed to her—and Marc would be damned if she'd tell them they were naked on a jet plane. His girl would get the most decent proposal he could devise. Lord knows he'd had enough time to plan one.

Yet he still had no idea exactly what he would say. Nothing sounded right despite having practiced a dozen versions.

Angelina knelt and retrieved her dress, a souvenir from their day trip to Firenza, slipping it over her curves. Good. Maybe now he could think more clearly. He didn't want to mess this up.

He surveyed the small but opulent cabin. A U-shaped sofa with a chess game laid out on the coffee table in between. Six leather executive chairs for passengers. The fireplace seemed the most romantic place. Taking her hand, he led her to stand in front of the fire.

Marc stared down at her a long moment until she wrinkled her brow. "Why so serious?"

"Angelina, there's something I've wanted to ask you for a long time but never found the confidence to do so—until now."

Her hand flew to her mouth, and tears formed in her eyes before he could even start.

"*Amore mio*, I chose this time and place because we are an equal distance between the homeland of my childhood and the place I've lived now for the past two decades. As I told you, I have no strong sense of home in either place. Lombardy and Colorado are mere geographic locations on a map."

Angelina's expression grew quizzical as she lowered her hand to her side, but her lips continued to tremble.

Marc stroked her cheek with his fingertips. "One thing I've learned with you—and even more during the time I was separated from you—is that I have only one home. Wherever you are."

Tears spilled from her eyes, and he brushed them away.

"*Tesoro mio*, you have given my life back to me."

No, too trite.

"*Scusa.* I'm nervous." He took a deep breath and started over. "*Tesoro mio*, you've helped me learn to live life fully for the first time ever. You have nurtured me, kicked my ass, and loved me like no one before."

Angelina framed his face with her hands. "Oh, Marc, you're so easy to love."

"That's debatable."

She grinned. "Well, I did have to peel away a few layers to find the real you."

"You saw past my flaws and weaknesses and loved me anyway." He reached into his suit pocket and retrieved the ring. A glance at his watch told him now was the time and place.

Marc took her hand and knelt on one knee. Tears flowed with abandon now. He cleared his throat, hoping not to blow this again.

"*Amore mio*, will you marry me?"

Shit. He'd forgotten something very important. He held up his hand. "Wait. I'm sorry. There's more."

She nodded, seemingly too overcome with emotion to speak anyway. He hoped he could finish without losing it himself.

"Angelina Cristina Giardano, you would do me the greatest honor if you would choose me to be the man you agree to share the rest of your life with, if you would allow me to love, honor, and protect you, to provide for you and any children we are blessed with, and to share all of the moments—good and bad—of the rest of our lives."

Okay, now that sounded like wedding vows. How could he...

She launched herself into his arms, and he held her tightly before easing her to her knees beside him. Her hug seemed to be the answer he wanted, but he wasn't finished yet. He separated their bodies and framed her face with his hands.

"As your Dom, I also promise to guide you, to do everything possible to help you reach your highest potential, and to give you whatever your heart desires that lies within my power and your best interests. My life would be complete—everything I've ever dreamed of—if you agree to stay beside me."

Angelina pulled his face toward hers and kissed him, short-circuiting his brain. When he could think again, he stared into her eyes. "Is that a yes?"

"Of course it's a yes! On all counts, Sir."

Marc's eyes filled with tears, but he didn't care. Through a throat suddenly closed off he whispered, "*Grazie, amore.*"

Remembering the ring, he took her hand again and slipped the sleek, elegantly carved platinum ring over her finger. He knew she wouldn't cook with an elaborate gemstone ring on her finger without constantly removing it. This ring, he wanted to stay on her hand more often than not. He kissed the ring before standing and pulling her to her feet again.

"Angelina, I've been trying to find the words to ask you to marry me since New Year's, but until now, I never knew what to say. Well, as you can see, I botched it a bit."

She shook her head. "Those were the most beautiful words anyone has ever spoken."

"I've changed so much this year—for the better, I hope. But I finally understand what it is I want—I need—and what I have to offer you."

She nodded. "Oh, yes, Sir. You most definitely have a lot to offer. I'm just glad you can see it now."

He smiled, a little more relaxed. "I'm finally beginning to understand who I am, why I act the way I do. I'm no great prize for womankind, but you, *mio angelo*, you have made my life complete by accepting my ring—and my heart. I will do everything in my power never to disappoint you…ever again."

*   *   *

Angelina couldn't tear her gaze away from Marc long enough to look at the ring. She'd never seen him so at peace, despite his nervousness. How could he think she would not have accepted such a heartfelt proposal?

When she'd seen a momentary flash of anxiety in his eyes, all she could think was *"trust me."*

"Marc, I would be honored to remain a part of your life for the rest of time."

Tears dampened her cheeks, but she dashed them away.

"Cuor mio. Marc, you will always be my heart. Always."

He pulled her toward him and kissed her until she lost her balance, sending them both tumbling onto the fur rug. She bumped her head on the coffee table and giggled as he cradled her, checking her forehead for injury.

"If I bring you back to your brothers with visible bruises, Rafe might rescind his reluctant blessing."

She pulled away and grew serious. "You asked Rafe for his blessing?" That's what Marc had talked with her eldest brother about? *Wow.* That he would brave the lion's den to make such a request warmed her heart, but knowing he'd done so even before he'd completely made his peace with the past during this journey of discovery melted her to the core.

Marc grinned. "Well, he balked at first. I think I'm going to be on probation for years, maybe decades—or perhaps until I give you the first few babies—before he will believe I can make you happy." He sobered. *"Amore,* I promise I will spend every hour of every day making sure I achieve that mission in life."

"What, giving me babies?"

He drew his brows together, replaying his words probably. Realization dawned. "No! I mean, of course I want us to have babies one day, but I meant my mission to make you happy."

"Good, because having babies will be one of those details you'll need to consult with me about." Angelina hadn't really thought about being a mother until she'd spent so much time with Marisol this spring. Nothing would please her more than to give Marc a house full of tiny D'Alessios.

Marc grinned. "Duly noted." He pulled her face to his and pressed his lips against hers. She opened wider, allowing him to deepen the kiss.

When his hand trailed to her breast, she pushed him away.

Angelina cleared her throat before she could speak past the tears. She had some words to say, too. "Marc, being your true partner is all I've ever wanted."

"Before any children, we'll need to decide where we'll live. We'd quickly outgrow your—."

"Oh, Marc!" She wrapped her arms around his neck. "You said, 'we'll need to decide.' You really have changed!"

His chuckle rumbled against her breasts. "I'm trying, pet. I can't promise I'll always think to consult with you before I act—I do have this tendency to make rash decisions—but something as important as where our *bambini* will be raised requires your input."

"As long as we're all under one roof, we'll be where we belong."

He nodded. "In the meantime, I look forward to a long honeymoon period in your house in Aspen Corners before we start making all of these babies. It's the perfect place for newlyweds. Reminds me of Mrs. Milanesi's."

She smiled, brushing a lock of hair from his forehead. "What will you do about your business in Denver?"

"Brian runs the day-to-day stuff, and there's plenty of wild areas to be found in your part of the state. We may even open a second branch of the store in Breckenridge. Or start a restaurant where you can attract guests from around the world to enjoy your fabulous cuisine. I have a need to…"

When he didn't continue, she quirked her head. "To…?"

"You said you wanted us to be equal partners, but what will that mean to our Dom/sub relationship?"

"I didn't say equal; I said *true* partners. There will be many times when we won't be able to maintain an equal partnership. We're both stubborn Italians, remember? And I would die if you didn't take me in hand from time to time to assert your authority over me."

He grinned. "Love to."

Angelina held up her hand. "But that's in the bedroom. Well, in whatever room we're having sex or getting kinky in. But *I* will have control over my own career. I'll probably need to have control over the household finances, too, because you truly have no business sense whatsoever."

"They're all yours."

She smiled. "Thank you, Sir."

He grew serious. "But when you submit to your Dom, you will behave and be a good girl."

"Yes, Sir. Most of the time." He swatted her butt. "Oh, you know you love it when I'm your naughty little brat."

He acknowledged her statement with a grin. "No, pet. What I love is punishing your brattiness. With you, I've learned what it means to have the responsibility of a Dom, not just the kink and fun. So you've been warned."

"Perhaps once a year, you'll allow Mistress A to see to your needs, as well, Sir."

His eyes smoldered, making her wonder if he hadn't enjoyed that a little bit. She certainly had. Angelina giggled. Maybe she was a bit of a switch.

No, not really. Being the Top was more work than she wanted to take on. She preferred to have him do all the planning and let her simply unclutter her mind—and feel.

As his wife and his submissive, she wanted nothing more than to devote herself to making this man happy. She bit the inside of her lip. "Sir, you've always been the perfect Dom—the heroic guardian angel—for me."

Marc grew serious. "I'm nobody's angel, *cara*."

She leaned in closer. "Marc D'Alessio, you've been a heroic angel to many. Ask Damián if you don't believe me. He told me once you were the reason he didn't kill himself after Fallujah. You didn't give up on Damián in the attack on that rooftop in Fallujah nor at the hospitals in Germany and San Diego. You even called Adam out to Balboa when you thought you might lose him to suicide."

He grew serious once more. "I've spent a lifetime playing the Dom—and the hero—but I'm not sure I ever succeeded. I know I did a lousy job of saving myself."

"That's because you needed me to save you, Marc. We saved each other."

"Thank you for letting me be a part of your life, *tesoro mio*."

Tears filled her eyes despite her smile. "You've been my special avenging archangel and owned my heart from the moment you rescued me from Allen, even if it took me a while to recognize you without the mask." She sobered. "Marc, life has no guarantees. We've both learned that the hard way. And lots of times we aren't going to have a clue what to do or why something is happening. But we have guardian angels watching over us now—my papa and your brother."

She stroked his cheek. "Don't you ever forget that, Sir. But I'm even more blessed because I have my angel here in the flesh, too. As far as I'm concerned, you're *somebody's* angel, Marc—mine."

Glossary of Terms
for *Somebody's Angel*

Alla mia bellissima ragazza—to my very beautiful girl, in Italian

Andiamo alla nostra tana—let's go to our lair, in Italian

Bambino mio—my boy, in Italian; *bambini* for children

Bebé—baby, in Spanish; an endearment that can be used for a lover or child

Cara—dear, in Italian

Cover—military term for head covering or hat

Cuor mio—my heart, in Italian

Desert Digitals—a description of the desert Marine uniform used by older Marines (also see MARPAT)

Devil Dog—term for a Marine

Dio—God, in Italian

DM or DMS—Dungeon Monitor or Dungeon Monitor Supervisor; a volunteer usually at a play party or club who ensures the safety of those in scenes/activities; while on duty, a DM should not be engaging in play scenes. A DMS oversees one or more Dungeon Monitors.

Dom/sub or D/s Dynamic in BDSM—a relationship in which the Dominant(s) is given control by consent of the submissive(s) or bottom(s) to make most, if not all, of the decisions in a play scene or in relationships with the submissive(s) or bottom(s).

Grunt—term for a Marine

Had My Six (aka Had Your Six)—has your back; watching out for you

Head—bathroom (Navy jargon)

IED—improvised explosive device (homemade explosives, often detonated by vehicles on roadsides in Iraq and Afghanistan)

In-Country—term used by military personnel to describe being in the country of deployment

Lido—Lidocaine, a topical ointment used as a numbing agent for stings, cuts, or burns

Maman—mother or mama, in French. NOTE: Savannah's mother was born in France and responded to Maman, as does Savannah with her daughter

Mamma—mama, in Italian (used only in places where Marc is actually speaking/thinking in Italian)

MARPAT—stands for Marine Pattern, a more recent term for the Marine uniform (also see desert digitals)

Merda—shit, in Italian

Mindfuck—Something that intentionally destabilizes, confuses or manipulates the mind of another person. Used in the BDSM lifestyle to make a submissive think something is happening that usually is much worse than what is actually happening.

Mio angelo—my angel, in Italian (*il mio angelo* in third person)

Mio Dio—my God, in Italian

Muñequita, mi—my little doll, in Spanish

PsychO/Psycho—Navy jargon for a psychologist (Psych Officer)

Rack—bed (Marine term)

RACK—Risk Aware Consensual Kink. This is a BDSM scene that is negotiated ahead of time and doesn't need to adhere to the standard of Safe, Sane, and Consensual (SSC). Most still have a safeword, unless the participants have a high level of play experience and trust built.

Safephrase—a phrase agreed upon prior to a BDSM scene that can be used to end (temporarily or completely) a play scene

Safeword—a word agreed upon prior to a BDSM scene that can be used to end (temporarily or completely) a play scene

SAR—Search and Rescue

Scusami—I'm sorry, in Italian

Semper Fi (short for **Semper Fidelis**)—Marine Corps motto; Latin for "always faithful"

SERE Course—an intense training program teaching Marine and Navy personnel the tactics for survival, evasion, resistance, and escape

Sí—yes, in Italian

SNAFU (snafu)—Situation Normal, All Fucked Up

Sono nel bosco—I'm in the woods, in Italian

Spazzolami i capelli—brush my hair, in Italian

SSC—Safe, Sane, and Consensual kink scenes with a safeword that doesn't carry the level of risk some edgeplay does.

Subspace—A state of mind that a submissive may enter, particularly after intense activities and/or (depending on the person) intense pain play, characterized by euphoria, bliss, a strong feeling of well-being, or even a state similar to intoxication. Thought to be related to the release of endorphins in the brain. The euphoria associated with subspace may last for hours or sometimes even days after the activity ceases. (Source: Xeromag.com)

Tesoro mio—my treasure, in Italian

Total Power Exchange (TPE)—a relationship in which one person surrenders control to another person for an indefinite duration, and in which the relationship is defined by the fact that one person is always dominant and the other is always submissive. One of the more extreme forms of power exchange. Sometimes referred to as lifestyle D/s. (Source: Xeromag.com)

Twentynine Stumps—a derogatory term used by Marines who served or trained at the base in Twentynine Palms, Calif.

About the Author

Kallypso Masters writes emotional, realistic Romance novels with dominant males (for the most part) and the strong women who can bring them to their knees. She also has brought many readers to their knees—having them experience the stories right along with her characters in the Rescue Me Saga. Kally knows that Happily Ever After takes maintenance, so her couples don't solve all their problems and disappear at "the end" of their Romance, but will continue to work on real problems in their relationships in later books in the saga.

Kally has been writing full-time since May 2011, having quit her "day job" the month before. She lives in rural Kentucky and has been married for 30 years to the man who provided her own Happily Ever After. They have two adult children, one adorable grandson, and a rescued dog.

Kally enjoys meeting readers at national romance-novel conventions, book signings, and informal gatherings (restaurants, airports, bookstores, wherever!), as well as in online groups (including Facebook's "The Rescue Me Saga Discussion Group"—send a friend request to Karla Montague on Facebook to join if you are 18 or older and don't mind spoilers. Kally also visits the Fetlife "Rescue Me! discussion group" regularly). She hopes to meet you in her future travels whether virtually or in-person! If you meet her face to face, be sure to ask for a Kally's friend button!

To contact or interact with Kally,

go to Facebook (http://www.facebook.com/kallypsomasters),
her Facebook Author page
(https://www.facebook.com/KallypsoMastersAuthorPage),
or Twitter (@kallypsomasters).

To join the secret Facebook group Rescue Me Saga Discussion Group, please send a friend request to Karla Montague and she will open the door for you. Must be 18 to join.

Keep up with news on her **Ahh, Kallypso...the stories you tell** blog at
KallypsoMasters.blogspot.com
Or on her Web site (KallypsoMasters.com).

You can sign up for her newsletter (e-mailed monthly) at her Web site or blog, e-mail her at kallypsomasters@gmail.com, or write to her at

Kallypso Masters
PO Box 206122
Louisville, KY 40250

Get your Kally Swag!

Want merchandise from the Rescue Me Saga? T-shirts and aprons inspired by a scene in *Nobody's Angel* that read: "Master Marc can put me in culinary bondage anytime." A beaded evil stick similar to the one used in *Nobody's Perfect*. Items from other books in the series will be added in coming months. With each order, you will receive a bag filled with other swag items, as well, including a 3-inch pin-back button that reads "I'm a Masters Brat," two purple pens, bookmarks, and trading cards. Kally ships internationally. To shop, go to http://kallypsomasters.com/kally_swag.

Excerpt from
Captured Innocence

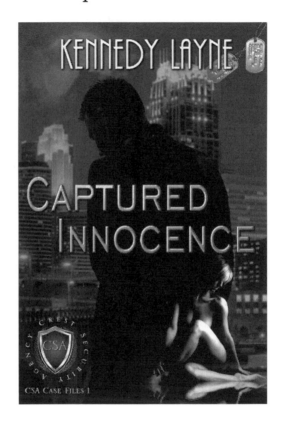

Captured Innocence (excerpt)

"**S**ir, wait." Lauren lifted her head upon hearing the nurse's tone coming from outside of the curtain. The emergency room was busy for a Friday night, but the staff still ran a rather tight ship. Maybe it was the police coming back to ask more questions. "You aren't allowed back—"

The curtain was yanked aside, revealing Connor Ortega. His presence never failed to leave her breathless. No man had the right to look like him. His blue eyes zeroed in on her and she instinctively wrapped her fingers around her wrist. *Ouch.* The action brought her out of her reverie for two reasons. One, it helped stabilize her feelings and two, her wrist hurt like hell.

"Connor? Why are you here?"

"Do you want this gentleman removed?"

Lauren glanced at the nurse holding her discharge papers. A frown marred the woman's haggard face. She hadn't been the most pleasant. After Lauren had discovered she was closing in on the end of a twelve-hour shift, she didn't blame the nurse for her fatigued attitude.

"No, she knows me." Connor stepped into the room. Lauren prevented herself from looking for something to throw. This back and forth between them only further fueled her irritation. She didn't need more bullshit right now. What she needed was for him to go back where he came from. He'd somehow upset the balance of her daily routine and she needed it back desperately. "Where are the police?"

"They left. Connor, how did you know I was even injured?" Lauren asked, still wondering what he was doing here.

"Left?" Connor turned to address the nurse and Lauren felt her irritation with him return. It had only been two days, but he seemed to have a gift when it came to raising her ire as well as her...maybe she had hit her head a little too hard. "Is she being released?"

"Yes."

The nurse ripped off the top sheet of her clipboard and pushed the paper into his chest in what could only be an act of dismissal. Nurse Broomhilda actually smiled as she paused before launching into what seemed like a drill sergeant impression. Lauren would have thrown her hands up in disgust if she thought she could handle any more pain.

"I'm glad to know that she won't be alone this evening. She hit her head pretty hard against the cement. We tried to get her to stay the night for observation, but she insisted she'd be fine. I can see where she learned that trick. Here are her discharge papers. It wouldn't hurt to wake her every couple of hours. No sex, buddy boy. Got that? She should eat light and there is to be no alcohol consumption. The rest of the directives are included on the discharge order and she should make a follow-up appointment with her doctor. See that she does that."

"Thank you, *Sergeant*." Connor returned her smile. Lauren resisted the urge to roll her eyes, knowing all too well it would only make her headache worse. "I'll see to it that she follows orders."

Lauren's heart skipped a beat at the double meaning of his words, but chose to ignore it. There was no way in hell he was coming home with her. She'd resisted calling him for two days and would continue to do so, for both their sakes. In her experience, as well as by observing customers on a daily basis, a true Dom didn't date vanilla girls like her. She turned and picked up her purse out of the chair, realizing that her hands were still trembling from the attack. Connor's presence didn't help anything at all.

"What happened?"

Lauren slowly faced him, and only then noticed the nurse had left. It was now only the two of them in the tiny emergency room area. Still not understanding why Connor was even here, she pulled the strap of her bag over her shoulder with every intention of leaving. Lauren couldn't help but wince when her wrist started to ache from the movement. It wasn't her issue that the nurse misunderstood why he was here. Bottom line, her mugging had nothing to do with him.

She was surprised when Connor stepped forward, crowding her space. What shocked her even more was when he laid down the papers he'd been given and gently took her hand, exposing her wounded wrist.

"Lauren, I asked you what happened."

A feeling of utter provocation overcame her at the sound of his voice and she found that she needed to get away from him before he changed her mind and she took him up on what he offered. If he would just stop coming around her, Lauren knew she wouldn't have a problem with ignoring these overwhelming feelings of longing that he stirred within her. She tried to pull back her hand, hoping that he would release it. She should have known better.

"I was mugged," Lauren said rapidly, hoping the faster she spoke, the sooner she could leave. She continued to stare down at their hands as his fingers encircled her wounded wrist, not wanting to look into his bright blue eyes and get sucked in. Her emotions were unstable and she didn't want to do anything stupid. "Someone must have heard me scream and called the police. Within moments of the guy attacking me, I heard sirens. He ran off. They called for an ambulance. End of story. Can you please move?"

"Look at me."

That was the last thing she wanted to do. Before Lauren even lifted her gaze, she felt tears sting her eyes and berated herself for it. She didn't want him to think she was some weak woman who couldn't handle herself in a crisis. And that annoyed her even more. Why should she care what he thought anyway? Unable to prevent herself from following his command, Lauren connected her eyes with his and saw his immediate sympathy. His warm grip seemed to stop time in her small world. She could only barely perceive that around her the planet continued to spin as they were trapped in this moment. Why did he care? That was all it took for a tear to escape.

"You're fine," Connor murmured, gathering her up in his arms. Lauren couldn't suppress the sob that escaped her chest. His warmth enveloped her and though she knew the safety she felt was illusory, that didn't stop her from relishing in his embrace. "I've got you, Red."

*   *   *

The *Rescue Me* Saga

Masters at Arms & Nobody's Angel (Combined Volume)
(First in the *Rescue Me* Saga)

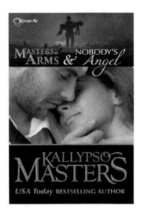

Masters at Arms is an introduction to the *Rescue Me* Saga, which needs to be read first. The book begins the journey of three men, each on a quest for honor, acceptance, and to ease his unspoken pain. Their paths cross at one of the darkest points in their lives. As they try to come to terms with the aftermath of Iraq—forging an unbreakable bond—they band together to start their own BDSM club. But will they ever truly become masters of their own fates? Or would fate become master of them?

Nobody's Angel: Marc d'Alessio might own a BDSM club with his fellow military veterans, Adam and Damián, but he keeps all women at a distance. However, when Marc rescues beautiful Angelina Giardano from a disastrous first BDSM experience at the club, an uncharacteristic attraction leaves him torn between his safe, but lonely world, and a possible future with his angel.

Angelina leaves BDSM behind, only to have her dreams plagued by the Italian angel who rescued her at the club. When she meets Marc at a bar in her hometown, she can't shake the feeling she knows him—but has no idea why he reminds her of her angel.

Nobody's Hero
(Second in the *Rescue Me* Saga)

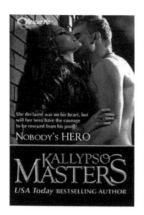

The continuing romantic journey of Adam and Karla from *Masters at Arms &* *Nobody's Angel*, which ended in a dramatic cliffhanger that sets up the opening scene of *Nobody's Hero*.

Retired Marine Master Sergeant Adam Montague has battled through four combat zones, but now finds himself running from Karla Paxton, who has declared war on his heart. With a twenty-five year age difference, he feels he should be her guardian and protector, not her lover. But Karla's knack for turning up in his bed at inopportune times is killing his resolve to do the right thing. Karla isn't a little girl anymore—something his body reminds him of every chance it gets.

Karla Paxton fell in love with Adam nine years ago, when she was a 16-year-old runaway and he rescued her. Now 25, she's determined to make Adam see her as a woman. But their age difference is only part of the problem. Fifty-year-old Adam has been a guardian and protector for lost and vulnerable souls most of his life, but a secret he has run from for more than three decades has kept him emotionally unable to admit he can love anyone. Will she be able to lower his guard long enough to break down the defenses around his heart and help him put the ghosts from his past to rest? In her all-out war to get Adam to surrender his heart, can the strong-willed Goth singer offer herself as his submissive—and at what cost to herself?

Damián Orlando and Savannah (Savi) Baker also will reunite in this book and begin their journey to a happy ending in *Nobody's Perfect*.

Nobody's Perfect
(Third in the *Rescue Me* Saga)

The continuing story of Savannah Gentry (now Savi Baker) and Damián Orlando from *Masters at Arms & Nobody's Angel* and *Nobody's Hero.*

Savannah/Savi escaped eleven years of abuse at the hands of her father and finally made a safe life for herself and her daughter. But when her father once again threatens her peace of mind—and her daughter's safety—Savi runs to Damián Orlando for protection. Eight years earlier, Savannah shared one perfect day with Damián that changed both their young lives and resulted in a secret she no longer can hide. But being with Damián reawakens repressed memories and feelings she wants to keep hidden—buried. After witnessing a scene with Damián on Savi's first night at his private club, she begins to wonder if he could help her regain control of her life and reclaim her sexuality and identity.

Damián, a wounded warrior, has had his own dragons to fight in life, but has never forgotten Savannah. He will lay down his life to protect her and her daughter, but doesn't believe he can offer more than that. She deserves a whole man, something he can never be after a firefight in Iraq. Damián has turned to SM to regain control of his life and emotions and fulfills the role of Service Top to "bottoms" at the club. However, he could never deliver those services to Savi, who needs someone gentle and loving, not the man he has become.

Will two wounded people find love and healing in each other's arms?

Somebody's Angel
(Fourth in the *Rescue Me* Saga)

The continuing story of Marc D'Alessio and Angelina Giardano.

When Marc d'Alessio first rescued the curvaceous and spirited Italian Angelina Giardano at the Masters at Arms Club, he never expected her to turn his safe, controlled life upside down and pull at his long-broken heartstrings. Months later, the intense fire of their attraction still rages, but something holds him back from committing to her completely. Worse, secrets and memories from his past join forces to further complicate his relationships with family, friends, and his beautiful angel.

Angelina cannot give all of herself to someone who hides himself from her. She loves Marc, the BDSM world he brought her into, and the way their bodies respond to one another, but she needs more. Though she destroyed the wolf mask he once wore, only he can remove the mask he dons daily to hide his emotions. In a desperate attempt to break through his defenses and reclaim her connection to the man she loves, she attempts a full frontal assault that sends him into a fast retreat, leaving her nobody's angel once again.

Marc finds that running to the mountains no longer gives him solace but instead leaves him empty and alone. Angelina is the one woman worth the risk of opening his heart. Will he risk everything to become the man she deserves and the man he wants to be?

Connect with Kally on Substance B

Substance B is a new platform for independent authors to directly connect with their readers. Please visit Kally's Substance B page (http://substance-b.com/KallypsoMasters.html) where you can:

- Sign up for Kally's newsletter
- Send a message to Kally
- See all platforms where Kally's books are sold
- View excerpts of Kally's work on your web browser, tablet, or smartphone
- Download free samples of Kally's eBooks

Visit Substance B today to learn more about your favorite independent authors.

Made in the USA
San Bernardino, CA
15 May 2014